THE FLAME EATER

By

BARBARA GASKELL DENVIL

Cover design by
EVM

ALSO BY

BARABARA GASKELL DENVIL

SUMERFORD'S AUTUMN

BLESSOP'S WIFE

THE FLAME EATER

A WHITE HORIZON

BETWEEN

THE WIND FROM THE NORTH

THE SINGING STAR

FAIR WEATHER

FOR ANOUSHKA

CHAPTER ONE

The curve of his thigh skimmed the melting candlewax. He sat amongst the platters, the rolling cups, the crumbs and scattered food, watching the reflections from the chandelier play along the polished pewter. He swung one leg, tapping his foot against the side of the table. His other foot rested on the body lying beneath.

A small flame hissed as the toppled candle stub extinguished in the spilled wine, for the table setting had been ruined in the struggle. Cold pork crackling and crumbled honey cakes lay strewn beneath the swing, swing, tap, tap of his foot, and the red wine puddled with the red blood, seeping to the edges of the rug.

The man stood eventually, looking down at the corpse as it sprawled, tongue protruding, eyes glazed. From the fallen wine jug, the trickling Burgundy dripped to the gaping mouth below. The man watched and smiled, but finally shrugged, clearing his thoughts of whimsy as he bent to finish his work and start the fire. As the first little flame rose amongst the piled napkins, the man turned and strode from the hall.

Outside the stars were singing. So he knew he had done the right thing.

They found his lordship's charred remains within the hour. The messenger set off just minutes later, riding hard for the castle and his lordship's father.

....

The curve of his thigh, sleek in fine grey wool, rested peacefully against the table, avoiding the mess of pottage. Another table; a far smaller table, gouged along its outer edge, one leg wedged with splintered willow chips to keep it stable, a smeared slime of onion and smashed turnip across its surface and the faint smell of smoked bacon rind. Another candle stub hissed, extinguished in thick trickling soup. The drip, drip of the sour green slid from the table to the ground where it was absorbed, not by the dry beaten earth but by the neat white apron of the woman lying there, her legs askew and her mouth slack lipped and open.

The body did not bleed, as the other had. Around the neck were black bruises, the marks of fingers, and the welts of a leather belt.

In the deepening shadows, the hearth was cold and no faggots were stacked. The cauldron hung empty, the poverty apparent. What food was now wasted, its spilled remains already congealed, was all there had been.

A chicken pecked at the woman's outstretched hand, accustomed to more active fingers that scattered seed beneath the old table.

The man stood watching a moment. Then he buckled his belt back around his doublet, pulled it tight and readjusted the clip on his hat, flicking its small brim from his face. As he strode from the tiny dark chamber, he looked back once and smiled.

The fire he lit took hold almost at once, surging up the walls into the flimsy rafters, and sucking at the wattle, the daub and the thatch. Scarlet and gold roared upwards, gathering force and threatening the tenements close by.

The man was some distance away when the fire discovered the woman's body, and claimed her grey frizzled hair, her careful little headdress, her outworn clothes and her tired old flesh.

....

Eyes down, feet together and hands clasped neatly in her lap as the low winter sun warmed the back of her neck, the young woman waited. Her mother said, "Look at me, Emeline. I want to make sure you are not glowering. And when you promise to obey me, as you certainly shall, I need to see the willing obedience in your expression."

Emeline said, "You know I'll obey you, Maman."

"And don't fidget with your fingers, Emma. Idle hands make for idle thoughts. It is high time you were married."

She had not raised her chin, and still spoke to her fidgeting fingers. "But he is dead, Maman, as we all know."

"Don't be absurd, child," said the baroness. "You understand me perfectly well and will now marry the wretched man's brother, since your father has not the slightest intention of allowing all that tedious negotiation to be wasted. The families will be affiliated, whichever brother is the target. And since Nicholas is now heir to the title, it is him you shall have."

The baroness's eldest daughter sat in silence for a moment, her gaze studiously blank. Finally she mumbled, "But I hate him. Everybody hates him. Do you mean me to marry a murderer, Maman?" and then wished she had not said it.

The Baroness Wrotham was standing very straight in front of the vast fireplace, and as she drew herself straighter and taller, the wind whistled down the chimney and black smoke gusted out in a small ball of fury. "May the Lord forgive me," said her ladyship, "if I strike you one day, Emma, but if you ever say such a thing in public, I will have your father thrash you again. No doubt once you are married, young Nicholas will beat you for me. Murder is a monstrous allegation, and is almost certainly untrue. At least – there is no legal accusation as yet. And you cannot possibly hate a man you have never even met. Besides, the deal is done and the bride price practically agreed. Our families will be properly aligned to the benefit of both, and you will prove yourself dignified and obedient while accepting your Papa's decision with ladylike compliance. In other words, you will behave as you never have before."

"Peter loathed his brother. He said Nicholas was deformed and mean spirited and lewd. He said Nicholas was sour as a quince and coarse as a bramble weed."

The wind was rattling the casements and the little flames across the hearth flared and sank. The baroness had to raise her voice. "What has any of that to do with it? If you do not like the man once you marry him, you will allow a suitable period to pass, produce the obligatory two sons, and then refuse to admit him to your bed just as every other good woman in the land chooses to do with a husband she dislikes. I will hear no more, Emeline. The matter is settled."

"He's probably the sort of man who would try to force me."

"Then good luck to him," sighed her Maman. "If he ever manages to force you to do anything at all, I must ask him how he achieves it."

"I liked Peter."

"Then Peter should not have got himself killed. You may consider yourself remarkably fortunate to have been almost affianced to one man you imagined you liked, which is certainly more than ever happened to me. But since you were never wed to Peter, and the settlement was not even finalised, there is no difficulty in arranging your union with the brother. Not even a dispensation will be required."

The sun had faded and now the wind was whistling outside. "Peter was murdered."

The countess gathered up her short velvet train and tossed her small stiff headdress, preparing to march from the room "Peter - Peter - I am tired of hearing of a matter now quite inconsequential. His death was no doubt sheer carelessness. And if it wasn't, then I am entirely uninterested. Your Papa would be very cross with you for questioning God's will. And you know quite well how your Papa reacts when cross."

"How can he know it's God's will for me to marry the wrong brother?"

"Your Papa knows everything," murmured her mother. "The priest has never dared argue with him, and nor will you."

Upstairs, Emeline recounted the conversation. She folded her arms across the warm window sill, rested her chin on her wrists and gazed out across the hedged garden, the wind blown meadows and the Wolds beyond. Her sigh was heavy with regret at being both misunderstood and mistreated.

"I suppose I sympathise," said Avice from the shadows of the bed curtains, "but if I were not your sister, I would say it was a very good match and you should be grateful. A castle, no less. His papa once sat on the Royal Council, so you'll go to court with new gowns and drink from real gold and silver. I doubt Papa will ever find me an earl's son. I shall probably get the seventeenth son of an alderman."

"You can have my earl's son."

"Don't be pouty, Emma. One day you'll be a countess. And he's rich. Richer even than Papa." She cuddled up against her sister's side of the bed, enjoying the softer, larger and grander pillows. "You're not thinking of - disobeying - are you?"

"Don't be silly. I just thought Maman would consider my feelings for once. Take my preferences - at least into account - and perhaps speak to Papa on my behalf."

"What good would that do? Papa has never changed his mind about anything - at least, not since I was born. And anyway, you really liked Peter. You were so happy to marry him. The brother can't be so different. And you'll get a new gown for the wedding feast."

Emeline sighed again. "You know exactly how it happened, Avice. Once Maman told me a match was being arranged for me with the heir to the Chatwyn title, I was honoured. Of course I was. Then I was introduced to Peter, and he was so handsome and charming. I just knew, right from the beginning, I was going to love my husband. So tall, and gallant and kind. But Peter talked a lot about his brother. He despised him."

"Well," said Avice, testing the bouncability of the mattress, "we shall meet this horrid creature next month and find out just what he's like at last. Since we're all invited to the castle, it will be six whole days and nights of incredible luxury and roast venison and new gowns and beeswax candles and real foreign wines and huge sugar subtleties and fur lined eiderdowns and all the things Papa won't let us have."

"With the wretched Nicholas paying court to me, and me having to be polite."

"You can pull your fingers away, and simper. I always wanted an excuse to simper. But simpering at the swineherd's son just somehow wouldn't be worth it."

"I'm more likely to spit," said Emeline. She returned her gaze to the heather pale hills on the horizon. "I wonder if Papa will make the horrid man accept a smaller dowry. Peter was hanging out for everything he could get. He admitted it. We used to laugh about it. I hope Papa makes Nicholas take a pittance."

"It will be our Papa and his Papa," Avice shook her head, "and nothing to do with anyone else."

"I know." Emeline slumped lower on the window seat. "But how can you bargain top price for a husband who is ugly and rude with a horrid temper and sinful habits?"

"And horns and a forked tongue? Wake up, Emma. His father's an earl. Nicholas will be an earl. Earl's always get what they want. Goodness knows if Nicholas actually wants you, but he's going to get you anyway. And maybe a few sinful habits might be fun."

The sleet angled sharply through the trees, turning the paths first to churned mud and then to ice, the ruts solidifying. The horses slipped and danced, pulled into snorting single file. Their breath steamed, their riders swore. The cart wheels leapt, axles groaning, hurtling Lady Wrotham from one cushion to another as she held onto her headdress and bit her tongue and wished she had chosen to ride. The litter's low hooped confines swayed as the base planks rolled, the rain outside pelting against the waxed canvas and drowning out the neighing, the cursing and the sullen stamp and plod of hooves beyond.

Epiphany not long past, the January weather already smelled of snow. The small cavalcade was soaked, tabards and surcoats sodden, hats wilting over slumped shoulders, the horses' bridles jingling and the wet reins squeaking between gloved fingers. Overhanging leaves collected the unrelenting torrents, then surrendered them, dumping sudden rivulets upon those riding below. The five men at arms had trotted a little ahead, clearing the way. Baron Wrotham, very stiff in the saddle, was followed closely by his two daughters and their ladies, braving the winter weather, flush faced and squint eyed in the cold. The clatter and slosh of the household trundled behind.

Four long days' journey, two aching nights in small wayside taverns, and the main family stayed over for the third night at the Ragged Staff Inn on the road from Dorridge, buried their noses in hippocras and hot possets, were too wet, bad tempered and tired even to complain, then bundled their aching limbs between well warmed sheets and slept on past dawn the next day.

During the long night, the rain stopped. A brittle white sparkle tipped each scrubby blade of grass along the hedgerows for a bright frost and a clear sky lit the morning.

Six hours later they rode from the forest's edge down into the wide valley's cradle where the castle walls soared golden from their waters. The portcullis was raised, and the drawbridge lowered. A buzzard sat like a lone gargoyle on the battlements, peering below, picking her target.

....

A different day, a different place, but the curve of his thigh skimmed the deep stone window ledge, the elongated muscles enclosed in coarse brown wool, the swing of both legs out and over. Then the drop. Eight foot to the ground, landing light and lithe in the cobbled courtyard, adjusting, balancing, and pivoting for escape. A long fingered hand grasped a bundle of skirts - a man's wrist pushing from the frilled cuff, the shift emerging half torn from the gown's too tight neckline, the apron adrift, a man's boots beneath the bedraggled hems. Masculine body, wide shouldered, long legged. Feminine clothes; the soft pink of a servant's well worn livery.

He did not suit his skirts. Not a convincing disguise but there should not have been anyone to see. Instead there was someone. The befrocked gentleman turned his head, the straw hat darkening his face into shadow, and stared straight into the young woman's startled gasp. He grinned, shrugging, gathered his skirts up again and without a word strode off towards the stables.

She watched him go. Too brazen for a thief, too assured for a scullion, the Lady Emeline wondered who, in this castle of grandeur and disdain, dared prance in borrowed clothes, play the fool, and climb from windows. She had seen little of him, and more of his legs than his face, but thought she would recognise him if seen again. The profile had seemed elegant in its shadows beneath the absurd maiden's bonnet. But then he had turned his head. She had seen the flash of sky blue eyes, but also the pitted crevice of a scar slashing from lower lid to earlobe and dividing the flesh, a rut as deep, it seemed, as that along the winter paths. One blue eye was part drowned in iced milk. A disfigurement that, even from the shadows, marked a face as forever memorable.

....

"My son," said the earl, "apologies for his absence. Unavoidably called away. Sadly, since my elder son's death, the estate claims more of our time than we'd like, and Nicholas - well, Nicholas is Nicholas. I trust he'll return - eventually."

There was the very best Trebbiano, the sweeter Malmsey for the ladies, tansy cakes and candied raisins soaked in honey displayed on silver platters. Refreshments were served in the great hall, draughts retreating behind the thick tapestries, the fire blazing on a hearth almost as wide as the road from the forest to the drawbridge. It was a great carmine splendour. It also smoked and smelled of soot.

Baron Wrotham looked down his nose. "Your courtesy is much appreciated, my lord," he said and did not look as though he meant it.

The earl waved long plump fingers. "You'll be tired. The journey – the unpleasant weather – the roads were at least passable, I see. Good, good. You'll be needing to rest, of course. You'll be shown to your quarters."

Her ladyship tottered upright and curtsied. Her legs barely held her and she wished indeed to rest. She took her elder daughter's arm, and, effectively dismissed, they followed the bowing steward from the hall. Avice scuttled behind them. His lordship the baron remained. He had a great deal to say. It was some considerable time before he took to his bed.

But Emeline had very little to say before closing her eyes. The bed was wide and warm and soft but being squashed between her mother and her little sister, she was less comfortable than she had expected. Waiting until she heard her mother's gentle snores, she then quickly mumbled into Avice's ear. "I've no doubt the wretched Nicholas was sulking in his bedchamber. Scared of meeting me because I know he murdered his brother."

Avice sniffed, avoiding the sudden movement of elbows. "How does he know you know? And how do you know he knows you know? And if he's wicked, he won't care what you know. Wicked people don't sulk. I sulk. You sulk. He wouldn't."

"I don't sulk."

"You're sulking now just because your beastly betrothed isn't showing the slightest desire even to see what you look like."

"Go to sleep," said Emeline.

CHAPTER TWO

It rained again on her wedding day. There was thunder in the west, and its echoes rolled across the battlements.

They helped the bride into her gown. Emeline shivered, goose skinned. Her mother tightened the wide satin stomacher and Avice sat on the window seat, hugging her knees as she watched. Nurse Martha was combing her mistress's hair and the two dressers, who had been attending the baron's daughters since they were in nethercloths, shook out the great sweep of the velvet sleeves, brushed down the short train, and nodded with eager approval.

"Oh, mistress, you're as pretty as one of the good Lord's own precious angels," murmured the maid Petronella. "His lordship will be so proud."

Emeline opened her mouth and her mother pinched her sharply. "One word, Emma - one wrong word and I warn you, I shall tell your husband to thrash you on your wedding night."

"If he bothers to attend his wedding at all." Emeline gazed at the wilting stranger in the long silvered glass before her. The gown was more beautiful than any she had ever previously owned; gold embroidered satin and rich saffron velvet trimmed in murrey and laced with golden ribbon.

"Don't be absurd, Emma," sniffed her ladyship. "The bride price is agreed, and a shockingly high price it is. But the earl was adamant. Your Papa was quite worn out after the negotiations were complete."

Martha continued to comb Emeline's hair, which she would wear loose for the last time. She shook her head, and the russet curls rippled. "You mean he'll come for the money if not for me? But we were visiting here nigh on six days last month, and he hid the entire time. None of us met him and I've still never set eyes on him. He didn't even come to wish us goodbye. It wasn't normal. It certainly wasn't polite. And now this time - the wedding imminent yet no sign of him last evening after we arrived. He didn't even join us at supper. Does he eat with the scullions in the kitchens? Is he frightened of me? Or merely a clod with the manners of a donkey?"

"You will meet him at the chapel doorway," said the baroness. "Which is perfectly proper."

There were a hundred candles smelling of beeswax and sweet perfumed honey. The small altar was draped with silver cloth and the great silver cross, heavily embossed, reflected the candlelight. Outside the wind howled and the narrow arched window, its haloes and suffering saints momentarily sullen, rattled in its leaden frame with no sun to brighten the colours. The priest stood holding his bible, and around him the families had gathered in two small gossiping groups.

Just before the alcoved doorway, a tall man stood alone. He was dressed in black velvet, the doublet laced in gold, his hands clasped behind him, his head uncovered, and his face turned towards the corridor as though waiting for someone.

The baroness escorted her daughter. From the cold passageway Emeline entered the great golden aureole of candlelight, and recognised the man waiting there at once. The deep disfiguring scar which divided the left side of his face seemed more profound in the fluttering light, the long pit drawn black by shadow, but scarlet by candle flame. He did not smile and nor did he greet her, but turned as she came beside him, now facing the priest at the chapel entrance, and there, in a cool, quiet voice he took her for his wife, speaking the simple words of contractual intention. Mistress Emeline accepted, answering in whispers as prompted. The small ring was blessed, the castle chaplain nodded, murmuring confirmation in nomine Patris, et Filii et Spiritus Sancti, the families and a handful of friends clucked, adding blessings of their own, and the earl announced it high time they gathered in the hall for the feast to begin, or half the dishes would be cold as the stone.

The great hall was well warmed and well lit, the minstrels' gallery was filled with music and joviality, the tables were heaving with steaming platters and the twenty or so guests were already wellnigh cupshotten. Nicholas was drinking heavily. Emeline sat to her husband's right hand beneath the tasselled awning, ate very little, and drank nothing at all until his beringed fingers grasped her cup and filled it from the flagon, saying, his voice soft and lazy, "If you are to face me later, my lady, with anything remotely suggesting pride and composure, you should probably first drink everything on offer. And this being my father's castle, I promise the wine on offer is both palatable and plentiful." And then he refilled his own cup, drained it, and again looked away to talk to others.

More candles, the blaze from the hearth brighter still, a dancing liturgy of flame and shadow, and Emeline hunched in her finery, golden as the swaying lights. She ate only a slice of venison with prunes, for the food was highly spiced and her stomach refused the smell, the weight, the heat and the taste of it. But she drank as bid, while the minstrels played and some of the guests pushed back their benches and rose to dance. Nicholas did not invite his wife to dance. Behind his seat, standing neat in a livery far grander than the usual, stood the young lord's squire, who helped serve him. They spoke often though it was beyond Emeline's hearing. His father sat on his left side, but he spoke little to him, and more regularly to a solid gentleman sitting beyond the earl's bulging shadow. The earl bellowed for the wine jugs to brim again and again, and buried his nose within the rim of his cup.

Emeline heard little of any conversation. "Adrian? You here?" from Nicholas.

"I am certainly here, cousin, as you would remember if you stopped drinking long enough to do so."

"Stop drinking? As a permanent reminder of exhausting boredom, perhaps? Bad advice, Adrian, and far too late."

"Then be assured I am here and shall remain here," replied the solid young man. "And will no doubt help drag you to bed at the appropriate hour."

"Never needed your help, not with that nor with much else," Emeline's new husband grinned, consonants not yet noticeably slurred, "and never with anything as interesting as tonight is likely to be."

"Impolite and unnecessary, coz. At least remember your bride, Nicholas."

"Not likely to forget her," Nicholas was laughing. "Would rather spoil the fun if I did, don't you think?"

It seemed interminably late when her mother came to Emeline's elbow, signalling to take her upstairs. She then led her, suddenly deep in quiet shadow, along narrow stone corridors and steep steps and finally into the young lord's bedchamber. Emeline was dizzy, barely stumbling as she tripped on her saffron velvets.

Then the servants waiting at the doorway threw open the great creaking oak, and Emeline stood and blinked. A small fire deep within the hearth flared with a rush of scattered reflections, but there were also candles, everywhere candles, in sconces, on tables, a chandelier of ten small flamelettes and a huge silver candlestick beside the bed. She sank down onto the settle by the fire and wondered if anyone would pity her if she cried.

Her mother hauled her up. "Remember you are a Wrotham, my girl. Dignity, always dignity. Your husband will show you what to do, and you will obey him utterly."

"What," sniffed Emeline, "if he doesn't know what to do either?"

The baroness said, "Don't be ridiculous, Emma," and began to unlace her stomacher.

"But with that - face," Emeline whispered, "he will not have had - no girl would have - so perhaps he has never - either."

Her mother scowled and pinched her wrist. "Enough, Emma," and her bustle of maids hurried around, carefully removing all the sumptuous beauty they had heaped upon her just a few hours previously.

The bride grabbed her mother's hand. "Maman, tell me the truth. Is it so bad?"

"Nothing is ever as bad as the anticipation of it," mumbled the baroness. "And remember, child, you will be respected for your courage and your obedience, however frightened you may secretly be. And the young gentleman has drunk a great deal, for I was watching him, which may help him quickly to sleep. Doubtless he has no great experience of treating women with respect, for sadly his mother died when he was very young and he has no sisters. But I believe he is kindly natured for he ordered that you be allowed to prepare quietly, without parades or the snooping attention of the feasters. No brawlers are to be permitted into the chamber here, and no winking, sniggering revellers eager to watch the preparations for your wedding night."

"Perhaps it's himself he doesn't want being watched," muttered Emeline. She could hear her voice wavering with the odd distortion of her own vowels. "And I'm - well, I drank more than - that is, more than I ever have in my life before. So I shall try and go to sleep before he comes in. Indeed, I am very, very tired."

"You are very, very stupid," sighed her mother, "though I cannot blame you for drinking too much wine on such a day. But I can certainly blame you if you try and avoid your duty. Besides, you look very pretty in your shift, my dear, and your hair shines quite wonderfully in all this candlelight. If only your dear Papa would permit the burning of so many candles on these cold nights. But that is quite another matter - so clamber into bed now, my love, and see what a great high mattress it is too, and well warmed I am sure."

Needing a little help, and not only because she was quite tipsy, Emeline climbed onto the bed. It was wide, heaped and richly curtained, four great oaken posts carved and scrolled, hidden within a swirl of painted damask. A welter of pillows and bolsters wedged her straight, and she sat, staring into the exaggerated wealth of lights. Her mother rearranged the pillows. Emeline mumbled, "Maman, please snuff some of those candles. I feel as though - as though I am on display."

"As you are, my love, and as you are meant to be," the baroness pointed out, and began to shoo the other women from the chamber. "He will be here very soon, for I can hear voices in the far dressing room. Remember pride, dignity, duty and modesty." And she bent, kissed her daughter's cold cheek, and hurried out.

Emeline had time only to breathe deep, whisper one short prayer, and hope for courage. She was not even aware that he had entered from another door until he spoke.

He said, "You look cold, my lady. Has the bed not been warmed? Shall I build up the fire?" Making her turn in a flurry, staring at him. She had been sitting huddled, her arms wrapped defensively around her. Then he smiled, saying, "Or perhaps you are simply preparing for the inevitable attack?"

She swallowed hard. "Is it attack you intend then, my lord?"

He wandered over to the hearth, kicked the flames from glow to spark, leaned one elbow to the great wooden slab of the lintel, and regarded the shivering woman within his bed. His voice was no louder than the crackle of the logs. "Attack? No, attack is not my style, my lady." He paused, as if considering either his words or his behaviour, and to what extent he wished to be polite. The candlelight above and beside him accentuated the scar cutting across his face. Finally he sighed, and said, "You look - delightful, madam. And you were beautiful - in the chapel. I found -," and his voice trailed off as if further diplomatic effort was beyond him.

"Truly gallant, my lord, but unconvincing." Emeline sniffed, increasingly uncomfortable. Her head hurt. Her stomach hurt. She said in a hurry, "Perhaps you'd like to borrow the dress yourself one day."

He laughed and walked over, sitting to face her on the edge of the bed. He appeared relieved, as if her words had suddenly released him from some burden. But Emeline froze, expecting contact. He did not attempt to touch her, and instead, after a moment said, "Are you so frightened of me?"

She said, "I'm never frightened of anything."

"Really?" He smiled again, but the warmth no longer reached his eyes. His left eye was part clouded, spotting the bright blue with cream. Emeline wondered if his vision was blurred, or even entirely lost. "How - admirable," he continued softly. "I, on the other hand, have been frightened of many things over the years. Indeed, fear has more than once saved my life."

She gulped, and said, "Is that a threat?"

Her very new husband sat back a little in surprise. "How very challenging," he murmured. "My reputation appears to have preceded me. Peter, I presume." He gazed a moment at her scowl, then stood abruptly and reaching out, pinched the flame from the tip of the flaring candle beside the bed. The shadows suddenly moved closer. From the darkened dazzle he said, "I have not so far, I think, appeared threatening, though perhaps not entirely sober. Nor are you sober, my dear, and both conditions are no doubt my fault. So then let us treat this as the practical business that it truly is, and do our duty instead of prolonging a pointless conversation for which you are clearly not prepared."

"Practical business?" she mumbled, sinking lower beneath the flush of sable bedcover.

"Is that the way you wish to see it?"

Nervous and miserable, Emeline hiccupped and did not answer. Nicholas turned at once and, striding quickly across the chamber, attended to the various sconced candles and the smaller stubs remaining lit. He snuffed each one, then loosened the chain to lower the chandelier, and killed all the little flames until the shadows loomed in deeper and deeper, swallowing every detail into darkness. Only the hearth remained bright with a scatter of simmering crimson and a sudden shooting brilliance, slanting intermittent illuminations to the painted ceiling beams, then shrinking again into black. Through the prancing spasmodic firelight, he returned to the bedside and stood looking down despondently at his new young wife. "Which," he said, inhaling, "if we are to be ruthlessly practical, brings practical although undiplomatic questions. Without wishing to be - ungallant - I should ask you, my lady, whether in fact you are a virgin."

Emeline squeaked, flushed, and bit her tongue. Her scowl turned to glare. She managed to say, "How - dare you!" and dragged the bed cover up to her chin.

Nicholas shrugged. "I have no objection, either way," he said, studiously careless. "It would simply make a difference to how I take you."

Horror became confusion and she said, "Take me? Take me where, for goodness sake? The only place I want to go is to my own bedchamber, wherever that is."

"I was referring -" and he shrugged again, and sat once more on the edge of the bed, facing the quivering shadows within it. "I know you wanted Peter," he continued softly. "I am sorry. In some ways, I miss him too. But now we are wed, and must make the best of it, I am ready to try - not to make you happy if that is to be impossible - but to protect you, and hopefully to make you comfortable." He reached out one hand, but she shrank back, and he let his hand drop. "Very well," he decided. "Perhaps, all things considered, we should leave this - business - for another day." Then he stood slowly again, and crossed to the other side of the bed. He still wore his shirt, elaborately pleated linen long and loose over his hose. He sat beyond her sight, pulled his shirt off over his head, unlaced and tugged off his hose, swung his legs up and climbed beneath the covers. Emeline did not watch him, but felt the mattress sink, and wriggled further to the other edge. Finally, his breath warm on the back of her neck, he murmured, "I won't disturb you. No doubt you are tired, as I am. Have they shown you where the garderobe is situated, should you need it?" She remained silent, so he continued, "I expect to be gone in the morning before you rise, so will not see you until dinner. Sleep well." And the hushed quiet again absorbed the shadows.

She did not know she had slept until she woke much later, accepting that the headache must be a hangover, but also knowing the foul smell, and the sense of accompanying dread, were something else entirely.

CHAPTER THREE

The grate was dark and cold, the window shutters enclosing the chamber in night. But it was fire she could smell, not the little smoky ashes remaining, but something raging and blazing beyond her sight.

Emeline sat up slowly, shifting herself carefully and trying not to disturb the unfamiliar bulk at her side. The body, visible only as a darker shadow within the shadows, reverberated gently as it breathed. There was no other movement. Emeline slipped from the bed, adjusted her crumpled shift, and stood. She tiptoed to the hearth but saw no glimmer of life, yet the stench of burning was insistent. She could not remember which door led out to the castle corridors, so leaned her cheek against the one she thought correct. The smell seemed stronger. She pulled on the handle and opened the door.

She stood there a moment, turning once, then twice. No flaming danger shattered the darkness. Wide awake now, and too alert for further sleep, she followed the winding stone walls, feeling for discovery. Her bare feet were frozen on the cold hard stone, and she could hear the little flap, slap of her hurried footsteps on the slabs. For a moment there was no other sound, and then she heard something quite different. A distant roar disturbed the silence, as of waves on a beach, very far off but of an incoming tide. Emeline stopped, listening. The echoes were louder; the stink was rank. She took one pace more and stood at the top of a stairwell, dark curved walls and steps winding down into invisible black. Then, as she peered past the newel, the black below was splashed with light and a glazed vermillion shone virulent in the depths.

Emeline turned and ran. She had left the door to the bedchamber open for easy recognition, and now raced in. Her flurry woke him and Nicholas sat up, bewildered.

"There's a fire," Emeline croaked, "and huge flames down the stairs."

"I can smell it," Nicholas said, and was already out of bed. He did not stop to dress and hurtled from the room, shouting over his shoulder, "Stay here, shut the door, and I'll be back for you. Listen out for whatever happens."

She promptly disobeyed. The window gave access to possible escape, but would surely be too high. Frightened of being trapped, instead she grabbed the bedrobe her maid had left for her at the foot of the bed, tugged it on, tied the sash tight and hurried back into the corridor. Still dark, still cold, the passage whispered with a wisp of invisible fumes smelling of filth and destruction. She did not go towards the narrow stairway of before, but turned left, searching for other stairs and a different escape to the ground level. The darkness remained impenetrable, but she was glad of it. Light might mean flames.

Endless doorways, doors locked, passageways lost in gloom, Emeline held to the walls for guidance but discovered no way down. She called fire, knocking on closed doors, but no one came and she ran on, losing breath, losing direction. She had no idea where Nicholas might be, and saw neither him nor anyone else. Eventually she found more steps, steep, narrow and winding, but they led only upwards.

Emeline leaned back against the wall, panting, knowing panic would not help her, would cloud her judgement and obscure her choices. But it was panic she felt and could not control. The castle was huge and as yet she had seen little of it, but knew this was the Keep, the soaring central block. Below was the grand hall, directly beneath the earl's quarters and those of his son where she had been sleeping. This was backed by the kitchens and down again to the cellars of storage, wine and grain. The women's and guests' quarters where she had stayed the month before were spread throughout the castle's vast western wing, and there her parents and sister would be housed. She knew no path to reach it, nor if the way would be open.

She was running again when she heard the screams. Emeline stopped, felt a great heave of nausea and the weakening tremble of her knees, steadied herself against the stone behind her, and listened again. She did not think herself braver than any other, or more capable, nor the best person to come if others could not help themselves. But she returned to the steps leading up, raised her hems, and raced upwards. She met flames half way up. The billows of sudden heat exploded in her face and she fell flat, her feet scrabbling for traction while slipping ever backwards.

The roaring virulence swept over her head and was gone, a hungry dragon impatient and furious. Her hair was scorched, her face blistered, and she trembled, horrified at the startling and astonishing pain of heat, even that which passed and barely touched. Suddenly her fear, already considerable, was exacerbated. Afraid to go back down and afraid to continue up, Emeline sat on the stone step and breathed deep. The little crowd clambered down towards her, stopping when they could not pass, crying for her to run. Children mainly, and women. Then two men bent and lifted her, hauling her up and hurtling on down the steps with her between them. Emeline was mumbling, someone was shouting, a child yelled, "Lady, come with us."

One of the men said, "We knows the way, lady, and will get you out. Hold on." She held. It was a great burly arm, sweaty, and muscled, but she clasped it with desperate hope and was helped along a corridor, still dark and cold, until there were more stairs, wide this time and shallow, leading straight down.

Stumbling, each pushing against the other, the group raced downwards. But with a stink of hellfire and sulphur the flames came up to meet them, a raging wall of unbelievable heat that threw them back. The large man gripped Emeline's wrist and in minutes they were back in the upper corridor, searching for which way to turn. The man croaked into Emeline's ear, "Can you jump, lady?"

And she gasped, "I shall have to."

The rising flames were close behind them now and the roar deafened speech and screams and sobbing fear and everything except the frantic terror. Sparks flashed, shooting cinders and the luminous dread. The children, half naked, streaked ahead, leaping to a casement window where the passageway angled deep and sharp. It was not so high and not so narrow and scrabbling fingers pulled it open, flinging the frame wide. At once the children climbed, each helping to hoist the other onto the stone sill, and immediately disappeared one by one into the cold black nothingness outside. The wind gusted back, bitter as the star shine beyond, chilled flurries that cooled the burning faces waiting for their turn to escape.

The man shouted, "You next, lady. Them lads will catch you." And with two vast clammy hands around her waist, he launched Emeline upwards until she clasped the window ledge. She clung one moment, the freeze in her face and the bursting hell heat behind her, then up, legs over and no care for her shift hitched almost to her hips, and at once released herself into the depths below.

She was caught. First slim hands and small children's arms, but then a man's grasp, lifting her bodily. Immediately she stood on the cobbles as the children scrambled back and instead the muscled and naked arm around her was hard and supportive and she was staring into her husband's scorched gaze. He held fast and pulled her with him although she could hardly breathe, running until there was grass and a gentle rise of soft green where he released her, and sank down beside her. Behind them the slope dipped down to the castle moat, and the little gurgle of water was a wondrous relief.

Nicholas said quickly, "Are you hurt?"

She shook her head, though she was not entirely sure. Over his shoulder she watched the mighty silhouette of the castle Keep rage in blazing fury against a lurid sky. Flames shot like cannon from every window and a rancid black smoke swirled and wheeled in the wind. A million sparks flared and danced, caught in winter's bluster, flaring like burning stars against the sweep of cold reality behind. Emeline whispered, with no voice to speak louder, "Is anyone else hurt?" Then she sank back, resting her head on the damp ground and closing her eyes. She could still hear the horror, could smell it and taste it but the heat was just a distant threat in a sudden burst of flying ashes.

Nicholas looked down at her a moment, then straightened and, as she opened her eyes again, said, voice raised above the fire's roar, "There are other rescues to organise, and I must arrange relays from the well and the moat. Will you stay here and watch my father? He is hurt a little, but not too badly I think."

Wedging herself on one shivering elbow, Emeline stared around. For the first time she saw the others, taking note of who they were. Most were servants, many hurrying back to help douse the fire, others searching for their friends and families. Emeline recognised the smartly dressed squire, now soot stained and running, buckets in both hands. But the earl, fully dressed unlike his son, lay on his back, gulping and sobbing, terrified and half unconscious, his belly rising and falling fast, his eyes wide and wet to the sky. He was drenched, as if someone had thrown water over him, and his fine silks were ruined and ragged, all burned in tatters and blackened wet strips.

Over the noise of the fire and the gurgled suffering of the earl, someone was screaming. The sound was thin and high, like the wailing of a seabird. Emeline said, "Is that – is she – dying?"

"No one is badly burned. No one is dying." Nicholas stood and sighed, pushing the hair from his eyes. "Different people have different reactions to fear. We're all afraid. But there's a lot to be done and I have to go. Are you all right? Can I leave you here?"

She looked up again at Nicholas, now standing over her, and managed to nod. His body was thick in ash and smoke hung in his hair like bedraggled ribbons. His face was inflamed and the disfiguring scar was ingrained with dirt. He was, she realised, wearing only his braies, which were also badly burned and barely covered him. But it was his flesh she noticed more, for he was bleeding and blistered and his chest and legs and arms appeared to ooze as though the skin was preparing to peel quite away. It was as if, instead of clothes, he wore the destruction of the fire itself.

Swallowing hard, Emeline whispered, "Of course. But it's you who are hurt, not me. I think you should rest now, and if you tell me what to do, I can help."

The young squire hurried over, quickly recounting the situation so far, saying both wells were pumping and the staff organised in relays. Nicholas turned away from Emeline. "Stay here and comfort my father," and to the young man, "Get back there, David. Hurry them up. I'll be with you immediately." Emeline watched him stride off, a barefoot stranger, broad shouldered and long legged across the old cobbles back to the burning Keep.

She crawled towards the earl but did not know what to do for him. "My lord, are you in pain? You are safe now, I promise, and I think Nicholas has saved you. Is there anything you need?" Though had he asked for something, she had no idea how she would have fetched it. Instead he lay quivering and silent. When a page hurried over, promising to bring ale and other aid to the lord, Emeline was thankful and crept back alone to quieten her pounding head and her heaving stomach, stifling the fear she had recently claimed never to feel.

Above her, the great black emptiness of the night sky had turned a scorched and virulent orange, as if the clouds themselves were burning. Sparks still flew, spangles of threatening unreality as the peaceful dark transformed, stinking and hideous, its thousand fingers all flame. The smoke haze spiralled and fanned out absorbing heavens, stars and the now invisible contentment of the countryside beyond.

It was many hours later when the fire was finally extinguished. A steady dawn was a pale insipid hesitancy behind the swirling stench. A host of people, some crying, some hugging, hurried around Emeline and the earl on the grassy slope, watching the new day shimmer and wake beyond the destruction of their home. But the great stones still stood, and although the windows were now empty and where there had been glass it was shattered and gone, the walls had not tumbled and the huge wings of the castle's separate towers, the stable blocks, the guards' houses, the cobbled bailey, the smaller courtyards, and even the arched entrance with the machinery for the portcullis and drawbridge, were all untouched. Yet up the walls of the Keep were the scorched and blackened fingers marking the passage of the flames. And where wooden outhouses had backed the Keep with a ramble of pantries, butteries, breweries, storerooms and bakehouses attached to the kitchens, there the fire had consumed everything and left only smouldering sticks and a rubble of paving.

The earl was carried on a great canvas litter, four men to heave him on to it and six to lift it and bear him away. Emeline stayed where she was. Her eyes smarted as the putrid yellow smoke, carried by a gusting wind, billowed in gradually dissipating clouds, and coughed as she swallowed soot. But when the servants begged her to come under cover, and said they would lead her to where it was safe, she refused. It was only open air that seemed safe to her now.

The fear remained. She felt it like black stones filling her lungs and belly, and she smelled it amongst the ruin. At first she was dazed, waiting quietly without consciousness of time. But then, as the paralysis of terror faded, she began to shake, so violently that she could not stand. Finally she cried, at first unaware of it, and then uncontrollably so her throat hurt and she felt sick. The tears swept down her cheeks, streaking through the soot, and leaving her utterly exhausted.

Eventually it was the steward, whom she recognised although his face was covered in ashes and his clothes were scorched, who came to find her. "My lady," he said, bowing even though she was huddled at his feet. "I have been requested to inform you regarding your family, my lady, that they are well and their quarters quite untouched by the fire. They have been informed of your safety and have gathered in the western solar. I am further instructed to take you there, should you wish to join them." He waited a moment, and then added, "But forgive me, should you wish to see his lordship first, my lady, I will lead you to him instead." He paused again, before hurrying on, "I should warn you that the young lord is grievously injured, and will need some care, and for some time to come I fear. The castle barber is with him now, but the Chatwyn doctor is much injured himself and needs attention. A boy has been sent to Leicester to bring back both town doctors, though sadly we cannot know how soon they may arrive."

Emeline stood slowly, stiffening her knees and testing her balance. Then she took a deep breath while imagining her parent's inevitable questions. She could visualise her sister's frightened face, the avid interrogation, and the criticisms of everything that had, and had not happened, should she admit to it.

She sighed. "Then you had better take me to my husband," she decided.

It had not been the wedding night she had imagined.

CHAPTER FOUR

They had taken him to the western wing. Here, at the greatest feasible distance from the ruined Keep, the smell had barely invaded within, nor had any damage been sustained beyond one shattered window. The mighty oak doors had been shut fast against all danger, and although buckets had been filled from the moat and still stood adjacent, they had not been needed.

At her request the steward led Emeline to a large bedchamber usually reserved for guests, and there she entered quietly amongst a stream of bustling servants. They brought possets, jugs of water and clean cloths, linen towels, trays of herbs, fresh bandages and cups of hippocras. Emeline brought nothing but herself, but tiptoed to the bedside, and sat there on the stool placed for her.

The bed, unlike his own where she had passed the first half of the night, was neither wide nor deep. The covers were all pulled back and the patient lay exposed, flat on the uneven lumps of the fleece below, his eyes closed. The bed curtains, tied carefully away against the headboard, were dusty and of indistinct colour. Across the chamber a small fire smoked fitfully and Emeline felt that the smell of it alone would disturb a man already injured by flame. She said nothing, and watched where, across the other side of the bed, the barber surgeon was carefully removing his lordship's braies. She had never yet seen any man entirely naked. That the first should be her husband seemed fitting, but Emeline blushed, and lowered her gaze to her lap.

The surgeon called her attention back. "My lady, I fear you need doctoring yourself. Your hair – the welts –"

She raised her fingers tentatively to her face and whispered, "I didn't realise. But it cannot be serious. I think I am quite unhurt."

Removing each thread of ruined ribbon from the fastenings of the braies, the surgeon again concentrated on his work, lifting the scraps of material where the heat had almost seared the linen to the man's skin. Nicholas did not move and Emeline thought him unconscious. His breathing was steady though shallow, but where the skin was already shedding, his body was glazed as if boiled. The surgeon murmured, "This is not my proper business, my lady, and I am not qualified. But someone must help, for Doctor Ingram is sore sick and must be doctored himself. I can only hope the medick arrives from Leicester before our lord sickens further." He sat back a moment, the charred shreds held nervously between his fingers. "But one thing I can assure you, my lady, that no amputation will be needed as long as proper care is given now, for infection is the danger where the skin is broken, and evil humours may creep in." He looked up again suddenly, staring across the bed at Emeline. "Will you take over, then, lady? Have you ever nursed folk, and attended to your family? Do you know the use of herbs and salves?"

She did not. She said, "I will try and wash away the burning, and the ruined skin, and the ashes and soot. Will that help, do you think?"

"It may." The barber sank back in disappointment. "I had hoped another – I fear to do harm, you see. This is not my skill, my lady, nor know of any in the household who could do better except our apothecary, who is now tending his lordship the earl. Washing a body may bring greater risk, but his lordship will surely not catch cold with that fire still merry in the grate and all the windows well closed. Meantime I shall interrupt the apothecary and get him to the Spicery for ointments. A cream for burns first I hope, and if not, perhaps butter will suffice."

"I think," Emeline mumbled, "that all the kitchen outhouses are destroyed, and their contents with them. But I will do what I can," and leaned reluctantly over her husband, touching the great blisters across his chest. Some were raised, pus filled and virulent, others raw and bloody. She was glad he slept, both for his relief, and so she might touch him without his eyes on her, watching her embarrassment.

The barber hurried off, clearly thankful to relinquish responsibility and to search for a lardy poultice, goose grease, or anything someone might suggest as a treatment for a man badly burned. "'Tis likely Mister Potts is still with the earl hisself, my lady," he stated as he pushed past the other scurrying servants, "and I shall go there first. I will be back directly, with whatever he tells me will be efficacious."

Emma sat alone and regarded her husband's ruined body. The smooth swelling of muscles at the top of both arms was striped red raw, and his forearms where the veins stood in grazed prominence, were bloody. His legs were long, the thighs well muscled and the calves well shaped, but it was at the top of his legs she preferred not to look. Indeed, she pondered, immediately perplexed, why a man needed such complicated and unexpected appendages, and why the good Lord had decided to fashion man so differently to woman. For a moment she even wondered if, during the undoubted exhaustion of creation, God had experienced a sudden moment of juvenile hilarity and in a fit of humour had decided to make mankind a figure of fun, before then returning to the sane and sensible creation of the woman. With a small hiccup, Emeline silently asked forgiveness for such unholy ignorance, and wondered instead if Nicholas was simply malformed, and entirely different to other men. Peter had told her many times that his younger brother was misshapen and ugly, explaining that his sins were apparent in the meanness of his appearance. But Emeline, having finally met her groom, had presumed this described the terrible scar that marred his face, and nothing more. Besides, attempting to be honest with herself in spite of her shock, Emeline had to admit that a gentleman's codpiece, often ostentatiously prominent, certainly suggested that all men were equally oddly endowed. Now she trusted, although without much conviction, that once this man demanded she consummate their marriage, she would become gradually accustomed to such strange and unpleasant necessities.

Resting a bowl of water on her lap, she laid the washcloths on the edge of the mattress and proceeded to use each one to cleanse her husband's burns, discarding them once befouled. She washed across his torso, around the dark flat nipples and down to the hard plain of his stomach. As the ashes and the blood slipped away beneath her frightened fingers, she realised his skin was not all over burned, but where the blisters were worse across his arms and chest, the damage to his flesh was severe. When she touched there he sighed, as if even in his sleep he felt the pain. Her fingertips travelled light, not only for his sake but for her own, feeling the hard muscled strength of him strange. At least she knew her blushes were known only to herself. So, with nothing else for a poultice or even a bandage, she quickly laid the remaining strips of cloth over him, all soaked in the remaining clean water. She carefully covered the parts of him she found most hard to contemplate, and finally called for more water, pouring this across the ravaged arms and chest. The palms of his hands, being raw, she held for some time in the water before resting his hands, now wet and cold, by his side. Then she prayed, hoping that God would still listen to her in spite of her previous amazement and criticism concerning His clearly mischievous design of masculine anatomy.

Several times she poured more water, keeping the linen coverings soaked and cool, and trickled streams across his hair and forehead where his skin still seemed aflame. In all that time Nicholas lay motionless except for the patient rise and fall of his breathing, and Emeline was not sure whether he slept, remained deeply unconscious, or whether, perhaps, he simply chose not to return to a world of pain.

It was some considerable time later when the barber returned with the apothecary, though she still slumped at the bedside, hands clasped and eyes closed. The new man exclaimed loudly, "My lady! That water is shockingly cold. His lordship could catch the pneumonia, or a chill might threaten his weakened state. He must be kept safely warm."

Emeline sat up with a start. "But he is so horribly burned," she explained, "and has been heated to extremes. A little coolness on that poor weeping skin would surely be a relief?"

Mister Potts shook his head, appalled. "Sadly you have no medical training, my lady. But in the doctor's absence, I will do what I can. I have discovered cream and butter in the cow shed, and have already been treating his lordship the earl with both. But some remains. And once these rags are dried in front of the fire, I shall use them as bandages."

"So much sodden linen," scolded the barber surgeon, "has leaked onto the mattress below, and the bed is quite soaked. I do not know where a new mattress might be found."

"This one can be turned," said Mister Potts, "and I shall instruct the pages accordingly. But in the meantime we must build up the fire and warm the sheets."

"Poor Nicholas," sighed Emeline, relinquishing her seat. "I was only guessing I'm afraid – seeing the heat of burns and thinking cold water would counteract the pain. I see I was wrong. I hope I've done him no harm. Now I shall go and see to my parents. But I shall, I suppose, be back."

It was late that evening when she finally returned to her husband's temporary chamber. She had spent some uncomfortable hours with her family, and they had insisted she receive some treatment herself, with the singed tangles combed from her hair and the florid grazes on her face and hands smothered in pork fat. The steward had organised collections from the local farms and provisions had quickly been brought in, yet dinner had been a sad affair, taken in the Western solar and without the presence of any member of the earl's household. Emeline had then thankfully accepted her mother's advice, and had rested in her sister's bedchamber for the afternoon. Avice immediately felt tired too and had then taken advantage and asked a number of questions which Emeline had no intention of answering with any honesty, and tried to avoid answering at all.

"So what exactly," Avice snuggled up under the bedcovers, peering through the shadows at her sister's tired expression, "was it like?"

"The fire? It was terrifying and hotter than anything I could ever have imagined, and it roared like a beast. Now I need to sleep."

"I didn't mean the fire." Avice wriggled closer. "Go on. I'm not that much younger than you. You can tell me."

Emeline had sighed. "You mean – being married? Well – that is – it's exactly how you might imagine."

"But that's the problem," complained Avice. "I can't imagine it. What happens?"

Emeline made a wild assumption. "Kissing," she said.

"Is that all?" demanded Avice. "But some women say it's sublime and ecstatic. And some say it's horrid and it hurts. Then they just refuse to explain what it's really all about. But kissing is just drab and ordinary."

Emeline sat up suddenly shocked. "Avice! Do you mean to tell me you've already kissed a man?"

She giggled. "Well – a boy. In fact, two boys. One was the swineherd's son when I was six and it took me ages to catch him. The other was Papa's secretary two years ago, and he caught me. Not that I ran very fast."

"I shall inform Papa, and have the wretch dismissed."

"Don't you dare," objected Avice. "Poor little Edmund Harris. He's never done it again. Though I keep smiling at him."

"Well, if you want me to keep your secrets," warned Emeline, "then you must also let me keep my own. Now go to sleep."

More to escape her family than with any desire to do her marital duty, Emeline entered her husband's sweat infused bedchamber again late that afternoon and slowly approached the bed. It was already dusk, though the shutters had closed in the windows all day and neither draught nor light entered. Only one candle had been lit at the bedside, but the hearth was splashed with flame and a fiery brilliance illuminated the room. Two pages tended the blaze and another was sweeping the tumbled soot while the barber surgeon concocted a cup of simmering milk sops on a trivet over the fire.

The figure in the bed was no longer immovable. Nicholas was propped up against a mass of pillows, and was awake although he appeared fractious and uncomfortable. His legs were hidden beneath the bedcovers, but his arms and torso, heavily bandaged, were visible and it appeared he was still unclothed. He was speaking as she entered. "If," he said, "you think I will agree to swallow that vile smelling sludge, Hawkins, you are even more addle brained than I am at present. Bring me some decent wine, and then I might have the strength to leave this gaol and stagger to the garderobe instead of pissing my bed again." He turned to his squire and body servant, who was hovering diplomatically silent in the shadows. "David," Nicholas called. "is there no solid food to be had?"

The apothecary interrupted in a hurry. "My lord, it is on strict orders from the doctor. A goat's milk junket with white bread is the only diet to be followed for some days, with small ale permitted on the second morning. Indeed, Doctor Ingram has prescribed the very same for himself. Your constitution must not be over taxed, and no wine can be served."

"I am already," Nicholas said softly with an edge of menace, "broiled like a lobster, yet you encase me in greased linen armour, turn the bedchamber into an oven, and poison me with slop."

Emeline thought he looked extremely pale. Apart from the vivid cut of the scar across his face, his visible skin had faded to an icy pallor. She stepped forwards with a confidence she did not feel, and said, "It would seem you're already feeling better, my lord."

"Ah." Her husband looked her over, seemingly disappointed. "Not the doctor from Leicester, then? Therefore not the man I can threaten with disembowelment unless he prescribes me wine and an edible supper."

"I'm amazed you have any appetite, my lord," Emeline said, keeping her distance. "Earlier today I thought you near to death."

The patient smiled faintly. "Hoped to be a widow before the day was out, I suppose?" He leaned back against his pillows and momentarily closed his eyes. "My apologies for my recovery. But if I am repeatedly denied food, no doubt I shall oblige you soon enough."

Emeline mumbled, "I suppose you have some excuse for being bad tempered, my lord, but there's very little point being cross with me. I did try to help earlier on, but your Mister Potts said I made matters worse. I hope your mattress is not still - damp?"

"It is," her husband replied without compunction, "because I can't get out of bed to piss. But whatever you did to me earlier, I doubt it made anything noticeably worse unless you strapped burning logs to my body. No doubt the doctor will think of doing just that tomorrow. He has already turned this chamber into a cauldron fit for frying bacon. And," he turned back to the surgeon, "he left instructions for me to be doused with goose grease from the farm and alum earth straight from the Vatican lands, so I'm likely to slip bodily from my charming wet mattress at any moment. And if the wretched man dares come armed with his fleam, I shall personally set the dogs on him."

"Choleric," announced the surgeon in a voice of pessimistic prediction as he bent again to the mixing of his milky potion.

Nicholas managed to raise his voice. "If," he announced, "you have the effrontery to be alluding to my bad temper, Hawkins,

I can tell you this is nothing compared to how I intend behaving once I have the strength. Ask my squire David over there lurking in the corner pretending to be deaf. He'll inform you how good natured I invariably am. But assuredly my choleric disposition will worsen at the earliest opportunity."

"I think," Emeline said, "I should leave you to your rest, my lord. At least the chamber smells - most pleasant. Rosemary needles perhaps? And lavender?"

His glare returned in her direction. "It is only the Turkey rug which benefits from the strewn rosemary, my lady, and does me no good at all except, perhaps, cover the stink of piss and boiled flesh. And I must inform you I have always loathed the smell of lavender."

Emeline hung her head, feeling almost culpable. "Then I wish you a good night's sleep, my lord," she managed, and backed hurriedly from the chamber.

There was nothing else to do but return reluctantly to her parent's quarters.

CHAPTER FIVE

Three endlessly tedious days later, Baron Wrotham regarded his daughter. "You will sit immediately, Emeline. You have been raised with a strict adherence to duty and a clear knowledge of your place in society. You are therefore not a picklebrained country simpleton and I will not have you fluttering before me in this inconsequential manner. In truth, you should be on your knees in the chapel, praying for your husband's full recovery."

"The chapel is burned to the ground, Papa." Emeline reminded him, sitting quickly on the small stool at some distance from the hearth. She clasped her hands in her lap and attempted to look meek. "And so, of course, is my lord's bedchamber, and my own temporary apartments which were also in the Keep. Which is why I have been staying in the guest quarters with you and sharing a bed with Avice. I now intend approaching his lordship - if you do not object, Papa - regarding the possibility of establishing my own chambers somewhere else, as surely I would eventually have done in any case. Separately, that is, if such a space exists -well, unless -"

"I have passed some hours in discussion with his grace this afternoon," her father informed her. "His lordship still suffers from the results of the accident and expects to be bedridden for some days further, but he is a little recovered. Between us we came to the conclusion that, under these unexpected circumstances, you will return to Gloucestershire with me as soon as the journey may be arranged. Your husband will be unable to undertake any semblance of normal married life for some time to come, possibly months. Suitable accommodation can no longer be supplied at the castle. You will travel home with us at the earliest opportunity."

She stared at him. "But I'm a married woman now, Papa," she objected. "Surely I should stay with my husband? You are usually very strict about - duty, Papa, as you've just pointed out. Isn't my duty here now?"

He shook his head, dismissing her. "Yes, you are legally wed, Emeline, and having passed the first night fulfilling your conjugal vows, you may rightly consider that you belong at your husband's side. I commend you for your sensitivity. However, the earl and I are in accord. There is too much to do here, and once his lordship is able, he will return to Westminster where his presence is demanded at court."

"I don't see why that should affect me," she mumbled. "Nor why he would leave when his son is so ill."

"Your opinion is of no consequence whatsoever," her father pointed out. "But I must tell you that the country is under a great cloud for her gracious highness Queen Anne is seriously unwell. This is of considerably greater moment than your husband's condition or your own discomfort. Indeed, it is said the queen is gravely sick and is like to die. With no children now living to secure a peaceful continuance to the monarchy, parliament urges the king to look towards prospective alliances with the royal houses of Portugal and Spain, where marriages might be arranged with the heirs of Lancaster." The baron sighed, as though feeling the weight of these political decisions. He continued, "Your father-in-law has evidently taken on some responsibility for these negotiations, and must therefore return to parliament as soon as possible."

Emeline dared argue. "But this is my home now, Papa. As a married woman I have the right to make my own choices."

The baron frowned. "There will be no one here to attend to your needs or properly chaperone your presence. You will do as you are instructed, Emeline."

"Surely my husband will be my chaperone."

"Your husband will be many weeks in bed and under doctor's orders, madam. He may not even survive. Almost half this castle, including all the principal chambers, is utterly destroyed. Rebuilding may take years. You have no experience of running a household on your own, and few of the staff would even recognise who you are. There is no place for you here."

"I can learn, Papa. I can –"

"You can do as you are told, Emeline. I will discuss this no further."

It snowed in the night.

She had dreamed. The hush and bitter chill of snow banking the outer window ledges had frozen the draught, and she had slept poorly. Once again she awoke with misgivings and the dread of approaching danger, but this time there was no crackle of flame or renewed reminder of smoke. She did not know what she feared, but crawled from the bed, trying not to disturb her sister. Avice snored a little, snuggled tight with her knees to her ribs, and snuffling beneath the covers. Emeline was wearing her sister's shift, almost all her clothes having been destroyed in the fire, but her own bedrobe lay to hand and she pulled it on. She lit a candle from the hot ashes in the hearth, slipped out into the corridor, and tiptoed to the unshuttered window at the far end. It still snowed and against the high silver scatter of stars, the crystal flight seemed unworldly and unutterably beautiful.

Downstairs the west wing offered little comfort. Three privies stood in their shadowed doorless row where the wall behind led directly into the moat. There was a small solar used as a withdrawing annexe next to the steward's large cold chamber of household office. Beyond that were more stairs and a winding escape to the entrance hall below; a dreary space without more than a screen between table and doors to the courtyard outside, no tapestries on the walls, and no blaze warming the hearth. February dismals both within and without. Emeline pushed open the main door, which was unlocked. The wind blasted in, flinging ice in her face and immediately extinguishing her candle. She staggered back, but when she eventually closed the door, it was behind her, and she stood under the stars and the great swirling white storm. It seemed preferable, somehow, to the cloying sickness, endless demands and criticism within. The wild boundless cold represented a freedom of sorts, however sparse. And it was freedom she craved, with escape from the dominion of others, and her own choices respected. So she stood where no one would have condoned, and no one would have understood, but told herself it was her right because, although forced into marriage, she was now a woman who might decide for herself. Her bedrobe had no hood, but the snow spangling her hair seemed refreshingly soft, like kisses after the frizzled knots caused by the fire.

She walked out into the freeze and looked up at the huge silhouette of the Keep before her, its soaring battlements black against the stars. Its windows were blind eyes, and its doorway yawned emptiness, dark as pitch. Emeline carried no torch or candle now, but she approached the ruined stone, curious as to what, if anything, might remain within. She could not expect to recover anything much of her own, but might find, perhaps, the little emerald brooch her mother had given her on her betrothal, the rubies once passed down from her grandmother, and even the tiny gold cross presented long ago by her father when she first knelt at Gloucester Cathedral, taking Holy Mass. Now all the jewellery she owned was her little plain wedding ring, which she did not even want, and had not yet earned.

There had been no exploration during the three full days since the fire, with the task of clearing of less importance than supplying medicines, restocking the larders and setting up a temporary kitchen. Many of the servants had no quarters left to them and had to cram in where they could, while others had been forced to return to their families in the village. The turmoil had increased over previous days, and not declined.

Yet Emeline had not expected the rubble immediately within the doorway, nor the clammy layers of drifting soot, the nauseating stench, nor the sudden holes and gaps which let in a dusting of snow. She stumbled over burned wood, the charred remains of the three great feasting tables and their fallen pewter, silver and candle wax. There would, she supposed, be a great deal worth rescuing in time, and once cleaned some would not even carry the memory. But the destruction was far greater than the salvage.

The grand staircase she had climbed on her wedding night seemed lost in shadow, but the wide steps were stone and so had survived untouched. It was as she reached the upper floor that wisps of broken plaster began to rustle and flutter against her. Emeline brushed the encroaching fingers from her face and hurried on into the darkness. Then she stopped. The patter of footsteps continued just one heartbeat after she had paused, as if her own following shadow needed that one breath longer to catch her up. She shook her head, disbelieving, but started to run.

The bedchamber, which had been her husband's, stood open, its door hanging on broken hinges, the once heavy oak now little more than a crust. The window shutters had burned too, so that the faint glitter of a starry night seeped in, flinging a sharply angled luminescence across the floor boards, showing where cindered pits opened black to the ground below. No glass remained and the falling snow bedazzled like a thousand dragonflies caught in moonshine.

It was the same chamber where she had slept those few hours three nights ago, for Emeline saw and recognised the bed. She remembered the coffers, the window seat, and the carved settle before the hearth. So she stood there looking around and discovered her trunk, a small affair standing by the doorway to the garderobe, and although the surface was blistered and buckled, it was not entirely destroyed. She bent and opened it. But within lay shifting ashes and charred ribbons. Lifting the lid sent the sooty remnants into sad little flurries, and when she closed it in a hurry, they settled again as though sighing. Although inexperienced in the ways of fire, she accepted the incineration of her possessions. What little might remain of her clothes would be in her mother's care in the guest wing. Nothing else was left.

The bed's tester hung in three long strips, each scorched and blackened, blowing like accusing pointers in the wind. She reached out and stroked the tattered damask bed curtains she had once admired. At the touch of her finger, the ashes flew. The bed smelled of ruin, of burned feathers, and of memories other than her own. Scraps of fur like tiny singed tassels were scattered across the surface, and amongst them Emeline sat and hugged her knees, scrunching her frozen toes into the last puff of blanket warmth. It represented her adulthood, which might once have been the greatest celebration and a grand romance with Peter as her gallant groom. So she had returned to face the horror, trying to conquer the terror of the fire which still lingered in her silent moments. And now the shelter, however slight, was some comfort after all. Thoughts buzzed in her head like wasps, recreating her father's orders, her husband's weary anger, her own frantic disappointment.

She lay back. There would be ash in her hair and dirt on her bedrobe but when she washed in the morning, she would wash away the past. If Nicholas lived, she could beg an annulment, pleading non consummation. If she dared admit it. But then as a marriageable maiden, once more she would belong to her father. As a widow, should her courage allow, she might make demands, lead her own life, and even claim back her marriage portion.

The whispers crowded closer. They curled with her, surrounding her, reminding her, tempting her. She closed her eyes and tried to close her ears. So it was in the drifting, uneasy dross that she finally slept, within the cremation of her wedding night, and covered over by its charred remains. No embers burned, and the snow hush still gusted through the little window frame, but she did not wake. She did not hear the man approach the bed, nor feel the touch of his hand as he moved her shoulder, peering into her face to see if she was living or dead. Yet, disturbed by dreams, she sensed some threat, somehow aware when the man slipped his palm past the opening of her bedrobe and across her body, feeling the warmth of her breasts, and the soft rise of her nipples through her shift. But she did not hear the sharp intake of his breath as he touched her, nor knew that he sat there a while, watching her in both suspicion and reluctant hunger before leaving as soundlessly as he had come.

She might have noticed his boot prints once the morning light climbed high as the windows, but other things happened first, and solitary footsteps in the ashes were quite obliterated by the time she woke.

The dawn crept up behind the battlements of the western wing, and Avice shouted, "Maman, are you there? Emma has gone. She was here when I went to sleep, but she's disappeared. Have you sent her back to her horrid husband already?"

The baroness was already awake in the adjacent chamber and sitting patiently while her dresser unpinned her headdress, rearranged her careful curls, and covered them anew with a bright starched net. Now she stood in a hurry and pins scattered. She marched next door and stood looking down at her youngest daughter. "Avice, make sense for once in your life. When did she leave?"

"If I knew that," Avice pointed out, "I wouldn't have called you. I'd be keeping quiet to hide whatever she's secretly up to."

Her mother sighed. "If you ever grow up to become as difficult as your sister, Avice, I shall give up entirely and join a nunnery. If Emma had the slightest feeling of filial respect and social propriety, she would be thrilled with the marriage we've arranged for her. The girl is quite unnatural. When your turn comes, Avice –"

"I shall be only too delighted to get a rich husband," Avice insisted. "And I don't really see anything wrong with Nicholas. He might be nice enough once you get accustomed to him. He'd even be quite pretty if he didn't have that mark on his face. But Emma wanted Peter. And Peter wasn't very polite about his brother, you know. It was Papa's fault for arranging that marriage first. And how did Nicholas get like that anyway? Is it a battle scar?"

The baroness sat. "I have no idea how Nicholas was wounded, since the family will not speak of it. But he's far too young to have been at Tewkesbury or Barnet, and I believe he never joined the Scottish skirmishes. Now, it is Emma I'm more interested in. Has she gone to Nicholas, do you think?"

"In the middle of the night?" Avice shrugged. "I doubt it, though she said he kissed her before the fire. But she hates him and I don't think a bit of kissing would make her change her mind."

"Just kissing?" inquired her mother, raising a sceptical eyebrow.

"Kissing. Doing it," said Avice, "and now I think she's run away."

"Oh dear." The baroness went slightly pink and her shoulders slumped. "It is possible of course. Poor Emma. She was so upset at the thought of marrying Nicholas and then she was most put out yesterday when dear Papa ordered her to come back home with us. Though really, it is most contrary. If she doesn't want the man, then she should be happy to stay with her own family."

"Papa will be furious."

"Stop smirking, Avice," accused her mother. "I have absolutely no idea how I will tell him. He's not had an easy time lately, what with all this winter travelling and your sister's behaviour, and the earl's stubborn demands over Emma's dowry." Her voice sank lower. "You know, my dear, his lordship the earl is not at all a man of high moral standards, and I believe he drinks heavily and is rarely sober. Your Papa despises him."

"Perhaps the fat old pig fell on the candles and started the fire. Perhaps he's debauched!"

"I have no idea, and you shouldn't think such things." The baroness stood, took a very deep breath, and prepared to leave. "You had better get up now, Avice, since goodness knows what will happen next. Your Papa will certainly want to question you. I do wish I could avoid telling him."

"So you're more frightened of telling Papa than you are about what could have happened to Emma," noticed Avice. "But she might have jumped in the moat."

"Highly unlikely. She would never be so obliging," sniffed the baroness.

"Well, I hope not," nodded Avice, "since she's wearing my very best shift."

The baroness quietly went to her husband's bedchamber and admitted the truth. The baron, cold with anger, alerted the steward, who informed the earl, who told his son.

The day was rising in the cloud sullen sky, lighting the first reflected dazzle over the night's snow cover. The earl hauled himself from his bed, thumped into his son's sickroom and announced, "The chit's run away from you, Nick m'boy. Disappeared in the small hours. Forfeited her dowry."

Nicholas blinked one eye and smiled. "First good news I've had for some time," he murmured. "Perhaps she's hoping for an annulment. With luck she's run off with that damned Leicester doctor who wants to starve me and suffocate me with lard."

The west and east wings, being the only parts of the castle buildings unaffected by fire, were now overcrowded and offered little or no place to hide, but both were immediately searched from battlements to cellars and at considerable length. But there were no signs of unaccounted females in any place.

Orders were then issued to search the castle grounds from the guards' entrance, the stables, the kitchen gardens and on through the outlying sheds rumbling with cattle and goats. The scullions were sent to tramp along the banks of the moat both within and without the great walls, and the dairy maids, laundry maids and brewsters were sent to check the far block of privies by the outer boundary. The steward questioned the night guard, who swore that no one had passed through the main gates since the previous afternoon, nor had a single soul crossed the drawbridge. Anyone wishing to leave the castle unseen would have had no choice but to swim the moat. The steward had turned quite white at this, and quickly returned to report to the earl. His lordship grunted and asked about footsteps in the snow, and the steward regretfully announced that since it had snowed heavily for some hours, all previous footsteps had been obliterated and buried, leaving nothing to show the passing of a young lady, and no other signs except the little black star prints marking morning's first hungry ravens and the tiny paws of the castle's population of busy mice. Now, of course, the snow was churned by the feet of every single Chatwyn servant, and no secrets remained in view.

So finally they went to the ruined Keep, which was the only place still unexamined, and they crept unwillingly through the blackened smoke filled chambers and the cold dark corridors, being the very last place they expected to find her.

CHAPTER SIX

"Must care for you after all," grumbled the earl. "The brainless wench slept the night in your old bed. Wrapped in dirt and ash when they found her, looking more like a spit boy who'd fallen in the grate. Liverich came to tell me - as if I'd be pleased to know."

"You should be," announced his son. "It's surely preferable than discovering her corpse down the well. The water's not particularly clean as it is. But it appears you've wed me to a madwoman, my lord."

"Humph," sniffed his lordship. "Peter liked her well enough."

"That's part of the trouble," said Nicholas. "And precisely why I didn't want her in the first place, as you damn well know. So if you're thinking the girl crawled into my old bed for sentimental comfort or romantic memories, then you're much mistaken."

The earl shook his head and trundled over to the window seat. "You mentioned an annulment earlier. Don't tell me you were too pissed that night?"

"I have no intention of telling you anything at all, sir," his only remaining son informed him. "This is my business alone, and will remain so. And if the doctor permits it, I suppose I should now go and visit my errant but rediscovered wife."

"Don't recommend it, m'boy," said the earl. "Probably has a damned parcel of weeping women with her, all praying and complaining no doubt. And you've no legs left worth speaking of. You'll not be allowed out of bed for another month."

Dragged from his pallet, the apothecary, aghast, quickly agreed. "My lord, I beg you, my lord, your life could still be in danger. It has been just over three days, and your health remains at risk. You should not leave your bed except for the commode, and even that as little as can be arranged. If you will allow, I shall call for another bowl of goose grease, and will attend to your wounds again shortly. In the meantime, good white bread has been soaking overnight in goat's milk ready for the morning's repast - and I believe small ale can be permitted a little later -"

"That settled it," said Nicholas. "More than three days fastened to this hideous lumpy mattress have made me more lame than the damned fire has, and all I can smell is lavender and cattle shit. I'm not sure which is worse. So I'm going to visit my wife."

The earl narrowed his eyes. "This is wilful stupidity, and you know it, Nicholas. I doubt you even remember the girl's name. If you were a little younger –"

"You would beat me senseless as so often before, dear Papa, or when too pissed to hold the belt yourself, have someone else do it for you." Nicholas also narrowed his eyes, wedging himself up painfully against the bolster at his back. "But as you have so sensibly noticed, I am now a little too old for that, and you are a little too large in the paunch. I advise caution, my lord. And patience. For I now intend doing exactly as I wish."

Baron Wrotham regarded his daughter with an expression closely resembling that with which the earl regarded his son. Emeline sat hunch shouldered as her father stood over her. The baron said, "After Mass, and after thanking the good Lord and all the saints for your preservation during such worthless female hystericals, you will then beg my pardon, Emeline. I shall be waiting for you in my chambers."

Emeline nodded, keeping her eyes carefully on her lap. She had not yet been given the opportunity to dress, or even wash, and felt increasingly embarrassed. She mumbled, "Yes indeed, Papa. I am quite happy to beg your pardon now. For I am sincerely sorry, truly I am. I had a nightmare. I never meant to – inconvenience you, my lord."

"Your very existence inconveniences me, Emeline," said her father. "Even when contrite, you manage disobedience. But you will not thwart me, madam, and the longer you attempt wilful arrogance, the longer I shall call on the good Lord to punish you in an appropriate manner. So now, without argument, you will prepare yourself for Mass in the makeshift chapel below. You will cleanse yourself, clothe yourself modestly in one of your old gowns, and present yourself without delay at the Lord's altar. Our own family priest awaits you and Father Godwin is ready to hear your confession and grant absolution. After this, and not before, you will make your apologies to me as I have intrusted you. Following that, you will begin to prepare yourself for your return to Gloucestershire in two days' time."

"Two days? Not tomorrow?" It was a relief, and would allow a little more time for discovering further excuses.

"You are a fool, Emeline, as I have always known," her father informed her. "Tomorrow is a Sunday. I have never travelled on the Sabbath, and never shall, as you are certainly aware."

She hung her head. "I had forgotten which day it was - so much has happened."

It was as she pushed back the chair and stood, keeping the edges of her bedrobe meekly together and straightening her knees to disguise the trembling, that her very new husband walked in entirely unannounced. Nicholas limped heavily, and leaned on the shoulder of his page. His other arm was in a sling, his hands were thickly bandaged, and his face shone with both exertion and lard. His great sorrel bedrobe swept the floorboards as he struggled in, nodded to the baron, and collapsed on the high backed chair which his wife had just vacated. He stretched the more seriously injured of his legs out before him and, closing his eyes momentarily, said, voice rather faint, "Apologies for the improprieties, but perhaps I should not have left my bed after all." He then opened his eyes again, and smiled at Emeline who hovered before him. "You look delightful, my lady," he croaked. "Ashes and sackcloth suit you."

The baron interrupted. "My lord, I am relieved to see you so much recovered. Although from the doctor's reports, I feel sure you should still be abed for many days to come. I trust your good father has informed you that, under these unfortunate circumstances, we feel it best to take Emeline home with us for some months while you remain under doctor's orders. We shall leave this coming Monday, sir."

Nicholas looked up at his wife. "So eager to be gone, my dear?"

She shook her head and blushed, one eye to her father's frown. "It is not - nor my own -"

And Nicholas said, "Perhaps you intend applying for an annulment?" and then looked up at the page boy now standing intent beside the chair. "Get wine," he ordered him. "The cellars weren't all destroyed, I presume? Bring the best of whatever remains." He turned again to Emeline. "Well, madam? I know your feelings, and I think you know mine."

The baron coughed. "I do not consider this to be an appropriate time, sir, but am I to understand -?" and was interrupted yet again. The door was pushed wide as the pageboy hurried out, and the baroness and Avice promptly hurried in with the slightly tumbled appearance of those who might possibly have been listening outside the door. Emeline sighed and the baron scowled.

"Emma dear, and my dear Nicholas," said the baroness, recovering her dignity, "how delightful to see you well enough to leave your sickbed, though I hardly think -"

And Avice said, "Papa says Emma has to come home with us but she says she doesn't want to."

At which Nicholas raised one eyebrow, sat a little straighter and said, "How alarming."

"Emeline's wishes have nothing to do with this," said the baron with deliberation. "It has been decided between myself and his lordship, your esteemed father."

So Nicholas said at once, "On the contrary, my lord. My esteemed father's wishes are of no consequence whatsoever."

"Oh dear, it would be for the best, sir," sighed the baroness. "With the Keep and all the principal chambers destroyed and yourself so shockingly injured, I cannot feel that Emma should remain, and it having been only four days since the wedding -"

At which point Emeline took a step forwards, cleared her throat, blushed again, and announced, "I cannot go home, Maman. I have decided - and would prefer - and the fact is," with one wild look around at the hedge of impatient irritation surrounding her, continued, "I am - I believe I am - with child."

The little fire sizzled on the hearth as the wind blustered outside the window and was funnelled down the chimney. Smoke billowed and the small arid chamber became suddenly fogged and acrid. There was, for a moment, total silence until Avice began to cough and squinted, saying, "Gracious. Is that how babies happen?"

Her Maman said quickly, "Emma my dear, after just four days? I hardly think - nor would anyone - and this does not seem the moment for such delicate -"

Nicholas was watching his young wife in considerable amusement. "My apologies, but I believe I should like a quiet word with my wife in private. If everyone would be so good?" And waited as the baroness hesitated, then clutched her younger daughter's wrist, and left with one last desperate look over her shoulder.

The baron stood his ground. "My daughter is an innocent, sir, and has passed a night of disturbance and discomfort. Before that, there was the fire - the injuries - I fear she is unwell. I would prefer to speak to her myself first, also in private. I trust you do not object?"

Emeline stared from one to the other. Her father stood impregnable as she had always seen him. Nicholas sprawled, slack in the chair to which he clung. Bandaged, scarred and in pain, he could neither stand, nor should have left his bed. She had no idea why he had, since he showed little interest in where she had gone or why. But when he spoke, although his voice was weak, he said, "But I do object, my lord. It appears I have something of an intimate nature to discuss with my wife."

"It would seem," Baron Wrotham stared down at the semi prone invalid before him, "that under these delicate and unexpected circumstances, my daughter should speak first with her mother. My family priest is waiting for her downstairs, but that can wait if necessary. After she has spoken with her mother and then with myself, I shall, if you wish it, sir, send her to your chamber. So with your permission, I will now take her to my baroness."

The earl's son smiled broadly and slumped a little further within the chair. "No, I believe not, my lord," he said with genial deliberation. "You do not have my permission. I claim my wife's patience, and will detain her for only a short time before releasing her into the company of her mother."

As her father still made no noticeable effort to remove himself, Emeline clasped her hands very tightly around her soot stained bedrobe, stared at her bare toes, shook her tousled head, and said very softly, "Papa, I really have to speak with Nicholas."

It was after the baron, silent with unspoken fury, had marched from the chamber that Emeline turned to her husband. But he raised one finger. "Wine first," he said, as the page trotted in with a tray holding the brimming jug and several cups. "Some form of lubrication is always helpful in such situations." The page poured the wine, and was immediately dismissed. Emeline passed one cup and clutched the other. With both hands bandaged into paws, Nicholas clasped the cup with difficulty and drank deeply, watching her over the brim as he drained it. "After three days of sour milk slops," he said, "I escaped my bed for this more than anything else. But you've supplied a far greater diversion than I expected, madam."

"As far as I can see," said Emeline, slowly sipping her Burgundy, "you don't care about me one way or the other. You just wanted to annoy your father and mine."

He grinned. "Isn't that your own motive? I'm flattered to see you prefer my company to your father's, but I'm not so simple as to imagine you know yourself with child just three and a half days after a brief wedding night of complete abstention. I learned to tell a goose from a capon a good many years ago, my lady. And I might otherwise ask whose child you think you're carrying, but my dear brother died some six months gone, and you're far too trim for a woman more than six months pregnant. Therefore, as far as I'm concerned you're welcome to escape your father with whatever lies appeal to you, and find yourself a corner somewhere to sleep within this God forsaken ruin, make yourself at home and do whatever you wish. Meanwhile I shall patiently await the miraculous appearance of my heir."

Emeline hiccupped. "But surely, even just sharing a bed - I could be -"

"You could not," said Nicholas.

"And three days ought to be enough -"

"It isn't," her husband informed her. "Have you never discussed such matters with your mother?"

"Gracious no," whispered his wife. "Papa is very strict, you know, and if it isn't in the Bible, then it doesn't get discussed."

Nicholas was still smiling. "I wouldn't be surprised if it is in the Bible in some form or other. And even Peter explained nothing to you?"

Emeline glared at him. "Peter? Of course not. He would never have spoken of such intimate matters, and nor would I ever have permitted such a conversation. And you're rude and stupid and spiteful to infer such things and you seem to have a problem with envy, which I can understand, since Peter was so obviously more – but it's not dignified – or proper."

"Envy?" Nicholas attempted to wedge himself upwards with his elbows to the chair arms, but winced and collapsed back again. "Envious of Peter?" he demanded, his voice fading in spite of indignation. "Why, in all that's holy, should I ever have been jealous of Peter?"

"Every possible reason I can think of," said Emeline through her teeth. "And I'm just very glad if I'm not having your child. And what have geese and capons got to do with anything anyway, or are you just bad tempered because you're hungry?"

Nicholas stared at his wife. "No madam, I was referring to neither poultry nor dinner, and it's probably better under the circumstances if I don't explain what I was referring to." He winced again, and quickly nursed the hand he had been clenching. "But bad tempered I probably am," he continued, his voice now growing louder. "With some possible excuse, if you care to remember. Having been ordered to marry my brother's mistress, I'm then forced to pass a chilly wedding night until significantly warmed by my home exploding in flames. Upon which I rescue my sot of a father, who no doubt started the fire in the first place, am roasted alive and consequently confined to bed where a parcel of inferior and idiotic medicks argue over how little to feed me and how much to bleed me while stuffing every crevice of my body with foul smelling fats. I am obliged to sleep in some damned abandoned guest chamber without even a semblance of comfort, and am then threatened with an agonising death should I so much as attempt to leave that bed for the privy. Both my ignoble parent and my pugnacious father-in-law promptly treat me as a witless infant just because I cannot stand, and I am finally informed that my bride has managed to conceive a child without –" and Nicholas took a very deep breath and stopped abruptly.

Emeline was no longer listening. There was only one sentence which had penetrated her consciousness, and she stepped forwards, glared down at the man she had married, and flung the last dregs of her wine in his face. "How dare you!" she demanded, turned and grabbed the wine jug.

Nicholas laughed, which was not at all what she had expected, and did not placate her in the least. "No, no," he yelled, raising his arm as best he could. "A dreadful waste." A thin crimson trickle had merged with the goose grease down his face and he managed to wipe it away with the bandaged back of his hand. "Have pity. Our supplies are dangerously low," he said, "since so many butts were burned and I doubt there's much decent Burgundy left. This is at least drinkable. Find something else to throw at me."

She replaced the wine jug on the table, turned her back and marched to the little window seat where she sat heavily and finally said, "I wasn't. You have to know that."

"Peter's mistress?" He grinned. "Well, my dear brother was an inveterate liar, but I presume some of the things he claimed must have been true."

"He would never - ever - have said that. It is you who are lying." It helped that he clearly could not rise, stride over, nor strike her. She said, "Peter was good, and noble, and honest, and I do not at all believe him capable of inventing vulgar tales."

"I could tell you," Nicholas remained cheerful, "just how he described you - and vulgar would come nowhere near it, my dear. What of course he could never have suspected, was that one day I'd have an excellent opportunity of checking the truth of his descriptions for myself."

She leaned her cheek against the chill of the frosted window pane, for her face was burning. She whispered, "You're vile and I wish I'd never married you. And with Peter not a year in his grave - and you say such wretched things about him. And let me tell you, he told me all about you too - and I'm quite sure it was all true but none of it was vulgar because Peter was far too upright to speak vulgarities. And," she sniffed with a very small additional hiccup, "I loved him."

"Oh good Lord," sighed Nicholas. "Poor muddle headed little mouse. What you have no way of knowing is that you've had a fair escape. Not by marrying me of course, since I'm probably no better. But presumably you'd been dreaming those romantic tales of courtly love and King Arthur and Sir Gawain, and imagined Peter as another Lancelot as soon as my brother was introduced to you. Once wed, you'd have had a nasty shock. And remember this, I was also ordered into a marriage I had no taste for. I imagined - having believed - well, now I'm none too sure. But we'll somehow have to make the best of it and in the meantime you can sleep in peace. I'm about as incapacitated as a drowned worm and there'll be no pregnancies just yet, I assure you. I suppose if you say your dalliance with Peter was innocent, I'm prepared to take your word for it. And I can just imagine what delightful stories he told you about me. Some of them may even be true."

She hiccupped again. "I'm not a mouse," she said after a long pause.

"More like a rat at the moment," her husband observed. "If you've a predilection for sleeping in ashes and cinders in the future, madam, you can damn well sleep alone."

"I intend to anyway," Emeline said, standing abruptly. "I shall now inform my father that I choose to return home to Gloucestershire with him after all."

"No, you won't," grinned Nicholas. "I think I'll exercise my superior claims and keep you here. I need some sort of diversion while I'm chained to my bed. You'll do just fine."

CHAPTER SEVEN

"I am not a - commodity," she said with what dignity she could muster. "You cannot order me here while my father orders me elsewhere and your father wants me somewhere else entirely as if I can be pushed around like a gardener's barrow. I can make my own choices, and I may - or may not - decide to tell you once I've made up my mind. In the meantime, you can just go away. I think you're horrid."

Nicholas had not yet stopped grinning. "I can't go away. I can't walk without help. Besides, it seems a touch brutal to dismiss me since this is, after all, my home."

"Well, I shall go away," said Emeline. "And you can just carry on sitting here until someone comes in and falls over you."

He laughed. "Since you're so keen to hurry off, I presume you're eager to spend more time with your benevolent Papa before he leaves. He is leaving soon, I hope? Good. Unfortunately I can't banish my own since he still owns the place, but I can revert to ignoring him whenever possible."

"So it was him you were escaping that time you climbed out of the window in your best frilly pink skirts?" Emeline inquired with hauteur. "Or were you escaping me? Your prospective bride? Completely avoided and ignored, even after being dragged miles and miles in filthy weather just to be introduced to you?"

"Something like that." Nicholas shifted, wincing as he managed to straighten both legs. "As it happens my personal collection of gowns is rather a small one, but I needed a quick get away. Escaping you, I suppose. You see, I'd already had a full description from Peter."

Emeline flopped back down on the window seat. "Stop talking about Peter like that," she mumbled. "It's upsetting. I loved him very much and I still do and I've dreamed about him every night for a year and more and he was the kindest, most elegant and courteous man I've ever met. And I was so proud - so happy to think I'd be his wife."

"Should a dutiful wife inform her husband that she's still in love with his brother?" Nicholas was still grinning.

"I'm no dutiful wife," Emeline informed him without compunction. "You've never given me a chance to behave like one, and besides, if it hadn't been for that dreadful tragedy, it's Peter I would have married. It was wicked murder, I'm sure it was. I cried every day and every night for weeks. Then Papa said I had to marry you instead and that made it even worse. Even you ought to understand how awful that felt."

"Having to marry me? Simply frightful. I sympathise." He did not look too sympathetic. "But there's something you don't understand, my dear. We're a reprehensible family and there's not one of us worth marrying. Living alone up here without much access to feminine company except for a few servants and the village girls, has made us neither courtly nor virtuous. My father's a drunken bully, and anyway he's usually away at court. Peter and I ran wild most of our lives. My mother died when I was six, and in spite of regular beatings, any education in manners stopped then and there."

"But Peter was –"

"A saint. Somehow I must have missed that side of him."

The dream softened expression returned. "As a brother, no doubt you wouldn't have seen him in the same way. But I knew him better." Her eyes quickly moistened, catching the candle light. "When I met him the very first time, he knelt at my feet and took my hand, and explained – well, I suppose you will laugh at me. But I'd been a little frightened, you see, when Papa said my marriage was arranged. I'd lived a very quiet life because Papa is so strict."

Nicholas interrupted her. "The dastardly and ignominious Chatwyns with a strictly Christian Wrotham maiden? A mismatch from the start, my dear."

"It wouldn't have been, not with Peter." Emeline sniffed and began to search for her kerchief, which wasn't there. "No man had even touched my hand before – not like that. But Peter's touch was so delicate – so courteous. He told all about how he had asked for me specially, begged for me in fact, because he'd seen me once when he'd come hunting in Gloucestershire, and fallen in love from afar. So he begged your Papa to approve the match. And of course the earl had to be persuaded because he's an earl and we are inferiors, but Peter managed to talk him around because he thought

I was beautiful and was –," she paused. "There's no need to snigger. I know I'm not really beautiful."

Nicholas said, "Your father approached my father, not the other way around. Peter had never seen you in his life before the marriage arrangements were already begun. But he was pleased enough and it had nothing to do with beauty, I assure you. You're an heiress, my dear."

Emeline took a deep breath. "You are utterly and completely vile," she informed her husband. "And I loathe you."

"Poor benighted little mouse." Nicholas shook his head. "I suppose I shouldn't squash your romantic delusions, but if you're going to have anything to do with my family, you might as well face the truth. Your father wanted the match because he's ambitious. Has wealth and property but never got anywhere in politics, so wanted to affiliate with someone previously on the Royal Council and powerful in parliament. Simple as that. There was a friendship between your great grandfather and mine, which was the polite excuse used to initiate talks. But basically my father agreed because you'll be rich as Croesus one day. Not a hard sum. Even with your family as religiously devoted as a cloister of monks and mine as shockingly irreligious as a parcel of barbarian heathens, an alliance was expected to benefit both parties. Your poor little fluttering heart was certainly not taken into consideration, and Peter, being the heir, wanted your money. You might not want me, madam, and who's to blame you. But Peter – well, Peter – oh, never mind about Peter. I daresay one shouldn't speak ill of the dead."

Emeline sat through this speech with growing hauteur, waited a moment, pursed her lips, clasped her hands a little tighter, glared and said, "Did you kill him then?"

Nicholas stared back at her in utter silence. His animation and humour blinked out and a furious and growing anger flashed in his bright blue eyes. Then it gradually faded. His face, tired and still inflamed with the welts and blisters from the fire, seemed suddenly sad. "I won't dignify that question with an answer," he said quietly. "Especially coming from my own wife. If you want an annulment, my lady, you can explain the situation to your mother, and no doubt something can be arranged. In the meantime, I think I should prefer to be alone. If you see any of the servants, perhaps you'll be good enough to tell someone I need help returning to my bed. Now, I am sure your mother is waiting for you."

Emeline stood, blushed violently, and ran quickly from the room.

She did not go to her mother's chamber, nor search for her father or sister. She found a pageboy and gave orders for him to help Nicholas back to his quarters. Then she hurried outside.

It had stopped snowing some hours previously but there were places, banking up against the huge stone walls, where the white freeze lay unmarked and pure and beautiful. The air was spitefully fresh and the sky was low with threatened storm, but the stench of burning had been washed away and the world felt clean. Emeline would have wandered further, but she was cold and her feet were soon numb on the ice.

Beside the ruined Keep some of the rubble from within had been piled without in an ash grimed heap of stone, charred wood and tumbles of ruined utensils. Beside this, dark with interesting shadows, a narrow space wound between the sooty wall and the tossed rejections. Here Emeline squeezed herself, with no particular desire except seclusion. She did not wish to speak to those who would doubtless be looking for her, to be scalded or to be judged, yet had no place of her own for escape, neither bed nor chamber. So she hid in the dark and closed her eyes. She still wore only her spoiled bedrobe and her sister's shift and the cinders in her hair remained, but it was the cold that bothered her at last. She was crawling out from the little crevice when she heard voices and the passing of horses. Being in no way presentable, she crept back and stayed where she was. Through a crack in the rubble she saw only one strip of daylight, but nothing interrupted her hearing.

The voices were young. A girl said, "Look, it's only the central Keep, Adrian. So the fire didn't spread. But what of Nicholas?"

A male voice answered her. "Isn't that what we're here to find out?"

Hooves on the cobbles, a small retinue with the jingle of harness and the snorting of horses. Over the busy clatter, the girl answered, "Badly injured, the messenger said. If he succumbs - and after dearest Peter - what then?"

"Not dead yet, they say," sighed the man. "There's no need to suppose it. Nicholas is hardly so fragile to expire at a whiff of smoke."

"Nicholas fragile? Oh, hardly." The girl sniffed. "We all know Nicholas. Irresponsible. Feckless. But robust enough I suppose. Strong enough to run away."

"Run? He didn't run fast enough for once, if he's as injured as they say."

The horses' hooves were louder as they passed Emeline's hiding place. She glimpsed the flutter of tabards, the swing of a fur trimmed sleeve, the kick of spurs and a cluster of sleek bay flanks as the retinue rode on towards the stable block. Only faint voices echoed back. "And will the new bride be sad, do you think? Too pretty to be a widow so soon."

Then the man, "Married to that drunken wretch? She'd be better off widowed. First almost affianced to the other bastard, and now wed to this one. Each worse than the other, each as bad as their brute of a father."

The girl's last words, "Hush, someone will hear you, brother. And you must never ever say such things about Peter, especially now he's - gone. You know how I - liked him. And Nick is a coward, but not a brute. Just a fool under all the teasing and the mockery."

Then barely heard, the man's voice, "We are here, are we not? And have ridden all the way back here in spite of natural exhaustion? That, my dear, is manners. I will always behave as I should. But I do not have to love my cousins."

Distance claimed the voices beneath the retinue's calls for the ostlers. So Emeline sat very small and cried soundlessly into the ashes.

It was a long time later when she finally reappeared and that was because she was hungry, of which mundane realisation she was heartily ashamed. She had considered hurling herself into the moat but decided it was far too cold and it would be unfair to ruin her sister's best shift. She decided she would find something to eat first and then change into the oldest and most threadbare gown remaining to her before running away as best she could. How to achieve all this without being seen would be the greatest challenge, but the drawbridge was down, and the guards were certainly inside by the fire, probably with their noses in cups of ale. Once she approached the world beyond the castle, surely no one would see or stop her. She had it planned. It didn't go to plan.

The make shift kitchens had been set up at the back annexe to the western wing, where a small additional bake oven had been enlarged and the old stone chamber transformed with a central fire and long tables. Emma found it quickly since the smoke, there being no existing flue nor chimney, and the busy file of kitchen boys, made its position clear. But as she entered, two small scullions regarded her with deep suspicion. One growled, "Might be a made up kitchen, nor has the proper space nor pots nor hearth, but there's no dirty beggars allowed in here and that's a fact. Off with you."

Since the boy came only to her shoulder, Emeline stared back with dignity. "I am the Lady Emeline," she said, "and therefore your mistress, so watch your manners. I am looking - that is, I missed dinner. At least I think I must have. Is it over?"

"An age past," scowled the boy. "And you don't look like no lady to me. Them guards ought to keep the village wenches out 'stead of snoring in the warm all day. You'll get no crusts here, lest you come abegging for left overs after supper wiv the others. Now off wiv you."

Emeline could smell roast meat now going cold on the great spread platters, waiting to be served for supper that evening. It was almost a full day she had not eaten but she felt too weak to argue, and knew she looked exactly like the beggarly slattern the boys had taken her for. Her only consolation was in the hope that her parents, the earl and her husband were all worried sick about her second disappearance.

The kitchen had been warm. The blast of snow born wind outside almost made her change her mind but she wrapped her arms around herself and ran fast for the arched gateway, the guards' house and the great planked drawbridge.

A heavily muscled arm in chainmail stopped her half way across, and an enormous clammy hand grasped her arm, fingertips pinching hard. "Hey, mistress. Wot's you doing then, and where's you come from? Running away like a thief, and covered in soot. Bin crawling through them burned rooms, I expect, seeing just wot you could nick."

"Certainly not. I am –" and gave up. She knew quite well her identity would not be believed. "Oh dear," she said. "Look, I've nothing stolen on me. You can see I'm not carrying anything. Just let me go."

"Gawd knows wot you might have up your shift, missus," decided the guard.

Others came out from the shadows, interested in the capture. One said, "Let's 'ave a look then, girl. Lift them skirts and show us wot you got."

The first man shook his head. "Molesting some village trollop? The young lord would have your head on a spike, Noggins. Leave well alone."

"Please let me go," whispered Emeline.

"Not on your life," decided the guard. "You comes along wiv me, girl, and we'll see wot the earl thinks."

"You'll not be popular wiv his lordship interrupting him this hour o' the day," remarked another. "Still farting his midday bellyful, he is for sure, resting in his bed."

"I'll take her to the young lord instead then," decided the first guard.

"Won't be interested in wenches neither," said the second man. "Just wed, and part burned alive he is, poor bugger."

Emeline was struggling, but now surrounded by six armed guards, two of whom had a good hold on her, she pleaded, "Then please let me go, for I've done nothing, and I promise not to come back."

"Can't," insisted the first guard. "Mayhaps you was lighting fires. Mayhaps you lit that first one. Mayhaps you've silver up your shift. I ain't takin' no risks." And he began to march her back over the drawbridge towards the castle's western wing.

It started snowing again.

There were four people in Nicholas's chamber. They all looked up in considerable surprise as Emeline entered, a guard either side. Nicholas was sitting propped up in bed, a swathe of pillows behind him. Two chairs had been drawn to the bedside, and a girl wrapped in a velvet pelisse sat in one. The other was empty but a young man stood by the hearth, his elbow to the lintel and his foot to the grate. A page knelt at his feet, building up the fire, and two panting hounds lay on the turkey rug, basking in the flames' reflections.

"Caught running," explained the principal guard in a faintly apologetic voice. "Not sure wot to do wiv her, my lord, being as how there's still stuff to steal in the Keep, and damage to be done. But we didn't want to examine the wench wivout your permission, sir. Though looks mighty suspicious, she do, in all that mess and dirt, and no shoes and no hat."

Emeline stood very still and looked at no one. She stared down at her toes, and noticed how they had painted little black patterns across the polished floorboards. She could not hug her arms around herself since they were both clasped very tightly by the men who had brought her, and she knew that her now filthy bedrobe had fallen a little open, revealing an equally filthy shift and the vague outline of her body through the fine linen. Her hair, thick with dust and other filth, hung improperly loose and bedraggled across her shoulders and down her back, and she was sure her face was besmirched, but she could not free a hand to wipe across her cheeks. Since she had previously been crying, she also supposed that the dirt on her face would be striped into sooty streaks, and she could even taste ashes on her tongue. She did not blush, for the horrible shame she felt had turned her to ice, and beneath the filth she was as white as the snow now falling steadily outside. She refused to raise her eyes.

The guards pushed her forwards a little, presenting her shame to their lord.

"A beggar, a thief and a maker of fires, if you asks me, my lord," continued the guard. "I've never seen a trollop so deep in sin."

"She does look rather dishevelled," agreed Nicholas with a delighted smile. "But you can leave her with me, thank you Rumbiss." He turned to his guests. "So, my dear cousins. Let me introduce you to my wife."

CHAPTER EIGHT

"I am laughed at and mocked by Nicholas," Emeline said, low voiced. "who has no consideration for my feelings whatsoever or even for my pride, which you'd think would reflect on his own. I'm stared at by his two cousins as if I'm an interesting but rather unattractive beetle for whom they feel some pity. Papa simply shouts at me, Avice just giggles, and the castle servants grab at me, thinking me a thief. So, Maman, what will you do?"

"Bundle you into the bath tub as quickly as possible," said her mother, hands on hips. "Honestly Emma, why do you insist on being so bothersome? Your Papa is furious, and he has every right to be. He believes you are bringing shame on us all."

Emeline sniffed, and said, "I don't care, Maman. I don't care what all these horrid people think. The earl is a beast and his son is just a liar - and a horrid mean pig."

"I have ordered the tub set up in here in front of the fire," said her mother firmly, "and old Martha will help you wash your hair. I shall see to it that you have some of your old clothes to dress in afterwards, which is a shame, but all the precious new gowns and shifts were burned. All that remains are your old things left in my own trunks. You may have to borrow something of your sister's, and then I shall escort you to your husband's chamber. You will apologise to him for your recent absurd behaviour, and whatever he orders you to do after that, you will obey."

"He doesn't want me," said Emeline, going pink. "Except to laugh at."

"Consider yourself exceedingly lucky that he only laughs instead of beating you raw, my girl." The baroness remained standing, looking down on her daughter's soot blackened curls. "The poor man must wonder what sort of imbecile he has wed. At least he did see you beautifully gowned at the chapel."

"And I don't want him," Emeline mumbled. "So I shall come home with you and Avice on Monday, and just do my best to avoid Papa."

"Too late," announced the baroness. "You husband insists you remain at the castle. So he does want you. What he wants you *for* is another matter of course."

They were interrupted by the troop of scullions who set up the linen lined barrel beside the hearth, and the stable boys carrying buckets of steaming water. So the bath was filled and the steam rose to the ceiling beams where it formed small drops of watery condensation along the painted rafters, and turned the entire chamber into a moist and clammy dungeon of mesmerising mist. Emeline sat, refused to watch and stared out of the window, even though the small panes were immediately fogged and completely opaque. The baroness bustled off to arrange the appeasement of her own husband and new clothes for her daughter, while the family's ancient nurse loomed over the proceedings, sponge and soap in hand. There was at least the consolation of good Spanish soap perfumed with flowers and herbs, water which was truly hot and strewn with dried lavender and whole cloves of spice, and Nurse Martha held a real sea sponge and not simply a wet drab of cloth. This was a castle of lavishly wasted luxury, clearly quite opposed to the abstemious strictures of the Baron Wrotham's household.

"Well now, my sweetest mammet," Martha held out both arms, "I will scrub you soft and pink all over and dust you with pounded cinnamon. Come to me, my duckling and I will sing as I scour."

The shift and bedrobe were discarded and Emeline hopped into the scalding water, sank deep, and allowed the tingle to release all the chill and the tension from her body. The warmth absorbed her, and she closed her eyes. Her nurse wielded the huge scrunched sponge, but Emeline kept her eyes shut. This heat, unlike that which had ripped the flesh from her cheekbones and chin, and which had turned the ends of her hair into tight singed tousles, was soothing and lapped her in comfort. Steamy ripples pressed against her breasts, turning her nipples soft. She sighed in pleasure.

It was dark outside now, and the shutters had been lifted into place. The chamber was enclosed by steam, and the candles and wax tapers hissed and spat, objecting to the condensation. The room was well lit, another luxury. The cost of upkeep must be enormous. Emeline decided Nicholas might well need her money in time. If she stayed.

She had missed supper, being in no fit state to present herself at the dining table and knowing that apart from the earl himself, there would be the guests. Two cousins, who, although they had been present at the wedding, remained strangers. Peter had spoken of both in the past, kindly of the girl, less so of the man. The next day Emeline expected to face them again, but for tonight she hoped to be left in peace. Apart, perhaps, from apologising to her husband though only if she was forced to it. He would be dining in his chamber, again forbidden by the doctors to leave his bed.

So it was a great surprise, though not a pleasant one, when Emeline heard a voice above the splashing of her bath water, and snapped her eyes open in a hurry.

Nicholas said, "Very pretty, my lady," and she blushed, quickly submerging herself up to her neck. Nurse Martha stopped mid scrub, sponge and dripping arm raised, and hurriedly curtsied.

He was leaning against the door jam, supported on the other side by a sturdy wooden crutch. His pageboy hovered behind him, but Nicholas grinned, and with a word over his shoulder sent the boy away. Then he staggered in, discovered the chair, sat as though he might never again be able to rise, and stretched both one leg and the crutch out before him with a sigh.

Martha said, "My lord, shall I continue, my lord, or shall I leave you with my lady?"

"You have to stay," said Emeline, trying to squash down further into the soapy water.

"You can leave," said Nicholas. "I'll call for you once I've finished here. I shouldn't be long."

Emeline gazed disconsolate as her servant swiftly obeyed her husband and scurried off, busily drying her arms as she closed the door behind her. Emeline, now invisible up to her chin and trying not to blow bubbles, glared at her husband and said, "For someone who is supposed to be near death, you manage to hobble around surprisingly well."

"I do, don't I?" grinned Nicholas. "Courage and fortitude, of course. But actually it's the bed. An inferior palliasse with inferior covers and a miserable set of damp flat pillows. I crawl out of it at every available excuse. The latest excuse happened to be you."

"How delightful," sniffed Emeline.

"Sarcasm," smiled the invalid, "is entirely lost on me, madam. I am too simple a soul for that. But I agree, delightful is an appropriate word, or it was when I first saw you. You have now disappeared into scum. A shame."

The steam was beginning to evaporate and Emeline wondered how long she would be kept there. She managed to speak without sniffing. "If you would say whatever you came to say, my lord, perhaps I can then continue my bath before I catch a cold," although it was difficult to keep one's dignity while hiding underwater, knees scrunched, in considerable discomfort. And he was right about the scum.

"As it happens," continued Nicholas without noticeable interest in her request, "I can now state without doubt that one of the things Peter frequently described about you was, in fact, completely inaccurate. I can also confirm that what you yourself told me this morning is equally inaccurate. You are not pregnant, madam."

"If you just came here to embarrass me –"

"I had no idea you were in the bath," Nicholas pointed out, "though I suppose I might have guessed. You certainly needed one. I was actually spoiling the habit of a lifetime by behaving quite altruistically. I'm told you had no supper. You certainly missed dinner. And I doubt you were present for breakfast since I gather you were still asleep in the Keep. So I came to invite you to a small private supper in my bedchamber before retiring. Rather nice of me, I thought, since all you do is keep running away and getting excessively dirty."

Emeline blushed. "If that was all – you could have sent a message."

"I told you," Nicholas explained, "I wanted any excuse to get out of bed. It's now four days trapped and tortured by doctors. I've had enough. So come for supper and cheer me up by insulting me and telling me how sorry you are to have married me. That cheers me up no end. Besides, the supper's already been ordered and you must be starving."

"You have your cousins to keep you company," Emeline mumbled.

He shook his head. "Adrian's a loose knucklebone, and Sissy's a baby. Besides, after travelling backwards and forwards for days, they've both gone to bed. They left here after the wedding feast and just managed to return home before hearing about the fire and deciding to travel back here to make sure I was well and truly dead. But they gave me a good idea before they went to bed, and it's something I'd like to discuss with you as soon as possible. So do you want some cold pork, apple codlings in treacle, sugared raisins and cold salmon stuffed with spiced leeks and onions? Or not?"

The wave of unsurmountable hunger swept immediately and painfully from her throat to her toes. She muttered, "I am a little - that is, it is a whole day since I ate anything at all."

"That decides it," decided Nicholas. "I can't help you out of the bath, I'm afraid, but you should come and eat at once. Having my wife expire of starvation in my own home and practically at my feet would be too much of a scandal even for my father to contend with."

The baroness entered at the appropriate moment, tottering beneath an armful of materials, and her two maids followed closely, each clutching towels, combs, hairpins, stockings and garters. "Oh, Nicholas," her ladyship noticed in surprise, "I would not have expected - nor do I think it wise, sir - and during the late evening chill too. Not that I wish to interrupt you, naturally."

"You're not," said Nicholas. "I would be leaving, except that I need my page in order to get back to my own room. Perhaps you'll be good enough to call him for me. Your daughter, once dressed I presume, will then be joining me for a late supper."

In a neat combination of her mother's stockings and little starched headdress, Martha's best linen shift, which was far too large, and her very oldest plain dun blue gown without secondary sleeves or any trimmings, Emeline entered her husband's bedchamber and felt immediately reconciled by the glorious perfumes of food. She sat at the little table which had been set before the hearth, and was already laid with platters, folded napkins, polished cutlery, and a dented candelabra. At least a dozen other candles had been lit and the small hearth was bright with fire. The flickering brilliance was lurid across Nicholas's face where the previous scars combined with the oozing blisters of burned flesh, many small massed scabs and the partially healed welts. The sheen of medicinal goose fat was, however, no longer evident. He lounged at the table, propped in a heavy backed chair opposite her own. He smiled and said, "You'll have to serve, my dear. I'm incapable and I sent the boys away. I need to talk to you."

This sounded ominous, and the endearment made her suspicious. Emeline began to serve, saying, "There are so many candles, sir. Do you need the light brighter because of your - that is - if sight is a problem? My father is very thrifty with good wax candles."

Nicholas tapped his cup. "The wine, if you wouldn't mind," and then drained what she poured for him. "Now, my lady. You eat, and I shall talk. First, no I'm not blind as well as burned, mutilated and mistreated. You've been politely controlling your curiosity regarding my fascinating disfigurements, I presume? But my sight is fairly good, all things considered. Certainly good enough to notice that your father's equally parsimonious with his daughters' clothing. What has happened to status and fashion in Gloucestershire, may I ask? I know most of your clothes were destroyed, but surely you still had a trunk of clothes remaining in the guest wing."

Emeline stared resolutely at the flagon and poured her own wine. It was hippocras, and the steam rose in a spiced spiral. Deciding she could not now ask any further explanations regarding her husband's unusual appearance, she said instead, "Do you *know* how to be nice? Or are you rude to *everyone*? Yes, Papa is very careful about waste, and he doesn't believe in extravagance except sometimes for formal occasions. For instance, my wedding gown cost a great deal, and I'm very sad it's gone. And yesterday Avice lent me her best shift, and I sort of ruined it, so today I only have my very oldest clothes left. But I thought you had something important to discuss, not just being horrid about my family and what I'm wearing."

"I liked you better wearing nothing," said Nicholas, holding his cup out for a refill. "But I'll buy you whatever you want once life gets back to normal. Not that having you around will seem normal of course. My family has always been profligate, and I've no intention of changing. So spend what you want. I always do. Money and property's never been a problem, and you bring a fair purse with you too."

"That's vulgar," Emeline mumbled, eyes on her platter.

"Truth - that's all," said Nicholas, the smile fading. "Something you seem to have a problem with, madam. As you've pointed out, romantic dreams don't suit me at all. I don't have the face for it."

"I didn't mean to offend you," she said in a hurry, filling his cup again. "But Maman and Papa say that I do speak without - well, never mind what they say. The thing is, I never met *anyone* until I met Peter. Not men, anyway. I don't even have any real cousins, except for one in Spain and Papa won't talk about him because he's nearly foreign. Our neighbours are just country bumpkins and a few tradesmen who come to the house sometimes, and Papa's lawyer and his secretary who is rather a silly man, though Avice likes him. Then there's the local priests and the others in our private chapel and the monastery just a mile away, and sometimes we hear them singing." She paused, disconcerted by her husband's glazed expression. "Am I boring you?" she asked faintly.

"I was simply wondering," remarked Nicholas, "whether all that was a clumsy attempt at an apology, or just an exercise in self pity?" Since she glared at him and made no answer, he pointed to the wine jug, said, "Help yourself. You probably need it," and drained his own cup for the third time. "Now," he continued, "since we both suffer from objectionable fathers, the castle is half in ruins, you have the composure of an affronted flea and the brain of a half starved sparrow, and now I'm about as useful as a shocked virgin, I intend taking up an offer from my cousin. Adrian is a pompous little prig and probably has even less intelligence than you do, but his suggestion is fairly sensible. So in about six or seven days or as soon as I'm capable of riding, I've agreed to take you to Nottingham where they have a reasonably comfortable house with a few spare bedchambers. There I'll get a decent night's rest in a comfortable bed, get a doctor who can think of more interesting medications than spreading me with putrid lard while shoving his fleam in my groin, you can get your hands on some more flattering clothes, have your own bedchamber, and enjoy some more congenial company while comparing Peter's more saintly qualities. Sissy thought she was in love with him too. The female capacity for self delusion can be quite amazing."

Emeline sat with her spoon in one hand and her cup in the other, her mouth slightly open, and eventually muttered, "Sissy?"

"Sysabel," nodded Nicholas. "My cousin. Adrian's sister. I've told you who she is several times before, but no doubt your attention was floating around elsewhere at the time. You were probably busy planning your next escapade into the nearest pile of cinders." When she still did not answer, he continued, "Of course, there won't be too many cinders available in Nottingham, except the usual fireplaces. But don't worry. There's a nice wide river for you to throw yourself into when you get tired of talking to me. The River Trent, if I remember rightly. It's waiting, just for you."

Emeline straightened, put down her spoon with a clatter, and said with dignified menace, "If that is a threat, my lord –"

"Oh, good Lord," muttered Nicholas. "Why do you insist on seeing threats everywhere? No, I've no particular desire to tramp along the damned riverbank in the snow, looking for my wife's corpse." He managed to reach the wine jug, and refilled his cup with only slight spillage. "Now," he said with a renewed smile, "Have some apple codlings. I notice you seem particularly fond of them, and indeed, they're very good. The kitchens may have burned down, but luckily the cook himself did not."

Emeline ignored the apple codlings. Besides, she had already eaten six of them. "Since we are invited to visit your cousins, I am clearly pleased to accept, my lord," she said with the quiet dignity she was carefully practicing. "I trust you will tell me when the journey has been arranged. I merely wish to point out that I have no travelling clothes, nor any other possessions left to take with me. Is it a long way from here to Nottingham, sir? I do have my own little palfrey in your stables, though I cannot be sure Papa will let me keep her. I certainly have no wish to be an – inconvenience."

Nicholas grinned suddenly. "Too late," he said. "As for the journey, it's just a few hours as long as we have no wretched litters or carts to drag along with us. I'll fix you up with some clothes before we go. There's a tailor and a couple of seamstresses somewhere in the castle, and there'll be time enough since I doubt I'll be able to ride for a few more days. Just make sure you don't choose some frumpy juvenile nonsense such as you're wearing now. You can talk to Sissy in the morning and she'll explain whatever you need to know." He stretched, winced, drained his cup again, and sighed. "Now I feel I've suffered enough, and I need to get to bed before I fall. I assume you won't want to share my bed, since you've a predilection for sleeping in some very odd places. Mind you, this bed is fairly odd too, but there's nothing I can do about that for the moment. But apart from anything else, you smell of lavender, which I dislike intensely."

Emma clenched her fists and stood, flinging her napkin onto the little table. "The bath water was scented with lavender, my lord. I didn't choose it. But my hair is still wet so the perfume remains."

"I might even put up with the smell if things were different," said Nicholas. "But they're not, and I'm not, and you're not. And while I think of it, I should warn you I'm naked beneath this wretched grease smeared bedrobe, so if you wish to preserve your maidenly modesty, madam, you'd do well to let me stagger to my bed alone."

"I most certainly intend to leave you entirely alone," said his wife. "Indeed, I shall keep as distant as possible until it is time to travel to Nottingham. At which time, I expect you will inform me of your demands, which I shall dutifully obey. In the meantime, my lord, I wish you a good night."

CHAPTER NINE

The castle did not feel in any way her home, nor did it welcome her. So Emeline was sad to wave her family goodbye, although she had claimed beforehand that she would be glad to see the back of them. She expected to miss her mother a little perhaps, but was not prepared for the black hole of loneliness that swallowed her thoughts after only a brief absence.

The last two days with her mother and sister had involved a late bustle, materials brought from the town markets and spread for inspection with the tailor and the seamstress awaiting each breath, each exclamation. Avice had said, "You must choose that green satin, and the pale grey velvet. What grand gowns you'll have. And oh, Emm, that glorious gold damask. Gold embroidered in gold all shot with gold, and the whole gown laced in gold ribbons. Perhaps with a black satin stomacher? You'll be walking sunshine." Sighing, "I do so hope Papa finds me a very rich husband one day."

With her nose buried in the swathes of luxury on offer, Emeline had replied, "Really Avice, that's exceedingly shallow of you. As St. Francis said, riches are just extraneous interruptions and have no real importance. Clothes can't make anyone happy."

"Well, not if someone's busy sulking and just determined to be miserable and ungrateful," sniffed Avice.

Emeline said, "Papa is always lecturing us about greed and vanity, and he ought to know. Nicholas says Papa only arranged our marriage because he wants political power and influence but I don't believe it. Dearest Peter told me much nicer things. I can't see why Papa could possibly want power when he lives so far from Westminster, and has all those farms to watch over. Besides, he says the only power on earth is God's."

Tossing her curls and eyes to heaven, "So naturally, being so virtuous, you will decline any new gowns at all?" Avice sniggered. "And will either give them all to me, or send these gorgeous fabrics away at once?"

"I would never be so rude," replied Emeline carefully. "And besides, I have to wear something. But Papa says –"

"If you think so highly of Papa, then *you* can go home with him and leave me here with all the wonderful new gowns and shoes and feathers and silk stockings," objected Avice. "And don't forget you owe me a good linen shift with a proper fitted bodice."

"There won't be time to have it made before you leave tomorrow. I'll send it to you. Unless you come to visit me in the meantime. And I wish you would."

Avice had shaken her head. "Papa would never allow such expense again for months. Though Sissy says I can come whenever I want to. She's really nice. You'll like staying with her."

"She's a fourteen year old baby, like you. That's why you like her, and that's why I probably won't."

Avice continued to shake her head. "I'm turned fifteen now, remember! But I still like her. Even though she says all those silly soppy things about Peter too, so you two can sit through the long evenings by the fire and sniff and sob together about what a wonderful person he was and how he was wickedly murdered."

"At nearly twenty, I know a great deal about broken hearts," Emeline had pointed out. "What could she know of true love? And Adrian is pompous, and has conceited ideas."

"Just like you," said Avice. "And like Papa too. Even bishops enjoy nice expensive clothes but Papa says it's ungodly. Which reminds me, if Papa catches you looking at satins and brocades on a Sunday, he'll start seething again. And I do so want a nice cheerful trip home, and not one of those awful glowering angry ones. Maman will be moaning about the horrid litter and the bumps in the road, and there won't even be a sulky sister to keep me company."

They had left in a bright shower of rain with the first shimmer of a rainbow. The earl, emerging only as far as the bailey, had wished them a speedy journey and returned quickly to the warmth indoors. Emeline had stood out beyond the drawbridge to see them ride off, but once their shadows had quite disappeared and the rickety trundle and splash of their progress had faded entirely, she hurried to the bedchamber she had been sharing with Avice, stared from the window at the newly sullen sky, and cried quietly into the gloom.

The following day Sir Adrian Frye and his sister had left with their much smaller retinue. It was still raining, the rainbow had long since given up the fight, and for saying his goodbyes and good wishes the earl did not even risk getting his head wet. "We shall see you again within two weeks, my lady," Sir Adrian, already mounted, had assured Emeline.

Sysabel, water dripping from hood to lap and trickling from the horse's mane, had nodded. "But I believe Nicholas seems much worse these past two days, and has probably relapsed. Such a fever, and some of those horrid sores reopened. The doctor blames Nick's silly determination to get out of bed too early, and has warned him not to travel in case infection sets in, and then - well amputation would be the only way to save his life. It's a warning to everyone," she glanced dolefully at her brother, "not to indulge in foolish self indulgence. I'm told Nicholas saved his father's life, which I find very difficult to believe, but perhaps it was courage after all. But now, at the very least he'll be scarred forever."

"He's already scarred for life," Adrian pointed out.

Sysabel frowned. "All the more reason not to be scarred twice. Nicholas is always so irresponsible, you know."

On the fourth day of March, being the feast of St. Owen, the Earl of Chatwyn left his suffering son and his ruined castle, and with a sigh of relief rode south towards Westminster and King Richard's court. His smile widened as the battered shadows of his own home receded behind him and he began to hum to himself, ignoring the pained glances of his retinue. He left the castle depleted, for he took more than half his senior ranking household with him, half or more of the already diminished stores and in particular the best Burgundy. He also travelled with virtually all the castle's remaining movable comforts. His clothes and luxuries had also been destroyed by fire, but he had time to order more, with every intention of acquiring a lavish excess once he reached London.

The empty spaces he left behind him shrank quietly into desolation. Repairs and rebuilding had begun, but with a slow plod rather than a busy bustle, for the dour weather made efficiency difficult and there was no lord to chase the workmen. Nicholas, sweating in an overheated chamber beneath a sticky layer of medications, lay increasingly feverish, barely aware of his father's abrupt absence. He did not leave his bedchamber.

Emeline did not go to his bedside. She wandered alone.

The Keep, although no longer deserted at all times, still echoed with tumbling wood and plaster, and Emeline did not return there to search for any remaining belongings. Martha and her young maid Petronella had been left to attend her, but after a week of speaking only to servants and the castle's timid priest, Emeline was finally informed that her husband intended travelling to Nottingham on the 16th day of March, weather permitting, and that she should make herself ready to leave early on that morning. There was no accompanying suggestion that she visit him prior to departure. She spent some days organising the packing, since there was little else to do, and she now had several gowns and a good collection of additional finery to carry with her, each item grander than the next. She had only worn two of the four new gowns, and gold damask was hardly appropriate for sitting alone in the small dining hall, creeping sadly through deserted passageways, nor while huddling in her bed to cry.

It was late in the afternoon two days before departure when the body squire David Witton came with a message, asking if the lady would be so kind as to attend her husband in his lordship's private chamber within the hour.

She sat where she was with a lapful of stockings, garters and stomachers, looked up, immediately opened her mouth to say no, then quickly remembered her manners and changed her mind. She therefore appeared at the door to the bedchamber a little flustered and a little pink. The new gown she was wearing was also pink but Nicholas did not appear unappreciative.

"No more burn scabs I see, madam. Delightful, come in, shut the door and share my supper. You can't avoid me forever, you know." He was lying out on the bed, but relaxed and at ease, propped up against a welter of pillows and no longer beneath the covers. Indeed, he was dressed for the first time since the wedding.

Emeline gazed down at him. "You look better yourself, my lord."

"I shall never look better, as you very well know," Nicholas smiled. "But the burns are healed, except for a few remaining sores on my arms. Hopefully I won't relapse again. So although my doctors don' sanction it, I believe I'm now well enough to travel." He paused, adding, "I've left you sadly solitary these past weeks. But since you've also avoided me, I doubt you've any objections."

Emeline said, "My apologies, my lord. I considered whether to fulfil my wifely duty and visit the invalid. Then I decided my appearance would probably make matters worse, not better. I can hardly imagine you missed me."

"Miss you?" He shook his head. "I've not yet become accustomed to your presence, so there was nothing to miss. In fact, I'm barely acquainted with you, madam, or you with me. But I was kept informed of where you went and what you did."

"In case I slept in the Keep with the cinders, or jumped into the moat?"

"Both possibilities occurred to me."

She sighed, and sat on a stool already pulled to the bedside. "I suppose you truly think me a mad woman. I assure you I'm not. But you sent for me for some other reason than just to confirm my sanity?"

"I wanted to talk to you about the journey, and about my cousins," he said, nodding towards the small table beside the hearth where their supper was laid. "I also wanted to give you something." He swung his legs from the bed and stood, a little stiffly, a little awkward. "Come and eat, and I'll show you." She watched him walk across the room to the table, and did not offer her arm. He moved quietly, assured and straight, but he held to the furniture as he passed, leaning one moment against the bed post and then sitting heavily in the wide chair at the table's head. He wore a loose cote doublet, unlaced and unbelted, swinging open over a white pleated shirt. His hose were tight grey knitted silk, showing the long curves of his thighs and calves, with no visible limp to spoil their elegance. Emeline followed and sat opposite, watching him with interest. The flesh on his face was smooth and unmarked in the candlelight, except for the old scar. No blisters or grazes, nor sticky unction or greasy salves spoiled the pale clarity of his face and she realised, as she had not done previously, that his features were well defined and even, and that without the scar he would have been an exceptionally handsome man.

He waited, amused at her scrutiny. Finally he said, "Waiting for me to topple face down, my lady? Or hoping for signs of fatal infection?"

"Was I watching too closely?" She blushed again.

"I've been watching you too." He grinned suddenly. "Here," and he pointed.

Her lost jewellery lay on the table beside her empty platter. The emerald brooch was twisted and some of the gold claws holding the stones had broken, but the large ruby ring which had once been her grandmother's, was unharmed. It caught the firelight and glowed like blood. The gold cross from her father was not there and she assumed that the metal would have melted in the heat, but instead there was a flash of diamonds which she had never seen before. The brooch was large and elaborate, a sunburst spinning out from a diamond heart. She reached out and touched it, tentative fingertip to its raised centre, and whispered. "This is not mine."

"It is now," Nicholas said. "It was my mother's. It came to me when she died. I meant it for you as a bride gift but our wedding night presented little opportunity for love tokens. So take it now. Your own brooch suffered in the fire, I'm afraid, though it can be repaired in time." Nicholas reached for the wine jug, and poured two cups. "I sent a couple of men to search though everything and see what they could find. This was all they discovered of yours."

"The diamonds are - magnificent." It was unexpected and she struggled for words. "An heirloom, your mother's, which makes it more precious. And to have my own property back - is - kind."

"That surprises you?" He laughed. "You expect no kindness from me? Have I seemed so brutal?" He stretched, leaning back to ease his shoulders, but kept a good clasp on his cup. "We've not started too well with this marital business. And I'm no courtly knight, I'm afraid. Nor will I ever look like one." He once again drained his cup, saying, "But I'm capable of kindness, I believe, and shall be more active once we get to Nottingham. Adrian often entertains the local dignitaries, and the town's busy with shops and markets. And there're plenty of churches, if that's your preference."

"No more than is - proper," Emeline mumbled, staring bleakly from her husband's wary smile to the diamond brooch in her hand, up to the velvet cuff of her new gown and then to the honey cake now spreading its sticky syrup over her plate. She had lost her appetite. "I'm not like my father, sir. But perhaps just as - unbending. I'm aware I've not always been as polite as I might - as I should have been. Now you've been very generous, my lord. And I have not."

His smile was slow growing, and lit an unexpected sparkle in his eyes. He said, "How delightful, my lady, an unexpected excess of guilt, I see. So you admit you may have been uncompromising in the past?" Emeline nodded sadly. "And have wilfully misjudged me?" With a slight hiccup, she nodded again. "And behaved with a complete lack of modest humility?" Emeline reluctantly raised her eyes to his and nodded a third time. "Exhibiting rude prejudice and a shocking dearth of wifely sympathy?" She swallowed, shifted with discomfort and managed a small fourth nod. Nicholas bust out laughing. "What a hypocrite," he decided. "But it seems bribery will inspire miracles every time. A woman sees diamonds and suddenly becomes as biddable as a heifer led to the bull."

Emeline sat up straight again and glared. "You *like* being vulgar," she accused him. "I was trying to be nice, that's all. And the diamonds are beautiful but you can take them back if you think I can be bought. In future I shan't try to be polite anymore." She thumped her spoon back onto the table, pushed back her chair, and stood, shaky but defiant.

Nicholas continued smiling, which annoyed her more. He also stood, though slowly and a little hesitant, as though his legs did not yet obey him as readily as he wished. He took just three steps towards the bed, now standing between his wife and the door. "Intending to run away again?" he inquired. "But I'm not sure I'm ready to let you go." His eyes narrowed, the blue lights hooded, and said, "Come here."

Although the shutters were up, shrouding the room against the outside world, the light of the flames was cerise across the hearth, crackling aromatic amongst the logs and sparking up the chimney. Ten high wax tapers burned bright in their silver stands. The small chamber was vivid lit. Yet Emeline felt suddenly enclosed by shadow. She stared at her husband. He stared back. He was no longer smiling. She read menace, and remembered how her mother had warned of beatings if she did not behave, and of punishments to come. She could outrun Nicholas if she chose, for he still seemed unsteady. But such disobedience might lead to harsher beatings in the future, when his strength returned. So she said quietly, "My lord, I'm tired. I wish to return to my bed," and tried to read his expression. She had not seen him drink enough to be dangerous, but he might well have filled his cup many times before she even arrived. Drunken men were the terror of many families, and Nicholas had proved his taste for wine at the wedding feast.

Yet no longer seeming unsteady, although she was sure his legs still pained him, Nicholas stood very still, did not move, and repeated, soft voiced, "You can retire when I permit it, madam. Now, come here."

"If you mean to hurt me," she whispered, "I warn you, I shall fight back. I know it's not a wife's prerogative but I will defend myself. I'm not your chattel."

Nicholas stood his ground. "An amusing thought, madam, though in fact, that is precisely what you are. Or do you imagine me infirm, and easily overcome? It seems you do not know me at all. Now, for the third and last time, come here."

She took one deep and anxious breath and approached him slowly, as though she might turn and run at any moment. He waited, his eyes fixed cold on hers. At an arm's reach, she stopped, but he demanded, "Closer."

As she took one small step more, at once his hands took her, gripping her arms so tightly she winced. He pulled her nearer and tighter. His strength surprised and dismayed her but she stood still and pride stopped her from struggling or crying out. She thought his fingers would bruise her but she looked up into the fierce intensity of his blue gaze and did not blink. He watched her a moment. Then he bent his head down towards her.

Again he paused, his eyes so close she stared into the milky fleck across the iris where once she had thought him blinded by whatever had scarred his cheek. She flinched. Then, unable to outstare his unblinking concentration, she closed her own eyes, and sighed. His breath was hot on her face.

There was the sudden touch of his mouth on hers. And then he kissed her.

CHAPTER TEN

Nicholas felt the sudden melting of her body against his own, and he felt the creep of her fingers to his back, the growing intensity of her grip and then the tightening of her embrace. His own hands clasped her gently, pressing firm as his tongue explored the inner warmth of her lips. Finally pulling away, he smiled down at her. "You kissed me back," he murmured. "I had not expected it. How inexplicable women truly are."

Dropping her arms to her sides, she mumbled, "You - took me - by surprise."

"There seemed no other way. Is the punishment sufficient then, to fit the lesson?"

"No," whispered Emeline, and shook her head.

So he kissed her again.

One hand to the small of her back, his other around her shoulders, Nicholas leaned her against the bedpost, and there he held her, bending over her. She felt his weight hard against her, and peeped up into his smile. Then his voice tickled her ear. "Nervous, little one? Do you hate me still?" and very, very softly kissed from the lobe of her ear down the side of her neck to the dip into her shoulder, and there took the edge of her gown and pulled it aside, just a little, so the curve to her arm was uncovered, and the first swell of her breast rested beneath his palm.

She inhaled sharply and held her breath. His fingers stroked, slipping inside to cup her warmth, his thumb slowly circling her nipple. At once the nipple hardened, and stood erect. At first she pulled away, nervous of such unexpected intimacy. But then she hesitated, looking up into the hooded azure eyes above her. This was, after all, her husband. "Have you no answer, then, my love?" he murmured. "Or are you planning your revenge?"

She hiccupped faintly against his cheek and mumbled, "I - I can't think. I can't breathe."

His chuckle was part smothered as he pushed his fingers inside her cleavage and down between the growing heat of her breasts. He quickly unhooked the little scrap of gossamer linen which closed the neckline of her gown. Then, clasping both her bodice and her shift beneath it, he pulled abruptly. She felt the sudden chill of air against her breasts before both his wandering hands warmed her again, and whispering, his voice tickling against her ear, "So will you come to me naked now, my love, and be my wife at last?" But he did not wait for her reply, nor seemed to expect one. He swept her up, one arm beneath her knees, out of her shoes as he swung her back onto the bed and against the heaped pillows. He was immediately beside her, unclipping the banded stomacher and pulling it free so she was left unclothed almost to the waist, with her arms trapped at her sides by the sleeves of her gown.

"You're blushing," he smiled, as though delighted. "As prettily flushed as a new lit flame," and reached up, first unclipping the starched folds of her headdress, pulling out and tossing aside the pins until her hair fell long over her shoulders. Then his hands were on her breasts again, caressing and teasing while he kissed her more forcefully, his tongue pushing in over her tongue as his fingers pinched her nipples. "But now, my love," he said, "I want all of you." And he moved back, reaching suddenly beneath her arm to unlace her gown, pulling the cord from its loops. Finally clasping the hems of her skirts, he lifted them in one swift fluttering arc up her legs, eased the material from under her, scooped the bundled velvet higher, then over her head and off her arms. He sat back then, the gown and shift tumbled in heaped creases on his lap as he looked at her.

As her gown slid to the rug at his feet, Nicholas leant forwards and firmly uncrossed her arms as she tried to cover herself. "Oh, no, my love," he murmured. "No hiding." And he rested both his hands on her thighs above the tops of her stockings, stopping her as she squeezed her legs tightly together. "Look at me, little one," he commanded. "I won't hurt you. It's pleasure I offer, not pain. But tell me first, do you know anything of how this is done?" He waited, searching her eyes as she gulped, and shook her head, and looked quickly away. "Very well," he murmured. "And you have no brothers, and a father strict enough to keep you innocent as a fledgling. So have you ever seen a man unclothed?"

She blinked hard, tried not to blush, and whispered, "Yes. You."

Nicholas sat back surprised, eyebrows raised. The occasion was something he struggled to remember. "I was surely not that pissed on our wedding night," he decided, "and I'm quite sure I neither touched you nor danced naked around the chamber."

"The next day," Emeline mumbled, "on this bed when the surgeon was trying to dress your burns, and you'd fainted."

"Ah," Nicholas grinned, which Emeline thought was definitely in poor taste. "I was trying to rescue the old man and a parcel of servants and save what I could of the castle, and had to do it all in my braies," he said. "Damned stupid, when you come to think of it. So you came to visit while I was out cold, did you? I hope it wasn't too hideous an education."

"Of course not," she lied. "But I'm really not used to being - so can I - may I pull up the bedcovers?"

"Certainly not," said Nicholas. "If you're cold, don't worry, I have every intention of keeping you warm. And you, my love, should not be shy, since you're quite deliciously beautiful."

She mumbled, "Don't be silly."

He moved closer once more, and slid his hands up her body, slowly from her thighs up the spread of her hips, over the small curve of her belly, the valley of her waist, and again to her breasts. Then he bent, kissing her nipples, first brushing his tongue gently across, then taking them hard, one by one, into his mouth, nipping between his teeth. She gulped, and he whispered, "Deliciously, sublimely beautiful, believe me my love. Who has ever been fool enough to tell you otherwise? Your stubborn pea brained father? Certainly no one who ever had the pleasure of seeing you naked."

"No one *has* ever seen me - like this," she whispered back.

"Then I am honoured," he told her, "and flattered, and ultimately delighted, now knowing my entirely unmerited fortune." His hands were exploring, smoothing again across her body, then his fingers pushing up beneath her arm. "I like the curls you keep hidden here," he murmured, "and here," and his other hand rested just below her belly. "But you are still not quite as naked as I should like you," He tucked both hands between her thighs, gently probing them apart. Then, fingers first to one leg and then to the other, he untied her garters and rolled down her stockings, slowly as he watched his own movements, firm and unhurried down her legs. He flipped each warm woollen stocking from her toes, tossed it to the floor, and smiled. "And now that you're exactly how I want you," he decided, "I am distinctly over dressed myself." Still watching her, he shrugged his sweeping brocade from his shoulders to the rug, untied the loose cord of his shirt, and pulled it quickly over his head. She watched him as he watched her.

He was not how she remembered. The dark oozing scabs of the burns, the weeping sores and blisters had gone. In the candlelight she saw faint silvery scars, barely visible across the pale skin. His nipples and the silky hair sparse over his breast were dark, and the muscles of his body were smooth and sinuous. Emeline sat curled, trying not to show more of herself than she could conceal, but gazed at him, and said, "I think you are - beautiful - too, my lord."

He snorted, moving close to her again. "Not beautiful, as I well know, my sweet. But deft, and kind, I promise. And I won't hurt you." He embraced her quickly, one hand to the back of her hair, cradling her head against his shoulder. His other hand wandered to the dimples at the rise of her buttocks, holding her tightly to him. He felt her trembling and looked quickly down into her eyes. "Not frightened I hope? You told me once you were never frightened. Can you trust me at last?"

She said, still whispering, "I am - nervous. Just a little. You do - and touch where I have never - and not knowing how - or what to - expect."

"Then let me show you," he murmured, and keeping her firm to his chest, he began again to caress her breasts, pulling gently and pressing around the nipple as he talked, his voice like the last hum of the waning fire in the hearth. He said, "So as I touch you here, my love, and here, you feel me where I touch. But as I touch your breasts, you also feel me lower down, in those places where your body ignites, and where arousal touches more surely than I can." His fingers slipped, smoothing around her navel and down across her belly. "So you also feel me here," voice softening, "and here, like a hunger, and a need." He smiled into her eyes, and shyly she nodded. Then he pressed hard into the soft flesh at the base of her stomach. "Here, a throbbing deep inside, and then –" and his fingers pushed down between her thighs and touched very gently, so that she shivered as he said, "and you feel me here, both at the entrance and inside, don't you my sweet? Sensations new to you, sudden awakenings and depths never realised. For it's here I enter you, once you're prepared, and bring us both the pleasure of loving."

She swallowed hard, her voice tiny, "Enter - me?"

He tightened his embrace, then gently pushed one finger higher, just inserted within her, and whispered, "Inside here, my love, where you'll open for me." She drew in her breath and pulled away from him but he smiled and kissed her eyelids shut, saying, "But not until you're ready, and I have many ways of making you ready." Then he took one of her hands in his own, moving it down to his groin, and easing her fingers inside the stiffened codpiece and then within the folds of his braies. "This is me," he said softly, "and we are made to fit together."

She shook her head, puzzled, for this was not as she remembered him when he had lain injured and sick. She tried to find the words to ask, but at once his fingers, releasing hers, roamed again and he murmured, "Breathe, my sweet, and let me play. This is how I make you ready, and then nothing will hurt, and you will learn why this is called loving, as well as its other names."

She felt her head spin and her breath quicken, and she said, panting, "Should I do something too, then?"

"No, my sweetling, except open your legs for me. Close your eyes, think of nothing but feeling and wanting, and let me take you swimming deep. One day, when you're long accustomed to what I do and to what I want, then I'll show you other roads and other places, and guide you to do as I do. But for now this is not meant as an education. It's pure pleasure, so don't hide from me and forget first time blushes. I'll take you as far as you let me."

"I couldn't stop you. I don't want to stop you." She sighed, releasing her embarrassment, and when he moved down against her, prising open her legs, she did not resist. Then he laid his cheek on the cushion of her stomach, and with one hand to the curls at her groin, pushed first one, then another finger deep inside her.

She groaned and he looked up at once, saying, "You are very tight, little one. Does that hurt?" But she sighed, mumbling words he could barely understand, and he felt her inner muscles squeeze tight around him, and smiled. Then he moved his thumb, pressing at the entrance just above, moving softly and building friction. She lurched, jerking against him, and wrapped both her arms tight around his neck.

When Nicholas finally released her, sitting back to remove his hose, she blinked up, eyes wide. "It's all gone - cold," she whispered.

"Cold? Not here," he grinned, one hand again between her legs. "You are all aflame, my love, hot as pepper corms and moist as wine. And here," and he traced the tiny trickled of sweat, one finger following the trail from between her breasts down to her navel. "There is a snail's sheen of silver and in the candlelight, your skin is golden. So silver, gold, fire and wine - my feast and my delight."

"Kind words," she whispered shaking her head, "Is that the way of seduction? But now I feel more - naked - more exposed - more -"

"Vulnerable? And so you are, my own, but now I am vulnerable too, which is how lovers must be at first." And he unhooked his codpiece and pulled off his hose and braies, and came quickly back beside her, holding her tight.

She again snuggled into the protection of his embrace, her voice muffled against his shoulder. "Is this how all men are? It seems so - strange."

He laughed. "No, only me in all the world and all other men are different, and inferior." He took her hand, placing it over himself. "But not at all. Of course we are all alike, and not so strange, my sweet. Men and women are made to fit together, and bring pleasure each to the other. Trust me now."

She did. "I will." And began to discover that truth was so very much better than all the months of confusion and the endless dreams, the yearning, and the impatient waiting to learn what romance was really all about.

Emeline woke in the night, and found herself again in his arms. She was still naked, as he was, and she felt the unaccustomed strength of his body clasped to her back, his knees tucked behind hers and his arms tight to her belly and breasts. She sighed, and remembered what he had done to her before they slept, and smiled to herself as she sank again into sleep.

She woke the second time as her husband kissed her ear, and said, "Have I exhausted you so completely, little one? It's long past dawn."

"Morning already?"

"The usual time for dawn," he nodded. "There's light beer and manchet with cheese here on a tray. Eat and claim back your strength. We leave for Nottingham at first light tomorrow, so this will be a busy day." He wore a bedrobe, fur lined to his feet, but when he sat on the edge of the bed beside her, it fell open and he was naked. Emma had already cuddled deep beneath the eiderdown. Nicholas grinned, put the beer cup into her hand, and swept the covers from her body to the floor. "I forbid timidity. I forbid maidenly blushes. You've taken me as husband, and I've taken you as wife. The time for hiding is over. Or did you suffer at my hands last night?" He paused, his voice softening, and asked, "Did I hurt you after all?"

"No." She was blushing, in spite of instructions. "But - this is another day - and everything feels different."

He crossed to the window, taking down the wooden shutters, but turned and looked at her. "So perhaps I should repeat what I did then, so you no longer feel different, but once again the same? After all, I've been ill for a long time and have a great deal to catch up with." She wriggled, reached over and pulled back the eiderdown, looking meekly into her well covered lap. He grinned. "Don't worry, little one," he said, coming back to sit beside her. "You're sore, as I know you must be. And I can't spend all my days seducing you, no matter how I'd like to." He took her cup, put it down beside the bed and wrapped both arms around her. "You'll get used to me in time. You were beautiful last night. Sweet memories, I hope?"

"Oh, so very sweet." She clung to him, burying her head against his chest, hiding her face and trying to choose her words. "But - if that is how it's done - as I suppose it must be - how will I know if I carry your child?"

He smiled at the top of her head. "No doubt I'll know before you do, my love," he said, "and will tell you."

She mumbled, "Now you've said it again. Last night you called me that - over and over - *my love*. But you don't love me. You don't even know me."

"I love you while I'm making love to you," he murmured to her ear, caressing her tangled curls. There was a short pause, a restful silence as his hands then wandered a little below the bedclothes and found her breasts, creeping lower to her legs. "And I will learn to love you more," he said, "as I hope gradually you learn to love me."

She hesitated, then said simply, "I do already."

"That, my dear, is honest lust speaking," he grinned at her, "and the flush of a first climax. It will wear off very quickly the next time I annoy you."

"Will you annoy me?" Her heart beat had quickened.

His fingers rubbed gently between her legs and he pulled the covers from her once again, nuzzling her breasts and kissing her. "Without doubt," he said, "perhaps very soon. Before last night you thought you hated me. Now perhaps you think differently. A child's romantic notions - no more. Did you dream endlessly of romance with Peter? And now you find it suddenly with me? Yet once this first discovery of lust wears off, then perhaps annoyance will return. But for me, if we speak of love making then it's love making I want, with you as wet and sticky as I left you last night. So do I take you again, as I want to? Or think with my head instead of my prick, and leave you in peace to get dressed?"

"Oh, please don't stop. And besides," she murmured, "my dresser won't know where to find me,"

"Would she be so surprised to find you in your husband's bedchamber?"

Emeline admitted, "And first I should go - before anything else - to the garderobe."

He did not remove his hand, and would not let her hide her face. "Lean back, and let me explore you in daylight. I'll be gentle, I promise. But where a man would have trouble swiving when his bladder's full, with a woman it's different. The pleasure increases. Look, when I press up here, you feel it tighter and deeper." Emeline groaned a little, lay back and closed her eyes. Then she sat up with a squeak. He had stopped abruptly.

She tried to grab his wrist. "Don't you - won't you?"

"Modesty already abandoned, my sweet?" He stood, grinning and looking down at her.

She screwed up her nose. "You made me feel - and now you're just teasing me."

"Only two days more, and we'll have the peace and comfort to learn a good deal more about each other." He laughed, shaking his head. "Then you can decide whether you hate me or want me. Now eat your breakfast while I get a boy to find your maid. There's a lot to organise today, both for our travels and for the months of repairs to be undertaken by those left behind." He was moving away, but turned back. "I intend riding out a mile or so to see how the roads are for tomorrow, but so far it's a mild spring and promises a pleasant journey. The wild lilac's in bloom already in the hedgerows. Soon we'll see the first swallows on the wing."

Emma had tugged the eiderdown back up to her chin. "Oh, do you love the countryside too?" she said, peeping over the thick feather quilt. "I always looked for the first swallows over the Cotswolds back home."

He gazed at the now well covered bundle beneath his bedclothes. "Sadly swallows seem to be the only thing on my horizon at present. Modesty is evidently a hard habit to break after all, my dear. Now, how, I wonder, do I teach you to be a wanton, and encourage you to climb bare arsed into my lap?"

She giggled. "At the dinner table?"

"I'd have no objection."

The door clicked shut behind him. Emmeline waited, holding her breath. Then she kicked off the blankets, swung her legs from the bed, flung both arms out to the intruding daylight, and began to dance with the shadows. The shy sun's warmth spangled her body as she whirled. She was interrupted by the door opening again. "My lady?"

Petronella had never before seen her mistress wheeling stark naked and entirely abandoned, especially considering this was, admittedly her husband's, but still a gentleman's bedchamber. Emeline flopped backwards onto the bed. "It is," she sighed to the ceiling beams, "a beautiful day after all, Nellie. Such a beautiful life. And a truly beautiful world."

"I'm sure it is, my lady." Petronella eyed her mistress with misgiving. "Tis surely good to see you recovered from the sullens of recent, madam. I was worried, as was Mistress Martha." The maid did not admit that she still was.

"That," beamed Emeline, "was before I understood what real love was all about. Now everything has changed."

Just as predawn paled the stars on the following morning, Nicholas helped his wife mount her palfrey, swung his leg over his own bay's back, and waved the outriders on ahead. The litter with the lady's nurse and personal maid, the trundling cart of baggage and the four armed guards rattled slowly some way behind, for Nicholas hoped to make Nottingham by that evening and had no desire to ride at the same speed as the pack horses. The square young man Emeline already recognised as the squire David Witton, rode at the retinue's head, but sometimes Nicholas called to him, and they travelled some miles alongside, speaking quietly together.

Although left almost entirely in silence, Emeline watched her husband's strong boned profile, square shoulders and long legs tucked to his horse's flanks in complacent anticipation. Before the light had fully risen behind the trees, they were on the road leading east, and the dawn's increasing pastel luminescence was in their eyes. Nicholas remembered occasionally to ask his wife how she felt, and whether, being a country girl, she was content to pass long hours in the saddle. But, more accustomed to solitary pursuits and lonely journeys, he was generally a quiet companion, leaving Emeline to relive her memories. The birds were tiny black shadows in the lightening sky and the wind had sunk to breezes by the time Nicholas signalled to halt. The wayside inn was expecting them, arrangements having been made by the outriders, and stopping for bread, cheese and light ale allowed Emeline to stretch her legs and back.

They were back in the saddle having ridden a few miles more with the sun now climbing higher when, although without any threat of rain or creeping cloud cover, the light dimmed as though it might suddenly snuff out. Emeline stared upwards, pulled on the reins and slowed her pace. Nicholas called, "The next roadside tavern isn't far away. We may have to stop again."

She pointed. Nicholas came beside her, one hand to her horse's bridle as it backed, abruptly skittish. Where the sun's light had been vividly visible, now, in a moment's blink, it had begun to turn dark, edged aside by a steady return to night. The sun's brilliant circle was swallowed as if by a great black throat and hungry invading teeth. Rich blackness sank across the road and over the banked green roadside, the trees ahead and the fields all around. A star, just above the horizon's forested tips, flickered awake. For an instant the sun's circle glowed as a huge empty ring with one tiny and terrifying point of dazzle. Then was gone into startling pitch.

It was from the embracing shadows that her husband's hand came, taking hers in comfort, while his voice murmured, "Just an eclipse, my sweet. Don't look directly, but it's nothing to be frightened of. It is, I think, the moon that blankets the sun. But they say the moon always loses and light always returns."

"The moon is - so dangerous?" Emma blinked hard, rubbing her eyes. "I never knew. I thought it beautiful - in its rightful place."

"I'm no astrologer, my dear. I know only that with an eclipse the sun must dominate in the end, and those who study such things can predict them."

And she said, "But is it a portent, then? My father's priest says the Lord speaks to us by means of heavenly signs."

"I doubt the Lord would take such pains to speak to me, nor ever has," said Nicholas. "I've had no helpful warnings in my life before."

"The warnings aren't always helpful. Perhaps someone has died." Emeline smoothed her palfrey's mane, soothing it.

"There is always someone, somewhere, dying," said Nicholas.

CHAPTER ELEVEN

The lights of the great house awaited, dozens of flaming candles and the fires roaring across the hearths. A white linen cloth lay over the smaller table in the narrow vaulted hall, the platters set, spoons and cups of polished pewter ready for a late supper.

Sysabel stood prim to greet her guests, Adrian behind her. A finger's breadth taller, stocky and plain dressed, he wore no fur trimmings to his sleeves and no fur collar in spite of the winter weather, and although his thighs were solid muscle, they were snug not in knitted silk but in close ribbed wool. He was frowning. Behind him Aunt Elizabeth tottered to her feet, but having risen, decided the effort outweighed the necessity and sank once more to the cushioned settle beside the window's alcove.

"My dear Emeline." Sysabel reached for her hand. "We had expected you some hours ago, and were worried." Then frowning at Nicholas, "Or were you simply not bothered to get yourself from your bed until midday, Nicholas?"

"Perhaps you were delayed by that dreadful black shadow that wiped out the sun this morning?" Aunt Elizabeth wavered from her shadows. "Father Joseph took to his knees in the chapel for half an hour or more and has proclaimed imminent disaster."

Nicholas smiled into the candlelight. "The eclipse."

Tapping his pointed toe to the boards, "Don't attempt to educate us, Nicholas. We are all well aware of the phenomena."

"Clearly Aunt Elizabeth was not. Didn't you choose to enlighten her?"

"Something so absolute, the sun so completely blackened, is hardly common," Sysabel said. "I have never seen anything like it before."

"A harbinger," croaked the aged lady from the window side, dabbing emotion from her eyes with her kerchief. "Certain death and destruction."

"I thought the same at first." The steward had taken her cloak, and now Emeline pulled off her riding gloves. "Nicholas doesn't agree."

"Nicholas," sniffed Sysabel, "never believes in anything uncomfortable."

Nicholas tucked his gloves into his belt, shook out his sleeves and wandered over to the fire. "The eclipse set us back very little, and my squire had already warned me something of the sort was due according to astrologers." An elbow to the lintel, he turned his back to the fire's heat and regarded his small audience. "But when we stopped for dinner near Barrow, there was a great pile up of over turned carts in the road, horses frightened perhaps, and that kept us dawdling some time. Now we're little more than hungry pilgrims."

"No altar here, cousin. But if you're ready to do penance –"

"Thank you, Adrian. But sadly I have little to confess. Our pilgrimage is simply an attempt to satisfy our more wholesome appetites."

"I am," admitted Emeline, "awfully hungry. Starving, in fact." She hovered mid chamber, one eye to the waiting table and its empty platters. "Though we are, of course, only here for your most congenial company."

"My wife," Nicholas informed his cousins, "is permanently hungry. A challenge to the castle's depleted kitchens."

Emeline stretched the saddle weary miles from her back and her fingers to the fire's warmth. "Nicholas wouldn't let me stop for a proper dinner and I've eaten no more than a crust at that miserable tavern outside Burton. And that was hours and hours ago!"

Sysabel, a sudden whirl in mahogany damask, took her hand and brought her to the ready table. "How vilely misused, Emma dear. I may call you Emma? Then we'll have supper served before everything congeals in its dishes." She turned back a moment to Nicholas. "And it's a pleasure to see you both so comfortable now, in each other's company."

"Finally accustomed to my lovable self," explained Nicholas, still enjoying the warmth of the fire. "If I remember rightly, last time we saw you, my dear wife was covered in soot and no doubt planning to stick a knife in my back."

Emeline blushed and sat quickly. But Sysabel frowned and said, "One day I shall have to face marriage myself of course. I do not - welcome -"

"Enough nonsense." Adrian snorted, stepping immediately to the table. "My sister's tongue is frequently undisciplined. I hope you forgive her immaturity. And now - before it is entirely wasted -"

Nicholas wandered to the window, offering his arm. Aunt Elizabeth clutched his elbow and hoisted herself upwards. The train of her gown rustled across the woven reed mats. "All this tittle tattle. Talk, talk. Oh, the energy of youth. I am exhausted already."

"Discussion. The joy of great intellectual conversation, my lady." Nicholas seated his aunt, then sat himself as the serving boys entered with three tepid platters of buttered chicken livers, curdled cream cheese with floating wafers and a sad eyed mackerel beneath a cinnamon rash. Two candles on the table almost extinguished in a flurry as Adrian muttered a semblance of grace.

Then the trenchers were filled and flagons of wine emptied as Sysabel said quickly, "You'll take Adrian hunting tomorrow I hope, Nicholas, leaving me free to make friends with dear Emma."

"But who is the bait, and where the trap, I wonder," murmured Nicholas, helping himself to a slice of mackerel.

Emeline said in a hurry, "I could not dream of anything - nicer."

"In fact she dreams of anything and everything," Nicholas informed the mackerel, "and mumbles constantly in her sleep." He looked up at Emeline, regarding her with faint amusement across the table. "Much like a demented mouse. Though it's a shame," Nicholas was chewing thoughtfully, "about the food. Did your cook die recently, Adrian?"

"Simply that the guests," Sysabel pointed out, "arrived at least three hours later than expected."

"Stop muttering, dear," called Aunt Elizabeth from the other end, "and speak clearly or not at all. Not a word any of you young people utter makes any sense whatsoever." She tapped her spoon on the table. "Where's the boy? Where's the wine?"

"But at least it's a decent Malmsy."

"Which is all you would know all about, Nicholas."

"But we appreciate it – the invitation – very much. Don't we, Nicholas?" Emeline mumbled, a little lost. It was not the style of conversation she was accustomed to. Nicholas was grinning at her over the brim of his cup.

"Since the castle is no more than a stinking heap," Adrian said, pushing away his half filled platter, "I had little choice. I believe in doing my duty. Unlike others."

Nicholas appeared unoffended. "I'm strangely sorry to see the castle so ruined," he said, drinking slowly, as though thoughtful. "But I might take my bride to London in a week or so, once my legs obey me and I can face a longer journey."

"London?" Emeline was suddenly bright eyed.

"Ever been?"

She shook her head. "Is it as exciting as they say?"

"Turgid, filthy, noisy and decrepit. But the old man has a decent enough place in the Strand. We can stay there."

Aunt Elizabeth had dropped her napkin. Sysabel retrieved it. Adrian still frowned. "As a married man now, Nicholas, I trust you're planning to settle. Have you established some future home for your wife?"

Still grinning. "You disapprove of my irresponsible passion for adventure. coz. But what of your own? I doubt you regret earning your knighthood on the battlefield."

"I fought for my king and my country." Adrian put down his knife with a snap. "I hardly count that as a foolhardy risk."

"The Scottish skirmishes – a noble cause," Nicholas leaned across the table and refilled his wife's cup. "But I doubt we'll have another war now," He returned his gaze to his platter. "Our king governs with justice and moderation."

Dismissed, the serving boys hurried off with the half emptied platters and the doors swung shut. Adrian loosened the neck of his shirt. "We'll not discuss battles and bloodshed in front of the women, thank you Nicholas"

"Nor knighthoods and prowess, cousin dear? Perhaps you are right." Nicholas pushed back his chair, a scrape of wood on wood. "And for the moment your hospitality is - all I could possibly desire, so I'll not argue." He stood slowly, stretching his back, and smiled at Emeline. "But since the ladies are no doubt tired, perhaps it is time to retire? May I escort you, Aunt Elizabeth?"

She shook her head. "Foolish boy. I've no intention of travelling at this time of night. It is all your fault that we had such a late supper and I am quite tired out. Now I shall go straight to bed."

"I'll take you up, aunt," Sysabel stood beside her. "I am exhausted myself."

"Then I shall have the pleasure of escorting my wife, who is already half asleep at the table."

Adrian stood abruptly. "And I bid each of you a good night. But," and he crossed the hall to the bottom step where the wide stairs led up, "I have matters to discuss in private, Nicholas. Return here, if you will, before you retire to bed."

Emeline remained in the shadows a moment outside the door of the bedchamber they would share, the house being too small to offer separate quarters, and regarded her husband. Knowing Petronella would be waiting within, she did not yet open the door. Nicholas was smiling. "I won't be long, little one. Sleep sound, until I come."

She whispered, "Do you dislike Adrian, Nicholas? Should we not have come?"

He shook his head. "I've warned you before, my sweet. We're a disreputable family. Cousinly distrust, of course. Adrian has never loved me. But he believes he owes my new wife some consideration after the fire, so invited us here, as he was obliged to do. Now he intends to lecture me about my irresponsible behaviour, and I shall smile meekly and accept his words, since I'm a guest in his house."

"I've never yet seen you meek., Nicholas."

"In your arms later, my love, I shall be meek as an ox to the plough."

She was fast asleep, but woke in Nicholas's arms when everything happened. He had slipped in quietly beside her as she slept, and she had turned, wrapping her arms around him and nestling her cheek against his back. She wore her shift but he was naked, and the smooth knots of his spine became her pillow. She was listening to his small murmured pleasure as she drifted back into oblivion.

It was a louder, more strident sound that woke her some hours later and she sat up, frightened in the blackness. Footsteps pounded past the door and echoed along the corridor outside. Then sobbing, an urgent call, and more footsteps resounding above her head. Nicholas slept on. Emma pushed at his shoulder. "Wake up. Is it danger again?" and clambered out of bed.

Nicholas muttered, "It can't be morning yet," and closed his eyes once more.

"And if it's fire?"

Reluctantly he squinted up at her, wedging himself up on his elbows. "Nightmares, my dear. We are not a permanent furnace, I assure you, and I smell no burning."

"Listen," she said.

Someone was crying as a man recited his prayers, loudly as if in desperation, and people were running. Nicholas groaned and rolled out of bed. He grabbed up his bedrobe, and flung open the chamber door. Emma squeezed to his side.

A body lay in the corridor, huddled and shivering, half lost in shadow, her knees to her breasts, her shift soiled and her face hidden. Two men came running, one holding a torch, light and shade dashing from wall to ceiling and flushing across the body and floorboards. The other man knelt, whispering, "Is it the same, mother?" The huddled woman moaned and the man lifted her, cradling her against him as he stood again. "Then I'll take you back to bed," he whispered. "But we must be quiet not to disturb their lordships."

"Too late for that," Nicholas said from the doorway.

They stood facing one to the other, staring through the leaping shadows. It was the torchbearer who said softly, "My lord, forgive us. We had no choice. There is sickness in the house. Four of the household have fallen ill and fit to die. We feared to tell the masters lest we cause panic for no good reason. The signs are not yet clear, and the doctor is loath to come too close. But, my lord," the man paused, then sighed, lowering the torch, "we fear the worst. We fear the pestilence."

"Dear sweet Jesus," said Nicholas, and turning abruptly, pushed Emeline back into the bedchamber, closing the door hard in her face. "This doctor is resident in the house?" he demanded.

The torchbearer nodded, face white with fright in the torchlight, eyes staring as if afraid to blink. "And is already in attendance, for there are more sick as we speak, and everyone wailing. Terrified, they are, my lord, and for good reason. But the doctor looks from the doorway and will not risk to touch. Forgive me for speaking out of turn, sir, but if this is what we think, then you should leave, and all their lordships with you this night."

"There are inns enough to take us," Nicholas said at once, "but if the whole city becomes infected, then there's no escape. Get that woman upstairs. I'll alert my cousins." He faced Emeline again within the bedchamber. She had been lighting candles. He said, "You and Sissy must get out of here. I don't know what Adrian will choose to do, but I'll get you two to the Cock Robin out on the high road, and come back for the baggage."

"And if we get sick too?" She was shivering. "So shouldn't we stay? The doctor's here, not at the inn."

"We arrived just a few hours back," Nicholas said. "There's an accepted period for the spread of such contagions. We can't be infected yet, whether it's the pestilence or not. Though Adrian and Sissy are perhaps, who knows."

Emeline was already part dressed, and held up her arm for Nicholas to lace her gown. "Can anyone run from disease?"

"There's no point in staying," he said, pulling the ties tight and whirling her around to look at him. "This is not like the fire, and I'll not be practising heroics. There's no known cure, so no point whatsoever trying to nurse the sick. It's been proved infectious, simple as that. Who stands near enough, gets it, and who gets it, usually dies. I don't want you dead."

"I don't want you dead either. So forget the baggage. But there's Petronella, and Martha –?"

He shook his head. "I'll get someone to alert your women and get them all to the stables. But for us, in the middle of the night, fleeing and frightened with neither baggage nor retinue, and rumours of pestilence in the city travelling close behind us? Any tavern would bar its doors." Nicholas was hooking up her stomacher. "So grab what you can, throw what you want into a basket, get a change of linen and warm stockings, and wear your thickest cape. I'll get Witton to pack a bundle for myself while I go and wake Adrian."

She stared up, trembling. "Is it always death we have to face then? First Peter. Then the fire. Now this. And yesterday there was the darkness - the eclipse - the warning."

He brought her to him, both hands firm to her shoulders. "Listen, little one. You showed great courage during the fire. Now you'll do as I tell you, and find the courage to leave this place, and quickly. I won't risk danger again if I can help it, and having found you, I won't risk losing you."

"I wasn't lost."

"In a way, my love, you were. I didn't want you. You didn't want me." He grinned suddenly. "But we've changed our minds. So now we need to stay alive." He pulled on his hose and braies as he spoke, hooking the codpiece and then climbing into his boots. "What - too proud to run? I hope this is nothing more than a handful of servants frightened of the stomach ache. But I'm getting you out until I'm sure. And you'll obey me, my dear, or I'll carry you out over my shoulder."

The flurry and desperation seemed unreal. She whispered, "It's not pride, and I'm frightened too. But you're still too weak from the fire. You can barely ride, let alone run."

"With the pestilence at our heels, I can outrun a fox." He shrugged into his shirt. "I mean it, Emma. Have you never heard of outbreaks, and the desolation they leave behind them? It's not just death, it's agony and there's no husband will subject his wife to that if he can help it. I can help it, so we're getting out. Fast."

CHAPTER TWELVE

They were already slipping away, the scullions and the laundry maids, the cook, his assistant and the steward with his wife, two by two like ghosts in the moonlight, through the pantries into the small hedged gardens, through the back door into the lane, through the courtyard into the shadows of the stables and beyond. The ostlers were wakened, jumping up in alarm from the straw, scared and confused by the noise and the midnight bustle.

Aunt Elizabeth stood trembling as Adrian shoved his bundled clothes into a saddle bag, and ordered the horses saddled. "The pack horses too, and two carts," he told them. "Then I give you leave to get out yourselves if there's no one already sick. Get off back to your wives and mothers but be quiet about it. Alarm will alert the city, and I'll not have them try and lock the gates in my face."

"And what if we're wrong?" ventured Sysabel. "What if it isn't the Great Death?"

"Then we'll look like fools," said Nicholas. "But happy fools, and can ride back home in a week."

"I am not in the habit of looking a fool," Adrian said, turning briefly aside from the organisation of the carts and baggage. "If this was an enemy, I would face him, but no sensible man flails uselessly against disease."

"We're leaving our people," Sysabel whispered.

Nicholas shook his head. "Most have left already. The pestilence moves fast, and respects neither title nor virtue. You can't help the dead."

Adrian interrupted. "You should know better, Sysabel, as if I would ever desert our household if they had need of me. It's high time you realised I know best."

Nicholas said, "Those still able are running quicker than we are, and the rest are beyond help."

Adrian turned to him. "You said the Cock Robin out on the west road? But that's a small place with little more than two extra rooms and one spare stall for the horses."

"Then I'll take Emma on further," said Nicholas. "You'll be recognised at the local inns, and be taken in more readily. I'll bear south, and send a message back in a day or two. Take Sissy and get out now while I hurry up my own people. I won't leave any of them behind. We'll meet up again when all this is over."

The Lady Elizabeth shivered, confused, shaking her head, pins dropping from a headdress she had not been able to adjust. "You say our own people are already leaving? I have barely had time to dress. I called for my maid, but she never came to my call."

"Rats running from a sinking ship."

"The rats die too," said Nicholas, helping the widow up onto the front bench of the cart. "I passed through a village once where the dead outnumbered the living. Every shed was full of rats' corpses."

The larger of the carts was already filled, clothes and baskets thrown in as Adrian's secretary clambered to the driving bench. "Get moving," Adrian called, slapping the sumpter's rump. Then he and his sister were mounted and left at once, Sysabel waving frantically as they thundered across the courtyard cobbles and through to the road beyond.

Nicholas bundled his wife up onto the saddle of her part bridled palfrey. The four guards who had accompanied them from the castle were already waiting in silence, and the two outriders, bridles in hand, stood at the main gates, holding them open. David Witton was still absent. Nicholas said, "One moment only, my love, while I chase the last of our people."

The house was dark and no candles had been left alight downstairs. Nicholas called, quickly mounting the main staircase. His squire had been housed in the small closet room next to the bed chamber, and Nicholas went there first, striding down the corridor, calling as his own echoes followed him. The principal chamber lay in dishevelled gloom. Nicholas pushed open the door to the annexe beyond. "My lord?" David Witton was leaning over the narrow pallet but looked up, startled.

"Without speed," Nicholas said quickly, "escape becomes pointless. We are waiting." He stared at the shadows moving in the bed. "Who is that?" he demanded.

"My lord, forgive me." David shook his head. "Her ladyship's women took the back stairs some minutes past and will already be at the stables. I was at the moment of leaving - but forgive me - against orders, my lord, I stayed only to see these children - two kitchen boys who came searching for help. It was Martha, her ladyship's nursemaid, brought them here. They are - very sick, my lord."

"Sweet heaven," Nicholas muttered, "do you choose infection, man?" He stepped forwards and crouched over the pallet, peering at the two children curled there. One did not move but moaned very quietly like the distant wail of a water bird. The other was flushed, tossing violently. Over his shoulder Nicholas said, "Light candles then, for pity's sake. I cannot help if I cannot see."

David said, "My lord, this is dangerous work. I would never have stayed had I not believed myself safe and my death not yet destined." But he lit two candles, and brought them to his master's side.

The children lay half entwined on the narrow mattress, the sheet in disarray, the straw dishevelled and tossed to the floor. One boy now lay still. The other flung off his covers, his body contorted as he cried out. They wore only their shirts, skinny legs bare grimed beneath. Nicholas sighed, and lifted the quiet child's shirt, uncovering him up to his waist. The buboes were visible both sides of the groin. Great dark uneven swellings shone glossy in the candlelight, and one pulsed as if living, more alive than the child whose scrotum it devoured. Nicholas whispered, "It is the pestilence without doubt, and I have no means of easing it. I am no doctor, but I've seen this before. David, get wine. There's a jug in the chamber next door, for I left it there myself."

The man returned immediately with the jug and two cups. "Is this for yourself, my lord, or for medicine?"

"Neither." Nicholas poured a cup and held it to the boy's lips, supporting and soothing him. "Hush child, drink and trust God." He turned back to David, saying softly, "Insensible with drink, pain eases and death slips in unnoticed. The church would not agree, but I'm no good with prayers and understand wine better. But this second child is burning. There must be a bowl or jug of water in the garderobe. Get it, and cloths if you can."

The child wailed again, and Nicholas leaned over him, bringing the cup of wine to his lips. His limp and sweat soiled shirt was open at the neck, and across the little shrunken chest the rash of the Great Death had already spread in purple bruises and flat blackened stains. The wine spilled a little, oozing from the cracked and bleeding lips, but the boy swallowed and fell silent. There was dried blood around his nose, and more on his legs, leaking from beneath the hem of the shirt. The other child was also bleeding now, from nostrils, gums and anus.

David returned with water and rags. "My lord, you must not touch the children, nor think to wash them, if that is what the water is for. If someone must – then let it be me."

"And if you catch the disease, what difference will that make?" Nicholas said. "For then you'll surely pass it to me just the same." He took the cloths, and cooled the boys' faces, necks, and small bodies. "I've long respected your desire to help and do good, as you know, David. Though sometimes – as now – it's a conviction that brings as much trouble as benefit." As he touched the quiet boy, he drew away, sitting back on his heels. "This little one is now dead," he whispered. "We brought no relief after all." He looked up, then stood abruptly. "Is there no one else left alive in the house?"

David shook his head. "I think not, my lord, unless some other poor soul lingers on in the attic, or in the kitchens where the scullions sleep."

"Dear God," muttered Nicholas. "How can I risk infecting my wife, simply to bring a last moment's comfort to a child I do not know? You're a damned fool, David. We should have left at once."

"It was my own intention, lord, but it's hard to ignore children sobbing in pain."

The older boy squinted painfully into the candlelight. As he spoke, he spat blood, and more trickled from his eyes. "My brother is cold, my lord. He needs the blankets more than me. And can you spare him more wine?"

Nicholas said softly, "Your brother is now asleep. Leave him be, child. Here, finish the wine yourself." He knelt again, offering the refilled cup. He asked, "When were you first ill, since you are now so – very sick? Do you remember?"

The boy was drinking, gulping as though desperately thirsty, and when he answered, his voice was slow, guttural and slurred. "A day or two. Maybe three. Alan was sicker. I never told no one, and hid in my bed. Was that wrong, my lord? I didn't want to be thrown out to the gutter."

"You've done nothing wrong, child," Nicholas told him softly. "Close your eyes now, lie back and dream sweet dreams. When you wake, you will be better and the pain will be gone. You will be safe with your brother."

He stood again, speaking under his breath, ordering his body squire to leave at once, to get to the stables and lead everyone waiting there out onto the highroad, heading south. "Reassure them, but travel slow. Tell her ladyship I'll catch her up before she reaches the county borders."

"My lord, you'll stay?" David stuttered. "Even now, when you know the danger, and one child is already gone? You must know I cannot leave you, my lord."

"Quiet," Nicholas said, "and do as I say. I won't desert a child so near to death. He has as much right to comfort as any other, and I can give him that."

It was some time later when Nicholas returned to the stables. All the stable boys had run, taking the other horses with them, but Nicholas's great bay remained fully saddled and kicking at the straw. Nicholas mounted and, heels to the horse's flanks, immediately galloped out through the manor's gates and down the wide hedged road beyond.

A fine drizzle misted the night, drifting in a silver haze beneath the stars. The moonlight was fading as he caught up with his own party a mile further south. Hearing the galloping hooves, they stopped and waited. The sumpter, head down beneath the rain, slowed as the rattling wooden wheeled cart swerved to a halt with a bounce of baggage, bundles and frightened women.

Emeline turned and rode back towards her husband. Nicholas held out both hands. "Don't touch me," he ordered. "You must not come too close. The fault was mine, but I will make amends."

CHAPTER THIRTEEN

The line cut thin, the great blackness divided by a new born horizon. The slice widened. A pale grey slipped through, leaking daylight into the pitch of night.

The inn sheltered beneath the trees, a rambling assortment of buildings banking the road at its junction with the southern route towards London. As the dawn stretched into rose petal pink, the inn's stables were a yawning bustle of waking ostlers, and the tavern doors were pushed open, brooms busy to the threshold. Nicholas dismounted and signalled his men to make sure the horses were fed, watered and scrubbed down. Within half an hour Emeline took a breakfast of bread, cheese and ale in their bedchamber overlooking the fields at the back of the first floor. Nicholas stood watching her.

He said, "I'll sleep on the pallet. You won't touch me or come close to me until I'm sure. In six days or a week's time I'll know if I've escaped. Or not."

She stared gloomily at him. "What can you do? And how will you know?"

"It starts with a fever, as almost everything does. But if it's the worst, then within an hour I'll be burning up. The rash comes fast, livid spots spreading like decomposing flesh under the skin. First red and sepia. Then purple. Then black. Everything bleeds. Nose, teeth, tongue, eyes, ears. And lower down. Then finally the buboes start swelling up, great dark lumps at the neck or the groin." Nicholas sighed, crossing his arms and leaning back against the wall. "But long before that happens, you'll be gone. I'll have sent you back west to your father."

"It must be terrifying."

"It is," he said simply. "The lucky ones fall unconscious and stay that way until the body rots and they die."

"Then," she flung down her napkin and pushed her platter away, "I must stay and nurse you. How could I leave? Does anyone ever recover? Are there medicines?"

"Listen." He shook his head. "Nursing doesn't help. Enough wine to send me insensible is the best idea, as long as I don't just vomit it back. I know doctors who treat it with tansy and willow bark but I also know that doesn't work. Bursting the buboes simply causes more pain. People can die of pain alone. So death can take hours - or days. Some of the lucky souls recover, but most die. And you won't have any choice about leaving. I'll order Witton to chain you to your horse and gallop off with you. Either that or I'll ride out into the night on my own to die in peace by some roadside."

"You couldn't." Emeline glared at him, eyes glistening. "I'd - I'd -"

"What? Kill me?" He smiled, cold eyed and still keeping his distance. "There's no surety about this, my dear. I've not given up hope. There's always the possibility of a reprieve - just perhaps - since I spent so little time with the children. And there are stories - many stories - of families who are stricken and die, yet where one or two, even staying close, keep their sanity and survive. But until I'm sure, I won't risk you touching me."

Emeline knotted her fingers, staring down into her lap. "Why, Nicholas, when you knew exactly what it might mean? You should never have risked staying - or touching. And especially if you knew you couldn't really help."

"It was stupid," he said. "But it's not the first time I've done something I've regretted later. This time I had reasons - stupid reasons - memories I should have ignored. Saving my father's miserable hide from the fire came close to killing me instead of him. And I've come closer other times too. Indeed, I've led a charmed life of close escapes. Perhaps it's time to pay the price."

Emeline shivered. "I pray there's no such charge." She looked up at him suddenly. "But how do you know so much about this vile illness? You told me you visited some village after the pestilence had passed. But you stayed? And saw what had happened when there might still have been risk? And now - to do exactly the same again?"

"I lied." Nicholas slumped down onto the window seat, abruptly turning his face to stare through the old polished horn and out to the new day. He scratched absently at his wrist, as if he had been bitten, but barely heeded it. "There was no village," he said. "I have a clearer memory than that of the pestilence and how it kills. I was a child, but I'm unlikely to forget. It was how my mother died, and my little sister, and my baby brother with them."

"Dear God."

"God is not always so dear." Nicholas turned back to her. "Now, no more talking. I'll send Martha in to get you to bed while I go downstairs for a jug or two of wine. Once I'm a good deal less sober than I am now, I'll come back and sleep on the pallet by the hearth. Meanwhile you should sleep until dinner time. Maybe I'll join you for that, though I'll not be sitting beside you."

"I can't sleep. And I won't be able to eat."

"I don't believe it." He stood and stared across at his wife hunched small on the edge of the bed. The curtained shadows half enclosed her. "I've watched you eat a good few times," he said, "and your appetite never wavers. And you sleep sound too, while you mutter through your dreams. So climb into bed, my love, and dream of salmon poached in ewe's milk. Apple codlings in syrup. Roast capon stuffed with raisins and spices. Onions broiled in honeyed mead. And jellies of course, with custards and stewed rhubarb. I'll order a late dinner served after midday."

She paused a moment, feeling suddenly cold. "Get tipsy if you want, Nicholas," she whispered. "And then come back up to me. But if you slip off alone and leave your wretched squire with orders to get me back to Gloucestershire, I swear I'll not go. I'll scream the tavern down and search every hedgerow on my knees until I find you."

He stopped at the doorway, staring back at her. "And this from a reluctant bride who hated her husband?" But then his voice shrank, until she could barely hear him. He murmured, "I must do what I think best, and always will, my dear."

She stood in a flurry and took a step towards him but he held out his hand, stopping her. She demanded, "Promise me, Nicholas. I won't sleep until you promise. Tell me you won't leave, and promise I'll see you at dinner."

"I'll promise anything you like." Nicholas sighed, leaning back exhausted against the doorframe. "Now go to sleep, Emma." He watched her a moment, opened the door and slipped immediately out into the passage shadows.

He took the stairs quickly and strode into the small back tap chamber where he ordered not a jug or two of wine, but a single cup, which he drank at once. He then ordered quill, ink and paper, wrote carefully, covering both sides of the paper and afterwards covering one side again, crossing the lines. Then he spoke at some length with his body squire, passing him the folded paper he had written, before sending David back up to bed. Finally he took his hat, cote, and cape, and strode out to the stables. His earlier orders had already been obeyed and a fresh horse was waiting for him ready saddled, its panniers laden full. Nicholas mounted, gazed back once to the first floor windows of the inn, then rode across the cobbles and back onto the road, heading south. It was still raining.

Emeline awoke late. She knew she had been crying in her dreams, for her eyelashes were stuck together and her head ached. She was shivering, although the bed had been well aired before she climbed into it. Now she sat up, looking around. She did not know what time it was but a steady trickle of sallow light leaked through the splintered boards of the window shutters. The chill was persistent. The small fire had gone out and the narrow pallet bed, set beside the hearth for a servant or companion, was empty. The blankets had not been disturbed and no one had slept there since it had been prepared.

At the small dining table set in the private chamber below, a cloth, spoons and napkins had been laid. No one sat at the table and no one waited for her there. The innkeeper poked his head around the door, bowed, and said he would serve dinner immediately as instructed. "As instructed?" demanded Emeline. "By whom? And where is he? Has he eaten already?" But the innkeeper was gone and she sat, knotting her fingers and twisting around at each twitch of noise.

Finally serving boys brought in five wooden dishes holding salmon poached in ewe's milk, honeyed codlings, roast capon stuffed with raisins and spices, broiled onions, jellies, custards, and stewed rhubarb. Emeline burst into tears and pushed her platter away.

His lordship's squire knocked quietly and entered, bowing to the young woman sobbing into her napkin. Carefully keeping his distance, he cleared his throat. Emeline looked up and stared at him. "Your master is a liar and a cheat," she declared through gulps. "He promised. He lied, didn't he? He's gone away."

David Witton bowed once more and still keeping his distance, handed her the folded and unsealed paper which Nicholas had given him. As she read, he replied, "My lady, his lordship was most apologetic and has ordered me to beg for your forgiveness on his behalf. I have known him many years, my lady, and if you will pardon me for speaking without permission, I know his lordship as a man of exceptional honour, great courage and undoubted kindness. I would give my life for his. Most willingly. He has experienced at close quarters the pain and misery the Great Mortality brings. He was adamant not to bring any risk of infection, not to you nor to those others of our people, even to the visitors at this inn and to any who may pass. He would not have - given false assurances - without good reason, my lady. And the fault is mine, not his. Two dying children were brought to where I was and I could not resist - could not deny them help. His lordship found me there, and - but you know the rest, my lady. The good Lord grant his lordship has taken no contamination and will be restored to us without delay."

"Here he writes of London." Emeline looked up at the squire. "How long ago did he leave? Well, we'll follow him there. Get everyone ready, Mister Witton, we depart in an hour."

Witton shook his head and bowed once more. "Forgive me, my lady, his lordship guessed you would say as much. I am forbidden to permit it and I have never disobeyed his lordship, nor mean to. He asks for a dignified privacy in which to consider and make his own decisions. If he had stayed, the risk would not only be to yourself, but to a hundred others. I am therefore instructed to lead our remaining party west to Gloucestershire."

"I also intend making my own decisions," Emeline said, biting her lip. "So, if not to London, we go back to Nottingham, to the Cock Robin, and Adrian and Sysabel. At least with them I can hear as soon as - and have company who understands - and be my own mistress."

The squire sighed. "His lordship also forbade such a move," he explained apologetically. "My master has informed me that no single building ever absorbs the pestilence alone. Death spreads, my lady, and will be raging throughout Nottingham in a day or less. They will either bar the gates to us, or welcome us in to share their burden and their graves. His lordship's cousins, having been previously in close contact with the miasma of the disease, may already be sickening. If not, they will understand what is happening around them, and will leave. Forgive me, my lady but I will carry out his lordship's orders. We depart for Gloucestershire at first light tomorrow."

"Without me," said Emeline, standing and glaring at him. "You have no power to force me, and I choose not to return to my parents. I will go where I wish."

"You will not, my dearest," said another voice behind her. "You will ride with us to safety on the morrow," Martha said, "as his lordship has instructed. It is right and proper, and you know it and will not argue, not with me nor with those who love you. And now, my own precious, you will eat a little, and cry a little if you must, and then come upstairs with me while I dress your hair and sing to you."

White lipped, Emeline gazed back down at the scribbled message in her hand. "He says he'll come and get me when he's sure he's all right," she mumbled. "But what am I to do if he doesn't come? Believe him dead in a gutter? Will I never know?"

"He has promised to send regular messages," David said.

"Promised? I don't believe his promises anymore." Her fingers curled around the screwed paper. "If he can lie about this - of all things. So his mother died, and the other children. So he has terrible memories. But he didn't die. He was there, but he survived. And so, I suppose, did Peter."

"I understand, being the eldest son," the squire answered, "the young Lord Peter was sent away at the first signs and went to stay with his father at Westminster. But it is true, Lord Nicholas remained and survived. I am told he was a little unwell but not for long. Then the pestilence moved on, leaving the child alone to mourn the passing of his family."

"If he dies this time," Emeline whispered, "I will never, ever forgive him."

The journey west, laborious through mud and overflowing fords, improved a little as they headed into the setting sun and its steadily later hour. Finally the weather brightened and a mild spring breeze bundled the clouds into small fluff puffs across the blue.

It was Avice who first ran from the house to the busy stables, grabbing at her sister's arm. "I heard you were coming, but I didn't believe it at first. Then Papa said you were just hours away, so of course I knew it was true. So why did you leave the castle? He's got rid of you already?"

The baroness stood at the doorway. "Avice, be quiet. Come indoors at once, Emma. Hippocras and oat cakes will be served in my chambers. Avice, you may come up too, but only if you promise to behave with dignity."

"I don't believe in promises anymore," muttered Emeline.

"Which is just as well," said Avice, dancing alongside. "Since I have a *great* deal to say, and keeping dignified and quiet would be *quite* beyond my power."

Emeline stood gazing at her mother and sister, and knew she was crying when her mother stepped immediately forwards and embraced her. "My dearest, has it been so hard? Whatever has happened, remember this is your sanctuary and you are safe with us. At this very moment, your Papa is in the chapel, praying for you."

"Praying I won't stay too long."

The baroness sniffed. "There's no need for childish retorts, my dear, whatever problems you have been facing. You are not the only one to suffer you know. We have recently heard the most terrible news, for her sovereign highness the queen is dead these several days gone, and the court is deep in mourning."

Emeline blinked. "Of the pestilence?"

"Oh, good gracious no," her mother said, pulling away. "I believe it was the bloody cough, although we have not heard all the details of course and rumour rides a faster horse than truth. I met the dear lady on only two occasions, but she was most beautiful, and most gracious. I hear the king is devastated."

"It is a cruel and wretched world," said Emeline.

She was bustled indoors, her cloak taken, and led up the staircase, Martha close behind, and Avice calling, "If you shut the door against me, I will scream."

Then the baroness, turning aside, said, "I must see to the arrangements first, my dear, and will be with you shortly. Wait for me upstairs, drink some spiced wine while it is still warm, and please rest." There was a small fire lit and hippocras steamed in its earthenware jug, the shutters were down, a bleary sunshine searched the chamber's distant corners, and Emeline sat on the padded settle close to the hearth, wiping her eyes on her sister's proffered kerchief. She could not rest, but resisted Avice's questions until finally her mother reappeared, and sat beside her. Clearly the baroness had been informed by the servants something of what had happened.

It was after a long but erratic explanation that the baroness leaned back in her chair and sighed. "A sad tale, my dear, but it seems young Nicholas has behaved with chivalry as he should. To bring you into danger would have been wicked. I trust we see him again soon."

"But he wasn't right, Maman. Everything was wrong." Emeline shook her head a little wildly. "He was the one who explained the terrible danger and insisted on running away. Then he contradicts himself and insists on looking after two children he'd never seen in his life before."

"Saving sick children! How noble," breathed Avice. "Just like Sir Lancelot."

"I'm sure Lancelot never did anything so silly," sniffed Emeline. "Certainly not in the stories I've read. And anyway, Nicholas never saved anyone either. The children died. And now perhaps he will too."

"Now use a little common sense, my dear," said her mother, refilling Emeline's cup. "You say the poor boy's mother and siblings died right in front of him, and him just a child himself. The horror of that would certainly make him decide flight was the only solution when faced with the disease once again. Confronted with the pestilence, every man flees. But then to be confronted with two little children in such pain, and of course to remember his young brother and sister who he was unable to help at the time. It must have been a bitter test, Emma."

"If you stop crying," complained Avice, "you could come to my bedchamber and tell me everything. It all sounds like such an adventure."

"I think I am going to cry *forever*," sobbed Emeline.

"But I am certainly comforted," her mother continued, once again taking her in her arms, "to hear how well you've accustomed yourself to marriage at last, just as you should. Now you must pray for young Nicholas to be saved. Besides, your father will wish to hear your story."

"I don't want to see Father Godwin." She shook her head, laying it against her mother's shoulder. "He'll lecture me for hours. And I don't want to see Papa either. He'll lecture me too and I haven't done anything wrong. I'm horribly miserable and I want sympathy, not lectures on doing my duty. If Papa needs explanations he can ask Nicholas's body squire instead. David Witton is very self righteous, but he's incredibly loyal to Nicholas. I saw nothing of him on the journey, but he must be around somewhere."

"Mister Witton never arrived, my dear," her mother told her. "Indeed, I have been informed that once he saw you safely on your way, he left the party. Still following your husband's instructions, I presume, and I imagine he set off at once for whatever meeting place was previously arranged. He might also carry the seeds of the illness I suppose, so could not come here. He must be staying with your husband, either to look after him while he is ill, or to accompany him back here when free to do so."

CHAPTER FOURTEEN

The Earl of Chatwyn's heir entered London through the Moorgate shortly before midday. Mounted, and his squire close behind, he pushed through the squash, threw a halfpenny to the suddenly cooperative gatekeeper, avoided the young woman leading two bleating heifers down to the Shambles, nodded to a twittering bustle of frocked priests as they elbowed their way under the low gateway, breathed a small sigh of relief, and finally followed the road leading through the city, trotting down Broad Street towards the strident excitement of the markets easily heard three lanes back. But once into the wide glow of welcoming bustle, Nicholas did not dismount, nor take interest in the stalls and their clamorous barter. His horse trotted on, keeping to the central gulley. David Witton rode just a half pace behind, with more of an eye to the shine and glamour of London's thoroughfares than his master.

It was as they approached the northern shadows of The Tower that Nicholas slowed, almost ambling, the horse's hooves echoing on the damp cobbles. Along Seethinge Lane and immediately to his left was a sharp angled alleyway where he turned abruptly, dismounted almost at once, and then led his bay to the back entrance of a tenement building sharing its stables with two others almost identical. He and David stabled their horses and paid the keeper for three days in advance, hauled the stuffed saddle bags over their shoulders, entered the immediate bleak darkness of the open doorway beyond, and mounted the stairs.

There was a low planked wooden door to the tiny occupancy on the third floor where they stopped, and stooped to enter. Most others of the dwellings within were simply curtained, loose screened or open to each other, and so unintentionally communal. Without greater division than a threadbare drop of unbleached hessian long turned stiff and black, or the unwieldy swing of an old leather blind, the oppressive dark was the only form of privacy. Families led their lives in permanent struggling enmity, one encroaching neighbour to the next. The weary insults and squabbles wove mutter and complaint into a constant chant, soon sufficiently familiar to fade into unnoticeable inconsequence, as does the sound of water flowing continuously over pebbles, becoming finally unheard.

Few dwellings boasted the status of the privacy which a solid barrier brought, and as Nicholas closed the little door behind him and slammed home the heavy wooden bar on the inside, so the murmur of discontent was blocked. David Witton sighed, leaning back against the flaking plaster. He said, "I never thought to come back here, my lord, and never wished it. Yet now it's the fourth time. I pray it will be the last."

Nicholas smiled. "Not the right prayer, my friend. You wish us dead so soon? The prayer I'd suggest is for living long enough to return a hundred times, and on into the future."

"If we live at all, my lord," David objected, "I mean to give this place away to some other family in need."

"Then let us clean it up, worthy of the gift to be," Nicholas said. "There are cobwebs, ashes, old candlewax, mouse shit and dirt of every kind. Did we leave it last time in such squalor? But the small comforts I remember supplying, have disappeared beneath the grime."

"The stools are stacked beneath the back window, my lord." David whipped the oiled rag from the wall, revealing the window beneath, and the stools beside it. The draught immediately whistled through the loose parchment covering the unglazed opening. "Platters, cups, jugs and pans on the shelves over there. The three pallet beds are heaped next to the hearth. The cauldron is still hanging on its chain, and, as far as I can see in this wretched gloom, a small pile of faggots is ready for your tinder box, my lord."

"Candles?"

"Some were left, as far as I remember." David crossed to the shelves he had indicated and returned, holding two candles and a handful of burned out stubs. "If you see to the fire and the light, I'll unpack our saddle bags."

"Unpack the food first."

"A pottage then, my lord? Shall I use the pork scraps and leeks you bought in Hendon Village?"

"No, you won't," said Nicholas. "But I will. I'll do the cooking myself. As I remember, your cooking is bad enough to frighten a starving rat. Which is near enough to how I feel."

"No rats here, my lord. In this tenement, they'd be eaten themselves before twitching a whisker."

He smiled. "Light the fire then, David. We need comfort, not talk."

David looked down sheepishly at the empty grate. "If you wish it my lord, but you know I have trouble ever getting a flame to spark, and all my attempts end in shame."

Nicholas laughed, knelt and reached for the faggots, twigs and tinderbox. The first tiny flames sent the shadows flying. There was just one chamber, thin plank walls held together with iron nails, gaps stuffed with rags, and the space within little larger than a public privy. The old door and the doorway it closed were low, far lower than most men's heads, cheaper to build and helpful for conserving heat. This was the corner of the tenement building where the third floor quarters huddled around the central and roofless staircase, its iron steps open to the sky above, its sides flanked by the desperation of London's poor. Nicholas spread two pallet beds against the walls and dragged one of the stools closer to the little hearth. The chimney, rising through all floors above and below, had neither flue nor draw, so smoked with a dry persistency which blew back and coloured everything drab, but warmed the room, and also helped warm those above where families who had nothing to burn could still huddle close to the chimney breast where the smoking heat of flame swirled up from below.

David brought water from the butt outside the door, which caught rain from the roofless square above the stairs. "There's a toad in the barrel," he said, "and not much water. No doubt the neighbours have been helping themselves."

"Having been months since anyone lived here, they'd be mad not to. Unless the toad drank it. But I doubt stewed toad would add much flavour to the pottage." David was scrubbing the leeks as Nicholas prepared the pork rind. "So I intend eating what I can first, at least sufficient to keep myself alive until I die of the Pestilence. After dinner I shall dutifully examine my groin for signs of buboes, bed myself down on that flea ridden straw, and sleep for a week."

"I suggest sleeping for just two more days, my lord." David brought the wooden ladle from the top shelf. "In two days or less we will know the truth. In three days, if God is good, we can go home."

"Home? I no longer know where that is. But we can go to Gloucestershire to collect my wife," Nicholas sighed, "if she will still speak to me by then. Wives - duties - families - and all the paraphernalia of responsibility which I once thought to ignore forever, is now mine after all, and I must remember to remember it, if I live. In the meantime, once I know I won't spread enough contagion to slaughter every lord from monarch to mayor, I intend visiting my father."

"Your father?"

Nicholas chuckled. "I've avoided the man for most of my life. Times change, David."

"You've taken a new interest in family loyalties, my lord?"

"I've taken a rather sudden interest in power, wealth and position." Nicholas sat back on the settle, leaving the ladle resting in the cauldron of slowly simmering pottage. "And there's no other way to get it than through the Westminster Court and that parcel of self serving hypocrites, and my father in particular. Unless I decide to horrify the old sot and take up trade. I suppose I could always go to Flanders and trade in best Burgundy. If I brought plenty back, he'd forgive me."

"My lord, pardon me," David said, taking up the broom again. "But I, more than most, know full well how involved in politics you have been in the past, but always in secret and never for profit. Surely your great family wealth, the property and lands, and the power of your esteemed father, are already -"

"Enough for any sane man, but not for me," Nicholas interrupted. "Since I have never been sane, as you're very well aware, David. But the marital status changes a good deal, and my virtuous wife is not the woman I once thought her. She deserves better than me, but since she can't have it, deserves a better me than I have attempted to be so far. So although staring death in the face yet again, and through my own fault as usual, it now occurs to me that since I have hopes of becoming a family man after all, duty looms."

David's mouth twitched slightly. "A dastardly prospect I presume, my lord?"

Nicholas smiled, once again peering into the cauldron. "I'm a changed man, David. That is - either a reformed one - or a dead one. Either way, the change will presumably be noticeable. His highness, being a man of honour and justice, will supply what I'm after. He knows exactly what I've done for him in the past, though always incognito. This time I need the recognition. And dearest Papa will either be invited to my funeral - or to celebrate my knighthood."

"You don't seem particularly fearful of death, my lord," David said, sweeping the dirt and ashes out through the crack beneath the door. "Nor for the first time. Yet most men fear death above all else."

Nicholas looked around at his squire, and his smile faded. "I should fear facing hell's fires, or Purgatory for eternity, perhaps? No - I've never much valued life before and therefore saw no point in fearing death. Now - perhaps - that's changing too." He sighed. "She should have a husband to respect, not despise," he murmured, although more to himself than to his squire. "And for once I should like to live, and earn that respect."

As twilight thickened, the narrow window slit, sealed in old parchment, remained unshuttered, but a rag, hooked to the protruding nails of the frame, kept out the threat of moonlight. The darkness was complete once past sundown, and not wasting their candles, both men slept before evening was through. Curled tight to the straw, Nicholas scratched vaguely, turned, sighed, heard the faint snores from his squire's pallet, turned again and slept.

They were both awakened, not by dawn, but by a violent vibration against the door, the rattling thump of bodies hurtling, falling and finally kicking. Someone called, "By thunder and blight, won't no bugger have pity?"

Nicholas rolled over, found himself on the cold floor, and sat up wearily. "Are you awake, David?" he demanded.

"How could I not be, my lord?"

"Then go and murder the neighbours," muttered Nicholas.

His companion crawled to the door, reached up and removed the bolt. Before the door was fully open, two men tumbled through, each with his hands around the other's neck. Both then stumbled to their feet and one stuffed his knife back into his belt and regarded his hosts. "This place is always kept empty," he remarked with conversational interest. "Didn't reckon on finding folks. You rent, or just squatting?"

David said, "I own it, as my father did before me. But I don't normally choose to live here, for obvious reasons."

"Had a choice, nor would we," agreed the second man. "So why come back?"

"None of your business," Nicholas said, unmoving. "So get the hell out."

The second man sat down beside him on the floor. "That's a mighty fine shirt, mister, for a gent has to sleep on the ground," he said, squinting through the shadows. "Fine linen, by the looks of it, and well bleached. Stole it, did you?"

"I did," Nicholas sighed, moving a little further from the smell of unwashed toil. "I also stole a good steel sword, and with which I'm very well practised."

"Now, now," said the first man, also sitting since a small circle was all the space available. "We quarrels together right enough, being brothers, which is normal. But we don't have no quarrel with you."

"And," said the other, stretching an appreciative finger, "them hose is the best I reckon I've ever seen. Silk, is they? And tight knitted?" His own legs, fat, squat and spread out before him, appeared swathed in a matted bulk of ill fitting buckram. The man shook his head, accepting the three pairs of eyes now concentrated on his plump thighs. "I only got the old sort," he acknowledged, "like me Pa afore me. Cut whole from a piece, shaped to a longer leg than mine and a larger foot into the bargain. Sewed up one side each leg, and neither stretch nor comfort to be had. Tis a fashion long gone for those with the coin to escape it. Now yours, my friend, being the new stretchy knitting, and worth a fair penny –"

Nicholas leaned back against the wall. "I have a headache," he said, "and a sore need to sleep. Take the remains of our pottage if you want, and go and eat it elsewhere. I don't intend relinquishing either my shirt or my hose, and I feel an urgent need to be left alone."

David looked up suddenly. "A headache, my lord? How bad is it?"

The first intruder blinked and recoiled. "A lord, is it then? So what sort of lord comes here to live in the slums?"

"A sick one," said Nicholas quietly. "So I advise you both to leave." He turned, resting back onto the rough straw mattress.

David had crawled over, staring down at him. "Could it be, do you know?"

"I doubt it," Nicholas answered. "But get those two idiots out, David, and let me sleep."

But David frowned. "I've known you ten years since you were bare sixteen years, my lord, and you've had two headaches in all that time." He turned to the intrigued intruders. "There's a candle on that shelf, and an oil lamp beside my bed. Light them both from the fire, there should be spark enough left. I need light, and I need quiet."

On his knees by the mattress, the first man held the oil lamp high. "Well now," he said. "Seems you've been in the wars, my friend, with a scar on your face fit to break bones. Reckon it ain't no wonder you've a headache. But I'm pleased to meet a real lord," he announced cheerfully, "what I never have afore. The pox, is it? Influenza? Or the dysentery? My old Ma died of the yellow pox some years back. Stank terrible, she did."

David ignored both men, but was frowning, bent over his master. "My lord, you cannot sleep yet. I must know."

Nicholas turned his head from the light and closed his eyes. "The headache is worsening," he admitted softly. "And I am hot, and sweating I think. The flame hurts my eyes. Leave me, David, and let me sleep. I shall know the truth by morning."

"The morning will be too late. I will search out a doctor now, if you need one."

"At midnight? Go to bed, my friend. No doctor can cure the pestilence."

The man holding the oil lamp recoiled. "Pestilence, you say?"

His brother came forwards, holding the candle and its pale flame. "Now then," he said. "I'm Rob, and this is Harry, and there's been no pestilence round here for a good few years. Don't reckon there's no cause to fear it now. Aches of the head now, that's common enough, be it from too much brewed ale or wine, and being woke in the night by two ruffians from the next hole along, well, that'll do it every time."

"Throw the buggers out," groaned Nicholas. "Let me die in peace."

Rob thrust David aside. "No point arguing the cock's spur on it," he said at once. "If it's the pestilence, I shall recognise it, for I had it once, and came through safe. Most doesn't, but I did, and can tell the signs. So, Harry, get that lamp up higher and stop quivering like the flea bitten tadpole you is, whilst I examines our new friend."

Harry shook his head. "I ain't never had it, and don't want it now, thanking you all the same. Friends, brothers or no – I'm off." And he dropped the oil lamp on the ground and hurried out through the half open door, closing it hard behind him.

Rob sighed as David took up the lamp. "Where's you been, then, lords and all, to catch a thing like this and bring it here to us?"

"My apologies," David said, "but I must point out how you burst in here uninvited. We had no intention of speaking to anyone, or risking anyone's health but our own. Five days gone, we were in close contact with some who died, and others who sickened. We've travelled a long cold journey to leave our friends safe from possible contagion, and had no thought to bring it here."

"Caught it a long way off?" nodded the man, lifting shirt and blanket from Nicholas's body. "That's good news, I reckon, and maybe it won't spread. Now, let's have a look."

Nicholas lay quiet, eyes closed. His breathing was shallow now, gurgling a little in his throat as gradually he seemed to sway between consciousness and sleep. But his body was unmarked, and the muscled symmetry of his chest was smooth in the flickering light. David exhaled, and sat back on his heels. "There are no signs – no rash – no swellings – nothing like the two wretched boys that died."

"Maybe too early," Rob said, his hand to Nicholas's forehead. "But this bugger's burning up. Fever comes first."

David sat in miserable silence for one moment, then stood abruptly. "I'll stoke up the fire," he said, "and try to stop the draughts."

"That's what them doctors tell us," wondered Rob, "but is it right for a gent already on fire to warm hisself beside more flames? I reckon we should leave it be. But he needs beer or some such to drink, for the next sign is a thirst so terrible it cracks lips and splits the tongue."

"We have ale," David said, taking up one of the saddle bags from a corner. "But we brought only as much as we could carry, and intended it to last three days until we felt safe enough to leave this place. And wine too - but that has another purpose. To die - in such pain - can at least be avoided, my master said, if enough wine is drunk to fall unconscious."

Rob shook his head. "Keep the wine for later then. But get that ale. Nor it ain't three days you needs to worrit about, is it? 'Tis now, and this gent needs ale to drink and water to wash him cool. You gets it then, and I'll do it."

"He's my master, and the man I love," David said quietly. "Which is why I am here, to live or die by his side. And I shall do whatever is necessary to keep him safe."

CHAPTER FIFTEEN

It was impossible to tell when dawn turned to day. No rosy light bathed the room nor sped sunbeams across those fitfully sleeping. So the disturbed night led them to waking late, and it was Nicholas, still uncomprehending, his fever exacerbated, that finally woke them. He drifted between sleep and a plaintive, questioning murmur. "Is it true?" he asked. "Is it come?" Then he turned away and slept quietly, but suddenly woke once more, and tried to sit. "She is calling for me," he insisted. "And the little ones are silent in their cribs. Does she know they have gone?"

"My lord," David said, leaning over him, "You must sleep. There is nothing to worry about, nor need to think on for now."

"Call me then," Nicholas sighed, "when she wakes."

Rob had been snoring, half propped against the wall. Now he blinked one sticky eye. "Make sense, does he, your gent? Or is it babble he's talking?"

"Babble. Memories. Delirium," David sighed. "So he is worsening. Yet I still feel strong. I have no fever - no headaches - no weakness or rash. So I will be nursing my lord from now until - until whatever comes. You should go, before you take greater risk."

"I'll go when I'm ready, and I ain't ready," decided the other man. "Thing is - grand lords, whether living nor dying - and folks appearing sudden in the night - it's interesting, you might say - in a mighty dull world."

David was washing his master's face and neck, the water rolling down into the opening of his shirt where the sweat glistened like oil. He said, "If this wretched business seems interesting to you, then your usual life must be dull indeed."

"Well, as it happens," admitted Rob, "apart from quarrelling with me brother - dull so it is. And I can never rightly remember what them quarrels is even about afterwards. 'Tis a grey world and a grey life. No work to be had nor for pay nor for dinner, so all them dreary hours is spent chasing just enough to keep alive." He paused, scratching his groin. "You say your Pa had this dump afore you? Old man Witton, was it? Worked at the charcoal in the old woods out beyond St. John's, didn't he? Bit of a bastard, but then, aren't we all! Being your name's David, reckon I remember you as a little lad. Never liked you much. Whined a lot, you did. 'Spose you was hungry, like the rest of us."

David had pulled the cloth from the window, and a greasy pale ooze was puddling across the floorboards. "Yes, I'm David Witton," he said, "And I certainly remember being always hungry. But I don't remember you."

"Robert Bambrigg. Ten year older, more or less, and ten year wiser no doubt."

David smiled faintly. "Probably true, since you were wise enough to stay right here, and I was foolish enough to leave, to travel, to educate myself and finally to find employment at Chatwyn Castle in the Midlands."

"The Midlands, eh?" Rob shook his head. "Don't trust them northerners. Funny lot." He thought a moment. "Though your Pa were a funny bugger too, if I remembers right. Weren't it your old man stuck your Ma's hand in the fire when he found her pissed, passed out downstairs with her skirts up round her neck and some old beggar climbed on top, with you as a little lad bawling your eyes out beside her?"

David stiffened, his expression changing. "As I told you, I left. I had many reasons for leaving."

Rob interrupted abruptly. "Your gent," he said, squinting through the gloom, "reckon he's not too well again. Worsening, pr'aps."

Nicholas appeared agitated, his eyelids fluttering as though in dreams. He spoke suddenly, crying out. "She is bleeding - from here - and here. Her mouth is full of blood. Her eyes bleed. Her fingers - look - the nails peel away and there is blood beneath." And then he was silent again and slept as though unconscious.

David dropped to his knees beside Nicholas, fingers to the collar of his shirt. "It's the marks of the pestilence. Vile, creeping bruises." He thrust his hands under the shirt's hem and pulled it up. Both men peered down. David sighed again. "Bad. But not as bad as I'd feared. The marks are shallow and light, and there are few of them."

The rash, a dusky sepia in the low light, dappled the skin in shadows, creeping around the rise of his chest, fading out below the arms, more lurid across the ribs. Flat blotches, some larger, others smaller, uneven and misshapen, straddled his upper body. His nipples stood like tiny brown islands in a weeping sea of poisons.

"Nort to do but wait," nodded Rob. "It'll get worser. Or it'll get better."

Nicholas groaned in his sleep, wandering through an inconclusive misery, grasping at sudden visions, then losing his way in darkness and confusion. He believed he struggled, climbing hills of rock and shingle where his bare feet slipped, and tore on jutting stones. Turning aside, he saw his mother beckoning. But when he followed her, she collapsed dying at his feet, calling out for her babies and for the help he could not bring her. Then finally he saw another woman, russet haired and dark eyed. He could not remember her name or who she was, but watched as she smiled, and came close, and lay beside him. He slipped his hand inside the open neck of her gown, his fingers tingling at the firm smoothness of her breasts. Then pain convulsed him, and a burning heat, and he drifted into delirium again.

The new day was as cold as the night had been but they did not build up the fire at once. Instead they plugged the gaps beneath the door and around the window, using the straw fallen from the third pallet bed. Yet as the chill crept around them, draughts quickly reassembling through the straw plugs, finally David said, "It's fire we need after all. Will you light it?" Rob piled the ready faggots, creating a small dazzle across the hearth. David then boiled water, and reheated the remaining pottage for their dinner. The freeze ebbed and Nicholas continued to sweat. He moaned a little, and tossed, eyes firmly closed, while muttering to himself. When the wind gusted outside, the building swayed, creaking like a ship under sail, its planks and boards shifting and shifting back. The window frames rattled and bursts of dust hurtled down the chimney, twice obliterating the fire. Finally, during the afternoon, the winds quietened as a hazy sunshine took its turn.

David sat long hours, clenching his fists, knuckles white. He and Rob talked sometimes, quietly and with no particular purpose except passing time, for waiting was the only possibility, and waiting in silence created the whispering ghosts of hopelessness; the other contagion.

The busy lives of the cramped dwellings echoed from outside, thumping from stair to overhead and back again. The noises reverberated continuously, the wailing of small children and cursing of those older, the ringing of pot on trivet and the clang of ladle on cauldron, the endless squabbling, a husband's fist sending his wife to the ground and the heavy thwack of her falling body, then the cursing again, complaints, and tearful pleas of forgiveness. David sat hunched over the pallet where Nicholas lay. Rob trotted from hearth to table, and from stool to mattress.

Biting his lip, David muttered, "There is no change. It has been a long time with no result."

"Better no change than a worse change."

"I need to know." David looked up, bleak. The flesh of his face seemed to hang wearily as if it now lacked the strength to stay tight to its bones. "I show no signs - no illness. Yet I sat by the dying boys before his lordship came. Should I not have sickened first?"

"Ain't no knowing how it spreads, nor what makes one get it, and another not." Rob sat cross legged on the ground beside him. "The air, some says. It's in the air. But you both left that air behind long back. Maybe your lord swallowed the air, and you didn't."

"He touched the boys. I did not."

Rob shrugged. "Some folks burn the clothes after a death. Is that because of touch? Or because the air's in the folds? Not even the doctors agree. 'Tis a shame for them nice hose and fancy shirt, if theys what holds the pestilence to the body."

"Should we strip him then? Burn everything? He's only recently recovered from a fire that near killed him, so it would be an irony and for what? Guesses? I do not know." David shook his head. "My lord believed there was a set time between contact with the disease, and showing signs of catching one from the other. Five days he said, six at the most. Seems he was right on that."

"A gent can count. Doctors and priests - they sees more of the sick than the rest of us - and they reckons on the days between sick and sicker too. I heard three and I heard six as the time it takes to grow inside afore showing." Rob shrugged again. "But I ain't sick. And you ain't sick."

Nicholas breathed with a steady and guttural wheeze, and did not open his eyes. The shadows, pale in the sallow light seeping through the window, crept in and shrank back, moving and assembling around the bleak and empty corners. Across the hearth the flames burst bright, then crackled low into spark and spit. Sudden warmth and sudden chill, light then dark, and through it all his breathing, rhythmic and hoarse, marked the day's passage.

"You're not sick," David told Rob, "because you never saw the two dying children up north. If you catch it at all, it would have to come from my lord, and the days between catching and showing have not yet passed. For me it's different. Surely I should have been ill by now, if I had it."

"It's enough to make me head spin," Rob objected, "like sums in the market. A penny for this and a penny for that - well, it's gonna cost two penny. I can do that. But when it's a pie, hot and juicy, with a stalk of radish, a cup o' beer and a basket of cabbage greens - well, that's got to be added all together. Head spinning stuff - like this. So many days to catch and so many days to wait. Then is it touch or swallow, or is it the air over your head or the doublet off your back? Well - I'm telling you - I don't bloody care. I ain't got it. I never got it last time and I ain't gonna catch it now. The pestilence don't frighten me."

"Don't mention hot pies," mumbled David. "Is that watery pottage hot yet?"

Rob staggered back up to his feet and peered into the cauldron. "Simmering. Hot enough. Don't smell particular appetising, but food's food and it's two days without none so I'm starving. Where's your trenchers?"

"There's no bread, neither fresh nor stale for trenchers. But platters are here," and he brought two over, and spoons for them both.

They conserved their candles for the small room took light when the little fire blazed, but the gloom dragged into the dismal hours of a dismal afternoon, even when sunshine flickered sometimes through the cloud. It was near supper time when Rob marched off to speak to his brother, but returned quickly, saying only, "Well - like I said afore. 'Tis a dull life for dull folks." He looked across at David, and at Nicholas beside him. Rob said suddenly, "By the by, your gent's waking."

David leaned over in a hurry. "My lord?"

Nicholas had opened his eyes, frowning as he tried to wedge himself up a little against the sweat sodden bolster. "David?" He rubbed his eyes, trying to focus. "Is it dinner time? I smell food, but I've no appetite for it. Has something happened? Have I been trampled by horses? And who the devil is that?"

"More a saint than a devil." David smiled, immediately reassured. "It's my neighbour, Rob. Don't you remember him from last night? But you've been ill all day, my lord, and dinner time is long gone, with the pottage you smell long eaten. Through all that time you've been unable to sit, unable to speak, and the pain, I believe, has kept you unconscious. That at least was a gift of salvation. But now it seems you are a little - just a very little - recovered. I pray that's true."

Nicholas fell back on the straw, lost again within the shadows. His voice was soft, as though he had no strength for louder. He murmured, "I've been ill then? Nor fight nor battle? I hurt in every limb, as though kicked and battered."

"My lord, with your permission, I'll examine you. Where does it hurt?"

After a pause, Nicholas said, "Everywhere," and closed his eyes.

David searched him, once more pulling up the soiled shirt, and calling for Rob to bring a candle. With trembling and gentle care, he traced the flattened muscles across his master's chest, barely touching and quickly drawing back. Finally he said, "It's true. I'd swear the rash is already fading, and the bruises beneath the skin are pale and shrinking. There are no new marks and the flush and heat is lesser too. There are without doubt neither buboes nor swellings of any kind."

"Your fingers at my groin," Nicholas told him faintly, "are most disconcerting. Whatever you've lost, my friend, you will hardly find there."

"But my lord," David insisted, "I feared the worse. And some hours ago the marks of the pestilence, although never fully developed, were clear enough to see. But now the rash is almost disappearing. My lord, we are all saved." He sat back on his heels, breathing fast, as though excited. "There's little bleeding. And no diarrhoea."

Nicholas tried once more to sit, failed, and fell back again, closing his eyes. "But I see the world through scarlet streaks and my lips are cracked. My throat burns and I have a terrible thirst. Every bone in my body spites me."

David hurried to pour ale, and held the cup to his master's lips. "Beer for the thirst, my lord, then wine for the pain."

Nicholas drank, winced, but drained the cup and said slowly, "The pestilence for sure then? And *you* are safe, with no signs – no fever?"

"Nothing, my lord." David refilled the cup.

"And you?" Nicholas looked up at Rob, now relighting the fire after another fall of soot. "I forget the name, and have no notion why you're here. Are you ill?"

"Nor a hair nor a feather," Rob assured him. "I was in the Clink ten years back, and the pestilence had the poor buggers dropping like fleas in a flood, both them behind the bars and the keepers alike. But me – no. I got a sore head and a nose bleed, and that were all. This time I reckon on the same. It's the good Lord, far as I can see, that don't want me mucking up His nice clean heaven nor dragging through purgatory complaining too loud and setting up a beer stall. So's the worser I curse and steal, the safer I am."

Nicholas smiled weakly. "An interesting thought." He drank the second cup of ale, and leaned back again. "The same, I suppose, might apply to me. If you call indiscriminate dalliance a sin, then I've sinned my share. But I feel half dead, and death might be preferable to the way I feel now."

"You won't die while I'm here to prevent it," objected David. "And you're better, my lord, a whole mountain better I assure you, at least than you were some hours back."

"I could not feel worse," Nicholas said.

"Them buggers in the Clink," Rob told him, "was screaming and wailing. I saw one poor wretch, just a little mite he was, but then so was I at the time. His whole scrawny body went to mush. Black bruises outside and no control inside. Bowels like water, and that weren't pleasant in a small space. And bleeding – well, there weren't no place he didn't bleed from in the end. Common blood first, red as you'd expect but then dark and smelly.

He lay on his straw, crying. Weeping blood he was. Then blood out his arse and his prick, his gums and his ears. So nasty, it put me off crime for a twelvemonth."

Nicholas gazed up at him, blue eyes hooded. "An eloquent description, my friend. But I have my own memories of the suffering this disease brings, and to those I loved. If I die, then so be it. But I have no wish to listen to the horrors of times past."

"My lord," David again held the cup to his lips, "the day is almost over and if you are in pain, you should sleep. Sleep is always a good medicine. So next I'll bring wine."

"Have I already slept for days?" Nicholas wondered. "I remember a procession of dreams, passing ghosts and a feeling of dread." The twilit shadows were growing heavier through the lightless window, and his bed was left in darkness. He closed his eyes. "The light burns and the dark is most welcome but now the thought of sleeping is dreary, not restful. I've no wish to dream of misery and foreboding."

David shook his head. "I doubt you were asleep at all, my lord. You were ill, delirious at times, and unconscious at others. Now, perhaps, you can sleep as a healthy man does, and wake refreshed."

"Healthy? Perhaps." Nicholas sighed. "But the pain in my legs and back is severe, so I'll sleep to escape, and take the wine you spoke of. But am I recovering, or will I worsen in the night? Have you checked for buboes?" He slipped his hand up around his neck, feeling, fingertips tentative.

David shook his head at once. "I checked, my lord, and there is nothing but the rash." He again lifted the sweat grimed shirt. "Here," and touched, very gently. "The wretched rash of pale bruises still cover your chest. But only that."

Nicholas winced when touched, then peered down, though through the gloom and the pain in his eyes, he could see little. "Painful – but no worse than other pains," he sighed. "And I could weep for a bath."

"Not possible here, my lord."

Rob was sitting a little apart, the wine jug in his hand. "There's the bathhouse not more than a stride away. But that's more for the pleasure of other things, as you might say. 'Tis more whores than soap you'll find there."

Nicholas drank the wine brought to him, and tried to smile. "I've no strength for that - nor for much else at present. And I pray I've passed the vile sickness to none of you, whoever you are. So I'll sleep again. Perhaps all of us will wake to a bright new day."

CHAPTER SIXTEEN

Not the next day, nor the next, but in three more days Nicholas woke without headache or rash remaining, stretched both legs, flexed his toes, and breathed deep. The air was still with a mild warmth, recognising spring. The fire had gone out and the smell of the soot and the sweat sodden straw beneath him were nauseating. But he did not feel ill. He felt joyously alive. His muscles obeyed him and at his first attempt to stand he remained on his knees only moments before rising. David was instantly beside him. Nicholas stretched. "It's a good morning," he said, "Let's have that foul curtain down, and see the sun."

David obeyed. "Your voice is strong, my lord. This is a wonderful awakening. But it's too soon, I think, to be out of bed."

"But there is no bed," Nicholas pointed out. "That heap of rank effluence counts as neither mattress nor pallet. I've no doubt ruined it myself, with shit and sweat - but ruined it is." He looked up suddenly. "And who on earth is that?"

"Never thought meself so easy forgot," said Rob, ambling over. "But seeing as how we've met a good few times now, reckon I might as well introduce meself again. I'm Robert Bambrigg, your lordship, being a neighbour in this tenement. And a right helpful one too, as it happens."

"Then I'm very much obliged to you," said Nicholas, leaning back heavily against the support of the wall. "What have you done exactly?"

Rob thought a moment. Then he said, "Well, come to think of it, not much. But I were willing."

"He kept me company," David interrupted, "and stopped me going insane with worry. He may have done little to alleviate your suffering, my lord, except to hold a candle when I needed it, and light the fire when it blew out, but nor could I do more myself. And his presence stopped me falling into dread and madness, convincing myself you were dead or dying. He showed courage too, and did not run."

"Then I'm doubly obliged," Nicholas said. "And it seems luck has blessed us all, since neither of you show the marks of illness, and I am, without doubt, recovering. I can believe it now." He accepted the cup of warmed hippocras which David had prepared, and drank deep. "It's strange, though," he continued, "that the pestilence is such a terror, and each outbreak kills so many, yet we three have escaped as if this room carries some special charm."

"This room? But this is the worst slum in the city, my lord." David smiled, drinking his own hippocras. "My father always said folk would be better off in The Tower dungeons than living here - but for thieves and whores, well, this is almost freedom."

Rob nodded with sympathy. "On the run too, he was, my old man."

"This discussion of criminal brotherhood, fascinating though it is," Nicholas murmured, "is of no immediate importance. My recovery, if that is what it is, echoes what happened when I was a child, and that interests me more. So what saved me then, and what saves me now? And you, David? And this other wretch? And beyond even that, what happens now? Am I safe to meet with others yet? Do I carry sickness in my clothes?"

"I'll burn your clothes if you wish, my lord."

"These are foul now, and certainly should be burned. I have others in the saddle bags - but should they all be destroyed? And what of Adrian, and Sysabel?" Nicholas sat forward again, blinking in the increasing daylight. "I left them in Nottingham. I thought to keep them safe from me, and me from them, since any one of us could have caught the thing. It spreads like smoke through the air, they say, so is all of Nottingham infected?"

"Shut away here, my lord, and speaking to no one, we cannot know."

"They will know at court," Nicholas said. "After tomorrow, unless I relapse, I shall go to see my father, and find out. And at court there are others I need to see, and matters to decide. I cannot risk asking to see his highness at this point, and in any case I doubt he's at Westminster. But I may approach Kendall or Brampton. Then, once I'm strong enough, we're off to Wrotham under Wychwood."

Rob frowned. "Ain't never heard of no place like that."

"Gloucestershire," said Nicholas, "and my wife."

"Which reminds me, talking of wives," nodded Rob, "you knows, I suppose, of the queen?"

The court was deep in mourning. Where there had always been music, now there was silence, the echoes of footsteps or the gentle murmur of reverential sympathy. Where there had been dancing and laughter, the pace was now careful and sedate. Where there had been colour now there was shadow, and where there had been hope, now there was none.

The Earl of Chatwyn regarded his son with vague distrust, and said, "I cannot say you're that welcome, tell the truth, my boy. This whole place has been as dark and dismal as the inside of my boot, and drunken feasts all cancelled this ten days and more. The king, poor soul, is as wretched as I've seen him. They got on well, you know, him and his consort. He misses her. Rides out with his falconer most days, I hear, to get the wind in his eyes and his mind on other things. When there's no royal duties, he spends his time in silence. And it's dark blue, black or morado we're wearing as you should know, boy." He eyed his son's rich green velvets. "That cote could be taken for an insult - and what's more - it needs a brush and a swab. You're not looking your best and if you must come here uninvited, at least I expect you to do me credit."

Nicholas had been standing politely in his father's presence, but now sank heavily to the chair beside him. "You've finished complaining, I hope?" he muttered. "My apologies for the clothes - it was the best I could do. As for everything else, I feel myself lucky to be alive. You came close to running out of heirs altogether."

The earl leaned back, tenting his fingers over the large black damask swell of his belly. "Been fighting again, my boy? Or got pissed and fallen off the battlements? And where the devil's that silly little wife of yours? Not flung her in the moat already, I hope?"

"I've decided to like her after all. She's growing on me. But there have been other complications." Nicholas briefly informed his father of recent events. He offered no details. "Since Chatwyn Castle was a seething hulk of soot and rank discomfort, I decided to visit Adrian. Unfortunately the pestilence hit Nottingham some two or three days before I did. His household was dying under his nose, though the fool didn't know it. I caught the damn disease. I sent Emma to her father's and came south to die alone. Not alone exactly since Witton was with me as usual, but I made sure no one else could catch the foul thing from me. I was sick, but not badly. Witton saw me through it and caught nothing himself. I seem to have the luck of the devil, since this is the second time. Now I need to know what's going on in the city, and I'm planning a change in direction for myself. So I came to you."

The earl narrowed his eyes, pushing instinctively back in his chair. "The luck of the devil? Perhaps. But also the devil's intentions, it seems. You will leave this place now, Nicholas, and take whatever vile humours you carry with you. Do you mean to come here - of all places - and to me of all people - and risk bringing the pestilence with you?"

"I carry nothing." Nicholas remained where he was. "It's five days since I've felt as fine as a summer's day. Whatever spreads this thing has gone. The companions I have are well, and so am I. I came here in good faith, and in need of advice."

The earl stood in a hurry, kicking away the chair and stepping back to the wall behind him. "My advice is to get out - to leave immediately," he said at once. "And if you will not move, then I shall. The court is already a place of black regrets and mourning. You wish to bring more misery? You should never have come."

Nicholas sighed. "You ran last time too, I remember, though took Peter with you. You left the rest of us to die. Three of us did."

"Your mother," puffed the earl, "was already - the signs were clear - and the smaller children - she could have left if she wished. If you think to pass the responsibility - and after all this time - and want to poison me now with the same spreading sickness? For what - for revenge?"

"Your breath stinks of wine. No drunken feasts while the court's in mourning? But there's wine still to be had in your quarters." Nicholas stood slowly, and went to the door. "Go get pissed again, father. You have a better excuse now, and can drink deep to forget me - and the fate that awaits you."

"The doctor," stammered his father. "Send for a medick. Call him."

His son smiled, cold eyed. "But the doctor cannot help you, Papa. There's no cure for the sickness you've already had all your life."

The corridors of Westminster Palace whispered with banners of deep purple and fluttering black curtains. Still in mourning after her grace's death, the footsteps were hushed, the minstrels were quiet, and no feasts were celebrated. Nicholas walked quietly, leaving his father's quarters and those more illustrious passageways where long windows looked out to the gardens and the great sconces flared with torchlight. He then headed into the narrow corridors, those less lit, less windowed, but busier since more minor nobility inhabited the lower echelons than the higher.

He had no difficulty finding his uncle's chambers. They were small, cramped, and at the back of the palace where the gently drifting perfumes of horse shit and mashed turnip announced those quarters of convenience only to the stables. Jerrid Chatwyn was not unlike his elder brother the earl, but, as the earl liked to point out, had never sat on the Royal Council. They had much in common, however. Jerrid was now slumped before the small grate and its little cheerful flames, a large cup in one hand, and the wine jug in the other. He was snoring.

"The family failing reigns," remarked Nicholas, entering without being announced. "Pissed and passed out."

His uncle opened one bright blue eye. "What else to do, my boy, when denied ordinary entertainment, and lacking the coin for other pleasures. Even the Winchester Geese have lately put up their prices, you know. It don't please me, but probably pleases the wretched bishop as he raises the rents."

Nicholas sat without being invited, and stretched his legs to the fire. His knees were aching and his lower back throbbed. He sighed, and said, "Don't tell me you can't even afford the washhouses?"

"Don't trust those washhouse females. Half an hour in that putrid water, and you come out with spots on your prick and your purse cut." With a yawn, he edged upwards and regarded his nephew, "Not that you've a scarcity problem in that direction of course. How's the new wife?"

Nicholas grinned suddenly. "Had little enough opportunity myself lately, uncle, wife or no wife."

"Heard you objected to the match. One of Peter's cast offs, I understand. That bad, is she?" Jerrid Chatwyn passed the wine jug. "There's cups somewhere, boy. Help yourself."

Nicholas did. "As it happens, I was mistaken." He drained the first cup of wine and winced slightly. "I should never have believed Peter in the first place."

"Your dear brother, God rest his soul," Jerrid shook his head, "never told the truth unless quite sure the truth would hurt someone more than the lie."

"Brothers don't sit well together in this family. I shall make sure to have only one son."

"Drink up, Nick. Sobriety don't sit well with this family either."

The warmth of fire and wine were easing the growing pain in his back. Nicholas sprawled, and drank. "No shortage of the grape, then Uncle? The queen's passing doesn't seem to have affected you after all."

Jerrid snorted. "Illustrious circles, Nick, and all too rarefied for me. Hardly ever met the dear lady. A Neville, as you know. She'll be much missed in the North."

"I met her highness on a few occasions and as queens go," Nicholas said, sipping his wine, "I believe she was well loved both north and south."

"Oh indeed, north - south - east - west, m'boy. Better than the last one at any rate," muttered Jerrid. "She and her family caused no end of trouble after the old king died. And before, come to think of it."

"You seem to think me an infant," sighed Nicholas, putting his cup back on the table beside him. "I'm not so young I don't remember what happened just two years ago. You may also remember I had a very small hand in quelling the situation on the king's command. Not that he was king back then."

His uncle chuckled. "I'm not that pissed. I know some of what you've got up to over past years - what with your secret dealings, and all that time spent with the little Princess Cecily - and no doubt a good deal more you've never told me too. You've never told your father any of it, have you? Not that I blame you for that.

My fool of a brother could never keep his mouth shut any more than your brother could."

"Enough," sighed Nicholas. "I tell my family as little as possible since I trust none of them. And now, since you serve a thoroughly inferior Claret, I can only believe you're as paupered as you say you are. Don't you cadge off your dear brother anymore, sir? Or has he finally learned you never pay him back?"

"I've never borrowed a penny from your father," objected his uncle. "I beg yes, I ask politely. Finally I demand. But as for promising to pay back, I'd not be such a fool. Sadly, he's stopped giving. If it weren't that the king pays, I'd never have afforded to dress in quality black, or eat more than rye bread. You see before you a broken man, Nicholas. A blight on the house of Chatwyn, I'm afraid. So the next time his highness sends you off on some special business, you'd better take me with you. Then I'll have the chance of more than an inferior Claret."

"The house of Chatwyn," smiled his nephew, "is a blight in itself. My father's a reprehensible old bore, you're a penniless picklebrain, and both of you are permanently pissed. I'd take advantage and get pissed myself if this was a better brew, since less than half an hour back my dear father neither welcomed me nor offered me so much as a cup of ale."

Jerrid shook his head. "A sad business it is, being the younger son. You should know, my boy, since you expected to inherit nothing until last year. Better you than Peter, I say, but he was your father's favourite of course. Now the queen. They say there were portents. I was asleep when it happened, but I hear there was an eclipse when she died."

"I saw it."

"People stared, ran out into the street to look, and now there's reports of folk going blind. Medicks blame the astrologers."

"Her death was expected?"

Jerrid spoke to the cup as he refilled it. "Was ill last year, but they thought it was influenza. Then coughing blood - well - who knows! The boy died last year of course - the little prince, poor child. The king went half mad at the time, they say, and her highness never the same since. So when she was ill many said it was a natural consequence. But she got better. Celebrated Christmas with a little extra bounce. Then February, she was sick again. The

Council started planning to negotiate with Portugal. They knew, you see. You cough blood - you're on the way out. Your father knew - parliament knew - I knew. No doubt the king knew. Perhaps the queen knew."

Nicholas shook his head. "Spare me a list."

"Well, your father got busy. Princess of Portugal - another in Spain. Both Lancastrian heritage. Diplomatic necessity, and should keep everyone happy. Even that other silly little princess, Edward's eldest girl Elizabeth whose been asking for a husband for months. Well now she's got her wish. King marries the Portuguese princess - his niece marries some Portuguese prince, keep it in the family. Something has to be set up, after all. A new king less than two years crowned - now no wife - and no legitimate children. Disaster. Parliament authorised the negotiations and your father's on orders to sail. He'll be off to Lisbon next month. Proud of himself he is, the bugger. No doubt Brampton will go with him, but I say Parliament is tipping the scales towards failure, choosing a Chatwyn. One word from my drunken sot of a brother, and any father would rush to lock his daughter away in a nunnery."

Nicholas sighed again, rubbing his knees. "A bit soon to foist another queen on the poor king, isn't it? Queen Anne barely cold in her grave!"

"It'll take a year or more to finalise. Need to start early. Point is -" Jerrid said, draining his cup, "my dear brother was knocked off the Royal Council long since, yet still gets the honourable positions."

"He won't like Portugal. Too hot. Though I believe the Jerez is the best quality, so that'll console him. And if he travels with Brampton, he'd best mind his manners or he'll be sent to his sickbed."

Sir Jerrid regarded his nephew. "Don't look too well yourself, my boy, come to think of it," he decided. "Been off your porridge, have you?"

Mentioning the pestilence no longer seemed wise. "Winter weather," Nicholas said with vague abandon. "But that's not why I came, uncle. Nor to gossip about the problems of widowhood. I had quite another motive."

"Well, and here was me thinking you came for the pleasure of my company," Jerrid said. "Not widowhood yourself already I trust, m'boy? Or is it the other direction, and an heir on the way to increase the ignominious Chatwyn bloodline?"

A sudden smile, almost secretive, softened the glimmer of pain around his eyes. Nicholas said quietly, "Not yet. There's been no - and an inappropriate beginning. But she's a sweet little thing. I've grown rather fond of her." He looked up again. "But that's not the business I came to discuss either."

"So you'd better tell me the worst, my boy. Just so long as it's not to beg or borrow, for I've not a farthing, nor half a saddle blanket to spare."

Nicholas pulled his chair a little closer to the fire. "I'm asking, uncle, but not for coin nor favours. Not even for myself, but for an investigation in the National interest, suggested by Sir James Tyrell. In fact, join me in what I'm planning, and I'll do the paying."

CHAPTER SEVENTEEN

Emeline said, "It's eight days ago since I sent cousin Adrian a message. If he bothers to reply at all, then his letter should come tomorrow." She waited for the tirade, muttered, "I'm afraid I sent one of the village carters, so Papa will be cross with me I suppose," and stuck out her lower lip.

"One day," sighed the baroness, "that lip will fall right off, Emeline. I shall have it swept up and cast out for the pigs."

Avice nodded vigorously. "And if Papa wasn't so mean, and bought us some of those gorgeous coloured rugs other people have on their floors nowadays, then at least your lip would have a softer landing."

"I sometimes wonder," said Emeline, "why I bother talking at all."

"And I wonder," said her mother, "why I listen. This cousin Adrian you speak of is a virtual stranger to you. On arrival here you distinctly informed me he was a dull man of prim proprieties. And what is more, he is probably dying or dead of the pestilence by now. What conceivable message have you sent the poor man?"

Emeline sat in a hurry. "I'm trying to find Nicholas. He said he'd write and tell me how he is and where he is. He hasn't. He may be dead too."

"I thought you *hated* him."

"He's my husband," Emeline glared at her sister. "I'm doing my - duty. Even Papa can't complain about that. Besides," she admitted, very small voiced, "I don't hate him anymore." The glare turned moist. "Not even a little bit."

"You're lucky, my dear," sighed the baroness. "To be reconciled to an unwanted husband so soon after the wedding is - fortunate indeed."

"I *am* fortunate," Emeline sniffed and hung her head. "He's nicer than I expected. Perhaps what Peter told me was all a mistake. Brothers you know - like sisters - they tease - and say things they don't mean. It seems Nicholas isn't how Peter told me at all."

"Just don't admit any of that to Papa," Avice sniggered. "He'll sympathise with duty, but not with actually *caring* –"

She was interrupted. The door swung open with considerable force and Baron Wrotham stood in the shadowed doorway, staring down his nose as his eldest daughter. "Your principal *duty*, Emeline," he informed her, "is, at present, to your parents who are housing you, and to whom you owe eternal honour as the good Lord informs us all." The pale spring sunshine streaking through the small solar window did not reach the doorway and the baron remained framed in sombre disapproval. "And now," he continued, "it has come to my attention that a written message has been dispatched at my expense, without it first being presented to me for approval."

The silence created its own shadows. Finally the baroness took a deep breath, and said, "I approved the message, James. You were not at home. I therefore took it upon myself to authorise the carter, his fee, and the delivery of a message I considered quite proper."

The baron narrowed his eyes. "Indeed, madam? And what, precisely, did this quite proper message contain?"

He held up his hand as his daughter began to answer, and looked firmly at his wife. The baroness answered her husband's gaze. "Addressed formally to Sir Adrian Frye, it was a request from Emeline regarding the whereabouts of young Nicholas. You are perfectly well aware, my lord, that Emma has heard nothing since her husband rode off alone to London, fearing for his life. Naturally she is worried."

"Approval during my absence might be acceptable, had I been informed immediately on returning to the house," the baron informed her. "And this Adrian Frye is a creature of little consequence. Any such message should have been addressed to the earl. Only the father has the right to pronounce upon his son's whereabouts."

"Adrian has *some* consequence," dared Emeline. "He was knighted, after all."

"If you believe that your marital status gives you the right to contradict or argue with me," the baron pronounced, "then you are, as usual, deluded, Emeline." He paused, looking around the chamber with hauteur. "And should this young man make any attempt to reply, and to divert you from your womanly duties, you will ignore him. Am I understood?"

Emma hunched, staring at her toes. "You wouldn't want me to be impolite, Papa? And I must - Nicholas that is - and surely he is my first duty - and since he might be ill -"

"His wellbeing is indeed your duty," said the baron with withering patience. "I have lectured you sufficiently over the years, I believe, Emeline, and see no reason to repeat myself. But evidently you have insufficient intelligence, being female, to realise that any inquiry regarding the son should come through me, and be addressed to his father."

"Even from his wife? And even though his papa is at Westminster and may not even know that Nicholas was in contact - or that he might have fallen ill?"

"If the Chatwyn heir is sufficiently remiss not to inform his father of such a momentous situation, then that is, no doubt, his own affair," pronounced the baron. "How my daughter behaves is, on the other hand, at least while she resides in my home, most assuredly *my* affair. You will behave with propriety at all times, Emeline, and queries regarding the son, if they cannot be directed to your husband himself, must instead be directed to the earl."

"I suppose so, Papa."

"I intend travelling to London this week," stated the baron, turning on his heel with a sweep of damask sleeves. "After the tragic death of her royal highness, may our great and merciful God take pity on her soul, I intend paying my respects at court before then continuing to the capital on business. I shall visit his lordship your father-in-law, and broach the subject of your husband's predicament."

Emeline stared at her father's diminishing shadow. She looked up at her mother. "Is he - right? I cannot believe, as his wife, it could possibly be improper to send a message to his cousin." Her mother looked unexpectedly cowed, so Emeline sighed, and said, "It doesn't matter anymore. But thank you for taking the blame about the message."

"Since your papa is, it appears, thoughtful enough to absent himself within the week," decided the baroness quietly, "I do believe, should any reply from Sir Adrian be delivered during the next few days, we may consider ourselves free to deal with it as we decide best."

Avice grabbed her sister's arm. "Thoughtful? It will be bliss. Five days or more to Westminster. Two days at court. Then three days at least in London. Five or six days to return, and it could be seven if he's tired. Oh, wonderful! Papa will be gone nigh on three weeks. I think I shall tell Martha to brush out my best blue silk."

The upstairs solar was a drab little chamber though not bare of furniture. Although it lacked tapestries, arras or mural, there were two sturdy chairs, two solid stools, an uncushioned settle, and a window seat. The hearth was neither large nor adorned, but it gave sufficient space for a cheerfully crackling blaze. It was in the light of the fire that the baroness stood gazing at her two daughters as their faces began to thaw, to brighten, and in their smiles, to express a new dawning pleasure.

The baroness raised one finger. "I know," she said, "but it must not be said. Three weeks indeed? But what we feel, my dears, is one thing. As long as nothing disrespectful is spoken aloud, then I feel we are entitled to our silent, and shared, opinions."

The day following the baron's departure, the expected reply came indeed. It was Sir Adrian who brought it himself. His approach, since three well dressed and unknown riders arrived in the village demanding a hot dinner at The Flag and Drum, was announced by a breathless youth who had run for a mile to warn his lord of strangers on the road.

The baroness informed her elder daughter. "Good gracious," said Emeline. "Thank the lord Papa is not at home," and fluttered to the grand hall to await her cousin by marriage, carefully rearranging her hair pins as she ran down the stairs.

Adrian had not brought his sister with him. "She is not in the best of humours," he told his hostess, "and I instructed her to remain at home. Many of the servants expired during that unfortunate outbreak, and we are now sadly understaffed. So Sysabel and Aunt Elizabeth must busy themselves to reorganise the household, hardly an exhausting task." He was stiff, a little uncomfortable, yet he had come, and remained polite. The baroness had already built up the fires in her husband's absence, even though the April showers were light and the spring warmth shimmered over the Cotswolds. Immediately upon her guest's arrival, she ordered larger and more elaborate meals from the kitchens, and lit more candles than she had ever risked before.

Adrian sat in the blaze of candlelight, his dun brown hair turned gold and the square simplicity of his face etched into the interesting shadows of determination. "But I have heard nothing," he admitted. "In all this time no message from Nicholas has been delivered. It seems he is as irresponsible as always. We have encountered our own considerable difficulties, being informed of devastation in Nottingham and the Great Mortality sweeping through the poorer quarters. It was some considerable time before I felt it safe to venture home, and on arrival discovered the household had been virtually abandoned."

"How, how - awful," whispered Avice, gazing wide eyed at Adrian.

"We were still in extreme discomfort," Adrian continued, "when your letter arrived, my lady." He bowed slightly to Emeline. "Appalled at what might have happened to Nicholas, I came at once."

"But," sighed Emeline, "you've no idea how he is? Where he is?"

"I shall attempt to discover both where, and in what condition," Adrian nodded. "My cousin is most reprehensible not to have informed you before now."

"But if he's dead -?"

"He had his secretary with him? And if both are ill, there would be all the greater impetus to send a message."

There was the consolation of a hearty supper, good wine, and the unaccustomed pleasure of warmth and light, but Emeline drifted unsmiling, played with her food instead of eating it, and drank far too much.

"I think," said Avice later that evening, though no one had asked, "that Adrian is quite *beautiful.* And *handsome.* And so kind. He is an *exceptional* gentleman."

"You," said Emeline, "are a silly little beetlebrain just like Sissy. I admit Adrian's been exceedingly kind in coming all this way, but frankly he's plain and square and not very clever. And I don't like the way he picks at Nicholas."

"Well," said her mother, "he seems very willing to try and find out what has happened. Though speaking of what has happened, I do find it a little odd that your Papa chooses to travel to London at such a time. April can be such a wet month. Of course it isn't as if he was summoned to court, and her highness, poor lady, died over a month ago so paying his respects is now a little overdue. He has left on what he calls business rather often lately, yet I had not the slightest knowledge of there being any such thing previously."

"Don't mention Papa," Avice begged her mother, "just when I was enjoying myself. Anyway, perhaps he has gone to visit the stewes in Southwark."

Baroness Wrotham turned in a hurry and slapped her youngest daughter's hand. "Avice, I should have you flogged. First for knowing about such things - and then for speaking of your father in such a shocking manner. There is no humour in flagrant vulgarity, nor in the most appalling disrespect. If your Papa were here, he would take his belt to you."

"Well, if Papa were here, I would never have said it, would I!"

Emeline was staring out of the window. "Papa is the last person in the world to behave - well - him of all people - as if he would. But I was thinking of Nicholas. I mean, I don't know him very well yet. What if he has simply run away from me?"

"To a bawdyhouse?"

"Stewes and bawdyhouses," exclaimed her mother, "are from this moment forbidden as a subject of discussion. I am shocked, Avice. Indeed, I am horrified. Of course Nicholas has done no such thing."

"Well," whispered Emeline to her lap, "I just wonder if he has."

Entertaining Sir Adrian broke the monotony and soon the gentle entrance of May, the sunshine on the opening flower heads in the hedgerows, the calling and swooping of the birds and the sweet smells of blossom and briar rose, helped rid the estate of brooding melancholy, opening shadows to light. Recovering from the tedious journey between Nottingham and Gloucestershire,

Adrian and his two retainers spent several restful days at the Wrotham manor, wandering daily into the village of Wrotham Under Wychwood. He was generous with praise, and promises.

"The kindness and comfort I find here," he told his hostess one morning, "are tempting me to prolong my visit, my lady. But I must leave and fulfil my promise to discover Nicholas and his fate. I shall leave tomorrow."

So that evening after bidding her cousin good night and thanking him for his care and interest, Emma scuttled to her bedchamber, threw off her little gauze headdress, uncoiled her hair and climbed into bed with relief. "Thank goodness," she muttered, hugging her knees while scrunched up under the counterpane, sheet pulled to her chin. "At last the pompous bore is leaving, and soon I shall know where Nicholas is."

Avice cuddled beside her, having crept from her own bedchamber moments before. "How can you say such things?" she demanded. "I am *in love* with him. He is Sir Lancelot embodied, but more handsome, and kinder. The *nobility* of riding all the way here - and all the way to London - and risking his life and limb both on the road and perhaps because of the *pestilence* -"

"Honestly, Avice, you are immediately in love with any man that appears between the ages of nine and ninety," her sister complained. "If all you can think of is childish nonsense, then you can go back to your own bed."

Avice scowled. "It used to be your bed too, and you know how lumpy it is. Now just because you've got the guest chamber, you think you can order me around."

Emeline glared back. "Here's me worried sick about Nicholas, and your wretched hero Adrian sits around here eating all our food and buying Maman silly little gifts so she weakens at the knees and gives him the best wine, when he should be riding at full gallop for London."

"I wish he'd give me little gifs."

"That would be most improper."

"Who cares about boring old '*proper*'? I wish he'd *seduce* me. I wish he'd *abduct* me. I dream of him *kissing* me. And it's *wonderful*."

"This," Emeline sniffed, "is even more ridiculous than the swineherd's boy or Papa's secretary. At least they were frightened of you. Who knows what Adrian might do if you tempt him. You know what the priests say."

"I don't know what the priests say," insisted Avice, "because I never listen to them."

"No one," declared Emeline, "could fail to hear Father Godwin. His voice is like thunder."

"Oh, all right," admitted Avice. "So the horrid old man spits and sneers about a woman's wicked sins, and how feminine vice tempts honest men away from their moral determination. Well, I only wish it was true. I've been trying to tempt nice young men for ages and ages and they take no notice of me, What's *wrong* with me? Am I so ugly? Papa says I'm plain and everything else is vanity, but I think he's just being mean because people say I resemble Maman, and she's *beautiful*."

"You're very pretty," relented Emeline. "But you're a baby and have no idea what seduction's all about."

"*Really* pretty?"

"Avice, of course you are but all I can think about is Nicholas. I miss him. What if he's sick? What if he's gone to live with his mistress? What if he's *dead*?"

"Has he really got a mistress? With that horrid scar?"

"What scar? Oh – yes, that scar." Emeline sighed. "I had meant to ask him how – but it seems so rude, you know, and now I've virtually forgotten all about it. He is actually terribly attractive once you forget about the scar. And he has such wonderful fierce cheekbones, and a wonderfully strong jaw, and those wonderful brilliant blue eyes."

Avice shook her head. "Perhaps his mistress did it with the carving knife when she discovered him in someone else's arms. "

"It is rather odd," said Emeline after a moment's agonised pause, "when I realise how little I know about my own husband. Peter told me things – but now I don't think they were true. And when the marriage was arranged and I asked questions, Papa said it was none of my business. I always thought that was a little unfair. And then of course with the fire, and Nicholas being horribly burned, and me being angry – well we didn't really see each other for weeks."

Avice squinted into the bed's shadows. "So you've changed your mind from hating him to adoring him without even knowing anything about him."

"Avice, go back to bed," sighed Emeline. "At least now I'm a lady and I know my own mind. You just enjoy dreaming about one man after the other, when you don't even know what love is. You're just longing to be in love with anyone. It's because of all those silly romantic stories you read. Lancelot and Igraine. Papa would burn them if he knew." "Maman knows. She gave them to me."

Emeline gazed into the empty space across her sister's shoulder. "I might be living the romantic stories myself," she murmured, "if only life had been a little kinder. I could be in his arms now. But now he might be lying somewhere all alone in agony. He might be dying. He might be dead.

CHAPTER EIGHTEEN

The curve of his thigh skimmed the trestle where two wine cups had been left, the flagon already empty. A fine white cloth covered the table but the meal was long finished, the platters had been cleared and the stools drawn back. There was no evidence of household servants, but the small downstairs had been left neat and clean.

It was a simple house but not impoverished, and the remains of a generous fire still flickered within the recesses of the hearth. The chamber reflected and absorbed the dance of warmth, light and shadow. Only the gentleman who had recently forced his way inside now occupied the space, but there were noises from upstairs, echoes reverberating; voices, and laughter. The bumps and thumps, since the upper floor was the same planked barrier as the ceiling below, shuddered and the walls shook.

The uninvited visitor sat silent for a while, listening. He did not smile. His movements were quiet and careful, smothered by the upstairs sounds, so when he climbed the stairs and entered the upper chamber, he remained unheard.

A splash of late afternoon sunshine slanted through the window, angling past the rooftops outside. The beam lit the woman's face. She was plump, pretty and young. She giggled, "Oh, Jamie, how naughty. How strong. How exciting. But surely you cannot do it again *already*?"

The man who lay beside her on the bed was elderly and somewhat scrawny, but animated. He was naked and so was she and his head was buried between her breasts. His voice was therefore muffled. "With you, my pigeon, I can, and I shall." His head moved lower.

"Oh, my big strong man, have pity on my poor weak female body," the woman panted, arching her back.

"Big, and strong indeed, my piglet," the man mumbled. "And this time it shall be my way. You know how I like it."

As he crawled downwards over the humps of dishevelled sheeting, his face now hidden in the folds of her belly while breathing the heat of her sweat, his hands remained firm on her breasts, the fingers digging hard into the soft heaped flesh. He clung, as though fearing to fall if he released her. The girl squeaked, "Oh Jamie, that hurts," and the man sniggered.

"I pay enough to keep you here, Bess, and I shall take you as and how I want. Now, my girl, roll over." She was obedient, and rolled. Her buttocks bounced upwards, and the elderly man slapped each one, making her squeal again.

"Naughty, naughty, James." Her giggles disappeared into the pillows as he climbed gleefully astride.

The quiet intruder stood listening and watching from the doorway. The two in the bed saw nothing but each other. What they did now absorbed them so entirely, the possibility they could be interrupted while in the seclusion of their private bedchamber, did not at all occur to them. They did not see the knife, even when the sunlight turned the blade to topaz.

Eventually, as he retraced his steps down the stairs to the chamber below, the unannounced visitor spoke very softly to himself. "There is little more ungainly, more incongruous, or more shameful," he murmured as he wiped the soiled blade of his knife on the tablecloth, "than an adulterous lecher fornicating with a whore. Hypocrisy once again must pay the price."

He bent a moment beside the hearth, and flung the crumpled and now bloodstained table linen to the flames. The smoke billowed and the little sparks shrank back, then flared anew. The white cloth flapped as a draught gusted down the chimney. Like a bellows, the air urged on the flames. The cloth raged, catching alight and turning flicker to blaze.

Still bending by the grate, the man moved back a little, the heat too sudden in his eyes. But he caught the corner of the burning material and swept it out so the fire spun like molten gold, and licked each thing it passed, infecting like the contagion of disease until small fires had kindled in every corner. Some fizzled, finding little fuel. Other sparks hissed, and grew. One wrapped around the banisters, and discovering old dry wood, leapt up the steps.

It was silent now, upstairs. The previous jolly vulgarity had been quenched. As the flames licked and climbed, they found the bed, its half open curtains and its sprawled occupants. The two bodies lay quite silent now, one half covering the other, their nakedness almost concealed beneath the blood.

There were no stars to signify the deed by song, for it was bright daylight. But the man had no doubts. He smiled at last, and quickly left the house, closing the door firmly behind him.

....

From the comfortably snug corner of his exceedingly cluttered chamber, the Earl of Chatwyn pursed his lips, clutched his wine cup, and regarded his nephew with faint distrust. "No damned reason I can see," he said, "so why should I either know - or care?"

The court at Westminster remained partially in mourning. The deprivations of Lent had been more dour than was usual, and only days after the queen's great Abbey funeral, Easter Friday had seen grief not only with regard to the usual religious traditions, but also on a state and personal level. Now six weeks since her grace's death, black was still the eternal shadow, the tapestries remained covered, feasting was curtailed, and as the sunbeams dappled the gentle river's pollution, so couples walked the banks in quiet contemplation, other entertainments not yet resumed. His royal highness was back at business. Those first wretched days of desperate escape out on the heath when the March winds blustered and the falcons stooped to the dash of the hare, were all the king had permitted himself. Even those had been interrupted by the necessities of the season, and his gracious highness had performed the duties of Palm Sunday and Maundy Thursday with bleak solemnity and a bowed head.

Adrian stared back at his uncle. "Because my cousin's wife is worried, sir, as she has every right to be, and is hoping I will find him for her. I had naturally assumed you would know where he is, and more importantly, whether or not he is ill."

"Wretched boy *was* ill. And," the earl muttered, scratching his head, "he had the damned temerity to come here when barely recovered. I sent him off, tail between his legs. The queen hardly cold in her tomb, and my own son threatens to bring the pestilence into the very confines of the palace. I myself could have been infected. I didn't ask the fool his plans nor where he was staying. Not with me, that I can promise."

"At the Strand House, perhaps?"

"Go ask your Uncle Jerrid," grumbled the earl. "I've no interest in it. The boy's alive, that's all I need to know. Like I said - I sent him off properly crestfallen, and asked no further questions. Didn't answer any, either, nor will I yours."

"It is hard to imagine Nicholas crestfallen," sighed Adrian. "He is a difficult man to crush. Even ill, I can hear him laughing at his own expected demise."

"Wretched boy," snorted the boy's father. "Takes after his fool of a mother."

"You're planning a move yourself, uncle? Back north?" Adrian looked pointedly around at the piled clutter, the folded shirts and twists of silken hose prepared for transport.

"Royal business. Spain next week. We have a king without a son, nor any wife to provide another. It's marriage we need to promote, now the funeral is over."

"Spain? I heard the negotiations were with Portugal?"

The earl frowned, scratching absently inside the open neck of his shirt. "They were. They are. I expected - but Brampton's already gone to Portugal. Well - better him than me since he speaks the language."

"Since he's Portuguese."

"Well, there you are then," muttered the earl. "But the king wants a bride to combine the York and Lancastrian bloodlines. Stop any future jealousies or new hostilities. He's battle weary, and has had enough of death. So Brampton's off to Portugal, and I'll be talking to the royal house of Castile."

"She's very young," remembered Adrian.

"The Infanta Isabel - yes. All the better for breeding. A good match if I can pull it off. The Portuguese female is a good deal older, which might be a handicap. After all, the king needs an heir, not just a handsome wench in his bed."

Adrian straightened his back. There was no place to sit, and the chairs were heaped with packing bags. "But the Portuguese are particularly keen, I've heard. They're offering the cousin Manuel for the old king's eldest daughter as a dual arrangement."

The earl paused, frowning. "You surprise me, m'boy. Know a good deal more than I'd have expected of a northerner. But yes. The king promised her a fine match back when her wretched mother let her out of Sanctuary, so the chit needs a husband and she's keen. They dream of romance, these silly young females, eager for a man between their legs. But this time it's simple politics. The Portuguese want in, offering a double bargain so Castile will be pushed out."

"So instead you'll do your best to push Castile in and keep Lisbon out instead?"

The earl eyed his nephew with vague surprise. "You certainly know a lot about something not yet known to many," he said sharply. "D'you come here to find young Nicholas, or to sound me out about the king's marriage negotiations?"

"Marriage? Monarchs?" Adrian smiled, narrow eyed. "I don't give a cock's feather for either, nor do I understand the joy of intrigue, uncle. I prefer straight speaking to kissing the feet of foreign diplomats." He turned, grasping the door handle. "So good luck with your flattery and lies. I'm off to do my family duty and find Nicholas for his wife."

The village lanes, pebbled in limestone, wound like trails of melt water from the hills beyond. Each led to the village square where the local stalls were packing up. Without a licence for a foreign market but too far to walk for Gloucester, the farmers brought their radishes, parsnips and cabbages every Saturday while the baker brought his ready milled flour, and weighed it in front of his customers where it could be seen he added neither grit nor sawdust to cheat them. The village stocks, empty as always, stood at a distance.

The butcher already had his shop facing the big hollow yew tree, but he sent his lad to set up a stall on the green where he sold chitterlings, glossy washed tripe, and sheep's intestines ready stuffed. The old widow from across the wooded slopes brought the bundled faggots she had collected, tied in red twine, for though Wychwood was no forest at all, there were trees ready enough to drop their branches in the winter winds slashing sharp through the valleys. Behind the stalls, the goose boy stood eyeing the swineherd's son, while the geese, feet tarred black and feathers all aquiver with fury, eyed the scrawny little pigs, mother red eyed as she kept her squealing piglets barricaded safe behind her bulk. The swineherd's son held his stick raised and his feet firm planted, ever protective, while the barefoot goose boy was glaring and pugnacious.

It was a warm morning but the wind was gusty and the low clouds threatened rain. There was the smell of fresh cut grass in the air and the perfumes of new baked bread, custards, lilac blossoms, egg crusted pastry and the last of the previous year's apples roasted and dipped in honey. Then a scatter of old dry straw flew up from beneath the butcher's stall, with a tang of stale spilled offal.

Avice wore pattens to protect her shoes, but Emeline wore bright new leather boots with a lining of rabbit, the trimming peeping at her ankles. Avice linked her arm through her sister's, her eyes bright and ardent with envy, resolutely fixed on Emeline's feet. Emeline said, "I know what you're looking at, Avice. But there have to be *some* advantages in being married, you know." The sudden sunshine lit the trimmings on her hood, gilding the lemon velvet. She patted her sister's small ungloved fingers. "But if Nicholas is safe, and comes back to me strong and shining, then I shall buy you a pair of boots too, and old Tom Thompson in Leather Alley will make them for you."

The tooth puller, looking up with misgivings at the dark rolling clouds suddenly obscuring the sun, quickly wiped the blood from his hands and his pliers onto his apron as he slung his stool over his shoulder and set off for the tavern with the morning's tenpence jangling in his purse. Stalls thumped as their owners folded them up for the day, striped canvas flapping in the breezes. The little pink sow trotted quickly off behind her master, tiny hoofs clicking on the pebbles as she guided her brood, unable to count far enough to notice the lack of two precious piglets sold for Brother Alfred's cauldron. Then the clouds closed as a last sunbeam slanted through, sparkling across the grass as each stallholder and each hurrying customer set off for home in time for their midday dinner.

The wind blew Emeline's hood from her head and she pulled it back and tugged it low, her hand flat on top of her head. Laughing, the sisters ran up the lane as the rain began to pelt, huge sloppy drops on their skirts and shoulders and bouncing up beside their feet, the dust turning quickly to mud. "Hurry," shouted Avice, "or our pies will be sodden."

"We should have eaten them right away."

"Eating while walking - and in front of the market folk? In public, with gravy on our chins, and even licking our fingers? How positively shocking. Papa would be horrified."

Avice giggled and Emeline shouted back, "Then thank all the saints that Papa is still far, far away in London, and will not be back for at least another week."

Up the lane and sharp left, both keeping a tight grasp on the basket where the pies were wrapped in damp linen, oozing perfume. Over the little slope, and down the alley between Master Lumpton's milking sheds and the kitchen garden's rosemary hedges. Through the big turfed courtyard leading to the stables, into the smaller cobbled courtyard backing the pantries and kitchens, and finally up the steps to the back door, and home. It was raining heavily now and the sky lowered in thunderous charcoal, promising to turn rain to storm. So, hurtling inside and slamming the door hard behind, shaking out soaked hems onto the worn slate tiles, stamping mud from their feet, and tearing off the dripping headdresses with their sodden gauze, pins flying.

"If you waste expensive pins " Avice mumbled, stooping to collect those fallen.

And Emeline twirled in one delighted circle, arms outstretched and hair uncoiling, laughing, "But Papa is not here. How delicious. What freedom. Come on, I shall race you upstairs and we can eat our pies by the fire. Your chamber or mine?"

"Mine," said Avice. "It's the furthest from the chapel, and besides I need to change my shoes."

"I need to change *everything*." Emeline made a dash for the stairs. "I will put on my bedrobe and come to your room in just *minutes*. Besides, I still think of it as my room too." Both girls hurtled up the back stairs, Avice pushing past and Emeline squeezing in front again. "I have *won*," she yelled on reaching the upper corridor, "and claim my right to first bathwater. You can have the tub *after* me, but I promise to finish before the water is cold."

"Well hurry *now*," grumbled Avice, "or the *pies* will be cold."

Emeline scrambled up the passageway to her own chamber at the far end, where the sound of the rain pelting against the window was an echo in the shadows. She pushed open the door and hurried inside.

The arm slipped silently from behind her, well muscled but silk clad, taking her firmly by the waist. A strong, long fingered hand swung her around. Dark hair, thick and as silky as the luxurious sleeve, was against her face. Two brilliant blue eyes blinked, then glinted below hooded lids as the face pressed against hers, and she was kissed, hard and long and as forcefully as surprise would allow.

Nicholas murmured in her ear, "And now, my sweet, and now –" She was pushed deeper into the shadows and only his eyes lit the gloom. His hands were on her breasts, probing the damp satin. He whispered, "I see your nipples standing erect when your gown is wet, and your breasts are cold. Even in this half light I see you." And his palms cupped her body, still easing her backwards towards the bed. The fire had not been lit and the huge mattress, its embroidered covers and feather pillows deep shaded, stood like a great curtained archway, the charmed entrance to dreams. Nicholas tossed the curtains apart and laid his wife back so she tumbled down and the rope paillasse swung and creaked beneath. Nicholas chuckled. "The ropes need tightening. But first I'll see if I can loosen them further." He released the curtains and they moved together again like heavy screens, enclosing the bed in darkness. "Now," he said, "let me remember you as I've tried to picture you for these past days."

Fingers deft and quick, he had untied the laces beneath her arm and was unclipping her stomacher. Then one hand was in her hair, thick damp coils just released from their ribbons and caul. "I like your hair," he murmured, fingers combing and ironing away the raindrops, "but it's your shorter curls I want now."

"You – you are – back," squeaked Emeline, flinging both her arms around him.

"Rode in an hour gone," Nicholas told her, "and found you out. Managed to be polite to your mother for an hour, then pleaded tiredness and came up here to wait for you." He grabbed her hand and held it tight between his own legs. "I've thought of nothing but bedding you for the past twenty miles."

He released her hand and put both his to the hems of her skirts. She mumbled, "I have been dreaming too - wanting -," and immediately he swept her skirts up to her waist, bundling the folds beneath her and laying his face on the warm flat plain of her stomach. His breath tickled, and his fingers crept at once, playing in the thick curls at her groin.

"Open your legs," he whispered, "and let me in."

She gasped, "I want you so much - so very, very much, but there is Avice waiting for me in her bedchamber -"

"I don't care if the Pope is waiting for you," his voice now muffled against her, "you are mine, my sweetness, and I shall have you now," and he pushed her legs apart, and pressed his fingers up. "No doubt I smell of the saddle, but you smell of summer rain, and that's how I want you."

Trapped by swathes of clothes, Emeline trembled. The mattress groaned. "Oh, Nicholas, I am so - utterly - delighted - let me -"

But he interrupted her again. "Go where I lead you, my sweet, that's all I want. But I'll have you naked." He leaned back a moment, laughing at her. "Trussed like a pullet for the skewer. How apt."

She tried to sit up. "Nicholas, you are shameless."

"Should I be ashamed of bedding my own wife? Isn't this what marriage is for?" He pushed her back down, half kissing, half undressing her. Finally he pulled the gown from her arms and tumbled it off over her head. He lay beside her then, tucking one leg between hers. He smoothed his fingers down across her breasts, first very, very softly, and then firm, as though he meant to dry her with his palms where her skin was still damp.

"But it is *daytime,*" whispered Emeline, peeping up at him.

"If I wait for night, I shall have already expired with impatience," he whispered back. "Are you still so timid to face me in daylight? But I like how the shadows across your body slip and slide. You're a beautiful woman, my Emma. Don't hide."

"Papa would be terribly shocked - it is forbidden, you know -"

"If your infernal Papa were not so damned parsimonious, you would have a bed that did not squeak and cringe, and a mattress with more down than bumps."

"Oh dear," Emeline mumbled, "This is the very best guest chamber, where my mother insisted I stay this time. I used to share a horrid little bed with Avice."

He lay back, smiling across at her. "Do I shock you then? Must I learn a gentleman's manners?"

Emeline shook her head. "I am just so happy you have come back. I was *so* frightened, wondering what might have happened, and it has been such a long time. Have you been *terribly* ill?"

"Devil a bit," he told her, watching cheerfully as she tried and failed to pull the bedcovers across herself, "I got the barest skeleton of infection, and threw it off quick enough. Seems there's no pestilence strong enough to floor me. But I took advantage of the time in London, and planned a few adventures to amuse myself. Then I thought of you. I came here simply to take you away with me."

There was a slight pause and Emeline sat up abruptly, staring at him. "*Adventures*? Then you *thought* of me? You've been perfectly healthy, and enjoying yourself in London while I've been heartbroken and sick with worry? And you promised to send messages and have sent not one single word. I even thought you might be *dead*."

"Would be a rare devilry capable of killing me off."

"I might do it myself."

He laughed. "And this is marriage too, I imagine, with a wife to plague me, and scold me endlessly and spoil all my plans?"

"You didn't even *miss* me?"

"I missed you, yes indeed my sweet. I missed you every night, with my prick hard against my belly and no soft place to put it."

She hurled the pillow first, and when he laughed and threw it off, she jumped on him with both fists, punching at his ribs. He grabbed her wrists, forcing her arms back and she winced. He was still laughing but his grasp on her was like iron and her arms throbbed as he forced her back. She gasped, "You wouldn't – you won't - and I will never forgive you for these horrible weeks alone thinking you in pain - I couldn't even eat -"

Which is when Avice knocked on the door outside and called, "What *are* you doing, Emma? I am starving and our pies are going cold."

CHAPTER NINETEEN

Nicholas called, "Eat the pies yourself, brat. You won't see your sister again until supper." Footsteps scuffled, then silence returned. Nicholas regarded his wife. "Well, my love, seems your appetite has barely suffered after all. So, is it London together? Or do I take my fill now, and then ride off alone again into the moonlight?"

Emma collapsed, staring up at the inside of the old linen tester above. "This is so confusing. Have I been making a fool of myself - waiting and praying for you? And all the time you have been - gallivanting - without *shame*."

"I've not taken another woman during that time, in case that's what you're thinking," he answered cheerfully. "Does that help?"

Sniff. "Just because you've been too sick."

He shook his head, still laughing. "Three or four days sick and a couple more feeling like a scalded hedgehog. The rest of the time I had my mind on other things. I've my own life to lead, my dear, or should I wear my wife around my neck at all times, like a baldric?"

"You could at least have sent the message you promised. Your promises are as unreliable as the wind." The wind had begun to whistle and the rain was heavier, thrumming against the window so that she had to shout over it. "You - you're a man without decency or honour or substance - and now I'm ashamed to be in love with a horrid brute who does not care for me at all."

"You're not in love with me," Nicholas told her curtly. "You don't even know me. You imagine yourself in love simply because I *made* love to you. You're infatuated with sex and romance, that's all. So come here."

"I'm *not* infatuated," Emeline protested loudly as the rain poured with renewed force. "I'm not an idiot. And I know you're not in love with me, but you might at least show me some - kindness - and - respect."

"I respect this," he said, both hands hard to her shoulders. half lifting her as he brought her firmly into his embrace.

"And I won't fight with a naked woman." She found herself held so fiercely, she could not wriggle nor barely breathe. "Hush," he told her, "or your sister will be discovering more than your miserable father would approve of. Now I've other uses for all your energy."

"I don't want to anymore," wailed Emeline.

"And that, my girl," Nicholas said, "is just the challenge I need." He had pulled her astride him, holding her nakedness tight to his leather and velvets, making no attempt to undress himself. Her own arms were limp, refusing to embrace him, but he took no notice and grinned, one hand firm to her buttocks, the other caressing her breasts, pulling and pinching, then leaning down to kiss her nipples. Between her legs she felt the stiffened rise of his codpiece, and against her belly the padded peplum of his doublet. She could not move away from him, her legs forced wide and the strange pressure of the heavy materials against her. He continued to explore with fingers and lips, and his warmth warmed her as she felt the steady wave of arousal mount in her groin.

But where he held to her buttocks, his fingers also probed, and Emeline was shy, whispering, "Don't -"

And he lifted his face up to hers again, and smiled, and said, "Oh, I shall, my love. I shall what I will, but as I enjoy you, so I shall take you with me, and teach you the joy of the both the simple and the forbidden."

His kisses travelled, a sensuous brush of his mouth against her skin from ear lobe to nipples and down between her breasts to her navel, his head nudging her ever back. Unable to go except where he permitted, she was now arched over, her legs spread and her body exposed while he watched, and continued to smile, so she mumbled, "Please -"

He interrupted, "Yes, it pleases me." And suddenly he released his support, pushing her even further backwards. Then with both hands he grabbed her ankles, whipping them up to his shoulders so she squeaked, wriggling away. "Oh, no," he murmured. "You'll stay where I put you."

Blushing fiercely, she mumbled, "I feel - invaded -"

He leaned forwards a little, his eyes very bright. "You want me to love you? Like this I adore you. You're very much mine, and this is how I teach you passion, instead of modesty." He rubbed his palms over her feet, one on each of his shoulders, as if warming her or quickening the circulation of her blood, firm and strong over her toes and soles, then to her ankles, lingering over the little sharp twist of her bones, and hard and fast along her calves. His thumbs pressed behind her knees as he gazed down, grinning at her, then his fingers smoothed the insides of her thighs, slowly now, tempting and tantalising. "Lie still, little vixen," he whispered to her. "These are my desires. One day you'll tell me yours." And his fingers reached her groin, stopped there and then, very, very slowly, began to circle, rubbing either side, his thumbs pressing in. She felt the sudden cold metal of his signet ring, and flinched. He did not pause. Then abruptly one thumb and finger pushed inside, the other hand rubbing at the point of entry so she jerked, gripped suddenly by sensations she could no longer avoid. "Oh, yes, little one," he murmured. "Now – close your eyes and trust me. I won't hurt you."

She shut her eyes tight, and felt him lean over so her legs were pushed up higher, and then his face was pressed down and the slight rasp of his chin prickled against her skin and the hot slide of his tongue was where his fingers had been. Now his hands slipped beneath her, again holding her up very closely against him while he breathed in her scent, making her gasp and twist as he kissed and discovered where else to kiss, and which kisses made her breathe faster.

He paused, leaning back again with a slight sigh, and said, "You are deliciously tight, my dear. It is such a sweet challenge." And again she felt the sharp chill of his gold ring against her flesh, and the mounting tides she did not know how to resist became internal storms and she shuddered, shaken and crying out. He smoothed beneath her eyes, then across her lips. "This is the taste of you," he whispered. "It is utterly delicious. See?" And he held her tight until she had calmed, and lay still in his arms.

Then he kissed her forehead, and slipped from beneath her, saying, "Now I must be naked too, to feel the velvet skin, and the cool softness, and the warm rise of your breasts."

She had no words. She curled back against the pillows, catching her breath as she watched Nicholas undress. He seemed leaner than when she had last seen him, and the sleek slide of muscles and sinews in his arms and legs seemed more pronounced. His hair, dark as the charcoal in the brazier, had been cut short, but he had not shaved and his jaw was dusky with stubble. As she watched him so he watched her, tossing his doublet and shirt to the floor and bending to unlace the waistband which joined hose to braies. When he was naked he stood a moment, then came to her slowly. When he spoke, his voice was a tiny hot wind on her belly. "Now, my sweet, you'll do as I say, for it's my turn and I want you more than I've wanted anything for a long, long time." He moved her gently, as if she was incapable of moving herself. And then he kissed her, first on the mouth with his tongue pushed between her teeth and his breath in her throat, and then he kissed her breasts while his fingers once again crept to her groin. "Squeeze," he told her. "You have muscles inside here, strong enough to break wood. Discover them. Squeeze my fingers." His eyes were so bright, she couldn't look at him, and turned away. But with one hand to her cheek, he turned her back. "No, don't avoid me. Learn about your body. Then learn about mine. Squeeze, as if restraining your bladder. That's right. Again. So you control your own rhythms, and will bring me a pleasure I'll have no voice to describe."

He pushed inside her so suddenly, she grunted and he smiled. "First slowly, little one, and when you catch me up, then fast and hard, and you'll squeeze, then relax, then squeeze again." He continued to watch her, his smile tucked in deepest delight, and his eyes intent on her reactions. Finally, for just a moment, he rammed hard and very fast, then stopped, inhaling deep, and sank down against her, gasping for breath and trembling as though utterly spent. He whispered, "Sweet Emma," and stayed still inside her, gradually calming his breath and body. Finally he moved away and sat up but brought her up with him so they were facing each other, legs entwined. Immediately he flung both arms around her and cradled her head against his shoulder. "And that," he told her softly, "is my road to love. Now – little one – will you come to London with me?"

"Of course I will," she whispered. "I'll come anywhere with you. And I'll share your adventures."

"I'll arrange some."

Emeline smiled into his shoulder. She had very little idea what an adventure might be like, but simply living in London sounded adventurous enough. "Would you," she whispered, "help me dress? Or do you want to sleep?"

"Neither." He looked her over, his smile widening and his eyes bright again. "I prefer you naked. I like the feel of you. And I'm not tired. A few moments with you curled against me like this, and I shall want you again."

She ventured, "Don't you want any supper?"

"I intend having a very satisfying supper, but my food is here, not downstairs." He grinned suddenly. "But I suppose you're hungry as usual."

"Starving."

He laughed. "Get those crumpled rags off the floor then and I'll dress you. I'll take you downstairs, be polite to your Maman, eat something, come back upstairs, and have you instead of damp wafers and subtlety."

"My father doesn't let us have subtleties. Sugar is too expensive."

"Then, my little love, since you are sweeter than sugar, we are in accord for once. Now - grab your gown and I shall try to make you respectable again."

It was a late supper. Nicholas lounged at the table, ignoring the several platters placed before him. The baroness pointed to the apple codlings.

"My dear sir, my cook steams the best codlings in Gloucestershire, a favourite of Emma's, but you've not eaten a thing. Are you tired, perhaps? Or not yet entirely well?"

"Your daughters' appetites are proof of your cook's expertise, my lady," Nicholas said. "And I am neither tired nor unwell. Simply that I have eaten so well for many days past, it's a pleasure to rest the appetite for a day."

"Then I'll eat the codlings," Emeline said, looking up at the page standing dutifully behind her shoulder.

Nicholas passed her the codlings. "And I expect to leave within the next few days," he continued, "and, sadly, may miss your good lord's return, madam. My affairs in London will not permit too long a delay. Naturally I should be devastated to miss him, but no doubt I shall meet up with him on some other occasion."

"My husband," frowned the baroness, "went to London most precisely on your behalf, my lord. Having received no word, Emma was fearful for your health. Her Papa undertook to search for you, and to visit your esteemed father for news of you. I expect him back within a week or two at the most. I believe he would be sorely disappointed if you had already left before his return, sir."

"Ah." Nicholas sighed. "The business of manners. Then I shall stay a few days longer, my lady, and at least hope to pass the baron on the road, and to wave, perhaps, in the passing. But I have matters of some urgency, and once Emma is ready to accompany me, we will be gone." He looked across at his wife, who was sitting beside her mother. "It will not take you *too* long, I imagine," he suggested hopefully, "to prepare for the journey?"

"Oh, not long at all," she said, gulping down the last bite of codlings.

Avice looked from one to the other. "I wish I could come. It would take me less than an hour to be quite ready. In fact, I could leave now."

"Avice," warned her mother.

"Well," Avice declared. "So it would. I have only two decent gowns and two shifts, since someone unmentionable ruined my best one. And I have only one cloak and two pairs of shoes. There's three pairs of stockings and three ribbon garters, one horrid old bedrobe, and –"

"Avice," her mother interrupted her again. "That will be quite enough."

"Under the circumstances," said Nicholas with a waning interest in his sister-in-law's scant collection of apparel, "I'm surprised the baron didn't manage to find me in London, since you say he intended visiting my father. After the first few days of illness when I was obliged to stay elsewhere – I took up residence in the family house on the Strand. A tumbledown old heap my grandfather liked to call the Chatwyn Palace, but a good deal more comfortable than the castle, even before the fire. My father knew exactly where I was, though doubtless he's contrary enough to deny it to some. However, I hardly believe he'd not divulge my situation to my wife's father. I left London only four days ago, and rode hard for Gloucestershire. Yet his lordship most certainly didn't come calling before I left."

"Your cousin Adrian went to look for you too," insisted Avice. "You must have seen *him?*"

"Tragically, no," said Nicholas with a faint smile. "Have you sent half the countryside searching for me, then?"

"Only Papa and Adrian."

"How devastated I am to have missed them both," Nicholas said, smiling widely at his hostess. "Perhaps my father was distracted. He's about to leave the country, you know, and royal responsibilities invariably make him even more self important than usual."

The baroness leaned forwards. "How interesting, my lord. My husband hinted how he was hoping to accompany your good father at some point. Might I ask the nature, and perhaps the destination, of his journey? Unless, of course, they are matters of a confidential nature."

"They probably are," Nicholas waved one hand to the heavens. "Indeed, I'm fairly sure they are. But it's the king's desperate need for an heir, and some appropriate female to provide one. He wants English peace into the bargain, so he's dealing with the princesses of both Spain and Portugal. Lancastrian bloodlines, you see, to avoid future jealousies. We English are, after all, a contentious nation. So my father's off to Spain - which makes me think his highness is more serious about the Portuguese match."

Emeline blinked. "Your Papa, not that I wish to be in any manner critical, but is he the best person to employ as a diplomat in sensitive situations?"

"Good Lord, no," laughed Nicholas. "Which is why I imagine our good king is more serious concerning the Portuguese Infanta."

"And so soon after the queen's death," sighed Avice.

"Oh, he has no choice. However much he's mourning his queen, we the people shall never know. An heir is any king's first duty," said Nicholas, absently taking a small piece of bread from the communal platter, but playing rather than eating it. "I believe the Royal Council sent Sir Richard Brampton off to Lisbon some time back."

"The Portuguese negotiations may be secret," nodded the baroness, "but his highness was very public concerning those horrid rumours some weeks ago." Nicholas lifted one eyebrow. "Not, of course, that his highness had ever thought of marrying the young Woodville girl," the baroness hurried on. "His niece indeed!

A horrid thought, and such a religious man would never contemplate - but I was quite amazed that anyone else had started - or ever believed - such a shocking rumour."

"Rumour," said Nicholas, "oils the cogs that turn the wheel of fortune."

"Papa will not let us listen to gossip," muttered Avice,

Nicholas grinned. "Yet it seems this time that even in the wilds of Gloucestershire, the vine spread its roots. Because the Portuguese were negotiating with our Royal Council for a union between his highness and the Infanta Joanna at the same time as proposing a match between the Infantas's cousin Manuel and the old King's daughter Elizabeth, rumour managed to put the two together and whispered that King Richard was thinking to marry the girl himself. Since his crown is entirely due to her and her siblings being discovered illegitimate, such a proposition was absurd. But rumour thrives on absurdities, and it is possible that some malicious soul had his - or her - own motive for spreading those rumours. The king likes to cut through confusion, so made an immediate proclamation to stop the silly tattle at birth."

"Tattle indeed," blushed his hostess, "but it was your own dear cousin informed us, sir. Sir Adrian was here at Emma's request, you see, since she was frightened for your safety. And he discussed the king's marriage situation in some detail. I was shocked at the rumour he shared with us. As my husband often says, the common folk are always ignorant."

"The king marrying his own bastard niece!" sniffed Avice. "As if he would want to - with every foreign princess after his hand."

"As well as an heir, the king needs foreign alliances, and marriage is a good way of finding them." Nicholas shrugged, looking at his wife. "The proposed match is with the Portuguese king's sister Joanna, and that's an alliance worth more than gold. The beneficial union of disparate houses, you might say?" Emeline looked down quickly at her lap. "Though," Nicholas added, eyes narrowed, "how Adrian knew so much is a puzzle to me, since he is rarely at court."

"Perhaps the Lady Elizabeth *wants* to marry her uncle," suggested Avice.

"I believe the girl wants to marry someone, and is already enamoured of her proposed Portuguese groom's portrait," said Nicholas. "And for a girl of announced bastardy, the most royal Manuel is a flattering proposal. Young women, it seems," and he smiled again at his wife, "yearn for romance and call it love when they find it. But the whole matter of the king's marriage negotiations is secret, which presumably means everyone knows about it."

"Chivalry and romance and dreaming of marriages," Avice interrupted, sighing, "and wondering what it would be like. That's even more fun than a new gown. And the king is supposed to be terribly handsome. Any girl would dream of marriage to a king."

Emeline glanced up at her husband. "You seem to know rather a lot yourself, my lord. Perhaps you actually know the king in person?"

"Know his highness? I'm a lowly earl's son, and only recently his heir." Nicholas said, studiously regarding his empty platter. "How should I speak with kings, while stuck in that monstrosity of a castle up north?"

Emeline paused, watching him a moment, then said, "But you haven't actually denied it, I notice. And I know perfectly well how much you love that monstrosity of a castle."

Nicholas grinned. "Shall I be indiscreet then? Shall I admit that my recent adventures have involved this very situation?" He shook his head, still laughing. "Oh no, I'm not off to foreign lands. But Sir James Tyrell asked me to investigate the beginning of the rumours. He's interested, as I am, in who might have started such gossip, clearly designed to cause trouble for the king. Knowing your friends is essential for any monarch, but knowing who wishes to build you problems is even more important."

The baroness stared and Emeline blinked at her husband. "You were actually working for his highness?"

"Not so unusual," Nicholas said. "Most of the younger courtiers, and many others too, offer service in such a way. Loyalty involves many different pathways. Tyrell, Lovell, Brampton, Howard, we prove our loyalty when we can."

"What did you discover?" whispered Avice, wide eyed.

But Nicholas shook his head again. "That's not something I can share," he smiled. "And should have said nothing at all. It's not a business I ever discuss with my family, and prefer to keep such matters private."

"I won't tell a soul," Avice assured him.

Nicholas shrugged. "They wouldn't believe you anyway. I'm the irresponsible coward and the family's shame. It's a useful position to hold onto."

CHAPTER TWENTY

They had ridden hard, first for the constable, and then, in company with the constable, for the sheriff. The sheriff had thrown down his quill and stared up in disbelief, ink blotting the parchment where he had been writing. But it was true, they assured him, and he must come immediately.

It was still raining. The rain had helped put out the fire, but such damage had been done that it took considerable time before the full scandal could be realised. The roof had tumbled in, then both floors and ceilings. The great bed had toppled from above to below and now rested, scorched, blackened and partially upended against the table downstairs. Not that there were any stairs anymore. But the two bodies on the bed remained visible, flesh burned and ruined, and their identities, though more guess than recognition, were noted.

"Lord have mercy," uttered the sheriff. "Dickon, get yourself off to Wychwood and inform her ladyship."

"It'll be dark, sir, by the time I arrive. And in this weather too."

"No choice, lad." The sheriff gazed at the sprawled and charred remains before him, and gulped. "But don't you go telling the widow just how he was found, mind. Use your manners and your common sense, now."

"But shouldn't it be you, sir, being the sheriff, and not me being the lowly constable, what informs her ladyship?"

"In this weather? Already I've a cold on the way." The sheriff declared, gazing at the charred bones and distorted limbs before him. Then he sighed, acknowledging the inevitable. "Very well, duty's paramount. I'll face the baroness myself, and my assistant can accompany me. Alert the guard. I want four armed men, and fresh horses. I'll time my arrival for the morning."

It was many miles distant and nearly an hour later when Nicholas regarded his wife through the shifting shadows of the unlit bedchamber. "So, what exactly has missing me entailed?" he demanded, grinning wide.

She thought a moment. "Wanting you back. Never feeling comforted. Thinking so much about you. Worrying myself sick - in case you were sick."

He shook his head. "Not good enough. I want descriptions. At night, for instance. Did you dream of the pestilence, of pustules and poxes? Or did you dream of lying in my arms, and of me touching where you want to be touched?"

"Yes," Emeline whispered, looking back at him. "Both those things. All the time."

They sat together before the window, although the sky beyond the small diamond panes was partly obliterated by rain and the stars appeared blurred, like the small muffled reflections of candle flames. The window seat was deep but uncushioned, and Nicholas sat in one angle, facing her in the other. Their eyes, intent on each other, did not notice the hazy mists of moonlight outside, or the small bluster of the wind in the treetops. Nicholas reached out and took Emeline's hand. "So when, in your dreams, I touched where you wanted me to touch -" he paused, then said, "where was it?"

Although the shutters had not been raised, nor had candles been lit, so in the darkness he could not see her blushes. "I cannot say," she whispered back. "I don't know any words for such places, and nor could I describe - only to say you know where - where you held and touched me before - that one special time - in the castle before we left for Nottingham."

He laughed, which broke the spell of hushful secrets. "You could explain if you wanted," he told her. "So instead take my hand," and he held his fingers out to her, "and put me where you want." She clasped his hand in hers as gently as if it might break, but he grasped her firmly back, rubbing his thumb across her knuckles. "Without shame - since there is none. Now show me."

She took a deep breath, released very slowly, and pressed his fingers against her breasts. "Here. You know it's here. I think you *want* to shame me, Nicholas. I've missed you terribly but you're so horribly - challenging. And I know you didn't miss me, but I don't care about that."

He was still grinning, and he moved his fingers, tracing them down from her breasts to her belly, and then tucking them firmly into the crease between her thighs. "And here?" he demanded. "So, thinking of me, and needing me, but not having me - did you touch yourself?" He had already removed her little headdress and uncoiled her hair, and now she wore only her shift, loose pintucked linen, cloud white and fine enough to show the outline of her body and the dark shadow of her nipples beneath. Nicholas leaned forwards, rubbing his cheeks against the warmth of those small shadows, and smiling up at her. "Without me to arouse you," he insisted, "how did you arouse yourself?" His fingers were still pushing between her legs. "Here? What did you do? Tell me."

"No." She shook her head. "I wouldn't - I couldn't. I thought about when you touched me there - I remembered - I imagined you coming home to me. But I never could have done such a thing to myself."

He removed his impatient hand, and kissed her. Then he leaned her back against the leaded window frame, watching her. "My dear, you were brought up by a father as different from my own as fathers can surely be. But believe me, there's no sin in pleasure."

Emeline gulped. "But self indulgence can be wicked. First there's duty and loyalty - and kindness - and respect for parents and -"

"Come here," he interrupted, and brought her head down against his shoulder. "Because I intend being very, very wicked." Nicholas wore a short shirt loose over his hose, long dark legs stretched, boots lying discarded across the bedchamber floor, his doublet thrown beside them. Her own gown was tumbled at her feet. Now he clasped her hand again, and brought her fingers to his groin where the stiffened broadcloth of the codpiece lay loose, and he pressed her palm there. "When I missed you, which I did," he murmured, "I touched myself, like this, as I want you to do now. With your small hand, it is so much sweeter."

"You only missed me - there?"

"Principally."

"I missed you in lots of ways. I kept remembering the laughter in your eyes, and how your face puckers when you smile. Do you mind me saying about it - here," and she reached forwards with her other hand, gently running her fingertips across his cheek where the scar cut deep and dark, dividing the flesh. "When you smile, and laugh, your face tucks up in two nice curled stripes, as if you're making fun of yourself\. I like that so much. I remembered it a lot while you were away."

He was so surprised, he released her. "What a strange thing to notice. And how perverse. I usually forget the wretched thing is there. But I've never expected anyone else to like it. Especially you."

She was momentarily affronted. "Why especially me?"

"Because," he said, leaning back, eyes narrowed, "that was one of the reasons, I presume, you hated me before we were married. Wasn't it? The ugly brother. The deformed one."

Blushing again, "No, well, not really. Peter told me - but I'd never seen you. I didn't know what he meant and he never explained very well. I suppose, thinking back to what he used to say, he was a little unfair."

"A *little* unfair?"

"You're laughing at me again. Yes, of course he was wrong." She sighed, and leaned forwards, taking her husband's hand again. "But I know something now, which I didn't realise until you went away. It's your eyes - and Peter's eyes. Both such bright vivid blue. But your eyes are so - full. They dance all the time with a hundred expressions. I can watch you thinking. Your eyes are so wonderfully alive. Peter's eyes," she leaned back again, and looked down, "they were just the same colour as yours, brilliant as jewels, with such beautiful black lashes, just like yours. But his eyes were empty. Perhaps he hid his thoughts. But they weren't starry, like your eyes. They just looked. Or they looked away. Open or closed. There wasn't anything else in them."

Nicholas chuckled, shaking his head. "No spiders? No battle banners? No blind wandering clouds?"

"No laughter."

"Peter was a complicated brother. He had some good points and we laughed together as children. He grew more difficult as he matured. But I thought you adored him." Nicholas stood quickly, then swept her up with him, carrying her to the bed where the covers were already dishevelled and haphazard from their love making before supper. He laid her against the pillows and sat beside her. "But it's not Peter I want to talk about now. It's us. And I want you naked before I close the shutters and lose the last moonlight." Where the bed posts rose straight and unadorned, the shadows swung in curtained folds, held by unravelling tassels, then falling straight and thick in dull sage, lined in cobalt blue. Nicholas reached over, pushing them further against the wall behind. "I want to see you. If I could find a candle, I'd light it. But in your father's house I imagine they're hidden, and certainly counted. So now, open to me." And he tugged her shift off over her head, the little cupped sleeves from her arms, and quickly flung it to the floor. He kissed her breasts, then wrapped his arms around her, hands closing on her buttocks to bring her tight against him, and whispered, "Now – you undress me."

Her voice was a tickle against his collarbone. "How?"

"Learn." He moved away abruptly and sat up, facing her. "Struggle. Discover. That's life. But unlike life, there's no punishment. Get it right, and I'll pleasure you with all my heart. Get it wrong, and I'll do exactly the same."

"Silly," she smiled. "tell me how, and then I can do it properly."

"I don't want proper." Nicholas grinned at her, and the tucks in his cheeks curled up as she had described to him. "I want you to explore," he said, "and find your own way to me." He shrugged. "I'm not wearing too much, as you can see. And a shirt is little different than a shift, after all."

"It's not the shirt that troubles me," she said. She peered, finding the small corded lacing at the neck, loosened it further, and pulled up the shirt from its neat hem, tossing it over his head and then tugging it from his arms. "See? That's easy."

"So – discover the rest of me."

His hose were dark, wide grey stripes on darker grey, knitting that clung to the muscles of his legs and enclosed his feet tighter than any shoe. Emeline touched the waist where the taut smoothness of his skin disappeared into the slim silken gathers. She slipped her fingers inside. She felt two thicknesses of material, though both were fine and soft and thin. Her fingers roamed, intrigued, down where his body was no longer visible. His skin was harder than her own softness, and a light tickle of hair covered it. Up across his chest, over the button nipples, his body hair was longer and as silken as the stuff of his hose. Being dark, it gleamed, even there within the shadows of the bed. Emeline hooked her fingers further within the waist of his hose and found the narrow end of the lacing. She undid the knot, and pulled the ribbon loose from its ties. The fine tight knit stayed clasped about his hips, but across the taut flatness of his stomach, she could pull it down, finding it attached to his braies, and she pulled them too. Gradually she eased both together down to his groin. The hair she had touched before now seemed to grow into a line like an arrow shaft, beckoning downwards towards thicker, blacker curls. She stopped.

"Undo the codpiece first," he grinned at her, "or you'll ruin me, my love."

She recoiled slightly, but fingered the bowl between his legs, and looked at him, questioning. "How can I ruin you that way?" she asked. "Last time you certainly didn't seem so delicate."

"As delicate as a meadow lark's egg."

"You're teasing."

"There's places where I'll risk injury, and places where I'd sooner not."

First she untied the laces holding the braies tight to the hose, then found the small ties which kept the codpiece in its place, allowing for hasty removal. She began carefully to slip it undone, whispering, "How confusing men are." And, very slowly, eased the hose down his legs. Once the knitted silk reached his knees, she paused"

Still sitting in front of her, he leaned forwards, his hands to her shoulders. His voice was very low now, and gruff, as if he had forgotten the laughter. "No stopping. Kiss me," he told her softly. "No, not like that. Kiss me there."

She blushed, "I don't know how to do such things. I might hurt you."

He swung his legs suddenly to the side, pulled off his hose and slung them to the ground. Then he took her in his arms. "I'm not so easily hurt, unless you mean to bite it off. Yes, I was teasing when I said I was delicate, though the scraping of stiffened leather is something I'd sooner avoid. So I'll teach you slowly, little one, lesson by lesson each time I bed you, and you'll learn not to be timid. But now I want you too badly to stop for education. So I'll swive, not talk, and the rest can wait."

"Do I disappoint you?" she whispered as his fingers sought her own secrets.

He chuckled, though his mouth was against her breasts and her hair was in his eyes. "In no sense and in no manner, my love," he told her. "I'm unused, perhaps, to bedding innocent virgins, but I'm learning too."

"You said - you touched yourself - when we were apart." She took a deep breath, but her voice faded out and she had to start again while he watched her, waiting and smiling. She mumbled, "If you show me how you do - then I can learn to do the same."

"But I can't suck my own prick," he said, and the laughter was back in his eyes. "A fine trick if I could do it, but I'll teach you in time. Now, breathe deep again, and I won't hurt you." He lay her back, straddling her, his fingers between her legs and his mouth to her ear. "And next time I'll show you other positions, but for now I'll keep it easy." He pushed her legs a little further apart, then entered her quickly, thrusting deep. "Now," he whispered, his own voice tightly under control, "put your legs up under my arms and around my back. Good. Link your ankles. Like this you'll hold me deep, and I'll discover all of you," and he pushed suddenly and hard, making her grunt. "Hurting?" he asked, but she shook her head, and he took his weight on his elbows, laid his head against hers, and forced deeper.

Each thrust was fast and hard before he stopped abruptly, sinking down on top of her, panting as if gasping for breath, and she felt him pulsing inside her. She squeezed around him as he had told her before. "Sweet Jesus," he muttered, and she smiled. Turning his head, he kissed her, his tongue searching out her tongue. She could taste the wine he had drunk for supper, and the rich fascination of his own spent desire. "Next time," he murmured, "will be better. I was impatient. Each time - I promise - will be better." And he rolled away, curled behind her, tucked the covers up across them both, clasped his hands around and over her breasts, and within one minute was asleep.

For some moments more Emeline felt his breath warm against the back of her head, and the heat of his body snug at her spine, his knees beneath hers. Then she too slept, and was not aware of dreams.

She woke to his kiss on her forehead, blinked and looked up. He was fully dressed, bending over her. "Your woman is waiting to dress you." He spoke softly, and smiled as though not to alarm her, and she saw Martha standing behind him. "There is some visitor of importance downstairs," he said. "And it appears we are both needed."

The shutters, since they had never been raised the evening before, still stood below, and the sun streamed through the little casement window. Emeline mumbled, "A visitor? We never get visitors."

"This one," said Nicholas, "is come to see your mother, but it seems she is confused, and also distressed. She has sent the steward for us." He waited a moment while Emeline blinked again, clearing her head of sleep. Then he said, "News perhaps. Pirates or portents, storms or secrets. Are you ready for the next adventure, little one?"

CHAPTER TWENTY ONE

Emeline sat up in a hurry, pulling the coverlet with her. "Visitors? Adventures? Is it morning? Then it will just be the butcher wanting to know what to deliver in time for my father's return. Or the smith with a special price to offer on horseshoes."

"Or the raker's assistant, come to swill out the privies? No, my dear, it is none of those things, or your mother would not be acting as she is. Dress, and be quick. Then hurry downstairs."

Emeline recognised the visitors as soon as she reached the lower sweep of the main staircase. The Sheriff of Gloucestershire stood solid, legs wide, as though expecting attack. His assistant, who was considerably taller, stood quietly behind. The baroness faced them, standing before the great empty hearth in the main hall. Nicholas stood beside her. He appeared to be supporting her, having taken hold of her elbow and with his other hand to her back. As the baroness saw her elder daughter approach, she went white and trembled.

"Emma, my dear. There is something which has happened - so very unexpected and very - very hard to fathom. But must be faced. Come here, my love."

She went, standing quickly beside her mother and her husband. She faced the sheriff, saying, "There must be something very wrong, sir. Is it Avice?"

Nicholas said softly, "Your sister is still asleep upstairs. It is better you know first."

"Then it's my father," Emeline said. "Tell me." The baroness appeared dizzy, and stood a little bent, swaying and barely upright, though Nicholas held her firm. He signalled for the sheriff's assistant to bring a chair, and sat his mother-in-law firmly down. He then moved to his wife's side, his arm around her waist. She looked up at him.

Quietly he told her, "Emma, your father was found in Gloucester yesterday, although there was some delay in informing us since he was not immediately recognised. It seems he is dead. It was not, I understand, a natural death."

Emeline stood a moment in appalled amazement. Then she whispered, "He was murdered? Like Peter?"

"Very like Peter," Nicholas said softly. "Now I must speak to these officials in private, and leave you to comfort your mother. I shall be back shortly. If you want me sooner, I shall be in the side chamber."

She looked up at him. "You call this an adventure?"

He said, "I would not have, my dear, had I known the nature of the news. But it will be," and turning, nodded to the two sheriffs who followed him from the hall.

Emeline waited until all the footsteps had faded, and a strange expectant silence leaked in where the sounds had been. Into the wandering shadows and the wilful hush, she drew out her kerchief, and came to kneel beside her mother's chair. "Maman," she murmured, "you will be safe, I promise. I shall always look after you. Please don't cry."

Red eyed and white faced, the baroness stared glumly at her daughter. "I am not crying," she said, her tears glowing gold in the slanting sunlight. "And I am not distraught. Nor do I need looking after. But I am deeply shocked. From what I understand, James deserved everything – I mean everything that came to him. For he was right in one thing. God brings justice, and justice is what your father received."

Emeline did not understand. She tried to take her mother's hand and was immediately pushed away. So she stood, and crossed to the staircase. "He's at peace now, Maman. You don't need to grieve for him." Then turned once, looking back, "I'm going up to Avice. I shall be back in just a moment."

But it was later when the situation was more fully explained. The baroness had ordered a fire lit large, hippocras heavily spiced and steaming for herself and her daughters, and had then joined her son-in-law in earnest discussion with the sheriffs. Emeline and Avice sat, cups in hand before the blaze.

"Grieve?" Avice said, glaring. "I *hate* him and I'm *glad* he's dead. I hated Papa when I thought he was sincere, and God loving, and stuffy, and mean minded. Now I know he was a pig and a hypocrite, I hate him even more."

"You don't mean it. Maman said the same. She doesn't mean it either."

"We do and so would you, if you stopped thinking you have to be loyal. Papa won't be sitting all smug with the angels. He'll be suffering hellfire and burning all over again. Now go away. I want to be alone. For ever and ever. I will *never* marry."

Emeline winced. "Not still dreaming of the gallant Sir Adrian?" Then she saw her sister's face, and swallowed hard, whispering, "I know, Avice darling. He was still our father."

"We were only ever happy when he went away somewhere," Avice mumbled. "And now we know what he was up to *when* he went away, so I never, ever want to think about him again. Or any man. They are all beasts."

It was Nicholas alone who travelled to Gloucester and stood witness to the identity of the burned and oozing corpse which had been discovered in the arms of his naked mistress. Sometime after the fire had been extinguished, it had been the signature on the property's bill of sale which alerted the local authority to the possible and awful truth, for it was Baron Wrotham who had bought the small backstreet house two years previously, and had immediately installed the young woman known to her neighbours as Bessie the whore.

The baron's face remained in part, although it seemed to snarl, with the jaw gaping and the teeth springing from the bone like little crooked mile stones. The gums had been all burned away and the tongue was a blackened stump protruding from the gaping throat. One startled eye stared out, the other a burned and hollow socket, but flesh hung, tattered and sticky, in sufficient determination to prove the man he had once been. His son-in-law knew him, but did not pity him.

The woman now lay stretched out close by. Nicholas shook his head. He said, "I will not know her."

The assistant constable bowed, hands behind his back. "My lord, we don't expect it. 'Tis the woman's little lad will come to claim her."

"You'll show a child his mother in that condition?" The naked woman had one remaining breast, one thigh, one leg and one arm. Her face, hair only ashes clinging to a scarlet scalp, was almost gone. Her nose had burned to a twisted lump of gristle, her eye sockets both empty and her mouth a fleshless scream. "Get someone else," Nicholas said. "Get the local priest."

The constable frowned. "The boy's fair twelve year, my lord, and being a whore's son, will know life's neither easy nor meant to be for those of his sort."

Nicholas untied his purse. "I'll stand witness myself," he said softly, "and will swear this is the woman you say she is. Here's money for her funeral. Show the boy a closed coffin, and tell him she's already been identified."

"You know her then, my lord?" The constable's frown deepened.

"If I say so, I imagine you'll not dare to doubt my word?"

Nicholas then sat an hour with the sheriff, discussing the slaying, how it was done, how afterwards it was disguised by flame and finally how it had been discovered. Still alone, he had then visited a small hovel in the back lanes of Gloucester. He did not return to the sheriff's chambers until mid afternoon, and it was nearly twilight before he left the city.

Baron Wrotham's coffin, draped in black velvet, trundled the old lanes and the primrosed paths, through the last sinking glow of sunshine and through the strengthening shadow. Beneath the breezes, the fluttering leaf, and the valley's gentle perfumes, the cart followed the roads north east from Gloucester to Wrotham under Wychwood, bouncing through ruts and ditches as the coffin rattled and groaned. The horses snorted, flicking flies with their tails, and passers by stopped as men took off their hats and bowed their heads. May blossoms sprigged the hedgerows, and the cattle were clustered beneath the trees' shelter, or waded, rump deep, in the cool green streams. The warblers were back from Africa, nesting in the high tree tops and singing for their mates, and across the empty and darkening sky a group of blackbirds, swirling arrows pitching and plunging, mobbed a sparrow hawk, each a dancing black shadow against the cloud. The hawk flew lower, disappearing then into foliage for the night. The blackbirds chittered, looking for a final territorial argument.

With his faithful squire at his back, Nicholas rode slowly behind the cart, controlling his liard hunter, its dappled flanks further dappled by the last of the pale sun. He rode so slowly that finally the sun sank behind the little hills and the sky billowed suddenly pink, dandelion yellow and cerise in their faces. It was gone midnight when he arrived back at Wrotham House, and immediately arranged for the baron's closed coffin to be laid before the altar in his own private chapel.

Father Godwin lit candles and knelt, muttering his prayers, but Nicholas hurried straight to his wife's bedchamber.

Emeline was neither asleep, nor undressed. She sat on the bed, playing with a cup of hippocras, twisting the small bowl between her palms as the warmth tingled through her fingers. She lowered her eyes as her husband entered the chamber. Nicholas threw his belt and boots to the empty hearth, and came beside her.

She had sat alone for most of the day. Now, since Nicholas remained silent, she said, "You didn't like him, and sometimes nor did I. But perhaps it's all a mistake."

"Your father's mistake."

She slumped, forlorn. "How do we even know it's him? Did they show you - did you recognise - even after the fire? This - this murdered fornicator can't be him."

"I saw him, little one, and knew him. I made the necessary arrangements. The coffin is now in the chapel downstairs with your priest, but will remain closed. You must take my word that your father died as we were told. Now your mother will arrange for his interment in the local churchyard."

Emeline whispered, "So it's really all true? He was found with a - prostitute?"

"Of sorts." Nicholas stood, and helped himself from the wine flagon. "Do you need to know all this?"

Emma stared up at him. "I need to know the truth."

Nicholas took her cup from her fidgeting fingers, refilled it, and drained his own. "There are no doubts, my dear. Those living nearby confirm he was there fairly often, and the woman was his mistress for at least three years - a Gloucester woman, widowed, with a twelve year son, though her son remained elsewhere. Your father evidently bought the house for her. Someone slaughtered them both and then set fire, presumably to hide his crime. Several houses in the same street burned and honest folk with them. Whoever hated your father enough, cared little for other deaths."

She shivered. "He was - hated?"

"Few commit murder for benevolent reasons." Nicholas came back to sit beside her. "There's no guess as to who did this, nor why. But the sheriff will investigate, and because of your father's title, someone will eventually be found to stand trial, guilty or not."

"Why say it like that?"

Nicholas shrugged. "I know a thing or two about local justice. Should I make it sound sweeter, to please you?'

He sat close but did not hold or comfort her. She whispered, "I don't want lies. But kindness –"

"It would be the same thing." Nicholas stood again abruptly and wandered over to the little table below the shuttered window. Again he reached for the wine jug. "There are things I can't tell you yet, my dear. But I'll tell you this. After the funeral I've three men to see. That may be where the adventure comes in after all."

Emeline slumped again, staring down miserably at her feet. "So I won't see you for another month or more?" she gulped. "And I'm to be abandoned again?"

"What small faith," Nicholas smiled. "I've promised you adventure. So I'll take you with me, if that's what you want. But you have the choice – to accept or refuse. And remember, if you choose to stay with your mother, then you abandon me."

"I'll come with you, if you want me. But I can't leave my mother yet. She needs – comfort." She looked up at him again. Her lashes were moist. "And so do I."

"If you hope for sympathy, my love, then you'd better stay at Wrotham. I'm likely to disappoint you."

"What's wrong with sympathy?" She straightened her shoulders, took a deep breath and glared as he yet again filled his cup. Now the flagon was empty. "All you do is drink. Do you *try* to get drunk? Is that what comforts *you*?" she demanded. "I know you didn't like my father and perhaps you don't like me either. But once you promised to be kind. I don't want adventure. My father's dead, and how it happened was horrible, and I'm trying not to think about what he's done and how he was found and what it all means. All my life I was frightened of him. I don't even know if I loved him. But I respected him. Now all the respect seems muddled up. I just want –" sniff – "a little comfort."

She had disguised the sniff but Nicholas came back to her at once and took her hand, rubbing his thumb across her small cold palm. "Silly puss. I like you well enough. If I didn't, I wouldn't be inviting you to come with me when I leave. And I'll wait until you're ready - a week perhaps, or more if I must. But comfort isn't something I'm used to giving, except to a lame horse or a bitch birthing pups. There's not a soul taught me the meaning of comfort once my mother died, and I've managed without it. Now it seems like an awkward thing - more patronising than kind. Perhaps it's something else I'll need to learn."

Emeline stared down at her hand, and his fingers wrapped gently around it. She mumbled, "Pretend I'm just a bitch then - birthing - whimpering. Is that so hard?"

He laughed, which didn't help. "I'd rub your stomach and scratch behind your ears and tell you you're a good dog. Then I'd take the pups, each one, and lay them at your teats. So not something I plan on doing with you, little one. A fine Burgundy eases pain much more, I promise."

"The jug's empty. You drank it all."

Nicholas put his arm warm around her shoulders, relenting, bringing her head down against his cheek, his other hand still clasping hers. "Listen, my sweet," and he murmured softly to her as indeed he might have to a suffering bitch by his hearth. "There's things I'm good at, more or less. Others, I'm unpractised at best." His arm tightened around her, and he caressed her neck, smoothing the hair from her wet cheeks. "Oh, I remember yearning for comfort when my mother died," he told her gently, "and when I helped lay my infant brother and sister in their coffins, I was helpless with tears. No comfort was given, for there was no one to give it, but I remember what I craved, and will try and offer that now. Even when Peter died - but that's another story best forgotten. So forgive me for being inept, while I try to improve." He kissed her ear, a damp tickle as he smiled again. "But adventure, pissed or sober, is the surest way to forget misery, and there I'm skilled enough. If you stay with me, then it's adventure we'll have. For now I can't explain more, except for starting with the three men I need to see."

"Which men?" she asked, peeping up as he once again drained his cup.

"First my father. You say your father went to London to see him. Did he arrive? Or not? I should know if anything is to be discovered. And my father is about to leave for Spain. I've questions of my own before he goes, since I doubt he'll return before autumn."

"But hardly adventurous."

"You don't yet know my father," Nicholas smiled. "But it's once I leave him I expect the fun to start."

"So then?"

"Then I want to talk to my cousin. Adrian offered to help find me too, I gather. Most obliging of him. And perhaps more interesting than I'd previously realised."

She was suddenly intrigued. "And the third man?"

"A very different creature," said Nicholas. "Name of Harry. I recently took his brother Rob into my service. Now I need them both. But that's not where the adventure comes in. It will start later."

CHAPTER TWENTY TWO

He blew in like a thunderbolt with his retinue almost outpaced and his feathers windblown flat to the velvet, nose pink, teeth clamped, horse foaming, and all the fury and pride of the Chatwyns in righteously indignant bloom.

The local boys from the village, sent to warn the Lady Wrotham that some fine and noble gentleman and his party were on the road under Wychwood, arrived too late. The gentleman himself was first to the stables.

"I won't be staying." The Earl of Chatwyn dismounted, threw his reins and his gloves to the stable boy, and strode the cobbles to the main doorway, already thrown wide. "But I've a deal to say and I'm as parched as a prune in aspic. Where's your wine and where's your mistress?"

Baroness Wrotham hurried out into the pale sunshine and curtsied. "My lord, I had not expected –"

"Well, of course you didn't," dismissed the earl. "I presume my son's here?"

Nicholas sauntered across the cobbles. "What a clatter and calamity," he observed. "What the devil are *you* doing here?"

"Follow me," said the earl.

Everybody did, with the lady of the house scuttling behind her guest, while Nicholas, nodding to his wife who stood bemused, ushered her inside with him and then closed the door firmly behind them all. The steward was immediately ordered away, and the small group entered the main hall as pages were sent for candles, wine and spiced biscuit. The earl did not take the chair he was offered, but took the wine cup in both hands. "Not some wretched diluted hippocras for the gullible, I hope? No, good. A thirsty ride," he explained. "Damned roads. Ice and snow in winter. Mud and swollen rivers in spring. Now it's wellnigh summer, and there's more dust than in the jousting lists." He signalled and his son obligingly refilled the cup, meanwhile refilling his own.

Nicholas said, "You've galloped all the way from Westminster?"

The earl ignored him and turned to the baroness. "Get rid of your servants, my lady. I've a matter of sensitivity to discuss."

Nicholas said, "Sensitivity? I doubt you know the meaning of the word, sir." He brought a chair for his wife and stood behind it as Emeline sat, her expression masked.

The baroness fluttered, standing alone and staring at her guest. The earl stood before her. "I intend arranging an annulment," he informed her abruptly. "I've someone scribing the papers right now. It'll be sent off to the Vatican next week."

Everybody gazed at him in increasing confusion. Nicholas said blankly, "But you're not married, sir."

The earl finally acknowledged his son. "Don't be a damned fool, m'boy. I'm here for you." He put down his empty cup, hitched his thumbs into his belt, and extended his lungs as his stomach swelled. He said, "Admitted to me after the fire that you'd never bedded the wench. Since then you've been holed up in London and struck down with the damned pestilence. Had that fool nephew of mine searching for you, so presumably you didn't return here for weeks. And no time for dalliance since then, I gather, what with sidling off to Gloucester, and whatever other odd business you've been up to." The circle of open mouths remained silent around him. The earl continued, "So I've every intention of finishing the alliance." He stared coldly at his son. "I take it, this is what you wanted, eh? Should have asked me before. I'm not pleased, but there's no way out now it's got this far. You never wanted the wench, and made that clear enough from the start. Well, now you've got your wish."

It took Nicholas a moment. Then he said, quite softly, "You're either drink sodden or luna pickled, sir. Is there a full moon? I've two answers to give you, but both will be given in private. Then I suggest you leave for Spain as soon as can be arranged."

The baroness had sunk to the nearest chair, but Emeline now stood, coming forwards. Nicholas took her arm, leading her back to her shadowed seat. "I don't understand," she muttered, looking up pleadingly at him.

"None of us do," sighed Nicholas. "Dealing with my father can be meaningless at the best of times. I imagine he's drunk as usual."

The earl twitched an eyebrow. "Your protestations don't fool me, m'boy," he said, raising his voice in irritation. "My trip to Spain is cancelled and that fool Ratcliff is being primed in my place. And it's this wretched business of yours has caused it, family scandals, with my son slaughtering half the neighbourhood, and accusations flying through the palace corridors. Are you mad, boy? And have the audacity to call me pickle brained, when all the world knows what you've done."

Emeline burst into tears.

Her mother gazed in increasing fear around the chamber, then began quietly to sob, both hands covering her face. From outside the door, a heavy thump rattled the floorboards, and a slightly muffled scream was silenced. Nicholas strode to the door and flung it open. Avice was huddled on the ground in the dark passage outside, blinking back tears. "Oh good God," said Nicholas.

Emeline glared at the earl, wiping away her tears with her kerchief and then loudly blowing her nose. "You have made my sister faint," she accused his lordship in a small and muffled voice. "And made my mother cry. And we are already so – worried about everything. Papa's funeral was just a week ago and we're still in mourning. And you're so wrong, so terribly, terribly wrong." She bit her lip with a sniff. "And I wish I was dead too."

"Live with my no good son much longer, and no doubt you will be," announced the earl. "Now listen to me, all of you. I'm not accusing anybody. Not that I don't know the truth, but that's a matter for the sheriff and I'll cast no aspersions. But the fact is, everyone knows. First Peter. Now the father-in-law. Only one person links the two. It's a nasty business, but I intend making the best of it. Splitting the two families as fast as can be – that's my aim now. Show the Chatwyns have no interest in the Wrothams, and cut out any motive for blind murder. Nothing shady. A properly arranged annulment, and the bride price returned without rancour. And you'll come back to Westminster with me, my boy. I'll deal with you myself, but I'll not have a son of mine with his head lying beside the block and all his Chatwyn blood draining into the sawdust."

Nicholas sighed. "If this is your idea of family loyalty and filial defence, sir, then I'd say you could have managed it better. First, I have no intention of obtaining an annulment, nor do I have the grounds. And secondly I have murdered nobody, nor had cause for that either. For someone who has ridden all the way from court just to clear your family name, you seem remarkably ignorant of the facts."

"I'm remarkably clear on one fact," roared the earl, crimson faced. "I'm bloody well aware that his highness has cancelled my trip to Spain, and put any royal business on hold for me until this scandal is cleared up. Any chance of patronage and glory has gone up the chimney with the flames you lit, you wretched worm brained idiot, and I'll not have another chance for a seat on the Royal Council next year because of you. The only way is to get you abroad before you're arrested."

Avice had crept within the hall, and was clinging to her mother, legs trembling. The baroness managed to say, "Please, my lord, I beg you - no more. You are wrong, I swear. Oh, mercy, this is all so disturbing - so shocking."

The earl remained a swirl of fur and velvets, sleeves sweeping the floorboards. Emeline stood abruptly, avoiding her father-in-law's furious march, and went to stand beside her mother and sister, one hand on the back of her mother's chair, the other around her sister's waist. She said, voice carefully controlled, "Nicholas, I believe you should take your father up to the small solar, and speak to him in private. I'll look after Maman. She can't deal with all this. You know she's still upset about - well, about everything."

"Speak to him upstairs?" Nicholas regarded his father with faint revulsion. "I'd sooner just throw him out."

At which moment the Wrotham House steward stepped awkwardly through the partly open door, and cleared his throat, saying, "My lady. I do beg your pardon for interrupting."

Every head swung around in expectation. "For pity's sake, Sherman," wailed her ladyship, "go away. Or get wine. I ordered the staff to keep out. So don't just stand there. Do something."

The steward bowed. "My lady, I regret to announce that you have another visitor. A young lady has arrived with her retinue, and is at present waiting in the withdrawing annexe. I explained that you were otherwise occupied, my lady, but she informed me that she has ridden a long way, and wishes to see you without delay."

"Oh good gracious," exclaimed the baroness. "Some silly village woman? And at a time like this? Who is it?"

"Another secret mistress, come to mourn her lover," muttered Avice.

The steward bowed again. "It is a Mistress Sysabel Frye, who begs leave to speak with you, my lady."

Emeline dropped her kerchief and Nicholas began to laugh. The earl, striding once again to mid floor with a flourish of crimson and a squeak of his boots, demanded, "That stupid niece of mine? What's she doing here?"

"Probably on a much more benevolent errand than yours, Father dearest." Nicholas grinned.

The baroness stood in a hurry, absent mindedly curtsied to no one in particular, and turning, hurried from the hall. Avice promptly took the chair left vacant, and started crying again. "I think," said Emeline, "I am going to be sick."

Nicholas, remembering to appear comforting, put his arm back around her shoulders.

The earl was glaring impatiently at his son. "All this feminine nonsense," he complained, "is of no matter whatsoever. You don't seem to appreciate the gravity of the situation, Nick m'boy."

"Oh, indeed I do," smiled Nicholas, taking his wife's hand. "Feeling sick can be a serious business indeed, and will probably interfere with what I had in mind for this evening." He squeezed Emeline's fingers in faintly amused apology. "As for you, Papa, I suggest you take yourself to bed as well. You need to sleep off whatever you've been chewing on for the past few days. I murdered no one, and can probably prove it if pressed since I imagine I was here in full view whenever it was done. Nor do I intend getting an annulment. I'm perfectly satisfied with my marriage as it happens, which is more than I can say for my parentage. Now, unless you want me to prove my violent tendencies and knock you down, you had better come upstairs with me. I'll find you an empty bedchamber and tie you to the bed if necessary."

"This matter isn't finished," spluttered the earl. "And if you think I give a damn about that silly little niece of mine - I just hope she's left her fool aunt behind."

Nicholas interrupted him. He released his wife's hand and strode across to confront his father. "Sissy is probably here to show this family has some manners after all," he said softly. "She knows her brother went off to find me, and won't know I've since turned up here. Now she'll have heard of the baron's death, and will have come to offer help and condolences. Something I doubt had occurred to you, Papa?"

"Help? Help indeed," scowled the earl. "I came to save your silly neck and extricate myself from this family pickle. If you think I'm going to sit peacefully in Westminster while the king wipes his hands of the Chatwyns, then you don't know me."

"Since I know you remarkably well," said Nicholas with a small impatient sigh, "I know full well you're interested only in preserving your position at court. If the king has cancelled your diplomatic mission to Spain, it's probably because he realised you'd make a raker's midden of it. You'd not be the first I'd recommend for organising a marital agreement on behalf of royalty. So he ordered you to ride to Gloucestershire instead, to give comfort to the Wrothams and your poor fatherless daughter-in-law."

"Well, well, that's as may be," sighed the earl, unbending slightly, "it's true his grace has his own quiet way of doing things. But if you'd heard the gossip flying north, south and west - and every wretched rumour monger whispering that it's my son who first killed his brother - and then his poor little wife's father -"

Nicholas had dragged his father upstairs when the baroness finally brought her new young visitor into the hall. The four women sat white faced as Sherman served hippocras and honey cakes. It was nearing suppertime, but the baroness had not yet asked for the table to be set, nor decided how many there might be to feed. She was hoping it would be fewer than she feared.

Emeline said, "It's totally delightful to see you again Sissy, and most kind of you to come." She was busy picking up the biscuit crumbs she had dropped in her lap. It was distraction she needed. "You have just missed your uncle."

"What a relief," said Sissy, accepting a cup of warmed hippocras.

Avice shook her head. "He's still here - upstairs. I suppose we can't hope he'll stay up there forever. He'll have to come down one day."

"I may go to bed early," Sissy decided. "It has been a tiring day, and travel is always so exhausting. Besides," she looked around, expecting confirmation, "I suppose he's drunk. Both of them, no doubt."

Nicholas faced his father through the long shadows. The room was small, but the twilight entering through the one casement window did not reach the corners. "I've no idea," he said, "whether this is the bedchamber you're supposed to be given or not. Since it's a miserable place with a dreary stench, it would be all you deserve, though presumably the baroness has ordered your bags to be dumped somewhere or other. But for the moment no one else is sleeping in this one, so we can at least talk in private."

His father pulled up a wide armed and cushioned chair and sat within it, ignoring the groan of unaccustomed wood to bulk. "Gloomy house," muttered the earl. "Light some candles, m'boy."

"I doubt I'll find any," remarked Nicholas. "My dear father-in-law was the thriftiest soul I've ever met. But I didn't kill him."

"If –" said the earl.

His son interrupted him. "I'm not entirely clear when it was done," he said wearily. "But at a guess, I'd say I was already here, probably in bed with my wife, and with enough witnesses to swear I was nowhere near Gloucester. Does that satisfy you? Or are you simply concerned with what others may think, and not actually bothered about my guilt or innocence?"

"The court thinks you did it." The earl stared glumly at the dust and horse spittle on his riding boots. "The whole of Westminster thinks you did it. The Council thinks you did it. And the king thinks you did it."

"The king won't think anything of the sort," said the Chatwyn heir without any visible signs of concern. "He's not the sort of man to jump to foolish conclusions, and besides, he knows I'm not the sort of man to have murdered my wife's father without strong motive."

"And how would he know that?" demanded the earl. "You're rarely at court, thank the Lord, so the king wouldn't recognise you from a damned Flemish pig salter."

Nicholas smiled faintly. "Never mind about that. It's you, dear Papa, who should know me better after all. Yet you seem curiously eager to convict me."

There was a pause. Then, "Peter," muttered the earl.

Nicholas sighed. "Yes, indeed. I rather wondered if you suspected me all along. I know you were disappointed it hadn't been the other way around. Peter did try to kill me once, of course. But I did not retaliate. Now I see we shall have to talk at some length."

"So where's the damned wine jug?" demanded his father.

CHAPTER TWENTY THREE

There were awkward silences across the dinner table. The earl's rank conferred the place of honour and Nicholas sat at the far end, which was how he liked it. The baroness discussed the recent mild weather, but only Sysabel took much notice of the conversation, informing everyone that it had rained for several consecutive days that week in Nottingham.

The courses were a little more plentiful and slightly more elaborate than had previously been served in the Wrotham household, for since his lordship's unaccountable death the baroness, initially a little surprised at herself, had begun to make her own choices. Encouraged by both daughters, she now consistently requested more appetising meals, and now she had not just one but three important visitors, she had ordered the kitchens to produce the best of whatever they had available and could put together in such a short time. There were, of course, apple codlings.

Avice, suddenly inquiring why everyone at Westminster Palace evidently assumed Nicholas had committed vile and heinous murder when they had no possible knowledge of the facts nor even knowing who Baron Wrotham was, was quickly glared into silence by her mother. But then Sysabel answered, "It's rumour, you know, that sprinkles the whetstones of every town. No one is too interested in truth when gossip is so much more intriguing. And Nicholas is hardly well respected - or trusted -" but she caught Emeline's glare, and her voice faded out."

Emeline said, carefully avoiding all eyes and staring down at the remains of an apple codling on her platter, "Is it - true then, my lord? That people at Westminster truly believe Nicholas guilty? Even of - his own brother's death?"

"Ah," said the earl, nose in his wine cup, "not a discussion for the moment, young lady." He drank deeply and looked up again, absorbing the variety of expressions fixed upon him. "Doubt my son will thank me for prolonging - as it were - that particular subject." He drank again, immediately looking around for the nearest flagon. Thankful to find one within reach, he appeared to relax. "Besides," he said as he refilled his cup, "No doubt the boy didn't do it after all. Says he didn't. We've talked – upstairs, as you know. Well, seeing as I can't vouch for one nor the other, I'll take his word for it."

"Generous of you," murmured Nicholas.

"Besides," the earl said, a little gruff, "'Tis true enough. The boy's not the sort to do such a thing." He looked up, his glare now fixed firmly on his son. "My boy Peter, he led our own troops up to Carlisle back in '81. Joined the skirmishes, and was commended for his leadership." The earl put down his knife with a snap. "Adrian, stuffy little cock a' poop that he is, did the same in '82. Saved some other fellow's life and killed a couple of reivers or something of the sort. Was knighted afterwards on the field by the duke himself." The earl still stared pointedly at his son. "Nicholas, now," he continued, "did nothing of the sort. Didn't volunteer. Didn't join his brother's muster. Didn't care to risk his precious life in the wilds of heathen Scotland."

Nicholas appeared remarkably unconcerned by these revelations. "So I'm clearly a coward who dislikes bloodshed," he smiled faintly. "And am therefore an unlikely murderer."

He excused himself immediately after the meal was finished and after a final thanksgiving had been led by the priest over the final course of wafers and hippocras, a family habit the baroness had not yet broken. As the table was cleared, the priest shuffled off, and the ladies joined the earl by the empty hearth in the hall, Nicholas bowed briefly and explained he needed to speak to someone outside. Emeline opened her mouth to ask who and why, but Nicholas left abruptly, marching outside into the deepening night.

Since manners and propriety precluded her from bouncing up and following him as she would have liked, she turned instead to her father-in-law. "My lord," she said, avoiding her mother's baleful stare, "I can offer my own assurances that my husband could not, *did* not, attack my father. Nicholas was ill, he was away, and then he came back to me. And how would he have known where my father went, when none of us had any idea at all?" She took a breath, smiled carefully and clasped her hands meekly in her lap. She then said, "But there are other matters I know nothing of. I should be most - grateful - if you would tell me, my lord."

"Humph," said the earl.

"There are things I want to know too," said Avice in a hurry.

"Avice, it is past your bedtime," said her mother. "Your new tutor is due tomorrow morning. You will have a great deal to do."

"I don't need a tutor," objected Avice, "I can read and write and I know everything already, even though Papa said I'd never learn to count past three. But he was wrong. About everything."

"Avice," threatened her mother, "Bed."

"Please, just one question," Avice pleaded, half rising from her chair. "I mean, he's family now, isn't he? So," she stood, peeping up with a small simpering smile, "I have always wondered how Nicholas got that - scar. If it wasn't in battle?"

The earl tapped his fingertips across his stomach. He was not accustomed to being surrounded by females, and it was many years since a pretty girl had simpered at him. "Well now," he said with magnanimous patience, "Not battle, no, not young Nickolas. He was twelve, you know. Most unfortunate."

"An accident?" Emeline leaned forward slightly.

"Accident? Well, yes. That's what it was." The earl seemed unwilling to continue.

"Oh do go on," insisted Sissy from beside him. "There's no secret after all. We have forgiven Nicholas long ago, surely?"

The earl humphed again, further confused. "Forgiven him? Didn't do anything to forgive, you know, not that time anyway. Not his fault. Must be fair. Just an accident, you know. Boys playing. Archery practise. Peter never meant it of course, but have to admit, it was Peter's fault."

Sissy gulped and shook her head. "Oh uncle, that's just not true," she said. "Of course I wasn't there, but Peter told me all about it later. They were out practising at the butts, early one morning. Peter said Nick pushed him, trying to make him fight. Naturally Peter refused. He was two years older after all, and knew he'd win. He just didn't want to hurt Nicholas, so he went back to shooting at the target. Nick ran right in front, goading Peter into fighting. Peter's arrow was aimed at the butts, but it hit Nicholas square in the face. Peter was so upset."

"I imagine," said Avice, wincing, "Nicholas was rather upset too."

Emeline shivered, staring at her husband's cousin. The earl sighed. "A nasty business," he said. "I heard the screams from the hall and ordered a couple of pages to investigate. Blood everywhere. I called my surgeon - fellow called Mannbury in those days - an excellent barber. He got the arrow out eventually. Nick was in bad shape for some time." He looked sharply over at Emeline. "Peter's story - well, he told it one way. But other witnesses told it a little differently. Nick was pretty sour about it of course. Pain - disfigurement - just a boy - I understood. But then, when Peter was killed, well it was years later of course, but I wondered. Revenge. Stands to reason. So proof or no proof, I had my doubts."

There was a small silence as the shadows lengthened. Avice grabbed back her abandoned wine cup and reached for the jug. Pewter clinked on pewter. "I think," said the baroness with a deep sigh, "it has been a long day. I believe I shall retire, my lord. Sherman will show you to your chamber, sir, and Martha will show you to yours, Sysabel, my dear. I wish you all a very good night."

Emeline escaped outside.

The stars were a cold shimmer in the darkness, and a glimmer of moonshine from behind the clouds spun pearl drops across the cobbles. She could not see Nicholas. Turning to go back into the warmth and her own bed, she suddenly changed her mind and headed instead in the opposite direction, wandering out across the courtyard to the stables. The familiar smell of horses, dry hay, snuggled sweat and fresh manure was strong in the sharp little breeze. One horse was awake, snittering and snorting, objecting to the disturbance. A medley of grooms boys snored, content in the warm straw. Then Emeline heard the voices.

Her husband's voice said, "I've talked to the boy already. He's half starved and terrified."

"All the easier to shake the truth outta the brat, then," said the other voice.

"Which is true," Nicholas conceded. "But the way it was done, I can't see it being him. Just a few questions should suffice. You'll soon discover whether he knows anything."

"You're too kind hearted, m'lor," muttered the other man. "No doubt the brat were after claiming the house and the coin he thought were in it."

"Then a little unwise to set fire to the place, and so destroy whatever he hoped to inherit, don't you think? No," decided Nicholas. "You'd do better to approach the child with food and a few pence for his next meal - encourage him to talk with kindness. He needs a friend. Threaten the boy, and he'll no doubt be scared into silence, guilty or innocent."

"But if you already don't reckon it's him, m'lor -?"

"No, I don't think it was him. Who it was - well actually I have an idea, but it's an idea I don't want to have," said Nicholas, somewhat obscurely. "So first I'll eliminate all other possibilities. Gloucester tonight. Then we're off to London."

Footsteps in straw, a shuffling of men, and the further disturbance of the horses. Emeline recognised her own palfrey's impatient whinny. The other man cleared his throat, seemed to walk away, then called from a distance, "Within the hour then, my lord?"

Nicholas said, "David's already packing my bag. You can wake one of these brats, and get my horse saddled ready. David's too - and yours. One spare for baggage."

"No outriders, m'lor? They say the roads is getting more dangerous now the baron's gone and no one sent to patrol the boarders."

"No outriders," Nicholas said, his grin obvious in his voice. "I want speed, not grinding propriety. I'll save your miserable hide for you if we get stopped by thieves."

The other man's snort sounded very like the horses. "Before midnight then, m'lor. Right here, ready saddled." And his footsteps disappeared in the direction of the outhouses.

Emeline stamped the three steps needed and regarded her husband with fury through the shadows. Her palfrey, smelling her familiarity, kicked at the stable door. Nicholas looked down in faint surprise. His wife glared up at him and said through her teeth, "I knew it. You're a vile, horrible, dishonest pig man. You promised to take me with you, but you're just running away from me in the middle of the night. Or is it your father you're running away from this time? Perhaps you'd like to borrow one of Nurse Martha's gowns? In either case, you're the miserable coward your father called you."

"Did I promise?" wondered Nicholas vaguely. "How unwise of me."

"You're always promising things and then you don't do it," she accused him. "Your promises are useless, worthless feathers in the wind. You - you're -"

"I probably am," grinned Nicholas. "But in fact I had every intention of asking if you wanted to come with me - mad escapes in the night being the stuff of all the best romances of course. Hardly proper for young ladies. But then, I'm not much interested in proper, as you might have gathered."

Emeline sniffed and bit her lip. "I don't believe you."

"Regarding what, precisely?" smiled Nicholas. "Being proper, or the romance of escape? Both quite true, I promise."

"There you go, promising again," she glowered. "And you know quite well what I meant. I think you're lying and I'm quite sure you meant to run away and just leave me a message to find in the morning, just like last time."

He took her hand firmly, leading her away from the stables and out into the little hedged garden and its neat paths, parsley sprigs and moonshine. "You speak too loudly, my love, and will have my father alerted and half the household gaping through the windows." He pulled her along until they stood together under a willow, its drooping leaf disguising their shadows. "Now," he said, "listen to me and don't interrupt. My father has every intention of dragging me back to Westminster to face my accusers and show an innocent face. Then he'll wrap me in fishing net and transport me bodily to Flanders or Portugal or some such. I've been avoiding the old man for years, and it's exactly what I mean to do again. A long sea trip most certainly doesn't appeal to me at present and nor do my father's attempts to bully me into his way of life. Simply refusing to take any notice of his demands is much like voluntarily running onto an unsheathed blade, or at the least beating one's head against the castle battlements. My only other form of escape would be to knock him down. But I won't do that.

He's too old, too fat and usually too pissed. Instead I intend disappearing. Then I intend discovering who slaughtered my brother and your father."

"Oh." She went pale, unnoticeable in the night's looming black, and mumbled, "But you don't know who it was, so how can you know it was the same killer?"

"Bloody murder doesn't happen every day, even in London's back alleys. When two people, linked by family, are killed within the same year and in exactly the same manner, then I have almost enough brain to see the probabilities."

"The fire –"

"Few know," Nicholas said, "since the details of Peter's death were kept as quiet as we could manage. But since I was first on the scene after the messenger arrived with the news, I know more than most. Peter was slaughtered a house in Nottingham – and his visit there was clandestine. His throat was cut, and an attempt was made to burn the body. But the fire didn't travel, and with his doublet doused in dribbled wine, went out. Your father – well, the similarities are clear enough."

"I don't want to know anymore."

"If you come with me," Nicholas pointed out quietly, "you'll be faced with worse truths than that. You'll be faced with discomfort, danger and surprise. Will you risk your reputation and your safety? I can guarantee your life, but little else."

She shook her head. "Your father thinks you're a coward. You're not, are you?"

Nicholas laughed. "My father doesn't know me. Nor do you."

"Then I'll gallop off into the night with you," said Emeline in a rush, "and find out."

"In which case," Nicholas said, "you'd better hurry upstairs and pack yourself a bag with as little as you think you can live with. Practical necessities, changes of linen, a warm cloak and no baudekyn gowns."

"I don't own a baudekyn gown. You never bought me one."

"I will, as soon as I have my brother's killer in gaol." One hand to her elbow, he was leading her back towards the house. "But I leave in less than an hour, with or without you. So hurry.

And for God's sake, don't tell anyone else or make enough noise to wake up my wretched father."

"And Martha? She's very efficient, and can pack in no time –"

Nicholas shook his head, pushing her forwards. "No Martha. No Avice, Sissy, or your mother. No servants and no secret whispered confidences."

Emeline now had the hiccups. "I have to come *alone*?"

"You don't have to come at all," Nicholas told her. "But if you do, you won't be alone. You'll have me, and once we get to London I'll set you up in the Strand House, and fill it with nursemaids and female companions to look after your things. But no females yet, nor anyone to slow me down. Leave letters for your family explaining what you've chosen to do – if you're entirely sure you want to do this – but try not to make it sound as though I've abducted you by force. My father would love something else to accuse me of. And don't tell anyone where we're going."

"I don't know where we're going."

"London eventually."

Just one moment longer she stood beyond the scuffle and busy smell of the stables and stared up into the face of her husband. "You'd sooner I didn't come, wouldn't you?" she whispered, the final hiccup swallowed back.

A couple of the stable boys were already saddling horses, hauling out the panniers and saddle scabbards while scrubbing down the young lord's great sleepy liard. Nicholas said, brusque now, "Of course I would. It would be far easier without you. But perhaps less interesting. Admittedly I'm surprised you want this, but hurry, or I shall leave without you anyway. If you're not back down here within the hour, I'll assume you've changed your mind and crawled into your nice safe warm bed. In which case, I shall blow you a kiss to your chamber window, and ride off into the night."

For one very short and chilly breath, Emeline realised she could not do anything so ridiculously absurd, dangerous, uncomfortable and positively shocking. Then she straightened her shoulders, shook her head, hiccupped again and said, "I'm coming."

"Well, you're a brave little thing," Nicholas smiled at her. "And I admire you for it, even though you're probably quite mad. Which means you'll fit nicely into my family. Now quick, quick - and remember, not a word to a soul. But for pity's sake get rid of those hiccups."

CHAPTER TWENTY FOUR

It was a huge and saffron moon behind the trees. Branches were black lace silhouettes, stark against the gold.

Nicholas rode a little ahead, speaking quietly with David Witton who kept close to his side. Emeline, tired now, trailed behind. The soft fur lining of her cape, hood up, tickled her ears. She breathed in the chill sting of night breezes, gazing forwards at her husband's back through the tiny mist of her own breath. The easy swing of his shoulders was rhythmic, dark in mahogany and beaver, his horse's tail twitching. The moon followed, always there, always watching, a fat sated Scorpio moon, pure gold, promising adventure.

Behind her rode the man Emeline did not know, a burly and quiet stranger, but who she had overheard talking to her husband an hour back when discussing his planned escape. The man led the baggage horse and was, she presumed, a servant, even though Nicholas had ordered her to bring none. He had also, she presumed, been told to ride behind her and protect her back.

Emeline had left the home of her childhood without interruption, and had tiptoed downstairs and out to the stables to find Nicholas waiting for her, her palfrey's reins in his hand. Down the old pathways and through the sleeping village, the horses kept to a brisk walk until they were past the shadow of the church steeple striped across their path. Then their pace had quickened and the moon had burst out from behind the clouds, shining like a burning torch. And so, taking the high road to Gloucester, they slipped away from the mundane safety of friends and family, and entered the world of possibility and doubt, risk and insecurity.

It was nearing dawn when Nicholas rode into the courtyard of the White Boar, and jangled the bell to wake the landlord. Beneath the indignant rustle of the little russet squirrels in the trees, a sleepy eyed ostler was bribed to unbridle and water the horses. Then finally Emeline clambered into a bed slightly musky and even more lumpy than the mattress she had only just become used to at home. At first she slept alone. Nicholas was downstairs talking quietly to his companions as the tavern keeper swept up last night's spilled ale as his wife piled yesterday's remaining cheat rolls into the oven for the unexpected gentleman's early breakfast. It was some hours later when the Chatwyn heir crept quietly into bed beside his wife, gazed at her crumpled bump under the covers, shook his head with tired amusement, and closed his own eyes. Outside the sun was now growing bright yet the wayside inn's early business did not disturb its sleeping customers.

Emeline woke and found she was being watched. Nicholas was sitting on the end of the bed, fully dressed, and regarding her with patient sympathy. She had barely opened her eyes when he said, "I have to go somewhere. This time I can't take you with me."

Having gloomily concluded it was unlikely her husband would be joining her in bed anytime soon, she had not removed her shift the night before. Now she was able to struggle up with impunity - staring into the day's pallid light. She glowered, mumbling, "So even though you brought me here, you don't really want me. Did you even bother coming to bed last night? And how long will you be gone this time? An hour? A day? A week?"

Nicholas grinned. "I don't do things I don't want. If you're here, and you certainly are, then it must be because I want you. And I spent several very comfortable hours wrapped around you this night - though it was past dawn when I came upstairs. You slept through all my caresses, presumably enjoying sweet dreams. I've no intention whatsoever of abandoning you in this dreary tavern for too long, but the person I need to see now is not anyone I could conceivably introduce to you. I shall be back before evening. Does that suffice?"

"Who?" she demanded. "Who is this creature who cannot even be permitted to set eyes on me? Who is it, and why is he so important that we've come all this way instead of going straight to London? Or is it a she? Do all the men of my family have mistresses in Gloucester?"

"If I had a mistress in Gloucester, I think I'd introduce you to her and then sit back and watch the entertainment." Nicholas was still grinning. "No, my dear. I'm going to see a boy, little more than a child. But you are staying here. If you try to follow me, I shall take you back home."

The small boy stood straight, shoulders back, hiding his fear as best he could as he faced his accusers. His hair, matted and pale, was in his eyes. He held his hands very still, fisted by his side. "Nort, m'lor, I swear it. Me Ma, I misses her terrible hard, m'lor. And him, well, I seen him little enough. Meant nort to me, 'cept more bread and beans on the platter. Weren't allowed to talk with the gent. Weren't allowed in that big house neither, 'cept after it were empty, and I were sent to clean up."

Nicholas frowned. "The big house? I know of none. Was there another? The house where your mother died was just two rooms and a shed."

"T'were big to me, m'lor. I ain't never lived nowhere 'cept here, and this be one room, no more and I shares it wiv the hens."

Nicholas nodded through the shadows. The single chamber was cramped although it held little more than a hearth with hanging cauldron, two stools and a straw palette in the corner. The floor was beaten earth and a wiry threshing of rushes held out the draught from beneath the only door. A tiny window was closed by oiled parchment, and the now blazing sunshine outside did not enter beyond a faint and gloomy glow. Nicholas said, "So you claim to know nothing of your mother's protector, nor anything of her killer? Her lover bought her the big house you speak of. Surely that interested you? You knew him to be wealthy? And are there enemies you know of? Family, perhaps, who criticised your mother's behaviour, and resented her good luck? Do you have a father, angry over his wife's adultery? And the baron? What of him? Was he ever followed here by those asking questions - or by someone wanting to know his direction?"

Throughout, the boy slumped wearily, barely comprehending. Eventually, since Nicholas had stopped speaking some moments ago, the boy mumbled, "I don't rightly understand, m'lor. T'were me Ma as brought me food every day and that were all I asked. Her days was her own to pass as she wished. And I ain't got no Pa. Never did."

Eyes narrowed in faint suspicion, Nicholas asked, "But you knew the whereabouts of the other house. So you went there. And you saw the baron?"

"I went there to clean and scrub, m'lor," the child answered. "When me Ma told me, but only after the grand gent were gone."

Nicholas sighed, resigned. "And when did you last eat?"

The child hunched his shoulders, unclenched his fists and looked down at his bare toes. "Don't rightly remember, m'lor. Three days, I reckon. I knows the baker's wife and she give me the stale bread when she has it left over."

"Giving you coin will hardly help," Nicholas said, untying his purse and taking out three silver pennies. "If I give you little, it won't last long and then you will starve again. Yet if I give you much, the locals will be suspicious and either steal it, or beat you for presumed stealing." He sighed, looking back over his shoulder at his forlorn companion. "You might join my company, and look after the horses perhaps. Do you know anything of horses?"

The boy's eyes glinted. "Nort, m'lor, ain't never had cause nor come near them big teeth. I looked after our chickens once, but me Ma strangled them and that grand gent ate them."

"Well, the little blighter's honest at least," muttered Rob from behind. "Coulda claimed a stable boy's skills, just to get the job. But told the truth instead."

"I'll do wot I's told, whatever you want, m'lor," the boy hurried on. "I can learn. I'm willing. I works hard when there's ort to do."

"I've no need of another servant." Nicholas looked him over. "But I dislike leaving you here with nothing to face but starvation. Board your house up, tell the mayor it's for sale - do what you want. But if you choose to come with me, it'll be neither comfort nor safety I'll offer. You'll get food twice a day, and a bed of sorts most nights. I'll work you hard and expect obedience. Make your own decision."

The child answered before Nicholas had finished speaking, and had fallen to his knees, hands clasped. "Wotever you tells me, m'lor, I'll do and be grateful - wondrous grateful - until me dying day."

Nicholas' mouth twitched. "Don't idolise me, boy. That wouldn't suit at all. And there's another complication. I travel with a lady who is my wife, and you'll treat her with the utmost respect. But she's not to know who you are. You are not to mention your mother to her, nor the gentleman who became your mother's lover. Do you understand?"

The boy shook his head. "Not rightly m'lor."

"Neither my wife nor any other person we meet from now on can know you are the son of the woman lately killed while in the arms of Baron Wrotham. That is precisely what I mean. Do you understand now?"

The boy turned the shake of his head to a nod, staring from beneath his increasingly tangled mop of dun hair. Rob said, "And wot is this urchin's name, anyway?"

Finally rising from his position of supplication, the child said, "Wolt, sir, being as me Ma called me Walter, if it pleases you."

"Don't please me none," decided Rob. He turned to Nicholas. "Does it please you then, m'lor?"

"Not particularly," Nicholas smiled. "But I doubt I'll remember it anyway. So, boy," he held out his hand, offering the three silver pennies, "I shall send Rob here to collect you before sundown today. In the meantime, eat and buy yourself some shoes and an oiled cape. Arrange whatever you wish regarding this house, and then wait for me. If you're not here at sunset, I shall presume you've changed your mind and have no wish to join me. In which case, keep the money and organise you own life."

"I'll be 'ere, m'lor, no doubt nor nuffin' save death'll keep me gone." The child was shivering, although the afternoon outside was warm.

"Well, try not to die," suggested Nicholas, "since that would seem a shame just as your life is about to improve." He thought a moment as he turned towards the door, then said, "Not that improvements are all that likely, come to think of it. But I won't let you starve."

Back out in the sunshine, Rob said, "You keep this up, m'lor, and we'll soon have a whole bloody retinue of ragamuffins and thieves."

"I have you," Nicholas pointed out, foot to the stirrup as he remounted. David had been waiting in the alley, holding the horses. "Might as well collect others of the same. Now – I need to talk to the sheriff. Then back to the inn."

The next day they took the road early and headed south east for London. Emeline did not remark on the addition of a skinny rag tail brat who clung astride the baggage horse, trailing well behind in the dust kicked up by other hooves. Magpies were chittering in the branches above their heads, and a sweet smell of hawthorn floated on the sunbeams. The party stopped midday for dinner, when Nicholas ordered apple codlings and watched his wife eat six. They did not stop for the night until late, and the tavern was a bedraggled affair with its thatch half tumbled and a scurry of mice in the upper beams.

Nicholas made love to his wife and kissed her gently as she regained her breath, tucking her in with apologies for the smell of mouse piss on the counterpane. He then retraced his steps downstairs to speak with David. Emeline was asleep when he finally returned to the small chamber, which is what he had hoped for. They left again very early the next day, just as a pearly dawn peeped over the still darkened hills.

They skirted townships and marketplaces, sometimes travelling the back lanes away from the jumble of traffic, ox carts and flocks of sheep, having no wish to advertise their party and their destination. But they stopped each day for food and retired to some convenient hostelry each night, never too late for a hot supper and a bed before the fatigue of travelling turned to utter exhaustion. But Emeline wilted as the horses plodded, and was glad when their road took them into shade and over streams where the horses stopped, thirsty and eager to drink. "Tired, my love?" Nicholas asked her as they dismounted in the cool by the grassy damp banks of the river they had forded. "Rest here then, or stretch your legs as you wish. There's ale in the sumpter's panniers, and oat biscuits too, if you want them."

"Tired? How could I be tired?" Emeline shrugged, leaning back against the mossy trunk of an oak, its roots in the shallows. "When the journey is so pleasant and so leisurely, and my husband so conversational and such an attentive companion that I'm barely conscious of being away from home."

"I know. We're all weary, little one." Nicholas smiled, but his face was grey and lined and there were purpled smudges beneath his eyes. The deep scar across his face seemed to have burrowed deeper, as if the flesh had shrunk around it. "But this is how I travel, if I travel at all, and indeed I've eased my usual pace only for you. Would you have us a month on the road, with all the local gossip recounting our names and direction and our presence known in every village before we arrive?"

"Would it matter?" She stared at the horses, noses to the water, and wished she might do the same with her toes. "I thought travelling with Papa was tiring, but it was never as - abandoned - as this."

He laughed. "You seem always to fear abandonment. So do you want our route known ahead and our arrival expected, with children running behind to beg for pennies every mile we ride?"

"It's a bath I want."

"When we reach the Strand House." He extracted the sack of ale and brought it to her. "First I need to make sure no one else is staying there, then I'll settle you in comfort at last. In the meantime, we ride, we sweat, we eat ill cooked meals at ill cleaned taverns, and we make good speed in anonymity. Should I have warned you of the disadvantages before you chose to come with me?"

"You did," she sighed. "I didn't really believe you. Surely we're respectable enough people, so I don't understand the need for anonymity. Are we robbers, to hide our names and titles?"

"When I leave you sometimes on the road, I go to meet others." He shook his head. "I have - I call them errands - call them what you will. For the business I do, I need contacts and friends in many places, and this is a useful time to reseal those friendships, which can prove important to me in the future. And those I meet up with are neither lords nor ladies, but invariably folk who prefer to keep their own identities quiet. So we travel my way, my love, whether you approve or not."

It was four days later when they came to the capital, and Emeline saw London for the first time. Not yet wishing to be recognised in Westminster or expected at court, Nicholas had first followed Watling Street from the west, and then branched north along Tyburn Way to the city wall at Newgate. The prison building and its great square gateway menaced those who entered London beneath its high iron portcullis, and the wailing, whining misery reeked into stone and earth and air all around. The place stank. Emeline shivered, keeping her palfrey closer to her husband's side.

There had been neither hanging nor visible remains at Tyburn junction itself, but each step of the road had seemed increasingly sad, as though only death claimed the path. They had crossed the River Fleet, busy with barges, but the water had slunk in smelly gurgles, brown as her horse's big weary eyes. Then the final stage, and Newgate prison's menace was gone into the sunshine.

She had been excited to come to London. Goldsmiths' Row gleamed and sparkled in the sunshine and even the cobbles had been swept clean. Traders sat within their little doorways, leather aproned, carving wood and polishing pewter. Some shops, so grand the doorways stood wide and customers wandered both in and out as if a palace awaited them, displayed gold and silver merchandise glimmering through the windows, window shutters folded down as counters. Emeline stared. Nicholas noticed her expression and said suddenly, "I'll take you there once we're settled. But other matters come first. They're not so pleasant, I'm afraid, but we've come for reasons other than shopping."

"I didn't say anything about shopping – I've never *cared* about shopping." Emeline stuck out her chin. "Papa always says –" and then she stopped. Since Nicholas offered no reassuring smile of sympathy, she said crossly instead, "But it's a horrid way into London. There are other gates, aren't there? Are they all so vile?"

Nicholas smiled then. "No. I chose the worst."

They spoke loudly, their voices raised, for London was noisy. A hundred chatterers, welcoming calls from vendors, children squabbling and dogs barking. A shopkeeper chased a dog from his shopfront with a broom, but the dog raised a leg and pissed on the broom's rushes. Ravens flew low to scavenge from the central gutters, and small gaudy selds had set up where the road was wider, leaving little space for the horses to pass. Nicholas dug in his heels, Emeline followed, and they trotted, hooves like cracking glass on the cobbles, pushing the shoppers aside as they clutched at their hats and their baskets. Then with a sudden turn right they entered Bread Street where cobbles ran out into beaten earth and the early morning bakers had already closed. It was quieter. They headed south.

Rob, directly behind Emeline, called out, "The tenement first, m'lor, or the Bear, to settle your lady?"

Nicholas turned and grinned, "You think I'm taking my wife to an ale house, my friend? I might as well leave her in Cock Lane or drag her up Seethinge Alley." David pursed his lips, riding to Emeline's left but staring adamantly ahead. Nicholas, now in front, grinned back at his wife. "There's the Swan, large and clean. We'll go there first."

"You've no need to say it, my lord," Emeline shrugged, tired. "You intend leaving me there while you travel elsewhere without me. May I expect you back before the end of the month?" She ignored the instant cackle behind her.

Nicholas said, "Almost positively my love. Even within the day. But where I intend going, you could not come."

She clenched her fingers on her reins and brought her horse alongside her husband's, leaving David Witton in the dust. "You seem to think me exceedingly delicate, my lord, and pretend I'm incapable of facing anything at all. I cannot meet this person, and cannot go to that place. But you bring me past the executioner's gallows and through a gateway of degeneration and horror." He continued grinning and did not answer, so she said, a little louder, "And you told me not to bring either my nurse or a maid so I'm entirely dependent on you. But you have three servants, and one is remarkably young. He only appeared when we left Gloucester, so was this the person you went to see when I was forced to stay alone in that nasty little tavern? I was not allowed to meet him - yet it seems you have brought him along with us so I have the pleasure of meeting him every day."

Nicholas chuckled. "My plans need to be adjusted from time to time. I'm an adaptable soul. Otherwise I wouldn't be undertaking this venture with a woman in tow. And as for the urchin, he's simply a waif I didn't want to leave to starve. Not the brightest brat, and only twelve years old, but he may yet prove useful."

"He's small for his age. What unsavoury use do you have in mind?"

"Roasted, I think, when we run out of food. But think, my love. Having no servants at all would hardly please you. I'd be expecting you to unsaddle the horses, and lead the baggage drey. I imagine you might complain."

"I would never dare complain, my lord," Emeline said coldly, "when you are such a polite and considerate companion yourself. Besides, I should be terrified you might leave me camped by the river, since you abandon me so regularly however pliant I try to be."

"Pliant?" hooted Nicholas. "You're as snappy as a pike and as doleful as a haddock, my dear, but far less biddable. But you'll share in all the adventures from tomorrow on, I promise you."

She raised an eyebrow. "Oh the surety of your promises again, my lord. How that fills me with faith and composure."

"Show off your composure now then, my love, for this is your hostelry for the next couple of nights." Nicholas waved an arm to his left where a long white limed building stood four stories tall and as grand as a mansion. "I've made no advance warning of arrival, so we must now pretend to be respectable or risk being turned away. But you'll like the place. The food's good, there's minstrels sometimes, no rowdy tavern below, and the chambers are spacious. Promise to let me wash your back, and I'll order a bath set up this evening." Emeline blushed, one eye to the three men of their company, now dismounting. Nicholas had stopped, and swung his leg over his horse's back, hopping down quickly, throwing the reins to David, and coming around to help his wife dismount. "Rob and the boy will take the horses to the stables. Come with me now, little one, and you can rest at last."

"Will you – rest too?" Both hands to her waist, he lifted her down to the hostelry's open paved courtyard. Then he took her arm and led her to the wide open doors and the flickering candle light within.

"Not exactly," Nicholas said. "I have other places to go and other things to do. But I'll join you for supper, I promise."

CHAPTER TWENTY FIVE

The sudden and violent banging on the door seemed so unexpected and threatening that Sysabel pulled the covers over her head. "What? What has happened? If it's Avice you want, she's not here anymore."

"No," Avice shouted from outside the door, "that's because I'm out here. You have to get up at once and come downstairs. Get dressed quick. Where's your silly little maid? Does she sleep like a drunken sailor too?"

Having no clear idea how a drunken sailor might sleep, Sysabel emerged from the bed's cocoon, and looked around. No one else was in the room and the truckle bed where her maid had slept, was now empty. She rubbed her eyes and said, somewhat plaintively, "I wish you'd come in, Avice. I have no idea what you want of me."

Avice poked her head around the door. "I just want you, silly. Everything is in chaos, your uncle is about to murder everyone and my mother's having hysterics in the hall. You have to get up. Don't bother dressing since your maid seems to have run off too."

They had shared a bed, Avice and Sysabel, since Emeline now occupied a grand guest chamber with her husband. But only Sysabel, tired after the previous day's journey, had slept in long past dawn. Now she mumbled, "I expect the girl has gone to try and get me some breakfast."

"No time for that. Other matters are far too urgent" said Avice with a grin of pure delight.

Within the echoes of the high ceilinged hall, the earl reverberated. He glared at the servants, at his miserable hostess and at his niece as she hurried into the room. "Let my damn fool of a son out of my sight for a few hours and every standard of decent behaviour crashes," the earl bellowed. "Has nobody any idea where that wretched boy of mine has gone?"

The baroness, recollecting her courage, murmured, "Nicholas and my daughter have taken only their own mounts and one baggage horse, my lord. Emeline's nurse informs me that my daughter took almost nothing with her, and practically all her clothes have been left behind. She took no maid and crept out without a word. But she is with her husband, my lord, and I can hardly complain. I am sure Nicholas will look after her."

"And just who will look after him, I'd like to know," roared the earl, unappeased. "He's as much sense as a raw cabbage, and is no doubt off doing something entirely absurd and irresponsible."

"Emma left me a note," ventured Avice with an ill concealed smirk.

The earl rounded on her and snatched the scrap of scribbled paper she was holding. His ruddy colouring increased considerably as he read. "No intention of obeying me, indeed! And off to solve the riddles of murder and intrigue, is he! As if the boy is capable of even tying his own hose around his waist, let alone solving genuine mysteries."

The baroness managed a few more proffered words. "Nicholas has taken one servant and his squire with him. David Witton is a respectable young man, I believe, sir. I have considerable respect for his intelligence, and he is obviously loyal."

"Anyone loyal to Nicholas needs their wits unravelled," declared the earl, throwing Emeline's careful apologies and explanations to the ground. "I shall leave here at midday, Madam, immediately after dinner. I shall then travel to London and hope to intercept the young fool before he brings more scandal and ruin to the family."

"Wine, my lord?" suggested Avice, stepping forward with her smile in cement.

"Don't interrupt, Avice," her mother frowned. "This is not your place."

"Place be damned," retaliated the earl. "Bring the wine. I need strength."

As soon as the earl and his entourage had clattered down the path from the stables to the Gloucestershire lanes towards London, Avice grabbed Sysabel's hand and dragged her back upstairs to her bedchamber which they had shared the night before. They sat together on the bed, hugging their knees, and Avice said, "We have to run away."

Notably unconvinced, Sysabel mumbled, "That's a *horrid* idea. You have a lovely house and a lovely mother, and just because your sister has been silly, it doesn't mean you have to as well."

Avice was disappointed. "But of course we have to. She's gone searching for murderers, so we need to follow her and be ready to help. And think of the excitement."

"Think of the danger." Sysabel shook her head. "Honestly, Avice. Only children chase excitement."

"I'm not a child," Avice pouted, "I've turned fifteen. And you're almost fifteen now, aren't you? So we're quite old enough to make decisions, and be brave, and help your cousin and my sister. Besides, we have to warn Nicholas that his father is out to catch him and beat him."

"He'll guess that already," Sysabel pointed out. "And I'm still only fourteen, but Peter said I was very mature for my age. And Adrian is out there somewhere already looking for Nicholas."

"That's it then," Avice insisted. "We need to help him too, since he can't have any idea of where everyone is and what they're doing." She was animated, grabbing at Sysabel's arm. "We know things that Nick doesn't, so it's our duty to tell him. Look, someone murdered Papa. I may not have liked my father very much but people just shouldn't go around killing people's fathers and getting away with it. And Nicholas said it was the same person who killed Peter. Now that ought to give you courage. You really liked Peter, didn't you? Well. We have to find his killer."

"We do?" exclaimed Sysabel. "Of course we don't if that's just what Nicholas and half the sheriffs of England are already doing. Which perhaps proves that it wasn't Nicholas who did it after all - though I had always thought - but now perhaps not. And," she sighed, extricating her hand, "I'll have you know I did a lot more than just *'like Peter'*. I was in love with him. And he was in love with me."

Avice screwed up her nose. "How was he in love with you? He was supposed to marry my sister."

"He didn't want to," said Sysabel with a sniff. "He wanted to marry me but his father wouldn't let him because he wanted an heiress in the family and I haven't any property at all. But Peter didn't care about money, he only wanted me. And he proved it."

"Proved what?"

"His adoration," whispered Sysabel, looking at her lap and blushing slightly.

Avice said, "He told Emma he loved her too."

"He couldn't have." Sysabel looked, up, eyes moist. "She must have - I mean, she was mistaken. And I suppose," she sniffed loudly, "it would be brave - and loyal to Peter - and maybe the right thing to do. Finding who killed him, I mean. Perhaps we *should* run away after all." She paused, summoning courage. "Peter would want me to do that, I expect. And he always told me I was brave - especially later when - but I don't want to talk about that. He must be in heaven, because he couldn't still be in purgatory because I've prayed for him every night for months and months, and anyway, he never sinned in his life so he's surely sitting on a golden throne at Holy God's right hand already. Do you think he can see me from up there?"

Avice brightened. "No doubt he's watching right now. That's it then, we make our plans this afternoon and we creep away tonight."

"Your mother will be horribly worried."

Avice continued grinning. "Not at all. She's secretly so relieved to be rid of Papa. She's already ordered three new dresses, and shoes with silver buckles. There's a cartload of the best beeswax candles due tomorrow, and the kitchens have doubled their rations. All the village traders are thrilled. Now she's talking of buying real books from the new printers, and a hat with a gold lace veil. I think she'll be just delighted to get rid of me too."

"But ladies don't run anywhere alone," sniffed Sysabel. "It isn't decent and it isn't safe."

"Ladies travel all across the country just with armed outriders and a few attendants. And even ordinary traders do. There's a big buxom woman who drives a cart full of ale kegs around Gloucestershire, and farmers' wives going to market, and the women who travel with the Mystery Players, and ------"

"But they have entourages and armed guards and proper guides." Sysabel stared wide eyed. "And they're all a lot older than we are."

Avice smiled. "We'll take your maid and my maid, and I'll ask old Bill. He's a sort of guide, and he can carry a sword. And we, as you pointed out yourself, are extremely mature for our ages."

It was not such a secretive or quietly organised escape, but it was achieved without either interruption or disaster. Avice had stuffed three bread roles, well wrapped in her spare shift, into a large bag, and Sysabel had secreted some of the cold meat from supper up her sleeve. Once the household was quiet, Mistress Avice and Mistress Sysabel, warmly dressed and holding a small candle holder each, crept downstairs followed by two maids, one elderly dresser, and a reluctant page. Nurse Martha had not been enlisted, since she would undoubtedly have disapproved and spoiled everything by informing the baroness at once. Outside, the maids and the page dutifully squashed the packages, bags and boxes into the sumpter's capacious panniers as two stable boys saddled the ladies' palfreys, and the one dour outrider, well bribed, temporarily ignored his arthritis and stuck his knife into his belt as he mounted his own elderly but impatient hunter.

Rattling and thumping, panting, gates flung shut, muttered complaints and the irritability of the disturbed horses echoed, only slightly muffled, through the stables. But it was not until the whole party left that anyone was alerted. The page, who had been obediently quiet while ordered to help with packing, now ran back inside the house to spread alarm in case he was later blamed for having helped the thoroughly improper behaviour of five women and one old man setting off for places unknown in the middle of the night.

The moon was now past its zenith, but it still squatted huge and golden above the tree tops. Having discovered that her elder sister had left behind some of her bright new belongings, Avice had taken advantage and was now wearing her sister's dark blue velvet cape with a fluff of white rabbit fur within the hood. Sysabel, dressed according to her brother's standards, wore a heavy worsted cloak in sturdy green and eyed her new friend with faint envy. The moon lit the girls' eyes with avid brilliance, Sysabel's light sky blue, and Avice brown as beef gravy, while the less enthusiastic servants followed in a small clump, eyes to their gloved fingers gripping tired to the reins. The armed guard rode a little ahead, looking occasionally over his shoulder with complacent contempt at his feminine following. But it was a quiet night, no thieves or marauders crossed their path, and only the pale passing of an owl shadowed the moonlight.

They slept in a tiny inn where they would not be known, and with the energy of anticipation, they both woke early and immediately rode into Gloucester. Avice stopped for some time at a double fronted shop in the main street where bundles of sumptuous materials were on show, and the tailor and seamstress ready at hand to help argue a fair bargain. But eventually, convinced by Sysabel that her funds were only sufficient for their needs on the journey, she reluctantly refused the offer of a lemon silk gown with heavy crimson velvet sleeves which had been recently been made for but rejected by another customer. Instead Avice agreed to ride on until supper time.

It was that following night when, discovering her maid in tears, Avice said crossly, "Oh very well, then. Sissy and I can share a maid. You and Petronella can ride back to Wrotham House in the morning and tell my mother I'm safe and on my way to London. But no one must come after us, and we'll be taking secret back roads and sleeping under the trees." Sysabel raised her eyebrows at this, but Avice hurried on, "Just tell Maman I'm happy and safe and I'm going after Nicholas. He'll look after me so she needn't worry. In fact, you'd better tell her we've caught up with Emma already, and then she'll be quite content."

"But mistress," quavered the maid, "that would be a lie."

"Oh, pooh," exclaimed Avice. "It won't be a lie tomorrow because by then we will have. So by the time you get back and talk to Maman, it'll be the truth."

The Gloucestershire lanes were puddled in sunshine and the leafy hedgerows they passed were sprinkled with blossom and the first flutter of butterflies. The little party ambled, old Bill in front, eyes half shut against the day's glitter, and the remaining maid dutifully at the rear. Sheep grazed the rolling foothills and breezes shuddered the valley grasses. With a buzzing of bees in the hedgerows, they breathed in the soft nodding smells of wild flowers, dusty lanes and new growth in the underfoot leaf litter.

But their pace, at first amiable, soon became interminable. Avice, Sysabel and Hilda began to hate their horses. They ached and their backs throbbed. They feared sun blemished noses and fingers crinkled from too long in riding gloves. They yearned for baths, for afternoon naps with the shutters closed, for hot dinners and cool wine, and the soothing comfort of their families. Avice missed her mother but sniffed into her kerchief and would not admit to it. Sysabel was equally as miserable, but at least had no mother to miss. Hilda the maid decided her life was over. Avice began to feel like the murderer she was hoping to uncover.

With a lack of funds, they stayed in the smaller hostelries and many times shared a bed with other wives and daughters travelling the same roads. They avoided river crossings because Avice did not want to get her hems wet, so they headed south east by the rising sun, with the general hope of one day hitting Oxford.

Folk said, "'Tis a terrible long way, Mistress." Or, "Make for the Little Mill, then the Big Mill on the stream, and then best ask for Witney, be it market day. If'n market day has bin and gone, then Witney ain't worth the visit. Best keep straight on." Finally, "'Tis Ossford Town has them big univestersy houses, where the clever folk go. You finds one o' them clever folk and ast him – for I've not left my village past the bakers' in the past forty year."

It rained and everything turned to swamp.

They did not catch up with Nicholas.

CHAPTERE TWENTY SIX

Nicholas stood at the wharf and watched the great sails dip and shudder, falling to the decks as they shed their streams of briny water. The sailors were bare foot, better for climbing ropes and not slipping on wet and salty planks, and their hands were practical and horned with calloused ridges, hardened against blisters and welts. But what they were bringing up from the hold was a different danger altogether.

The wind battered cob thudded against the old pier as the prow and stern were hard roped to the quay. The gangplank's end slid to shore, gradually the boards ceased to groan though the gale still whined through the loose rigging, and finally the men began to heave their captive towards his wretched destiny.

The bear whimpered, confused and unbalanced by the roll of the waves, little food and the smell of men. Heavily chained, it clanked from boat to land, shuffled to the wharf and stopped there, bloodshot eyes to the sun tipped clouds, thankful to recognise the surety of earth beneath its paws.

Those sailors hauling neither beast nor bundles were racing to the nearest tavern. Nicholas was distracted then, his eyes to the bear's lolling shamble and its huge brown furred bulk, thick with dirt and the sticky residue of old wounds. When he felt a very human hand creep to his belt from behind. Nicholas swung immediately, his own fingers steel gripped to the errant wrist. There was a sharp gulp from behind and the stranger's fingers went limp.

Harry Bambrigg lurched back, gulped again and mumbled, "'Tis you me lor, may the Lord God in His nice clean heaven forgive me. How were I to know it were you? Expectin' Rob, I were, but he ain't here."

"So you thought you'd make sure the walk down to the docks wasn't entirely wasted?"

"It's a fat purse you've got there, m'lor. You didn't ought to carry so much tempting coin around to lead poor honest folk into crime." Harry rubbed his wrist. "And you've a nasty grip on you, considering last time I saw you, you was sick fit to die."

Nicholas smiled. "Yes, I've a strong arm and you should remember it. I had a fair aim with the Welsh bow once, and no doubt a life of climbing out of windows also helps. So I'm quite prepared to protect my purse when needed." His smile turned to a grin. "But I didn't expect to have to protect it from my friends."

"Well, I'm proper honoured to be called a friend," said Harry, relaxing. "I'm just glad you didn't break my wrist, m'lor', which feels like you surely could've. That woulda spoiled me career real nasty."

"A failed career, I imagine," Nicholas said, "since your creeping fingers were as obvious as that poor wretched bear just offloaded."

Harry scratched his chin. "You've never bin to the bear pit in Southwark, m'lor? Nor set a wager for beast 'gainst hounds? Then you've not lived to the full is all I can say. And as for wretched, 'tis a beast with all the temper and cruelty of a Frenchie missing his dinner. Them buggers come from the forests of Calabria - and kills as sure as be killed, they tells me. Evil is as evil does, I say, and merits death."

"I consider the Southwark bear pits even more hideous than the Southwark brothels," Nicholas said.

"Can't afford neither," said Harry sadly. "Wish I could."

"Your brother," Nicholas told him without noticeable sympathy, "is waiting for us in the Katherine Tavern. I have a job for you both." He turned away, watching one of the cob's sailors striding towards him. "And I see the man I came to meet, who will tell me whether the job is urgent, or otherwise."

It was later that afternoon when Nicholas rejoined his wife. She was in the small private solar attached to the hostelry bedchamber, and she had been watching his approach from the adjacent window. She was therefore prepared, and when he entered the room she ignored him and continued with her supper. She had ordered her own apple codlings.

He said, "You don't seem overjoyed to see me," threw his gloves to the window seat, kicked off his boots and tossed them to the small empty hearth, and strode quickly over to sit beside her.

"Hungry as usual, I see? With luck we'll find the Strand House still employs its Florentine chef."

That made her turn towards him. "Oh gracious fortune, we're going there at last, then? So we really shall have a proper home and stop this hideous journeying and moving and sleeping in other people's beds?"

"Well, hopefully you'll be sleeping in mine."

She discarded the last apple codling into its syrup, and threw her arms around her husband's neck. "Oh – *wonderful*. It's been three wretched days in this horrid place, and ages and ages on the road, and before that it was Maman's and that lumpy bed, and before that it was more travelling, and Adrian's house for half a night until we were all threatened with disease and death – and before that –"

"The fire," nodded Nicholas, "and sleeping in the west tower with the smell of soot to flavour the porridge. What a delightful marital experience you've enjoyed so far, my dear. Didn't you believe me when I promised you adventure?"

"This isn't adventure. It's torture."

"Since I've been threatened with torture more than once, I can assure you it's something way beyond the boredom of travel, my dear." He grinned at her, spooned up the single apple codling she had discarded, and ate it himself. Mouth full, he continued, "And now I suppose I should explain something of what's been happening, and what will probably happen next."

"Your loyal squire," Emeline informed him, "has been explaining matters in your absence. At least there's someone in your employ with manners and intelligence who takes me seriously enough to tell me what to expect."

"How can I tell you what's on the next horizon when I don't know myself," objected Nicholas, "and if Witton has been explaining it all to you, then perhaps he should explain it all to me."

"And he told me all about the Strand House too," she smiled, remaining determinedly affable. "He said it used to belong to your grandfather, who left it to the whole family to use at will. And since your father was the eldest and inherited the title, he has prime claim, but he's not at the castle then he's usually at court so the house stays empty. Your uncle Jerrid, who sounds rather sweet, uses it sometimes, and so does Adrian. Your aunt Elizabeth used to stay there when she was younger, especially before her husband was killed at Tewkesbury. And Mister Witton told me you often go there, but it depends on the secrecy of your movements, and sometimes you prefer to go to a rather less salubrious address which actually belongs to him, close by The Tower. He says I wouldn't like it there, which is why you haven't taken me." Nicholas was frowning, so she hurried on, "What David Witton did not tell me was why on earth you like to be so secretive all the time. Why would you hide in a tiny little place belonging to your servant, when you could stay in a grand house amongst the palaces of the nobility?"

Nicholas sighed. "Probably because I'm pissed half the time, like my father." He smiled suddenly. "It's the only reason I've bought you some decent clothes of course - so I can borrow them from time to time."

"So," Emeline refused to giggle, "we remove to the Strand House tomorrow morning? Have you discovered whether Adrian is there already?"

"He isn't," Nicholas told her, "which is the main reason I'm prepared to take you there. The less I see of the rest of the family, the better. But I warn you, we'll receive visitors from time to time. Too many people know of the place. Even your wretched father knew of it. He kept hinting that he ought to be invited, since he wanted a close place to use for gaining access to court and the king's ear."

Emeline looked up, startled. "Don't tell me the king may come calling?"

Nicholas regarded her for a moment, eyes narrowed. "I wonder just how much Witton has actually told you, my dear. But in any case, his highness does not trot around to call on his subjects at whim. If he wants to see anyone, he summons them to court. But you will meet him, since I suppose I shall have to take you to Westminster Palace at some time."

Emeline's frown blossomed into a blazing smile. "Oh, gracious heavens. A new gown then. Baudekyn?"

"No doubt," grinned her husband. "And perhaps one for you too."

It dawned fine and clear, with birdsong, the church bells chiming for Prime, and the Thames at low tide. Sprats jumped in the shallows and the dragonflies dipped iridescent reflections from water to wing. The gardens all along the Strand sloped down to the riverbanks, grass sprigged with daisies. Emeline stood, her feet in the clover and her hands clasped in delight, gazing up at the long house. She exclaimed, "It is marvellous," seemingly transfixed.

"Then get inside," said Nicholas, "before it starts to rain."

Half bricked with a wooden framed central entrance, the house was full three storeys high. Peaked garret windows peeped beneath a proud slate roof with four groups of towering chimneys. The lower windows, overlooking the river, were large mullioned and bright, all fully glassed. Emeline breathed deep. "Oh, blessed miracles and bounty, there will be light."

"There'll be rain too," insisted Nicholas. "The sky's clouded over and those clouds threaten thunder. Harry and the boy are stabling the horses and Rob and David have the baggage in hand. Alan, my other man, is already based here. If you need anything, my sweet, while I'm not around, then ask Alan or David. I trust them both entirely. Now come quickly, my love, let me show you the Chatwyn attempt at comfort."

The rain began with a great sloshing downpour, huge heavy drops pounding on the roof and streaming from the overhang of the upper storey. The house had started to bustle and the grand door was flung wide. Against the outside thrum, the steward clapped his hands and summoned the servants from their apathy. Hippocras was set to warm, the fire was lit in the kitchen hearth, cauldrons unearthed and cupboards explored for supplies. The pantry woke, the buttery heaved into action, the spicery was dusted and the candles were aflame in the hall and in the sconces up the main staircase.

Emeline whispered, "You didn't warn them we were coming?"

"Certainly not," said Nicholas. "This is far more entertaining, tests the organisational skills of the household, and gives them all something to complain about afterwards." He turned as a page hurried to take his wet cloak, hat and gloves. "And tell Sanderson," Nicholas instructed the page, "we expect dinner within the hour, and an early supper to make up for dinner's inevitable inadequacies. But first of all wine, and plenty of it."

The page managed to smile, bow, and trip over a puppy racing to greet the newcomers. It slid the polished floorboards, tail swinging enthusiastically. Emeline found her fingers warmly licked as she reached down to slip out of her wet shoes. The house soon thundered with puppy enthusiasm as the rest of the litter discovered the new excitement, and as the storm grew outside, so the thunder escalated both within and without.

It was after supper, with parcels and panniers unpacked and two good meals digested, that Emeline said, "I love your house, Nicholas. Can we stay for ever?"

"Oh, without a doubt, and into a glorious eternity," he said. His feet, ankles crossed, rested on the low table where a candle gently smoked a wisp of honey perfume and two wine cups, one empty and one full, stood waiting. There was a small hole in one toe of his soft knitted hose. "But," Nicholas continued, "that's only until something interrupts us."

"So *not* forever then. And what will interrupt us this time? Fire? Pestilence? Your father? Battle, murder, the apocalypse?" She sat on the wide window seat, her gaze on the pelting sleety grey beyond the glass. "And who will be staying for such a short forever?" she sighed. "Both of us? Or only me?"

He grinned. "Yes. All of that."

So she turned and faced him. "Nicholas, I've told you I love you and I've told you I don't care if you don't love me. I'll be comfortable here, and it'll be interesting to try and be the lady of the house for the first time. There's all London to explore, and perhaps even the court. But I didn't come all this way to sit alone and give orders to servants and play with your dogs and wait and wait for you to come back." He did not answer at first, so then she said, "When I first told you I loved you, you said I couldn't, because I didn't know you. So how am I ever going to know you if you keep running off? I'm not your father. I don't carry a stick. I've no plans to murder anyone. You like me well enough in bed." She looked away again, staring at the rain. "Surely I'm not such a burden for the rest of the day."

He did not move, though his smile faded. Finally he said, "But you want comfort and you want sympathy, and I'm unpractised at both. Would you be content to ride through the night? Will you obey me if I tell you to sleep in a damp cellar? Can you go all day without food? Are you prepared to lose your reputation, and be known as the mad wife of a mad murderer? And even if you are prepared for all these things, how could I ask it of you?"

She looked up instantly and stared at him. "And when do you need to do any of those things yourself? And sympathy? I'd as soon expect angels to jump down the chimney. You talk of adventure, but you've never fought in battle. You talk of the king but you don't go to court. When something threatens, you just run away. You don't even care about being called a coward. And now you say you're going to find who killed my father, but you just pretend you're doing something clever and dangerous while you hide from me."

He was silent a moment, then spoke softly. "It's a mad bad world, my love, and every kingdom needs those who will surrender their comfort in order to help their king." He sighed, as if not intending to say more. But then he shook his head, and continued. "For instance, little one, I went to meet someone at the docks, who brought the message I'd been hoping for. There are those, but I'll name no names, who thought their lives at risk when King Richard first came to the throne. Some of them fled the country, and went to Brittany and France. Now there's one who regrets that choice, and wants to return. The king sanctions that return. The poor wretch attempted to sail back to England last November, but he failed. He was - let us say - dissuaded. Now the French hold him hostage. But I'm told he has found a way, and will try again."

She gasped. "You're going to help a - a fugitive?"

"A simple young man who discovered that foolish bravado and too much belief in his own importance, did him no good at all. Now he has learned that sitting in France at the side of the traitor Tudor is even more unpleasant than behaving himself at home. His mother has called him back. I have been asked to help, if he manages to arrive on our shores."

"You work for - the king?"

Nicholas did not miss the disguised sob, nor the candlelight reflecting the moisture in her eyes. He leaned back, gazing up at the high painted ceiling beams and their vaulted arches, addressing the trail of dust, out of reach of the cleaner's brooms. "Is it easier to think me a coward, little one? Perhaps I am. Does it matter?"

"I still love you." She fumbled for her kerchief and blew her nose defiantly. "I don't blame you for not fighting in the wars. I wouldn't want to go to battle either. But you've suffered too. It must have been terrible when your mother died. And then that accident with Peter's arrow."

Nicholas moved at last, placing both feet firmly again on the floor, and turning his chair to look at his wife. "Accident?" he said. "You asked who? Adrian? My father?"

"I didn't ask." Emeline blushed slightly. "But your father and Sissy were talking about it. It sounded - dreadful. Your father said you were ill for such a long time afterwards. And he said it wasn't really your fault."

"Good of him."

"I'm not prying," she said quickly. "I'm just - well - trying to be sympathetic."

"A good example," Nicholas said, standing abruptly and wandering off to find the wine flagon. He returned from the far table, jug in hand, and refilled his cup. "It proves how useless sympathy can be. And since you believe Peter was worthy of canonisation, I won't bother telling you the true story." He drained his cup, and handed the other, still full, into his wife's hands. "Drink," he ordered her. "It brings more comfort than words."

"I don't want wine." She shook her head furiously. "All I want is peace, and friendly company. In fact, right now all I want is a bath." And she replaced her cup firmly on the little table.

Nicholas stood over her, looking down with a frown that etched the left side of his face in disapproval, the scar burying deeper and catching the side of his mouth in a scowl. The he reached forwards, and took her wrist. "Come with me," he said softly, "and I'll give you bath, adventure, and sympathy as I know it." And he pulled her up on her feet, turned, and led her inexorably towards the great double doors at the end of the hall.

She squeaked, "You're drunk," as he raised one foot and kicked the doors wide. "Nicholas, you've no boots on. It's absolutely pouring, and there's lightning and thunder and it'll be so muddy and now it's almost night." Then she pulled sharply away, whispering, "Are you going to throw me in the river?"

He was laughing as he tugged her outside. "You want a bath? I'm going to share it with you."

He allowed her to pause one moment just outside the doorway as the heaving soaked blackness absorbed them. The rain pelted, slamming against them both, against the pale plaster of the walls behind, against the little bushes, herbs and paths, and against the great bending trees further down the slope. Nicholas walked resolutely into the storm and held Emeline close to him, one arm around her shoulders, the other hand gripped to her wrist.

No stars, no moon, only torrents of heaven's overflow and a small blustering wind. Suddenly lightning fizzled a twisting silver furrow into the darkness above, and the echo of a thunderous drumroll followed immediately. "I - am - drenched," Emeline croaked. "Please - where - why?"

He pulled her on. She felt the ooze of mud inside her shoes, wrapping around her toes. Where his fingers clasped her arm, the rain collected in rivulets. Her tiny gauze headdress began to slip down the back of her head, weighted by water. The neckline of her gown, velvet trimmed, sagged open and the rain found its own entrance. Her skirt hems slammed against her shins, soaked heavy. With no breath for complaints, she struggled and was hauled towards the riverbank.

The birch stood alone, low branches thick with dripping leaf. Nicholas stood beneath its damp shelter and its spreading shadows. Against the bark, the perfumes were loamy and rich. The rain, a little muted by the tree's overhang, was warm on the evening air as the faint sour smell of the river slipped up between the leaves. Nicholas pressed Emeline back against the trunk and lowered his mouth to hers. She tasted the water drenching her face and his, the wisps of her uncovered hair, and the heat of her husband's lips. He pushed his tongue into her mouth, tasting her as she tasted him. His body was pressed to hers, the sodden welter of his clothes further soaking her own. She caught her breath and closed her eyes. His voice was so tight to her ear that it was a hot breeze. "No one can see us from the house. I'm going to undress you. I want you naked in the rain."

She tried to shake her head. "Not here -," but he was grinning. Emeline stared at the tiny milky drops in his left eye as they caught the last crackle of lightning above and turned his bright blue iris into white flame. "You are – frightening," she whispered.

Nicholas snorted as his hands roamed. "Your nipples rise through the wet silk. So deliciously tantalising," and smoothing downwards, unclipped the wide band just below her breasts, then loosening her gown where it was laced beneath her arm. The deep V neckline was already gaping and finally he slipped the heavy material from her shoulders. It sank and crumpled to her hips. Beneath it, her shift stuck to her, outlining her nipples, dark as her gown. The linen clung. Nicholas slipped his hands inside, warming and drying her as the tree trunk scratched at her back. She stopped struggling.

His wandering fingers found the fastening, untied the ribbon and pulled it loose from its eyelets. Emeline stood uncovered to the dip where her navel rested just above the first hint of belly. The rain sluiced down her, discovering the swells and angles, making its own little pools and ripples as she shivered.

"Cold?" The increasing darkness remained warm. Even the summer storm did not chill the night.

Emeline shook her head. "No. Hot. Inside, not outside." Her hair was loose now, hanging in thick water logged ringlets, diverting the flow of the rainwater over her skin. Nicholas traced the rivulets, one finger down from her neck, curving out then pushing into her cleavage, down her ribs and to the round soft plane below. There the rain puddled until he tugged, and all her clothes fell sodden around her feet. She stood naked apart from her gartered stockings and her little mud squelched shoes, and he took her again in his arms and pressed her harder back against the tree. She could barely see him, too lost in fluttering leafy shadow, and his eyes, now heavy lidded, barely glinted. He said, very softly, "Do you want to please me, Emma?"

She whispered, "You have to teach me."

The lightning again interrupted, startling silver arrows bringing one short and sudden moment of visibility and a shatter of vivid reflections across the river. The Thames was rising fast, its waves white tipped. Then once again everything was dark as the thunder bellowed. Nicholas murmured half muffled by echoes and reverberation, "Touch me." He took her hand and brought it between his legs, one knee bent between hers, keeping her thighs apart. "Hold me, discover me. You're getting to know the rest of me, now know me here. Around first, then over, softly or tightly as you wish. Thumb below here, fingers wide. Down, then down to the base, then up again, pulling and tight. Every part is sensitive, just as you are, some places more than others. Find the places." His own fingertips were still running, exploring across her breasts, circling the aureoles, pushing up under her arms to the nestled curls, then down her body again to the richer, thicker curls at her groin. He cupped her there, his thumb to the opening, rubbing gently until she squirmed. Then he grinned and said, "Gloriously wet, my love, and not just from the rain. Look at me."

Her eyes flickered open, her lashes sparkling with rain and blinking back the falling drops. "I'm – soaked," she whispered.

"Oh, yes indeed you are," smiled Nicholas. "And now I shall share your bath, both outside and in. I shall take you standing up, but afterwards I shall carry you to bed and dry you, and tuck you in the warmth, and stay beside you until dawn creeps in."

CHAPTER TWENTY SEVEN

He had wrapped her in his discarded shirt to bring her in to the house again, up the wide stairs and through the dark corridor to the bedchamber. Here he laid her on the soft yielding counterpane of gold thread and white fur, removed his wet shirt from her, plumped up the pillows behind her and smiled. He was naked too, although he had draped his doublet over his shoulders. Now he threw that off and began to walk the chamber, lighting candles beside the bed and on the table. A flask of wine had been left there with cups beside, and he filled the cups and brought one to Emeline. The candlelight turned the wine to cherry, shot with as much gold thread as the bedcover.

He put up the shutters across the two windows, wandered into the adjoining garderobe and returned with some damp cloths and several towels. Then he sat beside his wife. He lifted her leg, bent it, rolled off her sodden stocking and brought her foot to his naked lap. He began to wash her toes as they curled, pressing down as she felt the rising muscles of his groin beneath her sole. "You're beginning to learn how to please me after all." He twisted the wet cloth between her toes, cleaning away the accumulated mud. Then he took a towel, and briskly dried where he had washed.

She said, "All my clothes are lying down in the storm. So are half of yours. What will the servants think in the morning?"

"That they have odd masters with odd desires, and so will gossip about us in the kitchens."

"You don't care?"

"Why should I?" He leaned across her, removed the second stocking and washed her other foot.

"There's mud everywhere," Emma giggled. "And your feet are worse than mine. You didn't even start with shoes on."

He bent over her suddenly, kissing her hard. "Not such a practical bath then?"

She sipped her wine, peeping at him over the brim. "So were you drunk, Nicholas? Are you still? Are you all the time?"

He laughed, throwing the mud crusted cloths to the ground. "Was I? No. Am I? Not yet. Am I always?" He paused, looking down at her. "No, little one, I am not my father. But life can be sadly disappointing, and a fine wine masks the sharper edges. Is that inebriation? I was intoxicated on our wedding night, and that was purposeful. Usually I prefer my head clear. You've not yet seen me entirely drunk."

"I was drunk on our wedding night too. That was the first time in my life and it was horrid." Emeline wrinkled her nose. "I had a dreadful headache afterwards and I still had to face4 all the horror of the fire."

"You should have drunk another cup. That's the best way to deal with fear and pain."

She reached up tentatively, fingers to the black scar down his left cheek. "That must have been – all those things," she whispered.

He sat back a moment, watching her as though wary. Then he said, "The surgeon took four hours to get the arrow head out. It had gone fairly deep, and because I was only twelve, he took pity and tried to make it easy for me. Yet I think his slow concern made it worse." Emeline tucked her fingers between his thighs, and he clasped his own hand over hers. "That's – comfortable, my love. Are you trying to encourage me to talk? Well, it's not so grand a story. Old Mannbury used a small pair of wooden tongs, something he found in the spicery I think, for cracking nutmeg. He fiddled around with the gash in my face, got both blades in and stretched the wound open with enough space between flesh, sinew and muscle to grab the arrow head with the points of some pliers, and wrenched it out."

Emeline gasped. "And it took four *hours*?"

"There was rather more to it than that," shrugged Nicholas. "First breaking off the shaft without jabbing the damn thing in further. Then dosing me up with wine, poppy syrup and henbane juice until my wits were wandering. Worse than simply being drunk, I can promise you, and the headache later was considerably worse too. But of course they still had to hold me down. I had black bruises up my arms for a month. And being what he supposed was careful, poor wretch, trying to stretch the opening far enough but not to rip my face apart. The apothecary cauterized the wound afterwards, and I think that was even more vile than all the rest. Only time I ever fainted until that damned fire after our wedding." He paused, as though blinking away memories, then smiled cautiously. "The doctors used great slabs of honey to keep the wound clean. A few times I woke in the night with ants crawling over my face. I had two ant stings on my tongue. That stopped me licking up the honey when it started to drip down my chin."

For a moment Emeline sat in horrified silence, summoning breath. Then she said, very quietly, "I am surprised you are alive at all, and that the scar isn't deeper." She paused again, looking at him and then away, her fingers hesitating across his cheek. "You don't like it, do you?" she whispered.

"Like it?" He laughed. "Why in God's good name should I?"

"I suppose," she mumbled, "you were terribly handsome before, and you resented it spoiling - well - you are still handsome, Nicholas. Terribly handsome if you don't look at the scar. And terribly interesting if you do."

"Silly puss," It sounded amused and affectionate, and he cupped her own cheek, smoothing back the loose curls of her hair behind her ears. "Do you think me so vain? It's the memories, and the lessons it taught me that I dislike. I found out a lot at that time. I suppose I grew up."

"I don't think you've grown up yet - all that talk of adventure." She paused again, then said suddenly, "Peter did it on purpose, didn't he? It wasn't the accident Sissy and your father think it was."

He shook his head. "Sissy believes what Peter told her. My father knows the truth but won't admit it."

Emeline said, "Peter did it because he was angry? Or jealous?"

"Both. We'd been sent to practise archery at the butts. Does this matter after all this time? Well, conceit apart, I was the better shot. I had double his skill. Just the luck of birth I suppose, and probably he was better at other things, though I can't remember what. He watched me loose my arrows at the target. I centred them all, and then all his missed. He turned and shot me in the face. Well, he didn't miss the target that time. I was too close."

"Did he want to kill you? Had you jeered, and laughed at him?"

"Strangely enough, no." Nicholas shrugged, draining his cup. "I'd known him a poor archer for a long time, and found the subject irrelevant. I rarely sought his company anyway, and just wanted the practise over, looking for my chance to get away."

"And so I don't blame you for never wanting to go to war after that." Emeline shuddered. "That would have put you off fighting forever."

"My renowned cowardice?" Nicholas swung his legs over and stretched out on the bed next to her, gathering her to his shoulder and lightly kissing her forehead. "Nothing is ever quite so simple, my love. I worked for the Duke of Gloucester throughout the Scottish campaigns, and have worked for him since. But it's easier to keep it quiet, and I achieve far more without my father's nose in my business. The duke - king now, of course - sent me to Berwick during the great siege. Pretending to be a smuggler of Scottish liquor, I infiltrated the castle there, and helped to break the standoff from the inside. And naturally managed to smuggle back Scottish liquors while I was at it. Then when the old king died two years ago and Edward Woodville sailed off with near half the royal treasure and all the fleet, I sailed with Brampton to help bring the fleet back. Later that year I had some small hand in squashing the Buckingham rebellion almost before it started. Oh - nothing grand - but I go where I'm sent and do whatever the king asks of me. I'm not alone, naturally. There's Brampton, Tyrell, the amazing Lovell, and plenty of others do the same, but it's not shouted by the town crier. Sometimes it's secret, sometimes not. Adventure, of course. But telling any of my family would ruin my work and displease the king. So don't whisper to anyone, my love, and if you prove a silent tongue, then I'm prepared to tell you what I do when I do it. Within reason."

Emeline proved her tongue was silent for some time, curled there against his shoulder with her arm around his waist and his fingers in her hair. Finally she said, "Now I know why I love you."

He laughed again. "And you couldn't love an apathetic coward? What a conditional and judgemental love, little one."

"Better than just loving you for that," and she pointed. "It's all you want *me* for, isn't it?"

"But I am apathetic sometimes, drink too much, and am a heinous coward when faced with my father's lunatic blunders, and a marriage I thought to be a tedious insult. Forgive me for that at least, my dear, for I was wrong. You are delightful, and I can speak with more than my prick, I promise."

"I don't trust your promises." She couldn't see his grin, but she knew it was there.

"Do you trust my prick more?"

"I like knowing you think me delightful."

"I must say it more often."

"Apple codlings are delightful, and a summer day can be delightfully delightful. Oh - a warm fire - a well aired bed - and a hundred other things. Delightful isn't outstanding. But if that's what you think me, I'm happy with it for now."

They were still entwined when she woke. Although the shutters closed both windows in planked shadow, a tiny line of brightness eased through one slit and Emeline knew the sun had risen. She wriggled free of her husband's embrace, but stayed a moment snuggled to his breast. She could feel the warm rhythm of his breathing and the steady soft pound of his heartbeat. There was a blush of damp at his shoulder where her cheek had lain, and the gleam of sweat stayed where they had been pressed close together. Even sitting now, and looking down on him, Emeline felt the same little warm dampness on her cheek. She leaned and kissed the place on his body, but he did not move.

She clambered down from the high mattress and went to the smaller window. The larger looked out to the river and the back of the house, but the smaller looked to the side where the herb garden led directly to the stables. She could hear someone crying, a harsh and guttural sound, then a man's voice shouting and another sound, perhaps of a slap.

When she looked back into the bedchamber, she saw Nicholas watching her. Bright blue eyes, like the glass in church windows. He was naked, unconcerned, stretched on the bedcover and warm enough not to delve below the feathers. "Seems I didn't exhaust you sufficiently last night. You're awake too early."

"It's past dawn - look." The knife cut of light through the shutters was beginning to dazzle. "The storm has all blown away and the sun is shining. But someone is crying in your stables."

"Disaster follows me, it seems. I will ask later. For now I want my wife. Then my breakfast. Finally my squire, and last of all my next adventure."

"I'm used to being up early." She came to sit on the edge of the bed, pulling the ties of her bedrobe tightly about her. "Papa always insisted we attend morning mass immediately after Prime, and then we had wafers and a little ale for breakfast. No more. He said eating would make us complacent and we'd forget our duties."

"Which I suppose is why you wake early and eat excessively. I have never known anyone else so fond of apple codlings."

"Never? And so surprising? Don't you usually feed your women, then?"

"You are an urchin," Nicholas remarked, then frowned. "Which reminds me, I suppose I know who is probably crying in the stables."

"More secrets?"

"I imagine this is going to be a busy day."

"Then I must dress too. But I have no dresser, no lady's maid, no nurse and no idea where to find one. Can I have servants now if we're going to live here for a while longer?"

"No doubt there's a parcel of women wandering this house somewhere," Nicholas said with vague disinterest. "Normally there'd be some poor wretch sleeping on the truckle bed from beneath this mattress, ready to defend me from thieves in the night, get me ale if I wake parched, comfort me if I have nightmares, and generally disturb me with his snoring. There might also be a scruffy page or two waiting to obey all my irascible demands and clean up the dog shit if those inexhaustible puppies disgrace themselves. There should also be someone else lurking in the annexe beyond the garderobe, ready to leap from his bed to warm my shirt as soon as I wish to get dressed, though I've no desire to have our lovemaking witnessed, even from beyond the bed curtains. You make far too many little gasps and squeals, and at the happy end you groan loudly as though in terrible pain. Small boys giggling from beyond the arras might put us both off."

An hour later Nicholas had entered the stable courtyard. Fully dressed but with his hair still uncombed, he strode past the assortment of busy grooms and fretting horses, and demanded the whereabouts of the new stable boy he had brought with him yesterday. Someone said, "Right there, m'lord. Got kicked up the arse. First by your lordship's hoby, and then by me."

"Ah," said Nicholas, running his hands through his hair, a form of grooming less effective than the horses', and peered down into the rummage of straw in the corner. "Boy? Hurt, are you? If you and my liard don't get on, I'd better get you some work in the kitchens instead."

"I's used to being beat," snuffled the boy. "But not whupped by them big horses. They got nasty hard feet, an' a lot harder than my Ma's." Nicholas conceded this probability while Wolt continued. "But I don't wanna turn no spits in no kitchens neither. I had a friend once, went to be a spit boy for the bishop. Burned all his fingers till they was just little sticky stumps."

Nicholas sighed. "When you decide what degree of discomfort you might manage to suffer in comparative silence, do let me know and I shall attempt to organise a suitable place for you."

But he was interrupted. A small clattering of hooves was entering the courtyard behind him, and a voice called, "Is that you, Nicholas? There's remarkably little organisation here, whatever else you're planning. The last time I stayed here the stables were fairly well staffed. You seem to bring chaos in tow, cousin. Is it intentional?"

Adrian dismounted, and signalled for his small retinue to do the same. He then waved the three men off to arrange their own quarters, and turned back to Nicholas. "Oh bloody Bedlam," exclaimed Nicholas. "I only moved in yesterday because you weren't here."

"Then I have come in perfect time." Adrian refrained from smiling. "I've come to talk of duty to you, cousin. There is a good deal to talk about."

"Then you can talk to my wife," said Nicholas. "She's been fretting for company for days."

"Ah, then your wife is here with you, Nicholas?" Adrian followed his cousin towards the house. "It was her I wished to talk about. She was worrying about you. So was I. I hear you had some slight contagion from the pestilence after all. Entirely finished now, I presume?"

"Well, of course it is," said Nicolas with some irritation. "Am I covered in black swellings and about to drop to the ground? That was weeks and weeks ago. If you must stay here, at least talk some sense. Now come and gossip with my wife. I have other things to do."

It was over a pleasant dinner served in the main hall that Emeline began to summarise her last few days on the road and in the hostelry by the docks. Nicholas was not present, and had politely absented himself with promises of an immediate return, which his wife did not believe. Chattering and animated with Adrian, apple codlings having magically appeared on a huge platter at her right hand, she was describing her first view of the Bridge with the massive beauty of The Tower's stone fortress beyond. She was, however, also interrupted, and it seemed far more alarming than Adrian's earlier arrival had been.

Baroness Wrotham swept into the hall, a bright scarlet coat over her arm, a tasselled turban swinging dangerously around her ears, and her vivid green skirts swirling with a determined silken rustle. She swooped on her daughter and the laden table, and threw her coat to an empty stool. "My dear girl," announced her mother, "you have had me chasing across the countryside, and near dead with the wind in my hair. I always thought those wretched litters your Papa insisted upon were too horrid to contemplate, but believe me, riding is worse. I am sore in places I cannot mention, and I never wish to see another horse. Now," she looked around, frowning. "Where is your sister?"

Emeline, mouth already open in astonishment, hiccupped. "Avice?"

"You have another?"

"Avice is at home with you," mumbled Emeline, "At least, you aren't at home, which you should be. But you shouldn't even know where I am. And I haven't the faintest notion where Avice is."

"If," warned her ladyship, "you are hiding her, Emeline, I shall – well, I shall think of something." She promptly sank to the stool where she had previously thrown her coat, and even in her new finery, began to look forlorn. "I have lost her, Emma. She ran away. But then I was told she was with you."

"And Sissy too?" gasped Emeline.

Adrian, who had remained in politely quiet disapproval until now, said loudly, "My sister? What has this to do with her? I ordered her to stay at home in Nottingham and learn her manners while reorganising the household after the devastation of that foul disease."

"Well, she didn't," said the baroness with considerable impatience. "The dear girl came to visit us, and I was most pleased to have her. Until she and Avice ran away, that is."

Adrian went as white as the tablecloth. "My sister would never act so reprehensibly, so irresponsibly –"

"Clearly she did," said the baroness curtly, "and my daughter left a silly note about going off to discover who murdered Peter." She turned back to Emeline. "Then two days later, while I was nearly dead with fear and worry, two of her little maids came riding back to say they had gone some way south east, but had been sent home as it cost too much to put them up at inns along the way. Sysabel's maid is still with them I gather, and that silly old groom Bill, who I kept meaning to retire since he is of no use to anyone. But he's evidently gone with them as a guide and protector."

Emeline clutched her mother's hand. "They are both babies. Avice could be anywhere. Lost in the hills. Attacked by animals. Abducted."

The baroness shook her daughter off. "Emma, don't frighten me. I'm already at my wit's end. Where is Nicholas? He has to ride out and find her immediately."

"I shall ride out and find them both," declared Adrian, standing quickly and throwing down his napkin. "I'll order my horse saddled this instant."

"And where will you go?" demanded Emeline.

Adrian paused, then waved a hand in the direction of the stables. "Why, out there - out beyond. I shall search the whole country."

"Send us a message when you get to Scotland," sniffed the baroness. "But I'm sure we can be a little more focused than that. I followed the road from Wrotham to Westminster, and I took several side roads and asked at every hostelry. No sign of course. So if they did not head for London, where on earth might they have gone? To search for James' killer. But who could they suspect?"

Adrian heaved back down into his chair and waved the other hand vaguely in a sweeping motion. "A madman. Some thief, perhaps? A jealous husband in Gloucester? Or some trader who held a grudge."

"The girls are definitely not still in Gloucester," insisted the baroness. "I not only sent half my household scouring every street, but I also informed the sheriff who sent out his constables. The girls had not been seen."

"Then back to Leicestershire," said Emeline at once. "To where Peter was killed, and clues might be traced. Perhaps a madman killed Papa and Peter both, but is madness so consistent? Yet if Avice and Sissy never took the road from Wrotham to here, then they must have gone in the opposite direction."

"Where will they stay?" wailed the baroness, reaching for her new embroidered kerchief.

"At my house in Nottingham," Adrian decided at once. "Sissy would have the good sense to take your daughter there, my lady, and that might have been her intention all along. To keep the proprieties, of course, in face of your daughter's impulsive whims."

The baroness looked up sharply and lowered her kerchief. "My daughter's irresponsible impulses, sir? Does your sister have none?"

"None, my lady. I have brought her up myself since she was quite young. Aunt Elizabeth being, let us say, a less reliable chaperone."

"Then a fourteen years child being passionately in love with her worthless cousin does not count as a whim, sir?"

A sudden voice behind the baroness said softly, "Which worthless cousin did you have in mind, my lady, since there are a number of us?"

"Oh, Nicholas," squeaked Emeline. "Thank goodness you're back. Look who has arrived. And there is the most dreadful news."

"That Avice and Sissy have scampered off into the wilds, and are now lost to us forever," smiled Nicholas, coming behind his wife and placing his hands somewhat protectively on her shoulders. "I was alerted to your mother's arrival by my squire, and came to discover the reason. I then questioned the woman Martha, who is my wife's childhood nurse I believe. She tells me your daughter left a note claiming she intended coming after me, and expected to catch me up quite soon. So she'd hardly be heading towards Nottingham, unless she lied purposefully to avoid capture."

"Oh," breathed Emeline in relief, "she wouldn't lie. At least, she would, but not over something like that. They must have got lost on the way, since old Bill wouldn't recognise a road from a puddle. And I'm so pleased you've brought Martha with you, Maman. So Avice can't be far off."

"When exactly did they leave?" demanded Nicholas.

The baroness thought a moment. "It has been so long - such a trying journey, I cannot be sure. Five days, perhaps? Six? A week?"

"Martha'll know to the hour," interrupted Emeline. "I'll go and talk to her at once." She hurriedly left the table, dropped her napkin, grabbed at her skirts and headed for the staircase. Her husband watched her departure with amusement.

He again turned to his mother-in-law. "Forgive me, my lady, you're naturally most welcome and I'll order the steward to arrange your quarters. I'll also organise two separate search parties and my squire David will head immediately for London. and alert the sheriff of the necessity for a more extensive alarm. I myself have been summoned to - and by - being a matter I cannot easily ignore. However, on my return I shall, depending on whatever has been discovered in the meantime, set out myself to find my cousin and my sister-n-law." He looked quickly to Adrian. "You'll want to ride at once, coz," he said, "but take some of my men if you've a mind to send out additional search parties."

But when he left the house shortly afterwards, only Emeline knew where he was going.

CHAPTER TWENTY EIGHT

His highness the king regarded the young man kneeling before him, and smiled. "Get up, Nicholas. I have business to discuss, and little time for discussion. Kendall will finalise the necessary details of course, and afterwards you'll see Tyrell. He will answer any remaining questions."

His grace sat at ease at the other side of the great table. Quill, ink, wax seals, papers and parchment scrolls were lined neatly at his right elbow. A cup of wine stood untouched by his left hand and a single beeswax candle was lit, the flame rising unchallenged and vertical, etching one side of the king's face in gold. His secretary, John Kendall, sat quietly at the table's far end, his hands clasped before him, remaining respectfully silent until otherwise requested. Nicholas said, "Sire, my apologies for arriving some moments late. I had family problems. I am, as always, at your disposal, your grace. Is this the continuing business of his lordship, the Marquess of Dorset?"

"Your delay is of no consequence," said his grace, "since my time is limited and I could not have seen you earlier. However, this matter is of some importance and must now be concluded, even with urgency. Now, as always, there is more than one single thread to follow. Henry Tudor himself is of little interest to me, and I would be tempted to overlook his impudence were it not for his mother, a lady not to be underestimated. Now I have news of escalation, and conspiracies. France is always dangerous. While Tudor remained in Brittany, he was kept under some semblance of control. But now that France is involved, control shifts."

"Will you have me travel to France, your grace?" Nicholas spoke quietly, disguising his reluctance.

The king looked up, smiling gently. "No man willingly travels into French territory and into danger," he replied. "But it may be necessary, in the end. There is also the usual business in Burgundy, which you are aware of. Tyrell sails to Burgundy soon, and I may ask you to accompany him. You understand the situation there with my nephews, and afterwards can more easily enter France through her mainland borders. But first there are matters I want you to discover here."

"Tudor's last claim from France was treated here with utter ridicule, sire." Nicholas stood at ease before his king, hands behind his back. "Does your grace suspect anyone of having acted on such absurdities?"

King Richard nodded. "The French instigated and invented that claim, a nonsense even Tudor must have been embarrassed to sign. Calling himself a son of the late Henry VI, and so the direct Lancastrian heir? Our people laughed, of course. In this country we have full knowledge of our ancestors, their rightful children and their less rightful children. But the French kings keep their people in ignorance, with a country still beggared, peasants and serfs bare able to read and ready to accept whatever they are told. We English are not such fools to accept wild and impossible claims. As usual, knowing only their own standards, the French misunderstand us."

"The same has happened again, your grace?"

"Not entirely," said the king, and smiled. "What has happened is a little different this time." He leaned back in his chair, tenting his fingers and watching Nicholas over their tips. "You are already aware that Dorset is once again attempting escape from France, and following his mother's instructions, intends to desert Tudor and return to safe haven back at home. His first attempt last year was intercepted and the French dragged him back and held him hostage. I believe his second attempt will prove no more successful, but if he succeeds in reaching our shores, someone must be waiting, ready to help should help be needed. Lovell has taken the eastern shore. You will go south."

Nicholas bowed. "I will leave at first light tomorrow, your highness. On your grace's previous orders, I have already begun investigating the situation, and have been given to understand that Dorset, should he avoid recapture at all, with take ship for the port of Weymouth, or for some more secluded beach in that vicinity."

"I have been informed of another visitor to our green land," the king continued. "Christopher Urswick has been involved more than once in conspiracies and errands involving Tudor, and is once again expected. He brings a letter of uncertain information, directed, so I believe, to Northumberland. He will land on the south shore sometime over the next four or five days. If my information is correct, which I believe it is, this letter must be intercepted at once. The king nodded, without pausing. "Others have been alerted, but since you will recognise Urswick from past occasions, I consider your cooperation of particular importance. I expect you to intercept Urswick and take this letter from him. You will then deliver it to me, or to Kendall if I am not at court when you return."

"I am, as always, at your service, your grace."

"You need not depart so soon, Chatwyn," continued his grace, "Another two days, I think, and then head south. Detailed instructions will be explained by Kendall directly. For now foreign travel to Burgundy and to France must wait. It is the English countryside which demands your presence, my friend, and two separate missions, both of considerable importance, which I believe can be combined."

Not far distant at the Chatwyn House in the Strand, David Witton was, from memory, mapping the route from Southwark to Weymouth and England's southern coast, then listing those villages, towns and any smaller hostelries along the way which seemed of relevance to him. When a shadow slanted across the study's doorway, David looked up quickly, turning the parchment over so that what was written there was no longer visible. He could deal with the smudging later.

It was his mistress who had come, and he stood at once, bowing slightly. "My lady? His lordship is not yet returned."

"I know," Emeline said, sitting herself at the other side of the small table from her husband's squire and regarding him with what she hoped would appear as natural and friendly curiosity. "It is you I wished to see, Mister Witton." She smiled. "I have a question to ask you."

"Of course, my lady, if I can be of help." David sat again, smoothing back the hair from his face. "Though I must warn you –"

"Don't look so suspicious, Mister Witton." Emeline folded her hands neatly in her lap and smiled again, a habit she had acquired with her father when wishing to see particularly innocent. "I'm well aware of my husband's secret work and his loyalty to the king. How can I reassure you? Talking of Berwick, for instance, and the treasure taken abroad after King Edward's death?" She paused, smiling again. "You see, I fully understand my husband's work. So don't worry, I shall not be asking about anything you feel you cannot answer."

"My lady, forgive me." He appeared no less concerned than before. "What his lordship imparts is his to decide."

Emeline frowned. "This is something I cannot ask him. But we've spoken before, Mister Witton, and you've been ready to explain certain matters - the Chatwyn family, about this house, and the house you own yourself. My question is no more intrusive. You see, I know he's about to leave on the king's business. I simply want to know how dangerous this is going to be."

David Witton looked down at the parchment he had turned over, which now rested at his elbow. "My lady, danger is always inherent. Yet unknown. Nor does his highness speak privately with me so I can know only as my lord informs me."

"If I ask his lordship," Emeline said, her voice low, "he will tell me there is nothing whatsoever to worry about, and to sleep easy. But I need to know the truth, Mister Witton, or I will not sleep at all."

David cleared his throat. "I cannot say - not only because I cannot impart - but because I do not know." He watched her face cloud into disappointment, and relented. "Far less dangerous than the business of the Scottish wars and the siege at Berwick, of that I'm sure, my lady. But somewhat more dangerous, I imagine, than his tutorship of the Lady Cecily." He smiled, not noticing Emeline's surprise, and continued, "but my lord is no unpractised simpleton, my lady. He has never been afraid, not that I know of, not even of the pestilence. Nor would his highness send a man on any errand if he thought that man incapable of achieving its ends with success."

Emeline stood. "You have put my mind a little at rest, Mister Witton. I thank you." She turned to go. "I expect his lordship to return late tonight. Am I correct?"

"Indeed, as far as I know myself." David looked towards the small sunny window, as if his mind had suddenly wandered elsewhere. "The stars will guide him home, my lady," he added softly. "As they always do. His lordship may travel far, and face danger for many reasons, but as the astrologers will tell us, we follow a destiny as best we can. "He bowed briefly again. "May I also assure your ladyship, that whatever happens I will be at my master's side, watching his back, and doing everything in my power to keep him safe."

She smiled. "Thank you, Mister Witton."

"No thanks are required, my lady," he replied. "I would lay down my life for my lord at any time and without compunction. He is everything to me."

By late afternoon, with Nicholas and Adrian still gone from the house, Emeline was cuddled in her nurse's reassuring embrace, her mother sitting still beside them in the small downstairs solar. The windows were open to the sunshine and a soft humming of bees floated on perfumes of lavender, rosemary and apple blossom. Sunbeams played like small transparent lemon clouds along the window casements and turned the glass mullions from muted green to glowing hazel. The baroness squinted, eyelids heavy in the glare.

Martha said, "Hush my dearest lambkin. Your little sister is safe, I promise you. Avice has a better head on her shoulders than you realise, my dearest."

Emeline mumbled, "No she hasn't. All she thinks of is new gowns and romance."

"Quiet," said the baroness suddenly, half rising from her chair. "Someone is coming, and there's a deal of clatter and shouting outside. Is that just Nicholas returning? Surely he's no need to make such a drama of simply coming home."

Emeline jumped up and ran to the door as her mother ran to the window. "It's Avice, surely. I'll go at once to the stables – "

Cart wheels, the squeak of rusty hinges against wooden planks, a horse's high pitched complaint and the stamp of hooves on cobbles, the wheeze of an oiled hessian awning flapping in the breeze, cart wheels again and ostlers yelling. Far too much noise and baggage for the simple return of Avice and Sysabel. Then finally a woman's quavering objection. "My good man, I have not the slightest interest in your gout, your ineptitude or your very bad temper. Hand me down immediately. I must speak to his lordship at once."

"'Is lordship's not at home, m'lady," snuffled one of the stable lads. "But 'er ladyship be indoors. I'll fetch Mister Sanderson, wot'll h'escort your ladyship to the Hall."

Emeline arrived at the stables before Sanderson, and stood in amazement and disappointment, face to face with her husband's elderly and absent minded aunt Elizabeth. The lady shivered in the stable shadows, a little wobbly kneed from her exertions in climbing down from the litter. Her small lady's companion was holding her hand, helping her mistress remove her travelling gloves while she rubbed her fingers, bringing back a modicum of vascular circulation. The ostlers led the horses and travel worn litter away as the three guards, dismounting, bowed to Emeline as she gazed towards the Lady Elizabeth.

"My lady," she stuttered, "that is - you've come all this way from Nottingham, with the roads as treacherous as they are? You are more than welcome, but we were not expecting - though my mother, and Adrian of course would not have known, though he's out, and Nicholas will be back shortly. The earl," she added, "is mercifully still at court."

"Thank the good Lord for His consideration," sighed her ladyship. "But it is dear Sysabel I've come to find. You see -"

And Emeline said, "I know, my lady, I know. Are you chilled? I shall order hot spiced hippocras at once."

Beneath her watchful mother's eye, Emeline acted the hostess and organised wine, chambers prepared, places for the additional grooms, guards and servants, and ordered a hearty hot supper to be served in the hall for five of the clock or as close thereafter as could be achieved. There would, she said a little faintly, be two gentlemen and three ladies, always supposing Lord Nicholas bothered to come home at all. And if he did, he might not choose to stay too long.

They sat for two hours by the empty hearth, fidgeting with their cups and refusing refills. "Young Sysabel," sighed Aunt Elizabeth, "is a good girl. Still awaiting her betrothal arrangements of course, since her Papa died many moons ago and dear Adrian, while a most attentive brother, seems loathe to lose her company. He is inclined to be a solitary gentleman, and trusts only his sister." The lady sipped her hippocras. "Adrian has every reason to trust myself of course, but age is not ever kind, and I do not always remember precisely what it is he has asked me to do."

"He should do it himself then," muttered Emeline.

Her mother scowled at her. "Young Adrian will be back soon, I'm sure": said the baroness. "And my son-in-law is expected home later. He will say you should not have felt obliged - coming all this way - a horrendous journey for a lady of advanced - and in any case, my dear, you are most certainly welcome, and I shall much appreciate your presence. My daughter will make sure you are comfortable and without doubt your niece and my younger daughter will be found very soon."

The Lady Elizabeth blinked. "I woke one dull morning to discover poor Sysabel had left at dawn," she sighed. "Properly accompanied and guarded, and leaving me a contrite message naturally, but I could just imagine what Adrian would say to me about his sister's unsanctioned departure. I sent an immediate messenger to your home, my lady, in Wrotham. But within days the messenger returned, telling me Sysabel was no longer there. She had left quite abruptly in the company of Mistress Avice, and had not yet been traced. It was supposed that both young girls were intending a trip to London. I immediately made plans to follow." She waved vague and directionless fingers. "And here I am, though with no thanks to the state of the roads."

"Sissy and Avice," said Emeline under her breath, "ought to be whipped."

A flutter of silken gowns left the supper table for an early retirement, the ladies fractious and dreaming of their beds. A despondent and unfulfilled impatience seemed more wearisome than any imagined activity. Adrian returned almost immediately afterwards, spoke at length with both the Steward Sanderson and his own henchmen, and then took himself off to his chamber, quite unaware that his aunt was deeply asleep just ten steps further along the corridor.

It was very late when Nicholas arrived home. Emeline, though half asleep, was sitting up in bed, not entirely hopeful, but waiting for him. She rubbed her eyes as the door quietly opened, made sure it was indeed her husband, and whispered, "Thank goodness you've come. I was frightened you'd be out all night, or even all week, or simply be too tired to visit me. I need to tell you something."

Nicholas collapsed onto the window seat, stretching both back and legs. He was clearly exhausted. "That I'm a neglectful husband, and you're worried sick about your sister?"

Emeline watched the deepening shadows slink like bruises around his eyes, silhouetting his expression in wary uncertainty. Down the dragging scar his flesh seemed sunken and hollowed. His lips were tight and pale. Emeline inhaled, abandoned all the words she had been about to say, and instead said, "Nicholas, my own darling, you've been speaking with the king. I'm just so pleased you didn't have to ride off in the night on some wild dangerous scheme without even speaking to me first. But yes, I *am* worried sick about Avice. And now your Aunt Elizabeth has arrived here."

"Impossible." He had started to undress, as usual not caring to call for his valet, with an impatient tug at his doublet lacings and the open neck of his shirt. He kicked off his boots, shrugged both shirt and doublet together from over his head, and reappeared, blinking anew at his wife. "The woman lives a hundred miles away," he said. "She doesn't travel."

Emeline flexed her fingers and inhaled again. "My brain, pickled and sadly female as it is, is not entirely lost to me, Nicholas," she said. "Your aunt is definitely here and asleep in one of the guest chambers. Adrian had forbidden his sister to leave home, so your aunt was worried about Sissy's sudden departure. She sent a query to Wrotham, only to discover chaos and upheaval with everyone already disappeared, off busily chasing everyone else. So she came here."

Nicholas, warmly naked, rolled heavily into bed and took his wife immediately into his arms, tight snuggled against him. Her last words tickled his neck. He sighed. "So we have Adrian, your mother, and now my aunt. Is there anyone I've overlooked? Everyone is here in fact, except your sister and my cousin who are the cause of it all. It seems coming here was not so wise. I'd hoped for peace, and a chance to get to know my wife."

"Peace?" Emeline's smile curved into the identical curve of her husband's shoulder as she slipped her fingers around his waist. "You never promised me peace, Nicholas. I've had that all my life and it's far less attractive than people seem to expect. And I thought you were chasing adventure - not tedium."

"Peace can be surprisingly seductive. And relatives can be irretrievably tedious."

"At least your father isn't here."

Nicholas sighed. "I imagine he will be. I've been talking to his highness, as you know. The king has work for me - while offering his excuses for having indefinitely cancelled my father's mission to Spain."

"Your father knows. He blames you."

"Which is why he'll be delighted to discover me here, and come to berate me again. It's all that's left to him."

Emeline kissed his ear, nibbling at the short flat lobe. "Poor darling. And I suppose you can't tell him the king's given you the mission instead."

"Certainly not." Nicholas kissed the tip of her nose. "And nor will you. But it's not the same mission. I doubt I'm the type to successfully arrange foreign marriages and pretend proxy courtships. I'll tell you something of the rest tomorrow."

Alarmed, she whispered, "You won't be leaving so soon, I hope? Please tell me you have time first to look for Avice?"

Nicholas shook his head. "There's time. A little anyway. But for now, my love, I have barely the energy to open and close my eyes." His fingers slipped, caressing her back, following down the gentle bumps of her spine to the tuck between her buttocks. His palm cupped appreciatively, fingertips against her dimples. But as she murmured, speaking of love, Emeline realised that Nicholas was already very deeply asleep.

His eyes remained closed. Some hours had passed in dreaming, drifting between troubled memories and future fears, Nicholas immovable in soundless sleep, when the sudden interruption woke Emeline first. It now seemed almost a familiar commotion, the jangling upheaval from the stables, voices of men pulled abruptly from their pallets, horses stamping and snorting, those already asleep disturbed by new arrivals, the creak and squeak of gates opening and the echoes across the cobbles, sharp sounds in the night.

Emeline scrambled up in bed, and Nicholas awoke, opening one reluctant eye. "Already? Again? Nightmare or indigestion?"

"Listen," she said with wide excitement. "That's Sissy's voice. And that's Avice. They've arrived." She hurtled from the bedcovers, grabbed her bedrobe and tugged it around her shoulders, tied tight. Within minutes she had thrown open the great doors to the main hall, and took her little sister in a fierce embrace. "You are a horrible, horrible child," she squeaked, though Avice seemed too squashed to answer. "All England has been searching for you, and I shall never, ever speak to you again."

Nicholas was behind her. "I suppose," he said, yawning, "we'd better wake someone somewhere and order the wine warmed. Then I'm going back to bed."

Emeline did not return to bed until dawn. Finally, crawling back to her chamber, she discovered Nicholas had indeed deserted her. Her bed was empty though dishevelled, and so instead she welcomed both Avice and Sysabel into the wide warm luxury. All three passed the little of the night remaining curled close and breathing their simmering exhaustion into each other's ears.

It was not until dinner the next day that the entire gathering of recent arrivals met together.

CHAPTER TWENTY NINE

There had been some hours of excitement, bustle and noise, affectionate demonstrations, tired recrimination, apology and temporary defiance. But it was at the dinner table after thanks being given for the food on the platters and while the grace of religious blessing still reigned, that they sat in those moments of silence and stared each at the other, assimilating what had happened, and acknowledging what would inevitably follow. The fury and accusations were over and a general contentment had slipped in with the blaze of relief. Avice wore one of her sister's prettiest new gowns, and Sysabel, avoiding her brother's frown, wore another. The baroness, gloriously grand in a new gleaming fur trimmed gown of her own in bright cerise velvet, unclasped her hands and smiled broadly.

"Well, well, it appears," she said with a complacent sigh, "that everything is finally solved, and we are all safe. I shall never forget, Avice, the trouble you have caused. Your religious upbringing clearly gave you a good deal less moral circumspection than your father imagined. But since I know I was an exemplary parent, I hold him responsible. However, now we are here together with all the glories of London just a few steps to our right and magnificent Westminster to our left. I must admit I am not even cross anymore."

"I, on the other hand," said Adrian with some resonance, "am exceedingly angry." He frowned across the table at his sister. "I made my wishes plain when I left. You were to stay in Nottingham."

Sysabel attended closely to her platter, choosing a small salmon pasty and a manchet roll which she then did not eat. She mumbled, "I'm sorry, Adrian," rather faintly, "but I'm not an infant anymore you know. I wanted - and I needed to - so I did."

"Evidently," said Adrian with ambiguous emphasis.

Nicholas took three carefully carved slices of roast beef in mustard sauce onto his plate, added a small spoonful of chicken livers and raisins cooked in claret, smiled first at his wife, then extended the smile to the rest of his family, and said, "How delightful to be surrounded by so many unexpected and cheerful guests. I've never known this house so – animated. However, I am devastated to tell you all that I've two days at the most before I have to leave. You're all most welcome to stay and keep Emma company, but I imagine since, as you say, the original problem is now solved, you'll all wish to hurry home?"

"Certainly not," said Avice, thumping down her spoon. "We set off to find who killed Papa and Peter. And that hasn't been solved at all."

"I hardly see," said Aunt Elizabeth, absently patting her forehead with her napkin, "that you young people could manage any such thing. How does one find a madman? Do they hide under bushes? And how would you know if it is the right madman you discover anyway? I believe England is full of them."

"An evil man, not a mad man," insisted Avice. "Peter was killed in the same way as Papa, so Nicholas thinks by the same man. Someone wanted revenge, and planned it all carefully. We didn't even know where Papa was, but the murderer found him somehow. And no one could have got in easily to kill Peter. So not mad, just wicked."

Adrian stood, pushing back his chair with a loud scrape. "Assumptions, ignorance, undisciplined imagination. We know nothing. Even the sheriff knows nothing." He turned to Nicholas. "And you, you're running off as usual, just as soon as matters appear challenging? Deserting your wife once again, abandoning your whole family, and certainly your duty. What excuses have you to offer this time?"

Nicholas looked up from his well filled platter and smiled widely. "My reasons? Boredom? Irritation? Headache? But no, my dear cousin, I offer no excuses. I have never acknowledged either the desire or the necessity to excuse myself. I am simply leaving on my own affairs and will inform my wife, whose business it is, and no one else since it is not theirs." He then refilled his cup from the jug of Tuscan Trebbiano, and as an afterthought also filled Emeline's. "Drink up, my dear," he told her. "I believe we may both need a little additional insulation."

She drank obediently, then turned back to her mother. "Nicholas has to go away, Maman," she said. "I know he hasn't any choice. So can you and Avice stay a little while?"

"I am also not entirely sure," her mother told her, "that I believe your Papa's murderer could possibly be traced by a couple of girls barely out of the nursery. But I do have a certain interest in knowing who - and seeing the culprit hanged - and I've very little wish to return to the Gloucestershire gales."

"That's it then," declared Avice. "We're all staying."

Sysabel gazed warily across at her brother who had sat down again with an air of being long misunderstood and much mistreated. "If you wish to return to Nottingham, Adrian dear," she said with care, "since you have so many responsibilities there, then you should go. I'm perfectly well chaperoned here as you can see, with Aunt Elizabeth, *and* her ladyship."

Adrian opened his mouth but Nicholas interrupted. "Settled then. Adventure and intrigue, and all at my expense. What more could you ask, Adrian? Off you go back north, and leave the women to their hunt."

Emeline spoke in a hurry, fearing further interruption. "So, did anyone discover any clues at all? Do we even have any guesses? Did you discover anything on that mad romp through the countryside while the rest of us were half dead with worry?"

There was a clatter as Adrian once again took up his knife and spoon, and Nicholas reached for the wine. Avice shook her head but the baroness, quickly swallowing a mouthful of honeyed pears, took advantage of the short pause and said, "As it happens, perhaps I have. Chasing after you two girls, I had occasion to speak with the sheriff at Gloucester. He informed me of some interesting facts which I had not previously been told," here she frowned briefly at Nicholas, "and although I've no wish to repeat any unsavoury secrets, the female who was evidently slaughtered at the same time and in the same manner as my poor husband, had a grown son. This son has since entirely disappeared. Although becoming the inheritor of his mother's property, he has recently run away. I find that most suspicious."

Nicholas glanced at her, cup in hand. "With one's only parent dead under gruesome but mysterious circumstances, a child might run, don't you think, to search for protection elsewhere?"

"You know about him then," scowled the baroness, "since seemingly you know he had no father."

"Quite true, my lady," he replied. "I spoke to the sheriff at some length shortly after the tragedy occurred. I saw no reason to pester you with uncomfortable and entirely incidental irrelevancies. The child was devestated at the loss of his mother and was in no way implicated either in her previous immorality, or in her death."

"You presumably know a good deal more than the sheriff, then," said the baroness, "since he seemed to think it as suspicious as I did."

Nicholas shrugged. Sysbel sat up suddenly very straight and stared at him. "So you've no real interest in finding who killed your own father-in-law, Nicholas – nor in who slaughtered your own brother."

"My cousin, the sloven, the coward and profligate," muttered Adrian.

"As you say," nodded Nicholas cheerfully, shaking out his sleeves. "And not nearly clever enough to go hunting murderers across our wide green pastures. I shall leave all that to you ingenious females. Just don't lynch anyone too quickly. Fear can make the innocent appear guilty, while the guilty are invariably working very hard to appear innocent. I shall take an interest from afar."

"From afar tavern?" suggested Adrian.

Nicholas shook his head. "The quality and quantity of good wine is superior at my own table. But you should know, dear cousin, since you've been helping yourself to it for two days now." He turned to Emeline. "Do as you wish my dear. I have things to attend to now, if you'll excuse me. But we can talk in private this evening."

It was late when he came to her bedchamber and found her alert and waiting. She wore only her shift, with her hair still pinned high beneath a pearl trimmed net. She held out her arms and Nicholas sat on the edge of the bed and kissed the fingertips of both her hands. Then he stood again and began to undress. She watched him. Two candles were lit and the room was cradled in leaping shadows and the sudden lustre of dancing gold. The light toned and emphasised the muscles and taut sinews of the body, the dark hair, and the curves of bone and flesh. His skin glowed, and where the flat hardness of belly followed down to the groin, the silky hair began to curl and snuggle tight, deeper than shadow.

Emeline sighed and said, "Nicholas. Tell me the truth. Do you know who killed my Papa?"

His exhaustion showed. He turned to her abruptly. "I remember you once asking if I'd killed Peter. Is this the same question?"

"Don't be cross, my love. I know perfectly well you didn't. But you knew about that whore's son, and chose to exonerate him without any explanation."

"No." He sat naked beside her, smoothing his palm across her forehead as he began to unpin her headdress. "I've wondered, guessed at an occasional possibility, had my suspicions. But I've no real idea who killed either Peter or your father, and would certainly do something about it if I knew for sure. After Peter was discovered dead, I had months to ponder and puzzle. I had doubts and those doubts lingered. At one time I thought perhaps I knew. It would have been an inconvenient truth - a possibility I hoped mistaken. Indeed, I no longer believe it. I simply believe coincidences hide less coincidental intentions, and so I'm sure both men were slaughtered by the same killer. And although I don't know who it was, I have a fair idea of who it wasn't."

She frowned and shook her head. The last of the pearl pins cascaded. "Like the little boy who was crying in your stables yesterday?"

He regarded her a moment, then began to laugh. "How glad I am I married you, my love." He picked the scattered pins from the pillows and deposited them on the chest beside the bed where one of the candles was beginning to burn low. "You are right of course. The child is simple, young, and as much of a victim as his mother. Now also destitute. So I judged him innocent and offered him employment."

Emeline scrunched up her knees beneath the covers, avoiding pins. "So you've brought the son of my father's mistress into our household?"

"Yes, I suppose I have." He was still laughing. "Do you mind? You need never meet him. And he's not your father's son, in case you were wondering."

"You know so much?"

"I know the present threat to this country is greater than the threat to us from one small boy." Naked now, his clothes discarded across the floor, Nicholas stood again and went to the hearthside table where he filled two cups from the jug waiting there, and brought one to Emeline. "You're getting to know me, my love. You order wine, and have it waiting when you expect me to come to your chamber. So drink with me."

She took the cup. "Threats to the country? Are you trying to frighten me, Nicholas, or simply change the subject?"

"Neither. Drink up." He drank, sitting again, the mattress sinking as he stretched his legs, resting back against the pillows. His cup in one hand, he slipped the other around her shoulders, holding her close. "But you must know a little of what I do and where I go, so let me tell you I've spent most of the afternoon and evening talking with James Tyrell, and another part of it with the king's secretary Kendall. The problem is France. Invariably it is France. Now they're using that exiled son of Stanley's Beaufort wife, trying to set him up as claimant to the throne."

Emeline snuggled, though she lay below the covers and he stretched out above. "That doesn't make any sense, Nicholas. England has a king."

"Henry Tudor has never known what to do with himself," nodded Nicholas. "He claims an earldom forfeited long ago, and both titleless and landless, has drifted in exile for long dismal years. But France now has a plan. They've no more interest in Tudor than England has, but they have an avid interest in weakening and undermining English security. France knows our King Richard is no lover of French politics, and long ago refused a French pension, even when half the English nobility gladly accepted one. Our king is not a man to play games or accept bribes. So France distrusts him. Tudor will play along – it's in his interests now and he's started to imagine a more hopeful future for himself. More importantly, his mother will push him."

"To claim – what? I mean, he's nobody. I don't understand."

Nicholas stroked her shoulder beneath the eiderdown. "It's the old story of Lancaster against York, Lancastrian objections to our present Yorkist monarch, and Woodville malcontents uniting with various wandering exiles. Tudor has no claim anyway since the Beaufort line is legally barred due to original bastardy. Even ignoring that, which no doubt his mother chooses to do, there are sixteen or more in the Lancastrian bloodline before him, including the Portuguese Infanta whom our King Richard is planning to marry. But as England grows stronger, so France simply wants an excuse to batter at our coasts and weaken English power. False claimants and divisive threats are their principal artillery."

"Nicholas, you're not going to *France*?" He turned to look down at her, slowly pulling away the counterpane, the blankets and the sheet. He removed one last wayward pearl pin from its hiding place, and tossed the covers aside. She whispered, "Now I'm cold."

"I can see that," he said, his fingers tracing the swell of her breasts. "When you're cold, your nipples rise like little dark studs." He rubbed his thumb over her shadows, then pinched, teasing through the thin linen of her shift. "It happens exactly the same when you're aroused." He grinned. "But this time I think you're simply cold. Now what, I wonder, should I do about that?"

"So you *are* staying tonight, Nicholas? I got rid of my maid on purpose, and when Martha said she'd sleep on the truckle bed, I said no, even though I knew she'd be disappointed. You're not leaving too soon, are you? Not before dawn?"

"I have all night and all tomorrow." He leaned forwards, pushing her hard back against the pillows. "Now how much of that, do you think, can I spend with you in bed?" Then he kissed her, his mouth forcing her ever back, his tongue pressing between her lips. He tasted the wine on her breath, and the yearning in her throat. While he kissed her, he forced his hand between her breasts, pulling down the open neck of her shift so that she was part uncovered. His fingers continued to tease, first soft, then harder, then sharp, then gentle again. She moaned slightly and he smiled. Releasing her, he sat back and running his palms down her body and her legs, reached for the hem of her shift and drew it quickly up, tugging it off over her head and tossing it to the ground. In the sudden little breeze, the bedside candle blew out with a flicker and a blink.

The chamber sank into greater shadow. Now one solitary candle flared from its far corner, and the light travelled like a golden moth across the high beamed ceiling, scattering sudden illumination onto carvings, a moment's vivid face in a tapestry but lost again immediately, a splinter jutting from a slat on the window shutters, the swing of tasselled drape where the bed curtains were closed on one side to eliminate any draught from beneath the door. Emeline lay in the darker depths of shadow within the bed, though where she was now naked, her breasts and shoulders and belly caught in a faint saffron glow. Her smile remained lost in darkness. The drapes rustled as he moved, shifting to face her.

She whispered, "I'm not cold anymore."

He didn't answer. His fingers travelled her body just as the candlelight travelled the walls around them with exploration and discovery. He used his palms, flat where she was curved, soft as a tickle, then pulling back. He watched her expression, smiled at her sighs and waited until he knew the depth of her arousal. Then he dipped his finger into the cup he had set down, and with a trail of dark wine, painted her nipples in liquid rubies. The little chill droplets trickled from the tilted tips down across her breasts, a sticky snail's path in the flaring light and shadow. Then Nicholas bent, and licked, sucking clean and drinking his wine from her body. She shivered, but this time it was not from the cold.

When he sat up again, smiling at her, he said, "No sleep tonight, my love. I have other plans which will take us to dawn."

"Will it be the last time then, before you go?" He nodded, and kissed her again. The wine from her breasts was on his tongue and his lips, and now she breathed its perfumes from his mouth. And his kisses travelled too, softly down her neck to the curve of her shoulder, to her breasts again and the hard thrusting nipples, and on to each little valley between her ribs. He kissed her navel, his tongue very warm. Then to the belly, all around and across as if he was searching. On to the line at her groin where her hair tightened into thick little curls, the dark russet now streaked with gold in the changeful wayward light. His teeth nipped, pulling at the soft pubic hair, and then forced lower, kissing the small entrance between her legs as if it was her mouth, his tongue pressing within the lips, opening where she had been tight closed. She grabbed at his shoulders, pulling him back up to her. "Oh my love, don't leave me. I wish you were truly the fool they all think you. Act the coward, and stay here with me."

His fingers followed where he had kissed, pressing between her thighs and pushing just a little inside. "Here," he whispered, voice gruff as if his own passion made speaking difficult, "this is a nipple too, of sorts. It swells, and hardens, and pushes up, as if waking and sitting to stretch after a warm sleep. This way you tell me what you want, even without words."

"I don't have words. But it feels more like a dream than waking up."

"Sometimes waking is the dream."

"I don't like waking to an empty bed."

"Then tomorrow you won't, my love. You'll wake in my arms, and I'll call for ale and cheese so we can breakfast in bed, and if any strength remains to me, I'll make love to you again before you face your relatives."

"No morning chapel? No prayers? You face danger and a long journey. We should both pray for your safety."

"These are my prayers. And the bed is my chapel." He took her hand, bringing it between his thighs and wrapping her fingers around him. "Here, my sweetling, a prayer as potent as any other. Hold firm. Now pull a little away from my body. Not too much yet, or you'll lose me too quickly to temptation. Now, feel that ridge. Press your thumb under and up, gently at first, and see how the shaft hardens ever larger under your palm. We're both responsive to each other, my love, and can explore old ways and new ways."

"You call it a shaft. Like an arrow."

"Perhaps it is." He smiled. "There are other words I might use, if you weren't my wife. But an arrow sounds well enough."

"So, if I wasn't your wife, what would you say?" she asked, invisible blushes. "Is prick too vulgar? But it does so very much more than just pricking."

He chuckled. "Names don't matter. It's touch that tells stories. Vulgarities apart, my love, marriage is for learning and teaching pleasure, giving it, and receiving it, and remembering it when responsibility calls and the bed goes cold. Reliving it in thought perhaps, when alone and following cold paths and other duties, but missing the warmth."

"I don't want to think about being apart yet. Can I touch you here, down further, and below?"

"Kiss me."

"There?"

"Does that frighten you? Now, my own love, use your tongue. I have an opening too. Find it, and explore inside me as I intend exploring inside you."

It was more than an hour later when he released her, both of them exhausted. The last candle had guttered and the chamber slumbered in seething, panting blackness. Nicholas kissed his wife's trembling eyelids, and again pulled the warmth of the blankets up around her chin, tucking her in, and pressing close to her side. He fingered the dampness at her thighs, and smiled, and wished her sweet hours until they awoke together the next morning. "Then I shall want you again, I warn you, my sweet, just as soon as I reopen my eyes. Already I know how I'll take you, and how you'll sigh and moan, ready or not."

She whispered back, "I love you so much, Nicholas my dear."

"Then dream now, little one." He shook his head, still smiling. "And so shall I."

"Of mc, Nicholas?"

"God willing. In truth, it all seems a dream to me now."

CHAPTER THIRTY

Avice stared, shoulders hunched, and said, "You're all pink, Emma. And sweaty. But it was quite chilly last night. You must have much thicker blankets than me."

"Hush, Avice," said her mother. "You really are an ignorant child sometimes. You must take after your Papa."

"I don't," said Avice. "I'm just like you, Maman. And don't tell me no. I've seen all your wonderful new clothes since Papa died, and the lovely food with honey and raisins and proper spices, and real loaves of sugar in the pantry, and the hundreds of extra candles, and far less time spent in chapel. Father Godwin looks positively lost and lonely these days. And Maman, those sleeves. They're long enough to dust the floors, and there's real rabbit fur all the way up inside. So you see, you're just like me after all."

"It certainly isn't simple rabbit," said her mother. "And you will not mention wagers again, Avice, not even indirectly. Indeed, that's quite enough chatter for now."

Adrian interrupted. "I'm sure it will be a great disappointment to all you ladies," he said with firm deliberation, "to know that I've decided to stay. With Nicholas about to scurry off, I feel at least one sober masculine presence is imperative. I intend staying until I escort my sister back to Nottingham."

"How nice," said the baroness without noticeable conviction.

Emeline said, "Nicholas is out at the stables organising his departure. But he'll have supper with us before he leaves." She looked directly at Adrian. "You've been so very nice, sir, offering to come here and look for Nicholas when he was missing before. But I know where he's going this time. At least, I have some idea. Nicholas trusts me to stay on my own. And now there's Maman. So we can look after Sissy, truly we can. You don't have to stay."

"Searching for murderers and clues and such nonsense. Pooh," said Adrian. "And as for Nicholas' trust, I put no more store in his opinions than I do in my sister's. I must tell you, madam, London is a dangerous place."

"And I'm so looking forward to going there," sighed Avice.

The spring sunshine was sinking a little behind the gables. Moss had crawled over the stable thatch, merging with the reeds and oozing green shadows down to the neat clipped edges. Nicholas was leaning against one of the stalls, regarding his liard's impatience. The horse kicked at the stable door. Nicholas smiled. "I feel the same, my friend, and these fools make me all the more eager to be gone."

Rob was quarrelling with his brother, and the new boy Wolt was watching with the first smile he'd managed since leaving Gloucester.

"Pompous codsprick," spat Harry. "Just 'cos you took up with 'is lordship afore I did, don't make you no more special now. We's both needed, ain't we m'lord?"

"Desperately needed. Needfully desperate," said his lordship. "Otherwise I'd send you both back to the tenements with pleasure."

David Witton shook his head. "You're sure of this, my lord? It's an odd package we'll seem, I think, which could make us too conspicuous."

"And another package of oddments left indoors," agreed Nicholas. "Eccentricity is my destiny, it appears. But I know what I want, David, and this, sadly, is it."

It was David who later arranged the filling of two saddle bags and gave further instructions to the grooms. The boy Wolt regarded the baggage sumpter with misgivings. "You'll ride it, or you'll walk," David said, reading the boy's thoughts.

Wolt looked increasingly haggard for his twelve years. "No one shows no sympathy," he mumbled, "nor even for a poor motherless lad like me."

"Brainless whelp," said David Witton. "I'd shown you less sympathy than his lordship chooses to, a motherless child himself at a younger age than you, and who offered you employment even though you possess no skill of any kind except feeling sorry for yourself."

"Just shows, dun'it," said Wolt, retreating from the hooves around him. "Don't no one else care – so if I feels sorry for meself, wot's only right and just."

"And if I kicks you up the arse, 'tis only fair the same, since you gets on me bloody nerves." Harry turned from Wolt to David. "Since his lordship don't like explaining too much, maybe you'd like to give us some idea of where we're going later? Seems strange to me, leaving at dusk. The London gates is likely locked, and there'll be no way to get to the tenement after that 'cept by river. And with five horses, the river'd make less sense than all the rest."

"We're not going back to the tenements," David said. "We're heading south. It's the coast we'll be seeing, not the city. And a fair view over to France, perhaps."

Harry went pale in the sunshine, and nervously scratched at his neck. "Don't trust them Frenchies. Don't trust them big oceans neither. As for boats – there's not a sane man would trust one of them. We ain't going to France is we? For I might reckon on changing me mind and going back home."

"Take no heed," Rob interrupted. "My brother will do what I tells him."

"There are no plans for us to head for France yet," frowned David. "But there might just be plans for France to head for us. It's the possibility of French invasion we're investigating, and you'll keep that a secret for now by the way. No cause for panic."

Harry gulped, staring at Rob, who was grinning. "Don't tell me you ain't dreamed of bashing a few Frenchie heads from time to time," Rob said. "I shall have my knife right ready for the first foreign voice I hears."

"Which is probably why his lordship didn't tell you," nodded David, "and why I should not have told you either. So forget what I said and help me with these panniers."

With the sunshine oozing through the mullions, Avice and Sysabel remained only half awake, curled together on the wide guest bed, covers discarded. "Maman's idea," whispered Avice, "is interesting. This disappeared boy, the son of that dreadful woman. What if he killed Papa?"

"What would he do that for if your father was paying his mother?" objected Sysabel. "Disapproval? But I don't think sons of whores think that way."

"How many sons of whores do you know?" objected Avice, sitting up a little and rubbing her eyes. "But why would a whore's son from Gloucester want to kill Peter, and how would he even know Peter existed?"

"Peter would never have had anything to do with such people."

Avice sighed. "You know, everything's just too complicated. There's Emma - she was in love with Peter for ages and she hated Nicholas. Even after the wedding she thought he was hideous. Now suddenly she thinks he's an angel."

"Peter was the angel. Nicholas - well," Sysabel shook her head. "He's nice sometimes. But compared to Peter, he's very shallow."

"I never really knew Peter. But a little while ago I started thinking I was in love with your Adrian. Oh, don't laugh. He was so smart and wise and kind and I dreamed of romance. Romantic love sounds so - glorious. Dressing up and kissing and having a man really smile at you - wanting you. Instead of just sitting around being ignored and bored all day every day." Avice screwed up her nose. "But since getting here, Adrian's just cross all the time and I don't think he even likes me. He's not kind anymore. And I don't think he's wise either."

"He's not interested in women," said Sysabel. "He's too serious and he acts as if he's my father. I wish he'd just go away."

Emeline was upstairs and back in her husband's arms. "For brief moments only, my love. I have to leave as soon as the sun sinks. Before the London gates are locked, but not too much before."

"You've told me very little, Nicholas." she sighed. "Can't you tell me a little more? And you look so very strange in those clothes. It's disconcerting."

"But not skirts this time." He was laughing. "Just a little fustian and worsted. Unbleached linen and second hand wool. Does it prickle?"

"Yes, very prickly. I'm not sure I've ever been this close to such uncomfortable materials before. This must prickle even more inside."

"I'm thick skinned," explained Nicholas.

Emeline smiled into his prickles. "So who are you supposed to be this time?"

The shutters had not yet been raised. The sunshine streamed in, angled in a wide sweeping stripe of gold across the floorboards. They sat together on the settle, she resting her head on his shoulder. The window was behind them, its light warming the back of their necks. Nicholas stretched his darned hose and scuffed brown shoes. "Oh, anybody will do. The story will change in different places. A wandering doctor perhaps, selling tinctures and salves. David has packed me a bag of herbs and spices, including lavender which I could smell from the other side of the stables. I suspect him of mischief, since he knows I loathe the stuff and will throw it out at my first chance."

She sat up, startled. "But Nicholas, how can you? What if people come for medicines? What if they want to be bled? What if you have to examine them?"

"I'll cheerfully examine the women. I'll send the men to Harry for treatment. He's been bleeding folk for most of his life."

Emeline said, "Oh, Nicholas. Would you really? Being quite free to do - without a boring wife pulling at your lacings - will you? Knowing I shall never know about it."

His thoughts were momentarily focused elsewhere. Then he realised what she was asking, and grinned. "Oh, I imagine I can resist for a few days. So think the best of me, little one. And I shall miss you, and promise to avoid the temptations of lust and fornication."

"Promises again."

"I'll be busy, my love, with no time for pleasure except in my dreams."

Emeline reached out, cradling his face, her palm light against the long black scar. "Even when we're not making love, you still call me your love. But I know I'm not. I'm the woman you didn't want to marry. You don't have to pretend."

"I'm fast becoming accustomed." He took her fingers, moving them from his face to his lap. She felt the sudden quickening of his body, and was surprised. He said, "And pretending is what I have to do from now on. I'll be playing a different part. Adventure. Danger. But also border security, with a small hand, perhaps, in keeping our country safe."

She shook her head. "Are you a - *spy* - Nicholas?"

"Lord no." Nicholas stood abruptly, striding over to the window alcove where a small bundle lay; the last of his preparations. "Just a messenger - a man of small skills but trustworthy - one of the many the king uses. Then there's a troop of ordinary men - perhaps more intelligent than the rest of us - who do the king's bidding in even greater secrecy. Those are the spies, faceless and nameless. It's a spy who gave the information I'm now being sent to act on. It's a king's main responsibility to protect his country. He can't do that with sword and axe alone."

"Oh dear," mumbled Emeline. "Why would any man *want* to be king?"

"Many do. Many don't. Some seek power. Me - power doesn't interest me but action does. I've seen my father slouch too long at the ear of kings, hoping for recognition. So I don't want boredom either. I doubt our good King Richard ever yearned to be king, though when Bishop Stillington announced the old king's bigamy to the world, Richard of Gloucester was the direct heir. He had no choice once he was elected by all three estates. But I believe he was born to power. He handles it better than most."

She took a deep breath. "But I don't want you to go on dangerous missions."

"But I do." Nicholas dropped the small bundle at his feet and came back to the settle, sitting quickly again beside his wife, both hands to her shoulders. "I call it adventure, and that's a convenient word, but I stand for more than that, my love. And I'll be back, I promise. Meanwhile you can start believing my promises. If the king trusts me, you might as well too. Can you love a man you don't trust?"

"You don't even believe I love you," she pointed out. "You said I was just infatuated because you make me feel - and you know how you make me feel."

And he said, "I know what you love, my little one," and chuckled.

"You don't understand," she sighed. "I wanted something all my life. Dreamed of it. Yearned for it. Not just romance, and certainly not making love, since I didn't even know what that was. It was so much more than that. I thought it was Peter, of course. Our wedding was nearly planned, so it had to be him. Then after you made love to me, I realised it was you. All the dreams, all the wanting, all the coming alive and feeling safe, it all just happened in your arms."

He took her hand, squeezing her fingers. "Silly puss. So trust me then."

"But you go away so often, and I'm frightened you'll never come back at all."

"I'm not such a fool." Nicholas stood again, bending to kiss her briefly on each cheek and once lightly on the mouth. "The king wants a little exploration, questioning and poking into corners. His grace would send Brampton or Lovell if there was real danger expected. I'm little more than fledgling fodder, my love, a tadpole amongst toads." He stepped back, smiling. "But I'm hoping to meet up with two very different men, one a Tudor emissary bringing letters from France to Northumberland, and I mean to intercept him. And the other –"

But he was interrupted. From downstairs echoes rumbled, the slamming of doors, calls for the steward, then for Nicholas. Adrian's voice answered, but was shouted over. "I'll have you know this house belongs to me before all else," roared the Earl of Chatwyn, "and I'll be attended to, nor accept argument. So where's my boy? Where's that fool son of mine?"

Upstairs Nicholas nodded to Emeline and spoke quietly. "I'm away, and fast. If the old drunkard sees me dressed like this there'll be a thousand awkward questions and I'll never escape. You're the lady of the house, so deal with your difficult guest while I get out by the stables."

Emeline whispered back, "Is he drunk?"

"He's so habituated, it's hard to tell. But listen. Slurred, slovenly, and angry without motive. So yes, he's drunk, and I wish I was. Can you handle it, my love?"

"I can. I will. My mother and your father. Adrian, Sissy and Avice. What could be easier? What joyful entertainment it will be to be sure, while I'm desperately missing you and just longing to crawl into bed alone and dream of your return." And Emeline turned from him, running into the corridor towards the main stairs. She did not look back.

CHAPTER THIRTY ONE

It was another slow saffron afternoon. They sat in Emeline's bedchamber, still drowsy with the tired yawns of an interrupted night.

Eight women, and the chamber seemed almost crowded. Emeline curled back on her bed against the high stacked pillows. She had dressed a little grandly, hoping for confidence in face of her father-in-law's arrival. But now her curls were unruly and the pins of her headdress were askew in the wilting starched chiffon. Her sister sat beside her, knees scrunched up and arms around her knees, showing far too much ankle and a face quite flushed with tired excitement.

The baroness, sitting very straight in her chair, faced her daughters. On the opposite side of the bed, neat and quiet, Sysabel sat resting against the end post, the open drapes like a small cloak around her shoulders. Across the chamber on the wide settle where Nicholas had sat the night before to say goodbye to his wife, now reclined the Lady Elizabeth, complaining of exhaustion and headache. The maid Hilda stood silently behind, gently rubbing the lady's neck to ease strained muscles. Nurse Martha sat alone on the window seat, hands neat clasped, hiding her misgivings, the baroness's maid Petronella standing quietly in the shadows beside her.

The baroness said, "My dear girl, you are a married woman, a lady in your own right and mistress of your own household. How do I advise you now?"

"I cannot believe that would ever stop you, Maman."

"Very well," said the baroness, "I shall tell you exactly what I think."

Avice mumbled at her knees, "You think we're stupid and have to stop."

"I'm surprised to hear you consider yourself my judge and jury, Avice," said the baroness, "yet as usual you fail me. Indeed, I have every intention of staying here for some time, and of becoming involved in this entirely interesting enterprise. I may not have mourned my husband quite as rigorously as I might have done had he not been discovered in the arms of a prostitute, but even such hypocrisy can hardly be said to merit his murder. Someone has had the unutterable temerity to slaughter the Baron Wrotham and leave me a widow. If the culprit is still cowering but living, I shall do my best to uncover him."

Everybody stared at the baroness in considerable surprise. "So you're not going to *stop* us?" asked Emeline in amazement.

"I intend helping you," said her mother. "Now, is there quill and ink available, or must we organise in secret? I believe a written list, each of us adding a name or two perhaps, will survive better than simple whispers written on the back of my mind."

The Lady Elizabeth, with a faint aroma of apple blossom, shook her head in silent disapproval. "Paper," muttered Avice, "can be read by all and sundry. Minds can't."

"Then we must be a little more efficient than you anticipate, Avice," her mother told her. "A skill I have in abundance, although you clearly do not. A simple list of names without further explanation is hardly a hanging matter. And it must be kept safe."

"Everything for scribing is kept downstairs," Emeline said, sitting forwards in a hurry. "In the little annexe off the hall. But his lordship is down there, and I would really rather not have to excuse myself to him again. He was such a trial last night and nearly as bad this morning."

"Then we'll leave the earl in peace with his bosom friend the wine jug," said the baroness. She turned a little, then saying, "Martha, we are in need of paper, ink and pen. Emma will explain exactly where you might find these things, and you will fetch them and bring them back upstairs to us. If either his lordship the earl or Sir Adrian interrupts you, you will inform them that your mission is urgent and that you have been instructed to hurry."

Having written, the baroness passed the paper to Emeline, the ink still wet and leaving its own thin trail of leakage. First she had written the anonymous boy, child of the whore who had been murdered at the baron's side. Secondly the baroness wrote the name *Edmund Harris*, and Avice, who was now peering over her shoulder, squeaked, "Really, Maman, that's ridiculous."

Emeline waved the small page under her sister's nose. "Why ridiculous? Edmund Harris is Papa's silly secretary, isn't he? Well of course he helped Papa with the negotiations for my dowry when I was still expected to marry Peter, so he met Peter then. He also used to accompany Papa when he went away anywhere. So if Papa went to Gloucester to see that dreadful woman, then Edmund Harris would have known all about that too. Who else could have known about both? But I admit I'm not sure how that makes him an obvious killer."

"Not obvious - no." The baroness shook her head. "But he's an odd creature with very large eyes, and has often made me uncomfortable. Nor can I think of anyone else who could possibly have known where and when your wretched Papa visited Gloucester."

Sysabel frowned. "Who cares about a *secretary*?"

"Murderers have large eyes?"

"I simply find this young man too clever for his own good, and too involved in matters that should not concern him," said her mother. "He was always asking questions, and I mentioned his overzealous curiosity to James a few times. Although James approved him, I must say I never did. The creature has accompanied me on this trip, volunteering his services even though I had no need for a secretary and told him so, though brought him in order to keep an eye on him." She turned suddenly to the far corner and the studiously patient Petronella. "I wondered," she smiled, "whether a very clever young miss might be prepared to take an interest in this young man, and make friends with him."

Petronella stepped forwards and blushed. "If your ladyships says so, then I shall do it of course. But to make friends with a murderer?"

"I don't expect he's anything of the sort," said Emeline. "And Avice, you seem quite prepared to make friends with Papa's secretaries. I have an idea you know Edmund Harris quite well. Perhaps you should get to know him better?"

Avice also blushed. "If you're going to be horrid, Emma -"

Emeline interrupted. "So, now! Does anyone else have a suspicion, even a vague guess, and a name to add to our rather short list?"

"I have a name to add," mumbled Avice, turning away. "But I can't say it aloud."

"Saying it silently," her mother pointed out, "is unlikely to help. Or do you expect us to guess?"

"Names, names," murmured Aunt Elizabeth. "Such tedious things."

"I have a name," said Sysabel, very quietly as if ashamed to admit it. "You see, Uncle Symond, the earl, has a younger brother. Nicholas seems to enjoy his company although Uncle Jerrid's just silly and vulgar and resented the fact that Peter would inherit the title while he'd inherit nothing. Being a wastrel, rather like Nicholas himself," here she smiled apologetically, and continued, "he probably sided with Nicholas against Peter."

The Lady Elizabeth, who had appeared to be dozing, now opened one eye and looked sharply at her niece. But it was the baroness who objected. "Why in heaven's name," she said, "would such a man wish to kill my husband?"

Sysabel shook her head. "I cannot really answer that, my lady. But I have a small theory, if I might suggest it? I do not wish to speak out of place, but I expect it will be no surprise to Emma to hear that Nicholas was always most envious of Peter's skills and position. No doubt Nicholas spoke of this to his Uncle Jerrid, saying he wished Peter would somehow disappear. Thinking to help his favourite nephew, who knows what might have happened? Then you see, on his way to Wrotham after his time sick in London, Nicholas may well have seen and followed the baron. He would have been curious, perhaps, to see him in the back streets of Gloucester, and then discovered him entertaining his mistress. Well, being loyal to Emma he might have felt – and he does have quite a temper as I am well aware myself –"

"Are you suggesting your Uncle Jerrid as the killer," said Emeline suddenly going very white, "or are you actually suggesting my husband?"

Sysabel again shook her head. "I thought perhaps if Nicholas informed Uncle Jerrid, – and then, having committed murder already, killing Peter, you see, believed a second time could endanger his soul no further. Therefore, decided to do Nicholas another favour?"

Avice scowled. "You say Nicholas could have found out on his way back - but this murderous Uncle Jerrid of yours couldn't have known a thing about my Papa. Your uncle was back in Westminster."

"Uncle Jerrid comes and goes," sighed Sysabel, "and being of little importance he has no official position at court and has very small quarters there. He could have travelled back with Nicholas. How would we know?"

Emeline leaned back heavily against the pillows again. "Nicholas has never said very much about him, and has never taken me to meet him. He certainly never told me his Uncle Jerrid was capable of committing murder, especially for such inconsequential motives."

"If it happened, then Nicholas would have known. But he could hardly have admitted it."

"But," Emeline pointed out, "he didn't join us on the road. And Nicholas would never, ever condone such a thing."

"You must certainly remain loyal to your husband," Sysabel murmured.

Emeline bit her lip and turned hurriedly to Avice. "Go on then, Avice. Who is this one mysterious name on your list? Sysabel is - brave enough - to accuse her own uncle, not to mention implicating Nicholas. So you might as well speak out as well."

Avice sniffed, looked around, cuddled her knees a little tighter, stared down, took a deep breath and spoke to no one in particular. "Adrian," she said.

There was a short silence.

Sysabel's blue eyes appeared to brighten. Two little spots of colour shone like rouge in the middle of her cheeks. For a moment she seemed to swell, as though in preparation for something. Then she squeezed her eyes shut, fisted both hands, opened her mouth very wide, and began to squeal. Pitched high like a whistle, at first the sound rose and rose in a thin wail of fury. But then the squeal became a scream. Sysabel beat her fists on the counterpane, and stamped both feet on the ground. At her back the bedpost vibrated and the mattress shook. Both Emeline and Avice seated at the head of the bed, bounced in unison. Everyone stared wordlessly at Sysabel. Both maids backed silently into deeper shadows. Nurse Martha stood, anxious, awaiting orders. Aunt

Elizabeth sighed, muttered something no one could hear, and closed her eyes. Finally the baroness stood, came around the foot of the bed, stood over Sysabel, and abruptly emptied her cup of light ale over the girl's head.

Sysabel seemed not to notice. The thin liquid seeped amongst her blonde curls and formed two twinkling trickles down her face, finally dripping from her chin to soak the neckline of her small busted gown, turning the cream fichu dark. Sysabel continued to scream. So the baroness leaned forwards and slapped her sharply across the cheek.

The girl stopped screaming, looked up, gasped, catching her breath, reached for the fallen cup of ale and threw it directly at Avice. Not a bad aim and too close to miss entirely, the heavy pewter cup clipped Avice on the ear. Avice howled and hurled herself at Sysabel. Emeline caught her rushed offensive, both arms around her sister's waist. Hauled backwards, Avice struggled. Sysabel stood in a hurry, backing quickly from the bed's shadows. Behind her, apple blossom fading, Aunt Elizabeth hiccupped and began faintly to remonstrate. "These young people," she complained to the ceiling beams, "such excitement, such energy."

Martha stood, quickly strode to Sysabel and took her by both shoulders, turning her away from Avice. The baroness stepped forwards again, ignored her tussling daughter and claimed Sysabel from Martha's containment. "This is the most shocking behaviour, young lady," the baroness told her, "and you will never ever again behave this way in my presence." Sysabel sagged, looking down and saying nothing. "I hope that is understood," continued the baroness. "Loyalty to your brother, a disagreement on the facts, an explanation of his certain innocence, all these are the proper response. Indeed, I might have admonished Avice for being so outspoken. But this exhibition of temper helps no one" She looked across at Avice, who had relapsed back against the pillows. "I thought," she said, "you two young things were firm friends."

Avice sniffed and once again cuddled her knees. "We were. We are. But she said nasty things about Nicholas which isn't fair to Emma. And anyway, I used to really - like - Adrian. Now I don't. And I think he could have killed Peter, and Papa, and all sorts of other people if he wanted to. I wouldn't have said so in front of Sissy, but Emma told me to be brave. So I said it."

Aunt Elizabeth opened her eyes and stared bright blue accusation at her niece. "Standards," she said loudly and with unexpected clarity, "are being sadly eroded as we speak." She swept up her train, looping the pale pink damask over her lap as she turned to the baroness. "I apologise, my lady, for such unruly disregard of the proprieties." And back again to Sysabel, "remembering, young woman, that the reputations of the Fryes and Chatwyns, being ancient and noble houses, must never be undermined. And also remembering that you can be carried back to Nottingham within an instant, should I decide you have outstayed your welcome."

"Oh dear," mumbled Emeline. Sysabel had crumpled to the little stool beside the bed, and now sat regaining her breath.

"Then I believe it is time to go downstairs for supper," announced the baroness. "This discussion can be resumed later on, if everyone will stay calm and sensible. Sysabel, you must present your reasons for your brother's innocence, and we will all listen carefully, I promise you. Personally, I do not suspect him at all. It is the common man and the gutter dweller who more usually turn to crime. But we, who need be conscious of our station, must remember decorum. Nor do I have the slightest desire to have his lordship overhear our arguments, and perhaps involve himself. He would not be welcome."

"I shall take my niece to my bedchamber," decided Aunt Elizabeth, reluctantly staggering to her feet. "Help me up, girl," she beckoned to Hilda. "And come with us to help Sysabel rearrange her hair and look respectable for supper." She gazed sadly at the baroness, shaking her head. "A most unfortunate - my niece has a temper, my lady, and can be petulant. Our apologies. The child is still young, and without parents, has pleased herself too long. It troubles Adrian, and I have tried, on his behalf, to curb her tantrums. To no avail. I shall speak firmly to her before we join you in the hall."

The baroness waved her apologies aside. "No matter, no matter, madam. Everyone is hot, bothered and basted, since these are such difficult discussions, and the warm weather sends the blood to the head more quickly. I trust Sysabel will feel better after supper."

Lady Elizabeth's nose twitched, both eyes once again adopting an unexpectedly formidable glint. "Indeed she will, my lady," said Sysabel's aged aunt.

The baroness stood only a moment, the disputed paper crushed between her fingers. She looked at it briefly, nodded, and folded it small. Then she smiled and tucked it into the depths of her cleavage.

It was impossible to discuss anything further over supper. Swelling with suspicion and intrigue, the women glanced, smiled, glowered and indicated with always one eye to the solitary figure of the earl in their midst's.

Much accustomed to being left frequently and entirely alone by all his relatives, his lordship was not offended at having been abandoned all afternoon to sleep in his chair. His fuzz of greying hair had fallen across his face and he had snored gently until abruptly awoken by the clinks and clatter announcing the laying of the great table. He now appeared quite unaware of the unusual undercurrents seething around him. Sysabel, with her aunt unusually close at her side, appeared particularly subdued, her light blue eyes more than normally watery. Avice was also unexpectedly well mannered, attending in silence to the short prayer and then to her platter. Sir Adrian did not join them, and conveyed no excuses, but the earl seemed pleased enough to be surrounded only by women. "Spent my life surrounded by men, you know," he informed the baroness. "Sons, brothers. Been a bachelor for years. Nice to see a pretty face for a change."

"How tragic," sighed the baroness, "to lose your wife so young. Having now lost my husband, I do sympathise, my lord."

"Umm," said the earl. He signalled to the serving boy and pointed cheerfully to the platter of tripe baked in beef dripping and the half empty wine jug. "Should have been off to Spain," he continued. "Chosen specially by the king - emissary - marriage negotiations. The boy spoiled it, you know. Scandal. The king thought it better - well, the mission was a delicate one. Isabella of Castile. His highness aiming to combine his York with the Lancastrian dynasty of course, and stop all that old animosity. Spanish princess is fourteenth in line, you know."

"But the Portuguese Princess Joanna is third in line," nodded the baroness patiently. "So that is the marriage most seriously considered, I believe. And the Portuguese king is eager, and has offered his nephew Manuel for our young Elizabeth, King Edward's eldest daughter. Indeed, we all await the happy conclusion, and a wedding date set."

"Humph," said the earl and took his spoon to his platter.

Emeline nibbled a spiced oat cake, wiped her fingers on her napkin, and attempted to be polite although clearly her thoughts were principally on quite other matters. There were no apple codlings. "Such endless conspiracies," she said, with a brief and poignant glance at her sister. "Nicholas was talking about the line of succession recently. But the Lancastrians have surely stopped expecting to claim back power? After Tewkesbury so many years ago – then King Edward's long peaceful reign. And now King Richard –"

'Nicholas talking?" the earl said, nose reappearing abruptly from his cup. "Wretched boy doesn't know a Lancastrian from a pigeon. Besides, the whole pack is pretty much scattered. There's that traitor De Vere, and a few Nevilles muttering under their breath. But Nicholas should know better. Not that he ever knows better. No right to go disturbing a lady's peaceful nights with fears of bloodshed and battle."

Emeline blinked. "He was only discussing – and it was more a question of marriage – but surely there are many women who are most interested in politics – and some very notable and intelligent ladies –"

"Not a female's natural place, my dear, not at all," and refilled his cup.

"So I shall attempt to confine myself to proper female interests, such as the turquoise silk now awaiting the seamstress in my bedchamber," muttered Emeline with a secret smile. "So many – delightful prospects – awaiting in my bedchamber. Paper and ink, for instance. Lists of – let us say – possibilities. Idle pastimes perhaps, the following of – new paths, and the prospect of just exactly what we ladies intend to do about them. Would that seem proper female behaviour, my lord?"

The baroness sighed, and the earl smiled and said, "No doubt, my dear, no doubt. Sounds most respectable. Turquoise silk? You will look very pretty, I'm sure."

CHAPTER THIRTY TWO

"Never," said the earl earnestly, "been a man to air my shorrowsh, nor bewail my fate. Nor shirk my dutiesh, of coursh." His eyes failed to focus, but it was his daughter-in-law he addressed. "Been around, you know m'dear, and sheen shush dangers and shadnesh. Lived through it all, shtaggered on besht as may. Wife gone. Little babiesh gone. Peter - ah, Peter. The trashedy of it all, and shush a hard burden. I mish him, you know. Shpect you do too."

Emeline sighed. "I cannot claim to miss him, my lord. I barely knew him."

The earl shook his head, though the subsequent vibration spilled the overflowing wine cup which he still grasped. "Thought you did, m'dear. Like him, I mean. Peter shaid - well, no point r'membring now. Marriage. Never eashy. But you'd've been happy - wife, that ish - to my Peter. But you're a good girl, now making do with second besht."

Sitting a little straighter, Emeline looked around desperately for her mother's help. "I am proud, sir," she said, "to be wife to Nicholas."

"Ah. Young Nick." The earl was slipping downwards within the chair, his rump sliding forwards on the polished wood, his legs stretching further out. "Bit of a washtrel, y'know. I tried. Peter tried. No avail. Maybe it wash the businessh of hish mother. Hard to watch little babiesh die of coursh. Hurt him. Never wanted to do mush after that. Jusht making a damn fool of himshelf. Nor never close to me. Not obedient lad. Didn't like hish brother either." The earl sighed, struggling to stay upright. "Envy, y'know. Jealoushy. Competishon. Not unushual with boysh."

Emeline waited, trying to ignore the temptation. Finally, exhaling deeply, she relented. "Why, I wonder," she asked softly, "did Nicholas dislike his brother? I find it hard to believe, my lord, that jealousy motivated that dislike."

The earl managed to drain his cup, spilled a little down his velvets, and hiccupped. "Ah," he said with a conspiratorial nod.

"Peter older. Would've got the lot, y'know. Title. Cashle. Housh. Land." He thought a moment, but could not remember any other specific benefits. "Young Nick, well, into the church pr'apsh. Peter wash the clever one. Had all the girlsh falling at hish feet."

Unable to think of any tactful argument, Emeline turned, looking for escape. The baroness sat at some distance, Avice close at her side. Behind her Petronella stood in timid silence. It was the secretary Edmund Harris who was their sudden interest, summoned to stand before them and clearly taking this as a compliment. "Mister Harris," indicated the baroness with unexpected friendliness, "please sit down." He sat very upright on the most forward edge of his seat, knees together and hands clasped.

"It is, my lady, an honour. I am, I assure you, at your ladyship's service in whatever you might consider. I am experienced and qualified in Latin, scribing, in numeracy, in matters of basic law and justice, and in the keeping of records. I was, I believe, much trusted by his lordship the baron, my lady, and never had cause to believe myself out of favour."

The baroness bestowed a limpid smile. "Indeed, Mister Harris, I am sure that was true. You often travelled with my husband, I believe. You accompanied him on most of his journeys, to London and to Gloucester."

Edmund Harris nodded enthusiastically. "Indeed I did, my lady."

"In which case," continued her ladyship, still benign, "you would have some knowledge of where my husband went and exactly what he did."

Mister Harris began to glimpse his downfall. "That is true, within limits, my lady." He sat a little straighter and wriggled on the very edge of his stool. "Of course, whenever there was business of a personal nature, I was dismissed to walk alone." He frowned with some deliberation. "But never, I assure you, your ladyship, did I accompany the baron on his most private business, nor was privy to his personal affairs. I had no idea - no knowledge at all. I remained at the hostelry until his lordship returned and called for me."

"But," continued the baroness sweetly, "your skills would have been required in the matter of the house - purchasing the property where my husband later - died."

The young man nodded earnestly. "Indeed. That I did, my lady. But without knowledge of its use, I assure you, nor ever went there. I followed orders, and managed the paperwork in accordance with normal practice, and all in the chambers of the city clerk."

"How clever," said Avice, interrupting. "Now, I wonder if you'd remember what it cost, Mister Harris? How sad to know it's destroyed, and all that clever work of yours gone for nothing."

Mister Harris brightened. "Not an expensive property, mistress, but a loss all the same." He blushed slightly. "My hard work was simply part of my regular work, but I thank you for your consideration. Certainly the setting of fire to hide the crime was wicked destruction, and nearly all that alley, so I understand, went up in flames."

Emeline, on the other side of the hall, shifted slightly. The earl was patting her knee. Removing her knee from his vicinity, she looked to her other side where Sysabel sat quietly next to her aunt on the settle beside the long shuttered windows. Neither spoke. Aunt Elizabeth was half asleep and Sysabel, although her embroidery was on her lap and the needle in her hand, stared into space and showed no desire to move.

A sudden blink as the nearby candle flared in the draught. Aunt Elizabeth opened one eye. "Still here, my dear? Good girl. But such a warm evening. I am just a little drowsy, you know."

"Yes aunt." Sysabel stared straight forwards into the small bright flame. Slowly she lifted one finger, short, pale, the nail clipped low and straight. Then she reached forwards as if pointing, and pierced the centre of the light with her finger. The flame shuddered as if in recoil, then blazed anew. Sysabel watched as it crawled around the tip of her finger, licking it in fire. "But isn't it strange," she said very softly, "how much pain one person can bear, if they are obliged to."

The Lady Elizabeth yawned, eyes closed, and resettled. "Pain? Ah yes, my dear. But life is not always kind. Nevertheless, I shall make a point of telling your mother what a good girl you've been."

The flame was growing, lapping as if hungry now it had found food. Sysabel did not remove her finger. She said, "If you wish, aunt. But you may remember that my mother died nine years gone."

"Sweet, warm sleep," murmured Aunt Elizabeth.

Sysabel slowly pushed her finger down, flattening the wick until the candle flame was entirely extinguished and, with a small hiss, the light was gone. She smiled and retrieving her finger, examined it. The skin was dark and blistered all around and the nail had singed, melting a little in one uneven line. There was soft warm wax on the tip. She put it in her mouth, sucking away the pain as if savouring the taste. Finally she murmured, "Sleep sweet? One day, aunt. One day all of us will."

It was in the furthest corner that Nurse Martha sat. She had been knitting. Now the wool lay unattended in her lap. No one else was present in the hall except the hovering page, ready to refill cups. Adrian had left the house shortly after breakfast and had not yet returned.

The earl said, "You'll have shunsh too m'dear, with luck. Carry on the title, do the proper thing. P'rapsh young Nick will grow up in time - take reshponshibility, be the man hish brother would've been."

"Sons? Oh dear," said Emeline. "I think it's time I went to bed."

Although a cluster of candles had been lit, the drifting twilight elongated the angled shadows while, since the shutters had not yet been lifted, the windows echoed the rising star shimmer.

"Ish that late?" His lordship was surprised. "But you young thingsh - all that energy - besht shleep early no doubt."

Emeline was in bed when Avice came to her.

The door was pushed silently open, no creaking hinges or squeak of wood, just a faint breeze and the sudden scramble from corridor to bounce upon the mattress. "I'm running away again," whispered Avice, grabbing at her sister's knees through the bedclothes, "and this time you have to come with me."

Emeline opened her eyes, blinked, and elbowed herself up against the pillows. "Avice, go away."

"That's exactly what I'm going to do," Avice said. "I have an idea. But you have to come too."

Emeline rubbed her eyes. "For goodness sake, I'm at home. What am I supposed to run away from? We aren't prisoners, Avice. Are you mad?"

"Run away from what *might* happen. From mother. From the earl. From being watched. But it's what I want to run *to* that matters. Don't you see? Mother thinks Father's killer is some silly little boy, or that poor pickle brained secretary who's all so proud because he thinks mother likes him at last. Actually I think he thinks *I* like him too, and I used to but I don't know. He's prissy and cabbage eyed. Besides, I don't imagine he's capable of killing anyone unless he sticks his quill down their throats and drowns them in ink. But there's worse than that, because Sissy secretly thinks it was Nicholas and his uncle together who killed everyone. And I wouldn't be surprised if the horrid earl thinks it was Nicholas too."

"Oh, pooh."

"But I *know* who it was. And he's gone off. He keeps going off somewhere. I think he's trying to find Nicholas, and kill him too."

"Adrian?" Emeline felt suddenly cold.

"Of course." Avice lowered her voice. "Don't you realise, Adrian is the Chatwyn heir after Nicholas. First Peter is got safely out of the way before he could marry you. Then when the fire after your wedding didn't work, probably Adrian meant to wait so as not to look too suspicious. But now he knows you like your husband after all, so he has to act quickly before there are any children to push him out of line."

"Avice," Emeline muttered in threatening undertones, "you're the one who's pickle brained. Adrian is a respectable if stuffy young man and look how protective he is of his sister. And remember how he came all the way down from Nottingham when I wrote saying I was worried Nicholas hadn't retuned, and might be dying of the pestilence."

"Exactly," said Avice, wide eyed. "He was hoping to find Nicholas dead of disease - most convenient - contagion doing the job for him. But he ordered Sissy to stay behind - didn't want her in the way even though coming to see you would have made it more proper to bring her. He didn't want her here either, and was really cross when he saw her - well, murder gets harder if your sister is watching."

"So why leave her here then, instead of carrying her straight back to Nottingham?"

"Because," said Avice gleefully. "now he's too busy rushing off to do the deed."

"Visiting friends. Business. Trade. He's entitled to make a little money on the side, isn't he?"

"But he never does. He's not well off," Avice pointed out. "They live off that old aunt's money according to what Sissy said while we were away. So he's after the Chatwyn inheritance and quickly needs to take advantage of Nicholas travelling alone somewhere."

"Nicholas isn't alone. He has armed guards."

"Probably Adrian won't know that. He's too busy thinking of himself, and Sissy and getting enough money for an easy life and the castle and a decent dowry for Sissy too - otherwise she's nobody and no one important will marry her. But even if he does have to face armed guards, he can always ask Nicholas to walk off alone with him somewhere. I mean, Nicholas wouldn't suspect him, would he?"

Emeline took a deep breath. "Even if you were right, which you're not, why on earth would he murder Papa?"

"Perhaps because," here Avice paused, lowered her voice further, leaned over and mumbled, "Papa found out and Adrian had to stop him telling anyone. Or perhaps he just disapproved since he is stuffy, and he found Papa with a whore and got angry."

"He disapproves of adultery but he cheerfully approves of murder?"

"Well." Avice chewed her lip. "Alright, either Papa found out he'd killed Peter, and had to be kept quiet. Or perhaps with Papa dead, Adrian thought we'd be rich, and he could marry me."

"Avice, you're far too fond of thinking people want to marry you."

"They will if I'm rich. But I have to admit I'm not sure about why he killed Papa. Perhaps it was someone else and Nicholas is wrong about it being the same person." Avice leaned suddenly forwards again, one quivering finger to her lips. "Besides, there's more. Sissy told me other things too. Did you guess - well I expect you didn't. But she was doing it with Peter."

"Doing what?" gulped Emeline.

"You know what I mean. Beds. Kissing. What men do with their wives, only she was barely thirteen the first time. That was a year and a half ago and Peter was nearly thirty when he died. I think that's horrid. I mean, I did kiss that silly Edmund Harris when I was thirteen, but he didn't even want me to." Avice crouched lower as her sister stared back at her. "But that gives Adrian another reason for killing Peter. And I think it got worse. Maybe if I was Sissy's brother, I would have killed Peter too."

"Tell me. But keep your voice down," urgently, "or Maman will hear."

It was the next bedchamber where the baroness stepped out of her gown. The thick brocade was scooped up by Martha, who shook out the creases ready to hang on one of the garderobe pegs. The baroness sat on the bed, pulled up her shift and began to untie her garters, carefully rolling down her fine blue stockings. She pointed a bare toe, regarding a still neat foot. "I am not old, you know, Martha," she said softly. "James should have had a different wife - perhaps a little older - more sedate. Docile!"

"My lady." Martha pulled back the covers. Then she saw the small folded paper which had fallen as her mistress was unclothed. Martha bent and picked it up.

Her ladyship crawled quickly into bed. "My girls, on the other hand," she informed the pillows, "are positively infantile. Clearly James carried a streak of ill balance and an inferior bloodline. I can no longer guess what either of my daughters might do next."

Martha sat on the edge of the bed and began to unpin her baroness's headdress. She paused a moment. Finally she said, "Speaking of young ladies, I had wondered, and thought of saying something, my lady. But perhaps it is better left unsaid."

"Which one?" demanded the baroness.

Martha sat back with a handful of golden tipped hairpins. "Our young ladies are without blame and I speak no word against them, madam. There was something else, something I noticed this evening, which reminded me of the fire which devastated the castle after the Lady Emeline's wedding, and which might have caused both her death and that of her husband."

There was a sudden rustle of linen and feathers and the baroness sat up in alarm. "Tell me, Martha."

Martha shook her head. "Just wondering, my lady, and thinking that perhaps we have not considered the possibility of another culprit. I happened to notice Mistress Sysabel playing with – a candle flame. An unusual game for an innocent young lady, I believe."

The baroness again collapsed against the pillows. "The silly miss adored Peter. Why would she kill the boy?"

"They say she has a temper, my lady. And perhaps – just perhaps – there could have been a reason which she now wishes to hide."

"The girl is too foolish to hide anything. And if you mean she was having an illicit affair, which no doubt that supercilious young man was wicked enough to encourage, then she has hidden nothing, for I already guessed some time ago. But all the more reason not to slaughter the lover."

"But if he meant to cast her off once affianced to our young Mistress Emeline? Or worse, my lady, if the affair had results which needed the young gentleman's immediate offer of marriage but which he denied?" The baroness paused, considering. Martha nodded and continued, "You may guess my meaning, my lady. Illicit affairs can often have consequences most terrible for the poor girl, but often quite easy for the gentleman to deny and to escape. Such a situation might leave the girl – let us say – both desperate and – infuriated."

"Young ladies don't commit murder, Martha," declared the baroness. "And more importantly, Sysabel had neither motive nor opportunity to divest the world of my husband." She looked around a moment, as if expecting something to leap from the shadows. Then she lowered her voice. "You have the list safe, Martha? Good. But there was a name I could not possibly be seen to add to that list."

Martha held out the scrap of paper. "Shall I add it myself, my lady?" But the baroness shook her head.

"It needs no ink, and is no doubt quite nonsensical. But I have wondered, you know, just sometimes, why young Nicholas tries so hard to appear unnecessarily stupid, and such a terrible coward, when he is undoubtedly neither. Odd, don't you think, Martha?"

Martha had lifted the little pewter candle holder, ready to snuff the last little light. "I had noted it, my lady," she said quietly. And she blew out the flame.

CHAPTER THIRTY THREE

Nicholas rode south, crossing the Bridge moments before the gates were locked for the night. The sunny afternoon had turned to a mild evening and late shopping, the delights of the taverns, cock fights, markets and the Southwark Bear Pit, left folk hurrying home in both directions. Insignificant and unseen amongst the crowds, His mount, unlike the proud liard he usually rode, was a knock kneed but docile mare with a sweet nature, a shabby coat and a wispy tail trailing, bedraggled. The crowds elbowed, thickening as the gatekeeper began to rattle his keys. Nicholas leaned over and patted the horse's warm neck. "Cheer up, Bessie," he said softly. "We'll soon be out in the countryside, and you can show these lumbering oxen your heels."

A little behind him Harry muttered, "Leaving London, that's the biggest mistake. 'Tis only fools what leaves the big city and takes off for them windy skies."

"Least you can see what's coming in them open places," Rob pointed out from the back of an overweight and lumbering sumpter. "Which is more than can be said for them bloody Southwark alleys."

David Witton had been keeping an eye on Wolt and the baggage but now rode up close to his master's side, silently dismissing Robert and Henry Bambrigg to oblivion. His own remarks were heard only by Nicholas. "We'll be remembered by nobody here, that's for sure, my lord. A company of ill dressed clods on horses fit for little more than the Shamble's butchers, trudging out of town as dusk falls. But which hostelry do we choose to stay overnight, sir? The Southwark inns are a vile lot, but if we stop at one of the better houses then we'll pay considerably more than could be expected of folk such as us, and will look out of place."

"Too nice, are you David, to stay in a slum for a night?" Nicholas smiled. "I seem to remember us staying often enough in your tenement room when I had reason to keep out of sight. Is that so much better than the Southwark taverns?"

"But it was my own, my lord, and could be kept clean. In Southwark there's more fleas than whores, and more whores than cutpurses."

Wolt, shuffling behind them all, led the baggage horse but preferred the use of his own feet. His first very short acquaintanceship with the great city of London had not impressed, but at least he was pleasantly surprised by the Bridge. In Gloucestershire he had seen several bridges but they were small wooden planked affairs which swayed when crossed, but at least were so short they could be run over in half a breath. The bridge of London, however, was made of soaring stone and sat on nineteen mighty pillars. It did not sway, it carried great hosts of people and animals all at the same time, and was so rich with houses and shops that you could barely see past them to the river below. The river could, of course, be smelled, so one knew it was very much there. Now beneath the massive iron portcullis, below the spikes for traitors' heads above the gate, the small party crossed the bridge into Southwark and immediately quickened pace.

The inn was not one of those along the main route which travellers had long taken on pilgrimage to Canterbury. Nicholas had chosen a small bustling hostelry in a shadowed alley where the customers were still drinking heavily long after dark. Jerrid Chatwyn was waiting for Nicholas, sitting back against the wall, legs spread over one of the pallets, cup in hand. He waved to the larger stool. "There's beer, and there's cold pork, black bread and cheese. Help yourself, my boy. Tuck in, all of you. But I've already helped myself to the two best blankets."

"Knowing, of course," grinned Nicholas, tossing his small bundle to another of the pallets, "that the biggest lice, fleas and spiders always nest in the best blankets."

"I shall squash the lot," replied his uncle, "as I snore my way to dreams of soft white arms, heaving breasts and a sweet plump mouth searching for mine." He nodded to David, but eyed the other three with amusement. "Been exploring the rubbish tips again, Nick my boy?"

Wolt muttered into his shirt collar, "I ain't no raker's snotboy, I's respektibal."

Rob, however, was not offended. "My tenement's bin called worse afore now," he said. "But we seen his lordship proper looked after when he come there sick as a castrated cockerel with the pestilence."

Leaving the confines of Southwark the next morning as the dawn hesitated behind the black silhouetted treetops, a slow lime wash of creamy pastels splashed with gold, the small party headed across open scrub and fields to the winding lanes, the little chilly streams and the stretching haze of southern England. Skirting townships, they took the narrower paths then left the roads completely and took the horses through farmland onto paths barely scratched in the earth and under the fluttering shade of the woodlands. Eventually it was a bluster of coastal wind that brought them the perfumes of stinging brine and the tang of the sea. A meadow lark was singing, but in the distance were the high wild calls of the gulls.

Nicholas smiled. "We are nearly there. Do we sleep here in the open tonight, and keep watch? The grass is dry and the stench of the fields is behind us." He dismounted, pulling out a well wrapped parcel from his saddle bags. The previous night's wayside inn had supplied a simple supper packed for the morrow, and now they sat under the trees to eat.

"I've no objection to a well fertilised field," Jerrid said, clamping a wedge of cold bacon between two slabs of dark bread. "Manure in, manure out. And it's manure we're chasing, far as I can tell."

"I doubt the good marquess would be pleased to hear your description of him, uncle." Nicholas grinned, drinking his wine straight from the leather sack. "Urswick, on the other hand, can presumably be described no other way."

"A turd amongst turds," nodded Jerrid. "How pleased I'll be to meet him again."

"If we manage to intercept him," David said. "Remembering he's evaded us more than once before."

Nicholas, his uncle and David Witton lounged, talking softly together as the sun sank low. "Christopher Urswick, a good Lancastrian chaplain, and loyal to his lord and that lord's mother," Nicholas sighed. "Yes, I've met him before. He loathes me, of course."

"Fears you."

Nicholas smiled back at his uncle. "Perhaps. Since his loyalties make him our enemy."

"Because his loyalties lie with that young fool Henry Tudor. Or more particularly to his lady mother who inspires such loyalty. She's indomitable. Her servants adore her."

"Loyalties are never simple," murmured Nicholas.

David looked up suddenly and frowned. "Loyalty is never so complicated, my lord, being my lifelong cape and my chosen armour. Loyalty first to God, then to the anointed king, and then to my master. I know where my loyalties lie, and I sleep well because of it."

"Which is why I call you friend," Nicholas smiled. "But remember this, if Urswick has the sense I think he has, that wretched letter he carried will already have been passed on to the messenger entrusted to deliver it in the north. So we are looking for strangers, furtive or belligerent, and not the good chaplain himself."

A little apart, Rob and Harry leaned against the ant infested bark behind them. The conversation they now heard was the first explanation they had been given of where they were going, and why. Rob looked up and said, "This be for our ears too, is it m'lord? There's folks to be killed or captured prisoner?"

"Which is precisely what you're here for," Nicholas said. "Since I have no clear idea of their numbers. Crossing in secret from France, they'll not be many. But once here, we could be looking for one man, or ten."

"No matter the numbers, m'lord," grinned Harry. "If that's the job, then I'm ready. My line, you might say."

Nicholas shook his head. "It's the king's business we're on, and no rout. If there's a fight, I want no wanton slaughter."

Jerrid spoke softly, as though reciting old stories. "Urswick's no fool, and nor is the woman who rules him. We're speaking of a man originally sent to Flanders with money and secret messages from Tudor's mother, who evaded all our royal guards, spies and envoys, and got himself right where he wished and into the hands of John Morton, the hypocrite of Ely. Urswick came backwards and forwards a few times it seems, and always without us knowing until afterwards. Then he was the wretch who somehow warned Tudor when Brittany's duke was about to take him under house arrest. Morton sent out the alert, Urswick carried the news, and Tudor got away to France. That Tudor's now in French favour with enough plots up his arse to turn turds into custard, is largely thanks to Mister Urswick."

"So it's this Urswick you're after?" Harry rubbed his nose. "Ain't never heard of him. And this Tudor - not rightly heard of him neither."

"Once of no account whatsoever," Nicholas answered, "now, with French backing, he is fast becoming a dangerous man."

"But it's the mother supplied the ambition," added Jerrid.

"Urswick, on the other hand," Nicholas continued, "is simply a messenger, who will pass his responsibility onto another messenger. We have reliable information that he's bringing with him a letter from Henry Tudor addressed to the Earl of Northumberland. This is, somewhat incongruously, a request from Tudor to marry with one of the Herbert girls, who are the earl's sisters-in-law."

"We're here just to stop a bloody wedding?" demanded Rob, aggrieved.

"A little more than that." Nicholas smiled as he helped himself to bread and cheese. "His highness finds it highly suspicious that an exile and enemy feels it both safe and advantageous to himself to approach one of England's senior nobility on a private matter such as this. Seemingly he expects Northumberland to back him in making a good marriage, in spite of having neither home nor title to offer a bride. Certainly Urswick would be an interesting guest should we manage to intercept and take him. But it's just how friendly and involved the Earl of Northumberland has become with Henry Tudor that is of far greater importance."

"Northumberland. I've heard of *him*." Harry was pleased.

Wolt, sitting alone, had heard of none of them, but smiled, assured of companionship. "Loyalty," he mumbled to himself. "Traitors. Kings. Grand lords and foreign countries. Me Ma'd be proud, I reckon."

The sun was setting behind the trees with a smudge of pink beyond the clouds, and a sudden streak of vermillion. The horses were loosely tethered and grazing as each man kicked out a place to lay his saddle blanket and lie warm wrapped in cloak and shaded by leaf. But they still talked as twilight hooded the treetops and the darkness folded them into greater secrecy.

Nicholas lay on his back, staring up into the first hint of star flicker. He clasped his hands behind his head, murmuring into the growing darkness. "Then there is a different matter entirely, involving someone else you have all surely heard of," he said. "The Marquess of Dorset is being held hostage in France after having once attempted escape. It's his own damn fault he's there in the first place, but some months ago his mother recalled him, having finally made peace with King Richard."

Even Wolt had heard of the king. Pleasantly stuffed with bread, cheese, bacon and light ale, he put his thumb in his mouth and closed his eyes.

The gentle hum or voices reverberated as the night deepened. The wind was shuffling in the trees. "The wind murmurs and moans along the shore," Jerrid said, curling tight beneath his thin blanket and thicker cloak. "But tomorrow may bring danger. Or it will bring a small boat and Dorset the passenger, if he and we are lucky."

Harry thought a moment. "Dorset's mother was the queen," he decided.

"Until her marriage was discovered bigamous."

"When she flounced into sanctuary."

"But," Nicholas said, "last year the lady was told something in secret concerning her younger sons, the king's sons declared illegitimate but who then disappeared. Some thought them dead."

Jerrid laughed, half smothered within his cloak. "When their mother was told differently, she immediately tried to persuade her various relatives to leave the ignominious Tudor camp and return to King Richard's court. Dorset obediently attempted exactly that, but was betrayed, captured on the French borders and taken back into French custody. Another of Urswick's fingers in the pies of conspiracy."

Rob was interested. "And this so called differently, what the lady were told, m'lord? And what would it be, that secret, then?"

"That secret remains a secret, my friend, and I have no intentions of telling you about it," Nicholas answered softly. "It is a matter at present too dangerous, and the lives of others would be at much risk. Eventually it will all become known, though not yet. But now we have word that Dorset will make another attempt to escape back to England. And so we are here for two men. One is a tentative friend, the other a committed enemy."

"Dorset was an enemy but now he ain't," muttered Rob from the shadows beside his brother. "This bugger Urswick weren't no enemy but now he is."

"We'll have to try not to kill the wrong one, then," grinned Harry.

Jerrid laughed. "Changing sides according to one's temporary benefit, one's temper, one's sudden hopes or sudden affronts, well that's the English way it seems. There's half the English nobility have made their fortunes and their titles by changing sides every few years. Loyalty? That can change too, with a little bribery or a few threats, real or imagined."

By the following morning, a thick fog had rolled in from the sea. The little village of Lympne was swathed in low cloud and even the church steeple could not find its way to heaven. No welcome for men choosing to sleep out of doors, it was therefore within the tiny local tavern's half timbered attic that Nicholas slept that night, disturbed by fractious dreams and his companions' snoring. So it was to a moonless and clammy mist that he woke dry mouthed, and set off downstairs to find a jug of ale and clear his head.

It was simply luck. But luck can rule the world.

Four men were leaving the stables, leading their mounts and slipping out under cover of night in a fog that obscured the stars. Sheltered by the doorway, Nicholas watched, suspicious. Only one voice, blurred by distance and caution, muttered, "We've an hour, no more, before the tide changes. So move yourselves or we'll miss him."

Within minutes Nicholas shook his uncle awake. "I must remember to thank my wife," he said, pulling on his cape, gloves and baldric. "She disturbed my dreams and sent me downstairs at the perfect moment to hear what I believe is the answer we've been waiting for. Up, all of you. We've an appointment on the coast, and very little time."

"Our hopeful Marquess arriving after all?"

Nicholas shook his head. "No. If Dorset arrives at all, then once on English soil there's no one meeting him except ourselves. What I overheard were four furtive ruffians expecting a secret arrival under cover of dark. It's Urswick I hope to meet now."

Half a mile beyond the cottages and lanes, Nicholas called halt on the scrubby cliff edge before trudging the downward path to the gravel banks below. The party had dismounted, ready to lead their horses, careful of rock fall or the slip of mud beneath tired hooves. And more insidious now; the risk of missing a boat out at sea, unseen in the gloom of rolling damp.

But then over the sounds of the sea Nicholas heard at once the breathing and the fumble of waiting men. He turned, pivoting, calling to alert his companions, his long knife immediately in his hand well before the first man reached him. They came out of the mist, a sudden dash from the bush tangled undergrowth. Three men, three knives, three pairs of muscled arms, boots kicking and the tearing of fustian on brambles. But they were three men outnumbered, since Nicholas led a group of five, not counting, as he did not count, the boy Wolt who was quickly out of sight beneath the trees.

The attackers used ambush and surprise. Forced backwards with a knife thrust into his eyes, stumbling, rebounding, Nicholas smashed the blade away with his own. His arm bent back by a man less tall but twice as wide, Nicholas gave ground, immediately grasping the second knife hidden within his belt, jabbing it to the back of his assailant's neck. The man lurched, staggering as the knife ripped down and along his shoulder blade. Then David took him from behind.

Two more ran at Jerrid, Rob and Harry. Nicholas yelled, "It's a diversion. Finish them - quick."

Jerrid, laughing, yelled, "No more scars please, Nick m'boy. I'll slaughter this bastard first, then come help with yours."

Nicholas swerved, one leg forwards to dislodge and trip, feet dancing, slipping over the grassy hollows, yelling back, "I've no need of you. See to your own."

The clash of steel on steel, and Harry shouting, "Filthy scut, dare cut my brother and I'll shove your scrotum up your arse," Then, "Come on, Rob. Can't we throw the bugger off the cliffs?"

Only moments later Nicholas and Jerrid, panting hard, looked down at the two sprawled and bloody corpses. The third, although wounded, had finally sliced at Jerrid's thigh, wrong footed him, then thrown down his knife and run. Harry had started to follow, then saw his brother injured and hurried back.

"This was a diversion." Nicholas wiped his knife on one of the fallen men's backs. "We were five strong men, young, and dressed much as these wretches were themselves. Not worth robbing nor the risk of three against five. So! Why attack?"

"But you told me four men left the tavern stables for the coast." Jerrid pulled out his kerchief and roughly staunched the bleeding from his thigh. "So a diversion, but a strange one."

Nicholas kicked over the body of the dead man at his feet, rolling him face up. He proceeded to rummage through the man's clothes within the rough tunic, shirt and boots, feeling for packages, but found nothing hidden. Then he nodded to Harry. "Give a good look to the other," he said. "Perhaps I've no cause for suspicion, but I'm suspicious all the same. Now I regret not having chased down the wretch that fled."

"If these were Urswick's men," said Jerrid, "they'd have avoided us, not purposefully drawn our attention."

Nicholas shook his head. "No. They knew exactly who we were, and these three risked their lives, planning to hold us up while the fourth man galloped away either to meet the boat, or already with Urswick's letter safe inside his shirt." He marched over to where Wolt shivered in the shadows, dutifully clutching the tethers of the horses. Nicholas took his horse's reins, leading it back to where Jerrid still sprawled on the grass. "You can't ride yet, uncle, but I can. David, come with me. I know the direction, and even in this murk I can follow a speeding horse and hear it too."

"And what if Urswick's boat hasn't anchored yet?"

"Keep a watch on the cliff top until I get back." Nicholas swung his leg to the stirrup and mounted. "Urswick would recognise me, so if the boat comes while I'm away, you're better without me." He looked down at his uncle. "That's a nasty gash on your leg, sir, and needs cauterizing."

"It needs nothing of the kind," snorted Jerrid. No more than a scratch. You'll have no rival for your own scars, my boy. Get off, then, and follow your suspicions. Harry, Rob and I will stay and watch the coast."

His horse was not bred for speed, but it was strong and dogged over rough terrain. Nicholas knew exactly the path a man would take for the north, and eventually Northumberland. And he knew where to cut across the fields, and head the other man off. Within moments he had outpaced David, and was gone from both sight and sound.

CHAPTER THIRTY FOUR

While waiting for Avice and Martha to accompany them into London, Emeline walked with Sysabel, silently remembering another rendezvous in the same place, love making in the rain, and willow shaded passion. They skirted the herb plot with its perfumes of sweet thyme, and followed the clipped hedges down to the placid swell of the Thames. No pier stood close to the house, and no wherries crossed at that point, so no splash of busy oars interrupted them. Only a swan, dipping, fishing and resurfacing caused eddies amongst the little bubbles of escaping fish. The brown waters were patterned with floating debris but this was too far upriver for the raker's tipped deposits, or the wail of hunting gulls. Emeline gazed out to the far bank.

"I'm sorry we upset you yesterday, Sissy, talking of Adrian that way," sighed Emeline. "It must be particularly hard for you to talk about, since I imagine you miss Peter very much."

Sysabel stared down at her toes. "I do," she said. "It's kind of you – most understanding – even though you must feel the same about him yourself."

"Although Papa's death was hurtful, I can't claim to miss him." Emeline shook her head. "Peter's death was equally evil of course, but I never really knew him well."

"You did," blinked Sysabel. She looked up but paused, staring at her companion. "That is, forgive me, I don't mean to be rude. But being affianced –"

"We never were." Emeline began walking slowly back towards the house. "The negotiations were never finalised. Of course, I thought him handsome and charming, but we met only a few times. Perhaps I was a little infatuated, but that was only a juvenile dream. Now I'm married to a man I love."

"I see." Sysabel sniffed. "So you think my dreams are juvenile."

With a deep breath, "No, Sissy dear, I understand from Avice that you went far beyond the juvenile. Should I not mention it? But we are all friends together, and I would never criticise. Nor will I ever tell my mother or your aunt."

The tears which Sysabel had been resisting now overflowed. "As long as you say nothing," she whispered, "perhaps it's a relief. And I know about you too, because Peter told me, so you've no need to try and hide it from me. I shall tell no one of course, not even Avice if you prefer. But Peter explained everything. Was that disloyal of him? But you see, we were so very much in love. He was resisting his father's attempts to make him marry you. He always promised to marry me, and had already written to the Vatican for a dispensation, since we are cousins." She gulped. "When he died - it was the end of my world."

Emeline stiffened. "Peter told you he'd *bedded* me?"

"He told me everything - always," Sysabel murmured. "He felt so terribly guilty about such unfaithfulness, but he said - well, I'll say no more."

"Perhaps," suggested Emeline with controlled fury, "he told you I had encouraged him and he couldn't resist or it would have been rude? In fact, he probably told you I undressed and then jumped on top of him?"

"I'm glad you don't mind admitting it," Sysabel said shyly. "We shouldn't have secrets between us, you and me and Avice. We need to support each other in such terrible times."

"I'll go and see if Avice is ready yet," Emeline said in a hurry. "It's too - well, we'll talk about this again later."

It was back in the bedchamber and the sun glazed window looked out on the paths where Emeline had recently walked and talked with Sysabel. Now gazing crossly at her sister, Emeline said. "Aren't you even properly dressed yet? I need to get out. I need to walk, very fast, and I hope it rains."

"I'm not ready because it's still early," complained Avice. "So what did the silly girl say to upset you?"

"She admitted what she'd done. Then she told me what Peter told her about me - and it's *disgusting*. So I told the stupid girl that Peter was a liar and a cheat. She didn't believe me."

"You should have slapped her."

"I wish I could have slapped Peter."

Avice giggled. "Then she'd think *you* probably killed him."

"I'm beginning to wish I had." Emeline, arms crossed tight, was hugging herself and feeling more than usually self protective. "Nicholas hinted - told me a few things - about Peter and the lies he used to tell. And you know his awful scar. That was an arrow at really close range, and Peter did it on purpose."

"No point getting all upset with Peter now," sniffed Avice. "After all, at the time you *did* think you were in love with him, and you used to talk on and on about him as if he ought to be sainted, just like silly Sissy does. If Nicholas had told you about the arrow back then, you'd have believed Peter too, and thought it was Nicholas who was lying. And when Peter died - well -"

Emeline slumped, dejected. "And now I despise myself so much. But I was young and horribly ignorant, and flattered by his attention. I believed every stupid word he said, and he said lots."

"But presumably," Avice, having already dismissed Petronella's dutiful attentions, was attempting to do her own hair, "he never told you he got his baby cousin pregnant and had to arrange to get rid of the baby in secret in some horrid back street? But you should find out if Sissy told Adrian."

"Because if Adrian knew, then he'd have killed Peter?" Emeline pushed Avice onto the little stool in front of the garderobe mirror, and helped with the hairpins. "For that and the inheritance too? And then perhaps - so disgusted with Peter's immorality - and then discovering Papa - but isn't it all very, very farfetched?"

"Adrian didn't come back last night. His precious sister he cares so much about is here, but he's disappeared."

"So of course he's off murdering four or five other people?"

"You'd better hope not," said Avice. "Since your Nicholas is certainly next on his list."

St. Paul's Cathedral, the Eastminster, was only a short walk from the city gate and could hardly be missed even by those who were not familiar with London's interweaving streets. The massive wooden steeple brushed the clouds and its echoing bell called the city's faithful to their morning prayers. Martha walked ahead beside Emeline, Avice and Sysabel followed through the crowds. Petronella, awed, crept behind, curtsying reverentially to the alabaster saints within and the shadow of the high altar beyond.

The noise increased. As the priest spoke, so did a multitude of others. A young lawyer was conducting business below a mural of the banishing of the moneylenders from the temple, and a young woman to the left of the great nave was selling stitched crosses for the vastly exaggerated price of a penny each. Two beggars wearing their Tom o' Bedlam badges sat in a side chapel, hands outstretched.

They stayed only for Mass, then tumbled out into Watling Street and the pale sunshine, giggling and catching at each other's ribbons as they chased down the great stone steps. Martha smiled attempting to restore only a semblance of order. "Young ladies," she murmured, "need fresh air and a brisk walk before the temptations of a well laden table. Petronella, you will keep up, and carry the basket. Stop looking behind towards the Ludgate for we are not leaving the city yet."

Avice passed the empty basket to her maid. "Are we keeping you from young Edmund Harris, Nell, or is there something else you want to rush home for?"

Petronella blushed. "Forgive me, mistress. But it's London, and all the wickedness my mother warned me about. Never go to the big city, she always said, for there's more wicked blasphemy and sin in every street than you'll see in the rest of England."

Martha patted the maid's hand. "Stuff and nonsense, girl. This is a city of kings, of wealth, of justice and government, of piety, and of the best shopping in the world. I have not been here since I was a young girl, and their ladyships have never been here at all. You we will therefore set off for a pleasantly informative stroll."

But it was in the gloom of the back alleys that Sysabel suddenly stopped and refused to go any further.

A light drizzle hovered between roofs and cobbles but the sun sparkled on the wet tiles and the rows of little windows reflecting rainbow prisms. But one small alley led off the other street, and just visible from where Sysabel stood, a ragged opening gaped between the neighbouring buildings. Beams stood blackened and stark amongst the uncleared rubble.

Emeline had seen such destruction before, though over an even greater and more devastating area, and she stopped behind Sysabel, also staring. Martha stepped forwards, nodding, and reaching for Emeline's hand. "No dear, no need to walk here. There are often fires, they say, with cooking in cramped quarters and no proper kitchens in the smaller houses. And all fire spreads quickly."

"There's no smell here anymore," whispered Emeline. "It was the smell of the fire I hated most of all."

Martha looked suddenly towards Sysabel. "No smell here, my dear, since I imagine this fire was put out - a year ago. Folk here are poor and cannot afford to rebuild. But the fire is old. Perhaps - ten months gone?"

But Sysabel clenched her small hands and said, "You brought me here on purpose."

"Who? Why?" insisted Avice, pushing at Emeline from behind. "Oh, do come on. There is not a shop in sight. It's silk and velvet and gold I want to see. This place is quite horrid and if there was a fire, then it's just as well."

"It was there," Sysabel said, her voice louder and more desperate. "I won't go there. I won't walk past."

Martha pulled Petronella aside, and waited a moment as if expecting something. Then she said, "The fire was long ago, and the house is now quite gone. We don't need to go past."

Avice mumbled, "What's the matter with you Sissy? What's where?"

But Emeline said suddenly, "So near to St. Paul's?"

Sysabel was crying. "I remember that horrid little hovel on the corner there, with the church across the other side and the graveyard spread just behind. It was because - knowing what was going to happen - and seeing the gravestones - it has stayed so strongly in my memory. Then I had to walk past and I was crying so hard I didn't see much more." She didn't seem to realise she was crying again now.

"Lord have mercy," whispered Emeline. She reached out but Sysabel suddenly turned and ran. Martha stepped between as the sun sprang through the clouds, lighting the alleyway as if sudden torchlight blazed between the houses.

Sysabel stopped and flung herself into Martha's arms. She wailed, "It's there, it's there," and buried her face against Martha's shoulder, crying uncontrollably.

Emeline mumbled in desperation, "We can't appear in public like this. What shall we do?"

"We go home, my dear," Martha said. "And as quickly as possible."

Having doubled back into Carter's Lane and from there to St. Andrew's Hill, they now stood a little west of the great cathedral. It was a narrow alley divided by a central gulley with sour water overflowing in sloppy leaking trickles. On both sides the houses stood uncertain, as though tentatively upright and held in place only by their neighbours. Here, against London ordinance, most of the roofs were still thin thatched, and the water butts standing at the doorways were mostly broken, their copper rings fallen away. It was a place of rank smells and dismal darkness for the sky seemed little more than a pale streak between leaning rooftops and jutting buttresses. The black charred threat of old fire hung unrepaired and barely disturbed where a row of six houses had been gutted, leaving little more than stark timbers without plaster and a tumble of sticks fallen from unsupported beams.

No longer trying to run, Sysabel was cowering, refusing to move in any direction and pointed one quivering finger. Avice understood, glared, and said, "*Here*? Peter brought you here himself?"

"Oh no." Sysabel twisted from Martha's embrace, reaching tentatively for Emeline. "It was a young man in his employ, but I don't remember his name and I never saw him again."

"Peter sent you with a *servant*?"

"Poor Peter, he could hardly have brought me himself. What if someone had seen us? He was so sad, and so contrite. And I was - terrified."

"But is it the same house that has gone in the fire? Five - no six houses ruined." Now Emeline held Sysabel tight. "Sissy dear, those dreadful memories must be forgotten, for half the street has burned with them."

Sysabel remained white faced, trembling within Emeline's embrace. "I shall never forget," she said. "It is not a thing anyone - could - forget."

They took her home. The streets had emptied, and the Ludgate was quiet. There were no raucous groups staggering off to the taverns, no dismal plodding sheep down from St; John's pastures heading towards their slaughter in the Shambles, no more bustling housewives off to the cheaps and markets. A desultory stream were returning from St. Paul's, clutching their prayer books, and a few young men were out courting in the sunshine, hailing wherries for a pleasant river crossing and an inexpensive way to impress a girl on her one morning away from her mistress's watchful criticisms. The Strand was dozing and even the birds were quiet. They entered the Chatwyn House through the back way past the stable block and Martha, nodding quickly to Emeline, whispered to Petronella to take Sysabel straight to her bedchamber.

They were interrupted. "Well now," roared his lordship, into the echoing silence, "a fine time it is for dinner and a little pleasant company." Suddenly aware that his niece was looking less spritely than usual, he reached out to pat her arm. "What is it, miss, with the long face on such a fine day? Is no one ready to keep me company at the table?"

Sysabel stood very still, pink faced and red eyes, and attempted a mumbled apology. Emeline said quickly, "Your niece is not feeling very well, my lord. I think it best if I take her up to her bedchamber. She needs to rest."

"Sick?" demanded the earl, disappointed. "Not that I'm sure what she's doing here in the first place. First Nicholas disappears like the pesky dunce he is, then young Adrian takes himself off without a by your leave, and now this silly chit gets herself into a miff. What is it then? One of those ridiculous feminine complaints?" His voice swelled as though fuelled by the silence.

"Very sick," Sysabel muttered, hurrying for the stairs.

"Better call your Maman," sighed the earl, shaking his head at Emeline. "Wretched women and their wretched problems. I can't deal with such nonsense."

Sysabel gazed up at her uncle. Quite suddenly her expression of tremulous misery solidified into cold contempt. Then fury flushed, and she clenched both hands, stamped both feet, squeezed her eyes shut, opened her mouth, and began to wail. She was still clutching her little book of hours and a blue ribbon sewn into a cross which she had bought in the aisle of the cathedral. Both these she now flung to the floorboards. Breathing fast, her cry reached a pitch and then sank. The small primrose bosom of her gown filled and shrank as she tried, and failed, to catch her breath.

Martha had already hurried upstairs to prepare a warm posset for her charges, and Petronella had hurried behind her. Petronella now returned to the stairwell, peering down from the upper corridor. Behind her peeped Hilda, Sysabel's own maid. The earl was outraged, immovable and wordless. A small group of servants also stopped momentarily and stared. A page had been bringing a brimming jug of spiced hippocras, which he now dropped. Steam spiralled up from the Turkey rug. Hilda came stumbling down the stairs, and behind her appeared the baroness, having heard the commotion from her bedchamber.

"It's her nerves, m'lady," Hilda mumbled as she rushed to her mistress.

Petronella burst into tears. The baroness thrust her out of her path and took Sysabel by both shoulders, forcibly leading her up the stairs. She briefly looked behind. "I shall be down directly for dinner," she announced. "But Mistress Sysabel will not. Emeline, please instruct the servants accordingly. Hilda, you will come with me. And Avice, tell Martha, I will see her afterwards. My lord, I hope you will excuse us."

"Tragedy and agony," said Avice with wide eyed admiration.

"More female upsets," muttered the earl with vague distraction.

CHAPTER THIRTY FIVE

A vibration of hooves and the first streaks of dawn slipped like warning fingers from behind the trees. Then suddenly the whole horizon flooded with light as Nicholas, leaning low to his horse's neck, concentrated only ahead. He could smell the dust rising, and now he could see it. Three echoes in the night, ever closer across the heath; David behind, the feeing messenger ahead. Nicholas, knees tight to his mount's flanks, thundered from the mist and into the light's glowing haze. The diamond splash of hooves through the stream, the parting of the scrub and heather, and Nicholas leapt.

The messenger tumbled, unsaddled and hurtling, two men rolling together onto the wet grass.

David spun his mount and caught the reins of Nicholas's panicking horse. The other reared, flung up its head and bolted.

Nicholas grappled, holding his bruised assailant flat, his body heavy across the other, quickly used the hilt of his short sword and clubbed the messenger, one quick strike to the head. The man sank unconscious. Nicholas immediately examined, exploring through the rough clothing, and found the package at once. A leather pouch tucked deep inside the opening of the shirt and strapped from shoulder to waist. Nicholas cut it free and pushed the soft leather through his own belt.

"It's the right letter indeed, sir?" David called.

Nicholas nodded, strode over and retrieved the reins of his horse, mounting quickly. He turned, swerving back the way they had come. "It's right indeed, my friend." An amiable canter with two tired horses, they headed back to the coast as the clouds turned lemon and the horizon glowed iridescent. "The first task completed," Nicholas grinned, leaning back in the saddle and stretching his back. "An easier success than I expected. I thank you, my friend. I thank my much beloved uncle and I thank those two energetic brothers. But most of all, I have the undoubted pleasure of thanking my wife."

David turned, momentarily puzzled, expecting a sudden appearance. "Your lady, my lord?"

"I missed her," Nicholas murmured, though more to himself than his companion. "She troubled my sleep and I woke to hear four men creeping out at night, talking of tides."

"That one won't be catching any more tides, my lord."

"I didn't kill him," Nicholas pointed out. "There seemed no need. But he has lost his message and his horse and faces a very long walk if he still aims for Northumberland."

It was not quite as far, but certainly a considerable distance to the Chatwyn House on the Strand, where his much appreciated wife was more than usually troubled.

Sysabel said, "I just want to get away. I want to run and run and run, and jump in rivers and climb hills and smell the flowers in the fields, just as we did, Avice and me, when we ran away before." She shook the pleats from her shift, laying it across the garderobe chest ready for Hilda to take down to the laundry girls the next morning. "So I'm going to do it again. Run away, I mean."

Emeline said, "It didn't work out so successfully last time.

"Your Nurse Martha must have known," glowered Sysabel. "She took me there on purpose."

"How could she know such a thing?"

Sysabel flopped back onto the bed. "Aunt Elizabeth knows, you see, I mean about what happened. She was the only one who knew, because she saw me in my shift and guessed about the baby. So even though she's half loony and asleep most of the day, she tries to tell me what to do, which annoys me."

"She's supposed to. She's your chaperone."

"She's just a silly old woman. Either she told on me or Hilda snitched. So I'm going to run away. And if everyone's worried, then I'm glad." Expecting argument, Sysabel hurried on, "I won't face my uncle again after today. He'll poke and probe and tell me I'm stupid, and I refuse to be all obedient and sit there meek and mild like a little baby while he enjoys himself being a bully. Adrian says that's what ladies do, but he's wrong because real ladies tell everyone else what to do." She paused, biting her lip. Then continued, suddenly subdued. "And today - seeing that place again - it was horrible. So I'm running away tonight."

Emeline stood at the window, watching as the enclosing darkness turned the brown river waters charcoal and stifled the last of the breezes. "So you can tell," she said, her voice drifting a little like the day waning into twilight, "when a woman is with child? The body changes? The mind changes?"

Sysabel glared. "I don't want to talk about that now."

Avice sat down beside her. "Alright. I've been thinking about this already. I want to run away again too. So I'm coming with you."

Emeline remained at the window. She spoke to the darkening sky outside. "Maman will murder you. She wanted to last time."

"No she won't," said Avice, "because you won't tell her."

"So she'll murder me. And there'll be another corpse to bury."

"Then come with us," whispered Sysabel. "We aren't babies, really we aren't and we won't get lost this time. We're very grown up, or we wouldn't be brave enough to do it. Last time wasn't that bad and nothing terrible happened. I'm going to find Uncle Jerrid and accuse him of killing Peter. And then I'll find Adrian and show him the proof."

"Petronella and Hilda will come," nodded Avice, "so it won't be just us alone. Old Bill will come again too, if we pay him."

Emeline sighed. "You really think all this running away will help you find murderers?"

"Nicholas runs away all the time. Running away makes sense when staying feels like being in prison."

Avice interrupted. "Emma, you know exactly what I think and how I'll prove it." She looked directly at her sister. "Just as I was telling you before about who needs warning and who's in danger. You really should come with us."

"You mean Adrian?" Sysabel sat up straight, her face suddenly white. "You think he's in danger? Then we have to leave right away."

"I never thought the world could be so horrid." Emeline turned, staring first at Sysabel and then at her sister. "Papa was, well, we know what Papa was. But he made the world feel safe. All we had to do was go to chapel and confess our sins, and then we were happy again with God looking after us."

"I never had anything to confess," sighed Avice. "It was so disappointing."

"I only ever confessed that I hadn't confessed for a whole day."

"But now we know Papa had plenty to confess. I wonder if Father Godwin knew everything about that horrible woman all the time." Avice took a deep breath. "So, are you coming?"

The pages came in to light the candles and put up the shutters, but once they had left, Emeline was suddenly decisive, marching immediately to the door. "I have to speak to someone and it can't be Maman. Then I'll make up my mind. Maybe I will come with you after all. And if Nicholas never forgives me for not behaving like a lady, then I'll tell him I only did it to try and save his life."

Emeline quickly closed the door and hurried along the corridor to the narrow back stairs. It was to a tiny closet chamber that she crept, snugly tucked away on the upper storey. There, amongst half unpacked clothes chests and materials spread for darning, for brushing and for stitching, Martha held her tight, both arms clasping Emeline cushioned to her breast.

"Did you," whispered Emeline, feeling once again very young and safe, "know already? Did you really take us to that place on purpose yesterday? Why? To make Sissy admit everything? Or something else?"

"I knew indeed, my sweetling," Martha breathed soft and cinnamon, "for that silly young lass Hilda told of it some time back when they first arrived in Wrotham. She's no more notion of keeping her mouth shut than a magpie singing in the bushes. I took the poor child past that place, thinking I'd a duty to inform you and her ladyship, but with the secret's not being my own, I wanted to cause neither trouble nor strife."

"Do you," suggested Emeline, voice smothered against her old nurse's apron, "really feel sorry for Sissy? You don't, do you?" She sat up a little. "Do you just think it's all a terrible sin?"

"Now what would you have me say?" Martha frowned, patting Emeline's shoulder. "Would you have me give the lie to the almighty Church and all those holy priests, and perhaps say there's no sin in loving? There's sin of course, but whose sin is it? The little girl child, who was as ignorant as the dew on the daisies? The poor midwife who does a service for those miserable girls, and saves their wretched bodies from the torment and the shame of bearing a bastard child? Or is it the seducer who bears the sin, a full grown man like as not, who knows and does it all the same, putting his girl at terrible risk without the kindness nor the offer of marriage?"

"Yes. It was Peter's sin." Emeline sat straight now. "How I hate him. First he used her, and then sent her off for the slaughter."

Martha clicked her tongue. "And so someone slaughtered *him.*"

Emeline sniffed. "Peter told me he'd loved me from afar, told me he'd begged his father to arrange our marriage, told me he dreamed of me every night. It was such a lie. He only wanted me for my money. But I was so infatuated – just like Sissy. He told her he loved only her. But then he got her with child, and sent her off alone to kill it. I'm lucky. It could all have happened to me. Every horrible detail."

Martha's arms bundled her back close. "Don't cry, my lambkin. You knew no better, and just believed the handsome young man at your door, as all of us do before we learn better."

She peeped up at her nurse, suddenly curious, "Were you ever in love, Martha?"

"With my mother and with my father as is proper, and with you, my own poppet, you and your dearest little sister. My precious children you are both of you, and have never wanted another."

"But you don't like Sysabel, do you?"

"I might blame her for ignorance and a head full of fluff and nonsense, and even blame her for believing the words of a villain instead of the words of her priest. But stupidity is no sin. I believe the good Lord will forgive, since all the poor lass dreamed of was love and has surely been punished enough. But," and Martha paused as if waiting for holy intervention before saying, "the girl is - impetuous. A little doom willing, perhaps. And seems unbalanced as a door does when its hinges are broken."

Emeline rested her head back on Martha's swelling apron. It smelled of bleach and starch and honey treats. "Yes, the screaming and wailing and flying into tempers. Or did the misery of it all send her insane? She thinks her greatest punishment was losing Peter."

"That was her reward, and God's mercy."

"I cannot imagine what she went through. The fear and the shame and the pain afterwards. And Peter didn't have to face any of that."

"Perhaps the young man had his own demons to face, my lambkin. What do we know of the blackness in any man's heart?"

"And the fire? It's always fire, isn't it. Did you know that the place you took us - where Sissy had been - was already gone? Burned?"

"How could I, little dearest? I had never been there and knew only the place Hilda had told me. More tragedy perhaps, more death." Martha wrapped both arms tighter, keeping Emeline against her bosom. "I took your little sister from your mother's body," she murmured, "and washed and swaddled her while the midwife thought your poor Maman might die from the agony of it. But women are stronger than they think themselves. Yet having an unformed babe cut from your body - now that's a battle wound even worse than the birthing of a living child for there's the tragedy of loss, and it must be done in secret with no one to give comfort and not even the freedom to scream."

It was another voice entirely which answered.

"Women die every day in childbirth," announced the baroness from the doorway, and both the other women sat up in a hurry and stared around. The baroness walked into the centre of the little chamber and regarded her daughter with an aggravated frown. "I have no idea why you are here, Emeline, and I find it most inconvenient."

Emeline stuck out her chin. "We all come to Martha for comfort and advice. That's why you're too, isn't it, Maman?"

"Don't be petulant, Emma," said her mother. "Whether you need comfort or not, I presume you've been talking of young

Sysabel. Yes, yes, I know all about her. With a maid who cannot keep her mistress's business in silence - and the Lady Elizabeth looking for a confidante. Indeed, Mistress Frye is in need of a far stricter guardian. And since it seems we now have suspicions regarding Mister Frye -"

"Well, it makes more sense than poor Edmund Harris. But it's Avice who thinks Adrian is the murderer. She says it was for Peter's inheritance."

"Nonsense," said the baroness with a wave of her fingers, "there were far better reasons for murdering Peter than that."

Emeline hiccupped and disengaged herself again from her nurse's embrace. "Does everyone know things they never told *me*? Are you suggesting you knew what a dreadful creature Peter was, while continuing with my marriage arrangements regardless?"

"Really Emeline, don't be absurd." The baroness waved away imaginary cobwebs. "You know how impossible it was to change your Papa's mind about anything. But I assure you, I had my own plans and would have put matters right."

"So why *are* you here, Maman?"

The baroness sank suddenly to the little chair beside the settle where Emeline and Martha sat. It held a pile of her own stockings ready for darning, but the baroness accommodated herself on top. She said, "The same, my dear, the same. Looking for common sense amongst the knots and muddles. Needing a little comfort, and a good deal of advice. Thinking of killings and widowhood, of unwanted marriage and the cruelty of man."

"And of pain," whispered Emeline, "and degradation. And pitying poor little Sissy even if I'm not sure I like her either."

Martha's voice faded to a little murmured tickle over the top of Emeline's curls. "There's few girls would choose such pain, but with a babe on the way and no husband to give it a name, pain is the only choice. An experienced woman will give herbs first, a mixture of acid and sweet, and all stirred in ale over the fire. But if that does not bring a result -" Emeline cringed, curling back again further into Martha's embrace, "then there's penny royal, hyssop and rue, and maybe, if she knows her business, there'll be marigold, tansy and ivy, a pinch of mandrake root perhaps, and white poplar for the pain. If the girl has good money to pay, there may be a spoonful of treacle and even syrup of poppy. But whatever is paid, there's no surety, and with enough poison in her belly to vomit the day through, the babe in her womb may still hang on to life, poor mite, and not knowing its mother wants it dead."

"That's' - what happened - to Sissy?"

Martha frowned. "Now, what a question to ask me, my sweetling, knowing I wasn't there and have never spoken to Mistress Sysabel on any subject, let alone that one. But we can be sure it was something of the same, and in the end it must have worked."

"You are speaking only of herbs, Martha," sighed the baroness. "But it can be far worse than that."

"Truly, my lambkins, not just herbs. For if they work, then there's the grinding and the pulling and the pain inside like to die or split apart. Then there's the bleeding and the weeping, the dragging on the back as though breaking, and the punching within the belly as though all the innards are screaming. And still it may not work, and there's the poor lass lying with her knees to her belly, and the inner fire burning her up, and the vile taste of what she has to drink, and all the effort not to spew it back. Then, if still nothing has washed the sin away and the poor unborn creature lives on, its tiny innocent fingers clutching onto hope, then there's the knife. In the end, it's the knife, like as not."

The baroness looked down into her lap. "Poor young girls. Poor children."

"Cutting up into her womb with her and the child screaming both. Then she has to crawl all the way home, poor lass, trying to hide the pain and the bleeding for she'll be cast out if the secret leaks - with the priests watching and holding up their crosses all ready to call her a wicked whore, and her wretched mother and father with the whip ready - and her weeping for months afterwards for the loss of what she's killed, and the dreams of how she might have loved her own tiny baby if it had lived, and, bitter in shame and regret, fearing what the Lord God will say to her when she dies herself."

"Martha -?"

"And after the knife scrapes the womb empty, it stays empty forever. No babe can grow in a womb where the knife has gone before," Martha said, sitting up with a deep breath. "But no more questions, my sweet lambkin. Your poor daft nurse has spoken enough of what she knows nothing about, and will say no more. Just to offer - a word perhaps - to give sympathy to those who have suffered these things, and not to condemn your poor little friend for what I doubt she could help and will never forget."

"I'm glad someone murdered Peter." Emeline looked across at her mother. "So who do we think killed him *now*? Adrian?"

The baroness was still staring into her lap, and spoke softly. "Yes, Adrian. Or this unknown Uncle Jerrid. It could even have been Sysabel herself."

"To murder Peter, yes. But not Papa."

"How many are there with a motive to rid the world of both?"

Martha sat quietly now, nodding as if she knew, but could not say. Emeline stood, staring back at both women. She felt suddenly quite cold. "So, tell me."

The baroness looked up. "I have discounted young Edmund, and certainly the unknown boy cannot be considered any longer. I had a moment's suspicion of his lordship, your father-in-law. Absurd of course. But who else?"

"Just Adrian."

The baroness stared at her daughter. "Or Nicholas."

Emeline stared back. "Or you," she said.

They left that night.

CHAPTER THIRTY SIX

The tavern buzzed, boots slipping in spilled ale as the doors continually swung open, slammed shut, opened and shut again. The whistle of the coastal wind, wood against plaster, the sudden shiver, then shut in warmth again. Voices, laughter, the topple of a body and the quick fingers of a cut purse, the candlelight catching the polish of chipped earthenware, and the grasp of clammy hands, torn fingernails and palms grimed with the day's toil. The fallen tallow and the stale crumbs from two days' suppers, the jangle of coins, each penny cut into its farthings, a man's wage buying a pot of beer and a smile from a friend before he staggered home for his supper, or simply a hungry belly and a lonely bed.

Nicholas looked into the shadows and said, "So you know this?"

"Not for sure," said the other man. "But he never made it to the boarder. When he didn't come, I crossed through into France myself, but never rode as far as Paris. When I doubled back from Flanders, I thought I'd find him already heading to Brittany. But when there was still no sign, I caught the next boat."

Jerrid nodded. "So Dorset failed again."

"Poor bugger. Desperate to defect from Tudor's little group of traitors, yet cannot make his escape."

The small man lowered his voice. "But Spudge confirms his lordship got the message. Not regarding his brother and half his family were caught in conspiracy and executed, now he's taken his mother's word and wants back home. Took his mother's letter – confirmed he'd be making a second attempt – asked to be met and wanted an armed escort. But he's well watched, he says, has been warned, and feels the danger of it. Knows Tudor doesn't trust him anymore. Nor does France."

"France doesn't trust anyone. It's French policy."

"Nor can anyone trust France," David muttered. "That's policy too."

"When he failed to get away last November, the bloody French laughed as they took him hostage. It'll be worse for him this time."

Jerrid nodded. "That French boy king's too ambitious for his years, and his sister regent is too damned clever, too damned sour, and has wed a wolf."

"Bugger France," objected Nicholas, "I'm only interested in England's monarchy, and keeping it safe. Will Dorset keep trying? Or does he now admit defeat?"

"He'll try again," said the small man. "Given a year or so, perhaps he'll manage eventually. Spudge tells me his lordship's miserable, squashed between the elbows of Tudor and French ambition. And he wants his Maman."

Jerrid groaned. "All right. We'll give him another week."

They sat, five men facing each other, Nicholas, Jerrid, David, and the two strangers, boots to the bench opposite, faces obscured by intention, by shadow, and by their cups. The tavern was crowded but few took notice of those deep in private conversation. Cursing in French, Breton, Cornish, Kentish and Flemish, port slang and the crudities of men long at sea. Drunken men speak loud, and curse louder. Dialect and language were interwoven with shadow and the inevitable shifting layers of coastal smells; driftwood and crusted weed, damp brambles and windswept reeds, old oyster shells scattered underfoot, fish scales basted to boot and cape, stale beer, rancid cheese, warm sweat, bad breath, unwashed bodies and the great overwhelming swell of ocean brine. As the door rattled, was pushed open and kicked shut, so the wind carried its stories and its chill, while the men squeezed further into the tavern and clutched their cups.

"And Urswick?"

"That part of the business is now over. Urswick himself got away," Nicholas said softly. "But his letter did not. I have the pouch inside my doublet, and my knuckles still itch from the bristles on the messenger's chin. The wretch himself I let free since I'd not enough men to arrest and hold him. Two of his companions are dead."

"I'll take the news straight to my Lord Brampton," said the small man. "Will I take the pouch as well?"

"No," Jerrid said. "My nephew and I will take the letter to Westminster and the king ourselves. You should return to

Brittany. If Dorset makes another attempt to escape from France, he'll need all the help you can offer."

"I will, my lord. And the letter - if you've seen it - is as expected?"

Nicholas sighed. "It is. From Tudor to my Lord of Northumberland, asking for backing and recommendation in the matter of marriage. The king will not be pleased."

"He's long mistrusted Northumberland," Jerrid said. "The Percies - the Nevilles - old jealousies - old rivalries and each loathing the other. Back when his grace governed the north, Northumberland sat quiet, nursing his grievances. But he never forgets."

"Damned Northerners."

"While you Southerners," grinned Nicholas, "are all fair minded lovers of forgiveness and justice."

"We are, my lord. Though I'll make an exception for Henry Tudor. That young man will make more mischief yet."

"A man of mischief indeed. Aiming to wed a wealthy Herbert girl, and into Northumberland's own family? It's a grand ambition for a landless exile. But I thought there was another ambition? To wed one of the old king's daughters, wasn't it? Some declaration from Brittany of wanting to wed Elizabeth or Cecily?"

Nicholas shook his head. "Indeed, it was what he wanted, though the dowager made no agreement. Her daughters may be declared bastards, but they're still daughters of a king and now one is due to marry a Portuguese prince."

"Perhaps," Jerrid shook his head, "Tudor heard the rumour put around that our king planned to marry his niece - taking the elder girl Elizabeth for himself? And so Tudor thought he'd need to look elsewhere?"

"Perhaps." Nicholas leaned back. "But I've an idea those rumours were spread by Tudor's mother herself, or at least by her friends and household. Of which Urswick is one."

It was outside in the stables where the first attack came. Wolt was crouched beside the straw bales, avoiding hooves and crying, nose and tears dribbling onto his knees. Harry stood over him, one fist raised. "If you keep snivelling," he threatened, "and if you tells me just once more time how you misses your Ma, I'll shove this fist right down your gullet."

The blow came immediately, the rock to the back of Harry's skull and the boot to his groin. Wolt stopped crying, stared into the face of the attacker, then scrambled silently back behind the straw. What he saw had made a great deal of sense and so, frightened, he remained very quiet. Not daring to wriggle, he peeped between the bales as Harry was searched then kicked aside. Four men, small, busy, intent, fingers exploring, shaking heads and backing off, were quick and efficient. Eventually when the intruders had left and been gone long enough to seem safe, Wolt crept forwards and stared around him.

He bent over Harry, listening and touching, frightened to face death yet again. But Harry was breathing, a forced and guttural wheeze. Hesitating a moment, Wolt looked over towards the tavern. It was still open with the raucous echo of singing, of drunken men laughing and swearing and reminders of the familiar pleasant evenings he had once spent in such places with his mother and her friends. He sighed, then ran straight for the second stable block where he hoped Rob and perhaps his masters would already be preparing for departure. He could hear the horses neighing and snorting, a close reminder of what he feared and disliked.

It was dark. The stars blinked sleepy from behind the clouds and even the gulls slept. The wind blew Wolt's hair into his eyes and he did not see the man hiding behind the water butt until it was too late.

The singing was too loud. Nicholas smiled, edging past the crowd as the last drinkers tumbled from the open doors into the little courtyard outside. Three men, arm in arm, were in chorus. "Oh, the long golden curls, soft virgin's ringlets both here - and down there -" with great laughter and approval from their companions.

Then Jerrid called and pointed. "Nicholas, get over there. What the devil is that?"

Nicholas knelt, turning over the small crooked body lying on the beaten earth. When he laid it back down, his fingers were sticky with blood. "Sweet Jesus," Nicholas whispered, "has the child been out here dying while I sat drinking inside?"

"He's dead then?" Jerrid came beside, kneeling in the dirt.

"He's still warm. But yes, the boy's dead. A long knife to the back, well aimed below the ribs." Nicholas stood, looking around. "Find Harry and Rob. But watch out for any further attack." He lifted the boy from the hardening blood puddles and the dirt, and carried him towards the smaller stable block. Already he could hear the grooms boys shouting and the disturbance of the horses. Jerrid followed. David ran ahead, pushing open the loose hinged doors, calling for Harry and Rob.

Rob stumbled up from the straw. "They got the boy? And someone got my Harry down with a blow to the head. But my brother's no weakling. He's coming round now, with a mug of ale to bring his wits back. Bastards were after that letter, I reckon."

Nicholas laid Wolt's small thin body on the ground beyond the reach of hooves or boots. The two stable boys stared and David pushed them back. "My lord, you're sure he's beyond help?"

"Poor little urchin. He's beyond any help I can give him except arranging for a decent funeral."

"That'll hold us up, my lord."

"The boy had no advantages in life. I meant to do him a kindness by taking him on, but it's proved no kindness in the end. The least we can do is say a prayer and see him into consecrated ground." Nicholas stepped back and looked over to where Rob cradled Harry. "You're not badly hurt? Then tell me exactly what happened."

Harry groaned. "I'd just told the little bugger to stop snivelling," he muttered, "and then knew no more meself. My bloody head bloody hurts and I can't see nothing straight."

"Can't see nothing anyways," complained Rob. "Since it's bloody dark."

Jerrid nodded to one of the stable boys. "It's light we need," he said. "Light the lantern, boy, and let's see the state of these wounds." Wolt's small crumpled face was white, his shoulders now rigid. Down the back of his shirt the blood had streaked the grubby linen in huge viscous stripes. "But I judge it a quick death," he looked to Nicholas, "if that consoles you. Someone stuck his knife where he knew it would kill fast. Well practised, I'd say."

"Frenchies," Harry shook his head and wished he had not.

One of the stable boys said, "Them heathen foreigners wot don't talk no proper language was here, for I heard them. Gabbling away, they was, though t'weren't nothing no decent Christian soul could understand." The boy pushed forwards into the spreading circle of light. "I reckon they couldn't understand nor each to the other, they just pretends since they don't know no English, only jibber jabber. Only one proper word they shouted and more than once too, being murder, like a threat and a promise. Murder! Murder! Right nasty."

"What else did you hear?" Nicholas demanded of the boy.

"Gabble an' bumps," said the stable boy. "I were up in the straw and thought it better to stay there."

The tavern had closed its doors for the night, but above it Nicholas had rented a bedchamber, and they sat there while awaiting the local doctor, the stable boy having been sent running to bring him from the village. Harry lay nursing his head where a pear shaped swelling protruded from the straggles of hair. He still found it hard to focus. "They was searching me for summint," he insisted, "since me shirt's all rucked where them sticky French fingers has been." Rob sat beside him, cross legged on the sagging mattress. David watched from the window seat and Nicholas sat talking to Jerrid at the other end of the bed.

Nicholas said, "So we're content to guess they were after the letter we took from Urswick? But is that the most likely answer?"

"Perhaps." Jerrid leaned back against the bedpost. "What else would they search Harry for?"

"Simple thieving? Looking for a purse?"

"But they made no attempt to take his boots or his knife."

"And then killed the boy, because?"

"Not to carry tales nor say what he's seen," said Rob from his brother's side.

"Seen what? How could the child recognise a pair of French cut throats he could never have seen before?"

"And why slaughter the most insignificant of all? What reason to knife a snivelling brat with his elbows out of his shirt sleeves?"

"Urswick's no fool," Nicholas said softly. "He got away when I thought him taken - but he made no attempt to get back the letter he'd carried - and abandoned it without care. Not as a coward, since he's clearly otherwise. He clearly saw no benefit in risking his life to retake it." He paused, looking to his uncle. "Yet someone else has - and even killed for it. I'm not sure what to think."

"There was no sign the boy had been searched," Jerrid decided. "His clothes were neither hitched up nor pulled aside. Harry - yes. Wolt - no. But someone knifed him anyway."

"Then this was all to do with Dorset's escape, my lord?" David asked, frowning.

"For what reason? Dorset has not yet even arrived in the country and in fact we know him still held by force in France."

"Them Frenchies just like killing us decent God fearing folk," nodded Rob. "They don't need no special reason."

"After Wolt is buried tomorrow morning," Nicholas said, standing quickly as the candle guttered, spat and sank into liquid wax, "we'll move west along the coast. The first time Dorset planned an escape through Flanders. Now he aims for Brittany. So if he comes at all, which I doubt, it will be nearer to Weymouth where he makes land. But we need to use our wits, my friends, not just our legs. There's something happening here that makes no sense to me, but I intend finding out before heading back to London."

Jerrid frowned at Harry's spread legs. "So we're doomed to damp mattresses for at least another week."

Nicholas nodded. "While I dream of knives in the dark, and the awful weight of guilt."

Many miles distant, his wife was riding, well wrapped, hooded, and head down, the damp country lanes leading away from the city. Beside her rode her exhausted younger sister, and further behind trailed their maid Petronella. Ahead Sysabel rode beside her own maid Hilda, and leading some way ahead rode a slump backed and solitary man, silent beneath the moon. It was a little ahead of him that their single outrider rode, a younger man who had, as soon as he heard the plan from Bill, insisted on accompanying them. Sysabel looked behind and waved one neat little gloved hand. Emeline waved back. Avice yawned. The night was not cold but tiredness brings shivers and a sharp little breeze blew through the treetops. Old Bill had led them quickly away from the grand houses of the Strand, cutting up beside the Fleet and its narrow sludge, avoiding the bent tiled gables of the gaol and its stench of depression and hopeless anger, aiming for the open fields beyond St. John's and the orchards of Piccadilly.

"It's so annoying to have to ride north," said Avice, "when we all want to go south. But I suppose that's the disadvantage of leaving at night. London's gates are all locked against us."

"We could hardly leave in the morning," said Emeline. "I can just see mother's face - and the earl's scowl - as we all trot out and say goodbye because we're off for an adventure to catch murderers. And anyway, it was all your idea in the first place."

"I like adventures. But I'm so horribly tired."

Emeline smiled. "I'm tired too but I'm going to save my husband's life."

"And that silly Sissy thinks she's off to save her brother." Avice sniggered. "It should be quite a battle."

"Sissy secretly thinks Nicholas is the murderer. She says he and Jerrid are two feathers off the same wing."

"A raven's wing? Scavengers and squabblers."

Emma clutched tighter to the reins. Her horse slowed. She allowed the space between herself and Sysabel to lengthen. Then she looked at Avice and whispered, "Martha was telling me about abortions, though I can't guess how she knows. I mean - well - Martha! She's so calm and kind and sensible."

"Martha always knows everything."

"And she's *capable* of everything. I mean, she's strong and clever and she'd so anything if she thought it was right."

Avice was puzzled. "What do you mean?" and edged her horse a little closer.

"She knew about Sissy already because Hilda told her. Now *there's* a silly goose who needs watching. If she was my maid, I'd be furious."

"Was Martha angry at Peter - doing things to Sissy when he was supposed to be marrying you?" Stirrup to stirrup, Avice whispered to her sister's ear. "I never liked Peter even when you were silly about him. Now I know how right I was"

"You only disliked him because I told you he was wonderful. If I'd told you he was a pig, you'd have stuck up for him. Just as you did with Nicholas at first."

"Oh, pooh," sniffed Avice. "I just have better taste than you."

"Like Edmund Harris."

"You know," said Avice, "he's not so bad really. Maman says he's being very polite and she's disappointed because she wanted him to be the murderer."

"Maman says she's given up on him being the culprit. And you'll think I'm quite mad," Emeline whispered, "but I was wondering about Martha." Avice stared open mouthed, and Emeline hurried on. "Well, she said how the sin was all Peter's - not Sissy's at all. And if she knew about Papa"

Avice sniggered. "Martha's much too nice to kill people. And Peter died almost a year ago. Martha didn't know anything about what he'd done back then."

Emeline shrugged. "But he was courting me and she never approved - and told me to be careful when I said how romantic he was."

"I think," Avice decided, "she has secrets. She was probably young and beautiful once and had a romantic love affair and nearly had a baby and learned never to trust men."

The moon hesitated between clouds, a slim crescent, its reflection wavering in the muddy puddles underhoof. A silvery vapour shifted through the trees ahead, threatening rain.

"If it rains," Sysabel called back to Emeline, "we must find a hostelry for the night."

"We'll find one anyway," Emeline replied, raising her voice. "The nights can be dangerous on the highways. Bill will find us a respectable inn."

"Bill," muttered Avice, "wouldn't know an inn from a ditch, and doesn't know what the word respectable means."

"Then we'll stay in a slum," sighed Emeline, "which will all be part of the adventure."

CHAPTER THIRTY SEVEN

The earl chewed his next mouthful of cold beef, dripped the juices onto his fine red silk doublet, and nodded to the page to refill his cup from the jug of claret. "Pretty. Black hair, nice wide hips. The boys, well they took after me with their blue eyes. But Alice, hers were deep brown. I liked that."

"How terribly sad, the manner in which she died, my lord."

"Certainly was for me. Coming home to shadows, empty corners, young Nick crying night after night."

The baroness stared. "Did Peter - not - cry?"

His lordship sighed. "A brave lad, my Peter. And of course it was Nick as suffered the most, having been with them all. A six years child with his Maman cradled in his arms, watching her cough and spit her way to delirium. She was buried before I got back home, so I never saw. Nick arranged it with the priest. Affected the lad of course. And the little ones too. Philippa, my little girl, three years old, and loved her big brothers. And the baby John, who bare knew life before he knew death. Nick carried each one out to the graveyard, insisted, the priest said, but couldn't carry his mother. She was too big for him. Cried, he did afterwards, telling me he'd laid the little ones in their coffins but couldn't carry his Maman. Could only lean over and kiss her cold face."

"My lord, it must haunt him still."

"So there's an excuse," the earl sniffed, reaching quickly for his cup, "when the boy runs from trouble and won't face what might hurt him. But it's twenty years gone since that time, and he must grow up and have children of his own. She's fine young woman, your daughter, and must make her husband accept his responsibilities."

After a snug night and a bright glossy morning of clear summer skies, fresh bread rolls still warm from the oven and butter golden from the churning, it was some time before her ladyship learned that the morning was not an auspicious one after all. She was informed by Martha.

Immediately the baroness ordered her riding clothes laid out, her horse saddled, a small baggage trunk packed, the litter rolled out and made ready for Martha and the luggage, five outriders prepared, armed and waiting, and Petronella warned that she must accompany her mistress.

"Petronella has gone already, my lady. She went with the other party."

"Damnation," said the baroness for the first time in her life. "Then drag young Bess downstairs, tell the wretched girl to wash behind her ears and then push her into the litter with Martha."

She then marched back into the hall and interrupted the earl's morning snooze. "Do whatever you wish, madam," said the earl, elbowing himself upright in the chair. "It's madness, one after the other, is all I can say. I've no interest in riding off into the rain after madmen and even madder females."

"It is not raining, my lord. The sun is shining. I trust the day will stay bright, and I shall catch up with my daughters by evening." The baroness paused. "I do not ask for your company, sir. But are you unconcerned for your niece?"

"The girl's a fool. I've been saying it for years. Go ask that feeble sister of mine if she wants to go galloping off into the wilds after her charge. She's the chaperone, since young Adrian is another who's conveniently left the stable door open on his responsibilities."

"I cannot imagine the Lady Elizabeth galloping off anyway, my lord. But she should be informed."

"Used to like a good gallop when she was younger," remembered the earl with a wistful glance at his widened midriff. "Never married." He sighed. "Affianced once, but the treacherous bugger was attainted and m'father put a stop to the wedding. Lizzy sulked for years."

The baroness set off to the Lady Elizabeth's chamber. She did not stay long, returned to her own bedchamber to change her clothes, then descended to the stables. "There will be a delay," she sighed, "for the Lady Elizabeth intends to accompany us in the litter." She nodded to Martha, saying quietly, "She will not be an easy companion, I imagine, and will slow our pace. But the poor dear decided anything was preferable than being abandoned alone with her brother."

"His lordship does not intend returning to court, my lady?"

"I have an idea he's out of favour there. He blames Nicholas and the scandal of James's violent death, but I doubt it's that. It's far more likely that his highness saw the earl drunk once too often, and has simply stopped offering him commissions. I doubt there will ever be another seat on the Royal Council."

"I shall attempt to keep her ladyship entertained as we travel, my lady," said Martha with little conviction.

"She'll be bringing her own maid." The baroness shaded her eyes, looking over the cobbles to where the leather hooded litter was being hitched to the sumpter. "Joan, I believe, and fat as that barnyard cat we called Joan back in Wrotham."

"Then at least should her ladyship feel crushed and faint, I can help revive her."

The baroness turned away. "I shall personally murder both my daughters when we catch up to them," she said. "And you need not bother to try and revive them."

By nightfall, Emeline and her small party was already heading into southern England. It was the solitary outride, Alan Venter, who had forced the pace. Avice, Sysabel and their maids were quickly wearied. Old Bill had objected. Emeline had not.

"I was tired when I left home," moaned Avice. "Now I am *exhausted.*"

Emeline said, "The journey is a nightmare. Arrival is the only goal, after all."

"That new man Alan is the one who keeps making us hurry. But he's no friend of Bill's. They quarrel all the time."

The small wayside tavern was their second stop, and they had managed a reasonable supper. The bedchamber contained one large palliasse which they would share, and pallets for the maids. "The roads are full of holes and the drizzle has soaked through to my bones," Sysabel mumbled, pulling down her stockings and shaking the drops from their toes, proving her case. "I hate your Alan and silly old Bill both."

"These pillows are flat," Avice pointed out. "The mattress is lumpy. There's no garderobe and the chamber pot isn't even clean."

"What complainers." Emeline stood by the little window, looking out on the stable block below. "Wasn't it originally you two who wanted this so called adventure? I only agreed to come because of Nicholas, and now I'm the only one not complaining."

"That's because you've got Nicholas to look forwards to. Sissy only has her brother, and me - no one."

Petronella was collecting hot bricks from the kitchen to bring up and warm the bed. Hilda was helping her mistress to undress. Emeline already in her bedrobe, remained by the window. She said softly, "I wonder what he's doing now. Where he's sleeping. If he's thinking of me."

The baroness's party was falling behind. Their pace became tedious as the litter lumbered through potholes and stuck in the mud. There was the necessity of stopping for dinner, then supper, and finding hostelries of superior quality for food and finally for bed. One of the outriders caught a bad cold and had to be sent home. Bess spilled hot spiced hippocras on the baroness's riding gown, and the bright sunny morning had turned to torrential rain once they passed Reading.

It was through the rain that Jerrid stared at the long misted coastline and the disappearing streak of horizon beyond, and said, "It's time we were leaving."

"Two more days."

"He's not coming," Jerrid said. "The poor bastard is hostage to the French again in Paris, and they'll not let him out of their sight, not even to piss. We have the letter to Northumberland, and we know Urswick is beyond reach. Why delay?"

"Because I gave the king my word."

"Nicholas, his highness has more sense than most. He'd be the first to tell you to leave." Jerrid sighed, turning back and taking up the reins again. "There's Tyrell heading off for Burgundy any day, and his highness will be organising that, not bothering about Dorset."

"Burgundy again? Yes, of course, I'd forgotten." Nicholas grinned at his uncle. "Richard originally intended sending me, but decided to be kind and permit my new bride sufficient time to get to know her husband before he was whisked away again."

"So forget the whisking, my boy. We've wasted enough time here. It's time we headed back to Westminster."

"I'm tempted. Indeed, more than tempted."

"The new bride again?"

"That's the temptation."

"Then we head north tomorrow at dawn. At least as far as Southampton and the Fox and Pheasant, decent ale and the best inn for miles around. I'll inform the others."

Nicholas paused. Finally he said, "But I'm missing something, uncle." Remounting, he turning his horse back towards the road. "Something obvious to do with the boy Wolt's murder, and I'll kick myself afterwards for having missed it. I simply hope we won't all suffer for the mistake."

The small hostelry just two miles north of Southampton had proved more than usually comfortable. Emeline's store of coins was running out, but now being so close to Weymouth, she had ordered apple codlings for supper and had gone to bed more cheerfully than usual. But through the night the wind took force, whipping through the treetops, turning rain to squall and squall to storm. Branches smashed against the bedchamber windows and the shutters shook and rattled. The moon blinked out behind the rush of tumbling clouds, and the world turned black. Then light returned in one vivid slash of white. The skies exploded, then closed tight again with rolling thunderous vibration.

The five occupants of the hostelry's large attic bedchamber awoke startled. Petronella whispered, "My lady, water's pouring in through the window. We'll be drowned in our beds."

Avice sat up and poked her sister. "You can't sleep through something like this, Emma. Try and stop the shutters leaking. Can we stuff the gaps with blankets?"

Emeline yawned and rolled over. "It's just a storm. I can't stop the rain raining and we need the blanket ourselves. Leave me alone, I ache all over and I never want to see another inn, and especially never another horse."

"It must be nearly dawn anyway," Avice declared, hopping out of bed and running over bare foot to bang on the rattling shutters. Puddled had formed beneath, trickling across the floor. "I'm hungry. Let's get some bread and cheese and start the day."

"We can't ride out in this weather," Sysabel objected. "Where are we anyway?"

"Nearly Southampton."

Emeline frowned. "Wasn't that yesterday? But we can't just stay here. I'm nearly out of money. How about you two?"

Sysabel sniffed and shook her head. "I have a shilling tucked in my garter. But I was saving that in case I have to go off alone to find Adrian."

"Don't bother looking at me," sighed Avice. "Where has the money gone?"

"Down your throat. Ale and food. And even hovels cost something. So we need to keep moving on. Once I find Nicholas, everything will be alright."

"Ride through this storm?"

"We'll have to leave as soon as it passes. I can't afford another night here, in case we have to wait days in Weymouth."

"I have a tiny gold cross I can sell," Avice said with a small hiccup of reluctance. "Though it was a gift from Papa, and now he's gone – even if I'm glad he's gone –"

"You won't have to sell anything," said Emeline firmly. "And nor will I. But we *do* have to face a very muddy ride later this morning. Our guides won't complain, at least Alan won't. He's always in such a hurry. He'd ride through the apocalypse."

Once the rain had stopped, although a mist of sporadic showers drifted, spangling the air while the new risen sun sparkled like candlelit crystals along the hedgerows, the party left and headed south once again. But the roads were awash and in places were flooded. Roads of beaten earth had churned into ruts and ridges between dank boggy pools and great slides of slime heaved down the little slopes and hillsides. The ravens were cawing from the treetops, with a great flap of wet wings spread wide to dry, and a straggly black strut as they challenged each other for the best dripping perch.

The five women and their two guides left the tiny hostelry shortly after midday and a light dinner. The horses were fractious, frightened by the storm and a night of panic. Alan Venter was tired. He had been up with the horses. Bill was sullen.

"The land will be boggy after last night," Alan had warned, "Then we've the Wey to cross and the ford could be underwater. I may have to find another path."

"Oh, for pity's sake," called Sysabel, stretching her aching back and sighing. "Hurry then. And promise me this is the last day I'll be stuck to saddle and stirrups. I shall smell like a horse myself by the time I see my brother."

"I shall look like one," sniffed Avice.

"Ladies, we've just one day left, but the horses are ill rested, so I beg you, keep close and don't trail off behind."

"A real bath tonight," Emeline called to the others. "I promise, a hot bath for everyone, even if I have to sell my boots."

"I'll sell this horrid horse."

The storm's dreary echo of misty drizzle damped shoulders and coated the horses, soaking their manes. Then a pallid peeping sunshine turned every sparkle golden and a great sweeping rainbow blinked, reformed, took courage and claimed the open path within its arch. The light turned turquoise and lemon. The lanes were bordered by fields, neat ploughed after spring sowing, and ditches filled with the night's water and the little swimming beetles, crickets and long legged spiders which had escaped the storm but not the marshy drains. Puddles the size of monastery ponds kept the horses wading up to their fetlocks, snorting, or stooping to drink. The sun was high when Avice called, "Mister Venter, it must be time for dinner, and not an inn in sight. Will there be one do you think?"

And Alan turned, saying, "I've been told of the Fox and Pheasant not far from here, mistress. Though it's likely to be expensive."

But Alan Venter stopped abruptly. Before them the lane opened into a crossroads, and onwards from their own roadway, three more choices of path led off from a tall post topped with a wooden cross and a thin rope noose dangling in the swirl of mist. At ground level the open square was trampled mud, purpled and thick with a reflected sheen under the strengthening sunshine. The cross flung its shadow, and the shadow of the knotted noose encircled a smear of ripples, as of warning and of threat.

And on the other side, crouched on his haunches, a thick built man stared, his eyes hidden beneath the sweep of his hat. He was armed, and his sword lay unsheathed across his knees. One hand held to the reins of his horse, a bandy legged and mottled grey, an old sumpter past its prime which chewed, bent, and chewed again with a gummy drip of saliva. To his other side stood a dog, an Alaunt mastiff, yellow and ridge backed, wide muzzle and tired eyes, its lower lids hanging red. It shook its head, slime flying. But the man barely moved.

Alan's horse refused the muddy pools and backed, bracing its front legs and snorting. Alan pulled on the reins and called out, "You'll doubtless know the way to Weymouth, my good man. Will you tell me which path to take from here?"

The man smiled, still sitting back on his heels. "Aye, I'll tell you, but it'll cost. And it's worth a penny or two, seeing as the wrong way will take you straight to my brothers, and there's six of them and all hungry."

"Shit," said Alan very softly. Then aloud, "And your price? You'll see I lead a party of defenceless females, and want no trouble nor mean to make any. I ask only a pointer to the right road, and don't find that a task worth too demanding for a local."

"Ten shillings, nor a farthing less," called the man, still grinning. "It's the cost of knowing the road and a deal more, for the wrong road sees you dead in a field and all your pretty mistresses on their backs with their skirts up to their necks, for me and my brothers ain't had nor a decent meal nor a decent fuck in a week or more."

Alan braced his shoulders and reached for the hilt of his sword. "No need for that language, since we've not threatened you, nor refused to pay." His feet were out of the stirrups, but his hands remained tight on the reins.

Old Bill followed the lead and tumbled from the saddle, but he kept well back. Close behind and her voice trembling, Emeline whispered, "Mister Venter, I don't have ten shillings. I have barely two. But we have a little jewellery between us, and though I'd hate the loss, I will gladly pay rather than risk such danger."

Alan dug in his spurs and forcibly edged his horse one step nearer to the cross's shadow. "We're not rich travellers," he called to the man. "Will you accept what we can pay? We'll cause no trouble, I promise you."

"But it's trouble I want, seeing as it amuses me," chuckled the man, "and I've no objection to a good fight, and welcome a brawl. You, my friend, I can kill in an instant, between me and my hound here, and I'll soon have you swinging dead from the rope. Then I'll do what I like with the women, and take from them whatever I wants. So you've nothing to bargain with, man. Pay, or fight."

Bill heaved, exhaled, summoning courage, and called, "Two of us to one o'you, and though looking old maybe I does, but I fought in battles afore you was born, and can still wield a knife and throw a good aim." But the dog sprang forwards, pulling against his leash, and started to bark.

Petronella was crying, her ungloved fingers fidgeting at the reins, ready to turn and gallop for her life. But the man laughed and stood, short, square shouldered, large hands still holding to his horse. He had pulled the dog back and now held to its collar, his sword now thrust through his belt and his eyes hidden beneath the old straw hat. Alan frowned. "Since your brothers aren't here, it's you against me and my friend here. Maybe your hound's a mauler, but these ladies have husbands not far off, who will hear any call."

"You've asked the way to Weymouth, being plenty far enough away for no folks to hear no girl's screams." The man shrugged, as if tired of the argument. "But my brothers, well they'd hear my whistle if I cared to make it, and would come running before Varmint here had you by the throat, mister. So make your choice, and if you means to pay, then make it quick before you tries my patience."

The horses snorted and the wind shuffled in the trees beyond the clearing. The threadbare noose swung a little in the wind, then settled. Emeline whispered, "I'm not frightened, Mister Venter. He's alone and we could be long gone before his brothers come running. If you judge that unwise, then offer the jewellery. My little broach is worth far more than ten shillings."

Alan said, "My lady," but paused. One of the horses, urged forwards with two small feet to its flanks and a screech that startled them all, pushed past then stopped suddenly and reared, panicked, hooves to the edges of the muddy pools. The halt was so abrupt that its rider, unseated, hurtled into the air, skirts flying, and landed heavily in the dirt. So Sysabel sat up in the slush, her little headdress of gauze netting toppled over, half blinding her, and her gown spread around. She scrambled to sit upright, gazing back then forwards. Twice she tried to rise to her feet but the weight of mud stuck to her skirts and she lost balance and fell more heavily into the boggy swill. The man on the opposite side was laughing loudly. His dog growled, but was held back.

Old Bill groaned and stumbled forwards as Alan Venter leapt from his saddle and stood, boots to the slime, reaching out, both hands stretching towards Sysabel. Too far out of reach, she tugged at her skirts, lost footing and slipped. The mud was more bog than pool. "Mistress," Alan called, "it's a quagmire. You struggle, you'll be held ever tighter. Stay calm if you can, mistress, and reach out to me."

Emeline gasped and dismounted, cautiously feeling her steps. Old Bill took her elbow. "Careful mistress, 'tis marsh, it is, and more dangerous than it looks." Avice was silent, staring ahead, and Petronella and Hilda clung to their mounts, crying and terrified.

Sysabel turned, frantic, grabbing at nothing, sucked ever deeper. She kicked and the bog sucked again, great gulping dark mouths of slime embracing her. She began to scream, pummelling at the surface mud as the wet earth splashed back, coating her face and arms in filth. The thief continued to laugh. Alan stepped further into the swamp, each step cautious. He nearly touched her. Sysabel stared, mouth wide and screeching.

Emeline led her mare forwards. "Mister Venter," she called, breathless, "if you hold to me and I hold to my horse, then we are braced. Can you go a little further then, even into the muck, and grab her? Then we can haul you both back."

Avice jumped down beside her. "I'll help. I'll hold the horse and lead it backwards."

The stranger beneath the cross called, "No, little mistress, come to me, for now I'm nearer. And ready I am, for my little house stands close, and there I'll have you naked as a babe and wash your flesh clean enough for bedding. One little push more, and come to Varmint and your friend Reggie, seeing as both of us is hungry." The dog was barking, straining against its master's hold. It snapped and snarled, dripping saliva. Sysabel's screams broke as her breath deserted her.

"The murderous thief can no more come to you through this bog, than we can, or be caught as the bastard he is," Alan shouted. "Take no more account of the fool, and do as I say ladies. It's calm will save us all." He turned to Emeline. "Yours is the best solution, mistress, but rather than your hand, I'd sooner take Bill's in case I pull you in."

Bill stepped forwards, holding tight to his reins and reaching for Alan's hand. Sysabel's screams wheezed, her face white, and she heard nothing but the sucking squelch. She managed to find her knees, attempted the crawl, hands flat, one knees forwards, and with a gurgle of turgid water fell flat on her face. "Heaven help us," cried Emeline, "she'll drown in mud."

Alan took Bill's clammy grasp and inched into the mud, each step a slow laborious struggle against the weight of deep wet marsh. The watching stranger stood, legs braced to grab, one hand outstretched. But Sysabel was unreachable by either, her screams silenced, though her hands scrabbled to wipe the thick paste from her nose and mouth. The dog pulled against restraint. "Mindful of the bog I is all right," chuckled the man, "but not my Varmint. Light enough, he is, to take a good bite from them fair plump tits. My pup to them puppies."

Alan had almost reached Sysabel, but was now sinking, his ankles deep in the slurping muck around him. Then, to Emeline's right, there was a moving shadow, a call, and the sound of hooves. She yelled, "Who is it? Help us." The two other paths, unreachable but open beyond hedge and bog, stood pale in the sun and one now echoed with arrival.

Alan turned. "No, my lady, for if it's this creature's brothers as he promised –"

"There are no brothers," Emeline shouted back. "I'd swear to it. That pig thief is a bumpkin and a liar. Just get Sissy safe, then throw the bastard into the bog to drown." Avice struggled to take her sister's hand but Sysabel, managing no more than a grunt and squeak, was still trapped and flailing.

Then from the right hand path the galloping shadows grew huge and the first horseman appeared, shouting, "Hold still," and dismounted, boots heavy to the mud, one hand tight on the reins, the other to the woman half swallowed in mire, unrecognisable for filth. The western roadway had brought him far closer. The man reached Sysabel's waving wrist. "Hold still, my dearest girl, I have you." And caught, his grasp firm and tight, then calling to the two men behind, "Here, take control. I have the reins, Lead the horse back and you'll pull us both free."

The second rider took the horse's bridle and calming the beast, led it steadily backwards. Sysabel held tight now, safely within an embrace she welcomed. The slick streaming mire gulped and released, losing suction. The man led Sysabel to dry land.

Alan Venter, trampling his own way out to dry land again, called out, "We'll find a way to reach you, sir, and thank you for the rescue. But we may need to double back in order to reclaim the lady to our party."

The new arrival bent his head, looking at the girl in his arms. He ignored Mister Venter. "My dear girl," he said softly, "this is both miracle and hell hole. What, in the good Lord's name, are you doing here?"

And Sysabel laid her head on her brother's shoulder and whispered, "Oh Adrian, only looking for you. And you've found me. God is kind after all."

CHAPTER THIRTY EIGHT

As Adrian carried his sister to the waiting horse, his two companions trotted forwards. One leaned down over his horse's neck and threw a rope, spinning it to land directly at Alan's feet. Alan caught the rope, wrapped it three times around his forearm, clutched tight and was pulled slowly and carefully to the western path. He stepped from the mud beside Adrian and Sysabel, breathed deep and thanked his saviour.

The rider retrieved and rewound his rope, nodding to Alan. "Surely only a brigand," he said, staring at the great cross in the square and the man still hovering uncertainly beneath it, "watches a man facing death and leaves him to his fate."

"May I know who to thank, sir?" Alan asked. "And to bless for saving my life?"

The man smiled. "My name's Christopher Urswick," he said, "and I might need that blessing, for I'm leaving the country on the morrow, and if there are more storm like that last night, I'll be using this rope to lash myself to the mast."

The lout, his horse and his dog, had now quickly disappeared into the long shadows of the southern path. "Look," Emeline pointed, "If you've a liking to be a hero, then catch that thief, for it's all his fault that Sissy nearly died, and our guide too. He was going to rob us and rape us and now he's getting away, no doubt to do the same to others"

It was Urswick's silent companion who turned his horse and leapt the high bramble hedge between the paths, galloping south. Adrian still held Sysabel, cleaning her face and hands with his cloak until both of them seemed creatures of the earth, thick with black slime. Sysabel was now weeping, great heaving sobs as she clung to her brother.

There were noises coming from the southern roadway, the howling of a dog, a thud and a man's howl, more desperate than his dog's.

Emeline sat down very suddenly on the path, buried her head in her hands and began to cry very quietly to herself. Avice came to sit beside her, both arms around her sister. Petronella sat shivering and terrified behind them, still clutching to her horse's reins, but Hilda dismounted and came to kneel beside Avice, saying hesitantly, "You'll be ruining your gowns in the mud, my ladies. Let me help, if I may."

The third man, his sword bright stained, returned at a gallop and began to cut a great wedge into the bramble thorn hedges that separated the western lane from the northern, making a way for the horses to pass without again approaching the turgid and hungry swamp. Mister Urswick strode in to help, chopping down with both sword and knife to widen the space sufficiently for a horse to pass without scratches and welts. Coming together one by one the group thanked each other, exhausted but deeply relieved. Avice whispered, "I have never fainted, not ever. But I think any moment now –"

Mister Urswick said, "Mistress, you're safe with us. And since Sir Adrian has found his sister, you know to trust us. The Fox and Pheasant is just a short ride from here. We stayed there last night, and will be glad to escort you there now."

Emeline sighed. "What bliss, sir. Food. Bed. Bath. I thank you all, and with all my heart."

It was three hours later when Sysabel slumped back in the bath tub, the barrel well worn and smooth within its planks and copper hoops. Her face appeared pink scrubbed above the rim, eyes blinking in the day's shimmer through the small window. "It is," she decided, raising the sponge so that scented water poured over her hair, trickling in hot ripples down her cheeks, "the most terrible – and then the most wonderful – of all things. No nightmare could ever compare. But I am the most blessed – just when I thought myself the most cursed."

Petronella and Hilda were bustling between upstairs and downstairs, trying to brush the dried mud from their mistresses' gowns. Small sighs and sniffs came in regular measure from the one huge bed where Emeline and Avice were curled, wearing only their shifts. The fire was lit and the bath stood before it. Avice squinted through the steam. "It was most peculiar. Did you *know* Adrian would be *just* there and *just* today?"

Sysabel pulled a face. "Of course I had no idea. But when he went away, he said he had business in Weymouth. He had to meet someone there, that Mister Urswick I suppose, and said he might have to wait so he didn't know how long he'd be away." She slumped a little lower into the water, her shoulders sliding deeper under steamy lavender swirls. "But I always *told* you my brother was a hero."

Dolefully, "I know Nicholas is around here somewhere too, and I do wish he'd just appear like Adrian did."

"Nicholas," sniffed Sysabel with a splash, "if he ever made it this far in the first place - and why would he - is probably lying drunk in an alehouse with Uncle Jerrid beside him. But Adrian isn't hurt, and that's all that matters to me. I was so worried in case - I mean Nicholas - and Uncle Jerrid - and the awful things that could have happened."

Emeline paused and the silence lengthened. Then she said very softly, "You really thought my husband only came down here to murder your brother, didn't you? You really did. Probably you still do, even though Adrian is obviously quite safe. It does seem odd that they both separately came to the same area. But Sissy, tell the truth. Why in heaven's name makes you think such villainy of Nicholas? He is such a - kind man."

Avice suddenly rolled from the bed and marched to the bathtub as Sysabel sank lower, soapy swirls and the day's debris floating around her chin. Avice said, "Adrian was good today. *Really* good. But then he was hardly going to ride by and see his sister drown in mud, was he? Maybe he's a hero after all, but that doesn't make Nicholas a murderer."

As Sysabel spoke, she blew bubbles on the water's surface. "I never said Nicholas," she mumbled. "I only said Jerrid. But if *you* suspect Adrian again, especially after today, then I shall never - ever - absolutely not speak to you again."

"Mister Urswick and his friend were heroes too," Emeline interrupted. "Are they Adrian's friends?" Sysabel shook her head, water droplets spinning. "But do you think that thief's corpse has been left on the road for anyone to fall over?"

"I don't care," said Sysabel. She waved a soapy arm towards the garderobe, calling, "Hilda, I've finished. Come here and dry me. Then," smiling, "I want a long, long rest. A good supper. Then sleep all night. Adrian has given me money so we are rich and can do what we like. Then Adrian will take us home."

"I don't want to go home," Avice declared. "I'm hunting for murderers."

"Then stay here," glared Sysabel. "But not me. Your silly Alan Venter proved quite stupid, didn't he, leading us to swamps and robbers! Well, I've had enough of all of it."

"You go home if you want to," Emeline said firmly. "But it was that dreadful storm made the marsh and Alan risked his own life trying to rescue you. And why you ever went flying into the mud in the first place, I have no idea. What did you think you were going to do, screaming and riding headlong? You get very overwrought sometimes, Sissy - and that doesn't help anyone. So you can have your rest, but I need fresh air and I want to think. Avice, will you come with me?"

Avice sniffed. "I wanted a bath. I *need* a bath."

"That bathwater is far too dirty now," Emeline scowled. "Perhaps we can both have a fresh one later this evening after supper."

It was a small private parlour where they met for supper. Emeline, having discussed her own personal preferences with the landlord's wife, ate her apple codlings and kept her head down. Avice and Sysabel, enjoying a far better meal than they had lately been accustomed to eating, filled their platters with roast pork, tripe stuffed with sardines and raisins, and drank the best wine. Adrian refrained from scolding his sister and her companions for riding across the countryside unchaperoned by any respectable retinue yet again, and instead seemed content to act the gallant hero, with constant glances at his own companions. The Fox and Pheasant was a large hostelry, with a half dozen ostlers, three well equipped stable blocks and even better equipped kitchens. But when there was a commotion outside and the sounds of other guests arriving, Urswick pushed away his platter of braised tripe and looked up, distracted.

"It's late," Urswick said. "Remember, Frye, I've a boat to catch - other duties and another master waiting, though it's the wrong news and not what he's hoping for."

"The boat's due tonight at Southampton?"

Urswick lowered his voice, "I'll not discuss my business here. Finish your wine, sir, and we must be off."

Sysabel looked up in distress. Waving a lavender scented arm, fingers wafting good Spanish soap. "Going? Again? Already?"

"Only for a day or two, Sissy." Adrian sighed. "You'll all stay here in comfort until I get back. It's urgent, or I'd not leave. But you need a rest I imagine, and will barely notice the time passing until I'm here again to escort you home."

Emeline was using the same soap with clean hot water when Petronella peeped in to the bedchamber and whispered, "My lady, it's Bill, poor mite, and as sick as can be."

"Not surprising," said Avice, looking up from her stool beside the bathtub.

"Oh, Lord have mercy. Another disaster?" Emeline emerged from the soap scum. "I'll finish here and be out directly."

Alan Venter and Bill were sleeping in the loft above the stables. Petronella climbed the ladder, clutching her skirts above the scattered straw, and peered, though keeping her distance, at the large spread figure. She turned and frowned at Emeline whose head popped up at the top of the ladder. "He's all hot and red and shivering, my lady. He has a horribly snotty nose and he's dripping like a conduit. He says Alan has gone for the doctor."

Bill, aware of the bright eyes staring from the shadows, attempted to speak. Instead, he sneezed. "Is it only a cold?" hoped Emeline.

"Alan Venter thinks it may be the influenza, my lady, being as we were caught in the rain and the mud almost all day.

"Alan Venter," glared old Bill from his sweaty straw pallet, "ain't no proper guide, nor a proper groom. You wait a bit and I'll be right as pottage. I only brung Alan 'cos he kept on and wouldn't take no gainsaying. But he's a city lad and don't know ort but London streets."

"It's just as well he came," frowned Emeline, "and he has led us well."

"Said he had to look after the lady or his lordship'd come back and behead the lot of us," Bill muttered, wiping his nose on his shirt sleeve. "But I reckon there's sommit sticky about him."

There was considerable bustle and noise from below, more horses brought in by the ostlers, the shaking of rain from tails and manes, the grooms shouting for oats and hot bran, blankets and brushes. Emeline shook her head and hurried back down the ladder. Halfway across to the shadowed peace of the trees beyond the courtyard, she bumped into Alan Venter himself.

"I've called, and hope the local medick's on his way," Alan said. "But forgive me, lady, you shouldn't be out here alone. There's much afoot as I know too well."

Emeline regarded him with confused suspicion. "It's a respectable hostelry, Mister Venter. And since I'm the senior within this group I consider it my responsibility = but I'm also desperate need of peace and fresh air. And now," she moved a little deeper beneath the trees, "you can tell me why you are actually here, Mister Venter. I've been told you actually insisted on accompanying me on this journey, through loyalty, perhaps to his lordship. But my husband had no idea I ever meant to travel anywhere or leave home at all."

"M'lady," he told her. "I'm under orders. It's many years I've been with his lordship and often journeyed with him, but this time I was told to stay put and look after his lady, being as how he's well used to danger, and always ready for the worst."

She was pleased. "So you've travelled with him in the past. Do you know where he is now?"

"I can't say, my lady, though he's gone south, as you know. May not be far from here right now. Though last time I travelled with his lordship, t'were north to York and Berwick and beyond."

"Berwick? The siege? My husband told me a little - but I didn't know he had his own men with him."

"Not many of us, my lady. Just David Witton, and me. But this time he left me behind to watch for his lady. Which is what I've been doing, and will do. And now, with your permission, I'll be off to see to your groom and whatever he's sickening from, lest it's a contagion. And don't you go near him, m'lady, for influenza can kill."

"I shall go for a walk," Emeline said firmly, "whether you approve or not, Mister Venter. My head is spinning. My sister is still in the bath, Hilda and Mistress Frye are discussing conspiracies and intrigues in private, and I feel quite nauseas myself."

"But it's late, and if you're not feeling well, my lady –"

"I shall be perfectly well if left alone for an hour to think," she declared and walked off into the crisp moonlit path beneath the trees and away from the hostelry.

Swept into a private parlour by the obsequious landlord, Nicholas sank down onto the cushioned settle and regarded his uncle. He had retrieved his sword and other belongings from his saddle bag, and now slung them to the table. He was far better dressed than had lately been his habit, having now decided his mission was virtually complete, and it was again possible to lodge at the best inn in the area. "David, book us a late supper as well as a bedchamber, and make sure it's the best bed they have. I've a backache worse than any wretch spending the day in the stocks, and a hunger fair wicked to swing on the gallows."

"You may smell like a felon, m'boy, but I see no reason for you to think like one," Jerrid said. "We've spent enough time on the road to break a man's back, but you're young. It's me should be complaining."

"You do," Nicholas said. "I simply need a wide bed, an aired mattress, and a very hot bath without sprigs of stinking dried lavender."

"My lord," the landlord bowed, "The bath is at present set up in another chamber, but as soon as it is free I will arrange for it to be emptied and set up in your lordship's chamber."

"The best chamber you have, and the softest beds."

"Alas, my lord," the landlord backed apologetically, "the best bedchamber has already been taken. But there is another of excellent quality, and I shall have the finest linen laid, and warm the mattress."

"Then three of us will share the room," Jerrid nodded, "and we've two out at the stables can sleep in the straw."

"And supper will be served here shortly, my lords."

Nicholas smiled with surprise at the apple codlings in warm honey, finished his tripe and roast pork, drained his cup, and followed the landlord upstairs to the chamber prepared on the second floor. It was a warm evening after a wet morning and outside a plover was calling before sundown, a shrill clarion disappearing into echoes as a hazy twilight shimmered across the fields beyond. One great oak just outside the hostelry's courtyard spread it shadow across the cobbles, slowly turning to silhouette as the shadows faded into the gloom. Within the chamber, Jerrid threw himself full length on the bed without removing his boots, and David tested the truckle bed, announcing it softer than most.

Nicholas looked across at his uncle. "Get your boots off, you'll have mud on the blankets."

Jerrid stretched, two hands to his back. "I doubt I could bend sufficiently to reach my feet. You'll have to put up with a little more mud, boy."

Steam spiralled in a thick mist up to the beams as Nicholas quickly undressed, waving away David's willing attention. The heat from the tub spun webs of dewy droplets vaporising against the window shutters. Nicholas tossed his well scuffed boots to the warmth beside the hearth, unlaced his doublet and pulled it off, hauled his sweat stained shirt off over his head, loosened codpiece, braies and hose, rolled them all off, throwing them atop the increasing heap, and climbed immediately into the bath tub. The half barrel stood tall enough for a good immersion but was unlined and Nicholas sat carefully, cautious of splinters. As the scalding water enveloped him, he sighed deeply, rested his head back against the brim, and closed his eyes. "The Fox and Pheasant, is it? Well it has my blessing."

"My lord," David's voice, "shall I take the clothes for brushing down? Or shall I stay and help wash your back?"

"The clothes probably need delousing." Nicholas shook his head but did not open his eyes. "Everything from my groin to my toes scratches or itches - and from my neck to my groin I'm encased in flea bites from every slum tavern we've stayed in. At least I'm dressing in my own comfortable clothes from now. But much as I'm eager for home, I'll not desert the last chance for Dorset to make the crossing."

Jerrid voice, muffled by pillows, sounded half asleep. "Dorset's not coming, I'm convinced of it. The good marquess was never the brightest of the Woodville brood, and no doubt the French king and his wretched sister have Dorset wrapped safe like a moth in a cocoon, and I swear he'll not be opening his wings again for a long, long time. Now I'm for home."

"We saw a small ship far out through the rain this morning."

David nodded as he scooped up his master's discarded clothes. "But it was out of sight once we climbed down the cliffs, and his lordship never turned up at the arranged point. Unless perhaps he was cutting across country. He'll be a frightened man."

"If we desert him, he'll be a dead one." Nicholas sighed and sat up, emerging again from the water and steam. He was, strangely enough, suddenly thinking of apple codlings. "So I'll stay here one more day, since the hostelry is comfortable enough, but only one. Tomorrow I'll start one last search from here to coast, and dig around the local area to make damned sure we've not missed the poor bugger."

Jerrid yawned. "You want yet another day here? You admire their bathtubs so deeply?"

Nicholas stretched an arm, pouring soap on the sponge. "It was something else came to mind." His feet sprang suddenly visible above the water's murky surface, to be washed one by one. "That sad little child's death. It still makes no sense. Why knife the boy and leave the men alive?"

"But since then it's been quiet as the grave."

"It was the grave I was thinking of," Nicholas stared back at his uncle. "There's something going on along this coast, and it's French inspired for it's French they speak. The groom said Wolt's killers spoke a foreign language. Amongst the rigmarole he couldn't understand, he twice heard them speak of murder."

"So not foreign - but English."

Nicholas shook his head. "Merde. It's French for shit. These were French assassins - but were they sent for us? Or for someone a deal more important?"

"Dorset?"

"Maybe just French pirates. They raid this damned coast at will."

"I have no idea. But I'd like to find out. I owe it to the king. And I owe it to the dead child."

"Then enjoy your bath, m'boy, and prepare for tomorrow," his uncle said. "But I don't see how you'll discover much in one more day. I'm as tired as hunted hare, and I've a suspicion one more day will turn into another, and then four or five."

"If my bathwater doesn't disgust you uncle, you'd best make use of it. I'm finished." Nicholas stood, climbing naked from the steam. He left wet footprints across the floorboards, retrieved the thin linen towel from the stool, and proceeded to dry himself. "But I promise not to delay past common sense. Just time enough to satisfy my sense of justice."

"You'll catch cold, not justice, boy," Jerrid said. "Get into bed. Is the water still hot? Then I'll certainly make use of it, and will leave it warm enough for David if he wants."

Nicholas grinned at David. "He smells of wet leather and horse sweat. So the bath's obligatory, even if it's near cold by then."

"I'm more than willing, my lord, especially in preparation for a ride back to the Strand." David looked up, clasping the clothes Nicholas had thrown in a heap. "And to face his lordship the earl."

"My father?" Nicholas pulled on a clean shirt from his pack. "Hopefully he's back at court. I certainly wish it, for my wife's sake as well as my own."

"I look forward to being back at court myself," Jerrid said, quickly undressing and leaving his clothes neatly folded on the stool. "Come on, boy. You think too much. Get yourself into bed."

"Should I think less? It's like a continuous mutter I can't be free of. I want home - sweet Jesus, I want home - but I don't like mysteries I can't solve." Nicholas had walked across to the window, but now turned, wandering instead to the bed. "But you're right, uncle," he said. "And you're right about something else. I'll not delay past tomorrow, Dorset, French assassins and storms in the night be damned. And that's also for my wife's sake as well as my own."

But had he gone to the window and looked past the half closed shutters, he would have seen his wife, her cape clasped tight around her, walk resolutely past the spreading oak tree outside, and disappear into the moon dappled shadows beneath.

CHAPTERE THIRTY NINE

Emeline walked on, wandering into the little copse of beeches beyond the courtyard and away from the road. The Fox and Pheasant had been built on a rise where the Dorset countryside undulated, looking from its ridge down to shallow slopes, then sweeping into equally shallow valleys. The previous night's deluge had eventually dried under the sun, though the thicker undergrowth remained sodden and the grass where the trees shaded the ground was still springy with damp.

As usual she was thinking of Nicholas.

Beyond the clustered beeches the land dipped suddenly and a small stream ran through the grass below. Emeline walked to the higher edge, looking down. The stream was still running high, partially overflowing its banks, though the buttercupped grass sloped, so escaping waterlog. A man, small and very thin, was filling his bucket at the stream, bending over, one knee to the flowers. Too late in the evening to wish being seen by strangers, Emeline remained under cover, wondering if the flashing dancing spring was fresh enough to drink. She had rarely drunk water unless first boiled, but the stream looked cold and clean enough to drink. Then she realised something.

The man below her appeared unable to rise. He had filled his bucket, not too heavy since it was not so large, yet could no longer lift it nor get to his feet. He rose once, stumbled, and fell again to his knees. He knocked the bucket and it began to spill, then rolled. He reached and caught it, hugging it to his lap, and began to sob. From where she stood, Emeline could hear the guttural misery and for a moment thought of her own retainer Bill, sick above the stables. The world, so full of sorrow and murder, seemed suddenly a sad and lonely place, worthy of a man's tears.

She began to climb down, slipping a little on the damp slope. Although the man might be embarrassed to be seen so helpless, it was help she thought he needed. The moon, half full and sprinkling pearly reflections across the stream's weedy reeds, showed a young man acting as an old one, stumbling, his back bent and his strength feeble. Remembering the thief at the swamp, she was nervous of tricks and of trusting those who might lead her into greater danger. Yet as she watched the man again leaned forwards to fill his bucket but toppled, almost falling into the water. Emeline paused, then made her decision.

As she arrived beside him, he looked up and stared, eyes wide as if alarmed. Emeline mumbled, "I'm alone, sir, and only wish to help. To carry perhaps –" though her voice faded out.

He appeared more frightened than reassured. "Get away," he wheezed. "I need no help." He was very young, even handsome, but his hands were wrinkled and he could barely rise from his knees though he steadied himself, both hands to the ground.

Emeline said, "Should a woman not help a man? I thought perhaps you were ill. I simply wanted to help." He didn't answer so she continued, "The water looks good enough to drink. I could carry it for you. A companion of mine has recently been taken ill. Influenza, perhaps. Are you also – unwell?"

He peered around as though watching or wondering, then his voice sank to whispers. "It's my poor wife needs help, lady, and thank you. If you've no fear of infection, we'd welcome that help."

Frowning, she said, "No one welcomes infection, sir. Is a doctor in attendance?"

He managed a small smile. "In attendance? No, lady. There's no doctor in our village."

"A doctor was called for my companion, so one must be nearby." She shook her head. "Though it's very late, sir. I'll carry the bucket willingly, but not too far, and forgive me but I'd prefer not to come too close. Then I'll return to where I'm staying and send the doctor after you."

He lived in a village nearby, he said, and his own home was on the outskirts. His wife would be so thankful. A man with a wife then, and since he had not asked for help, and had at first refused it, Emeline felt no threat. She filled the bucket from the stream and did not find it so heavy. The man walked very slowly and a little behind her, hobbling across the grass to the pathway, and dragging his feet. He was dressed in an unbleached shirt long over baggy felted hose and wooden clogs. He seemed poor, but she had no purse on her to give him. She could at least, she thought, pay the doctor before she sent him on to visit the man's wife. But now she felt she had gone far enough. She stopped and set down the bucket.

The footsteps were already close before she heard them. The man heard, again seemed frightened and fell suddenly to his knees. Footsteps along the pathway out of the shadows, and within a heartbeat they were surrounded, five men brandishing sticks. The sick man bowed his head and began to cry. Emeline stared around her, now equally frightened. "If," she said loudly, "you are thieves, then you're remarkably stupid ones. You can see this poor man is ill and hasn't anything to steal, and I carry nothing but water in a bucket."

The men scowled. "You'll not accuse us of thieving, mistress," one said, "nor act grand when tis only our duty we're doing, and risking our lives at that."

"Bring your water," said another, pointing with his stick. "and follow us, but no running, mind, for I've authority to stop anyone - even females - from running off."

Emeline did not understand. "How foolish. Why should I run off? And this man is incapable of it, for he's sick."

"Sick - indeed he is," said a third man, "and if you're not a fool yourself, lady, then you'll know how and what of, and should guess our orders, and the need for them."

Now more confused than frightened and more angry than confused, Emeline refused to move. The man she had gone to help remained on his knees. The ties of his shirt had fallen open. She looked down. She saw the rash, its dark bruises rising up the muscles of his neck and covering the pulse at his throat. She felt suddenly very cold, as if packed in ice. Emeline whispered, "Is it - the pestilence?" The man continued to cry and did not look up. She asked him, "But if it is, even if you needed help, how could you want to infect a stranger, someone who was kind and so deserved kindness in return?"

The man spoke between sobs, and did not look at her. "Did *I* deserve this?" he gasped. "Did my *wife*? I took our baby son from her body just four days ago, for no other soul would enter our home, and yesterday morning our little boy was dead. My Maud is dying too, but in an agony of thirst. There is nothing left in the house so I came only to get water for her. But I cannot carry the bucket. At least let her drink before she dies in my arms." His voice weakened but he continued in a rush, as if he had to explain what he had suffered. "At dawn today I buried our pretty baby Dickon," he said, "though he never had the benefit of a Christening for our priest is dead, nor has a consecrated grave, for I'm forbidden to leave the house." His voice was lost in tears. "Will the merciful God refuse him heaven, when he had no time to sin, but only time for pain?"

The five men grunted, shaking their heads and pushing at him with their sticks, refusing to touch him with their hands. "Get you home, Ralph Cole, and take your bucket. Let your wife drink while you say your prayers, but don't you leave your house again."

Emeline took one deep breath. "I'm sorry for you, and for your wife," she said softly, "but you should have warned me. I'll say my own prayers for you and your wife and son. But now I must get back to my own family."

There were five sticks, two at her back, one each side and one at her face. The tallest of the men shook his head again. "Tis the abbot's orders, and the only way, he says, to stop the Great Mortality in its fury. God sends what punishment He will, and tis up to us to do the penance. Without us, there's fathers will run off and leave their sons dying. There's daughters will scream and hide, with no care for the mother left writhing in pain. Deadly fear it is, and must be controlled. All the folk of our village will stay where they belong, and that's our orders. So you'll come with us."

They wouldn't touch her, keeping their distance, nor stand close enough to breathe her breath, but they herded her with their long sticks as though she was a wayward goose wandering from the flock. Emeline felt the panic rise into her chest like great black wings. She stared, shrugging away the sticks, trying to step back. "You've no right. I'm not one of your villagers and I have no sickness. I met this man just moments ago, and barely touched him."

"Barely touched?" one man answered. "Isn't it enough to stand side by side? In our village there's those as has touched no one, but only stood close in church. Father John, he took confession, nothing more, and on the other side of the screen, but was caught like a flea trapped in an armpit. We buried him two days gone, poor priest, and since then it's the whole village is dying. We've bare one cottage or two without the wailing and the pain."

"My brother died three days ago," mumbled the fat one, "and now his son's sick as a field mouse under the plough."

One of the men glowered. "At first there was six of us told to keep the village shut up tight, with no one in and no one out. Then Blackie got sick. We buried him yesterday and now we's only five. Me - I'm strong as an ox. But from us five, we'll go, one by one. A merry dance, I reckon, waiting for Mister Death to come slipping under the door."

Emeline started to speak but found she was crying so hard that none of her words made sense. She remembered what had happened to Nicholas and the haunting memory of his family's tragedy, then how he had feared having caught the pestilence himself, what his decision had been, what he had insisted upon, and how finally it had been all right. With a freeze of ice down her back, finally she managed to ask, "How will I know - if I'm sick?"

"It's the rash first," said another, and pointed with his stick at the man crying, guttural and distraught at her side.

"First I have to explain to my family." She wondered if she could escape, or if they would stop her and beat her, and if she could risk carrying possible death to Avice. Perhaps even to Nicholas. "At least if I can write a letter."

The fat man sniggered. "And who gets to deliver it then, and where to, and who finds the paper and the pen?"

"But my mother is Baroness Wrotham and my husband - his father is the Earl of Chatwyn. I can't just - disappear."

They didn't believe her. "And dressed like the queen herself as you are, mistress, with sweat and stains on your gown, and holes in your shoes."

She was pushed forwards, three sticks hard to her back. "I'm simply travel worn - and was at the Fox and Pheasant –," but her voice trailed off. She whispered. "If I come with you, where will you put me?"

"With him." The first man nodded, pointing again with his stick. "Or you sleeps in the monastery if they lets you. They won't let none of the rest of us in, but with you not from our village - well, maybe the monks will take pity."

The fifth man was frowning. "She ain't from around here," he said, scratching his head. "Her clothes says she's no lady, but there's no laundry maid wears a gown like that neither. If she ain't touched no one, I reckon we let her go."

"But if we let her go, she'll tell all around and have half the countryside running in panic. I'm doing as the abbot says, and there's no one will spread not sickness nor tales with me to stop them."

Emeline could feel the chilly trickle of tears down her cheeks, and the tremble in her knees. She would not let herself fall and whispered, though only to herself, "I only wanted to help."

"Which is what we's doing the same," the last man nodded, slow and apologetic. "'Tis a terrible death, mistress, and can have a whole county in their graves in a week. So we keep it close, we keep it quiet, we keep it in the village, and we keep the other folk safe."

"I'll carry the bucket and take water to the sick. But I don't understand." Emeline looked up, facing the first man. "How long have your people been dying? Have you sent for a doctor? How long is there between touching someone, and getting sick? I'm staying at the Fox and Pheasant and no one there knows anything of this." And then she thought of Old Bill lying sick and feverish, and once again her voice trailed off.

The man nodded. "The landlord and his missus, they knows. But they won't say. They'd have no business left, with folk running for their lives. Best say nothing – and there's not one soul yet has died there. It's close as close all right, but close don't mean touching. Like Restlebury Village not one mile away, yet not one man, woman nor child lies sick there. Which is why we's keeping tight shut away – the sick stays at home and no spit nor snot spreads beyond our lanes. Nor doctor will come, for they knows there's nort they can do 'cept sicken their selves."

Another interrupted. "Old man Hammond went for the doctor when his daughter got sick. No one knew it were the pestilence. But the doctor never come. Was scared, he was, and right to be when he heard what the sickness sounded like."

"Little Lizzy Hammond, she were the first, five days back, and dead not long after. Five days of shitting bloody hell."

Emeline slapped his stick away. "They'll have paper and ink to spare at the monastery. I have to write to my sister. And in the meantime, I'll walk willingly, but not with your cudgels in my back or your threats in my face."

The last man, still wavering and apologetic, muttered, "Then give us your name, lady, and I'll take a message to the inn. If I tells the landlord, he'll tell your sister. Can't do no better than that. But first I must ask the abbot's permission."

Pallid and hesitant, the moon dipped behind clouds, and darkness shrouded the land. But they did not walk far. The first houses clustered around a green, but no window showed candlelight and no soul moved or opened their doors. Even the church bell remained silent. Across the square and beyond the thatched roofs and little brick chimneys, she could see the stretch of the monastery and its grounds. Nothing moved except the flutter of leaves.

The man beside her mumbled, "My house is here, lady. Will you come with me, even sick as we are, and help my wife as you said you would?"

"Dear God," whispered Emeline, "must I invite my own end?"

The tall man following her, still keeping what distance he could between them, said, "It ain't no choice, lady, for you'll not carry the pestilence back to the Fox, nor spread death beyond our village. Maybe we'll make sure a quiet message is took to the inn, but it's here you'll stay, and I reckon a roof over your head is better than just the wind and the stars above. At dawn, if you wants, we'll move you to the monastery."

It was little more than a croft, with a narrow flight of creaking steps leading from the one room below to the one room above. It was below where the woman lay on a straw pallet, tucked all around with two thin blankets, and the open fire flickering in sinking ashes close by her toes. The hearth was a stone slab with no chimney, so smoke filled the space and all the room seemed to swirl in a thick and dirty haze. There were shelves and stools and a small table with crooked legs, but they merged into the smoke like little shadows, barely real.

The woman lay silent but her eyes were open. They were bleeding. Her husband knelt beside her. "I've brought water," he whispered, "and will get your drinking cup. No ale, for there's no stalls on the green no more and Daisy Green won't be brewing, for the lass is sick as you. But this is water from the stream, and safe to drink." The woman spoke, but Emeline could not hear or understand her. "Her name's Maud, and mine's Ralph," the man said, dipping the cup in the water bucket and then holding it to his wife's lips. "Drink my sweet." He lifted her head, but the liquid ran from her mouth and she could hardly swallow.

Emeline found a stool and sat heavily. The smoke was noxious and she could breathe only with effort. "It was like this for him," she whispered into the fumes of soot and misery. "Now I understand. He went through this. The black agony and the black terror." The weight of her own mounting fear was even thicker than the smoke. "He could have died too." She was whispering to herself, not caring if the others heard. "He was trapped, just as I've been trapped. And I'll face it with courage, just as he did."

The man frowned, looking up. "You're coughing from the smoke, lady. But my Maudie mustn't catch a chill. Doctors always say to stop draughts, and any sick chamber must be kept hot." He shook his head. "And we're used to the smoke, lady. All autumn, all winter, mostly all spring." Maud had managed to drink a little, and Ralph refilled the cup. He spoke over his shoulder. "Our beautiful little babe got it first, then my poor girl here. I got it two days later. But she's worse today. I reckon she'll go tonight. And once she's gone, I'll want to go too."

Through the sallow sepia swirl, Emeline stared at him. The rash was hidden beneath his shirt, his eyes and nostrils were clear. But his wife's suffering was visible. If she had once been as pretty as her husband was handsome, it was no longer evident. Her face was swollen and marked as though beaten and trickles of blood seeped from her eyes, her nose and her ears. Her hair was matted where blood stuck and as she drank, gulping as if it hurt her even though she gasped for water, her gums bled and her lips cracked, breaking into bright bloody beads. Her small pointed nose was crusted black in dried blood, softening as new blood joined the old. As she tried to grasp the cup, her hands trembling, her fingertips oozed blood from beneath her nails, and all her skin was patchy and dark.

Emeline wondered if Nicholas had looked like that. Then she imagined him as a child watching his mother and tiny siblings die. Finally she imagined herself covered in the rash of bruises, the huge black abscesses, and tasting blood in her mouth. She imagined never seeing Nicholas again. She felt bilious and began to cry.

Ralph Cole looked up. "Mistress?"

She shook her head, gasping back tears. "Give me something to do. Can I build up the fire? Are there more sticks outside?"

"I've had this fire constant for days," he said, "and they wouldn't let me out to collect wood. I meant to get some today, but couldn't even carry the water."

They watched Ralph's wife die. The moon slipped shy into the clouds behind the silent church steeple and a slow dawn peeped through. After a while Ralph hurried out to grab small twigs and handfuls of leaves from the grassy square nearby, and scrambled back before he might be seen, trembling and panting, bare able to walk himself. So the fire burned and smoke filled the cottage and the woman on the pallet began to moan. Her cry was so faint and so mournful that Emeline cried too, sitting on a stool near the fire with nothing she could do to help but warm her own helpless hands.

Ralph said, "Will the Lord God have mercy, do you think, lady? My wife is a good woman, and never did wrong to no one. We've been wed only a year, and was happy when she fell quick, being with child. Our little boy. She were so happy, and made pretty clothes all ready before he were born, with soft colours for the bonnet, and stockings for the little feet, a big fluffy blanket and best linen for the swaddling. And then, as my beautiful girl grew large and the birth was near, and we kissed and prayed the birth would be easy - then it all changed. He had no time to wear them pretty clothes, our sweet lad. Why did the Lord send the pestilence, when we done nothing but love each to the other, doing our work best as we could?"

"I don't understand either," Emeline whispered through her tears. "I wish I did."

"But you says you's a lady," said the man, squatting back on his heels beside his wife. "Being a lady, you should know more than simple folks." He sighed, disappointed, and took his wife's hand, holding it gently as she moaned, her eyes closed. "Every bit hurts, she told me before, like knives to her knees, and a flogging to her back. Like her insides was all screaming and falling apart. We had a potion of willow bark ready for the birthing, and juniper berries for the pain of the pushing. I bought wine too, to give hot with a little spice for I got a pinch of cinnamon though it cost my last pennies, but I wanted my girl and my new child safe. But she's drunk it all, my sweet Maudie, and there's no more to give."

Emeline came to sit on the ground beside the makeshift bed. She wiped away the tears and blinked back her own wretchedness. "Poor Maud. Poor Ralph I'm so sorry. If only I could get out, I could buy such things tomorrow, and come back to help."

"They patrols," Ralph said. "Night and day both. But now at least she has water to drink," he sniffed, clasping Maud's hand a little tighter, "She hasn't long, I reckon, then she'll be with our little Dickon. She were so sad, my poor wife, to lose her babe bare four days old. To carry a little one for all them months, and feel its squirming and its little toes kicking and that lovely big warmth inside, and then to bring him into the big bright world only to lose him forever. She told me often how it was. All for nothing. It isn't right. She wanted a little girl, and me, I wanted a son. But all we got were the pestilence and pain enough to die thankful in the end. Is there more pain, d'you think, in Purgatory? She's had enough, my dear girl, and don't deserve no more."

"I'm sure," Emeline said softly, "she will find only comfort, and her baby waiting, and no more pain forever and ever."

"That's good, then," Ralph said, his frowns softening. "I'll let her go, and be happy for her, and I'll pray for her all the day until I goes to join her." Emeline started crying again and Ralph hung his head "'Tis my fault," he muttered. "You should kill me for it, though I'm dying anyways. I just wanted the water, for my Maud cried so pitiful for thirst. But when I couldn't carry the bucket, so I thought of my dear heart and cared nothing for you, lady. I shouldn't have let you near me, and told the truth to you from the start. It were wrong, and I'm so sorry. But there's nort now I can do for it."

Maud Cole began to wail. Her moans turned to howls, and she opened her eyes. Her lower lids ran with blood. Ralph had a cloth, already badly soiled, and he wiped away the trails and trickles and the bloody tears, and whispered to her that he was near, and would hold her if she wished. But she tried to shake her head, choking on her own pain. Ralph licked a corner of the cloth and started to clear the crusts from her nostrils, helping her to breathe. He looked over at Emeline. "She has two great black lumps in her armpits, you see," he said. "And when she moves, they hurts so bad, 'tis like the devil's pinch. And there's another down in the soft part of her leg, and it pains more than all the rest. I tried to touch it once, to put on a slave I thought might help. But she screamed, for just the touch of a finger. When she gave birth to our little Dickon, she grunted and no more, for she's always been a brave lass. But with this, it's different. The pain's too strong."

The first pink flush of dawn had risen over the thatches and was shining full on the doorway when Maud died.

CHAPTER FORTY

The swell of briny tide was ebbing and the sand sparkled with salt. A jellyfish, like a small blob of melting wax, leaked its separate strands, washed up, its wilted arms reaching across the pebbled shallows. Gulls picked over the stones, snatching up the dead and dying. Clouds hid the sun.

"Back to the inn then," Jerrid said. "They say the Fox and Pheasant serves a plentiful dinner, but since the inn is full, if we're late we'll only get the left overs."

"We're already too late," Nicholas said. "We might as well finish the day out here, and head back for an early supper. Then it's one more night in this wretched place before heading home tomorrow at first light."

"For pity's sake," his uncle said, "you've searched every cove and every inlet. There's nothing to find here. I'm as hungry as a fox myself, and pheasant sounds like a good choice for dinner."

"The Fox will no doubt serve an excellent supper too."

The Fox and Pheasant did indeed serve an excellent supper, with a wide choice of platters. They were first at the table, and Nicholas chose corns of salt beef in a wine sauce with boiled onions, roast goose stuffed with peas, a small custard tart in lemon cream, duck livers with sage and garlic, a pattie of herbs, bread fried in beef dripping, and finally a dish of spiced leeks. There were no apple codlings.

David had joined them and was once again discussing with Jerrid the possibilities and probabilities concerning the attacks some days past, when Nicholas tossed his napkin to his platter and stood, stretching his back. "I'm for bed," he said abruptly. "Don't wake me when you come up."

Jerrid grinned. "Outdone by an old man, eh, boy? It's barely supper time and the sun isn't yet in bed, yet you're eager for yours?"

"I've better things to dream of than you have, uncle," Nicholas told him, "so have more reason to sleep."

With the light still finding some passage through the windows, he had no need of a candle as he headed for the stairs. But it was heavily shadowed and at first he did not recognise the woman walking down towards him. Then he recognised the squeal.

"Mercy," squeaked Sysabel, "It's Nicholas. What are you doing here? What have you done with my brother, you villain? And what have you done with poor Emma?"

Hearing the noise, Hilda had hurried down to her mistress, and it was her feet that Sysabel sat down on as she collapsed backwards onto the step behind her. Nicholas stared in bewildered alarm. He took the steps in two strides and took his cousin by her shoulders, shaking her. "Idiot girl, what are you talking about? Why in heaven's name are you here? And I've certainly not seen Emma. Where is she?"

Hilda burst into tears, Sysabel began to howl and Avice appeared at the top landing, shouting, "Oh, thank the Lord, it's really you, Nicholas. Oh, Nicholas, you have to save her."

Nicholas grunted, "What the devil?" and Jerrid and David rushed from the parlour as Avice ran down to where Nicholas was still holding Sysabel.

She pushed past Hilda and said urgently, "Somewhere private, quick, I have to explain everything."

They sat back at the table, platters pushed aside and food ignored. Avice hurried past the explanations of how and why they had all decided to leave the house in the Strand, abandoning her mother to his father's inevitable irritation, and added briefly how Emeline had been eager to find Nicholas and warn him of possible danger. With one eye to Sysabel, she did not dare say what they had thought the danger might be, but instead began to describe how, once settled in the Fox and Pheasant, Emeline had gone outside to see to their sick groom. Certainly Bill had seen her, but she had not returned to the inn and by ten of the clock both Avice and Petronella had gone to look for her. They had discovered nothing, and still with no sign of her, had been out all that day searching.

Once Avice had tumbled through her story, Sysabel said, "Of course it was Adrian who rescued us all yesterday. But then he went away with his friends and hasn't returned either. Now I know he's in terrible danger."

"What from? Magpies?" demanded Jerrid.

"From you," wept Sysabel, "and from Nicholas, and I know you've done something horrid to Emma."

"Emma," said Avice, her voice suddenly low, "has been taken hostage. It's only minutes past that I got a message from some village bumpkin, saying he had permission from some monastery or other. He said there's a village not far from here, and there's an outbreak of the pestilence with half the folk dead or dying. I have no idea why Emma is there, or why she would ever visit such a place, but the messenger said she can't leave the village, or she'll spread the contagion and must stay where she is. He left in a hurry. I just grabbed my cloak and was about to follow him when I heard Sysabel screaming at you."

Nicholas stood so suddenly his chair fell backwards, He turned to Avice as David leapt up beside him. "Avice, watch over this fool of a girl and don't let her leave. I'm going to get my wife."

"The pestilence? Don't bring her here," moaned Sysabel.

"Quiet," Nicholas ordered her, "or I'll have you silenced. Not one word of this must be spread to others. No hint to any one, remember, not to your groom, to the tavern staff, or anyone else. Now, which village?"

Avice shook her head. "He wouldn't say where. That's why I wanted to follow the man."

"I'll find her."

"But the pestilence. And Bill, our guide, is sick above the stables. Alan went for the doctor but the doctor refused to come."

"Alan Venter's here? Good. Jerrid, get my fool of a cousin into her bed, and keep her there. And what's this about Adrian?"

"He was here and he's coming back." Sysabel had stopped crying and was trembling with fury. "He'll - defend himself. With his life. And me too."

Nicholas nodded to his uncle. "I have no idea what the child is raving about, but no doubt you can deal with her, uncle. If Adrian returns soon, tell him to wait for me, as I may need his help. In the meantime, it's only Emma I'm concerned with."

He strode from the parlour and headed out towards the stables. Jerrid called to David. "You're going with him? Excellent. But you'd best get up to the bedchamber first and grab the boy's sword and cloak. I'll cope with everything here. You look after Nicholas."

"I always do, sir," David said, and left at once.

Without hope of escape, Emeline had remained at the cottage for most of the day. For two hours she had slept, but no more, her fear and her misery keeping her beyond tiredness. When she woke, she gazed past the guttering ashes, and saw the dead woman now held tight in Ralph's embrace. He had taken her in his arms as she died, the last pitiful gurgle of her breath all spent. Then he had leaned forward and clasped her, and rocked her, and began very softly to sing.

He looked once at Emeline. "It's our little lullaby," he explained. "We sang it to our baby when he cried, poor mite, though Maudie were losing her voice, and just croaked the words. Then she got the delirium, and I comforted our Dickon alone in the day, though gived him to her for feeding and then to hold all warm at night."

"I'm so sorry," Emeline whispered. "I'm so - terribly sorry."

"Don't be." Ralph looked down, wiping his wife's mouth where the blood had puddled, though was bleeding no more. "'Tis my fault you're here. You should hate me. But now I can hold my dear wife, and kiss her again. I couldn't before, it hurt her too much if I put just an arm around her, for it squeezed them terrible lumps and made her scream with pain. But now she's all mine. She were so beautiful when I married her. You couldn't tell it now. But that's how I still see her, and always will."

Emeline stood slowly, hugging herself, shivering although the fire still spat and flickered. "I'm going to try and get away," she said. "I don't think I'm sick yet but I won't risk going back to the inn or seeing my sister. If I manage to get away, I'll buy some medicines in the next village and bring them back to you."

Ralph said, "If them in Restlebury guess you come from here, they'll hang you."

"Doesn't everyone around here know each other? So they'll know I'm not a village girl. I'll make up a story. I'll say I've come from Weymouth. That's where I was going, before all this happened."

Ralph turned back to the limp body cradled against him. "Go to Weymouth, lady, and go now," he said, "afore they catches you. Don't you worry for me. I got two days more, I reckon, then will go to be with my Maud again. We can work our way through Purgatory together, and then we'll wake healthful and happy. One day we can run through the poppy fields like we used to. Will they have poppies, do you think, in heaven?"

"I'm sure they have great pastures of poppies, and roses, and buttercups," said Emeline, reaching for the door handle. "I'm going now. If they catch me, I'll be back sooner. If they don't – I'll come back with the medicines tomorrow. Some for you, and some for me."

No one saw her leave. Emeline closed the cottage door very quietly behind her. She stood one moment on the step looking up into the falling twilight, the wind in her face as she took one deep breath of freedom. Then she started to creep, a step, then two, keeping always to the shadows. She was under the cover of the trees within three breaths, and then deeper into the wooded slopes. The village she had left was tucked into a dip between rises, and the rises were thick with beeches. She avoided the dulling light and chose the damp shadows. She didn't care that she was lost. She wanted only to escape the patrol with their sticks and their sentence of death.

Her hems, still mud stained from the thief's boggy trap, now trailed in the undergrowth, sodden and heavy. and her ruined headdress barely clung to her head. Her thick russet curls escaped their restraints just as she escaped the village.

She was shivering and utterly wretched as she came through the trees onto the path. Not a path she recognised, just beaten earth and narrow, a ditch of muddy trickles either side and a view over the reedy grasses to the land stretched out beyond. It was growing quickly darker but the first glimmer of milky stars spun their sheen as the moon peeped, a hanging spoonful of silver behind the trees. Far off, and darker than the sky, Emeline saw the thin strip of ocean where she had hoped to find her husband, though no flicker of moonlight yet glinted on the water's sullen edge. She stared one minute longer, as if it brought her nearer to Nicholas.

Plodding along the pathway, she headed away from the sea. Ralph had told her the direction to aim for the next village, and she hoped eventually she might find someone to ask. As long as the patrols did not find her first. She had no purse, but she wore a broach she might sell, its tiny pearls and amethysts still pinned to her gown. She also wore, as always, the ring Nicholas had given her. She would do what she could in order not to sell this, but if death was so close, even such a precious token seemed of less importance. In the meantime, feeling ever colder and more miserable, she searched only for a place of cover where she might curl and sleep and for a few hours dream away the cloying stink of sickness and promise of death.

The sound of galloping horses was unmistakable, shaking the ground beneath her feet. Two men or more, racing through the night, and in their hurry would surely take no notice of her bedraggled shadow. The patrols had been on foot, but she did not know if there were others and it was too late now to risk danger. Emeline moved back against the little ditch, ready to scurry under the trees if the riders stopped. The first horse was a blurred and looming shadow, closing fast. An old horse, steaming and frothing, forced to run beyond its strength. The rider leaned low, urging his mount, and the hooves drummed, shaking the ground. She heard others further behind, but did not know or care how many. She stood quite still, her heels almost in the drain waters. It was so long now that she had been continuously frightened, she barely noticed the increase in her heartbeat.

Then the horse was on top of her, a bandy puffing bay doing its best for its master. The horse and rider came abreast, the reverberation so pronounced Emeline felt she bounced. She wrapped her arms around herself, bowing her head, unmoving, becoming a small part of the night.

The horse passed. But just three steps more, and swept around with a swirl of skirted coat and a whistle of wind, neighing, alarmed, thundering hooves and rearing in startled alarm; the rider turning his horse so abruptly it nearly stumbled. In a second he was out of his saddle, leg swung over the horse's neck and leaping to the ground. His boots hit the dust with a thump and a kick of dirt, his coat flashed white fur trimmings almost in her face. In the darkness Emeline staggered back, terrified and confused. Then she was in his arms.

"Dear sweet Jesus," said the voice she recognised, muffled into her neck, tickling her ear, forceful and urgent. Then the warm mouth was hard on hers, kissing her.

Emeline thought she might faint. "I'm dreaming. Or am I sick already? Am I delirious?" Nicholas held her so tightly she could hardly breathe, though not for one moment complained. His magical appearance, his reassurance and his protective strength smothered out the chill and all the fear was swept aside.

He said, "I'm real enough, my love, but are you?"

She peeped up at him and the moon reflected in the blue brilliance of his eyes. She whispered, "I was looking for you. And then everything went wrong."

"I've spoken to Avice. So although I know why you ran from the Strand House and my wretched father," he frowned, half delighted, half worried, "but this time – from the inn and even from your sister. Why run away again? And to run into danger. Of all nightmares, the pestilence."

"Oh, I didn't mean to," she mumbled. "I'll tell you everything. But I really, really need to sit down."

"You're sick?" She lost her footing and was lifted from the ground, her feet flew, his arms around her back and beneath her knees, carrying her as though she weighed no more than the bucket of water which had started it all. He said, "My horse will carry us both. I'll take you back to the inn."

She shook her head, then leaned it against her shoulder and said, "I can't. Not back there. And I can't come near you either. You have to put me down. I can't breathe on you."

"A little late for that."

"It's what you did and what I have to do. Not to risk anyone else –"

She struggled but he carried her to his waiting mare and tossed her up into the saddle. "I seem to have heard those words before," he murmured, "but you'll face nothing like that alone, my sweet." Then, his foot to the stirrup, he mounted quickly behind her, one arm to the reins and the other around her waist, and spoke directly to the back of her ear. His voice was a little warm breeze. "I'll ride slowly – the poor beast is exhausted anyway. In a few moments David and Alan will catch up with us. But I need to understand, and I want details."

She began to explain, but found she was crying. As the other two riders cantered into sight along the narrow lane, Nicholas waved them away. "Rob and Harry have taken the lower road," he said. "Find them and tell them to meet me back at the Fox."

After a while, Nicholas slowed his pace to an uncertain amble, and then stopped. Emeline was still trying to finish her story. She mumbled eventually, "But I've promised to go back to that poor man tomorrow. With medicines and something to stop the pain. And then I have to stay there, because it will be me next."

He kissed her ear and the back of her neck, and he loosened the reins so the horse again began to jog, a desultory trot along the dark path. Nicholas murmured, "Silly puss. Nothing like that will happen. I'll sort a way to fulfil your promise to your dying friend. But I want you back safe at the Fox, even if I have to smuggle you in. We'll need a separate chamber, something small and out of the way, with no questions asked. David can sort out clothes for both of us, and buy a supply of medicines. I'll keep you apart and in bed, so there'll be no contagion. The locals have all heard the rumours, but I've a habit of getting my way when I want it. I intend looking after you until we see whether there's danger or not."

She struggled out of his arms and turned to look at him. "You, of all people, I can't risk making you sick."

"Not me. I've twice proved myself against the pestilence, and if needs be I'll prove myself again." He sighed, then smiled, cradling her again against him. "It's the greatest horror of our age, greater than battle and the power hungry, greater than French threats and treachery, greater even than the pox and poverty. Every year it kills hundreds. It slips in quiet as moonlight, and in a week there's another village where new graves are dug across the land and the dying sob in desolation."

"I realised, back there," she mumbled, "how you must have felt. And I can't bring it to Avice or Sissy."

"No one knows how this infection spreads. Touch - breath - the air around - the clothes we wear. Or does our ever merciful God simply decide who will catch this filth, and who deserves to die in agony? But clearly He has no desire for me to sit at His feet, for I've survive it all. There's those who catch it and there's those who don't. I don't. Nor does David, for he's never even had a headache. So it doesn't frighten me, little one. Once you've passed the days of possible risk, as I promise you will, then I'll take you back home." He leaned over and kissed her forehead. "This nightmare will soon be over, I promise."

"You promise?"

"And from now on, my love, my promises will always come true."

CHAPTER FORTY ONE

Eventually they left the road. Nicholas dismounted, guiding his horse up through the beeches. Then turning sharply, they followed a thin track barely visible in the moonlight through the summer leaves. The hostelry stretched out on the rise, its smart thatch and beams creaking a little in the evening breezes, and its three chimneys gusting their smoke up to the stars. Alan was waiting outside the main stable block. He nodded, taking the horse, and whispered, "Bill's still sick, my lord. The others have talked of throwing him out under the trees, afraid of what he has, for rumours are rife. But he's still here, since no one is brave enough to touch him. If you ask me, my lord, he's suffering from the influenza."

Nicholas sighed. "That's well nigh as bad."

"I'll sort it, my lord. You get the lady safe. David has a chamber waiting."

David was at the hostelry door, holding it open. There was a sudden glorious warmth and the welcome of torchlight in the doorway.

"Up the stairs to the attic, my lord, if the lady can walk that far. It's the only chamber they had left, away up under the eaves. Little larger than a pantry, but it has a garderobe privy, a fair bed with soft pillows, and I've ordered the mattress warmed, a fire lit though the hearth is as small as a bean pod, and there's both a jug of decent Burgundy and some steaming hippocras waiting."

"I thank you. And the landlord wasn't suspicious?"

David smiled slightly. "If he was, my lord, I permitted no word of it. It's the Earl of Chatwyn's heir, come back with his wife and wanting privacy, I told him. He didn't dare argue, nor complain about the time of night. The nobility, I said, has their own habits and will brook no interference."

"Nor will I, since this is far too important."

Three flights up, then the final steps were steep, rickety and winding to the solitary attic chamber, once only used for storage but now the last resort for an overflowing hostelry. There

Emeline collapsed on the simple posted bed, leaned back against the heaped cushions and mumbled, "I promised Mister Cole back at the village –"

"That will have to wait for morning," Nicholas said, "though you're mighty obliging considering it seems to have been entirely his fault, and knowingly. But since nothing terrible will happen, we need not speak of it."

She shook her head, and said, "But if you'd watched his wife die, and him so caring –"

Nicholas said softly, "I watched my mother die. And I cared. I cared very much. I watched my little sister die. I loved her almost as much as my mother." He turned and continued speaking while pouring the hippocras. "They died in such pain and degradation." He handed Emeline one cup, then drained the other himself. "And my baby brother," he said very quietly. "All that pretty plump pink flesh sinking into dark bruises and loose wrinkled skin with no flesh left around his blood stained pleading eyes. He didn't understand, you see, why the pain was so terrible, and why I could not make it go away. I was only six myself, but I felt such guilt and wished I could suffer too, as if that would make it better for them. I watched them all die and could offer so little help, so I know exactly what you saw. I'm sorry you had to see it."

Emeline was crying again. "Will you watch me too, when I die?"

He paused, then spoke slowly, as if to emphasise the words. "You won't die. Emma, I shall forbid it." He had already removed her drinking cup and now refilled it. "I have to go down now, to explain the situation since the others will be worried. While I'm away, you will drink this, you will make yourself comfortable, and you will think of pleasure instead of pain. I shall be back very quickly. In minutes, no more, bringing your clothes, and mine, and anything else I think we need. We'll stay up here for just five days. Five days to wait and see. Five days to enjoy alone together, to talk, to kiss, and to think ourselves lucky to escape our relatives. And tomorrow, if you wish it, I'll buy medicines and take them to your sad widower."

She sat up again. "If you go there, the patrol will try and make you stay."

"No one," said Nicholas, "makes me stay where I don't want to."

She was asleep when he returned, but she woke, hearing his steps and the creak of the door. Still half drowsy, she heard him say, "Now we'll both sleep, my love. Your sister is greatly relieved, Sissy still awaits her brother, and my men know exactly what is expected of them."

Emeline snuggled next to him as he lay beside her and held her close. "You told them about the risk of the pestilence?"

He smiled. "You think me a poor liar, it seems."

She buried her head against the soft musty warmth of his doublet. "On the contrary."

She heard him chuckle. "Our own people know the truth, and will keep it to themselves. The servants at the hostelry know nothing, or we'd have panic and possible retribution. But in truth, we're not tucked away here because of danger and disease at all. We are here, my sweet, for all the love making we've missed these past weeks."

She thought of something, now properly awake. "And your Uncle Jerrid? He's not worried? He's not worried about staying with Sissy and Adrian?"

"What odd questions," Nicholas said. "Jerrid finds Adrian a bore and Sissy a fool, but no more than that, and he never worries about anything. He's a man who laughs sober, though prefers to laugh drunk. He seems to have been born with some part his elder brother missed, for my father growls sober and growls even more when pissed."

They slept warm. Nicholas did not make love to his wife. He lay some time thinking of her while she curled within his embrace, returning to the dreams he had interrupted. He discovered a strange peace, hearing the soft sound of rhythmic breathing and the little tickle against his neck. His hand lay across the dip of Emeline's breast, and beneath his palm he felt the strong steady beating of her heart. He listened to the little mutters of her dreaming, the small alarms and the complacent murmurs as she settled again. Sometimes her breathing became a tiny wheezing snore, and then she grunted, snug and satisfied by some dreaming pleasantry. Nicholas smiled, holding her to his own heartbeat, finding delight in her night time busyness.

It had been a long time, and he had missed the smooth tempting touch of her skin and the gentle swells of her hips to her belly and to the rise of her buttocks, the hollows of dimples and her other beckoning secrets. He had missed the heat of her naked breasts, the hard thrust of her nipples beneath his fingers, and the lush curls of the hair between her legs. He had missed the silk of her inner thighs, the eager push of her lips to his, her little gasps when he found her places of greatest sensitivity, then the enormous thrill of her climax. His own climax, for which he yearned, he dismissed, yet still he remembered, enjoying the memory, of touch and entrance, his deep pleasure in discovery, and the teaching of her which she accepted with such excited obedience. He had missed all the joyous lovemaking which had haunted his own dreams for those days and nights gone, but which he knew he could not now expect of her. So he lay quiet, thinking and remembering as he fondled, his hands careful across her half clothed body, as he kissed her cheek, though she knew nothing of it

When he finally slept, his dreams were less kind. It was his mother he dreamed of, and his siblings as they died, and the awful black fear of seeing the same again. And in his dream he realised that he had now, at last, found love again, and that the same end might accompany it. Being long past midnight, he slept late. It was David who woke them both, knocking, a little timid at the door. "My lord?"

It was nearly two hours later when David returned with the herbs and medicines Nicholas had instructed him to obtain, by which time Emeline was impatient for her dinner, to speak to her sister, and to hear all the news.

"The groomsman Bill is sneezing his beard off, my lady," David said, laying out the tubs and packets he had bought on the little table. "And there's not a victim of the Great Mortality I've ever heard with the sneezes. Every other horror including the cough and the delirium, diarrhoea and buboes, yes, my lady. But a simple tickle of the nose, no. So a man that sneezes does not have the pestilence, he has the influenza perhaps, or just a simple cold which he complains about far too loudly. There is no infection in this hostelry."

"As yet," whispered Emeline.

Nicolas inspected his squire's purchases. "Very well, David, there's enough here to dose a hundred of us. Now give me a few moments alone with my wife before I ride out with you to this wretched village and deliver a share of those medicines." David left as Nicholas turned to Emeline. "Well, little one, does the shopping expedition please you? And now, since it matters to you, I'll take whatever you wish to your undeserving Ralph Cole. But it means leaving you alone for an hour or three."

"It was me who asked you - and my promise to that poor man. But my love, I shall be ill with worry until you return, fearing you'll be caught and kept by those horrid patrols. The monks must be fierce indeed, and they intend no one to leave that village once arrived. What if you don't come back?" Emeline stood in a hurry, brushing down her skirts and reaching to straighten her hair. "Or perhaps, if you allow it, I might come too?"

"Allow it?" Nicholas grinned. "How timid and obedient you've become, my sweet. When did you last ask my permission for anything, making your own decisions to gallop half way across England and land yourself in more trouble than the entire package of wretched Woodvilles have managed since the old king's death."

"I'm being polite because I really want to come with you."

"So I'll answer you politely, my love. But the answer's no. What, and risk you coming in contact yet again with the damned pestilence? It'll be me and David alone will go since we've no fear of this sickness, having beaten it before. And we'll come back, that I can promise you."

"And so if you don't -" but she was interrupted.

The footsteps up the stairs, small vehement steps reverberating with determination, reached the bedchamber's small door. The voice was equally loud and equally recognisable. "If the child believes she can avoid me with silly stories of disease and death, then she is very much mistaken," announced the baroness. "She will immediately abandon all disabilities and ailments at this instant, pull herself together, and prepare her apologues."

David's mumble. "My lady, I beg you, if you could keep your voice down?"

"What? Whisper? Certainly not." The baroness thumped on the attic door. "Emeline, I demand you let me in and prepare yourself for a well deserved interrogation."

"Oh, bother and Bedlam," sighed the baroness's daughter.

Nicholas opened the door to his mother-in-law. "My lady, though the joys of seeing you here are naturally immense," he said with quiet amusement, "I cannot permit entrance. Allow mw to explain."

"Make her go away," moaned Emeline from the other side of the door.

Nicholas closed the door. "The risk is genuine, my lady," he told the irate baroness. "And it is imperative not to alert the staff here, or we will be asked to leave. Emeline needs warmth and comfort. But if you enter here, you may catch the disease yourself and even carry it to others."

"Oh, Lord have mercy." The baroness pushed past, entered the tiny attic room and stood central, eying her daughter. "I forbid it, Emeline," she said. "Do you hear me? It is utterly forbidden."

Nicholas, grinning, came behind her. "I have told her the same, madam. But now, if you'll leave my wife to me, I promise you she'll be as well protected as is ever possible since I have some experience of this disease and no fear of it. I'm sure she's not been infected, but in all decency, we need to allow for the possibility and keep our isolation." He led the baroness again from the room. "She's in good hands, my lady, I assure you. In the meantime it's Avice, I think, who is half delirious with worry."

It was a wary and hurrying Harry Bambrigg who later carried four platters, still steaming, and set them for Emeline on the tiny table. She ate her dinner alone.

Nicholas and David left the Fox and Pheasant and took the low road for the nearby village, its watching and officious monastery, and its lonely suffering. They saw no one else, but kept close and did not speak. When they came to the village, it was late morning, and bright with a smell of damp and peaceful warmth. But no movement disturbed the clustering houses, no market coloured the grassy square, no village shops were open, the church stood empty and silent, and only the sharp little wind disturbed the silence. The horses' hooves clattered down the lane, but no one came to their door as the shadows from the houses narrowed the path.

Ralph Cole lay on the straw pallet he had made up for his wife beside the fire. The fire had gone to ashes. There was no sign of the dead woman. He tried to scramble up as Nicholas entered. "In honour of my wife's promise," Nicholas said softly, "I have brought medicines. Your actions were dishonourable, but you are dying and I understand your pain. Some of what I bring will help that pain." He strode over, kicking the fire back to sparks. "So I've no kind words to give you. You tried to help your own wife at the cost of mine, and destined her to ostracism and possible misery. I'd not have come except for my lady's insistence. So thank her, who you might have killed, not me."

The man had no strength to plead, nor to apologise, not even to stand. He struggled to sit, gasping for breath. "Forgive me, my lord, before I die," he said. "I carried my Maudie upstairs, and she's all comfy on our bed like a queen sleeping. I was so scared I'd drop her, and let her tumble down them steps, but I managed it, and laid her all tidy. Them black lumps went away after a time, but the rash has stayed, and all her skin is spoiled. But I remembers her as she used to be, and that's how I pray she'll be when I sees her next."

Nicholas nodded. "I see you have the rash yourself, and the mark of a bubo growing under the jaw. I have brought two medicines to lessen that pain. One is the most commonly used, the other is the strongest. Use one, use both; the choice is yours." He opened the door slightly, looked out and signalled to David, instructing him to collect firewood. Back in the single chamber, the smoke had dissipated, but a smoggy stink smothered everything inside.

Ralph choked, gasping for breath. "I wish to God," he sighed, "I had this before, for my Maud."

"If there is still water in the bucket," Nicholas told him, "you must dilute the willow bark potion and take it weak at first, then afterwards stronger and undiluted as you feel you need it. But the poppy juice is very strong. It's here," and he placed the tiny tub on a stool, "for when you need it. I believe it will kill all pain, even the worst, but it could kill you too if you take too much." Nicholas turned towards the door. "What else needs to be done? Have you food?"

"I've no appetite, my lord," Ralph shook his head, "but have stale bread and a pot of old soup back there on the shelf, if I wants it. Which I don't, nor couldn't if I wanted, for it's swallowing, even for medicines, hurts my throat now."

"Then I'm sorry, but there's nothing else can be done for you." Nicholas knelt suddenly, speaking very softly. "You must cope alone now. But listen to me, for I know a good deal about this vile sickness, and you should follow the advice I give. The pain will get worse. Take the diluted willow bark now, it'll give you some relief, but that won't last long. Take it again when you need it. This evening take it undiluted and hopefully it will help you sleep. In the morning you'll know. You'll feel better or a good deal worse. If it's better, then you're one of those lucky enough to throw it off, as I did. But you show signs of a bubo growing, and that is not lightly thrown off. It you feel considerably worse, then you take the poppy drink. All of it. Then you stamp out the fire, you lie down and you wait to die. You'll sleep quickly, deep and dreamless. You will feel no pain, no pleasure. Nor have knowledge of day or night. You'll never wake. It's the easiest way." He paused, raising his voice a little. "Do you understand?"

Struggling, wide eyed, Ralph mumbled, "But my lord, you advise me to force my own passing, but this is a mortal sin. I cannot risk - and my Maud waiting at heaven's gates - I won't do anything to spoil -"

"Sin?" Nicholas interrupted. "It's this vile illness is the sin, dragging the innocent into an agony they cannot have deserved. I simply bring a medicine to relieve all pain. If you die peacefully in your sleep, then it's the Lord's gift. No guilt, no sin, no risk. The choice is yours. But do as I say, for otherwise you choose pain over peace, and there's no virtue in that." He turned abruptly. "Enough. It's time to leave while I'm still able."

Ralph Cole looked over to Nicholas, now standing by the door. "I'll do as you said, my lord, if you're sure it's not a wickedness. For I saw the pain my wife bore, and she were stronger and braver than me. Nor I ain't alone, not with my Maud waiting upstairs."

Nicholas pulled the door shut behind him, muttering, "If the man has any sense he'll take the poppy juice at once, and finish himself off before the pain's any worse," and he swung himself into the saddle. He waved to David who was waiting by the village green. "Time to be off, and quickly," he called.

It was a pale blue sky, almost cloudless and strangely benign. Yet it gazed down on a lifeless and tragic silence. But it was only moments before Nicholas was stopped.

The men spread out, blocking both the road and the grassy banks either side. On his liard, Nicholas might have leapt the blockage, but the placid old mare he was riding could barely jump a ditch. Nicholas once more sighed, and stared down at the angry patrol.

The tallest man stepped forwards, waving a stout stick. "What's this then?" he demanded. "Come to rob the poor dying folk as they lie defenceless, is we? There's no folk can leave the village, not for pity nor money, you can't. And be spreading tales, and carrying the pestilence wide and afar? No you won't, sir, grand dressed nor otherwise."

Nicholas looked down with some disdain at the tousled head below him. He said, "I am heir to the Chatwyn earldom, and you have no authority to keep us here, although I have some sympathy for your cause, its reasons and its aims. So I'll tell you I've a place set well apart from other folk, and have every intention of staying there until the sickness comes or time passes without sign of contagion when I and my companion will consider ourselves saved. We'll speak to no one else about the situation here, nor risk spreading it. You will therefore now let us pass."

The man scowled. The other four huddled, worried, muttering together. The horses kicked up dust, impatient. The first man, cudgel raised, did not stand aside. "We can't allow it," he said. "Tis as the abbot told us, not to let nor man nor child pass nor out nor in."

"Being as your lordship seemingly be a proper lord," said another, shifting uncomfortably in the dust, "mayhaps you could come tell the abbot yourself, sir, and let him decide."

A third man grabbed at the horse's reins and Nicholas swore. "Touch me again, and my sword will be at your throat," he said between his teeth. "I'll kill no man doing his duty, but you go beyond your rights."

Once again, they were interrupted. There was a call, loud and urgent. Every man turned and looked towards the village square. In the middle of the lane David stood, holding his fractious horse, but pointing back behind him. "Quick, you fools," he called. "It's fire. Every thatch will be ablaze in moments. Is there rainwater in the butts? Will you let your people burn?"

CHAPTER FORTY TWO

An interruption of almost similar magnitude spoiled the late morning dinner which was at that moment being served in the hostelry's small private parlour. Grouped around the table and already holding their tempers as they ate, were the baroness, her younger daughter Avice, her son-in-law's cousin Sysabel, and the ageing Lady Elizabeth. Joan, Bess, Hilda and Petronella were helping to serve since the hostelry staff were over stretched, and the ladies preferred the presence, under the circumstances, of those they trusted. Upstairs the family nurse, Martha, was reorganising the large chamber her mistress would now share with those existing occupants, Avice and Sysabel. It was at the precise moment of serving the roast beef slivers wrapped in smoked salmon beneath a herb crust, that the door slammed downstairs, a voice was raised, and everybody in the parlour put down their spoons and knives with a clatter and stared at each other.

"I don't give a rat's whiskers for your miserable hostelry, my good man," announced the Earl of Chatwyn from the corridor outside. "I'll thank you to remember exactly who *I* am. I've relatives staying here and my groom informs me that your stables are half full of the horses and other grooms from my own estates. You will therefore immediately show me where my relatives are at present housed, while you continue to arrange my bedchamber and a hot dinner. And if this place is simply too overcrowded to oblige me, then you had better instruct some of your other guests to move themselves off without delay into some alternative premises."

The baroness smiled apologetically at her companions, waved away the two remaining hostelry pages, leaned back in her chair, and addressed the hovering Petronella. "Please inform his lordship," she sighed, "that his son is at present absent but will return shortly, his brother Jerrid is resting in a chamber upstairs, we are already seated here enjoying a pleasant midday meal, and he is - naturally - most welcome - to join us."

The earl joined them. He eyed the laden dishes and scratched his head. "Been a tiresome journey," he admitted. "Left me a touch peckish."

"I shall order a new platter, spoon and napkin brought for your lordship," said the baroness. "You are clearly half starved, sir."

"Well, not exactly," admitted the earl. "Had an early dinner back at some pokey little inn along the way. But it's been a good few miles since then."

"The spiced calves' brains are very good, my lord."

He tried the calves' brains, along with nearly everything else, and regarded his hostesses with complacence. "Didn't mean to come," he explained, with a slight belch. "Used to travelling of course, though usually on the king's business, but I saw no reason to come cavorting through the rain and wind just to seek out the rest of my pesky relatives. Usually only too glad to see the back of them. It made more sense to stay at home and wait for them to come to me. But - well," he smiled with faint apology, "wondered if all you adventurous females might need an escort, or some such. Thought to do my duty. Besides," he added, "got damned dull, just waiting alone. So here I am." The earl lounged, ankles stretched out and crossed. He wore the fashionable short doublet usually admired by younger men, and his thighs pulsed large, muscles squashed together and forced into overflow.

The parlour, being a small back chamber, had only one very small window of polished horn which obscured everything but the falling drizzle outside. There were therefore two candles lit in spite of it being daytime, and one flickering spit of tallow illuminated the earl's jowls with unforgiving candour. The baroness regarded her new companion and wondered how it was that this coarse featured man had sired two such handsomely charming sons. She decided, as she had previously, that the late countess must have been a beauty. She further decided, with a smugly secretive smile, that her own family situation had been a similar one. She shook her head free of pointless fancies and said, "But you find us sadly disorganised, my lord. Nicholas was here earlier, but has now gone to fulfil some errand which I know nothing of. I myself arrived only recently and have yet to see young Adrian." She nodded towards Sysabel. "Though I am told he has proved himself a great hero and is much in favour. Now he has gone off on business with friends, but is expected to return either today or tomorrow."

"Adrian? Humph," decided the earl, pushing away crumbs. "He may well have gone off with friends, but genuine business in Weymouth is highly unlikely I'm afraid. No head for it, you know. And as for being a hero, he never managed to live up to his hero worship of my boy Peter. I expect he's off on some nonsense - well, his highness does use his more intelligent young courtiers from time to time. Looking into state matters and bringing back information. I am often employed on such subtle business, naturally. I wouldn't put it past Adrian, though I doubt he'd be considered a principal player."

"And Nicholas?"

"Madam," sighed the earl, "you must know the answer to that as I do myself."

"Perhaps," decided her ladyship, "I have just a little more respect for my daughter's husband than you do, my lord."

He waved a plump handful of beringed fingers. "I know my son," said the earl, "and for all a father's natural fondness, I have to admit the wrong one died. I miss Peter, Such a good boy. I have every reason to suppose he was destined for greatness, as I'm sure the king already knew. But Nicholas? He'll be lying drunk in some bordello off the coast, skulking away from duty and responsibility just as he hides from the cold north winds."

Sysabel, in spite of her Aunt Elizabeth's warning expression, interrupted. "I've no interest in defending Nicholas, uncle," she said, her voice a little tremulous, "although I believe he recently behaved with honour concerning Emeline. But Adrian is exceedingly wise, although naturally, coming from a noble family, he is not actually in business himself."

The earl sniffed. "No harm in a little trade sometimes, you know my dear. Wool through Norwich, even printing and books, something the king himself approves. But Adrian, well I doubt it. He's a clever boy, but not for business."

The Lady Elizabeth sighed. "If only there was something that brought in a little money –"

Avice snorted, and one of the candles blew out. "The only thing any of us should be worried about is Emma."

"If young Nicholas has deserted –"

The baroness shook her head. "My elder daughter is upstairs in one of the smaller guest chambers, my lord. But she is - unwell. A slight chill, no doubt. Nicholas is looking after her, and has forbidden anyone else from becoming involved. A risk of - infection, no doubt. At present he has gone to procure medicines but is expected back at any moment."

"Ah." The earl looked around the party of females, and frowned. "A chill?"

"A chill, my lord. But since the aged groom my daughters originally took with them as guide and protector has also gone down with some form of cold and is at present incapacitated, we are taking no chances as to infection and Nicholas has dear Emeline close closeted upstairs."

"And my wayward younger brother?"

"Uncle Jerrid," sniffed Sysabel, "is upstairs snoozing. I have no idea what he's doing here in the first place."

"Travelling with Nicholas," the baroness reminded her.

"Which," said Sysabel softly, avoiding all accusatory glances, "I find highly suspicious. They were up to no good, I'm sure of it. And my poor Adrian –"

The earl refilled his wine cup. "At the first sneeze," he declared, "I'm off. Can't afford to be getting sick, no profit in it, and besides, the king needs me. Hopefully it's just feminine sniffles. No harm done. But I need a decent chamber, and if there's none to be had then I suppose I shall have to share with Jerrid."

"He'll be delighted, I'm sure," muttered Avice.

"I believe," said the baroness, "I shall have another cup of wine." The earl released the jug, which he had once again taken up.

"I think," decided the Lady Elizabeth suddenly rousing herself, "I need a little fortification as well. Life is no longer as peacefully predictable as it once was."

"Was it?" sighed the baroness. "I don't remember."

Some miles south west, the drizzle was more welcome. There was the scorching, smoky stench of burning straw and plaster, and the combination of fire doused in low cloud and a mist of damp. Distant sounds, voices and alarm escalated. David remounted, watching the five men of the patrol race back along the pathway towards the village. He reached out, retraining his master, "Not back there, my lord. Now we need to get away."

Nicholas frowned. "You started this fire?"

"By no means, my lord. You know my dislike of fire, and you know why."

The simmering flames broke their confines and gusted, plumes of dirty smoke caught in the breezes. Whatever burned, burned soot and reeds, old planks, old thatch, and the bodies in each house lying dead or dying. The rotting remains of the pestilence and their sad empty houses were lit with new light. The breeze became a wind. The drizzle was a swirling silvery haze but the fire was stronger. The drizzle turned scarlet. Another thatch caught, two houses in from the Coles' cottage. Flames crackled, spitting their sparks high like dancing rubies, each fragmented, a game of tiny escaping explosions high against a dull grey sky. The next house, roofs attached, began to blaze and the flames ran along the thatches in little seeking tongues.

Nicholas shouted, "Damnation. Get here, David, quickly, before this spreads to the trees."

"We should leave at once, my lord. We have other duties and far more important. Your lady and then his highness –"

Nicholas frowned. "These poor miserable wretches have faced the pestilence. Must the survivors burn alive? If there's water, I'll help put out the fire. I've experience enough." He had already turned his horse. The mare snorted, her nostrils flared, smelling fire. But Nicholas urged her back towards the village.

David, again in the saddle, followed, heels to the reluctant horse's flanks. "My lord, is the aim worth the risk?"

"Come with me or not, my friend," Nicholas called back. "Your hatred of fire is something I well understand, so give your help, or not. But don't argue, when it's action we need." He was now well ahead, as suddenly the sky turned orange. Above the haze of gathering smoke obscured the leering virulence which varnished all the clouds as though they too were aflame. Only moments down the lane, Nicholas halted. "The horses are terrified," he shouted. "Stop here, David, and keep hold of my reins." He dismounted and ran.

Where the cottages huddled the fire spread unhindered, gaining strength and swallowing everything both within and without. First to Ralph Cole's, kicking open the cracked wooden door. One wall was already crumbling into soot, and showed the single chamber in a swirl of yellow smoke. Nicholas turned on his heel and strode back outside.

Around him there was noise and fear as hot and nauseas as the fire. There were screams, people running, a woman, her gown all in scorched tatters, crawling from the collapse of her home. A young man ran, his hair in flames. People, hugging, helping, shouting and panicking, racing or struggling to the open grass. David tied both horses' reins to an overhanging branch and followed his master. He marched among the scurry and chaos, offering help. Nicholas called for buckets, organising a line from butts to thatches and eventually a hope of salvation.

Within only moments those ten or more cottages grouped around the church and the grassy square were destroyed, lost in piled rubble, ashes, shattered beams, scattered iron pots and those few precious possessions now ruined. A bedstead, its strings all gone, stood broken legged in a mess of blackened fustian and feathers, its owner fallen through the burned base and now lying on the ground, a shrivelled memory of a life now cooked flesh, no knowing if this had been man or woman, or had died first of the pestilence, or later killed by fire. Eerie and echoing silences were shattered by falling walls and ceilings, the thunderous tumbling of timbers. Faint, distant and smothered, the moaning of someone left alive. Nicholas pulled the dead, dying and living from the rubble which had once housed them. Beside him the frantic patrol fought desperately to save who and what they could, five men working alongside Nicholas and David, checking each house as the wind swept up the flames and threw them like sheets into the rain.

The water butts were half full with wet leaves and insect larvae, little more than dirty puddles but water all the same. Buckets filled, trudged from scalding door to step. So the fire, slow pace by pace, was doused. Step by step and one by one some were saved. One man gasped, "God bless you, sir," and died, tongue out to taste the cool liquid as he heaved one last breath.

Then dark figures, a single line of black frocked monks from the monastery, alerted by the smell of fire, doggedly trudging the trail from their quiet haven. Nicholas beckoned to David, who was still checking the ruins of an adjacent house. "We'll leave," he said. "The monks and their patrol will finish what they can. We're no longer needed." David sank down a moment, gasping for breath. His hair was singed, his clothes blackened. Nicholas nodded, and helped him rise. "You're a brave man, my friend," he murmured, "to march into the flames you hate and fear." He supported his squire as they staggered back down the lane to where the horses had been tethered. A hazy twilight had turned the trees to silhouettes, the sky just grey pockets between the leaves. They had not even noticed the passing of time.

The Fox and Pheasant was quiet. The fragile drifting drizzle still blanketed the roof and its eaves, the tucked windows obscured in silver shimmer, and the sun was setting behind the clouds.

Avoiding all other sounds and all other chambers, Nicholas took the back stairs and climbed to the attic. He found his wife half drowsing, the long wait for him having turned to apathetic slumber. When she heard the door close, she blinked and sat up in a hurry.

"Forgive the delay," he sat beside her and took her hand. "There was more to do than we'd expected. Fire, and half the village destroyed. Unkind to you, little one, but I saved other lives; something I felt I had to do." He smoothed his thumb across her cheeks. "You've been crying."

She shook her head. "I thought perhaps that you couldn't get away. I thought you'd - never - get away."

"Foolish mistrust, my sweet. And before you ask, your friend was dead already, and is now at peace. I saw him before the fire and gave the medicines. I gave him poppy juice, and explained what would happen if he took a stronger dose. I hope that's what he did. We saved a few others, and some were saved by the men of the patrol. They were courageous, and did what they could, as David did, carrying out both the sick and the healthy from houses aflame and falling. I've a squire to be proud of." But he leaned down and kissed her smut marked cheeks, both arms still very tight around her. "And I've a remarkably brave wife too, and I'm proud to call her mine."

Emeline winced, whispering, "You're not cross with me for having left home before - for coming here - for bringing danger to everyone - so that you had to rescue me?"

"You imagine I'd be angry because you've not obeyed me? But you so rarely do, my love, I no longer expect it."

"And you said you're - truly - proud - of me?"

He kissed the tip of her nose which was fiercely pink. "I am exceedingly proud of my exceedingly courageous wife. I'm learning a great deal more about you, my love. And now we eat, we talk, we kiss, and finally we sleep."

She had decided not to warn him yet, but then she thought better of it. "Are you going down to order supper? Then I had better tell you who is here."

"A parcel of women, and most of them my wretched relatives."

"Not all of them women." She took a deep breath, and said, "Your father is here."

"Impossible. If you've heard his voice, then it's delirium or dreams."

Emeline shook her head. "He was tired of waiting alone in the Strand House, so he followed my mother's trail. The inn is full indeed. My mother tiptoed in to tell me all about it a few hours back."

"Oh, Lord." Nicholas sighed and stood. "Then I'd better face him. But he'll leave us alone once I whisper the word pestilence in his ear. I shall be back with food, wine, and ready to plump up the pillows for the night's deep and conscious free sleep."

"I shall dream of sickness and fire."

Nicholas smiled, turning at the door as he was about to leave the room. "I shall dream of you," he said.

CHAPTER FORTY THREE

They lay on the bed, half clothed, the dish of food between them, their wine cups on the small chest and their eyes on each other. Nicholas broke off a wedge of crumbled goat's cheese, and popped it into Emeline's mouth. She had been about to speak, but with cheeks suddenly full, she grinned at him, trying not to spit crumbs.

Nicholas laughed. "My poor sick and suffering wife. Clearly ailing. Will more wine help, do you think?"

"I'm probably tipsy already."

"Not nearly tipsy enough."

She wore only her shift, its fine linen clinging across her breasts. The neck was low, and where her nipples protruded soft and dark, it barely covered. As Nicholas moved his hand to her shoulder, he brushed over the swell of her body and smiled. As her nipples tightened, she whispered, "Is that not response enough?"

"Should I make love to my sick wife, then? Would that be selfish? Uncaring?"

"It would be kind." Emeline pushed the supper dish away and reached for her cup. "So must I be drunk, before you want me?"

"My dearest but foolish wife, there is never a moment when I don't want you." He took her cup and refilled it. "Drink. Enjoy our quiet moments for just a little longer. It's been a long time on the road, with cold winds and dirty taverns, straw beds and long hours in the saddle. While for you, my sweetest, it has proved even more challenging. Once this absurd scare is past, I'm taking you home. I plan a peaceful future, with children in the nursery and only rare visits to court."

He wore his shirt loose over his hose, boots kicked to the hearth and doublet thrown to the settle. Two candles were lit in a single stand but there was no fire in the grate, and the light was just a small golden flicker at their side. It reflected dancing fingers in the wine, the colour of flame. David and Petronella had been banished to other quarters, the room too small for servants, and the risk too great.

"And I've added to your exhaustion," Emeline whispered, "just when you thought you'd already done enough." She sipped her wine. "Did you do enough?"

"The young lord I was meant to meet never arrived. His escape was foiled, and the poor wretch is still held hostage in France." Nicholas sighed, his fingers now wandering inside Emeline's shift, encircling the firm warmth of her breast. "The other task proved more successful. An English traitor bringing a letter from the exile Henry Tudor, meant for delivery in the north. I met up with the messenger, stole the letter, and will take it to the king. The traitor lives and remains free, but that's no shame for he's well known to his highness, and is not a man easily taken."

"The king will be pleased then? Not disappointed?"

"He will be both. But complete success was not expected, and Dorset's failure was well nigh inevitable, being his second attempt. As for Urswick – the letter was more important than the arrest."

Emeline did not think it important at first. Her body tingled, warm tucked into the first stages of seduction. For many nights she had dreamed of caresses, as he had, and she had little interest in understanding the problems of security with France. So lying back a little against the pillows, she smiled, saying, "Another Urswick? But he has gone, and you are here, my love."

"Another Urswick?" His fingers slowed, pausing their exploration.

"The traitor you were looking for who brought the letter," She shook her head. "And then, of course, the other one is Adrian's friend."

Frowning, "Adrian was not alone? How many friends?"

"Just two, and no servants. If he had a groom or squire with him, then they were already back at the inn. But Adrian's friends were brave, and rescued us." Nicholas's fingers had now retreated, and she sat up, suddenly cold. "What's the matter? I told you about Sissy being stuck in that horrid marsh and Adrian riding by at that perfect moment. There was Adrian, and Mister Urswick, and the other was the brave Mister Browne who rode down the thief who tried to trap us."

"Urswick." The short silence seemed strained. Finally, very softly, he said, "Urswick? Are you sure?" Emeline nodded. Nicholas said, "Describe him."

She was worried now. "Tall, but not as tall as you, brown hair, lighter than yours and a little shorter than fashion. An ordinary man with very little to describe. Plain clothes. A kind smile."

"Did anyone," Nicholas asked carefully, "speak this Urswick's first name?"

"Adrian called him Christopher. He was nice."

Nicholas leaned back beside her, taking her hard into his arms, and speaking to the curls around her ears. "Dear sweet Lord have mercy," he murmured. "Must I challenge Adrian as well, then? Is it him I've been chasing without knowing? Have I been blind?" He paused, as she listened in horrified silence. Then he asked abruptly, "Where did Adrian and his friends say they were going? And how long past?"

"Two days gone," she gulped. "Urswick and Browne had a boat to meet and a journey across the water to make that next morning. Adrian was to see them safely off. He should be back soon, probably tomorrow."

"Then it's far too late to chase Urswick down." Nicholas said. He thought a moment, then smiled, though the smile remained cold. "I had no idea it might be my own cousin involved. But then, I warrant he has no idea it is me."

He turned, holding Emeline by her shoulders, facing her as if considering something. Then he released her and stood, abruptly pulling his shirt off over his head. He stood a moment, holding the shirt before he tossed it, his dark hair now tousled. The silk of black across his chest narrow striped the muscles of his breast and belly. The laces of his hose hung loose around his hips, the codpiece still in place, his legs tightly enclosed in the hugging soft knit of deep rustic green. Then he turned, wandering over to the candles standing on the stool beside the bed. He blew them out and the chamber blinked into shade. Nicholas became a shadow, half visible, half lost in suggestion.

"Come here," he said.

Emeline whispered, "There? Now?"

His voice was quiet, husky, almost too soft to hear. He said, "Yes, now. Here."

She heard the hint of menace in his voice. He had made love to her many times but this time, somehow, he had changed. The room was small; four steps and she was standing close so the heat of his body touched the tips of her breasts and her toes were against his. She mumbled, "You're angry."

"Yes. Do you mind?" He looked down at her. "But not with you. With Adrian. With myself." He grasped the shoulders of her shift and wrenched it down over her arms. The thin seams pulled apart, and the white tumbled linen floated to the ground at their feet. His gaze followed her nakedness, watching, not touching. His voice sank even lower. "If I hurt you," he murmured, "then you must hurt me back. Punch me and I'll understand."

She slipped her arms around his waist, her fingers clinging to the back of his hips. Still whispering, "It has to be love. Not anger."

"Then make me forget the anger," he said. "And make love to me." He stood very still, looking down at her, and his intensity had narrowed. The brilliance of his eyes was now heavy hooded, the muscles of his face tense, and the long scar down his left cheek seemed deeper, tighter, sinister, catching the flicker of the one remaining candle across the room. He said nothing more, but waited, watching.

With one hesitant fingertip she reached up and touched the tiny scars across his body where on their wedding night the flames had pricked and spat and marked him forever. Up his forearms, where the dark hair was sparse, there were a hundred memories of old fire. "So many wounds," she said. "Did the fire hurt you again today? I see no new marks."

Then he took both her hands in his, and brought them down to his groin. "Today I helped save others, and suffered nothing. Now it's myself I intend to save, but you must help me, my love, as I've taught you before, until the anger is all forgotten."

He brought her fingers to the closing of his codpiece, pulling at the hidden tie through its tiny eyelets which held the stiffened cup to the opening of the hose. Emeline took a deep breath and began very slowly and carefully to pull out the thin ribbon. Then she untied the band of his braies from around his waist, and even more slowly pulled his hose down over his belly and hips, smoothing downwards over the muscled curves of his thighs, the knees, the long slim swell of his calves, and finally, bending almost to the floorboards, she took them off over his feet. The braies and the hose and the codpiece fell away together, leaving him naked in his own shadows.

He stood easy, waiting a moment. But as she hesitated, he shook his head and pulled her close, lifting her a little, his hands beneath her arms, and pushed her back against the wall. She felt the hard cold planks behind her and shivered. "Cold?" He pressed against her and instead of the cold behind her, she felt the strength of him and the urgency. "Open to me then. I'll warm you."

She whispered, "I can't move."

"I move. Not you. Now open your legs."

He held her firm, her toes not touching the floor. "Don't let me fall."

"Fall?" he smiled, but all she saw was the sudden glitter of blue sparkle in his eyes. "Tonight you'll go where I put you and do what I tell you. I won't let you fall, and in a moment I'll carry you to bed. But first do as I say. Now open your thighs." She leaned her head against his shoulder, and did as he told her. He nodded. "Now reach down, take me, and put me inside you."

He had made love to her like this before. Their unions had been few enough and she remembered each one. Now once again she felt the tingle thread through her body, like the ties of his codpiece through its eyelets. She shivered again, though no longer from the cold, as her fingers crawled down across the taut muscles of his belly to the thick hair at his groin. "Further," he demanded. "You can hardly miss me, my love."

She did not miss, wrapping her fingers around him and guiding him between her legs. As she brought him close, he pushed immediately, battering his entrance. She squeaked, and he grinned, pushing again. Then balancing her against the wall, he hoisted her higher and with both hands beneath her buttocks, lifted and carried her, still inside as if speared, and brought her to the bed. Without releasing her, he laid her down on the mattress, his own weight on top. He quickly forced deeper within and she grunted, catching her breath.

"I said I wouldn't hurt you. Tell me if I do."

She whispered, "Not hurting. But unexpected."

He chuckled and pushed again. "Then squeeze tighter. Push up against me."

"I can't. I'm crushed."

"Poor love," he laughed at her, wedging himself up on his elbows. "Now push."

As she raised her hips, he forced in deeper, his hands beneath her and keeping her tight. When he stopped suddenly, unable to wait, she felt the pulse of him growing inside, the shuddering climax, and the explosion of silent energy. He made no sound except the hoarse release of breath, but it seemed a long time before his hands relaxed, his body calmed and he lay still against her.

Eventually he lay back, rolled her over away from him and tucked himself behind her, her buttocks to his groin and his knees beneath hers. Then he wrapped his arms around her, one hand to her breasts, and spoke softly into the back of her ear. She had thought to sleep, warm snuggled and feeling loved, and his sudden words surprised and alarmed her. "So, my Emma," he murmured, his voice sounding drowsy but his words were somehow harsh. "What did you do - ever - with Peter? Tell me."

Now she opened her eyes with a jolt. "So you're still really angry."

He still held her tight back against him. "No, not angry. If I was angry, I'd not dare to ask you. I'd not risk your answer. I'm merely curious. He told me, you see, being a bastard and a liar, what you were like. What he taught you to do, and what you wanted him to do. What you said. How you moved. He was wrong in almost everything. But I have wondered, sometimes, because of your passion for him back then, if something occurred between you after all."

"He never even kissed me." She pulled away, with the first tinge of her own anger only just controlled. "He played the gentleman. Oh, I thought myself in love. I was a fool. But I wouldn't ever have let him touch me. How could you - ever - think it?"

He tugged her back, almost roughly, one arm again across her breasts, the other around her hips. "Sometimes," he said softly, "when I make love to you, Peter's words echo in my head.

Thoughts slip sweat fuelled between us. It's as if he's still fucking as both."

"That's horrible." She wriggled around to face him but he held here firm, keeping her in his embrace.

His voice buzzed against the back of her neck. "Yes, absurd, and the absurdity is mine. Nor should I tell you, but it's tiresome, keeping those goading whispers out of my head. They come back when I least need interruption."

She bent down and kissed his hand, still clasped tight on her breast. "I hate even the memory of Peter. Why think of him now?"

His voice had grown softer, kinder, as his fingers traced between her breasts. "I missed you, little one, while I was away. More than I'd expected. Then the race to find you and the danger of the pestilence. Threat and loss are good lessons. But what I've now found in loving you, I don't intend to lose. Especially not to Peter."

"I thought it was Adrian you were angry with?"

"I let my father think the best of Peter. My cousins too. Other family friends. I didn't care. It even served my purpose at the time. But you, little one, I'd like to keep free of him." Nicholas kissed the back of her ear, and she felt the warmth of his breath. "Adrian doesn't know me, and that was my intention. I learned as a child to keep my thoughts to myself. But now I find that perhaps Adrian has done the same. I know nothing of his secrets."

"Like poor Sissy. Her secrets were the worst of all. And she still forgives Peter." Emeline sighed. "It makes me angry, thinking what he might have done to me, just as he did to her."

There was a pause. "Sissy?"

"Perhaps you don't know."

"I don't know." He sat up abruptly, pulling Emeline up with him so they both sat back against the pillows, his arm around her shoulder, her face nestled to the curve of his neck. "She was an infant, and still is. She thought herself in love with him. What more?"

Emeline paused, wondering who deserved her loyalty. Then briskly and quickly she decided. "I don't know who else knows. Obviously your father doesn't. I don't think Adrian does. But your Aunt Elizabeth knows, and of course Peter did. Now Avice and Maman do." She drew a deep breath and spoke fast. "So you should know as well. That Sissy was carting his child, and he arranged for her to have an abortion in some squalid little alley in London away from prying eyes."

"Dear God."

"You really didn't know?"

"I'd have killed him. Adrian would have killed him."

"Perhaps Adrian did." She sat up a little more, twisting to face him.

"Adrian was my principal suspect, even before this.", Nicholas nodded, and reached out again, searching for the wine cups. The room lay shadowed and warm with its billowing bed and the tiny window, the polished horn rattling in the wind behind its wooden shutters. Through the shadows, Nicholas found the cups and the jug, and poured the last of the wine. "Here, my sweet. It seems we've more to talk about than I realised."

She took the cup. "You've stopped being angry?"

"Curiosity kills anger. And this is important. Tell me about Sissy. Tell me about Adrian." He smiled as she drained her cup, then drained his own. "Now we're out of wine, my love, and must talk a little sober sense. You've proved surprisingly informative this evening; which I admit I'd not expected. I've been working for the king for three years of more – certainly since before he was king – and thought myself well aware of the subtle changes, the political necessities, the need for security after the '83 turmoil. And yet I've been blind to both my cousins, and even partially to my own brother."

The shadows receded as their eyes accustomed. "You think Adrian's a traitor? And a killer too?"

"You know I'd taken on the boy Wolt, the child left motherless after your father's murder. The boy was killed while under my protection, and I've not forgiven myself for that. The killers were looking, I believe, to take back the letter Urswick had brought. But why kill a grubby boy working in the stables?"

"Gracious, my love, what has that to do with Adrian?"

"Because it finally makes sense. Because if the men worked for Adrian, then Wolt would have recognised one or more of them from the Strand stables, and so had to be killed before he could carry tales and stand witness. But I was told the men were French. That distracted me. Merde, a French word. I was wrong.

Murder is an English word true enough, and with Nottingham accents which would have sounded foreign to those from the far south."

"If Adrian killed Peter, could he have killed my father?" The blankets lay around their waists but she was no longer cold. "You said it was the same man. But Adrian had no reason to murder my father. And fire, always fire. Why is there always fire, Nicholas?"

"It's the English plague, with every house a tumbled pile of rotting beams, insects rummaging in thatch, logs burning on unattended hearths and barely a decent kitchen beyond the palaces and castles."

Emeline shook her head. "It was the castle that burned on our wedding night."

"My father's fault, drunk at the table and the candles falling, no doubt. But it's usually the little places, and the folk with nowhere to run to that burn. Half of London is haunted by fire. A law was brought in, banning thatch and ordering new roofs on old buildings, but it's rarely been enforced. David's father was killed by fire. His mother was never sane after that, and neglected the boy. He still fears the flames."

"Oh, too many nightmares, too much misery. Is there nothing to cherish anymore?" She shuddered, sliding her arm around her husband's waist beneath the blankets. "And what if I'm the next nightmare, and you wake up to find me sick and bleeding? And I'll know I have just three days to live before I die in agony."

Nicholas leaned over her at once, his thumb wiping away her sudden tears. He caressed her cheeks and kissed her as he pulled the blankets gently back around her body. "That won't happen," he whispered. "None of that - not the pestilence nor any other sickness. Not now that I've fallen in love with you."

CHAPTER FORTY FOUR

They woke hungry, with morning seeping beneath the door. Nicholas yawned, stood, shook the sleep from his shoulders, stretched, then strode across and lifted down the window shutters, welcoming the fresh new sunshine. A diffused but blinking daylight already sat well above the horizon.

Then he sat on the edge of the bed, and regarded his wife. "You look sparkling, my love. No pains? No fears?"

Her voice was muffled by pillows. "Only about murder and murderers, and if we already live with someone who wants to kill us."

He tugged on his shirt and hunted under the settle for his hose. "I'm going down to get us something for breakfast. I can take yesterday's supper dishes down with me, you can't leave the room. But I can."

"Maybe you shouldn't."

"Cheese, manchet, bacon? Ale or wine?" He was pulling on his hose and retying the codpiece as he shoved his feet into his riding boots. "Damnable inconvenience, with half my clothes downstairs in the other chamber. I'll get David to sort the rest of them for me."

"If everyone knew it was the pestilence, and not just a chill, they wouldn't let you out of the room either."

"They would indeed." He grinned. "They'd be throwing the whole lot of us out on the cobbles. Now - cheese or bacon?"

"Both."

It was some time before he returned. He did not immediately explain the delay. Finally, she said, "So who was questioning you? Your father or my mother? Or were you questioning Sissy?"

"I'm hardly likely to accuse my baby cousin of flagrant immorality in the middle of a crowded hostelry while I'm more concerned with looking after my wife." Nicholas cut a slice of cold bacon and handed it to Emeline, then returned to the beer jug. "Besides, I simply feel sorry for the poor child. But she'll never talk to me about it, nor thank you for spreading the news. No, it was my father. He's in the way as usual." He looked up suddenly, frowning. "I wonder if I should one day ruin his complacence and tell him the truth about Peter." He shook his head, returning to the platter of cold food. "But he'd not believe me. And I'd gain nothing except his spite."

"So what," she swallowed and took another wedge of cheese, "are they all doing downstairs?"

"Haven't killed each other yet. Close, perhaps."

Emeline swung her legs from the bed and walked to the window, gazing out on the world she could not yet join. "So perhaps it's just as well I'm stuck in here." She smiled suddenly. "We're safe from our families, and the gossip, and the arguments. And even the fear and meeting Ralph taught me so much about what you went through and what you suffered." Then she sat down again, picking scraps of food from the eiderdown and hiding her face. "So I know you much better now. And I understand so much more."

He waved an accusatory arm. "Using the bed as a table as usual, crumbs between the sheets, and everything needing to be carried up four flights of stairs. But I see the advantages too, my love, having you to myself. And as you learn about me, so I learn about you. From now on I'll only go back downstairs when I've a purpose."

She sat, looking intently at him. "You said something last night. I wasn't sure what you meant."

He came beside her, winding his arms around her waist and burying his face in her hair. "I said a lot of things last night. And I treated you badly. Satisfied myself, probably at your expense. But I was angry about Adrian. Then I was tired, and had Peter muttering in my head. Angry about Sissy. And thinking of how I face Adrian once he reappears."

"What did your father want this morning?"

"Recriminations. The usual." Nicholas was laughing. "Me to shoulder my responsibilities and stop hiding in the attic. Bring my wife back to Westminster, and behave like a mature Chatwyn."

"What is a mature Chatwyn?"

Nicholas leaned back to where the remains of their breakfast now lay strewn. "Nothing unusual," he told her. "Wealthy, respected, ambitious, greedy, conceited, arrogant. Most of us drink too much, and that's largely due to boredom and a need not to think too deeply. Think too hard, and along come the doubts, conscience and uncomfortable memories. So my father drinks. I drink too. But I also discovered other opiates."

Emeline frowned. "What opiates?"

"What I once called adventure. Working for the king. Berwick during the siege, helping break the stand off from the inside. I acted as a casual tutor to the young Princess Cecily. Working undercover to negotiate with the dowager and get her and her daughters out of sanctuary. To explain what had happened to her sons, tell her Tyrell and Brampton were the occasional and financial custodians while her boys stayed safe abroad. The king uses many of his more able courtiers for such work. A common practise. Fulfilled my need for adventure. Keeping old memories at a safe distance."

"And Peter's opiates?"

Nicholas laughed, lying flat on his back on the mattress, the covers dishevelled beneath him, his hands clasped behind his head. "Peter?" He was smiling up at the beams and the bed's small faded tester. "Seductions and rapes. Secret violence and the spoils of story mongering and tale spreading. Watching the ensuing misery of others."

Emeline sighed. "There's so much to tell each other, but so little of it is pleasant."

He turned his head, looking at her. "I'll take you back to the castle later this month, once I've seen the king. My father will stay at court. Then I'll teach you pleasure, my love."

"But you don't know if we'll ever get there. Perhaps you have some special charm so you don't get sick. But that won't work for me."

Nicholas paused, frowning. "You'll live, because I need you," he said quietly. "What point in my survival, if it has to be alone?"

"You mean it?" Emeline sat up, staring back wide eyed. "That's what you said last night and I was hoping you'd say it again. But you don't mean it, do you! You're saying what you think I want to hear, because you're sure I'll die."

"When I'm telling you the opposite?"

"You're lying."

He smiled, sinking back against the pillows "Then clearly I must speak of the mundane, and of subjects where I shall be believed. There is, for instance, some small leggy creature up there, busy with its web and no doubt a hoard of spider children bursting from their eggs. Or whatever else spiders do to pass the time. Eat flies. There's flies and beetles enough up there to choose from."

Emeline laughed. "All right. You don't want to tell me to my face that I might be dying. And the hints about caring – about some growing affection – that's best not discussed either."

"Shall I tell you what I've been doing for the past few weeks?" He closed his eyes, slumped on his back, hands again behind his head. His voice softened. "Shall I describe all the wretched days of creeping in the shadows, wearing clothes that itch with fleas, and not caring to comb the lice from my hair? Attack, defence, knives from the mist. Days in shadows and nights in the dark. The boy was killed. I should have protected him, but it never occurred to me the boy would be a target, and I was too busy protecting myself. So, the bastard guilt and knowing he died for me." Nicholas opened his eyes suddenly and gazed up at Emeline who was staring down at him helplessly. "Oh, don't feel sorry for me, my sweet," he said, smiling. "It was one of the easier jobs I've taken on. I took no wound, and one part of the task was achieved successfully enough. Adventure after all, and I'll not complain about the life I chose myself. But this time the pleasure faded. Most of it seemed simply tedious." His smile widened. "And through it all, I kept thinking of you. I didn't ask to. It didn't help. But your face slipped constantly into my thoughts, your voice whispered into every silence. Your face pushed out Peter's whispers. Your smile stayed always at the back of my eyes. I missed you."

"You really *missed* me?"

"Quite horribly. And then, half mad with a dozen problems on my mind, I arrive at the hostelry where I intend staying in more comfort than usual, and come face to face with your sister."

Emeline put her hand over her mouth. "I'd love to have seen your reaction. You swore, didn't you?"

"At length. Then I demanded to know where you were. Avice told me everything. So I left at once, and rode out to find you."

"God was kind. You took the same lane I was on."

"I'd tried a dozen other lanes already." Nicholas watched her as the sun outside the window brightened, slanting abruptly across the bed and turning his eyes brilliant. "And now," he murmured, "the missing you and the thinking of you has grown into something deeper. This time alone with you in my arms - and the moments of fear when I imagine the loss of you - all leading to the words I use - which you doubt - but are now quite true."

"What words?" Hardly even a whisper.

"Words of love."

Emeline drew a deep breath. "It would be worth - the pestilence - to hear that."

He shook his head abruptly. "And now knowing Adrian's a traitor, is it easier to believe he's a murderer?"

"No." She sighed, accepting the change of subject. "There's a list. Sissy thinks it's Jerrid." Nicholas smiled and Emeline hurried on. "My mother thought it was some silly secretary of Papa's, but it can't be. She also thought it might be the boy you say was killed in your care."

"I know. Absurd."

"But, actually," another deep breath. "It could have been my mother. I mean, she really had a horrid life with my father and she's having such fun - and freedom - and spending - since he's gone. And now I know she guessed some things about Peter, and didn't really want me to marry him. But with father insisting, there wouldn't have been any other way to stop it except killing Peter. I mean, I can't actually suspect my own mother, can I? But she's strong, and determined, and she had more motive than others."

"Equally absurd." He had closed his eyes again. "Jerrid is too damned disinterested and never even knew your father. Your mother wouldn't have known where to find your father, since he was closeted with his mistress. As for finding Peter, that would have been even more impossible. Peter was also killed at the home of his mistress. A local woman living in Desford, a few miles from the castle. No one knew about that woman, certainly not Sissy or your mother. Nor Jerrid, who rarely leaves Westminster."

"The woman could have told ---"

"She died in the fire that followed Peter's slaughter. The same story."

"It could even have been Sissy herself. What if she discovered this other woman?"

"But hardly to slaughter your father."

"Why not? Another man cheating on the woman who trusted him?"

"Absurd."

"And my old nurse Martha. She adores me and Avice and my mother. She knew what Peter was like. She knew what my father was like. She always wants to protect everyone. And she's - clever. She knows things I don't know how she knows. She knew about Sissy before we did, because Sissy's maid told her. Everyone always confides in Martha. She could have known about my father in the same way."

"The servants always know more than their masters. But these killings weren't done by a woman. To set the fire, perhaps. But not the rest. Slashing a man's throat with a knife or sword? Neither man was killed from behind."

"Martha can carve a roast piglet with the same dexterity as any cook. I've seen her do it at home in the nursery when I was little. And neither man would have suspected - not until suddenly she pulled out the knife. Or she could have asked - paid - someone else to go with her. I think she has a brother."

"Still absurd. Who takes such risks, and tempts the executioner for simple dislike of one man for another?"

"A mad man. But I don't know any mad men. And there's no one really with an equal motive for killing both your brother and my father."

"Myself?"

Emeline glared at him. "Oh, Nicholas, don't tease me."

Nicholas rolled over and sat up. "All right, my sweet. It's a fine game to pass the time, choosing the assassin amongst our friends. So then there's Adrian."

"Yes, because of Sissy. And Avice thinks he had another reason, which now puts you in danger too. Inheritance."

"So he needs to kill me now, in order to inherit title, castle and wealth on my father's death." His smile slowly lit his eyes like sunshine. "Indeed, I'd thought of that. Adrian has few advantages, and very few funds to support either his own way of life or his sister's future. There's Aunt Elizabeth, but she has only her own small portion to pass on."

"You'll laugh at me," she looked momentarily into her lap. "But you know I thought you were in danger from Adrian. And that's why I travelled all this way to find you, because I thought I had to warn you. So Adrian's the favourite."

"Especially now there's the interesting possibility of him being in league with the French, and the Richmond exile."

"Unless his friend Urswick is another man altogether, and quite innocent. And Adrian killing my father doesn't seem to fit."

Nicholas nodded. "Perhaps only I had motive for both killings."

"Why would you kill my father?"

"We were talking of inheritance. The same applies. Once matters are finally unravelled, you and your sister will inherit almost all your father's wealth. Your mother will retain her dower lands and her own portion I presume, but I will have married more than an heiress. You're about to be a very wealthy woman, my dear."

"But as an heiress, there wasn't much difference. You just had to wait. And you're rich yourself, besides being your father's only heir. It's not the same as Adrian."

Nicholas smiled suddenly. "There were at least half a dozen occasions when I'd have cheerfully murdered your father."

"That's different too. So would I. So would Avice. So would Maman. But I know it wasn't you." Emeline sighed, clasping her hands. "But Sissy seems to think – and of course, she'd never suspect Adrian. We've all spoken about this together. And we all suspect different people."

Nicholas sat abruptly and reached for his cup. "I've doubted Adrian, then denied it for months. But now I know he dabbles in treachery. On this coast, at this time, there's only one

Urswick, my dear. But I, on the other hand, now have a great urge to kill several people all at once."

"Me? Adrian?"

"Most of the people I'd like to kill are dead already. Peter, and the motives are endless. Your Ralph Cole for putting you at such terrible risk. Sissy's parents for leaving their daughter a shameless fool. And the one person still alive - my father - for every bastard thing he's ever done, and in particular for how he misunderstood Peter."

"He never judged Peter, did he? Why?"

"Because Peter was the heir. Perhaps because my father associated the death of his wife with me. Simply because he's a blind fool. I have no real idea. I doubt my father knows now - or ever did."

"Well," Emeline looked back into her lap. "If I die, there's no else for you to blame. Just my own stupidity."

"I'm rather fond of your stupidity." He laughed. "You're an endearing little puss, my sweet. And by my reckoning you'd already be feeling tired and ill if the pestilence was taking hold." He kissed her lightly, then moved his fingers to her chin, lifting it and smoothing his hands gently beneath her jaw. "No swelling, no soreness. I don't believe there's any danger. You'll not escape from me that easily."

She stared back at him. "You really mean what you're saying?"

"That you've not caught the contagion - yes, of course."

"No." She blushed a little. "That you're really growing - fond of me?"

"Must I write it down? Must I swear it on the bible?" His arm was around her now, and he kissed her again, his mouth warm and quick against her cheek. "My sweet, if you weren't already my wife, I'd ask you to marry me."

"I'd say yes please."

"Since the wedding itself was as much a Chatwyn disaster as most of our family dealings seem to be, it's as well we're already wed. Now, my lady," he shook his head. "Do we speak of romance, or of murder?"

"Since we have to be locked in here alone together for days to come, perhaps both in turn." She paused. "How many days will it be, Nicholas – to be sure?"

"One – two – three – it's all a guess, my love. But if you were going to succumb, I believe you'd have a headache by now at the least." She began to answer but he raised one finger, interrupting her. "Hush a moment, my love. There's someone on the steps outside."

The creak of the stairs and the patter of footsteps seemed careful, almost surreptitious. Then Avice's whisper, "Emma, is that you? Are you alright?" Pause. Then, "Nicholas?"

Nicholas strode to the door and swung it open. "There's little point in your sister staying isolated if we greet visitors," he told his sister-in-law.

"It was you I wanted." Avice said, "Everyone is fighting downstairs. Your Papa says he'll throw your Uncle Jerrid down the stairs if another word is spoken about Peter, and Sissy is having hysterics and screaming at everyone and says you're a murderer. Maman is angry with everyone and has turned her back and says she'll go home tomorrow, and your Aunt Elizabeth slapped Sissy's face. Outside everyone is quarrelling too, with someone threatening old Bill saying he's just pretending to be sick, and the landlord is wringing his hands and muttering under his breath." She shook her head. "I thought perhaps you should come downstairs."

Emeline decided she had a headache after all.

CHAPTER FORTY FIVE

The Earl of Chatwyn was roaring like a gale through castle turrets, standing central in the little parlour and sharing his fury between the various members of his immediate family. His brother Jerrid half sprawled, smiling placidly around as though delighted to be the cause of such entertainment. The Lady Elizabeth sat tight kneed in one corner. Sysabel, facing her uncle Jerrid, stamped her foot and screeched her fury. Near the little doorway, the baroness was placating the landlord.

"It is quite beyond my power," said the baroness firmly, "and indeed beyond my interests, to make any attempt to quieten or appease his lordship. He is not a gentleman easily distracted." The baroness smiled. "But I imagine a large flagon of best Burgundy might go some way towards pleasing everyone."

"Yes, indeed, wine, your ladyship." The landlord backed, wiping his hands on his apron.

"Always a welcome diversion," nodded the baroness. "A large flagon. Perhaps two."

"You're just a horrid old man," squealed Sysabel, drowning out the landlord's acquiescence. "And I hate you."

Jerrid yawned. "The boy's gone. Why quarrel over him now, m'dear?"

"Because you said – you said –"

"Because I said he was a nasty little slime ball, and I'd have sooner coughed up phlegm and called that my nephew." Jerrid clasped his hands over his stomach. "But no point listing the lad's many sins. Not now he's being judged by a higher authority than my own."

"Peter was a saint," screeched Sysabel. "Truly a saint. And when I think what he had to put up with – a brainless coward for a brother, a mean and spiteful uncle, a fool for an aunt – and a drunken sot for a father."

The earl quivered. "Lizzie, if you don't take this spoiled brat away this instance, I shall personally give her the thrashing she deserves."

"Impossible to give the girl what she deserves," sighed the Lady Elizabeth. "Since we have neither stocks nor gibbet to hand."

"If anyone lays a hand on me," Sysabel shrieked, "I shall spit - I shall kick - I shall never speak to anyone ever again."

"What a mercy that would be," sighed her ladyship.

The baroness interrupted. "Should any one feel in the need of a placid moment or two, I have ordered wine. And it is, of course, approaching dinner time –"

But she herself was interrupted. Nicholas wandered into the little parlour, nodding sympathetically to the hovering landlord. Avice scuttled in behind her brother-in-law as he closed the door rather loudly behind the landlord's departure. He then faced the small group in the parlour. "What the devil's happening now?" he demanded. "Can no one in this hostelry even lie sick in peace? And is there not even a drop to drink?"

The baroness sniggered slightly. "I have this moment ordered wine, my lord."

"Excellent," Nicholas heaved himself into the nearest empty chair. "And does anyone wish to inquire how my wife is doing?"

"Simple sniffles. Chills," dismissed the earl. "Meanwhile your uncle risks far more than a common cold, he risks being knocked out and your damned silly niece risks a thrashing. And I've no need of you, wretched boy, to interfere. I can battle my own arguments without your pointless impertinence."

Jerrid grinned at Nicholas from the other end of the table. "Nice to see you, m'boy. Hope your lady's feeling better?"

"Fine - so far." Nicholas looked around the room and a temporary silence sank like unstoked ashes. "I presume my dear cousin hasn't yet returned?"

The earl shook his head. "Just as well. Hardly need another nit witted relative to tell me what I already know to be rubbish."

Sysabel sat hurriedly, squeezing up beside Avice on the bench. She mumbled, "Everybody's horrible," to her lap.

Nicholas nodded to her. "A vile family, as we all recognise, child." He paused a moment, then said, "So tell me, Sissy, about your brother's friend. This Christopher Urswick. Do you know the man?"

Sysabel looked up, surprised, and shook her curls. The earl, however, demanded immediately. "Who? I know that name. No friend of Adrian's, I'd be bound."

Glad to contradict her uncle without fear of argument, Sysabel said at once, "Oh yes he is. He's a very nice gentleman who helped save me from swamps and thieves. Didn't he, Avice? He was here with Adrian three days ago, but then he had to go and catch a boat leaving on the next tide. That's why Adrian had to go away again after he'd booked us all into this hostelry."

The silence lengthened. Eventually the earl looked to his son. "Is this true? Have you any idea, boy, who this Urswick is? Well, naturally you'd have no idea of the politics -enemies of the state - traitors -"

"I know exactly who Christopher Urswick is," Nicholas regarded his father with some impatience. "Especially since I've been chasing him for the past week." He turned to Jerrid. "Can you believe it, uncle? The man we've been attempting to locate and arrest, was here the day before we arrived, and was in company with my own cousin."

The earl, bewildered, stared around. The baroness, equally confused, took her daughter's hand. "I never met the man, but I've heard of his courage. Is he a criminal? How is that possible?"

"Quite easily, madam," Jerrid unwound himself from his chair and stood, glaring at his brother. "But it means we've a traitor in the family."

Sysabel screamed and fell backwards onto the Lady Elizabeth's lap, who squeaked and immediately pushed her off. "I have no idea," the lady said faintly, "what is going on. But everyone - absolutely everyone - is clearly mad."

"Probably true, aunt," nodded Nicholas. "But the facts remain clear. My Uncle Jerrid and I, along with a parcel of my men, have been down here for almost two weeks on the king's nosiness. Amongst other things, we were searching for a traitor, name of Christopher Urswick, who was bringing a letter from the Tudor exile to the Earl of Northumberland. Urswick is known to us, and has been working for the enemy for some years. We managed to intercept the letter, but the man himself eluded us. It's always been assumed he had helpful contacts over here, but who helped him this time was unclear. His men killed one of mine, and I'll not forgive that. Now I know who to blame."

Jerrid nodded. "It's been damned hard work, but the king's business is the king's business, and he trusts us. It's serious or we'd not have been sent. But to fail because of my own nephew – "

"We didn't fail." Nicholas stared at his father, who stared back, white faced and open mouthed. "We succeeded in taking the letter before it reached its destination, and that was the principal aim." He smiled suddenly. "So what shocks you more, Father dearest? Adrian's duplicity? Or the fact that I work in secret for the king?"

"I knew Peter –"

"Peter never did." Nicholas was still smiling, the slant of his facial scar curling as he smiled, though his eyes remained cold. "Oh. he went off cheerfully shouting gallantry during the Scottish skirmishes. Never achieved much, but he was willing enough. Meanwhile I was sent behind the wall into Berwick."

The earl spluttered, "The siege? Impossible."

Jerrid answered him. "Your younger son and I have been acting under the king's orders for the past five years, Symond. Peter didn't know. Nicholas couldn't tell you. For one thing, the work was usually secret. For another, we didn't trust you. Oh, not because of treachery of course. Just stupidity. And we trusted Peter even less."

The small scream was muffled as the baroness marched across to Sysabel and shook her into silence. The silence was interrupted by the landlord, serving wine. Everyone exhaled in relief and the clatter of cups replaced the furious tension. "Off with you," the earl pushed the landlord from the room. "We'll serve ourselves."

Nicholas was already serving everyone. "My lady?"

"Most certainly," said the baroness thankfully, accepting the overfull cup.

"Me too," begged Avice. "I'm completely exhausted and I don't know what anyone is talking about. And I wish I could go and talk to Emma instead."

"You can't," Nicholas told her. "Drink up. Your mother will explain everything to you later."

The baroness sighed. "Doubtful," she said, but was ignored.

Nicholas turned back to his father. "Your opinion of me never mattered," he said quietly. "But it was always wrong. And as his father, you're naturally entitled to your opinion of Peter, but that was always wrong too." He shook his head, but he was no longer smiling. "I doubt you believe me, and that doesn't matter either. The important matter at hand is that of Adrian."

The earl drank noisily and banged his cup down on the table. "The rest - whether lies or exaggeration, I need time to consider. But Adrian and Urswick! When's he due back?"

The Lady Elizabeth said calmly, "Later today. And since you failed to arrest this Mister Urswick, perhaps you'd better arrest young Adrian instead."

Sysabel stood up in the middle of the room, brimming cup in hand, and gazed around her. She appeared to swell, her face flushing from the neck upwards, until she appeared almost explosively crimson. She began to stamp both feet, a drum roll of fury, and then flung the contents of her cup directly into her aunt's face. There was once again an immediate silence as the lady blinked, streaks of Burgundy trickling from her stiff white headdress to her chin. Then Sysabel turned, and threw the empty cup directly at Nicholas.

Nicholas caught it. "No refill, perhaps," he smiled. "Shocking waste of good wine, you know. But I understand the problem. I imagine," he raised an eyebrow at his aunt, who was rocking slowly to her feet, "my cousin would be better retiring at this point. If you'd care to take her up to her room?"

The baroness pushed Avice forward. "Go with her, my dear. I imagine she needs a little comfort. Amongst other things."

"I don't want to," muttered Avice.

"Your wishes have absolutely nothing to do with it," sighed her mother. "So you will, for once, simply do as you're told."

A rustle of silk skirts and a flounce of forced compliance half emptied the parlour. It also interrupted the small group of hostelry servants who had been listening outside. The Lady Elizabeth turned once, saying, "I shall return for dinner shortly, and bring the girls with me. Until then I shall attempt to teach my niece some manners." The door shut again with a determined clank, Jerrid sighed with relief, and Nicholas grinned at the baroness.

"An interesting day, my lady. If it weren't for Emma's - chills - I'd say it was quite a delightful day."

"You're looking forward to accusing your cousin of high treason, sir?" But the baroness was smiling. "It appears you are quite enamoured of adventure after all, my lord, whatever it entails."

"And," Nicholas added, "since genuine adventure is proving harder and harder to find, I'm off to control my men out at the stables before they kill each other. May I leave my speechless father to your gentle patience, my lady?"

The earl was still spluttering. The baroness murmured, "With pleasure, my lord."

The sun was high and the day had improved. Nicholas stretched his shoulders, enjoying the warmth on his back as he walked towards the noise and bustle coming from the stables. One disgruntled traveller was departing and seeing Nicholas, scowled. "I'll have you know this was once a respectable hostelry, sir. But it appears as soon as the nobility move in, there's complete upheaval. A shocking lack of decent civilised manners. I doubt I'll be coming back here ever again, sir."

"Oh you'll be safe enough the next time," said Nicholas with cheerful abandon. "I doubt we'll be staying much longer. We've nearly emptied the cellars."

The horses were kicking at their stalls as four men were having a furious argument. The argument stopped mid word as Nicholas walked in. Alan Venter sighed. "Ah, my lord. A great relief, if I may say so, my lord."

David Witton was leaning against the far wall, keeping apart, smiling slightly. "Simply a clash of interests, my lord," he said. "Nothing to worry about."

"Worry?" demanded Nicholas. "Who said anything about worry? I'm thoroughly enjoying myself. Now - what entertainment have you miserable wretches to offer me?"

Harry and Rob released their hold on old Bill, and he flopped to the straw with a half strangled sniff. "These buggers bin accusing me o' all sorts, m'lord," he complained. "An' it ain't proper, since I don't even work for them, nor for no one here. From the Wrotham household, I is, and I were brought as guide an protector, I was, to the young ladies. And it ain't my fault if I gets sick."

"'Tis your fault if you makes such a moaning and pissing as to have folks think you got the pox or the pestilence," shrugged Rob. "And spreading rumours as to the lady getting the same. When all you wants is an excuse for a rest from your duties."

Nicholas laughed. "Is this all you beetle brains have been fighting over?"

"Not 'xactly, m'lord," said Rob. "It were more what Mister Witton were saying set us all to buggery. As to how we bin searching low and lower for that bastard Urswick, and him disappeared into them shadows, so it seems. And now we hear as how 'tis a member of your own family, m'lord, being that Sir Adrian hisself, what helped the traitor escape."

"And my beloved cousin," frowned Nicholas, "is likely to return sometime today. If and when he does, see if you can use more brain than you've shown so far, and question his henchmen. He'll have more than a couple with him, no doubt, since there were enough of them to knock you out and take down poor Wolt. And don't make your questions too obvious."

Alan grinned suddenly. "You mean, don't ask them if their master's always been a, and whether they're happy to go to the scaffold themselves for high treason?"

"Perhaps not." Nicholas turned, nodding to David. "You're not planning on sleeping in the stables from now on I hope, my friend? There must still be a truckle bed to be had in my uncle's chamber? Though now I'm afraid you'll have to put up with my father's presence as well."

"I have it already settled, my lord. But was called to witness the murder of this poor old wretch Bill by one of ours."

Nicholas turned and trudged back over to the hostelry, but stayed a moment outside, with the sunshine easing the muscles of his neck. He was smiling, but his own desperate tiredness was apparent. He did not return to the parlour, but he called to one of the passing kitchen boys and ordered more wine and a hot dinner brought up immediately to the attic chamber. Then he continued up the stairs.

His wife was waiting for him. She had managed to dress, looking herself again, and stood at once as he closed the door.

She said, "Nicholas. I have to say it. I'm terribly sorry. I lied."

CHAPTER FORTY SIX

"Peter kissed me," she whispered. "Twice. And I let him."

Nicholas stared at her a moment, then sat heavily on the bed beside her. "Sit, my love, and don't frighten the wits from me. I thought you were about to confess the first signs of the pestilence. Kissed Peter? I no longer care. As long as you didn't kiss his feet."

She didn't laugh. "And I have a headache." She sat beside him, propped by pillows. "But no lumps or rashes and I'm terribly hungry. And actually, it was three times." She drew a deep breath, blushing slightly. "I mean Peter was three times. But once was just my hand, and I don't think that counts."

"Tell me about the headache."

She was twisting her fingers, playing with the diamonds Nicholas had given her, turning the ring endlessly. "My head is pounding." She looked up, pleading. "But everybody gets headaches sometimes, don't they?"

Then he was pulling her closer and slipping one hand beneath her skirts, and his fingers moved to the white of her thighs above the garters of her stockings, and firmly pushed her legs apart. But he did not play or arouse her as he usually did. He bent to examine her and she blushed scarlet, but it was the warm skin at the top of her thighs he touched, pressing and tracing with his thumb. He leaned down and kissed her belly, his lips roaming across the soft swell, his tongue suddenly hot in her navel. Then he looked up, smiling, and said, "One thing more, my love, if you allow it." And he slipped the shoulders of her gown down a little over her arms, unclasped the fichu which closed the deep V of the neckline, pulled the straps of her shift off to follow her gown, and in the bright dancing sunlight, examined the pale skin of her breasts, the lines where her ribs pressed up through her flesh, and the small tucked warmth beneath her arms. Then he sighed very deeply, and murmured, "Not one sign, my beautiful girl, not one threat of the sickness."

Embarrassed, she struggled to adjust her clothing. The palliasse creaked as the mattress readjusted. "And you don't care about Peter?"

"I've just had the most delightful experience of telling my father a little of the truth about Peter," he grinned back at her, "and some more about myself. The old man looked as stunned as a newborn sparrow. I relished every intake of his breath and every click of his tongue. He was longing to call me a liar, but Jerrid was there, confirming everything." He smoothed her skirts back down over her ankles. "And you, my sweet, are suffering from no more than the results of too much worry, too much tension, and too much anticipation. After some hours of headache, if the pestilence was indeed the problem, you'd be showing faint bruising and the beginnings of the rash at least. Instead, I shall find you some willow bark mixture to dull the pain, and order apple codlings for dinner."

"Oh, Nicholas."

"Though why I bother helping you redress, I have no idea, since all I really want to do is undress you."

She reclasped her hands, looking back at her lap. "He's still haunting us, isn't he! What he did to you as a boy. What he did to Sissy. And now, wondering who killed him."

"Don't we know?"

"So what will you do when Adrian comes back?"

"Enjoy myself, I imagine." But Nicholas had stopped smiling. He wandered over to the little casement window and its diffusing panes, and opened it, pushing the little iron frame wide. The sunlight doubled, a great billowing golden light into every corner, with spangles along the dusty beamed ceiling arches. "I plan on finally banishing these dark shadowed doubts and black looming grievances."

"I *have* been feeling - gloomy. I was so worried about you when Avice thought Adrian might have followed you down here to kill you. After all, you're the last barrier to his inheritance. Then weeks of thinking about murder, and finding out about Peter and Sissy, and Father of course. And now this, with the pestilence and that poor wretched couple dying in the village. I've been so frightened - and every little twinge seems like the footsteps of doom. And on - and on - and on. Everything is a nightmare with no soft fur linings."

He strode back to her. "What a fine family I've brought you into, little one, with the disillusion first, deciding you loved

Peter virtually on the eve of his murder. Then the order to marry his ugly and deformed beast of a brother."

"Oh, Nicholas, I know I was stupid."

"Peter's words, I'm sure, my sweet, just as he left me imagining I was to marry his outworn mistress."

Emeline sniffed. "Outworn?"

Nicholas chuckled. "Well worn, rather than outworn perhaps." He muffled her retaliation against his shoulder, taking her into his arms, then standing and pulling her up with him. "Do you dance, my love? Beautifully, I've no doubt. Well, we've not a rebec nor a knackerer's drum here to sweeten the rhythm, but it's time I danced with my wife. We've a sparkling future to dance into, my love."

"We do?"

Her upturned face was strained, and he bent and kissed the furrows across her forehead. "It was an inauspicious wedding night, it's true, but now we know better." Keeping her still clasped tight, he turned with her, the steps of courtly dance, though not with the required restraint of finger to finger. "I should have danced with you then, but was too pissed and too angry. At least here in private, I've no need to play the gallant or keep you at arm's length. I like the press of your breasts against me." His eyes, gazing down at her, were summer sky blue in the sunshine. "At court they like to remind us, you know, of chivalry. And so they warn us to tighten the lacings on our codpieces before leaping too high to the music. Loose ties can be a disaster, as you might imagine. Indeed, I've seen it happen. But with you here alone, my sweet, perhaps we should be already naked. I'm no ardent dancer, my sweet, but in fact I've danced my way through life, choosing whatever steps kept me light footed, avoiding all but adventure. And I've spoken my true thoughts or feelings to no one at all since I was six years old. Until now. I'm willing - if you wish to dance into the future with me playing the juggler at your side." He twisted her twice, arms high, then brought her back against him. "And let me tell you, my sweet, in case you still need to hear it, there's no woman sickening with the pestilence who can dance, remember the steps, keep her balance and breath, and still feel hungry afterwards."

She was losing her breath after all. "I'm starving."

"It's a drink I need." Nicholas released her, sitting back with her on the side of the bed. "So more crumbs in the sheets."

She was panting a little but her headache had partially cleared. "I feel - almost better." She drew a deep breath, calming her heartbeat and blinking up at him. "Not dreading the future, or wondering about murderers and traitors. Nor thinking about the past and the fire and the castle and you lying there all covered in ashes and raw bleeding patches."

He laughed suddenly, leaning back against the pillows and bringing her again into his embrace. "You slept in those ashes yourself, my love, and puzzled us all. Were you escaping? From your visions of a future with the monster of Chatwyn?"

"I was so miserable." He could not see her blushes, which were pressed into invisibility against his shoulder. "Not just because of you, Nicholas dear. It was your father and my father, and everyone telling me what to do when I didn't want to do any of it. The whole nightmare of the fire."

"So you chose to sleep in the ruins of our marriage bed, echoing the ruins of our wedding night?"

"I suppose you thought I was mad. First I was the immoral slattern, and then the crazy woman." She wriggled upright for a moment, frowning at him. "I was so horribly melancholy. Feeling so forlorn, I searched out the most forlorn place to cry in. And perhaps I was a little crazy." She shook her head, trying to remember. "But something happened I hadn't even thought of again until now. At the time I thought the Keep was haunted. Ghosts. Ghouls. Whispers. I heard a voice, or thought I did. And when I slept, I dreamed -only a dream perhaps - but someone seemed to touch me. I dreamed of encroachment and fingers prying. Dark eyes watching." She shook her head again, dismissing memories. "It was my myself I was running away from really. But the whispers frightened me."

"What words?" Nicholas was staring back at her. "If you remember whispers, my love, then try and remember the words."

"Most of it was rustles and muddled murmurs." She was whispering herself. "But afterwards there were words. *The stars are singing*. That's what I heard."

He paused, confused. "You heard singing?"

"No, no." she clasped his hand, as if for reassurance. "It's what the whisper said. Sibilant and very, very soft. It said, "*The stars are singing.*" And that's the last thing before I fell asleep. But even while I slept, I felt touch - fingers - inside my bedrobe."

"A vile thought, my sweet. Some half drunk servant, perhaps. Surely not Adrian, though he was there that night and I've no idea what time he left." Nicholas sighed. "But you're a deep dreamer and mutter in your sleep most nights. Little mumbles and squeaks, like the busy mouse I once called you. So you woke and remembered the dream, and thought it real. If someone touched you, surely you'd have woken furious. And who there, that night of all nights, would have dared? I hope, my sweet, only dreams, and thank the Lord for it." He looked up suddenly and smiled. "Now I hear footsteps on the stairs outside."

The tray was left at the door. Nicholas carried it in. Emeline clapped her hands and shrugged off the dismal past. "Apple codlings?"

He left her after they had eaten, kissing her cheek with apologies. She asked, "To wait for Adrian?"

"I'd hoped he'd be back by now. But until he is, I can't settle to much else, my sweet. If you were ill, that would take precedence. But you've eaten a dinner large enough for two, and I need to talk to Jerrid." He poured her another cup of wine, but took his own with him.

Downstairs Nicholas found his uncle and his father outside, talking quietly together beneath the wide fluttering shade of the oak. Across the stable courtyard and the grassy bank, he joined them as they turned, hearing his steps. The ladies had presumably retired to their shared chamber. Nicholas blinked through the sunbeams.

"My lord. No sign yet of my cousin?"

Jerrid shook his head but the earl turned quickly, thumbs hooked into the opening of his doublet. "Ah, my son, claiming more gallant deeds, no doubt. And what do you intend to do, my boy, when Adrian arrives? You've no proof I assume. What if you're wrong? You've been wrong more often than right over the years, whatever you may like to boast about now." He paused, eyeing first Nicholas, and then Jerrid. "Personally," he continued with belligerence, "I find it quite impossible to believe my nephew is a traitor."

Nicholas laughed. "You never fail me, Papa."

Harry, Rob and Alan were lounging against the stable doors as the hostelry ostlers led out two of the horses for grooming in the sunshine. There was a jangle of bridles, the slop of water over the cobbles and the clank of buckets. Jerrid yawned. "It's time you trusted your son, Symond, and gave up this phantasm of Peter the Great. And you've no admiration nor love for young Adrian, so why support him against your own son?"

"To call my nephew a traitor? And have another Chatwyn scandal to blush for?"

"Blushing? I've never seen it." Nicholas leaned back against the trunk of the oak, lit by dancing shadows through the foliage. "It's ignorance you should fear, Father, and turning blind stupidity to the steel at your throat."

"Yes, I know the name Urswick," the earl said, thrusting out his chin. "I'm neither ignorant nor gullible, impudent boy. But how many Urswicks are there in England? Adrian was knighted on the battlefield, and proved himself a loyal king's man. Been loyal to this family too, offering you a home after the fire, and looking after Lizzie."

"Aunt Elizabeth looks after him, and Sissy both," Nicholas pointed out. "Financially, amongst other services."

Jerrid interrupted. "Just how much do you know, Symond?" he demanded. "So let me tell you a little of what you probably don't know - which is what we've been up these past weeks." He lowered his voice, conscious of the busy grooms behind him. "If nothing else, you've heard of Henry Tudor, son of Stanley's wife, the Beaufort heiress. Her strong Lancastrian loyalties, fanatical some might say, inspire her son. But he's been an exile in Brittany and France for many a long year."

The earl tapped his foot on the cobbles. "I've been at court long enough to know all this. Indeed, I've known much of it from my cradle. But there's been little need to resurrect t those memories for many years."

"The king has spies in France," Nicholas nodded. "They send information, and there's been more of it lately. After many years of dismissing this Tudor byblow as barely worth the notice, now he's becoming more relevant. The French have him in hand, and the French will always make trouble for us where they can."

Jerrid nodded. "But Tudor's simply the grandson of poor mad Henry VI's French mother, result of a secret liaison the old woman had with a servant after failing to win the man she wanted. It was the Beaufort gallant she chased, but evidently ended taking a servant from her own chambers instead."

"She claimed she'd married the man," muttered the earl, still scowling.

"In any case the king legitimised the affair afterwards, welcomed the offspring as his own half brothers. He even arranged for the elder son to wed the Beaufort heiress."

"A woman of immovable determination, and a will of iron."

"Why are we discussing a past nonsense of no interest today?" demanded the earl.

"It matters, because that's why we're *here* today," said Jerrid with impatience. Thinking his dream of a union with the old king's bastard daughter was in tatters, Tudor wrote to Northumberland, asking him to broker a union with one of his own sister-in-law."

The earl was puzzled and shook his head. "A mumble jumble, boy, and as foolish as your other ventures. One marriage that won't happen, and another that can't. An exile with no money dreaming of a woman with plenty. Or is this letter a rumour like all else?"

"I have the letter Father, and have read it. The reason for suspicion is the surprising friendship between an exile and the good earl, who should by affiliation have nothing to do with each other, let alone plan a marriage which would unite them in a fairly close relationship."

The earl snorted. "And what has this to do with Adrian?"

"His highness authorised my uncle and myself to come down and intercept the messenger." Nicholas shrugged. "You may not see the danger in this exile's sudden friendship with one of the greatest nobles in the land, but the king does. And that's where Urswick comes in, for he was designated to bring the letter to this coast and then pass it to someone less conspicuous who would deliver to Northumberland. That letter is now, in safe keeping."

"But we were attacked twice," added Jerrid. "And one of Nick's boys was killed. Perhaps because he recognised one of Adrian's henchmen."

"Are we surrounded by traitors?" The earl stared around, raising his voice. "My own family? Northumberland himself?"

"The French, certainly, since we still hold Calais, though little else, and our previous kings laid claim to their throne and flourish the fleur-de-lis on our banners."

"The French," snorted the earl. "They've wanted revenge ever since old King Hal beat them into the mud at Agincourt and before. So they hold this exile hostage. Why should we care?"

"Hostage? Or honoured guest? Dorset is held against his will, not Tudor."

"Why would Adrian support the French? He's hostage to no one and was knighted fighting for king and country."

"I'll ask him," smiled Nicholas. "But I'll surround him first. Apart from myself and my uncle, I've four men with me, including my squire David. There's also the guide who accompanied my wife and Adrian's sister. Then there's a bunch of armed guards who came down with my mother-in-law and Aunt Lizzie. And there's your own entourage, Father dear, if you'll give them the order."

"To capture your own cousin? You'll hardly need an army, boy."

"He has a pack of ruffians with him, though some may have come with Urswick, and have left now, sailing back to France some days back."

"I've no intention of starting a war," said Nicholas softly. "I'll give my cousin a chance to explain. To exonerate himself if he can. But there's more than treachery to talk about. There's also murder, and that may involve more than words."

CHAPTER FORTY SEVEN

Nicholas paused, looking over his shoulder to the tiny open window where the breeze combined the dizzy sulphur of sunset with the rising moon's first silver puddles. He grinned at his wife, his eyes reflecting the sun's last flame.

"I need a bath."

Emeline shook her head. It was not what she had expected him to say. "We can't allow any servants in here to set up the tub. Nor carry buckets up all this way to the attic."

"I might smuggle you down the back stairs, empty all our relatives out from the ladies' bedchamber, get the tub set up in there, and settle to a long hot frolic."

"So you don't mean you need a bath. You mean I need one."

He laughed. "I imagine we both do. I've had only one bath since spending two weeks in the saddle, or on flea ridden pallets in lice ridden taverns. You've been playing saint in a village rife with contagion. I'd say that points to a good delousing and a hot soak as imperative."

"So really, you just want something to do while you wait for Adrian. You find sitting around doing nothing as difficult as a small child forced to stay indoors."

Nicholas laughed again. "Yes, if I choose to blame Adrian. Which I might as well. The wretched man is late. I expected him this morning. Now it's well nigh evening."

"What hour does the sun set in late May?"

"The sun sets late. The moon rises early. And I shall make love to my wife, since she is not sick, nor even tired, having done almost nothing all day."

Emeline was tired, though the headache which had earlier troubled her, had passed. She rested against him, her arm around his waist. "It's fresh air I need, and to walk in the sunshine." She was still in his arms when they heard the horses on the cobbles outside, the call for the ostlers, the neighing of horses and the squeak of saddles as men dismounted.

Nicholas looked up, eyes bright. Emeline groaned. He traced very slowly down her cheek with the ball of his thumb, following the gentle swell of her smile, slipping his fingers around beneath her ear to the back of her neck, caressing where the long thick hair curled and fell across her shoulders. Then he bent and kissed her, eyes open, breath warm. "Shall I go?" he whispered. "Or stay, and show my wife that I love her?"

The bed curtains, a limp flutter of dyed linen, swung back as Emeline sat up, wedging herself on one elbow. "Love me? If you stay, you'll be thinking of Adrian, proving you love adventure more."

Jerrid had also heard the late arrival. Nicholas, part dressed and dishevelled from bed, stood beside his uncle. The clattering faded as the horses were taken into the stables, their saddles thrown off, their bridles unbuckled, and finally led to water, oats and hay. Adrian's five henchmen, stocky and thickset, followed the horses. Adrian strolled across the cobbles to the sudden torchlight in the hostelry doorway where Jerrid and Nicholas lounged, watching his approach. He was surprised. "You, cousin? And my uncle, not seen for months. And all here at such a time? I settled my sister and your lady here some days back, Nicholas, but didn't expect to see you here as well."

"Presumably not. I arrived shortly after you left." Nicholas smiled. "And quickly discovered I've an urgent desire to see you. Not reciprocated, no doubt. No matter. You must be tired. Come and have some wine."

"You're lucky not to find my brother waiting for you too, m'boy," Jerrid added. "For Symond's here as well. And Lady Wrotham. Together with your sister, and my sister Lizzie, 'tis a cosy family reunion, which lacked only your good self. And now complete."

Adrian frowned. "Something's wrong? Another death? Why such a gathering, and way out here, so far from Westminster?"

They wandered into the parlour where supper had been served earlier. A sleepy eyed scullion poked his head around the door. "My lords? We're closed for service, for most is already in their beds. It's late, my lords."

"Then bring us a couple of jugs of wine, boy," Jerrid said. "Then go back to bed and we'll serve ourselves."

Adrian said, "I'm ready for bed myself, sir. Too many hours in the saddle, and it's two hours I've been dreaming of a chance to sleep undisturbed."

Nicholas sat on the long bench, leaned back against the wall behind, swung one leg to the table, and continued to smile. But his eyes, heavy lidded, remained cold. "If we entertain you sufficiently, cousin, perhaps you'll stay awake long enough to entertain us in return. We've been waiting for you, you see. Avid anticipation, indeed. You should feel thoroughly flattered."

"Nonsense, Nicholas." Adrian sat, frowning at his cousin. "Such florid and pointless chatter. If you simply mean you wish to thank me for saving your lady three - no four days gone - then naturally I accept your gratitude. But there's no need for this display. I did only what anyone else would have done in such a situation."

Nicholas nodded placidly. "Anyone except myself, I presume," he said, "since I would have been far too busy trying to save myself."

"Even you would have stepped in to help, Nicholas."

"No need for gratitude then. How convenient. Especially since," Nicholas added, "were thanks obligatory, I should be in debt to your two friends, who have not returned with you, I see. How, I wonder, do I extend my gratitude to them?"

A slow suspicion glimmered in the back of Adrian's light blue eyes. He smiled quickly. "Ah yes, but no matter. They took ship for Flanders three days back, and I've no idea when I'll see them again. But they were - pleased to help at the time."

"Especially, perhaps, the genial Christopher Urswick?" suggested Jerrid.

The pause was barely noticeable. "Who?" Adrian shook his head. "You have the name wrong, uncle. Christopher Browne, and Francis Prophet were my friends. Traders I've done business with before, trying to make a little money since I have no lands of my own. I imagine my sister, or one of the other ladies, has mistaken the name."

Nicholas smiled more widely. "Trade. How - interesting, Adrian. Tell me, trading in what, exactly?"

The wine was brought, three cups and two flagons. Then the boy scuttled off and Jerrid poured the wine. "No shame in a little trade on the side," he said, passing the cup. "We all welcome some additional funds on the side. So what trade is it, Adrian lad? Wool, perhaps? Copper?" He drank deeply, then looked up, his mouth stained Burgundy. "Or," he smiled, "perhaps information?"

Adrian drank, taking time. "You're insinuating something, uncle, though I cannot imagine why. And you too, Nicholas. But I've no idea what, and I'm tired. The trade is dyed woollen cloth, and fairly lucrative as you must know. But I've no intention of discussing my finances with you, both of you as rich as Solomon without the wisdom. So I thank you for the wine," he drained his cup, and stood slowly, "but I'm in need of my bed."

"Well, you'll find my father in it," grinned Nicholas. "When he turned up here, there was limited space, so it's one chamber for the ladies, and one for the Chatwyn men. I'm up in the attic for reasons of my own. So go snuggle up with whomever you wish, cousin, but careful how you stretch your elbows,"

"I need sleep," Adrian shrugged, "and have no objections to sharing a bed." He placed his cup back on the table and turned towards the doorway.

"We're all tired, I think." Jerrid stood, wandering over to door, which was closed. He leaned against the jam, benign and casual, as though simply discovering a place of comfort. "But just a few words first, I think, before we all find out beds again."

"Since you're blocking the way, uncle, I presume those words are important?"

Nicholas swung his leg back to the floor tiles and sat forwards. The long bench creaked. "Important? Perhaps, cousin. You see, I know exactly who Christopher Urswick is, and exactly why he was here. When I asked about your companions, I hoped you'd convince me of an old friendship, or some coincidental and innocent encounter. Instead you denied him. Unwise, Adrian."

Adrian quickly crossed to the door and stood facing his uncle. "This is absurd. I know no one of that name, innocent encounter or otherwise. Now, I'm off to my bedchamber, whoever else may be in it. Do you intend to stop me forcibly, uncle?"

The door opened suddenly, but it was not Adrian who opened it. The earl stood in the passageway, glaring from the shadows into the low candlelight within the parlour. He glowered at Adrian. "So you're back. Good. I've questions, and every intention of getting answers." He pushed past, his large hand heavy on Adrian's shoulder. "So we'll sit together, we'll talk together, we'll drink together, and we'll settle this business before any more time is wasted or sleep interrupted." He noticed the two flagons of wine and nodded. "Some civilised attempt already made, I see. Well, come on, come on. No nonsense now. A discussion, quiet and friendly, that's what we'll have." Adrian was still hovering, Jerrid still blocking the only way out. "We're family," announced the earl, taking the full cup Nicholas handed him, "and we'll behave like family."

Reluctantly Adrian returned to the table and sat. Jerrid sat to his other side, keeping Adrian tight wedged between himself and the earl. Adrian sighed, and drank.

"Urswick," persisted Jerrid. "We all know who he is. So tell us why you've befriended a known traitor to the crown, my boy."

Two candles had been lit. One, tall sepia tallow, sat in its squat and solid stand, its flame undisturbed, smoke rising in a smudge of grey. The other candle was already half gone, a stub of wet tallow. Through smoke and flicker, Adrian's face was pale and lined with tiredness. "After five hours in the saddle, you accuse me of treason? Of a crime worthy of execution? What family gathering is this, to surround me at this hour, keep me from my rest, and talk of things I know nothing of?"

Four faces illuminated in fading light and flashing shadow. Adrian hunched over the table between his two uncles. Nicholas faced him. "You persist then, in denying knowledge of Christopher Urswick?"

Adrian looked up, anger controlled. "I've heard of no such person. I'm acquainted with no such person. And if this man is some petty traitor, what would you, of all people, know of him, Nicholas? You want recognition, perhaps, after all this time sheltering behind your brother's reputation? You pretend some special knowledge to make yourself important in your new wife's eyes?"

Nicholas leaned back, staring without expression at his cousin. Jerrid grunted. "We've angered you, it seems, Adrian? You expected never to be discovered, perhaps? You thought your family too unconcerned or simply too ignorant to notice your secret dealings?"

"Secret dealings?" Adrian stood abruptly, forcibly pushing his stool back and almost toppling the small rickety table. "How dare you sir. May I remind you that of all the family, I am the one knighted for services to the crown."

The earl shook his head. "Best face the worst and sort the accusations now, lad. Insults and denials won't do it, you know. Too serious."

Adrian was white faced. "No, sir. I'll not take accusations from this party of fools and drunkards."

"An innocent man accused, takes the time to explain and clear his name." Jerrid stood once again, sauntering a second time over to the doorway. "As your family, we'll be easier to convince, perhaps. You'll not leave this room, my boy, until we're satisfied with your answers. Best deal with those questions now, rather than later at a trial."

"A trial?" Adrian reached past Jerrid for the handle of the door. "You're all mad. I'm leaving, and you can keep your beds and your vile thoughts, for I'll find another hostelry along the road. I won't stay here and I've no desire to answer the questions of cowards and madmen."

Jerrid moved further to block the doorway, standing wide legged, arms crossed. Nicholas remained seated, but the earl stood in a hurry, turning from one to the other. "Is this necessary? I'll not take up arms against my own flesh and blood, but there's no escape, m'boy. You'll stay here until I know what's going on."

"Feeling trapped, Adrian? You could leap from the window," suggested Nicholas. "Or you could come back, sit down, and listen to sense." He regarded his cousin for some moments, then said, "Do you know that I have the letter?"

The pause echoed. Adrian's pale face flushed slowly scarlet, a blush that spread up from his neck like the dying of chicken feathers. He slumped, and sat. "What – what does that mean?" he whispered.

"You know exactly what it means," Nicholas sighed. "I intercepted a messenger riding full tilt for the north, and took from him a letter which I now hold, and will take immediately to the king on my return to Westminster. Two nights later your henchmen tumbled over mine in the local inn's stables. Apparently fearing recognition, they knocked out one, and knifed another. Just a boy, poor child, who had seen and recognised one of yours so had to be silenced. Your henchmen told you of this, no doubt but presumably you thought it an unfortunate coincidence that I was staying at the same inn. Once warned, you were able to avoid me. Believing me a wastrel, it never occurred to you that I was at Weymouth for reasons concerning the same business, as yourself, and in particular concerning your friend Urswick."

Adrian gaped. Jerrid smiled. "Your cowardly cousin has been following the king's orders for nigh on five years, boy. I have helped occasionally, when the matter at hand was urgent. So, well trusted by kings, but foolish we truly were perhaps - never to suspect you, nor understand your treachery."

"What was your job, then, cousin?" Nicholas asked. "To take Tudor's letter from Urswick, and deliver it to Northumberland while Urswick returned safe to France?"

"Treachery," spat Jerrid. "What act more vile?"

"Or murder." The door had opened again. Lady Wrotham stood in the doorway. In one hand she held a candle. In the other she held a small folded paper. "So Mister Frye, tell me," she asked as everyone else stopped speaking. Her voice echoed a little up the corridor and stairs behind her. "Why did you murder my husband?"

The earl stood again in a hurry, his stool clattering back behind him. "Is this true? Not only - but this too? And Peter?"

"What madness,' Adrian exclaimed, staring around him as the baroness entered and Jerrid shut the door behind her. "Madam - sir - what do you think of me? I had no hand in either - nor even barely knew the baron -"

"But you know Urswick," said Nicholas quietly.

"And perhaps you also knew your sister was shamed and sullied by your cousin Peter," said the baroness quietly. She placed the paper she had been clasping on the table. "Your sister's confession," she said softly. "Although she claims you never knew of it. Is she right? Or did you know, and defended her honour by murdering the man who got her pregnant when she was barely out of the nursery, and then forced her to a back street abortionist? And after killing one immoral bastard, did you decide to slaughter another? So finding my husband in the arms of his mistress, killed them too, and set fire to the evidence?"

"Oh, dear God," Adrian said, and leaning his arms on the table, closed his eyes and rested his head down on his arms in surrender,

CHAPTER FORTY EIGHT

Speechless, the Earl of Chatwyn stared at the baroness, tried to sit, discovered his fallen stool, and resettled himself with a deep sigh. Then after a moment he stood again and leaning over his nephew, shouted at the back of his head, "Did you know this about your sister, boy? Is it true? Is it *you* the coward, then - *and* the killer?"

The earl grabbed the back of Adrian's shirt, hauling him up. Adrian appeared to be weeping. "I didn't know," he mumbled. "But I guessed." He stared around, shaking off his uncle's grip. "I asked her, poor dearest Sissy. She wouldn't answer me. I wondered, I couldn't sleep, but I didn't want to believe so I shut the thought away. But it was there all the time at the back of my mind like a black stone." He glared at Nicholas. "But then she seemed alright. She was happy again. Running to Peter. I thought perhaps - it couldn't have been him. Would a woman still love a man after that?"

The baroness spoke quietly behind him. "Read her confession. She has written it this hour past, at my request. Sysabel admits her part and names Peter. She is trying to make good the evil done."

Adrian shook his head. "I can't read it. I accept your word."

"Did you kill Peter?"

Adrian gazed back at the earl. "May the good Lord forgive me, I didn't blame Peter. When my sister seemed better, I thought either I had been wrong and there'd been no wickedness done after all, or perhaps - perhaps being so small and young - her body had righted itself with God's kindness. But she adored Peter. I never liked him much, but how could he have been the culprit when she loved him still? It was Nicholas Sissy despised. So I thought - when I could bear thinking about it at all - I thought -"

"Sweet Jesus," murmured Nicholas. "You thought it was me?"

"I did," Adrian mumbled, shaking his head. "Forgive me. I thought it could have been - against her will - and in jealousy of Peter." He stared around again, finally facing the earl. "I always knew, you see, it must have been Nicholas who killed his brother."

Shuffling in the silence, the scraping of stools pushed back or pulled forwards. One candle guttered, sank, and blinked out. Lady Wrotham replaced it with her own. It was the earl who finally reached to the folded paper on the table and started to read.

But it was Nicholas who spoke first. "I don't believe you," he said abruptly.

"My Peter," mumbled the earl, refolding the paper. "Little Sissy."

"You're lying, Adrian." Nicholas stared, unblinking, at his cousin. "If you genuinely believed I'd raped your sister, got her pregnant, and then dragged her off for an abortion which might have killed her, you would have accused me, threatened me. You would have fought me. Ostracised me, announced my crime to my father and spat in my face. You'd hardly have brought your sister to my wedding, then invited me for a friendly visit after the castle fire."

"Your wife," Adrian mumbled. "She wasn't to blame for anything. I sympathised - poor girl. Already wed to you. Then the ruin of the fire. I felt obliged to offer a refuge."

"To have me in your house, and guest of your sister?" Nicholas shook his head. "And this already some months after you must have guessed about Sissy's predicament, and yet had done nothing. To me, you said not one word. You called me coward, but I never thought to call you that. Yet it would have been cowardice beyond possibility to think me guilty of such behaviour, then culminating in Peter's murder, and yet come to my wedding, invite me to your house, greet me with all civility and say not one word in anger."

"I couldn't be sure. I hoped it wasn't true." Adrian voice was unsteady. "Inviting you - I thought I'd see - see how you spoke to my6 sister and how she spoke to you. Try to find out the truth. I was ready - ready to kill you if I discovered the truth."

The earl interrupted, puzzled. "But if my Peter loved little Sysabel so well, why didn't he marry her? I'd have adjusted, accepted, stopped the negotiations with the Wrothams. Oh, a little bluster perhaps, a little shouting, and none too pleased. But with the girl expecting a Chatwyn child, a dispensation could have been asked and paid for. She and Peter could have wed."

The baroness took up another stool and drew it to the head of the table. She spoke quietly. "Peter never loved Sysabel," she said. "I came to know him later, and I doubt he was capable of loving anyone. He wished to marry my daughter because she's an heiress. Sysabel had no money, nor even a dower. I imagine Peter used her, despising her for being easy, and nothing more. When he discovered she was carrying his child, he sent her off to the abortionist with a servant. He neither collected her afterwards, nor contacted her for three weeks following, during which time she was desperately ill."

Nicholas looked again at Adrian. "Peter laughed behind her back, joking about her passion for him. I knew nothing more. But you lived with her Adrian. She was so ill, and for so long? And you claim you knew nothing?"

"I said I guessed."

"Simply a guess. But still did nothing."

The earl was going pink. "No one must ever know. The scandal would ruin us. Everyone must keep silent. What of this woman – the crone who performed –"

"She is dead," interrupted the baroness.

Nicholas looked up. "You know that, my lady? How?"

"More sudden suspicions, Nicholas?" Lady Wrotham smiled back at her son-in-law. "No, Martha informed me. I knew nothing of this until quite recently but evidently one of the old family retainers did. Martha was once my daughters' nurse, and has remained with us ever since. She has a manner which encourages confidences. Young Sysabel's maid told Martha a great deal. Thinking to bring the matter into the open, Martha took the girls past that particular street on a trip to London from the Strand House. The herbalist's house was gutted, and half the lane with it. Martha made enquiries the next day, and was told the old woman had been murdered. She was known to help girls in trouble. Her killing was therefore never investigated by the sheriff, and taken as justice for wicked immorality." The baroness sighed. "It seems these slayings are all much the same design, and all finish in fire.

Jerrid sighed, remaining slumped against the wall at the doorway. Nicholas still sat on the long bench, watching the others.

For some time he was silent. The earl sniffed loudly. "We're saying - murder. For what was done, if it's true, though I find it impossible to credit - sinful, of course, of both of them. Had I known - but it seems I misjudged." He stopped suddenly, sniffed again, and blew his nose loudly on the kerchief he pulled from his doublet lacings. "But murder? Revenge? Adrian?"

Adrian was now openly crying. "I would have. I should have," Adrian sobbed. "But I never did. I didn't want to - believe - it of her. Even of Peter. I blinded myself."

"You preferred not to believe it of her. Nor, it seems, of Peter. Yet apparently you were able to believe it of me." Nicholas remained unmoved. "Did you also blind yourself to high treason, my friend?"

"Muddles, mischief, lies and lunacy." Jerrid leaned back against the door jamb. He shook his head as the second candle spluttered, the tallow flared, and the stench renewed. "Sysabel and Peter. Adrian and Urswick. What wickedness have we uncovered?"

The earl stared, his eyes red rimmed. "My Peter - so wrong, so terribly wrong. And he never told me, never asked my help." He swallowed, half choking, then glared at Adrian. "And you slaughtered your own cousin? You killed my son?"

"Never." Adrian stood, panicked and desperate. "Alright. I know Christopher Urswick, and I know what he came here to do. I meant to take the letter north to Northumberland. My motives are my own business, and if you intend to inform on me to the king, I'll accept the consequences. But murder Peter - I never did. Nicholas killed his brother, and I know it. I've always known it." He was wild eyed and now he was shouting. "I said nothing and I let him get away with it, for I knew one of my damned cousins violated my little sister, and I hated them both. I hated - I hated everyone."

In the fury and the scuffle, with the earl now openly sobbing and Adrian throwing back his stool and marching once again to the door, Nicholas sat quiet, and smiled. He looked only at his father. And he spoke very softly. "I answer to no one else, but I will explain myself to you, Father," he said, little more than a murmur. "I knew Peter had seduced Sysabel, and I argued with him, asking him to leave her in innocence. He didn't care what I said of course, which I already expected. I did not denounce him for

I'd no idea she carried his child. I saw too little of her. And I did not kill Peter. To slaughter my own brother? Not something I could ever contemplate - never considered - whatever his crimes, however much he threatened, humiliated and hurt me. I grieved when he died. Not as much, perhaps, as you, Papa. But enough from one brother for another. His killer is someone else. There are several possibilities. It could have been the father of the girl he was with at that time, a Leicester magistrate, a wealthy man angry that his daughter had been ruined by the local lord."

"Nicholas, forgive me. I always thought it was you." The earl stared at his son through his tears. "I refused to accuse you - with sympathy, a little - I knew, you see, that Peter shot the arrow purposefully. But I always thought -"

"I accept that." Nicholas still spoke only to his father. "I was the obvious suspect. But knowing myself innocent, my principal suspect was Adrian. At first I thought the father of the girl - but he could hardly have murdered Baron Wrotham. Yet it was clearly the same killer. There could be no doubt of that. And so I thought of Adrian. Yet Adrian's friendship with Urswick and subsequent treason was something I did not suspect."

Adrian jumped up, shouting. "Neither killer nor traitor. Is it treachery simply to deliver a letter? The letter speaks of marriage, and says nothing against the king. Urswick is a man of God. Henry Tudor wrote the letter, but he's simply an exile - no murderous traitor. And Northumberland is loyal to King Richard." The earl stumbled up, reaching for his nephew, but Adrian backed and Jerrid came between.

"My lords." Lady Wrotham waved a cautious hand. "Quietly, please. The hostelry sleeps. It would be wise to let them sleep on. We want no interruptions."

"Perhaps," Jerrid nodded, "we also need to sleep on this whole affair. Decisions are always best left till morning."

"If Adrian decides to run -"

Nicholas shook his head. "He can't. He must speak to his sister in the morning. He knows the substance of her written confession, and can hardly choose to ignore it." Nicholas smiled suddenly. "Besides, my men will now have his men under guard. Adrian can go nowhere unless he goes on foot."

"Running barefoot from retribution?" Jerrid fingered his thin leather belt and the hilt of his knife wedged there. "I believe I can run as fast."

"I'm an innocent man, and will stay to face my sister in the morning," Adrian announced with furious deliberation, glaring at his uncle.

"And I will make one last visit to the stables," Nicholas said softly, "and ensure my orders have been carried out. And then," he smiled a little, "I shall find my own bed, and sleep deep with an untroubled conscience."

"Are you suggesting –?"

"A little more than simple suggestion, cousin."

"If *your* conscience is genuinely untroubled, Adrian my boy," declared the earl, eyes still moist, "then you've a conscience needs re educating." He pushed at Adrian from behind. "Indeed, it's a conscience needs a good thrashing. And you'll get up those stairs with me hard at your back, and sleep with me one side and your Uncle Jerrid tight to the other."

Emeline was asleep when Nicholas returned to the little attic bedchamber.

He stood a moment in the dark, watching the small blanketed body in the bed, and smiled. As usual she was muttering in her dreams, small murmurs impossible to decipher, a gentle mumble of unintelligible words. Then quite suddenly she called his name. Nicholas crossed quickly to the bed and sat beside her.

"What is it, little one? Bad dreams?" He stroked the side of her face, and realised she had been crying. "So many tears."

Emeline blinked and opened her eyes. "It's really you?"

"Who else? From now on, it will always be me."

"Oh, Nicholas." She struggled up from the bed's swathing warmth, breathing deep. "You were away so long and I was worried. I would have come down to see, but I thought everyone might scream '*Pestilence – be gone,*' and run screaming from me. It's all so horrible, Nicholas, and I feel so – dirty. But I'm not sick, not even a little bit unwell, really I'm not." She rubbed the sleep from her eyes and cuddled up tight to the warmth of his outstretched arms. "Was it – terrible – with Adrian?"

"Unpleasant." He smoothed the hair tangles back from her face, and the wet streaks from her cheeks. "Crying? For Adrian? For me? For yourself?"

"Oh yes, for everyone. Especially Sissy." She gazed up at him. "Don't you ever cry, my love?"

He shook his head. "I cried so much when my mother and little sister and the baby all died, I doubt I had any tears left." He thought a moment. "Though perhaps I cried when the surgeon ripped my face apart to pull Peter's arrow out of my head." He smiled suddenly. "Cried – or screamed."

She whispered, "Did you cry when Peter was killed?"

"No." Nicholas pulled her tighter into his embrace. "Lord forgive me, but I knew life would be a damn sight easier without him. Better for Sissy, and probably for a few other besotted females around the countryside. It certainly improved every day and every night for me. Peter was not an easy companion."

"And did you," she murmured, "think dying like that would serve him right for being so vile? And serve your father right for all his prejudice?"

Nicholas grinned widely. "Yes, I thought exactly that." He kissed the tip of his wife's cold damp nose. "But I grieved too, even missing him at times. We'd had pleasant moments together over the years." He frowned momentarily, the grin subsiding. "My father took no wards, so for much of my life Peter was my principal or only companion. We were close – once – as children." Nicholas paused again, then sighed. "I knew exactly where he was that day, where his latest mistress lived, and that he'd planned to be there overnight. So when news came of his death, I also knew I'd be the first suspect. But killing Peter was never an option, bastard that he was. So I went south, or north, anywhere to be away from him. Perhaps my work for the king was partly due to that. First escaping Peter. Then escaping the loss of him."

"Escaping? Or looking for adventure?"

"It was the same thing." The grin had reappeared. "Climbing out of windows. Dressing in disguise. Looking the part. Playing the game. The irresponsible younger son, with no prospects except those he forges for himself."

She sighed. "I won't ever stand in your way, my love, though I hope you'll never want to escape from me. But adventure –

working for the king – and if you find it sadly dull at home just sitting with me by the fire –"

"You are my adventure, little one."

"So sometimes you'll take me with you?"

"That's something we can discuss over that domestic fireside of yours." He swung his legs up onto the wide mattress, half across her snuggled billows. "Tomorrow will still be busy. Adrian has admitted dealings with Urswick. How deep he is with the exiles themselves I've no idea, but something must be done. Oh – not arrest I hope, nor official accusations, but he must be warned off, or made to face the king and ask for pardon. As for accusations of murder – that's another matter and he denies it. He would of course, whether innocent or guilty, but we've neither proof nor evidence. Sissy – well, that's something he must deal with himself."

Emeline wrapped her arm around her husband's naked waist. "Aren't you cold?"

He grinned again. "Perhaps. So keep me warm."

"No more fears of infection?"

"Tomorrow once matters are sorted with Adrian, I'll take you back downstairs," he told her. "But it's been sweet, having you here to myself. The pestilence – it's the curse every Englishman has to face at times, and we've been luckier than most. So we'll travel back to Westminster. I still have that wretched letter to deliver to the king. Adrian – I'll leave him to my father if I can, once the initial decision is made." He leaned back a moment, Emeline nestled to his side as he stared up at the ceiling beams and the bed's limp tester. "Strange," he said, more to himself than to her, "I never considered Adrian much in the past. Too busy avoiding the family and making choices for myself. But now – there's more to Adrian than I'd thought. And most of it I don't like."

Emeline was interested. "Well, he seems pompous and boring and bossy but nice to Sissy. Yet – if he's a traitor and a murderer – he's someone else!"

Nicholas smiled, his wandering hands discovering the rise of her breasts beneath the eiderdown. "Knowing him since I was a child clearly meant nothing, for I never knew him at all. Yet the bastard claims to have always thought me guilty – not only of killing my own brother – but also of raping his sister."

Emeline sat in a hurry. "He *what*?" she demanded. "How *dare* he?" She wriggled around, staring down at her husband. "*Raping* Sissy? *How* could he think such a thing? And if he really did believe that, *why* did he do *nothing* about it?"

"Just what I said." Nicholas pulled her back down and scrambled beneath the covers with her, their legs entwined. "Which is why I don't believe a word of it. There's something more to this." But he shook his head. "So have mercy now, my beloved, and give me leave to forget the dark memories and the sins of my family. I want to make love to my wife."

She gazed up at him as he moved over her, bright blue eyes shadowed. "You called me '*your beloved*', she whispered.

"Do you not yet believe that I've fallen in love with you?" His hands pushed down against her belly, pressing into the soft curls at her groin. His fingers probed.

She caught her breath on a sudden gulp. "Not just - *that* - part of me?"

"Every part of you."

"I don't even know - what it's called." She was losing her breath entirely.

"Oh there are names, my love, plenty of names, none of which I'll tell you. But it's a place I treasure." He leaned heavily over her, crushing her beneath him, and his eyes glittered just an inch from hers. "But it wasn't only this I missed while I was away, as I've sworn to you already. It was the soft slip of your fingers around me, the sweet warmth of your breath. The worried murmurs and mumbles you make in your sleep, and the bright dazzling joy of you when I see you wake in the morning."

CHAPTER FORTY NINE

David Witton straightened his shirt collar, pulled up his boots, tightened the lacings of his doublet and checked that both knife hilts were easy to hand and would be quick to draw. He took one deep breath and entered the stables. The horses, still snorting and kicking at the straw, were not yet settled, and one of the men, recently arrived, was filling buckets, while others unbuckled and heaved off the saddles and horse blankets. Five men, six horses. David watched a moment, leaning back against one of the stalls. He stuck his thumbs through his belt, and waited.

Alan Venter was already watching, waiting in the shadows at the stable's far doorway by the upturned barrows. Seemingly a casual wakefulness, he nodded, barely discernible. David smiled and raised one hand, four fingers spread. Again Alan nodded. There were four. So Rob and Harry were somewhere, hidden, alert, also waiting.

The horses gradually settled. The men continued to fold the blankets, hoisting sacks of oats and filling the trough. The water buckets were once again empty. One of the new arrivals called for an ostler. "Boy. Where's the boy?"

No one answered. The inn's stable boys had already been ordered to their pallets and were silent if not asleep. Alan sauntered from the shadows into the pooling moonlight through the open sided doorway. "You'll be the late arrivals, then," he said, kicking at the empty buckets. "I hear the Fox is overflowing with grand lords and their ladies these days. A couple of you look mighty familiar. So who do you serve, my friend?"

The other man stared, then shook his head. "My master's my business, and I'm no man's friend," he growled. "I'm pissing tired, and there's no bugger at this miserable inn to refill buckets nor help scrub down the bloody horses. What sort of place is this, then – to charge but not supply?"

"But I reckon I know some of you, and your master too." Alan shook his head. "You've been at the Chatwyn House stables, back outside London. So how come you're suddenly too grand to carry a bucket out to the well? Or perhaps you've an arm too weak to carry it back once filled?"

One of the other men grinned with a low chuckle as he settled the last horse into its stall. The first man scowled, flexing a fist. "Yes, I've seen you before. So you should know I'm no groom, nor bloody scullion to muck out some bandy old mare stinking of sweat."

Alan braced himself for attack before speaking. "Tis you stinking of sweat, my friend, and bandy as the mare, far as I can see. Fill your own bucket, for I'm no groom neither, and don't work for you nor your master."

It was one of the other men who immediately stepped forwards, both fists raised. "Making friends again, Francis? Give the word and I'll knock the bastard from one stall into the next." But David was already behind him, and had grabbed the man's arm before he could swing it, forcing his wrist up hard behind his back.

"More complaints?" David murmured. "What an unfriendly band of brethren it seems we have here, Alan, to disturb our righteous rest." He stared through the gloom. "And I know you too. You work for Sir Adrian Frye, if I recognise you correctly. Strange for a knight of the realm to employ such bad tempered servants." The three other men looked around. David abruptly released the man he held who tumbled to his knees, rubbing his wrist and glowering. David shrugged.

There was shuffling, indrawn breath, tempers rising. The horses, now abandoned half groomed, kicked, snorting and stamping, sensing unrest. One reared, knocking over the last full bucket. Water seeped into the straw. All five of the newcomers faced Alan and David. One also bunched his fists. "We ain't no brainless horse scrubbers, not that it bothers me for I'll do what's needed in times of needing. Maybe you remembers our faces from the Chatwyn stables, but we're fighting men, have been on important business and fighting were part of it, so watch your backs. One more word and I'll surely take offence. You stupid buggers be warned."

"Watch my back?" Alan snorted. "That's the way of brave fighters now, is it? Too cautious to approach the front, then?"

Which is when the first man swung his arm, full force from his shoulder, and aimed for Alan's face.

It was Harry who grabbed the arm from behind, twisting the man into a headlong tumble. Harry promptly banged the snarling man's head hard to the ground, punched him once to the jaw and again to the belly, sat on him, and wound the stout rope he was carrying around the other's flailing wrists, pinning them to his torso. "Louts and brawlers, is you then?" decided Harry with evident glee, pulling the rope tight. The prone man winced and grunted. "A lickle uncomfy, is it? Dear, dear, how awful sad. But then, tis proper unwise to go labelling yerselves as fighters, when yous no more than scufflers."

Alan already faced the others. "Come on then, my friends. Who's first? And which one of you bastards knifed our little lad, then? A child who did no harm to you nor no one else, but ended up dead for the pleasure of seeing one of your ugly faces."

"I also recognise two of you," David said, standing wide legged and ready beside Alan. "And you'll recognise me from the same place, for I know exactly who your master is, and what you've been up to. So which of you was so brave to slaughter an innocent child?"

The horses were now stamping and fretful, kicking hard, nostrils flared. Not only those six newly arrived, but those already settled into the hostelry stables now panicked. The earl's horse, a huge destrier of uneven temper, had been standing placid, asleep, his head bowed. He woke with a grumble and a hiss, memories of battle training remembered as he heard men shouting. The beast reared with two thundering front hooves crashing against the side of his stall.

Adrian's four remaining henchmen rushed Alan and David, but Harry was back and in seconds had another man down with a hard boot point to his knees and another to his groin. David, his knife now pressed to his adversary's throat, called to the descrier. "Calm yourself, Pallis. You know me. There's no trouble. Go back to sleep."

Above the stalls the hay loft was stocked with bales, sacks of oats and turnips, and the pallets of the hostelry's grooms. None now slept, but all covered their heads and kept flat down in the straw. The floor was half planked, then open to the stalls below. Rob jumped from above directly onto two of the newcomers. One hit his head on a rolling bucket, and, eyes glazed, slumped. The other fought back. Rob fisted him straight to the nose, his other fist to the eye. "Pit yerselves agin a backstreet fighter from London, would you?" Rob chuckled. "There's no Nottingham bumpkin will get his knee to my cods." The second man staggered and fell, eyes shut, mouth gaping, and was quiet.

Within a few moments of energetic concentration, there were five heavyset men lying prone on the ground, straw in their ears, horse dung in their hair, arms and legs thick roped and quite unable to rise. One was unconscious, another bleeding from a broken nose, but the horses gradually quietened, returning to an amiable supper.

David, Alan, Harry and Rob looked cheerfully down at their handiwork. David smiled slightly. "Though I seem to remember," he said softly, "his lordship saying something about subtle questioning."

"Oh well," Rob scratched his head. "No harm done. Least – maybe some harm to that bugger with the broken nose. But serves him right. The bastard tried to knife me. None too subtle, p'raps. But effective."

"His lordship won't mind," grinned Alan. "He'll just be sorry he weren't here to lend a hand."

His lordship was kissing his wife. The window shutters, raised and solid, kept the chamber enclosed in blackness and a whisper of warmth. But the bedcovers were thrown back and Emeline lay naked in the darkness, her arms wrapped tight around her husband's waist. As he entered her hard, her hands clasped lower. Nicholas chuckled softly, tickling her ear. "You've an arse as soft and round as rolled velvet," he told her. "I doubt mine gives the same satisfaction."

He was nuzzling the side of her face, the short evening pickles across his jaw scraping against her chin. She whispered, "I love your body, Nicholas. Long and lean and hard in some places and silky soft in others."

Wedging himself up a moment, he gazed down at her. "You surprise me, my love. I thought you still too timid to notice me one way or the other. Nor admit it if you did."

"I didn't. But now I do." The snuggled dark made the room feel smaller, more intimate, hiding the blushes and the shyness. "When you're dressed all grand, I'm proud to walk beside you. When you're undressed, it's an even greater pride I feel."

He grinned. "So? Better dressed? Or undressed?"

"I see other women looking at you, admiring, but that's just when you're dressed of course." She felt her toes curl, and smiled at herself, daring to say what she had long thought. "And I like thinking I'm the only one who sees you undressed," she whispered. "I am, aren't I, my love? And when you make love to me, your eyes glitter. I love looking at you."

"Only looking?"

"And touching." Her fingers, tentative but explorative, traced over his buttocks and down to the back of his thighs. "So much muscle," she murmured. "So much strength. I can feel the force and power of you, even here, where your skin is smooth. Rolled velvet wouldn't look right on you at all." She giggled, half smothered. "There's the long slight swell, dipping in at the sides," and her fingertips slid down across his back. "I like it because the muscles aren't all knotty. Some men look as though their muscles are stuck on afterwards and don't really belong to them. Yours are all lean under the skin. Almost glossy. You feel - polished."

He laughed, but it was husky as if his breath caught in his throat. "You have muscles I love too, little one, here, inside, where you close around me." He rocked gently against her, easing himself deeper within. "You squeeze, and those muscles take me straight to paradise."

She was losing her own breath. "That's just flattery. You exaggerate."

"No. Paradise indeed. Probably the only way I'll ever get there."

"You take me places too - places I never imagined. And I like feeling all that strength, when you're so gentle with me."

"If you only knew, my love, how tempted I am not to be gentle. Not gentle at all." His own fingers edged between their swear damp bodies, pushing down to his own place of entry, teasing and probing. One fingertip pushed inside, forcing deeper, and she gulped. "Too much?" He smiled, removing his hand, caressing between her legs, up and behind to her own buttocks and the dividing crease. "But I promise to go on being gentle, little one. At least until we know each other a good deal better."

"And you like me touching you - here?"

"Clasp my arse as tight as you like my sweetest and that pulls me tighter inside you," he whispered, his voice now softer, sultry as he pressed both from behind and in front. "But talking of arses, it's certainly yours I prefer. Round, pliable and dimpled. Now," and he pushed once more and climaxed at once, sinking down against her with a groan. She sighed, arms tight around his back, squeezing once more as she felt him grow and pulse within her, and surrendered to her own mounting delight.

After slow moments of gradually reclaiming breath, he rolled over, keeping her pressed against him, releasing her only from his weight as they then lay side by side. Then finally, slowly, he eased himself out from her and leaned over, resting her head against his shoulder as he kissed the top of her head. "Sleepy?"

"Umm."

His fingers smoothed down from her neck to her breasts, across and around, embracing her in warmth. "Not cold, little one?"

She paused, then whispered back, "I'm not cold. You feel like a furnace. I could forge horseshoes." Another pause, then, "I couldn't be - feverish, could I, Nicholas?"

He said, "No more than I am, my love." Then paused, before speaking slow and soft. "There's many thing bring pain in this sweet fresh world of ours. There's a thousand diseases, and a thousand tortures from the bitter punishments of the law to the pangs of childbirth. But I'd choose all of them sooner than face the pestilence. That pustulating growth of bleeding agony that eats the body whole, and leaves only a breathing hell in an empty rotting carcass. After four days of that, death is the reward, not the punishment." He turned to look down at her, although in the darkness he could see only the faint sheen of her eyes. Then he bent, pulling up the blankets which he wrapped around them both, tucking her in, swaddling her nakedness. "This sickness is not a thing you can mistake, little one, or be unsure. You have no contagion, no pestilence, no disease." He kissed her cheek, and then, lightly, her mouth. "Now my sweet and healthy beloved, sleep with me and we'll wake in ruddy welcome health tomorrow morning, ready to return downstairs together, and face my wretched cousin, my equally wretched father, my uncle, your mother, both sisters, and all the new day's adventure, whatever that may be." He chuckled softly. "And that may seem a pestilence of another kind."

She kissed his neck, which was where she was snuggled tight. "I like it when you call me beloved."

"Then sleep sweet, beloved," he murmured. "And forget the fears of the past."

CHAPTER FIFTY

The Fox and Pheasant served a cold breakfast. The private parlour and its table were overcrowded, each squashed tight to his neighbour, and Avice sat, carefully quiet while her mother's eyes, colder than those of the mackerel on her plate, warned her not to speak a word, even with Mistress Sysabel Frye's right elbow digging hard into her ribs. Sysabel was equally subdued. She ate nothing, sipped her light ale, and kept her eyes on her empty platter. The baroness was wearing a new gown of rose pink sarcenet, trailing sleeves trimmed in crimson velvet, and the neckline, also trimmed, deeper than a respectable lady of her age was normally expected to wear.

"I see," noticed Lady Wrotham, "that young Nicholas is absent."

"I expect, madam," nodded the earl, "the boy is tending to his lady upstairs. I have no idea why a few chills and sniffles are keeping her apart from us for so long, but no doubt she's better off avoiding the embarrassments of our recent sordid family affairs."

Adrian was not seated with the others. He stood in front of the empty hearth, his back to the table and its occupants, his hands clasped behind his back as he stared down at the cold shifting ashes. He spoke under his breath. "My dearly beloved cousin is no doubt once again pretending the hero by protecting his wife from murderous traitors."

"Actually," grinned Jerrid, "he's out at the stables, releasing your parcel of foolhardy henchmen, Adrian, since last night our men trussed yours up like piglets ready for the pot."

Adrian turned abruptly. "What? Attacked my men? How dare he?"

"So far, never noticed much he wouldn't dare," smiled his uncle. As Adrian strode from the parlour, and just before he slammed the door behind him, Jerrid called, "But not so innocent, your men, Adrian. Since one of yours killed one of ours back on the road some days ago."

The earl looked up in surprise. "What's this? More murder and mayhem?"

"A long story, Symond." Jerrid shook his head. "And a mean spirited one. Having taken that cursed letter from Urswick's henchman, we were waiting around to finish the other half of our orders from the king, when the servant boy travelling with us was knifed and left dead in the tavern courtyard. As far as we can guess, it was because he'd recognised one of Adrian's men from the Strand stables, and the bastard wouldn't risk his identity passed on to others."

"Since the man was also involved in the treachery at hand?"

"I believe so, my lady." Jerrid answered the baroness, frowning. "The boy was simply a child and innocent of everything except recognising his attacker. It's more than possible Adrian's companions are working not for Adrian himself, but directly for the exile Tudor."

The earl stood, throwing his napkin to the table. "Then I shall investigate this business myself," he announced. "I've my own outriders bedded in the long barn, six fine Leicestershire fellows ready to lay down their lives for me if needed." He bowed slightly to the baroness. "If you'll excuse me, my lady, I mean to get to the bottom of this." He took a deep and laborious breath, and his stomach swelled. "Never," he informed the table, "– never since my great grandfather's time – has there been a traitor to the crown amongst the Chatwyns – and there won't be now if I have to wring his scrawny neck to ensure it."

The Lady Elizabeth watched her brother leave, winced as the door slammed a second time, and sighed. "I never," she decided faintly, "thought of young Adrian as having a scrawny neck." She took a small slice of cold roast beef and began to cut it into tiny squares with her penknife. "I believe he has rather a thick and stubby neck. Don't you think so, my dear?" Sysabel declined to answer and kept her glare rigid on her powder blue lap. Her aunt sighed. "As for bad temper and brawling, my maid Joan is upstairs darning the hem of my best cloak, but if I called her I imagine she could sort them all out in an instant. A very fierce young woman, is my Joan, when roused." Once again she turned to Sysabel. "Isn't she, my dear. Has a fine thwack when required."

Sysabel had begun to bite her finger where she had previously burned the nail, holding it within the candle flame. Now she was gnawing on the tip so it appeared raw and red. Avice turned and slapped her hand away. "You'll make it bleed," she hissed. "Chew something else."

Sysabel immediately burst into tears. "You're all so - horrible," she sobbed. "To me and my poor brother. I wish I'd never come."

"It's nice to know we agree on something," said Avice.

"Quiet, both of you," ordered Lady Wrotham. "There may be matters of some importance to deal with today, and I've not the slightest intention of missing any of it. You two children will be sent to bed if you don't behave."

"I'm not a child," Avice objected. "I'm old enough for - for being married."

Her mother sighed. "What a tempting thought."

"And I might be," Avice retaliated, "if you arranged something honourable and bought me some nice new gowns so I'd look more - eligible."

"I'd marry you tomorrow, my dear," Jerrid said, pushing back his stool and bowing low with impressive elegance. "With new clothes - or without them, my dear."

Avice seemed a little unsure as how to react to this, and the baroness quickly interrupted whatever she might have been about to say. "It is thoroughly improper to speak of marriage and such matters - especially at breakfast. You will keep silent from now on, Avice."

"Just not at breakfast? It would have been all right to say it at dinner?"

Aunt Elizabeth nodded. "We are all family to be sure, and will take no offence. However," she looked around, "the principal difficulty is that of young Adrian. What a bothersome letter that must have been. Though why Adrian should wish to wed with the Earl of Northumberland, I have no idea."

Sysabel was still crying into her napkin. Avice glowered. Jerrid was grinning for motives uncertain to anyone else. The baroness folded her napkin neatly, replaced it on the table, and stood. "I am going upstairs," she said. "If anyone makes a sensible decision on any matter whatsoever during the next few hours, I should appreciate being informed. Otherwise, I shall remain in my chamber with Martha, who at least speaks some sense." She glanced briefly at her daughter. "Marriage," she said, "would do you a great deal of good, my girl. I shall begin negotiations immediately on my return home. Probably with a family of Scottish reivers, or perhaps a kindly warden from Newgate."

The stables were once again in uproar, and this time a group of sniggering grooms and the harassed hostelry landlord were looking on. Two other groups of men, intrigued by the noise and commotion, were watching from the cobbled courtyard, for both the Earl of Chatwyn's six outriders and Baroness Wrotham's four household guards had awoken to an eager awareness of the day's probable entertainment. Old Bill, still nursing his aches and sneezes, was keeping well hidden in the straw of the stable's half floored loft, peeping down without being seen, but several kitchen boys and the companions of an irate trader and his wife sent to arrange their immediate departure, were all hoping for a little drama before being ordered back to work. David, Alan, Harry and Rob grinned widely at their appreciative audience, having slept very well indeed, then waking to a pastel dawn of sweet balmy warmth and the anticipation of a promising rout.

One by one Adrian's henchmen were untied. They had not spent a comfortable night.

"So which one of you delightful gentlemen was it did the killing?" inquired Nicholas, leaning back against the main doorway, cup of beer in hand. "Is anyone courageous enough to confess? Or wise enough to implicate one of his fellows?"

There was a great deal of general noise, groaning, cursing, complaints and threats, but no noticeable answer to his question. Finally Alan said, "So we should execute the lot of them, then, my lord? To be sure to get the right one?"

"Or call in the law," suggested David. "And have them all arrested? Hanged, castrated and quartered for high treason?"

"I'm more for the do it ourselves execution idea, meself," said Harry with jovial anticipation. "We could do it proper. There's the stable block for mounting over there. Make a good rest for five pretty heads, it would, while I find the local woodcutter's axe."

There was renewed spluttering and swearing. The hostelry landlord seemed as agitated as the men under threat. "My lord, I beg you. You'll ruin me."

"Which would certainly be a shame," Nicholas admitted, "since you serve excellent apple codlings. But the dead boy was under my protection, and his death isn't something I intend overlooking."

The landlord sighed and turned back to his staff, clapping his hands and ordering the kitchen boys to the kitchens and the grooms to their duties. The grooms, although reluctant to leave the discussion and miss its conclusion, began leading out the horses, some for exercise, some for grooming, two for the departure of their masters. Once the stables stood comparatively empty, David said, "It appears Sir Adrian is coming to watch his men's ignominious destinies, my lord."

Nicholas turned, and smiled. Adrian marched towards him.

"This is neither the place nor the moment," Adrian said quietly, "to tell you what I think of you, sir. But you'll release my men this instant. I'm leaving. We'll talk in private back at the Strand."

Nicholas shook his head. "Might as well insult me here as there, cousin. I'm used to my family's insults and since I know them all based on ignorance and coming from the ignorant, they matter not one shit. We've less privacy here, it's true, but these good people already have a fair idea of what's afoot, and deserve to know the consequences. So tell me what you think of me by all means. But you're not leaving yet, cousin, and I might point out, you're somewhat outnumbered."

"Outnumbered? Four bullies and your own brave self, Nicholas?"

The earl spoke suddenly and loudly from behind him. "And my six men, lad, watching on now, just waiting for my word."

Adrian did not raise his voice. The fury in his face remained cold and the muscles around his eyes and mouth tensed, white knotted. His pale blue eyes turned black. He addressed only Nicholas. "Buffoon and coward that you are, spoiled and petted, born rich as a king without so much as a spit in the porridge to earn all that wealth! While I've had to struggle from birth with not a penny to my name, both parents dead and leaving me with a half brained sister to protect into the bargain. Yet I was the one knighted while you skulked behind your brother, a creature even more loathsome than yourself." His words slid like seething, bubbling slime, long contained and now released. "I've held my temper for many long years," he spat, "waiting to tell you the truth. Yet still you hide behind your henchmen and your father's power. And you dare threaten me?" He raised his voice at last, speaking also to his uncle who stood at Nicholas's back. "You've not one breath of proof against me – not one hint. As you've told me yourselves, you took the letter from Urswick long before I arrived to join his company. I'll say I had no knowledge of it. Christopher Urswick was previously chaplain to Henry Tudor's lady mother, and a man of distinction and respect and I've every right to speak to a man I've known some years as a man of God." Adrian looked around then, speaking to all those who crammed close, attentive and listening. "There's no treachery in knowing a man and as for the letter you've stolen, I've never seen it nor touched it. As for murder," he turned back to Nicholas, "it was you who vilely slaughtered your own brother. I had no hand in it. You're the cowardly killer, cousin, and you know it even if you've not the courage to admit it."

Even the crowd was silent, though with a shuffling of feet and indrawn breath. Nicholas spoke first. He had come armed, and his hand now rested on the hilt of his sword. But he was smiling. "Long held hatreds long disguised, it seems, cousin," he said softly. "So your endless complacent pomposity hid bubbling envy, and the well nurtured jealousy of the inept. A bitter destiny perhaps, as son of the youngest son, your father a drunken sot who left his children penniless and bare educated. But the fault's not mine, Adrian, for you to nurse such seething jealousies. Killing Peter – a coward's act from someone who likes to shout that word at others. As for treason, I know the truth whether or not I can prove it. So fight me, cousin, and prove your talents and your courage now."

Adrian threw out both arms. He was clearly unarmed. "You rape my sister. Murder your brother. So now kill me too, Nicholas."

Nicholas spoke over his shoulder. "Give him your sword, Father."

"My boy, this is hardly the way –." But the earl unbuckled the scabbard from his baldric and with two steps towards Adrian, presented the sword's hilt. "Your choice, nephew," he told him. "But don't be a fool and leave the matter to the law." He nodded to Nicholas. "You've a deal of right on your side, boy, and I don't doubt your motives. But don't kill him."

Adrian took the sword from his uncle's clasp and held it, point high so the steel caught the wavering sunbeams. He scoffed, "Kill him? Who? Your idiot son kill a man knighted on the battlefield for his courage and his skills?"

"Not such a bad swordsman, my Nicholas," muttered the earl, looking around him. "Maybe not always said it myself, and maybe should have. But young Nick's always been the best archer and the best swordsman in the family. But beware, both of you, for we'll have the sheriff, and half the countryside down on us within minutes. 'Tis not the place, boy."

"I'll avenge my king, my own reputation, and my brother's life," Nicholas said, drawing his own sword. "And to hell with the law and the countryside both." He looked back briefly at his father and his cluster of henchmen. "No interruptions, no interference, no defending heroics. Leave this to me.

Some of the horses, led out for grooming, were coming back. The young grooms halted, watching, not willing to pass. The landlord, shepherding the scullions, had already hurried from the courtyard. A horse neighed, another snorted. Then Adrian stepped forwards. 'Beware – fool. You've never yet seen my unbridled temper."

Nicholas's voice remained even but the smile had faded. "Surprisingly, perhaps, since you claim to believe so much against me," he said, "But now I am more than a little angry myself."

There were other footsteps, somebody pushing through the crowd. Jerrod called out, "He's not worth it, boy. Leave it be, or you'll end up taking the blame yourself."

"I invariably do," said Nicholas, and sidestepped with sudden speed. Adrian's sword swung straight, aiming into unexpected empty air. Nicholas, now behind, took him at once around the neck with one arm, muscles straining through the fine linen of his shirt sleeve. His sword countered Adrian's, clash to clash and flashing sparks of reflected sunlight. Nicholas forced his cousins head back and hissed directly into Adrian's ear, his spit on Adrian's cheek. "I could kill you now. Just one little thrust. But I want a better fight than this. Show me what you can do, cousin." And he released him at once, hurling him sideways.

Adrian stumbled, righted himself, and tightened his clasp on the hilt of his uncle's sword. He turned, spinning back to face Nicholas. "Bastard. Trickster."

Nicholas laughed. "Come show your cowardly cousin how to fight with honour, then." He bowed, then danced backwards. "Though if you want a straightforward face to face slash and batter, you'll be dead at my first blow. And remember, I'm also the younger son, or was until you murdered my brother. And I'd have had a little sister to protect, if the plagues of hell hadn't stolen her from me. Few men grow old without some share of misery. So show me your pathetic grievances, and play the hero, sir knight."

Adrian rushed him. He grappled Nicholas one handed, bringing the point of his sword straight to his cousin's chest. But Nicholas forced it down with his own steel, relentlessly inch by inch down across his thigh. Then he twisted his leg behind Adrian's unbalancing him, so Adrian's sword sliced first down his own leg, then rebounded. The blade scraped Nicholas's thigh, springing loose threads down his hose and a light graze against the flesh. Adrian's leg was deeply wounded and when he righted himself again, he found Nicholas's sword point pressed to his throat, and a long knife point to his groin. Adrian yelled, "Killer. Tell your father this is what you did to your brother."

"So easily infuriated, cousin?" Nicholas laughed, again releasing him with a quick shove backwards. "A few children's insults, and you lose all control and fight like a blacksmith's apprentice. So now face me square, and prove your skills."

Wide legged, sword raised, Nicholas waited. Adrian limped, adjusted, and stood four steps off, watching carefully. He raised his sword. Nicholas began to turn his blade, twisting it to swing in the sparkling sunlight. It thrummed faintly, cutting the breezes. Adrian's hand was trembling, the palm badly sliced. His leg poured blood, his throat bleeding from one small round cut. Nicholas's thigh was bleeding also, a thin trickle soaking into the wool of his hose. As he swung his sword right handed, he kept a grip on the knife in his left.

Then one of the horses bolted. Flinging up its head, ripping the reins from the small groom's loosened clutch, it snickered in alarm and made straight for the fence. The crowd parted, the groom squeaked and ran after. The other beasts began to mill, champing and fretting, twisting, turning, unsure. Two grooms grabbed, two horses reared, one kicked out and David moved aside, catching it by the tail. The horse pulled back and kicked, teeth bared. The earl yelled, "Watch out, Nick m'boy." Another horse reared and a stable boy fell, half trampled. The noise mounted, whinnying and spitting, shouting and frightened cries from the boys. The crowd half dispersed, some running forwards, yelling advice and pulling the boys from harm. A stall's planks cracked and split with splinters and another squealing horse.

Nicholas dodged. One heaving belly, black and bulging, wedged between himself and Adrian. Adrian looked around, desperate. "Run, then," Nicholas called, "It's your best chance." He raised his sword again, point it towards the oak tree and the path leading back into the hills. "Run," he laughed again. "As all traitors and murderers do."

The horses were frantic, avoiding capture. The stable boys were grabbing at manes, flying reins and the panicked flick of plaited tails. Nicholas ran past one, again facing Adrian. He grinned, and brought his sword hard down, its edge to a fallen and rolling wooden bucket. The bucket split immediately in two shuddering parts. Nicholas laughed. "Your skull next time, cousin? This sword can split a body in two, or cut through both legs with one stroke. What part would you choose, I wonder? Knees? Shoulder? Head? Shall I make two of you, cousin?"

Adrian shouted back, "Madman. Mad as your mad father." But he was panting, the words disjointed and breathless.

Harry was flat on his back, kicked by a horse, blood pouring from his chin and nose. Rob dragged him into one of the stalls, away from flying hooves. Alan and David were rounding up as many of the beasts as they could, dodging, advising, ordering the stable boys into moving lines to block the horses' escape. Jerrid, back amongst the crowd, was reassuring the landlord and two of the patrons. "Just a little misunderstanding," he said, wide and earnest blue eyed. "Conflicting loyalties, you know. Nobles of the land - never easy to talk out of some crusade or another."

The earl stood central, staring, red faced. He seemed stunned. Gradually the horses calmed, one by one led back to their stalls. David filled two buckets at the well and hauled them back to the trembling, thirsty animals, speaking softly, soothing them.

Adrian's five men had entirely disappeared along with their horses. Nicholas watched the last shadow streak beneath the low branches of the distant oak tree. When he looked back, Adrian had gone as well.

CHAPTER FIFTY ONE

Petronella combed her mistress's hair. "Very tangled, m'lady," she said with a sniff of disapproval.

"Honestly Nellie," Emeline objected, "sometimes you're worse than my mother. There's been nothing but sweaty travel and horrid little taverns for weeks and then the most awful danger. My husband's badly wounded, I've been terrified that I might have caught the pestilence and I've been shut away up here for four days without a bath, and you just think I should have done nothing but comb my hair?"

Petronella apologised with a faintly martyred sigh, and Martha looked up. She was brushing down Emeline's best gown with Fuller's Earth, and a small damp brush to the mud around the hem. Martha frowned. "The proper care of a young lady's appearance is never of minor importance, as I've taught you for years, Emeline. And his lordship has no more than a slight graze to the thigh. I doubt he'd be pleased to hear you call him badly wounded."

Nicholas was, in fact, thoroughly enjoying the compensations of the wounded, with best Burgundy and hot baked honey cakes served in the parlour downstairs. His father regarded him with unusual hesitancy. "You did well, my boy. Showed some skill - at least - bested that foolish cousin of yours, but luckily didn't kill him."

"I'd no intention of killing him," Nicholas waved an impatient hand. "I expected him to run. It's the easiest solution for all of us. Dragging him off to the sheriff and seeing him manacled in the Tower dungeons would be a huge exaggeration at this stage. High treason? Well, perhaps. Tudor's letter puts both him and Northumberland under suspicion, but it was no battle cry. It's Peter's murder which concerns me more."

A pause. "Did he? Can we be sure?" The earl drank quickly, choosing his words with unexpected care. "I've learned a good deal about you in these past two days, my boy, and I admit I've misjudged you. But I'll listen to no criticism of Peter. I didn't when he lived and I surely won't now he's gone. Now, as for his murderer?"

"I believe it was Adrian. But believing isn't knowing. I don't know. I can't know. Adrian denied it adamantly enough."

"And blamed you instead."

Nicholas shrugged. "An easy accusation for a guilty man. Perhaps even a genuine belief from an innocent one. But the sheriffs have been involved in both Peter's and my father-in-law's killings for some time now, and have no better answers than we do."

The earl sighed. "Adrian then."

Nicholas sat up, drained his cup and refilled it. "He can't run far. But even if he eventually returns home, what can we do? What can we prove?" He slumped again, lounging back against the rough plastered wall behind the bench. "But he's a man I never puzzled over, never understood, barely even saw before. I was never much interested and thought him dull." Nicholas smiled. "He's not dull after all. He's a mess of tidal rages, seething fury and bitter envy. All that disguised hatred bubbling beneath a dull veneer. Has he been working against us in secret for years, perhaps?"

"Turned traitor against the king, purely to spite us profligate and idle relatives, you mean?" Jerrid had wandered into the parlour, having smelled out the best Burgundy. "Where's the cups, Symond? I've been out talking to the men, and I'm parched."

The earl snorted and passed his brother a cup. "We were discussing young Adrian. Motives. But no proof."

Jerrid shook his head. "I'll not be killing my own nephew - but someone should. The boy's a menace. His father was a lout, for all he was my brother. And the mother was an ice cold wind. She cried three times a day every day - though perhaps with a husband like Edmund, she had good cause. As for the boy and all this well nourished envy, well, we're a wealthy family yet Adrian remains damn near penniless. Not that I consider myself a rich man, but I've more than he has. Did he hope to kill off Peter and then young Nick, and end up as the Chatwyn heir?"

"That's one of the possibilities."

"So where does that miscreant Tudor come into the picture? Trying to call himself the Lancastrian claimant to the throne, when he's as much royal blood as the hedgehog I used to play with as a boy in the castle grounds."

"Quiet little thing. But prickly."

Nicholas regarded his father and uncle with slight confusion. "Henry Tudor? Or the hedgehog?"

"Well, probably both," decided Jerrid. "But what has any of it to do with Adrian?"

"I imagine," Nicholas said, "that Adrian started taking an interest in the Tudor claims for the same reason a few others have. Adrian's a nobody with no hope. But bring in a new regime and new pathways might open, a new king, a usurper with small backing, needs new allies. Adrian could set himself up as a Beaufort loyalist and look for advancement, a title and a position at court."

"And spit in the face of the loyal York Chatwyns, whom he's loathed in secret for long gloomy years. A new royal line would likely frown at past loyalists who'd supported the previous dynasty. So Adrian could advance himself and stab us in the back at the same time. What better ambition?" Nicholas frowned. "Says he suspected me of ravishing his sister but never accused me. Well, it was safer to keep quiet of course since he couldn't be sure and didn't want to risk shaming Sissy if he turned out to be wrong. But by turning traitor and ushering in a Tudor dynasty, he'd revenge himself on all of us, whatever our guilt."

"Or he knew it was Peter which is why he killed him. Now he accuses you for simple spite."

The earl finished the last of the wine jug. "So we do nothing. With this threat, this treachery looming? We wait?"

"I don't mind waiting, but not here. I've had enough of this tavern," Nicholas shrugged. "Now Emma's over her - chill. So I'm back to Westminster and then to Leicestershire. I don't expect any of you to accompany me. That's your choice. I've backers and men of my own."

"Seems true enough, Nick, my boy. A trusty handful of men, as long as you do trust them of course."

Nicholas nodded. "To the death, Father. David's my squire of course, been with me half my life and has saved it for me more than once. You know him anyway, since he's been at the castle for years. So has Alan - nearly as long - nearly as bright - just as trustworthy. They've both accompanied me on various jobs for the king. Harry and Rob are later recruits, brawlers from the London tenements, both with the courage of a badger and the determination of a kestrel." His left thigh, heavily bandaged beneath torn woollen hose, was stretched below the table. The pain was minor and he ignored it. "And tomorrow I intend taking my men and my wife back to the Strand, and this absurd injury won't stop me riding." He looked to his father. "Apart from anything else, I've a letter to deliver to his highness. So will you travel with us, sir?"

They left on the morrow at dawn, a cavalcade including his lordship the Earl of Chatwyn and his clinking and dazzling entourage. The earl, his great destrier brightly caparisoned, rode at the head of the central body. A few paces behind, Nicholas rode beside his wife. Her ladyship Baroness Wrotham and her younger daughter Avice rode a little further in the rear, both in silence having decided that conversation was useless while reconsidering their particular grievances. The Lady Elizabeth Chatwyn travelled in the large covered litter, accompanied by her maid Joan, and the Wrotham nurse Martha. This lumbered and swayed, flanked by two men at arms and followed by the cart carrying a good deal of the ladies' personal baggage and also the other maids, driven by old Bill who disguised his sneezes on the sleeve of his tunic. Three other carts were piled with luggage and travelled slow. Trunks, coffers and parcels bounced at each rut in the road. Mistress Sysabel Frye, silent and subdued, rode directly behind the baroness, keeping pace while avoiding bringing her mount alongside. Leading the cavalcade and ensuring free passage and a clear way ahead, were the Wrotham guards and two of the Chatwyn beaters, bright liveried and well armed. Behind, with jangling grandeur, rode the remaining Chatwyn outriders, Harry and Rob Bambrigg who were arguing loudly with each other, Jerrid Chatwyn who was in conversation with the squire David Witton, and Alan Venter who kept back, but had one eye constantly on his master.

Streaming feathers, veils, and banners, the rattle of wheels and the squeak of leather, the splash of plumes and metal harness, the procession trailed for near on a quarter mile along the narrow country lanes with no pretence at speed and far more for comfort. It was a warm and sunny day with bright leafy trees sporting their spring growth above and to either side, and dewy spangles catching the sunshine from every cobweb and busily filled birds' nest. The breeze was gentle and just enough to lift the litter's canopy and flutter the ladies' little white headdresses and the gentlemen's proud feathers.

With the fine weather and the approach to summer, the roads were dry, the ruts worn deep and solid, the crossings of streams little more than a splash through a pebbled trickle, and even the rivers were easily forded. The carts lost no wheels, the horses kept their shoes, and the riders, little concerned for proprieties and status, stopped at the easiest reached of the wayside inns, and made no effort to save time. It was therefore quite some days before they arrived at their destination. The Lady Elizabeth stated that she would never again travel by litter or indeed by any other means but the rest of the party felt that the journey had been easier than most.

Sir Adrian Frye was not present and nor was he seen. His sister took care not to mention him and kept her conversation at all times polite and without substance. She said, "Yes please, aunt." Or "No, thank you, Uncle." She took bread, beef and dumplings on her platter at mealtimes and no one, therefore, noticed that she had entirely stopped eating.

The Strand House was accustomed to bustle and grand guests arriving with little warning, but they were unprepared for the family procession which arrived on the first day of June, announced only one day previously by two galloping household outriders. Uproar followed.

By the time their lordships arrived, it was calm again, beds were tucked, clean linen laid, and the kitchens were steaming with every spit turning and every cauldron set to simmer. But Nicholas only strayed long enough to change his clothes, order his hunter brought out from the stables, and then, accompanied by his uncle and three of his henchmen, rode straight for the palace at Westminster. The precious letter he carried was safe in a leather pouch strapped inside his doublet.

He was back within the hour.

Emeline said, "A month's travel, a child killed, discovering the treason of your own cousin, endless danger, fighting, disease, and a mire of expense - and what for? A ten minute audience with the king."

Nicholas grinned. "I didn't see the king. This is the eve of Corpus Christi and his highness is now on his way to Kenilworth. I saw Kendall."

"Well," she smiled, "you look good enough – for kings. It's a long time since I've seen you so grand." His sleeves swept the floorboards in great folds of cerise damask fully lined in black velvet, the edges trimmed in marten. The under sleeves, cut in three places with black silk, were saffron and the tight wrists then flared into cerise damask cuffs. His doublet, saffron brocade and laced in gold over a fine white linen shirt, was tight belted and stopped with a peplum so short it displayed the full length of his legs. Since Emeline was wearing her oldest gown and a posset stained apron, she felt a little out classed, and sighed. "I suppose," she said, "you have turned every female head in Westminster."

"I wouldn't have noticed." He was still grinning. "Actually, I was thinking of taking it all off. I want a bath."

"*Two* baths? In *one* day?"

"This one," he said, stripping off his riding gloves, "I intend taking with you."

"I don't remember you having a tub big enough for both of us."

"So I wash you first, and you wash me afterwards."

Half stripped, he bathed her with great intimacy, standing beside the well filled tub with his shirt sleeves rolled up, the suds frothing around his fingers and the steam turning to condensation against his forehead. He used a large sea sponge and perfumed Spanish soap. Briar rose, not lavender, as he pointed out. She laughed, lifting each foot as he commanded her. The bath was custom made instead of the half barrels she was accustomed to, and lined in softest linen with a padded cushion for her head. "Lean back," he told her, "and move as I tell you, lift as I tell you, and obey me as I direct you."

She stretched one leg clear of the heat, flexing her ankle and pointing her toes as ordered. "In everything?"

"In everything. Naturally."

She smiled and closed her eyes, soap bubbles on her eyelashes. The heat was sensuous and the fingertip caresses delicious, and she giggled as he massaged, pretending to wash. But his hands were firm as he scrubbed, dissolving the tiredness of difficult days past.

As she climbed from the tub, he lifted her and wrapped her in heated towels, drying her briskly between her toes, her thighs, between her legs, her belly, her breasts and beneath, then finally her hair, now a damp tousle around warm pink cheeks and sparkling brown eyes.

"And now," he told her, "you wash me."

The water still steamed, the soapy bubbles floating like lilies on a pond. Nicholas pulled his shirt off over his head, tugged down his hose and stepped naked into the bath. "So, obedient still, my love?" He sat and presented her with the sponge. "Or shall I obey you?"

Emeline washed slowly across his belly where the dark hair lay in a central line towards the groin. Over the strong bones of his hips to his thighs, and down to the muscles of his calves, then back again to his groin. When she brushed the sponge upwards once more to his ribs, he clasped her hands, and brought them back.

"Will you not wash me there?" he murmured. She bit her lip. So he brought her hand between his legs, the water pouring over him. He cupped her fingers beneath his scrotum, whispering, "Is this so strange to you, little one? We've made love often enough. You know how I'm made." Blushing, she used her fingers as he instructed, and explored, touching more firmly and washing each secret place, feeling how he grew larger and harder beneath her explorations. Then finally he climbed from the water and pulled her down onto the rug, both naked, both damp, and lay there a moment, staring at each other with the sinking light from the window catching the bright blue of his eyes and the softer brown of hers.

He kissed her nipples and stroked the swell of her breasts. She clung to his upper arms where she could feel every discovery of his hands, his fingers teasing between her legs as her hands sensing every twist and pull of his muscles. She smiled and said, "You still have streams of water and soap suds on your face. It's as if you've painted yourself, like children do sometimes, pretending to be demons or dragons."

Nicholas laughed and wiped across his own forehead, taking a thick smear of soap foam on his fingertip. He began to paint a thin warm line around each of her nipples so they seemed huge, and erect, and dark. Then, fingertip to her belly and downwards, he painted an arrow, leading deep between her legs. Playing, fingering and discovering, and smiling as she gasped and clung to him. Then, quite suddenly he rolled on top of her and pushed inside. As he entered her, hard and fast and deep, their wet bodies together like a slap, and stuck tight as he moved even further into her. She kissed him, pushing her tongue between his teeth, surprising him, tasting the smooth width of his tongue and the heat of his throat. Then she had no breath remaining for anything, and simply clung, panting fast.

"When we get back to the castle," he whispered to her, "I'll make love to you on the battlements. There'll just be the sky above us and the rolling clouds." He kissed her forehead, the tip of her nose, and both her eyes. "Once during the day, with the sun making your body gleam," he said, "and then at night in moonlight, with the stars reflecting across your breasts."

She whispered back, "Will the castle be repaired, then, Nicholas my love? Can we live there?"

He nodded, his words muffled now against her belly where he laid his head, murmuring to the curls at her groin. "Then," he said, "I'm going to make love to you in the forests beyond the moat, with the smells of good green summer growth, and the damp loam and the dry bark and the seeds all pushing up to search for the sunshine and the rain. I'm going to make love to you all day amongst the daisies until the moon comes up, and on through the night until you're too tired even to beg me to carry you back to bed. I shall roll you naked on the grass, and watch you gasp. And finally I'll carry you home and make love to you all over again."

His climax seemed leisurely, no longer pushing but pulsing within, holding her tight and still, a heartbeat of sorts but so strong that she cried out, making him smile.

It was afterwards, lying close and tired on the bed, that he said, "Each time, each touch brings you closer, little one. Less timid. I like it when you show you want me."

She spoke with her eyes shut, snuggling to the warmth of his body. "You want an adventuress."

"I think," he murmured, "I shall become domesticated instead. A creature of comfort and complacent arrogance. I shall keep my passion only for my wife's bedchamber."

She didn't believe him.

CHAPTER FIFTY TWO

No longer the gloriously meticulous aristocrat, no velvet, no damask and no fine dyed silk, Nicholas strode into the great hall of the Chatwyn house in the Strand, and regarded his wife.

"I've had word," he said. He wore laddered black hose with a small hole at the knee, a loose belted broadcloth tunic in drab blue, and an unbleached shirt below. These were the clothes he had long worn when travelling on the king's orders when requiring discretion and anonymity.

Emeline stared back. "What words? Who from? About what?"

"That might take longer to answer than you'd suppose," Nicholas said, pulling up a chair and stretching out his legs and the ill fitting hose. "Some old fellow unknown to any of us loped into the stable block this morning and informed Rob that a Sir Berendon Baker was hoping to speak with me later today." Nicholas was smiling. "Interesting don't you think?"

Since she found it exceptionally uninteresting, Emeline said, "Really? And who is he?"

Still smiling, Nicholas shook his head. "I know nobody by that name. But Adrian's home sits square in Berendon Place, Nottingham. Adrian's name is Frye, which denotes some obscure kitchen activity, as does baking. And the use of the knight's title, which means so much to Adrian's conceit, remains. I therefore presume it is him."

"So why such a mysterious message?" Having long been waiting for her mother and Avice to return from a shopping trip in the city, Emeline had spent the last half hour attempting to involve herself in some much despised needlework. Instead she had stared out of the window far more consistently than at her needle. Any discussion with her husband was a welcome distraction. She said, "For what possible reason would he give a false name? Especially if he wants to meet you anyway?"

"There are several possibilities," Nicholas said, the smile intact. "Either he considers me sufficiently stupid not to read the code and wants me to come galloping down, incautiously and unarmed, to meet my fate. Or he wishes to inform me that we need to speak, but without others present. All guesses, of course. Adrian is, perhaps, a little odd. I always accepted that I was. But he's worse."

"Perhaps he wants to say he's returning to his home in Berendon Place, and wants Sissy to accompany him. Baking - you know."

"Sissy's never baked anything in her life."

"But it's a female association perhaps - even though cooks are usually men - but at home, of course, in ordinary families - ovens and women - so he's implying he wants Sissy to go back to Nottingham with him."

"So why not say so?"

Emeline knotted her fingers. "So you think it's a trap?"

"This poor old dodderer who came to the stable block," Nicholas told her, "admitted he was paid a penny to bring the message. He was evidently given the information and the payment by a thickset fellow with a northern accent."

"Not Adrian then."

"But presumably one of his men. And there's more. I sent Rob immediately to the docks at Bilyns Gate where the message said to meet this Sir Berendon Baker. Rob saw Adrian entering a rent house backing the quay. Why there? Either he's still involved in treachery and is meeting some spy shipping incognito from France, wishes to catch a boat himself, or he's planning on employing the sort of cut purses who often hang around the docks these days, and he's ready for further family retribution. There are also more innocent possibilities. Perhaps he simply wants to contact his sister and the cheapest rental he could find happened to be at the dockside. I intend finding out which it is."

"Adventure again?" She put down her needlework. "I thought you hoped he'd run, and stay away."

"I did. I do. But if he's back I can't ignore it."

She paused, then said softly, "Can I come with you?"

He laughed. "If my wicked cousin simply wants to make sure his sister is thriving, then you'd be the ideal companion.

For anything else, you'd be in the way. I can't take the risk that you'd be at risk."

Emeline stood up in a hurry. "Adrian wouldn't hurt me."

"Even though he probably killed your father? Murdered my brother?"

"He might not even recognise me. I can wear old clothes, just like you. I well used to that, since my father thought that was how a modest young lady ought to dress." She paused, then said, "And what if I promise to stay out of the way? I'll only talk to Adrian if it's about Sissy. And if there's - fighting - danger - I'll run into the nearest church and stay hidden there."

"Sweet Jesus," Nicholas muttered. "I'd be mad to agree. My father would hurl me from the house if he ever found out I'd permitted my wife to join me on such business. Your sister would think me a lunatic and your mother would certainly want me thrown into Newgate. Even Jerrid would frown - and that's something he barely knows how to do. The king would probably send me off to Calais."

Emeline danced across and kissed his cheek. "So you mean I can come?"

"Well," Nicholas conceded, "I doubt Adrian plans on fighting or anything else too energetic after last time. And you could actually prove a calming influence. He'll hardly be inspired to act the hero, and will more likely want your help with Sissy." Nicholas grinned suddenly. "No doubt I should be shut up in Bedlam for it, but all right, you can come if you make those promises you mentioned. Any trouble, and you run straight into the nearest church. Perhaps you'd better pray for your husband's miserable life while you're in there."

"I promise." She twirled, skirts askew, arms out, smiling broadly. "Will I do like this? Shabby enough? Or must I poke holes in my stockings and drop pottage on my apron?"

"That hideous old gown of yours is ugly enough," he decided. "Remind me to have any remaining item of your old clothes burned once we get back to Chatwyn Castle and a peacefully elegant life without fires or murders." He took her hand. "But I want no cavalcade of attendants to alert whatever hole he's hiding in, so I'm taking only David and Alan with me. Enough to protect you, my love, should there be need of it. But you'll stay quiet and obey orders, and if anyone behaves foolishly and oversteps the boundaries of good sense, then it will be me alone as usual - not you, my sweet. Remember your promise."

"I've promised and I'll remember. I'm not the mad adventurer in this family," she laughed.

He looked her over with a slow smile. "I'm not so sure," he said.

A light sunshine turned the drizzle into a melted butter mist. The horses shook golden spangles from their manes. Over the small stench of the Fleet, fleet no longer, and through the busy Ludgate, four tired mounts and four slumped riders were heading east. No one observed such travellers of little note.

Where the roads were paved, the cobbles seemed glazed, their little wet stones sitting high between the trickling puddles, and the horses' hooves clattered with a damp thud and a spray of rain drops. Where the unpaved lanes lay deep in shade, the ground gradually turned to mud. Where they rode beneath the overhang of the houses' upper storeys, so the drip, drip of falling water seeped down the travellers' necks, then spilling over the waxed surface of their rain proofed capes into little rivulets dribbling from every stirrup. The houses leaned in, sharing their shadows, worn oak trusses now soaked, tired beams and cracked doorways leaking. But the day remained warm and the tall brick chimneys belched no smoke nor dancing cinders flying skywards.

The travellers passed the steeple of St. Magnus, the sunshine turning the church windows into haloed brilliance. Nicholas nodded and spoke quietly to his wife. "This will be the nearest church, should you need it. We're nearly at Bilyns Gate."

She whispered back, keeping her head down. "But surely Adrian won't be standing at the docks just waiting for us?"

"That," grinned Nicolas, "depends on whether this is simply an innocent desire to meet with me, or a complicated trap. He may not wait at all, since I sent no message in return to his invitation."

"Or there'll be some respectable gentleman tapping his foot impatiently - the real Sir Berendon Baker."

"In which case," Nicholas nodded, "I shall tip the wretch into the Thames for having dragged me out in the rain for no reason whatsoever."

It was the great blanketing shadow of the Tower beyond the loading bays that blocked out the sunshine and turned the river cold. Ships too tall to pass beneath the Bridge, stopped before it, and at Bilyns Gate three cargo ships, high masted carvels, were tight roped to the quay. The two wooden cranes cranked, unloading crates and bales. A swarm of traders pushed forwards, shouting, waving, each man concerned for his business and the cargo he had come to inspect. Their carts waited and the sumpters, heads patiently bowed, flicked their tails in the drizzle.

There was no immediate sign of Adrian, nor of his henchmen.

The noise hemmed in the dockside, one wall of busy warehouses behind, ropes thrown, streaming seawater, caught, and tied. Calls from deck to shore, calls from crane drivers to those carters waiting, calls from customs officials to ships' captains and from captains to wherrymen. The smells, sweet to some, were of brine and ocean weed caught on barnacles, cargos of fresh fish, dyed and treated hides and barrels of wine. The customs' wherry dodged the bow waves, heading out to those cogs waiting in line, a queue of three mid river, more ships hoping for space alongside the bay once their cargo had been cleared, their ballast dumped, their dues paid, and bribes carefully passed below deck.

Nicholas raised his voice over the bump and thud of one wooden hull to another and the complaints of those fearing damage to their gunwales. The crack of wet sail to mast, quickly lowered, the whine of sudden wind in the halyards and the thump of the boom. "The Cock Inn first," Nicholas called. "Steaming hippocras, and a dry place to wait without being too quickly seen."

The small alehouse was set back, a busy place for traders celebrating deals and for others waiting for ships overdue. Leaving their horses in the small stable barn at the back, Nicholas edged through and found a tiny table in an annexe, half private, seated his wife on the low bench and pulled up a stool for himself. The noise was larger than the space. Alan leaned back, elbow to the wall. David strolled off to order light ale, strong beer, and hippocras, if they had any, for the lady.

It was some time later when they realised that David had not returned. Emeline and Nicholas had been discussing their return to Chatwyn Castle. Not Adrian, not Henry Tudor, not the possible threat to national security, nor even the problem of what to do with Sysabel. It was dreams of an orderly future that seemed attractive now. "Whatever happens," Nicholas said, "and whatever my wretched cousin decides to do, I'll not stay much longer in Westminster. The king's in Coventry anyway, before heading up to Nottingham Castle."

Emeline was breathing in the sweat and stale beer from an alehouse overflowing around them. "Will we be able to move into the Keep again then, and will you have your own bedchamber back, Nicholas?"

"Not even fire can turn my childhood home to ruin." He shook his head, smiling again. "It's stood for five hundred years through war and pestilence and storm, protecting our family as well as it might. My forefathers and their forefathers have always lived there. Continuity, a sense of the land and the people, farming and hunting. Home. The castle will protect you too, and you'll be the mistress of it all."

She watched the animation sparkle in his eyes. "Yet so many of your memories there are - sad."

He shook his head. "I couldn't enter the nursery tower for years afterwards –. But it's not just memories. There's a sense of belonging. And it's more now. The inheritance for our sons."

"All ten of them?"

He hadn't heard her. "The castle gleams like polished brass under the summer sun. The battlements rise stark against a blue sky, the gatehouse walls drop sheer to the moat, golden stone reflected in the water, ripples as the swans dip, tails up, fishing. The calling of the frogs in the long evenings, the cries of the kestrels in the mornings. The banners fluttering like little wings in the breezes, the glass mullions echoing the dawn blinking dewy over the hills, the creak of those huge iron hinges as the outer doors open, welcoming me home."

"I didn't know," she whispered, "you loved it that much. It must hurt, then, to remember the fire and the ruin."

But at that moment, interrupting very quietly, Alan said, "My lord, 'tis some time, I reckon. Too long. Is Witton brewing the ale himself, then?"

Nicholas stood at once, his stool scraping back. "Watch the lady. Whatever happens, Alan, stay with her. If it's dangerous, take her to St. Magnus and then join me."

"Are you armed, my lord?" Nicholas wore no sword and no obvious weapon.

"Don't be a fool," Nicholas said, and strode out into the larger chamber. Within a breath, he had gone.

Emeline stared at Alan Venter. "I'm all right," she said quickly. "You should follow his lordship."

Alan shook his head. "Not yet, my lady. I'll obey orders as always."

Nicholas did not waste time searching the crowded alehouse. David would not have stood patiently waiting to catch the landlord's eye nor a waiter's attention. Outside the drizzle had turned to a fine veil of scattered silver for the sun had dulled, breaking through the clouds only in fragments. Those glimpses steamed the damp shoulders of his cape. Nicholas skirted the edges of the Bilyns Gate harbour where the warehouses towered and the alleys between lay in constant shadow. He crossed to the steps leading down to the water where the wherries bumped, unloading travellers, collecting those aiming for the Southwark side, and taking those both buying and selling upriver.

A thickset man was standing at the foot of the steps, looking across at a fishing cog rolling in from the estuary and the Narrow Sea beyond. Nicholas recognised the man's back, his hunched belligerence and his dark red cape over solid soled boots.

Nicholas stood above on the quayside, looking down. He called, "Not planning on buying fresh fish for your supper I'd warrant, Mister Prophet." The man turned in a hurry, scowling up. Nicholas nodded, smiling. "Awaiting the arrival of some messenger from France, I presume? Or perhaps even scouting out a vessel suitable to carry your master into Henry Tudor's welcoming embrace?"

"My lord?" The man shifted uncomfortably, half an eye up to the dockside, the other across to the fishing cog.

"And your master's friend, Sir Berendon," asked Nicholas, "where might I find him?"

Francis Prophet flushed beneath his hood. "Not for me to say, my lord. Nor have I heard of any such gentleman. I'm here - to meet someone, sir, and must ask you to excuse me. I'm on business which cannot wait."

"Codfish?" Nicholas smiled, staying where he was. "Sole? Or simply herrings, Mister Prophet? Or perhaps - just perhaps - a cargo of secret information?"

Hearing footsteps behind him, Nicholas expected the voice. "Can't leave well alone, even now, cousin?" Adrian demanded. "What brings you here, of all places?"

Nicholas turned slowly, "Why, you, my dear, who else? I received your message, after all. Was it not intended to bring me here?"

There were rain drops on the end of Adrian's feathers, his hat a little askew. "That message was for Sysabel, not for you, you fool," Adrian objected. "I hardly expected it to reach you, nor for you to understand it if it did. Do you always intercept my sister's messages?"

"Ah, sad inefficiency, cousin dear," Nicholas sighed. "You sent some ancient buffoon who passed your name, ineptly disguised, to '*his lordship*'. Indeed, it should have been my father who received your fascinating news, but since it was my own man who spoke to your jester, it was I alone who was then told. If your message was meant for your sister only, then it was poorly phrased and poorly executed. Next time send a messenger young enough to remember your words and direction. A sad waste of a penny, I imagine."

Adrian flushed deeper. "Does Sissy know of this?"

"She does not. And was not, in any manner, informed. She sits patiently in the house on the Strand, watched over by a parcel of female servants, hoping, I imagine, for you to climb through the window and rescue her. Your reputation for heroic rescues has, of course, improved over recent weeks." Nicholas continued to smile. "Along with your reputation for treason, of course, which has rather spoiled the final affect."

A young man had disembarked from the bobbing cog, and had climbed down into one of the small wherries. He was being brought to shore. Francis Prophet moved aside, ready for the passenger to disembark. Adrian said, "Well, Nicholas, since you're here, wanted or otherwise, then it's the ideal time for us to talk without anger or misunderstanding. I intend taking my sister back home, and no doubt you'll be pleased to pass her back into my care."

"Your attempts to distract me from the new arrival are a little too obvious, Adrian," Nicholas smiled. "If you wish to escort Sissy back to Nottingham, then I suggest you come to the house to collect her, as would be both normal and proper. I've not abducted the girl and naturally she's free to go. In the meantime, I'm perfectly well aware that you're about to greet someone you clearly don't want me to identify." He shook his head. "And before even that, I wish to know exactly where my squire is. David Witton. You know him. Where is he?"

The clouds had darkened, squeezing out the last flickers of pallid sunshine, and the rain was beginning to strengthen again, a soft rippled patter across the river waters. The newcomer paid the wherryman, and climbed the steps to the docks, followed by Mister Prophet. The four men stood looking at each other as the rain cloaked them.

"David Witton," Nicholas repeated. "Where exactly is he now?"

Adrian's pale blue eyes narrowed. "You think I've trussed the young idiot and carried him off to some dungeon? Don't be a fool, Nicholas."

"I would not once have believed it," Nicholas said, "but nor would I have believed you capable of treason. Now I tend to think you capable of anything, except, perhaps, intelligence. I'm guessing your brawler was sent to the Strand stables to inform Sissy of your imminent need to see her, and take her away. But your same brawler, one Francis Prophet I imagine, changed the message quite purposefully. He has no interest in your reunion with your sister. He was far more interested in getting me here to instigate some sort of quick annihilation. So before I throw your man bodily into the Thames, I suggest you find out what has happened to my squire. Otherwise, your new visitor may find he follows your henchman into the turgid waters, and enjoys a hearty mouthful of London's excrement for his dinner."

CHAPTER FIFTY THREE

The newcomer bowed, smiled very faintly, and kept his mouth shut. Francis Prophet averted his eyes. Adrian appeared belligerent but genuinely confused.

Nicholas read the signs. "Very well," he said. "I'll find my squire myself." He turned, but looked back. "As it happens, I'd guess your men don't work directly for you at all, Adrian, and are loyal either to the French or their puppet Tudor. I advise you to watch your back, cousin. You may think yourself the leader but you are not in charge here."

Strolling off across the cobbles, Nicholas waited neither for reply nor for questions. He knew exactly where to go, for Rob had already described the cheap rental where Adrian was boarding. Nicholas, seeing he had not been followed, quickly adjusted the hiding place of both knives within his belt and the sword strapped within the lining of his stiff waxed and weather proof cape. Then he pushed open the main door and ran up the short flight of narrow unlit stairs. The door to Adrian's rooms was locked. Nicholas waited a moment, listening. He then inserted the point of his shorter knife into the keyhole, and twisted. A hovel, cheap wattle and daub and a door of thin planks; the lock was equally lightweight. It clicked open on the second attempt and Nicholas entered silently into the musty shadows within.

There was one room divided by a low screen and the tiny window was nailed shut with scratched parchment, barely passing light. But Nicholas's eyes adjusted quickly. He stared back at the five men watching his appearance, four in surprise. David Witton himself did not seem surprised at all.

One man held David, still tying the ropes. The three others rushed Nicholas. Sword in one hand, the longer knife in his other, he retaliated before they reached him. David yelled, "My lord. Where's Prophet? And Sir Adrian?"

Nicholas did not answer. He was busy.

Her ladyship Baroness Wrotham and her daughter Avice were walking a little faster as they approached the Tower. It was raining much harder than they had expected, and Avice was regretting having suggested walking so far. Dragging a little behind, Nurse Martha and the maid Petronella were clutching their cloaks around their shoulders, one hand clamped on their heads to keep their hoods from blowing off. A little ahead, though already at a weary slouch, old Bill tramped faithfully on towards the huge shadows of the stone walls, the distant despondent roar of some monstrous foreign creature known as a lion, and the busy march of the Tower guards. The baroness, though sidestepping the crowds, gazed up at the thickening clouds and sighed. "I should have guessed," she said faintly, "that your idea this morning was on a level with most of your others, Avice."

Avice glowered. "You said you thought it was a good idea at the time."

"Maternal prejudice. I imagine. The blindness of fond hope."

"Mother, really. You've no notion of what maternal prejudice means. As for fond hope – it's just as unlikely. You simply wanted to see what the Tower looks like."

Her ladyship straightened her back. "Don't be petulant, Avice, or I shall leave you here to be thrown into the dungeons or eaten by lions. And I hear there's an interesting contraption known as the Duke of Exeter's daughter."

"Then I hope the duke is nicer to his daughter than you are, Maman." Avice stopped abruptly, looking across at the rising river waters to their right. "Well, I've seen the walls. Perhaps we could just go home now. I'm starving."

Bill was leaning against the long side of the adjacent warehouse, sheltering from drips. Hopefully, "Reckon tis well past dinner time, m'lady."

Martha caught them up. "The docks are just one minute's walk away, my lady, and the eel boats sell cheap at this hour. Then I could buy us some for supper if you'd care to see the bustle. Far more interesting, I imagine, than those cold turrets."

The baroness looked down her nose in affronted astonishment. "I can hardly imagine the sheer joy of being caught in the push and shove of a busy harbour, Martha, nor the even greater delights of carrying a basket of smelly fish all the way home across the city. But I fear I must decline."

"I want to go," decided Avice. "And Petronella can carry the basket."

"The great Tower," sighed the baroness, "is one of Christendom's most beautiful palaces. The White Keep, the silver moat, the vast council chambers and the royal apartments where every king for five hundred years has stayed to await his holy anointing." She stared up at the walls again, and lowering clouds above. "A place of gaiety and pleasure, but also of responsibility and wise political governance." She shook her head. "And instead it seems I have come to gaze at a pit of eels drowning in their own slime."

Although one of the three men now striding the riverside up Lower Thames Street was the younger brother to an earl, it was not at all obvious to any passer by. All three men, two of them short and thickset, the other tall and slim built but wide shouldered, were dressed as market traders and their short capes barely kept the rain from their legs nor their heads.

"Dammed weather," complained Jerrid Chatwyn. "What wretched dockside did you say the boy was heading for?"

"Bilyns Gate," muttered Rob Bambrigg, "what's no more'n a sniff and a blink away now, m'lord, as I reckon you already knows right well."

"I've been sniffing and blinking for the past hour," objected Jerrid, "and I'm tired of tramping through rain and mud. If the wretched boy needs his useless lifesaving, then let's hurry up and do it before supper."

"We ain't had dinner yet," Harry pointed out from beside and slightly below. "But there's a good few decent taverns round here does a tasty pottage and a good pot o' beer."

"Well, you should know," nodded Jerrid. "You both lived somewhere near here once, didn't you?"

"Tenement to the left," Rob said. "Docks to the right. Both smell the same."

In the small annexe within the Cock Inn at Bilyns Gate dockside, Emeline shook her head and stood in a hurry. "It's been long enough, Mister Venter. And since you can't leave these premises to go to his lordship's aid while you're supposed to be watching over me, then I shall have to come too."

Alan looked alarmed. The stool toppled back as he stood. "My lady, if I might escort you first to the little church we passed –"

"Certainly not," said Emeline. "I intend looking for my husband."

The rain now slanted, steel ice. Emeline stared through the veils, peering for some sign of Nicholas. Instead she saw Adrian. He was talking to another man, sheltering at the corner of the main storage shed and barely visible through sleet and bustle. Emeline set off towards him. Alan followed close, his huff of disapproval lost amongst the restless noise.

Adrian turned, swore, and, stepping forwards, managed to smile. Emeline said, "Where is he?"

"A delightful surprise," Adrian said with a slight bow, "I did not expect to see you here, my lady. The weather is not – but no doubt coming from Gloucestershire, you are accustomed. May I assist you with something, my lady, or perhaps you have a message from my sister?"

"I've a message for you, sir, but not from Sissy," Emeline informed him. "I came with Nicholas some hours ago, because *he* received a message from *you*. Or thought he did. What's all this silly nonsense of false names, anyway?"

Adrian frowned. "That message was never intended for my cousin," he said with an impatient nod towards his companion. "And I'm now much occupied, madam. I apologise if I seem unhelpful, but Nicholas left some time back and I have no idea where he went."

From slightly behind, Alan Venter cleared his throat. "I've a notion where, my lady, if you'll come away now." And Emeline scowled at Adrian, wished him a cold damp afternoon, and hurried away. "I know the rental where his lordship would be searching," Alan said, under this breath. "And I'll be off there now to see what's amiss. But you can't come, my lady. Not in no conditions, nor will I permit it."

Emeline thought a moment. "Go on then," she relented. "He's been away too long and must need help. But I shall wait at that other corner where there's some shelter, and they're selling eels from those big baskets. There's a lot of other women there and I shan't seem conspicuous, but I can see if you come back with his lordship and David."

Resigned and in too much of a hurry to argue, Alan ran to the building where Rob had already informed them Adrian was lodging. Emeline put her hood up and her head down and hurried to the baskets of live eels and the fishwives jangling their purses and objecting to whatever price was mentioned.

"And what," suddenly said a disastrously clear voice behind her, "are you doing here, my girl? When I'm fully aware I left you at the Strand not three hours gone?"

"Oh, Lord have mercy," stuttered Emeline. "Maman! I don't know whether to be pleased or horrified."

"You might as well be pleased," said Avice, grabbing at her sister's sleeve. "Since we're here anyway. And Martha. And Bill. And Nell. So what are you up to and where's Nicholas?"

"That's exactly what I want to know," said Jerrid Chatwyn, his voice booming from a few paces away as he strode across the open harbour towards them.

Rob pushed unceremoniously in front. "Has his lordship gone to the rental where I seen Sir Adrian?" he demanded.

Emeline nodded, turned, and pointed. "That's what Alan thinks. And he's just gone there too."

"Third floor," added Rob. "Can't be missed."

"Right then," said Jerrid. "No time to waste."

Avice and the baroness stared in amazed alarm. "No time to explain," Emeline said. "Come on."

They followed, Martha close behind and Petronella with Bill at a distance, as Jerrid pushed open the half broken door to the leaning four storey building, its frontage almost touching that of the little house opposite across the lane. "This hovel?" demanded her ladyship. "I am expected to enter *here*?"

"No, not 'xpected," said Harry, turning at the foot of the stairs. "Best not, in fact."

"Buy eels instead," suggested Rob.

"*I'm* coming in," insisted Emeline, picking up her skirts and running up the stairs.

There was a clatter and a squeak. A small boy hurtled down the steps from the echoing darkness. Avice grabbed the skinny bare wrist. The boy squealed. "Twenty -thirty - and fighting," and he pointed upwards. Avice let the child go and he ran. She took a step forwards but the baroness pulled her back.

"But Maman, Emma's up there."

"You are far too young and feeble," her mother informed her. "I shall sort it out myself. Are you coming, Martha?" She began a sedate climb.

Several things had happened at the same instant. Jerrid, Harry and Rob reached Sir Adrian Frye's rented chambers on the black shadowed third floor and found the door wide open. Before they were able to enter, one man rushed out. Limping badly and bleeding from a slashed leg and torn ear, he tumbled down the stairs, pushing aside those on their way up. It was lightless, with a smutty leakage of dark smoke from above where the city's effluent of coal fires and urine filled gutters leaked down the chimney and through the broken windows, and the stench of river, brine and fish from below.

The noises were of scraping feet, heavy breathing, the thump and creek of floorboards and the clash of steel. In one corner of the small squashed rented chamber, David Witton, pleading for release at the top of his voice, was bundled in an uncomfortable tangle of fish scale crusted ropes. Two bodies lay slumped on the floor, one dead, one half alive, his groans fading as he gurgled blood. Nicholas, feet dancing across the sprawling body, was fighting two other men. But his breathing was strained, his forehead was streaming blood and his knuckles on one hand were slashed to the bone.

He raised his sword again, parrying the steel thrust against him, but his knife now hung limp, his wounded left hand trembling. One assailant again raged forwards with a sudden shout and surge, the knife aiming for Nicholas, his face and his eyes.

Then the voice behind said softly, "Safe to back off now, boy. Step back quick. We're here now." Rob and Harry moved in, clutching at Nicholas, helping him back against the wall as Jerrid's sword slashed down, straight through one heaving shoulder, killing the other man instantly. Jerrid faced the last man as Rob freed David, quickly slicing through the ropes. Harry said, "And Alan, my lord? He were afore us."

Nicholas's voice was hoarse. "Up – there," he murmured. "Upper stairs. Go – help." He wiped the blood streaming into his eyes from the long wound across his forehead and slumped down, leaning against the wall and releasing his grip on both sword and knife.

Jerrid looked back over his shoulder. "Rob, get upstairs and find Alan. David, stay with our boy. Harry - here."

Jerrid and Harry killed the last man between them. David knelt over Nicholas. "He's fainting. Deep wound to the head. Lost a finger and might lose another. Exhaustion of course. But nothing to threaten his life."

Jerrod moved beside him. "Why the devil did he come so scarce accompanied and ill equipped?"

David looked up and shook his head. "Myself and Alan - it should have been enough, my lord. The message was a joke - his lordship barely took it seriously."

"He don't take nor life nor nuffing serious," frowned Harry.

Which is when Emeline appeared breathless in the doorway and said in a rush, "Where is he?"

"Here, my dear." Jerrid nodded down to where Nicholas sat, half conscious. But as Emeline hurried to kneel beside her husband, through the shadows behind with a thump and huge reverberation, a heavy set man tripped, hurtling down the stairs, and reaching out with both hands. Emeline turned in a swirl of muddy hems and faced the newcomer. He growled and pushed her aside with a wild kick at Nicholas. Emeline picked up the stool which had rolled on its side at her feet, swung it with all her force, and hit the newcomer over the head. He crumpled with a guttural sigh.

Jerrid clapped his hands. "Excellent, my dear lady. Well done."

"He wanted to kick my husband," agreed Emeline, once more on her knees beside Nicholas.

Alan Venter was behind, racing down the stairs, saw the newly prone adversary beginning to stumble back to his feet, and grabbed him around the neck. "Bastard Francis bastard Prophet," he muttered, which appeared to be an effort at explanation. He looked up at Jerrid. "Him and another. His lordship killed the one but Prophet is a harder bastard to trounce. Do I kill the bugger, my lord? Or hand him over to the constable?"

"Since the constable don't appear to be around," decided Jerrid. "Best kill the bugger."

Alan did.

Mister Prophet stared upwards at the sword which swept towards him, and opened his mouth to yell. He was dead before the sound emerged, his neck sliced in two. The mess leaked, splintered bone and the ravaged bloody brain lying exposed. Nicholas was half back on his feet and trying to focus. With her kerchief covered in his blood, Emeline had been cleaning his face when the baroness as Martha heaved into the doorway, staring in dismay at the bodies strewn around them.

"Good gracious," exclaimed the baroness with several steps backwards. "I feel a little superfluous." She stared a moment at the carnage, heaved, put her kerchief to her mouth and turned away.

"Water," said Martha, already rolling up her sleeves. "There must be a bowl here somewhere. A water butt? Cloths, bandages, a sheet to rip into strips? How many are wounded?"

"Nicholas," said Emeline at once, trying to stop him from staggering to his feet. "And perhaps David, though just rope burns. And maybe that horrid man lying choking over there."

The tiny dark space shed its shadows, figures quickly moving into coherent and visible symmetry. Somebody found a bowl, then a water hug. Martha knelt, adjusting her skirts.

"My lady," Jerrid addressed the baroness. "This fight is over, and well won. A single adversary lives - there," he indicated the groaning man, "but it seems Nicholas was alone at first, facing four, perhaps five men by himself. He's wounded. We need to get him out of here." But Lady Wrotham faced the doorway, and would not look back.

"Adrian?" Nicholas muttered, heaving himself upwards.

"Outside with some foreigner," Emeline said. "Does he know nothing of this?" She shrugged, both her hands to her husband. "Now stay still, my love. You're badly hurt."

"Not so bad." Nicholas blinked through blood and the insistent tying of ragged bandages. "Sore head. Sore hand. Nothing more. But if one of them is left alive, keep him alive. I need someone to question. There's more to this than I knew before. I need to know the rest."

David stood, brushing fish scales from his clothes, speaking to Jerrid. "We'd gathered in the alehouse, awaiting Sir Adrian. I saw Prophet in the main drinking room, just slipping out the door, and I followed him. Four of them jumped me, dragged me up here and trussed me like a capon for the pot. It was a trap, set and sprung. They were waiting for his lordship to come after me. He did, but by then I was unable to help him. Lord Nicholas fought against four of them, wounded one, chased one off, but was already badly injured."

Nicholas insisted faintly, "Not bad. Not so good. But not bad."

Alan was still catching his breath. "By the time I arrived, damned Francis Prophet and some other dirty bugger turned up too. I chased Prophet upstairs, trying to make sure his lordship didn't have yet another slavering bastard against him."

"Prophet - most dangerous," Nicholas said, again trying to rise.

"But now dead," Jerrid told his nephew. "Alan's work, with a little help from your wife."

Emeline smiled and clutched at her husband's unwounded hand. "I didn't do much. I wish I could have done more."

Nicholas, sight still blood blurred, stared up around him. "Now the place seems to be filled with females," he said vaguely.

"Please stay quite still, my lord," said Martha with magisterial command, "while I shall tend to these nasty cuts. I have no ointments with me, but a torn sheet makes fine bandages. We don't want to be left with any more scars, now do we!"

CHAPTER FIFTY FOUR

"The Tower," Jerrid said. "I want the best. The boy's sick. It's too far back to the Strand; an hour even on horseback. But no dirt lane barber will do, nor some grub streaked doctor more interested in hurrying off to his supper. The Tower is the best organised palace in the country, and there's a doctor and his assistant there worthy of ministering to councils and kings."

"But my lord, in these old clothes? They will think us beggars," David frowned. "The Tower is the busiest as well as most efficient - but also the best guarded."

"They know the Chatwyn name." Jerrid shook his head, leaning down to help Nicholas stand, yet half falling in his arms. "Brackenbury knows Nicholas and Symond both. After all, my brother was once on the council, and young Nick has a reputation with those who know. You'd best ride ahead, Witton. Tell them we're coming and why. I'll get the boy mounted and follow you."

Nicholas remained on the stool, his head back against the wall. He now wore a crown of bandages. His left hand was tied within a thick cloth mitten, yet the blood seeped through. Emeline stood next to him, her hand on his shoulder. The baroness had retreated to the doorway. "I shall go down and reassure my daughter," she said. "But since we're on foot, we shall follow at a distance."

"Oh, Maman. I'd give you my horse, but I must stay with Nicholas," Emeline said. "Perhaps you and Avice and Martha should go back home and warn the servants to prepare for him. Warm the bedchamber, have water and bandages ready, make a light supper. Gruel - and -"

"Apple codlings," murmured Nicholas.

"Yes, my dear, the household should be warned indeed. Petronella and Bill must return immediately to prepare the Strand House for his lordship. But," declared the baroness, "I intend accompanying poor Nicholas and my daughter to The Tower."

Alan bowed. "My lady, I ride a beast far below your station, but she's yours, if you'll have her. I can walk. It's no more than a spit to the Tower gates."

Nicholas groaned. "I need no chaperones. Get someone to guard that bastard in the corner, then someone else call the constable. He's important and I want him alive."

"Adrian," said Emeline with an undisguised smile, "will come back home here to a rather unexpected surprise." She counted. "Four bodies. And rather a mess. Dear, dear."

But Nicholas needed help down the stairs and it was a long time before he reached the horses waiting below. Harry had remained upstairs on his orders and Rob had gone for the constable and the doctor. David had ridden ahead to warn the authorities at the Tower, and on the baroness's instructions, Petronella and old Bill had set off for the Strand House to alert the household.

Alan, Jerrid, the baroness, Martha and Emeline, now accompanied by her animated sister, approached the three remaining horses. The baroness mounted Alan's docile mare, taking Avice up before her. Martha shook her head and stood solid, ready to walk. Nicholas was hoisted into the saddle of his own horse. Jerrid then helped Emeline mount. "No, no, I shall walk," he told them, "and lead the boy's horse." He took the reins, smiling up. "Not used to being treated as a feeble invalid, are you, my boy? But it's excellent practise, I imagine, if you intend keeping up this life of adventure. Just don't fall out of the saddle or I shall have to tie you on."

Nicholas grinned. "Not quite that infirm, uncle. But I seem to be missing a finger or two. I shall miss them."

"You've got eight others," his uncle nodded. "Dare say they'll suffice. Now," he looked around, "is young Adrian in sight?"

He was not. There was no sign either of Adrian, nor of his newly arrived companion. It had stopped raining. The eels had sold, carters were driving out of the dockside, wheels squeaking on wet cobbles, cargo bulging. Another carvel had come in to dock, its gunwales straining against the wooden quayside. Nicholas and his party turned their backs and rode slowly away from the warehouses, heading north east into the vast and brooding shadows of the Tower.

They crossed the moat at the Byward Tower, entering the inner ward. Patrolling guards, alerted to their arrival, escorted the party beyond the curtain wall to the physician's chambers where David was already waiting. The captain of the guard bowed, the doctor hurried to aid his patient, the horses were led away, Jerrid supported Nicholas across to the long sheeted mattress within the chamber of surgery, turned once with instructions to Alan, said briefly, "My lady, I shall inform you as soon as the physician informs me. But then I must see Brackenbury," and the doors were quickly closed.

Emeline stepped forward, but the baroness took her hand. "Not yet, my dear. Let the men relate their stories and complain of their injuries. I'm sure dear Nicholas is in very good hands."

"Well, Jerrid brought him here because the resident doctor is the best. And I believe Brackenbury is Constable of the Tower, and one of the king's most trusted. He and Nicholas are already friends."

"So Nicholas could hardly be better served. Meanwhile we shall wait, and wander the grounds."

Avice had thrown back the hood of her cape, adjusted her little headdress, and was peering around. "It has been an *amazing* day," she confided, shaking rain drops from her shoulders. "Maman has ordered me a new gown and it may even be ready by Thursday. It is a *real* lady's gown, Emma, and *just* as nice as some of yours. You'll see, because I shall wear it *all* the time. Then we had dinner at a very grand inn, with braised beef and proper Burgundy. After that it was even more exciting and everything happening with swords and running up and down stairs and Nicholas wounded. I'm rather glad I didn't see anyone's head cut in half, but it's nice to know that the bad people got killed. Such an unexpected thing to happen just when I was getting tired of walking. And now this. I do hope we can see the lions."

"You mean it's a lucky chance that my husband is wounded close to death?"

The open grounds, banked in grass beyond the cobbled bailey, seemed a maze of walkways and narrow crossings between the huge stone towers, great wooden doorways and guarded paths. The first week of June and the days were long but the rain had coated everything in a drip, drip of shadow. Small braziers had been lit, the flare of torches hung from doorways, flickering through the alleyways past towering stone. It was just as busy and almost as noisy as the dockside. There was a constant scurry of servants with a flap of maids holding on their headdresses as the wind swept up from the river, scullions rushing on duty in their new clean aprons, delivery men pushing a bumping rattle of laden barrows and marketeers' carts, a trudge of suppliers carrying great leaking baskets of fish, a troop of lawyers, their capes catching the breeze, and the endless tramp of the guards.

Martha now kept to Emeline's side. "I like a place," she said, crossing her arms and looking around, "that keeps order. Order means routine and routine means safe keeping."

"Order? That's true enough," nodded Alan. "There's authorities over authorities and everyone in their proper place with those that work for the lords, and those that work for the lesser folk, and those that work for those that work - and once you set your boots past the moat, then you're answerable to a hundred more and remembered by two hundred others. Even them ten gardeners has another ten working just on clipping them hedges and sweeping them paths. Day and night, it is, and night is more watched than by day."

Avice was hopping from one small foot to the other. "And the menagerie?"

"Across by the Lion Tower, mistress," Alan told Avice, "which is where the mint operates and is best not to go, being as there's gold and silver stored for the coinage pressing and a dozen guards to guard it."

"I'm not in the least interested in lions, and I shall wait here until my husband reappears or I am invited in," said Emeline sternly.

Seagulls, in from the estuary, were flocking along the stone parapets where the walls overlooked the Thames. High tide was seething up the river banks, surging towards the pillars of the Bridge. "Perhaps," suggested the baroness, raising her voice over the avian complaint, "we should await Nicholas in the church, my dear. A very pretty building they say."

Emeline sighed. "I suppose prayer is the right thing for such an occasion – but if Nicholas reappears and I am not here waiting –"

It was David who appeared first. "His lordship," he announced, "is feeling somewhat improved, my lady. And the physician suggests, should you wish to –"

"I most certainly do," said Emeline, and marched to the door. She turned once. "Take Avice and visit the lions and swans on the moat and the royal apartments and anything else you wish, Maman. I shall find you later."

The baroness sniffed. "I shall take your sister home," she informed her. "It has been a long day, the afternoon is fading, and we have walked enough. Since I now have use of four strong hooves, I intend beginning a leisurely stroll back to the Strand, which is where you will find me later, on, Emeline, should you deign to look." She nodded to Martha, and took her younger daughter's arm "I am looking forward to a hot supper."

Nicholas was seated on the bed, deep in conversation with the physician. He appeared to be blooming with health. He looked up as Emeline entered, and grinned. "We've been talking about the uses of blood and its circulation," he informed her. "Seems I've lost so much blood it will relax the heart, slow the circulation thus aiding breathing, and certainly do me good. Personally I just think it makes me wobbly kneed, but the doctor assures me I'm wrong. I shall now recover wonderfully and grow new fingers."

"Not quite, my lord."

Jerrid also lounged on the mattressed platform, looking perfectly comfortable. "But our boy will live, probably to a disreputable old age. Come in, my dear, and tell him to behave in a sedate manner while the rest of us go looking for the wretched Adrian."

Nicholas shook his now neatly bandaged head. "Leave Adrian. He's lost most of his men. I want that last one left alive, and I want him questioned by the ward sheriff. Hopefully Rob has that under control. Adrian can go hide his tail in France or sail off to the Spice Islands for all I care. I wish him joy of it."

Sitting now beside him, Emeline clutched his left hand. "But my love, you must be feeling horribly ill. You must come home and rest. I shall arrange for a litter."

"Litter be damned," Nicholas said with sudden asperity. "Must we pass our time nursing each other in turn?" He laughed, looking up at the doctor. "Make your announcement, sir. Am I fit to ride?"

The doctor was wiping his hands on a blood stained towel. "The gash in your forehead is now stitched, and the stumps of the fingers cauterized, my lord. You have two broken ribs but those will heal if you refrain from undue exercise, and the blow to your head which had caused some stunning of the wits, will clear as you rest. The skull appears undamaged and a headache may be the worst you'll suffer for it, sir, though you must keep both wounds well bandaged, use the salve I have given you, and do not use your left hand for at least two weeks." He nodded, untying his apron and folding it neatly. "And I advise you to contact your own medick tomorrow, my lord," he continued, "since there is always the risk of infection. But I believe a brisk ride home is quite acceptable."

The late sunshine was an earnest endeavour through the sullen clouds. Nicholas, his wife, his squire and his Uncle Jerrid stood on the steps leading down from the Beauchamp Tower. The rising tide of the river behind them was a steady slurp against the water gate. David brought the horses and assisted his master and mistress into the saddle. Nicholas straightened his back and shoulders, took up the reins and squinted into the low slanting sunbeams. "Home, then," he said, his voice stronger. "I'll wait for no one. The sheriff can come to me. But is Brackenbury in his chambers?"

"I'll report to Sir Robert Brackenbury." David nodded. "If I may offer you use of my horse, sir," he bowed briefly to Jerrid, "for your ride back to the Strand. Alan can walk ahead and I'll follow on foot."

Jerrid took the reins and swung his leg over the mare's back. "Sir Robert's a busy man. If he's not here, simply inform his lieutenant."

They left the Tower, its sunny greens and looming stone, three riders and Alan Venter leading the way. The streets were no longer busy, with shops packing up as day faded. The sun now slid behind them into corals, fast deepening to a crimson sunset.

At first they heard nothing, but they had barely passed from the observance of the Tower's patrols, when they were attacked. Six men had been waiting. A yell, a rush of feet and they appeared, racing suddenly from Water Lane to the left.

Jerrid's horse reared, startled. Nicholas whirled, his horse snorting in sudden panic as he drew his sword from within his cape. Alan drew his knife, lunging towards the assailants' leader. Nicholas lashed down, the sword found its mark but unable to hold the reins with his wounded left hand, his horse wheeled. Emeline reached out from her own mount, taking the frightened mare's reins as it circled as if to bolt. Nicholas yelled, "We're outnumbered. Emma, get under cover."

Jerrid was kicking off two men who were pulling him from the horse's back, dragging him to the ground. One boot found another man's groin, his sword to the same man's chest. "Bastards," he yelled. "Is there no one around to help? Set up a hue and cry. Call the Tower guards."

"We're too far beyond the walls -" Nicholas swayed, grabbing at both pommel and sword hilt. The man below him retreated, his shoulder slashed. Nicholas turned back to Emeline. "Get back, for I can't protect you. Ride back for David."

She had lost her headdress. Whirling, swirling, surrounded by shouting men and the thrust of blades, her cloak was cut and her hair escaped its pins, half blinding her. She leaned suddenly across, found the hilt of Nicholas's short knife within his belt, and pulled it out. With a kick of her heels she spurred her horse into the fray and stabbed downwards. A wild aim, it found one man's cheek and sliced through, grinding into his jaw. In fury, he jabbed back but Emeline's horse reared backwards as she clung on. She kept hold of the knife, dripping blood to her skirts. "For pity's sake," Nicholas yelled at her, "Emma, get out of here. Ride back for David."

Jerrid was on the ground and on his back, three men on top of him, while Alan grappled with another. Nicholas rode straight into the mob. The horse, forced forwards, trampled arms, legs and backs. Jerrid crawled free.

A man and his wife, passing by, ran for cover but two others raced forwards, shouting. Windows opened, someone screamed, a child peered from his upstairs chamber, cheering on both sides as his father ordered him to race for the ward's constable. A goat, its tether pulled loose, ran from an alley and butted the ruffian Nicholas had already wounded. Someone raced after the goat, and three more louts appeared from Water Lane, each armed. All three ran straight at Nicholas. Emeline was crying, hair in her eyes. She had lost hold of both reins, fumbling her grip as the horses swerved, avoiding feet and steel. Jerrid scrambled to his feet and kicked out, but his leg was caught by two grasping huge and filthy hands, and he was dragged back beneath a scrimmage. His horse, left riderless, bolted.

Thunder split the sunset's scarlets. The lightening dazzled for one blink, then night fell like an unchained portcullis. There were shapes moving through the murk, searching to discover which side - which part - who to support - while more appeared from laneways and doorways and their shadows merged - shouting and flailing - impossible to know who to help as citizens emerged from their houses wielding saucepans, jugs of water and kitchen knives. But with no one dressed as a lord, and none wearing the label villain, every man attacked every other. Yet some swore in French, and were well armed.

Emeline screamed, "Where are you?"

And, his voice disappearing beneath the hoard, Nicholas yelled back, "Get the bloody constable."

Now it was raining. Slashing through the confusion, suddenly illuminated by the white blade of lightening; the storm was directly above them. Someone she couldn't see gripped Emeline's arm. "My lady. Come with me."

She pulled away. "No. I won't leave him." She still had the knife, and waved it.

"It's me, my lady. David. I've sent some child and his father for the constable. I've set the alarm rolling from the Byward Tower to the conduit. But I can't help his lordship until you're out safe. He won't let me."

"I'm safe." Emeline shook her head, loose curls now streaming rain.

"You will be, my lady," David said, and grabbed the reins of her horse.

CHAPTER FIFTY FIVE

Rain pounded, blurring the way ahead, closing the night with ice. With David's firm hand to her horse's bridle, she rode up Hart Street, passing the old Crouched Friars' Priory, and into the narrow alleys beyond4. He was running, the horse's hooves fast and heavy in the puddles as Emeline held to pommel and mane. Both out of breath, both soaked, in minutes they passed Seethinge Lane and turned quickly right. Little more than a rutted track, but now a row of three tenements blocked the alleyway, all lightless as the shadows seemed darker than black and the high walls seemed to shiver with water. No braziers or lit torches hung from the doorways. No candlelight flickered within the windows.

"Here, hurry, my lady."

Emeline was frightened, and nearly as angry. "Where on earth have you brought me? And why? I insist on staying –"

"My lady." He was apologetic. "It was his lordship's orders. And the faster you settle here, the quicker I can return to help him. The attack was planned, and they outnumber us. Traitors, French backed. The constable has been called, though he may not be at home. I've alerted others. But Lord Nicholas thought only of you –"

Emeline slumped, catching her breath. She did not realise at first that she was crying. "Settle me, if settling me is so important, hiding me away where I can do nothing to help, but only sit alone in misery." She stared at the looming many storeyed building and its rough buttressed and ramshackle walls. "Where is this? It looks like a gaol."

She dismounted and David tied the wet and tired horse to the long hooked rail at the tenement's rear. He unlocked the outer door. Inside it was just as wet. No central ceiling closed in the stairs. Metal rungs, soaked wood, the clang and clank as they hurried up and the rain poured down. Only one upward climb to each storey, but the steps were narrow and steep. David, still running, supported the lady's elbow as she pattered, clutching at her sodden skirts, trying to keep up. "It's my old family home, my lady, once belonging to my father and now to me. I meant to sell after my parents were gone, but it's worth nothing in coin yet has had its uses over the years. Whenever his lordship, with Alan and I, came to London incognito or intending to keep out of sight, we came here. The place has been used - oh, many times. But it's not comfortable, my lady. Serviceable for an hour or two, no more."

The rain poured past the interminable stairs and there remained no solid balustrade to cling to. There was noise, half drowned by pelting rain, but constant as breath; a low buzzing hive of complaint and argument, creaking timbers as pliable as a ship's hull in the ocean, the persistent shuffle and rattle within a black background. At every stop where a corridor led off from the steps to the dwellings, there were curtains and old rags hanging from wooden rails, or leather flaps nailed over openings. Few doors, only doorways.

Emeline stared. "You were born here?"

"Yes, my lady. Here." He led her along a passage past other shaded entrances. Then there was a door, low framed but almost solid, with a water butt outside. David unlocked it and stooped to enter. "Mind your head, my lady. Now - there are candles on the shelf, and stools below it. I can build a small fire."

She flopped down on the stool he brought, tired from stairs and more tired from fear and desperation. "I can find the candles and light the fire myself. Take the horse. Get back to Nicholas. Tell him I'm safe, and go and save his life."

"I'll not argue with that, my lady." His face was white and worn. "It's his lordship means more to me than anything - his life more important than my life -" David turned and ran. The door swung and slammed behind him. The walls shook.

Emeline sat alone for what seemed a long time. A mournful hopelessness leaked through the gloom. Gradually she could see, though there was little enough for notice. The tiny chamber was dusty but the streaming cobwebs hung almost invisible within the relentless shadows. Eventually she found a small scattered pile of faggots and a tinderbox beside the little hearth. She lit a fire. The flames leapt, showing her nothing but it warmed her fingers and the soaked toes of her shoes. Beyond the thin walls the continuous noises reverberated. The murmur of belch, complaint and objection, the stirring of a wooden spoon in a metal pot, deep snoring, coughing and then someone was hitting someone else, and the someone else shouted and cursed. Many were words Emeline had never heard before. Then suddenly she sat up and stopped crying.

A galloping race of thoughts had interrupted the misery. Approaching the trembling planks of the wall that separated the Witton chamber from the one next door, Emeline tapped politely. There was no response. She banged louder.

"Oo's that?" demanded a woman's voice, as the other sounds quietened.

"My name," said Emeline, "is Emma, and I'm a - friend - of the Wittons. I wonder if I could - speak to someone - in fact to everyone - about something terribly, terribly important?" She told them everything at once, and she listened to a great deal in return. But there was little time for explanations. "My friends are outnumbered," she said, a little desperate. "Brave, but already wounded. Help is needed at once - or it will all be lost."

"There'll be naught lost with me at your back, lady."

"'Tis time to help our friends."

"Bugger the friends. Let's go have some fun."

It was still raining, even harder now, as they crept from the tenement, hurrying down the stairs and out into the storm. There was little wind but the sleet was persistent, closing the night into moonlessness.

Emeline led the group of David Witton's tenement neighbours from Seethinge Lane back down towards Harp and Water Lanes. Cautious, keeping low and careful not to arouse the Watch or other passers by, they turned each corner, huddled together, coming closer. With Emeline came twelve men, eight women and one following child with his thumb in his mouth. Muttering turned to whispers, then sank to silence except for the pelt of rain. Then finally noise began echoing back.

The fighting had stopped but it had clearly not finished as Emeline had hoped. As those from the tenement crept forwards, Emeline halted abruptly and peered around the final sharp street corner. Beyond it was narrow and little could be seen, but the sound of voices carried, even through the rain.

It was through the rain that Emeline stared, the others grouped tight at her back. She had seen Nicholas. He stood, unsteady and wavering, leaning back against the long brick wall of the storehouse behind. The overhang of the upper storey sheltered him, but he could barely stand. His forehead was once more bleeding heavily and the blood and the rain streaked his face in persistent stripes. It was Adrian he faced. Behind Adrian were eight men, none of whom Emeline recognised. Beside Nicholas stood David. She could not see either Jerrid or Alan. Adrian was speaking softly, half obscured by the rain which sluiced over his oiled cape and pounded on the ground around. He was unhooded, his hat was drenched and his boots squelched. But he was smiling.

"It is a pleasant change, Nicholas," Adrian said, "to see you humiliated, while I stand proud. You appreciate, I hope, the justice."

Nicholas wiped bloody streaks from his eyes. "I'm as uninterested in my supposed embarrassments as I am in yours, Adrian. You've finally won a battle of sorts here, though a battle of shame with louts, foreigners and traitors, and your own arrival coming only after the fight was safely over. Now it's the consequences which interest me. Do you have some plan or ambition? Or are you as caught in this trap as I have been?"

"Trap, Nicholas?" Adrian scowled. "You persistently imagine traps, like a mange ridden fox in a snare. There's been no trap. Only of your own making."

"Then you're a simpleton, cousin." His legs were sliding a little down, unable to hold him. Emeline understood his exhaustion. But she realised something else. He was playing for time. She thought she knew why, and held her own people back. "The men you suppose loyal to you," Nicholas continued, "made sure your message was misdirected. I was purposefully brought here, and ambushed. Twice. A trap then. Can you be sure you're not equally trapped?"

One of the men at his side growled something Emeline could not hear. David reached out, steadying his master, but remained silent. Adrian sneered, "There's only the result of your own arrogance. I've loathed you, your vile brother and that drunken sot my Uncle Symond since I was a ten year child. None of you ever gave a thought to me and my sister, though we were the penniless orphans in a family of wealth and greed."

"Self pity again, Adrian?"

"Once I thought you a cringing coward," Adrian said between his teeth. "Perhaps I was wrong in that. But I'm not wrong about your stupidity, Nicholas, nor your arrogance. Obnoxious avarice, brutality, conceit, and blind insistence on everything to your own benefit, even when those gains were my losses. Selfish to the end, like all your family."

"What has that to do with treason and loyalty to your country?" Nicholas straightened himself against the wall, strengthening his knees. "You have no Lancastrian sympathies. You've no friendship with Tudor nor his mother. Your parents proclaimed no loyalty to any foreign cause before they died. You've no genuine grudge against the House of York, nor against the king who knighted you on the Scottish Marches, much to your own pride. So your treason is simply a coward's revenge against your own family." Nicholas spoke slowly, both through weakness and a need to slow time. Again Emeline beckoned to the group behind her, her finger to her lips, asking them to wait.

"You know nothing of me," Adrian glowered. "Long years of ignorance, uncaring arrogance and playing the clown. You've no concept of my suffering."

"You join a treacherous cause simply because you're envious of your rich cousins?" Nicholas sighed, again wiping the blood from his eyes. "You'll back a cold hard man without a drop of royal blood in his veins, simply to reject whatever cause I support? Even if it means your own country destroyed? Heaven help us from English bitterness and French spite." He was slipping again, his knees buckling. "I despise you, Adrian," he said faintly. "Now do whatever you will."

"Kill you?" Adrian sniggered. "Too easy, cousin."

"You killed my brother. Why stop now?"

Adrian paused. He shook his head. "I loathe you all. I loathed Peter more than anyone else, with his claws into my poor sister and his filthy prick eager to escape its codpiece at any paltry opportunity. But I never killed Peter." He shook his head with a whirl of flying raindrops. "I know full well you killed him yourself, and probably your father-in-law as well. Yet your wretched luck continues. You married a woman who despised you just as she should have. Yet the witless girl has grown to love you, so I'm told. But your undeserved luck ends here, cousin."

Nicholas was too weak. David was trying to hold him up but he was bleeding copiously. Emeline thought he would fall. Whatever he needed to wait for, no longer mattered. She raised her hand, picked up her skirts and ran forwards as fast as she could. The crowd followed her, splashing through mud and puddles. Sudden shouts, a rush of shadows and shapes, stones thrown and the flash of steel through the streaming waters. Nicholas and David had been disarmed but Adrian's men, their swords raised, whirled, disorientated and alarmed, not knowing whether they faced the law, guards, or untold assailants. The crowd from the tenement carried cudgels and old bent arrows, honed kitchen knives and skillets, pots and steel butchers' hooks. Emeline held an iron poker. Adrian and his men were outnumbered four to one. Adrian stared, and dropped his sword.

Sudden and unexpected, the rush overpowered almost at once. Adrian toppled, down to his knees in the slush. One of his men disappeared beneath five flailing sticks, and roared once before he slumped unconscious, skull cracked. Another of Adrian's men faced three women, one with her carving knife in his face. It was thrust to the hilt into his mouth, through his tongue and down his throat. He gargled torn flesh and fell. A third man stumbled and went down, four pairs of large hands squeezing around his neck, strangling him into silence as an iron hook pierced one ear. Emeline wielded the poker, heavy as a blade, and smashed it over one man's head. Then she ran to Nicholas.

It had taken only moments. Nicholas also fell, but he fell into his wife's arms. Emeline kissed his blood streaked cheeks and held him tight. They sat together in the mud as the noise and violence spun around them, kicking legs, dancing skirts, wooden clogs, grappling hands and the wavering reins of one confused horse.

"Don't kill Adrian," whispered Nicholas, and fainted.

One last flash and crackle of lightening, a roll of thunder less distinct and more distant, and abruptly the rain began to ease.

The people crowded round. "Was that it, then mistress?"

"A fine tangle, lady, but not as profitable as we'd hoped. Eight miserable dolts and one fine gennelman without purse nor rings, what we can't even finish off." Then the man saw David and recognised him. "It's Witton, lads. Look. The little bugger from next door is here after all."

"I'm off back to own my little lad," one woman said, shaking her head. "Ain't no more fun to be had here and I were never no friend o' Howard Witton, nasty bugger he were, and Liz not much better."

"The son ain't like the father. David's a good boy, and a clever one."

"No matter," the woman said, wiping her hands on her apron. "I'm off. I ain't waiting round here 'till the law turns up."

"True, true." Some of the crowd drifted away, looking back only briefly. "So you look after yourself now, lady. Reckon we're not needed no more and will be gone afore the Watch comes this way."

"The Watch? Of course." It was what Nicholas had been waiting for. Emeline nodded, and without rising she thanked her new friends. "I hope no one is hurt?"

"A bruise, missus, no more."

"There's plenty of them other buggers hurt, and that's what was asked of us." David Witton's neighbour grinned. "But I reckoned on seeing them Bambrigg boys. Good boys they are, and useful in a brawl."

David was clasping hands, thanking and praising, knowing every soul who had come at Emeline's request. "The Bambriggs work for my lord now," he told them. "But both Harry and Rob are off on another errand. They'd have been helpful indeed, but when they were instructed to stay behind elsewhere, we had no way of knowing this would happen. We expected no organised attack." He smiled. "Didn't expect all of you to come either."

"Thanks to the lady," he was told. "Poor lass was in a right spin and said she needed help. Gave your name. So we come for you."

"Besides," added another, "we's always ready for a good fight."

Finally, David returned to his master's side. Nicholas was still only half conscious, blur eyed and dizzy. "It is hard," he murmured very softly, "to believe what I've just seen."

"All true, my lord. We've been saved by the ruffians from the tenement, roused and brought to our aid by your ingenious lady wife herself" And David knelt in the mud, his hands carefully testing where Nicholas had been wounded. As he examined, he began to explain what had happened at the end. "We thought we had beaten them, my lady," he informed Emeline. "After I returned here, riding your horse as you graciously instructed, I found the fight almost won. We finished them off quickly, my lord and I, and the locals who'd come to our aid thought matters done with, and left. Our attackers were fair beaten and those not hurt set off running. Two dead, but their companions carted them away. To the river maybe, being the best place for traitors. We thought ourselves free, and hoped for the Watch to come by at last, since it's close to their usual patrol. But both my Lord Nicholas and Lord Jerrid were badly wounded."

The rain was just a chilly silver trickle now, puddling deeper into the mud beneath them. Emeline sighed. "What happened to Jerrid?"

"We believed we needed only to return home as quickly as possible, and summon the medick. It was too late to return to the Tower, so Alan Venter took the wounded Lord Jerrid up before him, riding west. He hoped to alert the Watch on his way, but Lord Jerrid was near fainting, so they set off at a gallop. My lord and I intended the same, and I was helping him mount his own mare, when we were ambushed."

Emeline shivered, trying to adjust the soaked bandage falling from head to eyes across Nicholas's brows. "Adrian?"

"Indeed, my lady. There was just his lordship and myself left alone, when along comes Sir Adrian and a clutch of louts. It seems those that ran from us before had run only to call for help, and waited, I believe, to see Alan and Lord Jerrid leave so we'd be without hope of defending ourselves. And the Watch didn't come. We were hopelessly outnumbered, nine against two, and my lord barely able to stand."

Nicholas pushed David's administering hands away. "How is Adrian?"

Adrian sat alone, watching them. He seemed bemused and unable or unwilling to rise. He made no attempt to escape, and sat cradling his shoulder. His doublet was cut across the chest, its ribbons dangling beneath his cloak, but there was no sign of bleeding. Of his backers, three were dead, another dying. Two were badly injured and trying to stagger away from further retribution. The others had disappeared.

David murmured, "My lord, after this - the ruin - the treason - Sir Adrian cannot be left alive. He can never return home. To the sheriff, then? Or we wait a little longer for the Watch? Or I drag the constable from his bed?"

Nicholas murmured, "Let him go."

Emeline whispered, turning from Nicholas to Adrian, and then again to Nicholas, "But what if he calls for help as before? What if he attacks another time? You can't fight any longer, my love."

"Nor can he." Nicholas nodded towards Adrian. He held Emeline's hand but was looking beyond her. "Give me a moment more, my sweet, and then help me to my feet. We've still one horse left between us, and David will see us back to the Strand. I don't care where Adrian goes."

Now she looked to David. "Can his lordship ride all that way?"

David nodded. "In my experience, my lady, there's nothing his lordship can't do if he wishes it. But apart from the original wounds which have reopened, he's been slashed to the back of the head and deep across the knee. Perhaps more. You'll need to support him on horseback, my lady, while I lead the beast by its bridle."

Nicholas squinted up through the last gentle patter of the rain. He said, with almost a smile, "We were finished, you know, my love, before you magically materialised. David expected to die. I was already nigh dead."

"Life is always unexpected, my lord, as the wheel turns, whether with turns of fortune for the better - or for the worst."

"For the better," Nicholas murmured, "with my beautiful wife appearing from the shadows like some voluptuous Sir Lancelot."

Emeline smiled. "You must be feeling better, my love, to talk like that."

"Let us hope so," David said. "And hope too that Harry and Rob took that other traitor to the constable for questioning and are now back at the Strand. And more importantly still, that Lord Jerrid reached home safely and is being tended by the doctor at this moment, and did not fall in the gutter on the way."

"Jerrid is very fond of gutters," mumbled Nicholas. "But he survives. He always survives."

"And you, my love. You would have been all right in the end," Emeline assured him. "I was listening, ready to rush forwards, you know. I realised you were trying to delay, hoping the Watch would come."

"It appears," Nicholas said, "that the Watch was watching elsewhere. And now I'm going home. The other side of the city of course, and it will take me an hour, but I shall cling to that saddle, with your warm strong arms around me, my love. I want my own damned home and my own sweet wife and my own warm dry bed. I may never leave it again."

"I wish that were true," said Emeline. "But it will only be until the next adventure."

His horse had wandered, nosing the moss along the side of the empty storehouse and the weeds between the stones. David grabbed its reins, brought the horse alongside and with some difficulty, helped his lordship mount. Then Nicholas reached down, and Emeline bounced up before him, cuddled side saddle, one arm around his waist.

Adrian remained where he had fallen. He was propped, quite silent, against the low stone wall of the herb garden attached to the storehouse behind. He gazed up at his cousin, his pale blue eyes colourless in the night's shadows. Nicholas stared back.

Eventually Nicholas said, "Are you hurt, cousin?"

Adrian roused himself, as if he had been half asleep. "Not much. Your brawlers did little damage."

"Whereas your brawlers did a great deal."

The rain had almost ceased. It dripped from the overhang of the buildings along the lane, and hung faint like a silver sheen within the darkness. The clouds were separating and a first glimmer of stars peeped between. The faint pearly light pricked out the raindrops on Adrian's cheeks, spangling along his eyelashes. He sighed. "It would be easier if you killed me."

The horse was prancing, impatient. Nicholas soothed it, stroking its neck although his own hands were trembling. He remained watching his cousin. "I do not kill in cold blood. And I do not kill within my own family."

"Except for your leech of a brother."

"I'm tired of that repeated taunt. If you slaughtered Peter yourself, then you know the truth. If you didn't, though that seems unlikely, then my protestations of innocence are of no concern to you." He paused, then leaned down, saying quietly, "Get yourself out of here, Adrian. Find passage across the ocean to join Tudor's precious court of traitors if that's your wish. I'll not stop you. Or go back to Sissy, and try to reform your life. I'll not inform on you to the crown." His voice sank even lower. "But tell me this. What was this bitter battle for? Simply following your desire to eliminate the Chatwyns?"

Adrian croaked, half laugh, half sob. "Urswick came with letters. I went to collect them, and then deliver them as I'd been instructed."

"Just one simple request for Tudor to find a rich wife and align himself with Northumberland?"

Adrian shook his bedraggled hat and its torn feathers. "Other letters as well, which you never found. A whole walletful of them. Rallying support, demanding allegiance, declaring himself the rightful monarch, reminding some of favours long owed and Lancastrian loyalties long overlooked. Tudor's coming, Nicholas. He'll be king of England before the year is out."

"So the men who fought for you were Tudor's men. That means Frenchmen and English traitors."

"Men who appreciate and care for me. For *me*, Nicholas, not because of wealth or title, but because of loyalty. True friends. Unlike my own uncaring family. But they weren't under my orders, nor I under theirs." Adrian looked away, wincing as he touched his shoulder. "I've no funds to pay for that many henchmen. They protected me because we fight for the same cause. And because they respect me."

Nicholas nodded, and began to turn the horse. He looked back once. "Then let these respectable and respecting friends come back to collect you," he said, "otherwise it's the Watch will find you. That, or in the morning the dairymaids and swineherds will discover your remains dead from the cold. So best get yourself down to the docks and find a carvel heading southeast." He paused, holding the horse still. "Can you walk?"

Adrian looked away. "Why should you care?"

"Self pity again, Adrian?" Nicholas nodded to David to walk on, saying only, half to himself, "It is so often those who cannot summon pity for others who wallow in pity for themselves."

The horse walked slowly, keeping to David's careful pace. Emeline, with a lot to say and questions bubbling in her head, said nothing. It was not the moment. She sat sideways, one arm around her husband's back, the other tucked into his belt. He slumped a little, half supporting her, half allowing the horse its own choices. It was David who led.

They were some distance away when they heard the noises. The night had grown quiet and a slant of moonlight reflected in the puddles, lighting the wet cobbled silver. Stars peeped between the clouds. The storm had passed entirely. But clear in the new washed air were the sudden shouts, then the rattled gurgle of pain.

For a moment Nicholas frowned. Then he yelled, "Get back," and wheeled the horse back the way they had come.

Adrian lay where he had been before, but now, instead of being propped again the little garden wall, he sprawled flat upon the wet earth. The seeping mud squelched into his ears. His hat had fallen off and his hair was thick with filth. His eyes were closed. Nicholas tumbled from the saddle, half collapsing. One knee bent, standing only on one leg, he leaned down towards his cousin. Adrian's throat was sliced across so deeply that above the stiffened laces of his shirt, the gullet, sinews, flesh and blood oozed clear. A butcher's chop, impatient to kill and be gone. Nicholas whispered, "Adrian?" But Adrian was already dead. There was no longer any sign of the killer. "Finished, then," murmured Nicholas, "by those friends of honour and respect. By those he thought cared." He looked up at David. "We must arrange the funeral. But nothing can put right what has been done."

CHAPTER FIFTY SIX

With her shift a dazzling bleached white and the skirts over it a flutter of embroidered primrose, Avice sat, studiously draped in taffeta glory upon the settle. There was sunlight from the long mullioned window slanting across her russet ringlets, her little toes were well shod in pale blue kid, and the long curls of ribbons lacing her neckline, waist and cuffs were pretty pink satin. Her smile echoed the brilliance of her new clothes. She had rarely been more content.

"I am," she said, "not sorry in the least."

"I think Nicholas is," decided Emeline. "He shouldn't be. But he truly is."

"Of course he shouldn't be sorry. He should be jumping happily up and down just like me. After all, the horrid man sent a dozen armed traitors to get rid of him. Adrian killed his brother Peter, not to mention Papa, and then tried to murder Nicholas himself."

"Well," pondered Emeline, "we feel that way of course. But Nicholas knew Adrian from birth. He was his cousin, for goodness' sake. And after all, Peter was a vile creature who deserved to be slaughtered. As for Papa – well, I'd prefer not to think about it."

"Someone should kill Nicholas's own father; mean nasty man he is."

"It's a bit later for that now. And neither of us need see much more of the earl, even though he's my father-in-law so I suppose I ought not to say it. Meanwhile Nicholas is taking me back to Chatwyn Castle." Emeline regarded her sister with a widening smile. "And you have three new gowns and practically a dozen new shoes and shifts and bedrobes and enough ribbons to strangle yourself. What more can you ask for?"

"A husband. Maman says she'll start to arrange it after we get back to Wrotham, and she says Nicholas will help find me someone rich and handsome. After all, I'm an heiress. Not as much as you are, though second best is still quite cosy. But," Avice screwed up her nose, "I want someone *nice* who will *like* me. To think I once thought myself in love with Adrian. Ugh."

"And that silly secretary Edmund Harris, and the goose boy before that." Emeline smiled into her sister's scowl. "Don't worry. None of that is as bad as me, thinking myself in love with Peter. I should thank Adrian for having killed the wretch, otherwise I'd now be married to him."

There was a moment's pause. "Which is what made me wonder - you know," Avice switched to a sudden whisper, "if it wasn't Adrian after all. If perhaps it was Maman. Or Nurse Martha. Or both of them together. There's no one else had more cause to get rid of Papa and Peter too. And they're both so - well, determined. Capable!"

Emeline stood quickly, pushing back her stool. "We've discussed all these possibilities before and I'm not ever going to think about it again. It was all Adrian. Talking about Maman like that, Avice, is mean."

"It isn't mean. It's admiration." Avice smoothed the creases in her skirts. They turned to gold in the sunlight. "Martha and Maman together, just think of it. To protect you from Peter when Papa wouldn't listen to any suggestion about calling off the marriage negotiations. And then the fury when they realised Papa was living with his mistress, and spending his money on her when he wouldn't even let Maman have more than one candle in her bedchamber. All that hypocritical preaching about holy morality and being chaste and no new dresses. And there he was romping in piles of cash with naked women."

"Maman didn't know about the other woman." Emeline shivered in spite of the sunbeams on her back.

"What if she did? We wouldn't have known. She could have seen Papa and followed him one day. And both Maman and Martha would march into battle just as bravely as the king, I know they would. And just like in battle, it wouldn't have been murder. It would have been a righteous war."

Jerrid Chatwyn reclined in bored lethargy for a week in one of the spare bedchambers at the family house on the Strand, then ordered a litter followed by a cartload of bedding, medicines and wine barrels, and transferred himself back to his own rooms at Westminster Palace. His body, fit and honed during past years of joust and jest, healed quickly. But he was still in bed under doctor's orders when his elder brother, also keen to return to court, trundled in to visit.

"You're a fool, Jerrid," the earl informed him. "You could have been killed. All this absurd playing at gallantry and trying to make me look like a sluggard in comparison. I'm not impressed, not at all."

"I didn't do it to impress you, Symond," his brother informed him. "And my opinion of you never changes, whatever you might get up to. Nor do I expect to change yours of me. But you could pass the jug. My cup's empty."

The earl glowered, repositioned himself on the stool beside the bed, and topped up his brother's wine cup from the brimming jug of best Malmsey. "Damned fool of a brother. Damned fool of a son." He had topped up his own cup too, and now drained it for the third time. "The Chatwyn name's already been held up to gossip and slander. Now brawling in the streets, and young Adrian getting himself killed."

Jerrid raised an eyebrow. "Still thinking it was Nicholas who slaughtered Peter, are you, Symond? Or you've finally accepted it was Adrian?"

"Adrian. Nicholas." The earl shrugged and poured more wine. "What difference? I've lost my previous boy, my heir butchered, whatever devil's hand did the deed. So now Nicholas likes to show himself a hero, as you do, Jerrid. But I know you both better. Peter was my hero, poor lad. I'll miss him, you know, till my own dying day."

"Then you're a bigger fool than I even thought you." Jerrid turned away. "It's natural enough to care for your eldest son. But to merit Peter over Nicholas?"

"Nicholas? A smarter boy than I once gave him credit for, perhaps. But Peter? He was exceptional in every way." The earl stood, tossing back the stool. "I'll not listen to my boy criticised, but I'll tell you this, Jerrid, before I go. He'd have brought pride to the family, instead of this foolhardy mummery. Peter was a red blooded Chatwyn, and all the girls fell in admiration at his feet. No nonsenses of book learning or secret errands. No sneaking about the countryside in shoddy clothes and a false identity. Peter was proud to act under his own name, and show his talents." And the earl finished the last cup of wine, turned on his heel and marched from the chamber. The heavy door swung back on iron hinges and thudded shut.

Jerrid Chatwyn sighed, closed his eyes, and silently wondered if he would be strong and steady enough to climb from the bed, cross over to the table, and retrieve whatever little was left in the wine jug.

The baroness was organising her imminent journey. Petronella would stay with Emeline, while Martha would return to the Wrotham manor with the others. It was Sysabel who fell between the cracks.

The Lady Elizabeth sighed. "My responsibility, as always, I assume. I'll take the girl. But the sooner she's wed, the better. She gives me the twitches." The lady patted her stomacher, broad scarlet pleats over a small well filled belly. It was a long balmy afternoon, dinner not long over, and the sleepy sunbeams crept into everyone's eyes. "Yes, marry the girl sooner done the better is. But now," Lady Elizabeth murmured, "that duty is for Nicholas, with Adrian gone. And Symond's duty too, though he'll not stir himself, I'll be bound."

"Symond is snoozing upstairs."

"Symond is snoozing even when he's awake."

The baroness smiled. "You've a poor opinion of your brother, my lady."

"Who? Oh, Symond. Yes indeed," sighed the lady. "The family is much flawed. Once I had hopes for young Adrian. He seemed a bright boy. But his father, you know, was a gambler and a drunkard. Being the youngest he never inherited a farthing, but he came into a little coin when he married, for the wife was one of the Bridgeworth girls. Then he gambled her money. Cheated at dice I heard, but I cannot see the merit in cheating if you do not win even then. He was a bully too and my least favourite sibling when I was a girl. Silly little wife had not a pennyweight of sense either. Drowned. Both of them. A grand trip to Flanders, costs borrowed from Symond who hoped to be rid of them. Well, rid of them he was, for they had the stupidity to sail off into a storm. I washed my hands of them."

"You didn't," the baroness pointed out. "You ended up with Adrian and Sysabel."

"I was reasonably fond of them when they were younger," remembered Aunt Elizabeth with vague disinterest. "But then they grew up."

"Sysabel has not stopped crying."

"It will teach her the worth of prayer and duty," Sysabel's aunt announced. "And she may come to appreciate my own efforts as guide and chaperone a little more. She alone will inherit from me eventually, not that I have too much to leave and have as yet no plans to depart. But no doubt young Nick and Symond too will add something for her marriage portion."

Nicholas still kept to his bed, strictly commanded by his doctor. The half tester spread its painted silks across the headboard, surrounding him in gentle shadows. He watched his wife enter with relief. "Smuggle the horses around the back outside the window," he told her. "Alert the grooms to say nothing, warn the horses not to neigh, tell my doctors I'm fast asleep, grab some cheese for supper, stuff a flask of wine into the neck of your gown, take down the shutters, open the casement, find a nice long vine of hanging ivy for climbing, and we'll escape off into the countryside before the sun goes down. I think I should become a highway robber."

Emeline nodded. "I almost believe you."

"Have you any idea," her husband demanded, "how unutterably dreary it is stuck in this damned bed for days on end? I'm stiff enough to carve into a table. My only pleasure is stumbling out of bed to piss or cursing at the apothecary."

"Just two more days, my love. The doctor promises you can get out of bed and limp downstairs on Friday. I shall clear the spicery of lavender, and we shall have salmon and roast duck for dinner. A last celebration before we say goodbye to Maman and Avice."

He grinned back. His forehead was still thickly bandaged, his left hand was invisible beneath a wadding of linen, and under the covers his right knee was swaddled. He also had two broken ribs and a small wedge of flesh missing from his left earlobe. But, he assured everyone, he was now feeling exceedingly well. "I lost so much blood during those damned attacks, there was none left to feed the leeches once I got home. But bed rest isn't my favourite pastime as you know, my sweet, though you might think it is, the amount of time I've been tied to it over the year. Besides, I feel wretched about Adrian. And even worse about Sysabel."

"I hadn't realised before just how much your Aunt Elizabeth secretly dislikes the poor little thing." Emeline took a deep breath. "Should we bring Sissy to live at the castle, Nicholas?"

"She'd not thank us." Nicholas sighed. "She blames me for Adrian's death. A little unjust, but understandable for all that. And she can't look us in the eye now we know about Peter and the abortion. Besides," he shook his head, "she's still convinced I murdered the sainted Peter and ruined her life."

"Find her a husband then. Avice is hoping for romance too."

Nicholas grinned again. "Is a husband such a tempting prospect? And I hear Elizabeth, the eldest of the old king's girls, is near to tears fearing the negotiations for her alliance with the Portuguese prince will be put on hold while there's the risk of that miserable traitor Tudor about to cause trouble. The girl wants out of England and into sunnier palaces."

"You mean Edward IV's daughter? But she was declared illegitimate. And I didn't know you knew her."

"I don't." Nicholas stretched, half yawning. "But I know one of her sisters. When I was at court delivering that damned letter, Cecily assured me that Elizabeth wants both a man in her bed and an escape from England's miserable strictures. The Portuguese don't care she's illegitimate for she's a king's daughter, as pretty as a swan, and comes with a huge dower. More importantly, she means a powerful alliance between the two countries, since our king will marry their princess Joanna at the same time. It's a done deal once peace is ensured."

"We all dream of romance."

Nicholas leaned back again against the propped pillows. "You and I, we've been lucky, my dear, for all we originally thought ourselves cursed. Most men are simply after a rich wife. They spend all their time away from home and when they're forced into their wife's company, they either tumble her into bed or beat her for being a fool."

"So she must be a fool to believe in romance?"

Nicholas grinned. "Our king was a good husband, I believe, before Queen Anne died. He was devastated, you know, especially after losing his son the year before. But before Richard, King Edward spent no more than a faithful month in his entire life." Nicholas shook his head and laughed. "So much for romance."

"For a man who tells me he loves me," Emeline mumbled, looking down at her toes, "You're very pessimistic, my love. But you'll find a nice man, won't you, for Avice? She's such a sweet and trusting little thing, and is so hopeful."

She had seated herself on the side of the bed where the rumpled covers were thrown back a little in acknowledgement of the warm afternoon. Nicholas reached out and clasped her hand. "I've a couple of decent men in mind. Avice has a dower to attract half the kingdom, making her suddenly as beautiful as a princess."

"Maman will want to supervise the final choice. But," Emeline remembered, "Avice has some very odd ideas about Maman."

"Avice has some odd ideas about everything. I shall buy her a blue velvet cloak lined in sable and trimmed in gold thread. She'll be happy for evermore."

Emeline shook her head. "But poor Sissy says she'll never be happy again."

The sun through the half closed shutters was in his eyes. "I'll find her a good man, and eventually she'll love her children. In the meantime, my sweet, we'll be back at Chatwyn, and awaiting our own first child."

Emeline whispered, "And will you truly love me after that then, Nicholas."

He looked down at her, leant, and kissed her forehead. "Oh, my love. Listen to me." She peeped up, his breath warm across her eyes. His face was creased into pale lines of pain, tiredness and concern, but his bright blue eyes were earnest with care and sincerity. Then he smiled, and much of the pain seemed to fade. "I can't kiss you properly," he murmured, "or my bandages will blind you and I'll drip blood onto your very small nose. I can't caress you, for I have two fingers less for the task, and those that remain are as numb as a frozen trout. I certainly cannot make love to you, for I've a knee that won't bend or hold me up, I can't walk and I'm as dizzy as an impotent drunkard. So sadly I just lie here like a useless slug, bemoaning my fate." But he grinned, belying his own words. Then he gave the lie further, leaned down and kissed her lightly on the mouth. "But I swear to this, my beloved. I have learned to adore you, to treasure you, respect and admire you. You have saved my life both with your kindness, and with your courage. But more importantly, you've saved my life by being my wife, and by loving me when few others do."

Emeline blinked away sudden tears. "Oh, Nicholas."

"You've no idea," he continued softly, "how much I missed you on that last mad ride down to the south coast."

"Oh, Nicholas my love," Emeline repeated, clutching at his unbandaged hand and entwining her fingers with his. "It is wonderful - just glorious - to hear you say such things. But however much you missed me, my dearest, can have no comparison - none whatsoever - to how much I missed you."

"There is a poker, I believe," he told her, the smile lighting his eyes, "over there by the hearth, for I remember one of the pages poking at the fire before you turned up and I sent them all away. And I certainly remember how dangerous you can be with a poker in your hand. So arm yourself, my sweet, and we can battle over who missed who the most."

"I couldn't eat. I couldn't sleep," she insisted.

"A lie." Nicholas shook his head and the bandage slipped. "I have never known your appetite to diminish for any reason, and you sleep like a child in its crib, muttering in your dreams every might. I refuse to believe that even total misery could make any difference."

"Oh Nicholas," Emeline smiled through her tears. "I always dream of you."

Mistress Sysabel Frye lay very straight on the bed, her back flat to the feather mattress, her arms crossed over her breasts, her eyes closed. It was how she had last seen her brother. Gazing at him in the open lead lined coffin, she had wanted to lean over and kiss his cheek, but had been afraid, and done nothing. She had been crying for a long time.

Sysabel wondered if Adrian had ever known what she truly thought of him, and how she had never admired him as much as he surely deserved. She then wondered about her parents, whom she could barely remember, but hoped had loved her. She wondered about her own unborn and massacred baby, a little girl she had secretly called Sara, but which had never been baptised, nor had lived to know that her mother missed her. She wondered whether an unbaptised child would wander forever in Purgatory, as the priests had once told her. She wondered if she would ever have other children, and be free to love them as a mother should. But, since it would be the hated Nicholas and Uncle Symond who would find her a husband, she wondered if they would purposefully find her a vile man who would beat her and bring her more misery and no joy.

Most of all she wondered about Peter, and what life would have been like had they married, brought up little Sara as a Chatwyn beauty, inherited the grand castle and shared the joy that she now knew she would never know.

The tears which she had wept for many days continued to streak across her face, dampening her pillows and making her nauseas. So she wondered whether, once she was able to stop weeping, she might have the courage to murder Nicholas, and send him unshriven to join the brother he had wronged, and the cousin he had deserted.

But she knew, as she lay very still and stared into the back of her eyelids, that she would never have the courage. Not even to kill herself.

CHAPTER FIFTY SEVEN

The castle's stark granite, aged plaster, old oak and wide moat welcomed home its masters. No stench of fire, smoke or ashes hung in its winding passages or spoiled the new clean lime wash. Repairs blended, though less invisible perhaps where bright brick now jutted against the original grandeur of limestone, buttresses were pristine hewn, glass shone sunshine bright as new oriel windows jutted far larger than the tiny unglazed insets of before, and doors were fresh built and brass hinged. The household was waiting beneath the portcullis, excited, giggling and nudging one to the other, watching Lord Nicholas and his young wife come riding home, their entourage dazzling behind them.

Half a mile of baggage, servants and mounted guards with trumpets and banners trailed through the Leicestershire villages to the cheerful interest of the villagers. Sunbeams sought out the glint of bridle and spurs. Harry, Rob and Alan rode in the train, not as part of the armed guard but as retainers, their weapons tucked beneath their capes.

David Witton had remained behind, taken into Jerrid's service, although only while his lordship completed his recovery. "It will only be for a week or two," Nicholas told him. "But for now my uncle has need of a man he can trust."

"And you do not, my lord? Forgive me, but you still cannot walk unaided, and they say there may soon be war. There's talk of a French invasion, and I've heard that his highness already expects it."

"Expects it and has denounced Tudor as the traitor that he is," Alan Venter interjected. "Though most folk dismiss the danger as too small to worry over."

Harry, heel out of his hose, was hopping from stable to stall, collecting his belongings for the journey. Rob, seated on an upturned barrel, regarded his brother. "War? Who's worrying? We's ready. I never fought in them battles at Tewkesbury and thereabouts. I'll be keen to show my metal, my lord, and so will Harry."

Nicholas leaned on the crutch he still used. "There'll be fighting of some sort if the French have anything to do with it. They're holding Dorset hostage and there's clearly a reason for that."

"Payment will be the satisfaction of seeing England in disarray," muttered David.

"Who fears the flagging hopes of a few miserable traitors? Alan insisted. "And how many will follow? Five Welsh dreamers? Six vengeful reivers from the Scottish borders? Seven fools who've angered our king, so think they'll do better under another?"

Nicholas said quietly, "Northumberland perhaps, since it's to him that Tudor writes and asks to marry one of his wife's wealthy sisters?"

"And how about my Lord Stanley," muttered David, "who is wed already to Tudor's mother? And Stanley's wretched brother, who has never kept to the same side in any battle as he began it, lest he changes twice."

Nicholas began to limp back to the house, and even with the use of the crutch, dragged one leg and was unable to stand on the other. The bandage over his forehead had been finally discarded but the scar remained livid while his hand was still thickly protected. "I've no desire for war," he said. "And doubt I could even prove my loyalty if an invasion came. It will be months before I could ride to battle. Any call to arms before winter, and I'd be forced to sit at home like an old woman. With one hand cocooned and a damned great hole in my knee? I can hardly ride, let alone fight. Jerrid too. He's worse wounded than I am and has been ordered back to bed rest for the third time with enough fever to stew pottage. At least I can hobble around and make my wishes known."

"So I shall stay with his lordship, as you ask me," David nodded. "But if war comes indeed, sir, I ask to join it, and to answer the call in your place. Aiming to earn your pride if you cannot join the battle yourself, my lord."

"Enough battle talk." Nicholas turned again and, leaning on the stout wooden crutch, continued to limp back to the house. He called over his shoulder. "Only a week or two, David, then I'll send for you. In the meantime, tell my uncle he's lucky I've not sent him Hectic Harry instead."

Emeline was waiting for him outside the principal doorway beyond the stable courtyard. "Sissy is sitting upstairs clutching her parcels. She's sulking because she doesn't want to make the first half of her journey in our company. But Aunt Elizabeth seems happy to get back to Nottingham, and has started dreaming of weddings."

"For herself?" Nicholas laughed.

"It wouldn't surprise me. I think my mother is secretly wondering about a second marriage too. Though she also says the best chance any woman has to make her own decisions and rule her own destiny, is when she's a widow,"

"A rich widow. Though I cannot imagine your mother ever allowing anyone else ruling her fortunes from now on, married or otherwise" His smile widened. "And you know, I presume, my love, that you take after your mother. And that's no bad thing at all."

"I shall miss her. And Avice too. I hope they'll visit often though Wrotham is so far away. But," admitted Emeline, "I hope Sissy doesn't. I feel terribly sorry for her, and she'll be lonely without Adrian. But much as I love you, Nicholas, your family is rather a difficult matter. And I know it's shocking of me to say so, but I also hope your father doesn't come home too often either."

"He won't." Nicholas put his arm around his wife's shoulders and led her inside. "He's no reason to leave court now, especially since he's discovered what he thought was scandal against the Chatwyn name is actually Chatwyn pride and royal favour. Besides," Nicholas added softly, "he'll never learn to like me, you know. It no longer concerns me since I'm well accustomed to it. Peter will always remain the grand favourite, and now cannot ever grow to disappoint. So just poor Nick, scarred and foolish, is left to carry the name."

"I think I hate your father."

He leaned down and kissed her. "He's a poor sad creature, my love, pickled in wine and with all hope of a proud future lost. You should pity him."

The journey had been slow with tiring days in the saddle but wayside inns bright lit each night, relieved calls for the ostlers, easing aching backs with hot spiced hippocras and laughing at chickens underfoot in the straw strewn courtyards, boys rushing to stable the horses, the landlord hurrying out with smiles, trays of raisin cakes and steaming jugs of wine, Nicholas taking his wife in his arms and hustling her across the cobbles, late evenings talking and drinking over the supper table and then warm beds shared in comfort until the next morning dawned rosy, cockerels crowing outside the windows and the whole procedure starting all over again.

Now at last the castle beckoned. There were new born fluff ball ducklings on the moat, and a pair of scrubby cygnets keeping a watery pace behind their elegant parents. The herb gardens were flushed in emerald and the clambering briar roses were a fresh scramble of thorny perfumes. The gaping mouths of the stone gargoyles were toasted warm in the sunshine and polished glass spun green tinged promises across cushioned settles. Huge iron chandeliers again swung in the grand hall, its walls repainted with scenes of myth and chivalry, and the great feasting table was new carved with chairs and benches high backed and fit for royalty. The great Keep housed new decorated bedchambers with downy pillows, silken bed curtains and canopied posts. Most importantly the quarters for his lordship were newly positioned very close to those of her ladyship.

Summer settled across the farmlands and forests, with rolling clouds and the shrill whistle of the falcons. Crops ripened and fields turned golden. Pasture spread dry and green. Late June and the year of our Lord, 1485, and England was at peace, serene beneath the sun.

Emeline discovered the little stone steps she had run to on her wedding night when fire had ravaged the castle. She stood leaning against the solid newel, gazing up into the narrow shadows. The fire was only a memory now, and the misery of her marriage bed not even remembered. But some memories renewed others. It had been assumed that the earl, drunken sprawled at the table after the rest of the guests had retired, had knocked over some candles. His lordship had surely started the fire that had well near killed him.

But she wondered. For Adrian's carnage had always been accompanied by fire. Peter's murder was discovered when his body was half charred, extinguished only by the spillage of wine from the table. And her own father's murder had been half hidden within a mighty blaze. Even the home of the old woman responsible for Sysabel's abortion had been burned, and almost all the lane ruined beside. Coincidence was not always a coincidence. And Emeline knew that Adrian, before taking his sister home, had certainly been present at her wedding feast.

Her thoughts were interrupted. One strong arm slipped around her waist, breath hot against her cheek, and a half teasing whisper. "Does a faithful husband deserve some special manner of welcome when he brings his wife safe home?" His left hand was no longer bandaged, but the stumps of the two middle fingers remained swollen, angry and inflamed. Emeline knew the pain remained.

"It's not long since you told me you were an impotent drunkard." She smiled. "So *are* you drunk, my love? Perhaps just a little?"

"What ignominious distrust!" She heard his low laugh echoing up the chilly staircase. "I'm investigating the joys of sobriety, my sweetling. Come and test me." So he led her up the steps and she held his hand. Very slowly Nicholas dragged one leg, with a grip of the other hand tight to the balustrade, but then up again without pause. Suddenly there was a gust of bright fresh breeze in their faces as they stood together on the battlements.

The evening sun hung low, edging the treetops into silhouettes as the frogs began to call from the moat. Nicholas smiled and the slanting shadow stripes crept into the deep scar down his face, playing along the new shallow scar across his forehead. Emeline reached up, caressing the scars as she often did.

His right hand was tight over her breast. The neckline of her gown was deep, her cleavage covered by white gauze. Nicholas pushed his fingers past the velvet and the gauze, tracing her nipple. He nuzzled her ear. "Not cold, my love?"

It was a warm evening. She shook her head. "Am I ever cold in your arms?"

She felt the curve of his smile against her cheek, and his sudden pinch around her breast. The tight silk of her gown imprisoned his fingers, and limited his explorations, forcing his clasp ever deeper. His left arm was around her waist, her back hard against the stone wall. The breeze was no more insistent than his fingers. She closed her eyes and held her breath as she felt his hand push further inside the neck of her gown.

"Trust me," he murmured. "You won't fall. The merlons are too high." His eyes were as blue as the sky. Then abruptly the sky was no longer blue. A streak of ruddy carmine turned sapphire to rose petals. She felt the strange space between his fingers as his other hand pressed against her spine and then down to her buttocks, pulling her to him as he continued to play between her breasts, fingers first gentle around the aureole and then pulling at her nipples. "Your gown," he informed her softly, "is in my way."

She thought he might drag it off her, and whispered, "Someone might come past. The guards. One of the pages."

He grinned. "Not here. We're not expecting marauders or invasions just yet."

The sinking sun shot sudden arrows of rich crimson against the darkening indigo. Way above where the hazy, lazy clouds still floated as if on shallow streams, the light remained. But the vivid interruptions sweeping up from the horizon now reflected in the moat and the castle was turning to gold.

Emeline heard his breath becoming strained. Then as his fingers forced within the neck of her dress, his left hand sought entrance below. She felt the sudden draught. He was lifting up the hems of her skirts.

"Open your legs. Let me in." Now his eyes reflected scarlet.

Behind him, across the rising stone turrets, the Chatwyn banners flew in the breeze and from a tower's peak, an iron leopard, crouched to spring, swung obediently, pointing in the wind's direction. The sky was turning to purple as red shot through blue but faded into melted butter and cherry syrup's sweet trickling pastels.

Emeline stared up at her husband. Now both his hands were beneath her skirts and his fingers were cold on her thighs. She felt the rasping tingle of his jaw against her forehead. His hands crawled higher, pushing her skirts up to her knees. The pads of both his thumbs, smooth and strong, rubbed her inner thighs, then stopping suddenly. His breath was now strained. He seemed to pause, to regain his own composure. Then his thumbs started to move again. Suddenly she felt the scrape of stone against the back of her legs; her skirts pushed higher. His knee was between her knees, his foot pushed between her feet. She leaned forwards against him and he supported her. The wind was on her neck. Both his hands remained beneath her skirts, the silken creases now hitched almost around her waist while his fingers were once again busy.

She whispered, "I love you, Nicholas. I love you loving me."

The frogs were calling louder now and the shadows were deepening. The sky was soot coloured, but flashes of cinnabar gathered into sunset flames. Something flew overhead, dark and silent. The distant trees became black waving threads in the little wind.

She felt him pause again, one hand moving from her body, and knew he unlaced his codpiece. He entered her without warning, first his fingers and then immediately himself, thrusting hard and deep. She grunted. He caught his breath, then exhaled with a shudder of release into even greater pleasure. "Hold me too, little one. Touch me."

He had stopped pushing, remaining still and rigid inside her. She could hardly move, hardly think. So he smiled, pressed once more, deeper inside, and took her fingers in his. She felt his hand moist and warm from her own body. The top of her gown was pulled to the side, the velvet trimming becoming unstitched, the fichu quite gone and the cleft between her breasts uncovered. The rich pink circle of one nipple peeped out. She felt the breeze in her hair and knew her headdress was fallings, pins tumbling down to the cold pavings at her feet. The backs of her legs were squashed against the stone, her stockings pulled down, the garters untied, and now her raised skirts, bundled up to her stomacher, left her entirely uncovered. She did not care about any of those things. She could only care about the fire in her belly and the raging desire in her groin.

Nicholas pushed her fingers between his own legs, pulling her hand up to where he entered her. "Now. Put your finger inside yourself," he whispered. "Push inside. Push against me. Touch me where I touch you. Now, move your finger up a little.

Now down. Caressing. Discovering." His breathing quickened. "I'll push. But slowly. Very slowly. So use that beautiful little finger of yours, my own beloved. Feel me as I feel you. Feel where my prick pushes and swells. There's a ridge, and that moves as I fill you." His voice became barely a whisper. "Touching me in such a moment, you understand the heart of me. And you understand yourself, and how you squeeze and feel inside."

He leaned down quickly and kissed her hard as though drinking, as though desperate with thirst. She kissed him in return, reaching up to taste his tongue and his breath.

The setting sun slipped unnoticed behind the long crenellated towers. Stabbing ruby and topaz blurred and sank. The long twilight was settling. The frogs still called as the ducks and the forest creatures nosed into their nests, tree holes and burrows, safe for the night. Darkness swept in from the north. A thin pearlised slice of moon peeped.

Nicholas and Emeline saw none of it nor heard the soft hooting of a hunting owl. They remained within each other's arms, tucked oblivious to the other world, knowing only each other as they neared their own climax.

CHAPTER FIFTY EIGHT

The curve of the young man's thigh skimmed the platters, spoons and napkins still neatly tidy, still ordered, awaiting his lordship's appetite.

Only one toppled candle, not yet congealed, lay out of place. The pale melting wax had oozed into one thin stalactite pointing towards the shadowed boards below. The great table, set for a late supper not yet served, otherwise remained undisturbed for the attack had caused little disarray and no sound. His lordship, placid in his comfortable stupor, had felt nothing but the deepening of sweet sleep.

Yet now the lord of the Strand House, to which he had returned on leaving court for the day, lay silent upon his back, his corpulence in unashamed evidence as the velvet belly proudly rose, the codpiece, a smaller protuberance beneath, now a little askew, and then lay the muscular stretch of the legs, thighs spread apart upon the floorboards, shoes pointing to the small dancing flames of the lit chandelier above.

The Earl of Chatwyn's heavily jowled face appeared peaceful, but the hole in his throat was ragged and the subsequent bleeding had pumped across his doublet even to the padded shoulders before hardening and turning stiff and black.

David Witton replaced the much stained carving knife on the tablecloth, stood and looked around. It was time to set the cleansing fire, but he was momentarily reluctant.

The house had long belonged to the Chatwyn family; often repaired, enlarged and consistently adored throughout the generations. Lord Nicholas Chatwyn, now the earl although he could not yet know it, loved this house. David would not willingly do what might sadden his master. Every action, every studied detail, every killing and every blazing furnace had been designed only to help his master, and for no other reason. Now Nicholas would no longer be shamed or insulted by his great pig of a father, and could inherit the title he deserved. But he would be sorry to lose this grand house.

Mister Witton sat a moment, gazing down with pride at the destruction of the man who had so often caused Nicholas pain.

First in his service when Nicholas the boy was little more than sixteen, David had witnessed bitter years of turmoil and spite, wilful misunderstanding, unjust punishments and the harsh rejection of any affection or warmth. David had considered killing the foul old man many years ago, but had decided to wait. Protecting his master by killing that master's father was not an easy decision. Now setting the fire was an even more challenging choice.

But the stars were singing. Beyond the tall glass window and its gleaming diamond reflections, a hundred spilling stars shone their music across the paths and hedges below, even down to the glittering water's edge. There could be no mistake.

At first, followed by long months of doubt and self loathing, David had thought setting the flames to the castle hall had been a mistake of disastrous misunderstanding. At the time his master's enforced marriage to Peter's mistress, a woman of stubborn ignorance who had been taught to loathe her new husband, was a wretched business which David had believed he must end as quickly as he might. Finishing the union in fire and death had been the direct order from above. Then it had somehow proved wrong. For it was Nicholas who had suffered, rushing to save, to extinguish and restore, declaring himself the hero he surely always had been, but near dead from the flames. Not only, but now, with the marriage proved a success, it was hard to see why the order from the singing stars had been sent at all.

Yet David thought he understood. It was that very disaster which had burned away the hatred and ignited the love. The blossoming happiness of his master's marriage was, David decided, the direct result of the initial misery.

The wife, who had initially arrived at the castle in sin and immorality, had been cleansed also by fire. David had found her alone in the lord's bedchamber, bathed in soot and sleeping in ashes. He had caressed her, and even, he admitted, desired her, seeing her that way. He was aroused by her acceptance of the flaming destruction, and her own wickedness thus washed clean in embers. By wallowing in ash, she had acknowledged the filth of her past, and so was saved. And it was the stars, the fire and David which had saved her.

And so, one by one, by such acts of salvation never noticed and never seen by others, David Witton had continued to destroy any creature or cause which threatened his master. The flames that destroyed the village eaten by pestilence, where the guard had dared to threaten. The hypocritical father-in-law who had disrespected a man he should have felt overwhelmingly honoured to welcome into his own paltry family. The old witch who had murdered the unborn Chatwyn infant, and who, if left alive, might have stood witness against the family. Immorality, impropriety, and deliberate wickedness against the preaching of Holy Church. One of the most important, of course, was the eradication of the vile brother and his whore. And there had naturally been others. A valet caught stealing. A villager spreading gossip and rumour.

The stars were never wrong.

And there must always be fire, for fire cleansed. Fire had killed his own father, another brute without love, who had worked in the woods beyond London, felling trees for the charcoal furnaces and the casting of the cannon. David had been fourteen, still nursing the bruises his father gave him each evening, when one day the whole forest burned and his father with it. His mother, sodden in drink as always, claimed she had lit the fire, though David doubted it. It had surely been the stars, knowing best as always.

Then the year afterwards he had watched her burn when she tumbled cupshotten onto the hearth. The woman had screamed and disturbed the neighbours, but it had seemed a reasonable justice. And it had given David his freedom. Shortly afterwards, tramping north, he had found Chatwyn Castle and the master he loved.

So he took the spill he had folded ready, held it to the remaining candle flame, and then lowered it to the earl's flabby oozing carcase. The old man's hair was a frizzled grey but it turned dark, singed into carmine prickles. Springing into tiny dancing flamelettes, each with a perfect golden heart, while the sagging degenerate features turned to melting lard.

But the fire did not immediately spread, and the household would quickly smell the danger and rush to stamp out and douse the burning body. The house might yet be saved, even while the flames obeyed their destiny and the cleansing was achieved.

He hoped the threatened invasion from France would come indeed. His master, too badly wounded to join any battle, would be safe. But David, in his master's place, would have one more opportunity to prove his worth.

Backing slowly from the chamber, David turned to the door, did not look back, and strode from the house. On the morrow he would journey north again and back to Chatwyn Castle. He would take the news with him, of his master's newly inherited rank and rise to the family title; Earl of Chatwyn.

Outside the stars were still singing. David smiled.

ooo ooo ooo ooo ooooo

If this book has had any impact, please review on Amazon, Kobo, Goodreads etc. As they can make all the difference to an Author and would be very much appreciated.

ACKNOWLEDGEMENTS AND HISTORICAL NOTES

My novel is fiction and my principal characters are fictional. But I am, as always, strict concerning the absolute historical accuracy of my settings, background situations and various authentic figures of the past.

Anyone can make mistakes. I probably do, although unwittingly, and I apologise for any that may creep in. But I make every effort towards accuracy, and in this I am exceedingly indebted to friends who know more than I do, and to the many non fiction books which have provided for my endless research over the years.

Christopher Urswick is a genuine historical character, priest and personal confessor of Margaret Beaufort, mother of Henry Tudor who eventually became the first king of the Tudor dynasty. Urswick later supported Tudor's invasion, and before this acted as a messenger between the exiled Henry in Brittany, his mother in England, and John Morton who had escaped abroad in 1483.

Polydore Vergil, Henry VII's official biographer who obtained his information directly from his king, tells us that back in early 1485, following the persistent rumours that King Richard III was considering marrying his niece, Elizabeth of York, (a slightly absurd rumour which we now know as untrue since at the time King Richard was negotiating to marry the daughter of the King of Portugal, and the Portuguese Manuel to marry Elizabeth) Henry secretly sent Christopher Urswick to England with a letter for the Earl of Northumberland, seeking a marriage with any one of the Herbert girls, who were the earl's sisters-in-law. The letter was intercepted, Vergil informs us, and was never received by Northumberland. At that time this comparatively unimportant exile and proclaimed traitor was by no means an obvious candidate for marriage to a young English heiress, closely related to one of the greatest of the existing nobility.

Yet it appears that Henry Tudor had some expectation that his proposition would be acceptable to Northumberland, and that the earl would agree to negotiate Tudor's alliance within his close family.

This opens many questions, but these cannot be answered unless further documentation comes to light in the future, and I do not attempt to cover those points in my book. Christopher Urswick's presence in England as related in my novel, and the reason for it, is therefore historically accurate. As are the related movements of the Marquess of Dorset, and the situation relating to the king, Richard III, at that time.

I should particularly like to thank the eminently helpful and knowledgeable Annette Carson and her several important non fiction books on the subject and in particular *RICHARD III: THE MALIGNED KING,* which is a continuous source of both delight and expert information.

I should also like to thank my wonderfully patient and endlessly helpful family, in particular my daughter Gill and my granddaughter Emma, without whom I could not have published any of my novels.

Blessop's Wife
1483, and England is in turmoil. But there are those who work behind the scenes to bring peace, order and prosperity.
Tyballis escapes an abusive husband but finds herself in the midst of a great mystery. Who is Andrew? And what does he intend?
The King is dead. Rumour whispers. City backstreets are shadowed and dangerous with watching thieves, prostitutes and spies. But not all these characters are what they seem, and Tyballis finds new friends amongst those she would once have feared.
Andrew strides ahead. But Tyballis still does not know where he is leading her, nor from what direction the danger will leap next.

....

Made in the USA
Charleston, SC
25 February 2017